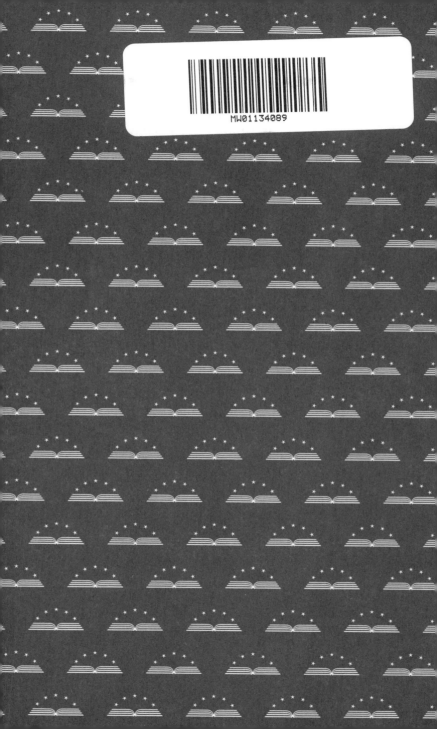

Library of America, a nonprofit organization,
champions our nation's cultural heritage
by publishing America's greatest writing in
authoritative new editions and providing resources
for readers to explore this rich, living legacy.

F. SCOTT FITZGERALD

F. Scott Fitzgerald

THE GREAT GATSBY, ALL THE SAD YOUNG MEN & OTHER WRITINGS 1920–1926

James L. W. West III, *editor*

THE LIBRARY OF AMERICA

F. SCOTT FITZGERALD: THE GREAT GATSBY,
ALL THE SAD YOUNG MEN & OTHER WRITINGS 1920–1926
Volume compilation, notes, and chronology copyright © 2022 by
Literary Classics of the United States, Inc., New York, N.Y.
All rights reserved.
No part of this book may be reproduced in any manner whatsoever without
the permission of the publisher, except in the case of brief
quotations embodied in critical articles and reviews.

Published in the United States by Library of America.
Visit our website at www.loa.org.

This paper exceeds the requirements of
ANSI/NISO z39.48–1992 (Permanence of Paper).

Distributed to the trade in the United States
by Penguin Random House Inc.
and in Canada by Penguin Random House Canada Ltd.

Library of Congress Control Number: 2021938720
ISBN 978–1–59853–714–7

First Printing
The Library of America—353

Manufactured in the United States of America

F. Scott Fitzgerald:
The Great Gatsby, All the Sad Young Men
& Other Writings 1920–1926
is published with support from

ROGER LATHBURY

Contents

THE GREAT GATSBY

Then wear the gold hat, if that will move her;
If you can bounce high, bounce for her too,
Till she cry "Lover, gold-hatted, high-bouncing lover,
I must have you!"

—THOMAS PARKE D'INVILLIERS.

ONCE AGAIN
TO
ZELDA

Chapter I

I N my younger and more vulnerable years my father gave me some advice that I've been turning over in my mind ever since.

"Whenever you feel like criticizing anyone," he told me, "just remember that all the people in this world haven't had the advantages that you've had."

He didn't say any more, but we've always been unusually communicative in a reserved way, and I understood that he meant a great deal more than that. In consequence, I'm inclined to reserve all judgments, a habit that has opened up many curious natures to me and also made me the victim of not a few veteran bores. The abnormal mind is quick to detect and attach itself to this quality when it appears in a normal person, and so it came about that in college I was unjustly accused of being a politician, because I was privy to the secret griefs of wild, unknown men. Most of the confidences were unsought—frequently I have feigned sleep, preoccupation, or a hostile levity when I realized by some unmistakable sign that an intimate revelation was quivering on the horizon; for the intimate revelations of young men, or at least the terms in which they express them, are usually plagiaristic and marred by obvious suppressions. Reserving judgments is a matter of infinite hope. I am still a little afraid of missing something if I forget that, as my father snobbishly suggested, and I snobbishly repeat, a sense of the fundamental decencies is parcelled out unequally at birth.

And, after boasting this way of my tolerance, I come to the admission that it has a limit. Conduct may be founded on the hard rock or the wet marshes, but after a certain point I don't care what it's founded on. When I came back from the East last autumn I felt that I wanted the world to be in uniform and at a sort of moral attention forever; I wanted no more riotous excursions with privileged glimpses into the human heart. Only Gatsby, the man who gives his name to this book, was exempt from my reaction—Gatsby, who represented everything for which I have an unaffected scorn. If personality is an unbroken series of successful gestures, then there was something gorgeous about him, some heightened sensitivity to the promises of life, as if he were related to one of those intricate machines that register earthquakes ten thousand miles away. This responsiveness had nothing to do with that flabby impressionability which is dignified under the name of the "creative temperament"—it was an extraordinary gift for hope, a romantic readiness such as I have never found in any other person and which it is not likely I shall ever find again. No—Gatsby turned out all right at the end; it is what preyed on Gatsby, what foul dust floated in the wake of his dreams that temporarily closed out my interest in the abortive sorrows and short-winded elations of men.

My family have been prominent, well-to-do people in this Middle Western city for three generations. The Carraways are something of a clan, and we have a tradition that we're descended from the Dukes of Buccleuch, but the actual founder of my line was my grandfather's brother, who came here in fifty-one, sent a substitute to the Civil War, and started the wholesale hardware business that my father carries on today.

I never saw this great-uncle, but I'm supposed to look like him—with special reference to the rather hard-boiled painting that hangs in father's office. I graduated from New Haven in 1915, just a quarter of a century after my father, and a little later I participated in that delayed Teutonic migration known as the Great War. I enjoyed the counter-raid so thoroughly that I came back restless. Instead of being the warm center of the world, the Middle West now seemed like the ragged edge of the universe—so I decided to go East and learn the bond business. Everybody I knew was in the bond business, so I supposed it could support one more single man. All my aunts and uncles talked it over as if they were choosing a prep school for me, and finally said, "Why—ye-es," with very grave, hesitant faces. Father agreed to finance me for a year, and after various delays I came East, permanently, I thought, in the spring of twenty-two.

The practical thing was to find rooms in the city, but it was a warm season, and I had just left a country of wide lawns and friendly trees, so when a young man at the office suggested that we take a house together in a commuting town, it sounded like a great idea. He found the house, a weather-beaten cardboard bungalow at eighty a month, but at the last minute the firm ordered him to Washington, and I went out to the country alone. I had a dog—at least I had him for a few days until he ran away—and an old Dodge and a Finnish woman, who made my bed and cooked breakfast and muttered Finnish wisdom to herself over the electric stove.

It was lonely for a day or so until one morning some man, more recently arrived than I, stopped me on the road.

"How do you get to West Egg Village?" he asked helplessly.

I told him. And as I walked on I was lonely no longer. I was a guide, a pathfinder, an original settler. He had casually conferred on me the freedom of the neighborhood.

And so with the sunshine and the great bursts of leaves growing on the trees, just as things grow in fast movies, I had that familiar conviction that life was beginning over again with the summer.

There was so much to read, for one thing, and so much fine health to be pulled down out of the young breath-giving air. I bought a dozen volumes on banking and credit and investment securities, and they stood on my shelf in red and gold like new money from the mint, promising to unfold the shining secrets that only Midas and Morgan and Mæcenas knew. And I had the high intention of reading many other books besides. I was rather literary in college—one year I wrote a series of very solemn and obvious editorials for the Yale News—and now I was going to bring back all such things into my life and become again that most limited of all specialists, the "well-rounded man." This isn't just an epigram—life is much more successfully looked at from a single window, after all.

It was a matter of chance that I should have rented a house in one of the strangest communities in North America. It was on that slender riotous island which extends itself due east of New York—and where there are, among other natural curiosities, two unusual formations of land. Twenty miles from the city a pair of enormous eggs, identical in contour and separated only by a courtesy bay, jut out into the most domesticated body of salt water in the Western hemisphere, the great wet barnyard of Long Island Sound. They are not perfect ovals—like the egg in the Columbus story, they are both crushed flat at the contact end—but their physical resemblance must be a source of perpetual confusion to the gulls that fly overhead. To the wingless

a more arresting phenomenon is their dissimilarity in every particular except shape and size.

I lived at West Egg, the—well, the less fashionable of the two,
though this is a most superficial tag to express the bizarre and
not a little sinister contrast between them. My house was at the
very tip of the egg, only fifty yards from the Sound, and squeezed
between two huge places that rented for twelve or fifteen thousand a season. The one on my right was a colossal affair by any
standard—it was a factual imitation of some Hôtel de Ville in
Normandy, with a tower on one side, spanking new under a thin
beard of raw ivy, and a marble swimming pool, and more than
forty acres of lawn and garden. It was Gatsby's mansion. Or,
rather, as I didn't know Mr. Gatsby, it was a mansion inhabited
by a gentleman of that name. My own house was an eyesore, but it
was a small eyesore, and it had been overlooked, so I had a view of
the water, a partial view of my neighbor's lawn, and the consoling
proximity of millionaires—all for eighty dollars a month.

Across the courtesy bay the white palaces of fashionable East
Egg glittered along the water, and the history of the summer
really begins on the evening I drove over there to have dinner
with the Tom Buchanans. Daisy was my second cousin once
removed, and I'd known Tom in college. And just after the war
I spent two days with them in Chicago.

Her husband, among various physical accomplishments, had
been one of the most powerful ends that ever played football
at New Haven—a national figure in a way, one of those men
who reach such an acute limited excellence at twenty-one that
everything afterward savors of anti-climax. His family were enormously wealthy—even in college his freedom with money was a
matter for reproach—but now he'd left Chicago and come East
in a fashion that rather took your breath away: for instance, he'd
brought down a string of polo ponies from Lake Forest. It was
hard to realize that a man in my own generation was wealthy
enough to do that.

Why they came East I don't know. They had spent a year in
France for no particular reason, and then drifted here and there
unrestfully wherever people played polo and were rich together.
This was a permanent move, said Daisy over the telephone, but
I didn't believe it—I had no sight into Daisy's heart, but I felt
that Tom would drift on forever seeking, a little wistfully, for
the dramatic turbulence of some irrecoverable football game.

And so it happened that on a warm windy evening I drove over to East Egg to see two old friends whom I scarcely knew at all. Their house was even more elaborate than I expected, a cheerful red-and-white Georgian Colonial mansion, overlooking the bay. The lawn started at the beach and ran toward the front door for a quarter of a mile, jumping over sun-dials and brick walks and burning gardens—finally when it reached the house drifting up the side in bright vines as though from the momentum of its run. The front was broken by a line of French windows, glowing now with reflected gold and wide open to the warm windy afternoon, and Tom Buchanan in riding clothes was standing with his legs apart on the front porch.

He had changed since his New Haven years. Now he was a sturdy straw-haired man of thirty with a rather hard mouth and a supercilious manner. Two shining arrogant eyes had established dominance over his face and gave him the appearance of always leaning aggressively forward. Not even the effeminate swank of his riding clothes could hide the enormous power of that body— he seemed to fill those glistening boots until he strained the top lacing, and you could see a great pack of muscle shifting when his shoulder moved under his thin coat. It was a body capable of enormous leverage—a cruel body.

His speaking voice, a gruff husky tenor, added to the impression of fractiousness he conveyed. There was a touch of paternal contempt in it, even toward people he liked—and there were men at New Haven who had hated his guts.

"Now, don't think my opinion on these matters is final," he seemed to say, "just because I'm stronger and more of a man than you are." We were in the same senior society, and while we were never intimate I always had the impression that he approved of me and wanted me to like him with some harsh, defiant wistfulness of his own.

We talked for a few minutes on the sunny porch.

"I've got a nice place here," he said, his eyes flashing about restlessly.

Turning me around by one arm, he moved a broad flat hand along the front vista, including in its sweep a sunken Italian garden, a half acre of deep, pungent roses, and a snub-nosed motor-boat that bumped the tide offshore.

"It belonged to Demaine, the oil man." He turned me around again, politely and abruptly. "We'll go inside."

We walked through a high hallway into a bright rosy-colored space, fragilely bound into the house by French windows at either end. The windows were ajar and gleaming white against the fresh grass outside that seemed to grow a little way into the house. A breeze blew through the room, blew curtains in at one end and out the other like pale flags, twisting them up toward the frosted wedding-cake of the ceiling, and then rippled over the wine-colored rug, making a shadow on it as wind does on the sea.

The only completely stationary object in the room was an enormous couch on which two young women were buoyed up as though upon an anchored balloon. They were both in white, and their dresses were rippling and fluttering as if they had just been blown back in after a short flight around the house. I must have stood for a few moments listening to the whip and snap of the curtains and the groan of a picture on the wall. Then there was a boom as Tom Buchanan shut the rear windows and the caught wind died out about the room, and the curtains and the rugs and the two young women ballooned slowly to the floor.

The younger of the two was a stranger to me. She was extended full length at her end of the divan, completely motionless, and with her chin raised a little, as if she were balancing something on it which was quite likely to fall. If she saw me out of the corner of her eyes she gave no hint of it—indeed, I was almost surprised into murmuring an apology for having disturbed her by coming in.

The other girl, Daisy, made an attempt to rise—she leaned slightly forward with a conscientious expression—then she laughed, an absurd, charming little laugh, and I laughed too and came forward into the room.

"I'm p-paralyzed with happiness."

She laughed again, as if she said something very witty, and held my hand for a moment, looking up into my face, promising that there was no one in the world she so much wanted to see. That was a way she had. She hinted in a murmur that the surname of the balancing girl was Baker. (I've heard it said that Daisy's murmur was only to make people lean toward her; an irrelevant criticism that made it no less charming.)

At any rate, Miss Baker's lips fluttered, she nodded at me almost imperceptibly, and then quickly tipped her head back again—the object she was balancing had obviously tottered a little and given her something of a fright. Again a sort of apology arose to my lips. Almost any exhibition of complete self-sufficiency draws a stunned tribute from me.

I looked back at my cousin, who began to ask me questions in her low, thrilling voice. It was the kind of voice that the ear follows up and down, as if each speech is an arrangement of notes that will never be played again. Her face was sad and lovely with bright things in it, bright eyes and a bright passionate mouth, but there was an excitement in her voice that men who had cared for her found difficult to forget: a singing compulsion, a whispered "Listen," a promise that she had done gay, exciting things just a while since and that there were gay, exciting things hovering in the next hour.

I told her how I had stopped off in Chicago for a day on my way East, and how a dozen people had sent their love through me.

"Do they miss me?" she cried ecstatically.

"The whole town is desolate. All the cars have the left rear wheel painted black as a mourning wreath, and there's a persistent wail all night along the North Shore."

"How gorgeous! Let's go back, Tom. Tomorrow!" Then she added irrelevantly: "You ought to see the baby."

"I'd like to."

"She's asleep. She's three years old. Haven't you ever seen her?"

"Never."

"Well, you ought to see her. She's——"

Tom Buchanan, who had been hovering restlessly about the room, stopped and rested his hand on my shoulder.

"What you doing, Nick?"

"I'm a bond man."

"Who with?"

I told him.

"Never heard of them," he remarked decisively.

This annoyed me.

"You will," I answered shortly. "You will if you stay in the East."

"Oh, I'll stay in the East, don't you worry," he said, glancing at Daisy and then back at me, as if he were alert for something more. "I'd be a God Damn fool to live anywhere else."

At this point Miss Baker said: "Absolutely!" with such suddenness that I started—it was the first word she had uttered since I came into the room. Evidently it surprised her as much as it did me, for she yawned and with a series of rapid, deft movements stood up into the room.

"I'm stiff," she complained. "I've been lying on that sofa for as long as I can remember."

"Don't look at me," Daisy retorted. "I've been trying to get you to New York all afternoon."

"No, thanks," said Miss Baker to the four cocktails just in from the pantry. "I'm absolutely in training."

Her host looked at her incredulously.

"You are!" He took down his drink as if it were a drop in the bottom of a glass. "How you ever get anything done is beyond me."

I looked at Miss Baker, wondering what it was she "got done." I enjoyed looking at her. She was a slender, small-breasted girl, with an erect carriage, which she accentuated by throwing her body backward at the shoulders like a young cadet. Her gray sun-strained eyes looked back at me with polite reciprocal curiosity out of a wan, charming, discontented face. It occurred to me now that I had seen her, or a picture of her, somewhere before.

"You live in West Egg," she remarked contemptuously. "I know somebody there."

"I don't know a single——"

"You must know Gatsby."

"Gatsby?" demanded Daisy. "What Gatsby?"

Before I could reply that he was my neighbor dinner was announced; wedging his tense arm imperatively under mine, Tom Buchanan compelled me from the room as though he were moving a checker to another square.

Slenderly, languidly, their hands set lightly on their hips, the two young women preceded us out onto a rosy-colored porch, open toward the sunset, where four candles flickered on the table in the diminished wind.

"Why *candles?*" objected Daisy, frowning. She snapped them out with her fingers. "In two weeks it'll be the longest day in the year." She looked at us all radiantly. "Do you always watch for the longest day of the year and then miss it? I always watch for the longest day in the year and then miss it."

"We ought to plan something," yawned Miss Baker, sitting down at the table as if she were getting into bed.

"All right," said Daisy. "What'll we plan?" She turned to me helplessly: "What do people plan?"

Before I could answer her eyes fastened with an awed expression on her little finger.

"Look!" she complained. "I hurt it."

We all looked—the knuckle was black and blue.

"You did it, Tom," she said accusingly. "I know you didn't mean to, but you *did* do it. That's what I get for marrying a brute of a man, a great, big, hulking physical specimen of a——"

"I hate that word hulking," objected Tom crossly, "even in kidding."

"Hulking," insisted Daisy.

Sometimes she and Miss Baker talked at once, unobtrusively and with a bantering inconsequence that was never quite chatter, that was as cool as their white dresses and their impersonal eyes in the absence of all desire. They were here, and they accepted Tom and me, making only a polite pleasant effort to entertain or to be entertained. They knew that presently dinner would be over and a little later the evening too would be over and casually put away. It was sharply different from the West, where an evening was hurried from phase to phase toward its close, in a continually disappointed anticipation or else in sheer nervous dread of the moment itself.

"You make me feel uncivilized, Daisy," I confessed on my second glass of corky but rather impressive claret. "Can't you talk about crops or something?"

I meant nothing in particular by this remark, but it was taken up in an unexpected way.

"Civilization's going to pieces," broke out Tom violently. "I've gotten to be a terrible pessimist about things. Have you read 'The Rise of the Colored Empires' by this man Goddard?"

"Why, no," I answered, rather surprised by his tone.

"Well, it's a fine book, and everybody ought to read it. The idea is if we don't look out the white race will be—will be utterly submerged. It's all scientific stuff; it's been proved."

"Tom's getting very profound," said Daisy, with an expression of unthoughtful sadness. "He reads deep books with long words in them. What was that word we——"

"Well, these books are all scientific," insisted Tom, glancing at her impatiently. "This fellow has worked out the whole thing. It's up to us, who are the dominant race, to watch out or these other races will have control of things."

"We've got to beat them down," whispered Daisy, winking ferociously toward the fervent sun.

"You ought to live in California—" began Miss Baker, but Tom interrupted her by shifting heavily in his chair.

"This idea is that we're Nordics. I am, and you are, and you are, and—" After an infinitesimal hesitation he included Daisy with a slight nod, and she winked at me again. "—And we've produced all the things that go to make civilization—oh, science and art, and all that. Do you see?"

There was something pathetic in his concentration, as if his complacency, more acute than of old, was not enough to him any more. When, almost immediately, the telephone rang inside and the butler left the porch Daisy seized upon the momentary interruption and leaned toward me.

"I'll tell you a family secret," she whispered enthusiastically. "It's about the butler's nose. Do you want to hear about the butler's nose?"

"That's why I came over tonight."

"Well, he wasn't always a butler; he used to be the silver polisher for some people in New York that had a silver service for two hundred people. He had to polish it from morning till night, until finally it began to affect his nose——"

"Things went from bad to worse," suggested Miss Baker.

"Yes. Things went from bad to worse, until finally he had to give up his position."

For a moment the last sunshine fell with romantic affection upon her glowing face; her voice compelled me forward breathlessly as I listened—then the glow faded, each light deserting her with lingering regret, like children leaving a pleasant street at dusk.

The butler came back and murmured something close to Tom's ear, whereupon Tom frowned, pushed back his chair, and without a word went inside. As if his absence quickened something within her, Daisy leaned forward again, her voice glowing and singing.

"I love to see you at my table, Nick. You remind me of a—of a rose, an absolute rose. Doesn't he?" She turned to Miss Baker for confirmation: "An absolute rose?"

This was untrue. I am not even faintly like a rose. She was only extemporizing, but a stirring warmth flowed from her, as if her heart was trying to come out to you concealed in one of those breathless, thrilling words. Then suddenly she threw her napkin on the table and excused herself and went into the house.

Miss Baker and I exchanged a short glance consciously devoid of meaning. I was about to speak when she sat up alertly and said "Sh!" in a warning voice. A subdued impassioned murmur was audible in the room beyond, and Miss Baker leaned forward unashamed, trying to hear. The murmur trembled on the verge of coherence, sank down, mounted excitedly, and then ceased altogether.

"This Mr. Gatsby you spoke of is my neighbor—" I said.

"Don't talk. I want to hear what happens."

"Is something happening?" I inquired innocently.

"You mean to say you don't know?" said Miss Baker, honestly surprised. "I thought everybody knew."

"I don't."

"Why—" she said hesitantly, "Tom's got some woman in New York."

"Got some woman?" I repeated blankly.

Miss Baker nodded.

"She might have the decency not to telephone him at dinner-time. Don't you think?"

Almost before I had grasped her meaning there was the flutter of a dress and the crunch of leather boots, and Tom and Daisy were back at the table.

"It couldn't be helped!" cried Daisy with tense gayety.

She sat down, glanced searchingly at Miss Baker and then at me, and continued: "I looked outdoors for a minute, and it's very romantic outdoors. There's a bird on the lawn that I think must be a nightingale come over on the Cunard or White Star Line. He's singing away—" Her voice sang: "It's romantic, isn't it, Tom?"

"Very romantic," he said, and then miserably to me: "If it's light enough after dinner, I want to take you down to the stables."

The telephone rang inside, startlingly, and as Daisy shook her head decisively at Tom the subject of the stables, in fact all subjects, vanished into air. Among the broken fragments of the last five minutes at table I remember the candles being lit again, pointlessly, and I was conscious of wanting to look squarely at everyone, and yet to avoid all eyes. I couldn't guess what Daisy and Tom were thinking, but I doubt if even Miss Baker, who seemed to have mastered a certain hardy skepticism, was able utterly to put this fifth guest's shrill metallic urgency out of mind. To a certain temperament the situation might have seemed intriguing—my own instinct was to telephone immediately for the police.

The horses, needless to say, were not mentioned again. Tom and Miss Baker, with several feet of twilight between them, strolled back into the library, as if to a vigil beside a perfectly tangible body, while, trying to look pleasantly interested and a little deaf, I followed Daisy around a chain of connecting verandas to the porch in front. In its deep gloom we sat down side by side on a wicker settee.

Daisy took her face in her hands as if feeling its lovely shape, and her eyes moved gradually out into the velvet dusk. I saw that turbulent emotions possessed her, so I asked what I thought would be some sedative questions about her little girl.

"We don't know each other very well, Nick," she said suddenly. "Even if we are cousins. You didn't come to my wedding."

"I wasn't back from the war."

"That's true." She hesitated. "Well, I've had a very bad time, Nick, and I'm pretty cynical about everything."

Evidently she had reason to be. I waited but she didn't say any more, and after a moment I returned rather feebly to the subject of her daughter.

"I suppose she talks, and—eats, and everything."

"Oh, yes." She looked at me absently. "Listen, Nick; let me tell you what I said when she was born. Would you like to hear?"

"Very much."

"It'll show you how I've gotten to feel about—things. Well, she was less than an hour old and Tom was God knows where. I woke up out of the ether with an utterly abandoned feeling, and asked the nurse right away if it was a boy or a girl. She told me it was a girl, and so I turned my head away and wept. 'All right,' I said, 'I'm glad it's a girl. And I hope she'll be a fool—that's the best thing a girl can be in this world, a beautiful little fool.'

"You see I think everything's terrible anyhow," she went on in a convinced way. "Everybody thinks so—the most advanced people. And I *know*. I've been everywhere and seen everything and done everything." Her eyes flashed around her in a defiant way, rather like Tom's, and she laughed with thrilling scorn. "Sophisticated—God, I'm sophisticated!"

The instant her voice broke off, ceasing to compel my attention, my belief, I felt the basic insincerity of what she had said. It made me uneasy, as though the whole evening had been a trick of some sort to exact a contributary emotion from me. I waited, and sure enough, in a moment she looked at me with an absolute smirk on her lovely face, as if she had asserted her membership in a rather distinguished secret society to which she and Tom belonged.

Inside, the crimson room bloomed with light. Tom and Miss Baker sat at either end of the long couch and she read aloud to him from the Saturday Evening Post—the words, murmurous and uninflected, running together in a soothing tune. The lamp-light, bright on his boots and dull on the autumn-leaf yellow of her hair, glinted along the paper as she turned a page with a flutter of slender muscles in her arms.

When we came in she held us silent for a moment with a lifted hand.

"To be continued," she said, tossing the magazine on the table, "in our very next issue."

Her body asserted itself with a restless movement of her knee, and she stood up.

"Ten o'clock," she remarked, apparently finding the time on the ceiling. "Time for this good girl to go to bed."

"Jordan's going to play in the tournament tomorrow," explained Daisy, "over at Westchester."

"Oh—you're *Jor*dan Baker."

I knew now why her face was familiar—its pleasing contemptuous expression had looked out at me from many rotogravure pictures of the sporting life at Asheville and Hot Springs and Palm Beach. I had heard some story of her too, a critical, unpleasant story, but what it was I had forgotten long ago.

"Good night," she said softly. "Wake me at eight, won't you."

"If you'll get up."

"I will. Good night, Mr. Carraway. See you anon."

"Of course you will," confirmed Daisy. "In fact I think I'll arrange a marriage. Come over often, Nick, and I'll sort of—oh—fling you together. You know—lock you up accidentally in linen closets and push you out to sea in a boat, and all that sort of thing——"

"Good night," called Miss Baker from the stairs. "I haven't heard a word."

"She's a nice girl," said Tom after a moment. "They oughtn't to let her run around the country this way."

"Who oughtn't to?" inquired Daisy coldly.

"Her family."

"Her family is one aunt about a thousand years old. Besides, Nick's going to look after her, aren't you, Nick? She's going to spend lots of weekends out here this summer. I think the home influence will be very good for her."

Daisy and Tom looked at each other for a moment in silence.

"Is she from New York?" I asked quickly.

"From Louisville. Our white girlhood was passed together there. Our beautiful white——"

"Did you give Nick a little heart-to-heart talk on the veranda?" demanded Tom suddenly.

"Did I?" She looked at me. "I can't seem to remember, but I think we talked about the Nordic race. Yes, I'm sure we did. It sort of crept up on us and first thing you know——"

"Don't believe everything you hear, Nick," he advised me.

I said lightly that I had heard nothing at all, and a few minutes later I got up to go home. They came to the door with me and stood side by side in a cheerful square of light. As I started my motor Daisy peremptorily called: "Wait!

"I forgot to ask you something, and it's important. We heard you were engaged to a girl out West."

"That's right," corroborated Tom kindly. "We heard that you were engaged."

"It's a libel. I'm too poor."

"But we heard it," insisted Daisy, surprising me by opening up again in a flower-like way. "We heard it from three people, so it must be true."

Of course I knew what they were referring to, but I wasn't even vaguely engaged. The fact that gossip had published the banns was one of the reasons I had come East. You can't stop going with an old friend on account of rumors, and on the other hand I had no intention of being rumored into marriage.

Their interest rather touched me and made them less remotely rich—nevertheless, I was confused and a little disgusted as I drove away. It seemed to me that the thing for Daisy to do was to rush out of the house, child in arms—but apparently there were no such intentions in her head. As for Tom, the fact that he "had some woman in New York" was really less surprising than that he had been depressed by a book. Something was making him nibble at the edge of stale ideas as if his sturdy physical egotism no longer nourished his peremptory heart.

Already it was deep summer on roadhouse roofs and in front of wayside garages, where new red gas-pumps sat out in pools of light, and when I reached my estate at West Egg I ran the car under its shed and sat for a while on an abandoned grass roller in the yard. The wind had blown off, leaving a loud, bright night, with wings beating in the trees and a persistent organ sound as the full bellows of the earth blew the frogs full of life. The silhouette of a moving cat wavered across the moonlight, and turning my head to watch it, I saw that I was not alone—fifty feet away a figure had emerged from the shadow of my neighbor's mansion and was standing with his hands in his pockets regarding the silver pepper of the stars. Something in his leisurely movements and the secure position of his feet upon the lawn suggested that it was Mr. Gatsby himself, come out to determine what share was his of our local heavens.

I decided to call to him. Miss Baker had mentioned him at dinner, and that would do for an introduction. But I didn't call to him, for he gave a sudden intimation that he was content to be alone—he stretched out his arms toward the dark water in a curious way, and, far as I was from him, I could have sworn he was trembling. Involuntarily I glanced seaward—and distinguished nothing except a single green light, minute and far away, that might have been at the end of a dock. When I looked once more for Gatsby he had vanished, and I was alone again in the unquiet darkness.

Chapter II

A BOUT half way between West Egg and New York the motor-road hastily joins the railroad and runs beside it for a quarter of a mile, so as to shrink away from a certain desolate area of land. This is a valley of ashes—a fantastic farm where ashes grow like wheat into ridges and hills and grotesque gardens; where ashes take the forms of houses and chimneys and rising smoke and, finally, with a transcendent effort, of men who move dimly and already crumbling through the powdery air. Occasionally a line of gray cars crawls along an invisible track, gives out a ghastly creak, and comes to rest, and immediately the ash-gray men swarm up with leaden spades and stir up an impenetrable cloud, which screens their obscure operations from your sight.

But above the gray land and the spasms of bleak dust which drift endlessly over it, you perceive, after a moment, the eyes of Doctor T. J. Eckleburg. The eyes of Doctor T. J. Eckleburg are blue and gigantic—their retinas are one yard high. They look out of no face, but, instead, from a pair of enormous yellow spectacles which pass over a non-existent nose. Evidently some wild wag of an oculist set them there to fatten his practice in the borough of Queens, and then sank down himself into eternal blindness, or forgot them and moved away. But his eyes, dimmed a little by many paintless days under sun and rain, brood on over the solemn dumping ground.

The valley of ashes is bounded on one side by a small foul river, and, when the drawbridge is up to let barges through, the passengers on waiting trains can stare at the dismal scene for as long as half an hour. There is always a halt there of at least a minute, and it was because of this that I first met Tom Buchanan's mistress.

The fact that he had one was insisted upon wherever he was known. His acquaintances resented the fact that he turned up in popular restaurants with her and, leaving her at a table, sauntered about, chatting with whomsoever he knew. Though I was curious to see her, I had no desire to meet her—but I did. I went up to New York with Tom on the train one afternoon, and when we stopped by the ashheaps he jumped to his feet and, taking hold of my elbow, literally forced me from the car.

"We're getting off," he insisted. "I want you to meet my girl."

I think he'd tanked up a good deal at luncheon, and his determination to have my company bordered on violence. The supercilious assumption was that on Sunday afternoon I had nothing better to do.

I followed him over a low whitewashed railroad fence, and we walked back a hundred yards along the road under Doctor Eckleburg's persistent stare. The only building in sight was a small block of yellow brick sitting on the edge of the waste land, a sort of compact Main Street ministering to it, and contiguous to absolutely nothing. One of the three shops it contained was for rent and another was an all-night restaurant, approached by a trail of ashes; the third was a garage—*Repairs.* GEORGE B. WILSON. *Cars bought and sold.*—and I followed Tom inside.

The interior was unprosperous and bare; the only car visible was the dust-covered wreck of a Ford which crouched in a dim corner. It had occurred to me that this shadow of a garage must be a blind, and that sumptuous and romantic apartments were concealed overhead, when the proprietor himself appeared in the door of an office, wiping his hands on a piece of waste. He was a blond, spiritless man, anæmic, and faintly handsome. When he saw us a damp gleam of hope sprang into his light blue eyes.

"Hello, Wilson, old man," said Tom, slapping him jovially on the shoulder. "How's business?"

"I can't complain," answered Wilson unconvincingly. "When are you going to sell me that car?"

"Next week; I've got my man working on it now."

"Works pretty slow, don't he?"

"No, he doesn't," said Tom coldly. "And if you feel that way about it, maybe I'd better sell it somewhere else after all."

"I don't mean that," explained Wilson quickly. "I just meant——"

His voice faded off and Tom glanced impatiently around the garage. Then I heard footsteps on a stairs, and in a moment the thickish figure of a woman blocked out the light from the office door. She was in the middle thirties, and faintly stout, but she carried her surplus flesh sensuously as some women can. Her face, above a spotted dress of dark blue crêpe-de-chine, contained no

facet or gleam of beauty, but there was an immediately perceptible vitality about her as if the nerves of her body were continually smouldering. She smiled slowly and, walking through her
husband as if he were a ghost, shook hands with Tom, looking
him flush in the eye. Then she wet her lips, and without turning
around spoke to her husband in a soft, coarse voice:

"Get some chairs, why don't you, so somebody can sit down."

"Oh, sure," agreed Wilson hurriedly, and went toward the
little office, mingling immediately with the cement color of the
walls. A white ashen dust veiled his dark suit and his pale hair as
it veiled everything in the vicinity—except his wife, who moved
close to Tom.

"I want to see you," said Tom intently. "Get on the next
train."

"All right."

"I'll meet you by the newsstand on the lower level."

She nodded and moved away from him just as George Wilson
emerged with two chairs from his office door.

We waited for her down the road and out of sight. It was a
few days before the Fourth of July, and a gray, scrawny Italian
child was setting torpedoes in a row along the railroad track.

"Terrible place, isn't it," said Tom, exchanging a frown with
Doctor Eckleburg.

"Awful."

"It does her good to get away."

"Doesn't her husband object?"

"Wilson? He thinks she goes to see her sister in New York.
He's so dumb he doesn't know he's alive."

So Tom Buchanan and his girl and I went up together to New
York—or not quite together, for Mrs. Wilson sat discreetly in
another car. Tom deferred that much to the sensibilities of those
East Eggers who might be on the train.

She had changed her dress to a brown figured muslin, which
stretched tight over her rather wide hips as Tom helped her to
the platform in New York. At the newsstand she bought a copy
of Town Tattle and a moving-picture magazine, and in the station drug-store some cold cream and a small flask of perfume.
Upstairs in the solemn echoing drive she let four taxi cabs drive
away before she selected a new one, lavender-colored with gray
upholstery, and in this we slid out from the mass of the station

into the glowing sunshine. But immediately she turned sharply from the window and, leaning forward, tapped on the front glass.

"I want to get one of those dogs," she said earnestly. "I want to get one for the apartment. They're nice to have—a dog."

We backed up to a gray old man who bore an absurd resemblance to John D. Rockefeller. In a basket swung from his neck cowered a dozen very recent puppies of an indeterminate breed.

"What kind are they?" asked Mrs. Wilson eagerly, as he came to the taxi window.

"All kinds. What kind do you want, lady?"

"I'd like to get one of those police dogs; I don't suppose you got that kind?"

The man peered doubtfully into the basket, plunged in his hand and drew one up, wriggling, by the back of the neck.

"That's no police dog," said Tom.

"No, it's not exactly a *police* dog," said the man with disappointment in his voice. "It's more of an Airedale." He passed his hand over the brown wash-rag of a back. "Look at that coat. Some coat. That's a dog that'll never bother you with catching cold."

"I think it's cute," said Mrs. Wilson enthusiastically. "How much is it?"

"That dog?" He looked at it admiringly. "That dog will cost you ten dollars."

The Airedale—undoubtedly there was an Airedale concerned in it somewhere, though its feet were startlingly white—changed hands and settled down into Mrs. Wilson's lap, where she fondled the weather-proof coat with rapture.

"Is it a boy or a girl?" she asked delicately.

"That dog? That dog's a boy."

"It's a bitch," said Tom decisively. "Here's your money. Go and buy ten more dogs with it."

We drove over to Fifth Avenue, so warm and soft, almost pastoral, on the summer Sunday afternoon that I wouldn't have been surprised to see a great flock of white sheep turn the corner.

"Hold on," I said. "I have to leave you here."

"No, you don't," interposed Tom quickly. "Myrtle'll be hurt if you don't come up to the apartment. Won't you, Myrtle?"

"Come on," she urged. "I'll telephone my sister Catherine. She's said to be very beautiful by people who ought to know."

"Well, I'd like to, but——"

We went on, cutting back again over the Park toward the West Hundreds. At 158th Street the cab stopped at one slice in a long white cake of apartment-houses. Throwing a regal homecoming glance around the neighborhood, Mrs. Wilson gathered up her dog and her other purchases, and went haughtily in.

"I'm going to have the McKees come up," she announced as we rose in the elevator. "And, of course, I got to call up my sister, too."

The apartment was on the top floor—a small living-room, a small dining-room, a small bedroom, and a bath. The living-room was crowded to the doors with a set of tapestried furniture entirely too large for it, so that to move about was to stumble continually over scenes of ladies swinging in the gardens of Versailles. The only picture was an over-enlarged photograph, apparently a hen sitting on a blurred rock. Looked at from a distance, however, the hen resolved itself into a bonnet, and the countenance of a stout old lady beamed down into the room. Several old copies of Town Tattle lay on the table together with a copy of "Simon Called Peter," and some of the small scandal magazines of Broadway. Mrs. Wilson was first concerned with the dog. A reluctant elevator-boy went for a box full of straw and some milk, to which he added on his own initiative a tin of large, hard dog-biscuits—one of which decomposed apathetically in the saucer of milk all afternoon. Meanwhile Tom brought out a bottle of whiskey from a locked bureau door.

I have been drunk just twice in my life, and the second time was that afternoon; so everything that happened has a dim, hazy cast over it, although until after eight o'clock the apartment was full of cheerful sun. Sitting on Tom's lap Mrs. Wilson called up several people on the telephone; then there were no cigarettes, and I went out to buy some at the drug-store on the corner. When I came back they had disappeared, so I sat down discreetly in the living-room and read a chapter of "Simon Called Peter"—either it was terrible stuff or the whiskey distorted things, because it didn't make any sense to me.

Just as Tom and Myrtle (after the first drink Mrs. Wilson and I called each other by our first names) reappeared, company commenced to arrive at the apartment-door.

The sister, Catherine, was a slender, worldly girl of about thirty, with a solid, sticky bob of red hair, and a complexion powdered milky white. Her eyebrows had been plucked and then drawn on again at a more rakish angle, but the efforts of nature toward the restoration of the old alignment gave a blurred air to her face. When she moved about there was an incessant clicking as innumerable pottery bracelets jingled up and down upon her arms. She came in with such a proprietary haste and looked around so possessively at the furniture that I wondered if she lived here. But when I asked her she laughed immoderately, repeated my question aloud, and told me she lived with a girl friend at a hotel.

Mr. McKee was a pale, feminine man from the flat below. He had just shaved, for there was a white spot of lather on his cheek-bone, and he was most respectful in his greeting to everyone in the room. He informed me that he was in the "artistic game," and I gathered later that he was a photographer and had made the dim enlargement of Mrs. Wilson's mother which hovered like an ectoplasm on the wall. His wife was shrill, languid, hand-some, and horrible. She told me with pride that her husband had photographed her a hundred and twenty-seven times since they had been married.

Mrs. Wilson had changed her costume sometime before, and was now attired in an elaborate afternoon dress of cream-colored chiffon, which gave out a continual rustle as she swept about the room. With the influence of the dress her personality had also undergone a change. The intense vitality that had been so remarkable in the garage was converted into impressive hauteur. Her laughter, her gestures, her assertions became more violently affected moment by moment, and as she expanded the room grew smaller around her, until she seemed to be revolving on a noisy, creaking pivot through the smoky air.

"My dear," she told her sister in a high, mincing shout, "most of these fellas will cheat you every time. All they think of is money. I had a woman up here last week to look at my feet, and when she gave me the bill you'd of thought she had my appendicitus out."

"What was the name of the woman?" asked Mrs. McKee.

"Mrs. Eberhardt. She goes around looking at people's feet in their own homes."

"I like your dress," remarked Mrs. McKee. "I think it's adorable."

Mrs. Wilson rejected the compliment by raising her eyebrow in disdain.

"It's just a crazy old thing," she said. "I just slip it on sometimes when I don't care what I look like."

"But it looks wonderful on you, if you know what I mean," pursued Mrs. McKee. "If Chester could only get you in that pose I think he could make something of it."

We all looked in silence at Mrs. Wilson, who removed a strand of hair from over her eyes and looked back at us with a brilliant smile. Mr. McKee regarded her intently with his head on one side, and then moved his hand back and forth slowly in front of his face.

"I should change the light," he said after a moment. "I'd like to bring out the modelling of the features. And I'd try to get hold of all the back hair."

"I wouldn't think of changing the light," cried Mrs. McKee. "I think it's——"

Her husband said "*Sh!*" and we all looked at the subject again, whereupon Tom Buchanan yawned audibly and got to his feet.

"You McKees have something to drink," he said. "Get some more ice and mineral water, Myrtle, before everybody goes to sleep."

"I told that boy about the ice." Myrtle raised her eyebrows in despair at the shiftlessness of the lower orders. "These people! You have to keep after them all the time."

She looked at me and laughed pointlessly. Then she flounced over to the dog, kissed it with ecstasy, and swept into the kitchen, implying that a dozen chefs awaited her orders there.

"I've done some nice things out on Long Island," asserted Mr. McKee.

Tom looked at him blankly.

"Two of them we have framed downstairs."

"Two what?" demanded Tom.

"Two studies. One of them I call 'Montauk Point—The Gulls,' and the other I call 'Montauk Point—The Sea.'"

The sister Catherine sat down beside me on the couch.

"Do you live down on Long Island, too," she inquired.

"I live at West Egg."

"Really? I was down there at a party about a month ago. At a man named Gatsby's. Do you know him?"

"I live next door to him."

"Well, they say he's a nephew or a cousin of Kaiser Wilhelm's. That's where all his money comes from."

"Really?"

She nodded.

"I'm scared of him. I'd hate to have him get anything on me."

This absorbing information about my neighbor was interrupted by Mrs. McKee's pointing suddenly at Catherine:

"Chester, I think you could do something with *her*," she broke out, but Mr. McKee only nodded in a bored way, and turned his attention to Tom.

"I'd like to do more work on Long Island, if I could get the entry. All I ask is that they should give me a start."

"Ask Myrtle," said Tom, breaking into a short shout of laughter as Mrs. Wilson entered with a tray. "She'll give you a letter of introduction, won't you, Myrtle?"

"Do what?" she asked, startled.

"You'll give McKee a letter of introduction to your husband, so he can do some studies of him." His lips moved silently for a moment as he invented. "'George B. Wilson at the Gasoline Pump,' or something like that."

Catherine leaned close to me and whispered in my ear:

"Neither of them can stand the person they're married to."

"Can't they?"

"Can't *stand* them." She looked at Myrtle and then at Tom. "What I say is, why go on living with them if they can't stand them? If I was them I'd get a divorce and get married to each other right away."

"Doesn't she like Wilson either?"

The answer to this was unexpected. It came from Myrtle, who had overheard the question, and it was violent and obscene.

"You see?" cried Catherine triumphantly. She lowered her voice again. "It's really his wife that's keeping them apart. She's a Catholic, and they don't believe in divorce."

Daisy was not a Catholic, and I was a little shocked at the elaborateness of the lie.

"When they do get married," continued Catherine, "they're going West to live for a while until it blows over."

"It'd be more discreet to go to Europe."

"Oh, do you like Europe?" she exclaimed surprisingly. "I just got back from Monte Carlo."

"Really."

"Just last year. I went over there with another girl."

"Stay long?"

"No, we just went to Monte Carlo and back. We went by way of Marseilles. We had over twelve hundred dollars when we started, but we got gypped out of it all in two days in the private rooms. We had an awful time getting back, I can tell you. God, how I hated that town!"

The late afternoon sky bloomed in the window for a moment like the blue honey of the Mediterranean—then the shrill voice of Mrs. McKee called me back into the room.

"I almost made a mistake, too," she declared vigorously. "I almost married a little kyke who'd been after me for years. I knew he was below me. Everybody kept saying to me: 'Lucille, that man's way below you!' But if I hadn't met Chester, he'd of got me sure."

"Yes, but listen," said Myrtle Wilson, nodding her head up and down. "At least you didn't marry him."

"I know I didn't."

"Well, I married him," said Myrtle, ambiguously. "And that's the difference between your case and mine."

"Why did you, Myrtle?" demanded Catherine. "Nobody forced you to."

Myrtle considered.

"I married him because I thought he was a gentleman," she said finally. "I thought he knew something about breeding, but he wasn't fit to lick my shoe."

"You were crazy about him for a while," said Catherine.

"Crazy about him!" cried Myrtle incredulously. "Who said I was crazy about him? I never was any more crazy about him than I was about that man there."

She pointed suddenly at me, and everyone looked at me accusingly. I tried to show by my expression that I had played no part in her past.

"The only *crazy* I was was when I married him. I knew right away I made a mistake. He borrowed somebody's best suit to get married in, and never even told me about it, and the man came after it one day when he was out." She looked to see who was listening. "'Oh, is that your suit?' I said. 'This is the first I ever heard about it.' But I gave it to him and then I lay down and cried to beat the band all afternoon."

"She really ought to get away from him," resumed Catherine to me. "They've been living over that garage for eleven years. And Tom's the first sweetie she ever had."

The bottle of whiskey—a second one—was now in constant demand by all present, excepting Catherine, who "felt just as good on nothing at all." Tom rang for the janitor and sent him for some celebrated sandwiches which were a complete supper in themselves. I wanted to get out and walk eastward toward the Park through the soft twilight, but each time I tried to go I became entangled in some wild, strident argument which pulled me back, as if with ropes, into my chair. Yet high over the city our line of yellow windows must have contributed their share of human secrecy to the casual watcher in the darkening streets, and I was him too, looking up and wondering. I was within and without, simultaneously enchanted and repelled by the inexhaustible variety of life.

Myrtle pulled her chair close to mine, and suddenly her warm breath poured over me the story of her first meeting with Tom.

"It was on the two little seats facing each other that are always the last ones left on the train. I was going up to New York to see my sister and spend the night. He had on a dress suit and patent leather shoes, and I couldn't keep my eyes off him, but every time he looked at me I had to pretend to be looking at the advertisement over his head. When we came into the station he was next to me, and his white shirt front pressed against my arm, and so I told him I'd have to call a policeman, but he knew I lied. I was so excited that when I got into a taxi with him I didn't hardly know I wasn't getting into a subway train. All I kept thinking about, over and over, was 'You can't live forever, you can't live forever.'"

She turned to Mrs. McKee and the room rang full of her artificial laughter.

"My dear," she cried, "I'm going to give you this dress as soon as I'm through with it. I've got to get another one tomorrow. I'm going to make a list of all the things I've got to get. A massage and a wave, and a collar for the dog, and one of those cute little ash trays where you touch a spring, and a wreath with a black silk bow for mother's grave that'll last all summer. I got to write down a list so I won't forget all the things I got to do."

It was nine o'clock—almost immediately afterward I looked at my watch and found it was ten. Mr. McKee was asleep on a chair with his fists clenched in his lap, like a photograph of a man of action. Taking out my handkerchief I wiped from his cheek the spot of dried lather that had worried me all the afternoon.

The little dog was sitting on the table looking with blind eyes through the smoke, and from time to time groaning faintly. People disappeared, reappeared, made plans to go somewhere, and then lost each other, searched for each other, found each other a few feet away. Some time toward midnight Tom Buchanan and Mrs. Wilson stood face to face discussing, in impassioned voices, whether Mrs. Wilson had any right to mention Daisy's name.

"Daisy! Daisy! Daisy!" shouted Mrs. Wilson. "I'll say it whenever I want to! Daisy! Dai——"

Making a short deft movement, Tom Buchanan broke her nose with his open hand.

Then there were bloody towels upon the bathroom floor, and women's voices scolding, and high over the confusion a long broken wail of pain. Mr. McKee awoke from his doze and started in a daze toward the door. When he had gone half way he turned around and stared at the scene—his wife and Catherine scolding and consoling as they stumbled here and there among the crowded furniture with articles of aid, and the despairing figure on the couch, bleeding fluently, and trying to spread a copy of Town Tattle over the tapestry scenes of Versailles. Then Mr. McKee turned and continued on out the door. Taking my hat from the chandelier, I followed.

"Come to lunch some day," he suggested, as we groaned down in the elevator.

"Where?"

"Anywhere."

"Keep your hands off the lever," snapped the elevator boy.

"I beg your pardon," said Mr. McKee with dignity. "I didn't know I was touching it."

"All right," I agreed, "I'll be glad to."

. . . I was standing beside his bed and he was sitting up between the sheets, clad in his underwear, with a great portfolio in his hands.

"Beauty and the Beast . . . Loneliness . . . Old Grocery Horse . . . Brook'n Bridge . . ."

Then I was lying half asleep in the cold lower level of the Pennsylvania Station, staring at the morning Tribune, and waiting for the four o'clock train.

Chapter III

THERE was music from my neighbor's house through the summer nights. In his blue gardens men and girls came and went like moths among the whisperings and the champagne and the stars. At high tide in the afternoon I watched his guests diving from the tower of his raft, or taking the sun on the hot sand of his beach while his two motor-boats slit the waters of the Sound, drawing aquaplanes over cataracts of foam. On weekends his Rolls-Royce became an omnibus, bearing parties to and from the city between nine in the morning and long past midnight, while his station wagon scampered like a brisk yellow bug to meet all trains. And on Mondays eight servants, including an extra gardener, toiled all day with mops and scrubbing-brushes and hammers and garden shears, repairing the ravages of the night before.

Every Friday five crates of oranges and lemons arrived from a fruiterer in New York—every Monday these same oranges and lemons left his back door in a pyramid of pulpless halves. There was a machine in the kitchen which could extract the juice of two hundred oranges in half an hour if a little button was pressed two hundred times by a butler's thumb.

At least once a fortnight a corps of caterers came down with several hundred feet of canvas and enough colored lights to make a Christmas tree of Gatsby's enormous garden. On buffet tables, garnished with glistening hors-d'œuvre, spiced baked hams crowded against salads of harlequin designs and pastry pigs and turkeys bewitched to a dark gold. In the main hall a bar with a real brass rail was set up, and stocked with gins and liquors and with cordials so long forgotten that most of his female guests were too young to know one from another.

By seven o'clock the orchestra has arrived, no thin five-piece affair, but a whole pitful of oboes and trombones and saxophones and viols and cornets and piccolos, and low and high drums. The last swimmers have come in from the beach now and are dressing upstairs; the cars from New York are parked five deep in the drive, and already the halls and salons and verandas are gaudy with primary colors, and hair shorn in strange new ways, and shawls beyond the dreams of Castile. The bar is in full swing, and floating rounds of cocktails permeate the garden outside, until the air is alive with chatter and laughter, and casual innuendo and introductions forgotten on the spot, and enthusiastic meetings between women who never knew each other's names.

The lights grow brighter as the earth lurches away from the sun, and now the orchestra is playing yellow cocktail music, and the opera of voices pitches a key higher. Laughter is easier minute by minute, spilled with prodigality, tipped out at a cheerful word. The groups change more swiftly, swell with new arrivals, dissolve and form in the same breath; already there are wanderers, confident girls who weave here and there among the stouter and more stable, become for a sharp, joyous moment the center of a group, and then, excited with triumph, glide on through the sea-change of faces and voices and color under the constantly changing light.

Suddenly one of these gypsies, in trembling opal, seizes a cocktail out of the air, dumps it down for courage and, moving her hands like Frisco, dances out alone on the canvas platform. A momentary hush; the orchestra leader varies his rhythm obligingly for her, and there is a burst of chatter as the erroneous news goes around that she is Gilda Gray's understudy from the Follies. The party has begun.

I believe that on the first night I went to Gatsby's house I was one of the few guests who had actually been invited. People were not invited—they went there. They got into automobiles which bore them out to Long Island, and somehow they ended up at Gatsby's door. Once there they were introduced by somebody who knew Gatsby, and after that they conducted themselves according to the rules of behavior associated with amusement parks. Sometimes they came and went without having met Gatsby at all, came for the party with a simplicity of heart that was its own ticket of admission.

I had been actually invited. A chauffeur in a uniform of robin's-egg blue crossed my lawn early that Saturday morning with a surprisingly formal note from his employer: the honor would be entirely Gatsby's, it said, if I would attend his "little party" that night. He had seen me several times, and had intended to call on me long before, but a peculiar combination of circumstances had prevented it—signed Jay Gatsby, in a majestic hand.

Dressed up in white flannels I went over to his lawn a little after seven, and wandered around rather ill at ease among swirls and eddies of people I didn't know—though here and there was a face I had noticed on the commuting train. I was immediately struck by the number of young Englishmen dotted about; all well-dressed, all looking a little hungry, and all talking in low, earnest voices to solid and prosperous Americans. I was sure that they were selling something: bonds or insurance or automobiles. They were at least agonizingly aware of the easy money in the vicinity and convinced that it was theirs for a few words in the right key.

As soon as I arrived I made an attempt to find my host, but the two or three people of whom I asked his whereabouts stared at me in such an amazed way, and denied so vehemently any knowledge of his movements, that I slunk off in the direction of the cocktail table—the only place in the garden where a single man could linger without looking purposeless and alone.

I was on my way to get roaring drunk from sheer embarrassment when Jordan Baker came out of the house and stood at the head of the marble steps, leaning a little backward and looking with contemptuous interest down into the garden.

Welcome or not, I found it necessary to attach myself to someone before I should begin to address cordial remarks to the passers-by.

"Hello!" I roared, advancing toward her. My voice seemed unnaturally loud across the garden.

"I thought you might be here," she responded absently as I came up. "I remembered you lived next door to——"

She held my hand impersonally, as a promise that she'd take care of me in a minute, and gave ear to two girls in twin yellow dresses, who stopped at the foot of the steps.

"Hello!" they cried together. "Sorry you didn't win."

That was for the golf tournament. She had lost in the finals the week before.

"You don't know who we are," said one of the girls in yellow, "but we met you here about a month ago."

"You've dyed your hair since then," remarked Jordan, and I started, but the girls had moved casually on and her remark was addressed to the premature moon, produced like the supper, no doubt, out of a caterer's basket. With Jordan's slender golden arm resting in mine, we descended the steps and sauntered about the garden. A tray of cocktails floated at us through the twilight, and we sat down at a table with the two girls in yellow and three men, each one introduced to us as Mr. Mumble.

"Do you come to these parties often?" inquired Jordan of the girl beside her.

"The last one was the one I met you at," answered the girl, in an alert confident voice. She turned to her companion: "Wasn't it for you, Lucille?"

It was for Lucille, too.

"I like to come," Lucille said. "I never care what I do, so I always have a good time. When I was here last I tore my gown on a chair, and he asked me my name and address—inside of a week I got a package from Croirier's with a new evening gown in it."

"Did you keep it?" asked Jordan.

"Sure I did. I was going to wear it tonight, but it was too big in the bust and had to be altered. It was gas blue with lavender beads. Two hundred and sixty-five dollars."

"There's something funny about a fellow that'll do a thing like that," said the other girl eagerly. "He doesn't want any trouble with *any*body."

"Who doesn't?" I inquired.

"Gatsby. Somebody told me——"

The two girls and Jordan leaned together confidentially.

"Somebody told me they thought he killed a man once."

A thrill passed over all of us. The three Mr. Mumbles bent forward and listened eagerly.

"I don't think it's so much *that*," argued Lucille skeptically; "it's more that he was a German spy during the war."

One of the men nodded in confirmation.

"I heard that from a man who knew all about him, grew up with him in Germany," he assured us positively.

"Oh, no," said the first girl, "it couldn't be that, because he was in the American army during the war." As our credulity switched back to her she leaned forward with enthusiasm. "You look at him sometime when he thinks nobody's looking at him. I'll bet he killed a man."

She narrowed her eyes and shivered. Lucille shivered. We all turned and looked around for Gatsby. It was testimony to the romantic speculation he inspired that there were whispers about him from those who had found little that it was necessary to whisper about in this world.

The first supper—there would be another one after midnight—was now being served, and Jordan invited me to join her own party, who were spread around a table on the other side of the garden. There were three married couples and Jordan's escort, a persistent undergraduate given to violent innuendo, and obviously under the impression that sooner or later Jordan was going to yield him up her person to a greater or lesser degree. Instead of rambling this party had preserved a dignified homogeneity, and assumed to itself the function of representing the staid nobility of the country-side—East Egg condescending to West Egg, and carefully on guard against its spectroscopic gayety.

"Let's get out," whispered Jordan, after a somehow wasteful and inappropriate half hour; "this is much too polite for me."

We got up, and she explained that we were going to find the host: I had never met him, she said, and it was making me uneasy. The undergraduate nodded in a cynical, melancholy way.

The bar, where we glanced first, was crowded, but Gatsby was not there. She couldn't find him from the top of the steps, and he wasn't on the veranda. On a chance we tried an important-looking door, and walked into a high Gothic library, panelled with carved English oak, and probably transported complete from some ruin overseas.

A stout, middle-aged man, with enormous owl-eyed spectacles, was sitting somewhat drunk on the edge of a great table, staring with unsteady concentration at the shelves of books. As we entered he wheeled excitedly around and examined Jordan from head to foot.

"What do you think?" he demanded impetuously.

"About what?"

He waved his hand toward the bookshelves.

"About that. As a matter of fact you needn't bother to ascertain. I ascertained. They're real."

"The books?"

He nodded.

"Absolutely real—have pages and everything. I thought they'd be a nice durable cardboard. Matter of fact, they're absolutely real. Pages and— Here! Lemme show you."

Taking our skepticism for granted, he rushed to the bookcases and returned with Volume One of the "Stoddard Lectures."

"See!" he cried triumphantly. "It's a bona-fide piece of printed matter. It fooled me. This fella's a regular Belasco. It's a triumph. What thoroughness! What realism! Knew when to stop, too—didn't cut the pages. But what do you want? What do you expect?"

He snatched the book from me and replaced it hastily on its shelf, muttering that if one brick was removed the whole library was liable to collapse.

"Who brought you?" he demanded. "Or did you just come? I was brought. Most people were brought."

Jordan looked at him alertly, cheerfully, without answering.

"I was brought by a woman named Roosevelt," he continued. "Mrs. Claud Roosevelt. Do you know her? I met her somewhere last night. I've been drunk for about a week now, and I thought it might sober me up to sit in a library."

"Has it?"

"A little bit, I think. I can't tell yet. I've only been here an hour. Did I tell you about the books? They're real. They're——"

"You told us."

We shook hands with him gravely and went back outdoors.

There was dancing now on the canvas in the garden; old men pushing young girls backward in eternal graceless circles, superior couples holding each other tortuously, fashionably, and keeping in the corners—and a great number of single girls dancing individualistically or relieving the orchestra for a moment of the burden of the banjo or the traps. By midnight the hilarity had increased. A celebrated tenor had sung in Italian, and a notorious contralto had sung in jazz, and between the numbers people were doing "stunts" all over the garden, while happy, vacuous bursts of laughter rose toward the summer sky. A pair of stage twins, who turned out to be the girls in yellow, did a baby act in costume, and champagne was served in glasses bigger than finger-bowls. The moon had risen higher, and floating in the Sound was a triangle of silver scales, trembling a little to the stiff, tinny drip of the banjoes on the lawn.

I was still with Jordan Baker. We were sitting at a table with a man of about my age and a rowdy little girl, who gave way upon the slightest provocation to uncontrollable laughter. I was enjoying myself now. I had taken two finger-bowls of champagne, and the scene had changed before my eyes into something significant, elemental, and profound.

At a lull in the entertainment the man looked at me and smiled.

"Your face is familiar," he said, politely. "Weren't you in the Third Division during the war?"

"Why, yes. I was in the Ninth Machine-Gun Battalion."

"I was in the Seventh Infantry until June nineteen-eighteen. I knew I'd seen you somewhere before."

We talked for a moment about some wet, gray little villages in France. Evidently he lived in this vicinity, for he told me that he had just bought a hydroplane, and was going to try it out in the morning.

"Want to go with me, old sport? Just near the shore along the Sound."

"What time?"

"Any time that suits you best."

It was on the tip of my tongue to ask his name when Jordan looked around and smiled.

"Having a gay time now?" she inquired.

"Much better." I turned again to my new acquaintance. "This is an unusual party for me. I haven't even seen the host. I live over there—" I waved my hand at the invisible hedge in the distance, "and this man Gatsby sent over his chauffeur with an invitation."

For a moment he looked at me as if he failed to understand.

"I'm Gatsby," he said suddenly.

"What!" I exclaimed. "Oh, I beg your pardon."

"I thought you knew, old sport. I'm afraid I'm not a very good host."

He smiled understandingly—much more than understandingly. It was one of those rare smiles with a quality of eternal reassurance in it, that you may come across four or five times in life. It faced—or seemed to face—the whole external world for an instant, and then concentrated on *you* with an irresistible prejudice in your favor. It understood you just so far as you wanted to be understood, believed in you as you would like to believe in yourself, and assured you that it had precisely the impression of you that, at your best, you hoped to convey. Precisely at that point it vanished—and I was looking at an elegant young rough-neck, a year or two over thirty, whose elaborate formality of speech just missed being absurd. Sometime before he introduced himself I'd got a strong impression that he was picking his words with care.

Almost at the moment when Mr. Gatsby identified himself a butler hurried toward him with the information that Chicago was calling him on the wire. He excused himself with a small bow that included each of us in turn.

"If you want anything just ask for it, old sport," he urged me. "Excuse me. I will rejoin you later."

When he was gone I turned immediately to Jordan—constrained to assure her of my surprise. I had expected that Mr. Gatsby would be a florid and corpulent person in his middle years.

"Who is he?" I demanded. "Do you know?"

"He's just a man named Gatsby."

"Where is he from, I mean? And what does he do?"

"Now *you're* started on the subject," she answered with a wan smile. "Well, he told me once he was an Oxford man."

A dim background started to take shape behind him, but at her next remark it faded away.

"However, I don't believe it."

"Why not?"

"I don't know," she insisted. "I just don't think he went there."

Something in her tone reminded me of the other girl's "I think he killed a man," and had the effect of stimulating my curiosity. I would have accepted without question the information that Gatsby sprang from the swamps of Louisiana or from the Lower East Side of New York. That was comprehensible. But young men didn't—at least in my provincial inexperience I believed they didn't—drift coolly out of nowhere and buy a palace on Long Island Sound.

"Anyhow, he gives large parties," said Jordan, changing the subject with an urban distaste for the concrete. "And I like large parties. They're so intimate. At small parties there isn't any privacy."

There was the boom of a bass drum, and the voice of the orchestra leader rang out suddenly above the echolalia of the garden.

"Ladies and gentlemen," he cried. "At the request of Mr. Gatsby we are going to play for you Mr. Vladimir Tostoff's latest work, which attracted so much attention at Carnegie Hall last May. If you read the papers you know there was a big sensation." He smiled with jovial condescension, and added: "Some sensation!" Whereupon everybody laughed.

"The piece is known," he concluded lustily, "as 'Vladimir Tostoff's Jazz History of the World.'"

The nature of Mr. Tostoff's composition eluded me, because just as it began my eyes fell on Gatsby, standing alone on the marble steps and looking from one group to another with approving eyes. His tanned skin was drawn attractively tight on his face and his short hair looked as though it were trimmed every day. I could see nothing sinister about him. I wondered if the fact that he was not drinking helped to set him off from his guests, for it seemed to me that he grew more correct as the fraternal hilarity increased. When the "Jazz History of the World" was over, girls were putting their heads on men's shoulders in a puppyish, convivial way, girls were swooning backward playfully into men's arms, even into groups, knowing that someone would arrest their falls—but no one swooned backward on Gatsby, and no French bob touched Gatsby's shoulder, and no singing quartets were formed with Gatsby's head for one link.

"I beg your pardon."

Gatsby's butler was suddenly standing beside us.

"Miss Baker?" he inquired. "I beg your pardon, but Mr. Gatsby would like to speak to you alone."

"With me?" she exclaimed in surprise.

"Yes, madame."

She got up slowly, raising her eyebrows at me in astonishment, and followed the butler toward the house. I noticed that she wore her evening-dress, all her dresses, like sports clothes—there was a jauntiness about her movements as if she had first learned to walk upon golf courses on clean, crisp mornings.

I was alone and it was almost two. For some time confused and intriguing sounds had issued from a long, many-windowed room which overhung the terrace. Eluding Jordan's undergraduate, who was now engaged in an obstetrical conversation with two chorus girls, and who implored me to join him, I went inside.

The large room was full of people. One of the girls in yellow was playing the piano, and beside her stood a tall, red-haired young lady from a famous chorus, engaged in song. She had drunk a quantity of champagne, and during the course of her song she had decided, ineptly, that everything was very, very sad—she was not only singing, she was weeping too. Whenever there was a pause in the song she filled it with gasping, broken sobs, and then took up the lyric again in a quavering soprano. The tears coursed down her cheeks—not freely, however, for when they came into contact with her heavily beaded eyelashes they assumed an inky color, and pursued the rest of their way in slow black rivulets. A humorous suggestion was made that she sing the notes on her face, whereupon she threw up her hands, sank into a chair, and went off into a deep vinous sleep.

"She had a fight with a man who says he's her husband," explained a girl at my elbow.

I looked around. Most of the remaining women were now having fights with men said to be their husbands. Even Jordan's party, the quartet from East Egg, were rent asunder by dissension. One of the men was talking with curious intensity to a young actress, and his wife, after attempting to laugh at the situation in a dignified and indifferent way, broke down entirely and resorted to flank attacks—at intervals she appeared suddenly at his side like an angry diamond, and hissed: "You promised!" into his ear.

The reluctance to go home was not confined to wayward men. The hall was at present occupied by two deplorably sober men and their highly indignant wives. The wives were sympathizing with each other in slightly raised voices.

"Whenever he sees I'm having a good time he wants to go home."

"Never heard anything so selfish in my life."

"We're always the first ones to leave."

"So are we."

"Well, we're almost the last tonight," said one of the men sheepishly. "The orchestra left half an hour ago."

In spite of the wives' agreement that such malevolence was beyond credibility, the dispute ended in a short struggle, and both wives were lifted, kicking, into the night.

As I waited for my hat in the hall the door of the library opened and Jordan Baker and Gatsby came out together. He was saying some last word to her, but the eagerness in his manner tightened abruptly into formality as several people approached him to say good-by.

Jordan's party were calling impatiently to her from the porch, but she lingered for a moment to shake hands.

"I've just heard the most amazing thing," she whispered. "How long were we in there?"

"Why, about an hour."

"It was . . . simply amazing," she repeated abstractedly. "But I swore I wouldn't tell it and here I am tantalizing you." She yawned gracefully in my face. "Please come and see me. . . . Phone book. . . . Under the name of Mrs. Sigourney Howard. . . . My aunt. . . ." She was hurrying off as she talked—her brown hand waved a jaunty salute as she melted into her party at the door.

Rather ashamed that on my first appearance I had stayed so late, I joined the last of Gatsby's guests, who were clustered around him. I wanted to explain that I'd hunted for him early in the evening and to apologize for not having known him in the garden.

"Don't mention it," he enjoined me eagerly. "Don't give it another thought, old sport." The familiar expression held no more familiarity than the hand which reassuringly brushed my shoulder. "And don't forget we're going up in the hydroplane tomorrow morning, at nine o'clock."

Then the butler, behind his shoulder:

"Philadelphia wants you on the phone, sir."

"All right, in a minute. Tell them I'll be right there. . . . Good night."

"Good night."

"Good night." He smiled—and suddenly there seemed to be a pleasant significance in having been among the last to go, as if he had desired it all the time. "Good night, old sport. . . . Good night."

But as I walked down the steps I saw that the evening was not quite over. Fifty feet from the door a dozen headlights illuminated a bizarre and tumultuous scene. In the ditch beside the road, right side up, but violently shorn of one wheel, rested a new coupé which had left Gatsby's drive not two minutes before. The sharp jut of a wall accounted for the detachment of the wheel, which was now getting considerable attention from half a dozen curious chauffeurs. However, as they had left their cars blocking the road, a harsh, discordant din from those in the rear had been audible for some time, and added to the already violent confusion of the scene.

A man in a long duster had dismounted from the wreck and now stood in the middle of the road, looking from the car to the tire and from the tire to the observers in a pleasant, puzzled way.

"See!" he explained. "It went in the ditch."

The fact was infinitely astonishing to him, and I recognized first the unusual quality of wonder, and then the man—it was the late patron of Gatsby's library.

"How'd it happen?"

He shrugged his shoulders.

"I know nothing whatever about mechanics," he said decisively.

"But how did it happen? Did you run into the wall?"

"Don't ask me," said Owl Eyes, washing his hands of the whole matter. "I know very little about driving—next to nothing. It happened, and that's all I know."

"Well, if you're a poor driver you oughtn't to try driving at night."

"But I wasn't even trying," he explained indignantly. "I wasn't even trying."

An awed hush fell upon the bystanders.

"Do you want to commit suicide?"

"You're lucky it was just a wheel! A bad driver and not even *try*ing!"

"You don't understand," explained the criminal. "I wasn't driving. There's another man in the car."

The shock that followed this declaration found voice in a sustained "Ah-h-h!" as the door of the coupé swung slowly open. The crowd—it was now a crowd—stepped back involuntarily, and when the door had opened wide there was a ghostly pause. Then, very gradually, part by part, a pale, dangling individual stepped out of the wreck, pawing tentatively at the ground with a large uncertain dancing shoe.

Blinded by the glare of the headlights and confused by the incessant groaning of the horns, the apparition stood swaying for a moment before he perceived the man in the duster.

"Wha's matter?" he inquired calmly. "Did we run outa gas?"

"Look!"

Half a dozen fingers pointed at the amputated wheel—he stared at it for a moment, and then looked upward as though he suspected that it had dropped from the sky.

"It came off," someone explained.

He nodded.

"At first I din' notice we'd stopped."

A pause. Then, taking a long breath and straightening his shoulders, he remarked in a determined voice:

"Wonder'ff tell me where there's a gas'line station?"

At least a dozen men, some of them little better off than he was, explained to him that wheel and car were no longer joined by any physical bond.

"Back out," he suggested after a moment. "Put her in reverse."

"But the *wheel's* off!"

He hesitated.

"No harm in trying," he said.

The caterwauling horns had reached a crescendo and I turned away and cut across the lawn toward home. I glanced back once. A wafer of a moon was shining over Gatsby's house, making the night fine as before, and surviving the laughter and the sound of his still glowing garden. A sudden emptiness seemed to flow now from the windows and the great doors, endowing with complete isolation the figure of the host, who stood on the porch, his hand up in a formal gesture of farewell.

Reading over what I have written so far, I see I have given the impression that the events of three nights several weeks apart were all that absorbed me. On the contrary, they were merely casual events in a crowded summer, and, until much later, they absorbed me infinitely less than my personal affairs.

Most of the time I worked. In the early morning the sun threw my shadow westward as I hurried down the white chasms of lower New York to the Probity Trust. I knew the other clerks and young bond-salesmen by their first names, and lunched with them in dark, crowded restaurants on little pig sausages and mashed potatoes and coffee. I even had a short affair with a girl who lived in Jersey City and worked in the accounting department, but her brother began throwing mean looks in my direction, so when she went on her vacation in July I let it blow quietly away.

I took dinner usually at the Yale Club—for some reason it was the gloomiest event of my day—and then I went upstairs to the library and studied investments and securities for a conscientious hour. There were generally a few rioters around, but they never came into the library, so it was a good place to work. After that, if the night was mellow, I strolled down Madison Avenue past the old Murray Hill Hotel, and over Thirty-third Street to the Pennsylvania Station.

I began to like New York, the racy, adventurous feel of it at night, and the satisfaction that the constant flicker of men and women and machines gives to the restless eye. I liked to walk up Fifth Avenue and pick out romantic women from the crowd and imagine that in a few minutes I was going to enter into their lives, and no one would ever know or disapprove. Sometimes, in my mind, I followed them to their apartments on the corners of hidden streets, and they turned and smiled back at me before they faded through a door into warm darkness. At the enchanted metropolitan twilight I felt a haunting loneliness sometimes, and felt it in others—poor young clerks who loitered in front of windows waiting until it was time for a solitary restaurant dinner—young clerks in the dusk, wasting the most poignant moments of night and life.

Again at eight o'clock, when the dark lanes of the Forties were five deep with throbbing taxi cabs, bound for the theatre district, I felt a sinking in my heart. Forms leaned together in the taxis as they waited, and voices sang, and there was laughter from unheard jokes, and lighted cigarettes outlined unintelligible gestures inside. Imagining that I, too, was hurrying toward gayety and sharing their intimate excitement, I wished them well.

For a while I lost sight of Jordan Baker, and then in midsummer I found her again. At first I was flattered to go places with her, because she was a golf champion, and everyone knew her name. Then it was something more. I wasn't actually in love, but I felt a sort of tender curiosity. The bored haughty face that she turned to the world concealed something—most affectations conceal something eventually, even though they don't in the beginning—and one day I found what it was. When we were on a house-party together up in Warwick, she left a borrowed car out in the rain with the top down, and then lied about it—and suddenly I remembered the story about her that had eluded me that night at Daisy's. At her first big golf tournament there was a row that nearly reached the newspapers—a suggestion that she had moved her ball from a bad lie in the semi-final round. The thing approached the proportions of a scandal—then died away. A caddy retracted his statement, and the only other witness admitted that he might have been mistaken. The incident and the name had remained together in my mind.

Jordan Baker instinctively avoided clever, shrewd men, and now I saw that this was because she felt safer on a plane where any divergence from a code would be thought impossible. She was incurably dishonest. She wasn't able to endure being at a disadvantage and, given this unwillingness, I suppose she had begun dealing in subterfuges when she was very young in order to keep that cool, insolent smile turned to the world and yet satisfy the demands of her hard, jaunty body.

It made no difference to me. Dishonesty in a woman is a thing you never blame deeply—I was casually sorry, and then I forgot. It was on that same house-party that we had a curious conversation about driving a car. It started because she passed so close to some workmen that our fender flicked a button on one man's coat.

"You're a rotten driver," I protested. "Either you ought to be more careful, or you oughtn't to drive at all."

"I am careful."

"No, you're not."

"Well, other people are," she said lightly.

"What's that got to do with it?"

"They'll keep out of my way," she insisted. "It takes two to make an accident."

"Suppose you met somebody just as careless as yourself."

"I hope I never will," she answered. "I hate careless people. That's why I like you."

Her gray, sun-strained eyes stared straight ahead, but she had deliberately shifted our relations, and for a moment I thought I loved her. But I am slow-thinking and full of interior rules that act as brakes on my desires, and I knew that first I had to get myself definitely out of that tangle back home. I'd been writing letters once a week and signing them: "Love, Nick," and all I could think of was how, when that certain girl played tennis, a faint mustache of perspiration appeared on her upper lip. Nevertheless there was a vague understanding that had to be tactfully broken off before I was free.

Everyone suspects himself of at least one of the cardinal virtues, and this is mine: I am one of the few honest people that I have ever known.

Chapter IV

O N Sunday morning while church bells rang in the villages alongshore, the world and its mistress returned to Gatsby's house and twinkled hilariously on his lawn.

"He's a bootlegger," said the young ladies, moving somewhere between his cocktails and his flowers. "One time he killed a man who had found out that he was nephew to Von Hindenburg and second cousin to the devil. Reach me a rose, honey, and pour me a last drop into that there crystal glass."

Once I wrote down on the empty spaces of a time-table the names of those who came to Gatsby's house that summer. It is an old time-table now, disintegrating at its folds, and headed "This schedule in effect July 5th, 1922." But I can still read the gray names, and they will give you a better impression than my generalities of those who accepted Gatsby's hospitality and paid him the subtle tribute of knowing nothing whatever about him.

From East Egg, then, came the Chester Beckers and the Leeches, and a man named Bunsen, whom I knew at Yale, and Doctor Webster Civet, who was drowned last summer up in Maine. And the Hornbeams and the Willie Voltaires, and a whole clan named Blackbuck, who always gathered in a corner and flipped up their noses like goats at whosoever came near. And the Ismays and the Chrysties (or rather Hubert Auerbach and Mr. Chrystie's wife), and Edgar Beaver, whose hair, they say, turned cotton-white one winter afternoon for no good reason at all.

Clarence Endive was from East Egg, as I remember. He came only once, in white knickerbockers, and had a fight with a bum named Etty in the garden. From farther out on the Island came the Cheadles and the O. R. P. Schraeders, and the Stonewall Jackson Abrams of Georgia, and the Fishguards and the Ripley Snells. Snell was there three days before he went to the penitentiary, so drunk out on the gravel drive that Mrs. Ulysses Swett's automobile ran over his right hand. The Dancies came, too, and S. B. Whitebait, who was well over sixty, and Maurice A. Flink, and the Hammerheads, and Beluga the tobacco importer, and Beluga's girls.

From West Egg came the Poles and the Mulreadys and Cecil Roebuck and Cecil Schoen and Gulick the state senator and Newton Orchid, who controlled Films Par Excellence, and Eckhaust and Clyde Cohen and Don S. Schwartze (the son) and Arthur McCarty, all connected with the movies in one way or another. And the Catlips and the Bembergs and G. Earl Muldoon, brother to that Muldoon who afterward strangled his wife. Da Fontano the promoter came there, and Ed Legros and James B. ("Rot-Gut") Ferret and the De Jongs and Ernest Lilly—they came to gamble, and when Ferret wandered into the garden it meant he was cleaned out and Associated Traction would have to fluctuate profitably next day.

A man named Klipspringer was there so often and so long that he became known as "the boarder"—I doubt if he had any other home. Of theatrical people there were Gus Waize and Horace O'Donavan and Lester Myer and George Duckweed and Francis Bull. Also from New York were the Chromes and the Backhyssons and the Dennickers and Russel Betty and the Corrigans and the Kellehers and the Dewars and the Scullys and S. W. Belcher and the Smirkes and the young Quinns, divorced now, and Henry L. Palmetto, who killed himself by jumping in front of a subway train in Times Square.

Benny McClenahan arrived always with four girls. They were never quite the same ones in physical person, but they were so identical one with another that it inevitably seemed they had been there before. I have forgotten their names—Jaqueline, I think, or else Consuela, or Gloria or Judy or June, and their last names were either the melodious names of flowers and months or the sterner ones of the great American capitalists whose cousins, if pressed, they would confess themselves to be.

In addition to all these I can remember that Faustina O'Brien came there at least once and the Baedeker girls and young Brewer, who had his nose shot off in the war, and Mr. Albrucksburger and Miss Haag, his fiancée, and Ardita Fitz-Peters and Mr. P. Jewett, once head of the American Legion, and Miss Claudia Hip, with a man reputed to be her chauffeur, and a prince of something, whom we called Duke, and whose name, if I ever knew it, I have forgotten.

All these people came to Gatsby's house in the summer.

*

At nine o'clock, one morning late in July, Gatsby's gorgeous car lurched up the rocky drive to my door and gave out a burst of melody from its three-noted horn. It was the first time he had called on me, though I had gone to two of his parties, mounted in his hydroplane, and, at his urgent invitation, made frequent use of his beach.

"Good morning, old sport. You're having lunch with me today and I thought we'd ride up together."

He was balancing himself on the dashboard of his car with that resourcefulness of movement that is so peculiarly American— that comes, I suppose, with the absence of lifting work or rigid sitting in youth and, even more, with the formless grace of our nervous, sporadic games. This quality was continually breaking through his punctilious manner in the shape of restlessness. He was never quite still; there was always a tapping foot somewhere or the impatient opening and closing of a hand.

He saw me looking with admiration at his car.

"It's pretty, isn't it, old sport?" He jumped off to give me a better view. "Haven't you ever seen it before?"

I'd seen it. Everybody had seen it. It was a rich cream color, bright with nickel, swollen here and there in its monstrous length with triumphant hat-boxes and supper-boxes and tool-boxes, and terraced with a labyrinth of wind-shields that mirrored a dozen suns. Sitting down behind many layers of glass in a sort of green leather conservatory, we started to town.

I had talked with him perhaps half a dozen times in the past month and found, to my disappointment, that he had little to say. So my first impression, that he was a person of some undefined consequence, had gradually faded and he had become simply the proprietor of an elaborate roadhouse next door.

And then came that disconcerting ride. We hadn't reached West Egg Village before Gatsby began leaving his elegant sentences unfinished and slapping himself indecisively on the knee of his caramel-colored suit.

"Look here, old sport," he broke out surprisingly. "What's your opinion of me, anyhow?"

A little overwhelmed, I began the generalized evasions which that question deserves.

"Well, I'm going to tell you something about my life," he interrupted. "I don't want you to get a wrong idea of me from all these stories you hear."

So he was aware of the bizarre accusations that flavored conversation in his halls.

"I'll tell you God's truth." His right hand suddenly ordered divine retribution to stand by. "I am the son of some wealthy people in the Middle West—all dead now. I was brought up in America but educated at Oxford, because all my ancestors have been educated there for many years. It is a family tradition."

He looked at me sideways—and I knew why Jordan Baker had believed he was lying. He hurried the phrase "educated at Oxford," or swallowed it, or choked on it, as though it had bothered him before. And with this doubt, his whole statement fell to pieces, and I wondered if there wasn't something a little sinister about him, after all.

"What part of the Middle West?" I inquired casually.

"San Francisco."

"I see."

"My family all died and I came into a good deal of money."

His voice was solemn, as if the memory of that sudden extinction of a clan still haunted him. For a moment I suspected that he was pulling my leg, but a glance at him convinced me otherwise.

"After that I lived like a young rajah in all the capitals of Europe—Paris, Venice, Rome—collecting jewels, chiefly rubies, hunting big game, painting a little, things for myself only, and trying to forget something very sad that had happened to me long ago."

With an effort I managed to restrain my incredulous laughter. The very phrases were worn so threadbare that they evoked no image except that of a turbaned "character" leaking sawdust at every pore as he pursued a tiger through the Bois de Boulogne.

"Then came the war, old sport. It was a great relief, and I tried very hard to die, but I seemed to bear an enchanted life. I accepted a commission as first lieutenant when it began. In the Argonne Forest I took two machine-gun detachments so far forward that there was a half mile gap on either side of us where the infantry couldn't advance. We stayed there two days and two nights, a hundred and thirty men with sixteen Lewis guns, and when the infantry came up at last they found the insignia of three German divisions among the piles of dead. I was promoted to be a major, and every Allied government gave me a decoration—even Montenegro, little Montenegro down on the Adriatic Sea!"

Little Montenegro! He lifted up the words and nodded at them—with his smile. The smile comprehended Montenegro's troubled history and sympathized with the brave struggles of the Montenegrin people. It appreciated fully the chain of national circumstances which had elicited this tribute from Montenegro's warm little heart. My incredulity was submerged in fascination now; it was like skimming hastily through a dozen magazines.

He reached in his pocket, and a piece of metal, slung on a ribbon, fell into my palm.

"That's the one from Montenegro."

To my astonishment, the thing had an authentic look. "Orderi di Danilo," ran the circular legend, "Montenegro, Nicolas Rex."

"Turn it."

"Major Jay Gatsby," I read. "For Valour Extraordinary."

"Here's another thing I always carry. A souvenir of Oxford days. It was taken in Trinity Quad—the man on my left is now the Earl of Doncaster."

It was a photograph of half a dozen young men in blazers loafing in an archway through which were visible a host of spires. There was Gatsby, looking a little, not much, younger—with a cricket bat in his hand.

Then it was all true. I saw the skins of tigers flaming in his palace on the Grand Canal; I saw him opening a chest of rubies to ease, with their crimson-lighted depths, the gnawings of his broken heart.

"I'm going to make a big request of you today," he said, pocketing his souvenirs with satisfaction, "so I thought you ought to know something about me. I didn't want you to think I was just some nobody. You see, I usually find myself among strangers because I drift here and there trying to forget the sad thing that happened to me." He hesitated. "You'll hear about it this afternoon."

"At lunch?"

"No, this afternoon. I happened to find out that you're taking Miss Baker to tea."

"Do you mean you're in love with Miss Baker?"

"No, old sport, I'm not. But Miss Baker has kindly consented to speak to you about this matter."

I hadn't the faintest idea what "this matter" was, but I was more annoyed than interested. I hadn't asked Jordan to tea in order to discuss Mr. Jay Gatsby. I was sure the request would be something utterly fantastic, and for a moment I was sorry I'd ever set foot upon his overpopulated lawn.

He wouldn't say another word. His correctness grew on him as we neared the city. We passed Port Roosevelt, where there was a glimpse of red-belted ocean-going ships, and sped along a cobbled slum lined with the dark, undeserted saloons of the faded-gilt nineteen-hundreds. Then the valley of ashes opened out on both sides of us, and I had a glimpse of Mrs. Wilson straining at the garage pump with panting vitality as we went by.

With fenders spread like wings we scattered light through half Astoria—only half, for as we twisted among the pillars of the elevated I heard the familiar "jug-jug-*spat!*" of a motorcycle, and a frantic policeman rode alongside.

"All right, old sport," called Gatsby. We slowed down. Taking a white card from his wallet, he waved it before the man's eyes.

"Right you are," agreed the policeman, tipping his cap. "Know you next time, Mr. Gatsby. Excuse *me!*"

"What was that?" I inquired. "The picture of Oxford?"

"I was able to do the commissioner a favor once, and he sends me a Christmas card every year."

Over the great bridge, with the sunlight through the girders making a constant flicker upon the moving cars, with the city rising up across the river in white heaps and sugar lumps all built with a wish out of non-olfactory money. The city seen from the Queensboro Bridge is always the city seen for the first time, in its first wild promise of all the mystery and the beauty in the world.

A dead man passed us in a hearse heaped with blooms, followed by two carriages with drawn blinds, and by more cheerful carriages for friends. The friends looked out at us with the tragic eyes and short upper lips of southeastern Europe, and I was glad that the sight of Gatsby's splendid car was included in their somber holiday. As we crossed Blackwell's Island a limousine passed us, driven by a white chauffeur, in which sat three modish negroes, two bucks and a girl. I laughed aloud as the yolks of their eyeballs rolled toward us in haughty rivalry.

"Anything can happen now that we've slid over this bridge," I thought; "anything at all. . . ."

Even Gatsby could happen, without any particular wonder.

Roaring noon. In a well-fanned Forty-second Street cellar I met Gatsby for lunch. Blinking away the brightness of the street outside, my eyes picked him out obscurely in the anteroom, talking to another man.

"Mr. Carraway, this is my friend Mr. Wolfshiem."

A small, flat-nosed Jew raised his large head and regarded me with two fine growths of hair which luxuriated in either nostril. After a moment I discovered his tiny eyes in the half darkness.

"—So I took one look at him," said Mr. Wolfshiem, shaking my hand earnestly, "and what do you think I did?"

"What?" I inquired politely.

But evidently he was not addressing me, for he dropped my hand and covered Gatsby with his expressive nose.

"I handed the money to Katspaugh and I sid: 'All right, Katspaugh, don't pay him a penny till he shuts his mouth.' He shut it then and there."

Gatsby took an arm of each of us and moved forward into the restaurant, whereupon Mr. Wolfshiem swallowed a new sentence he was starting and lapsed into a somnambulatory abstraction.

"Highballs?" asked the head waiter.

"This is a nice restaurant here," said Mr. Wolfshiem, looking at the Presbyterian nymphs on the ceiling. "But I like across the street better!"

"Yes, highballs," agreed Gatsby, and then to Mr. Wolfshiem: "It's too hot over there."

"Hot and small—yes," said Mr. Wolfshiem, "but full of memories."

"What place is that?" I asked Gatsby.

"The old Metropole."

"The old Metropole," brooded Mr. Wolfshiem gloomily. "Filled with faces dead and gone. Filled with friends gone now forever. I can't forget so long as I live the night they shot Rosy Rosenthal there. It was six of us at the table, and Rosy had eat and drunk a lot all evening. When it was almost morning the waiter came up to him with a funny look and says somebody wants to speak to him outside. 'All right,' says Rosy, and begins to get up, and I pulled him down in his chair.

"'Let the bastards come in here if they want you, Rosy, but don't you, so help me, move outside this room.'

"It was four o'clock in the morning then, and if we'd of raised the blinds we'd of seen daylight."

"Did he go?" I asked innocently.

"Sure he went." Mr. Wolfshiem's nose flashed at me indignantly. "He turned around in the door and says: 'Don't let that waiter take away my coffee!' Then he went out on the sidewalk, and they shot him three times in his full belly and drove away."

"Four of them were electrocuted," I said, remembering.

"Five, with Becker." His nostrils turned to me in an interested way. "I understand you're looking for a business gonnegtion."

The juxtaposition of these two remarks was startling. Gatsby answered for me:

"Oh, no," he exclaimed, "this isn't the man."

"No?" Mr. Wolfshiem seemed disappointed.

"This is just a friend. I told you we'd talk about that some other time."

"I beg your pardon," said Mr. Wolfshiem. "I had a wrong man."

A succulent hash arrived, and Mr. Wolfshiem, forgetting the more sentimental atmosphere of the old Metropole, began to eat with ferocious delicacy. His eyes, meanwhile, roved very slowly all around the room—he completed the arc by turning to inspect the people directly behind. I think that, except for my presence, he would have taken one short glance beneath our own table.

"Look here, old sport," said Gatsby, leaning toward me, "I'm afraid I made you a little angry this morning in the car."

There was the smile again, but this time I held out against it.

"I don't like mysteries," I answered, "and I don't understand why you won't come out frankly and tell me what you want. Why has it all got to come through Miss Baker?"

"Oh, it's nothing underhand," he assured me. "Miss Baker's a great sportswoman, you know, and she'd never do anything that wasn't all right."

Suddenly he looked at his watch, jumped up, and hurried from the room, leaving me with Mr. Wolfshiem at the table.

"He has to telephone," said Mr. Wolfshiem, following him with his eyes. "Fine fellow, isn't he? Handsome to look at and a perfect gentleman."

"Yes."

"He's an Oggsford man."

"Oh!"

"He went to Oggsford College in England. You know Oggsford College?"

"I've heard of it."

"It's one of the most famous colleges in the world."

"Have you known Gatsby for a long time?" I inquired.

"Several years," he answered in a gratified way. "I made the pleasure of his acquaintance just after the war. But I knew I had discovered a man of fine breeding after I talked with him an hour. I said to myself: 'There's the kind of man you'd like to take home and introduce to your mother and sister.'" He paused. "I see you're looking at my cuff buttons."

I hadn't been looking at them, but I did now. They were composed of oddly familiar pieces of ivory.

"Finest specimens of human molars," he informed me.

"Well!" I inspected them. "That's a very interesting idea."

"Yeah." He flipped his sleeves up under his coat. "Yeah, Gatsby's very careful about women. He would never so much as look at a friend's wife."

When the subject of this instinctive trust returned to the table and sat down Mr. Wolfshiem drank his coffee with a jerk and got to his feet.

"I have enjoyed my lunch," he said, "and I'm going to run off from you two young men before I outstay my welcome."

"Don't hurry, Meyer," said Gatsby, without enthusiasm. Mr. Wolfshiem raised his hand in a sort of benediction.

"You're very polite, but I belong to another generation," he announced solemnly. "You sit here and discuss your sports and your young ladies and your—" He supplied an imaginary noun with another wave of his hand. "As for me, I am fifty years old, and I won't impose myself on you any longer."

As he shook hands and turned away his tragic nose was trembling. I wondered if I had said anything to offend him.

"He becomes very sentimental sometimes," explained Gatsby. "This is one of his sentimental days. He's quite a character around New York—a denizen of Broadway."

"Who is he, anyhow, an actor?"

"No."

"A dentist?"

"Meyer Wolfshiem? No, he's a gambler." Gatsby hesitated, then added coolly: "He's the man who fixed the World's Series back in 1919."

"Fixed the World's Series?" I repeated.

The idea staggered me. I remembered, of course, that the World's Series had been fixed in 1919, but if I had thought of it at all I would have thought of it as a thing that merely *happened*, the end of some inevitable chain. It never occurred to me that one man could start to play with the faith of fifty million people—with the single-mindedness of a burglar blowing a safe.

"How did he happen to do that?" I asked after a minute.

"He just saw the opportunity."

"Why isn't he in jail?"

"They can't get him, old sport. He's a smart man."

I insisted on paying the check. As the waiter brought my change I caught sight of Tom Buchanan across the crowded room.

"Come along with me for a minute," I said; "I've got to say hello to someone."

When he saw us Tom jumped up and took half a dozen steps in our direction.

"Where've you been?" he demanded eagerly. "Daisy's furious because you haven't called up."

"This is Mr. Gatsby, Mr. Buchanan."

They shook hands briefly, and a strained, unfamiliar look of embarrassment came over Gatsby's face.

"How've you been, anyhow?" demanded Tom of me. "How'd you happen to come up this far to eat?"

"I've been having lunch with Mr. Gatsby."

I turned toward Mr. Gatsby, but he was no longer there.

One October day in nineteen-seventeen——

(said Jordan Baker that afternoon, sitting up very straight on a straight chair in the tea-garden at the Plaza Hotel)

—I was walking along from one place to another, half on the sidewalks and half on the lawns. I was happier on the lawns because I had on shoes from England with rubber nobs on the soles that bit into the soft ground. I had on a new plaid skirt also that blew a little in the wind, and whenever this happened the red, white, and blue banners in front of all the houses stretched out stiff and said *tut-tut-tut-tut,* in a disapproving way.

The largest of the banners and the largest of the lawns belonged to Daisy Fay's house. She was just eighteen, two years older than me, and by far the most popular of all the young girls in Louisville. She dressed in white, and had a little white roadster, and all day long the telephone rang in her house and excited young officers from Camp Taylor demanded the privilege of monopolizing her that night. "Anyways, for an hour!"

When I came opposite her house that morning her white roadster was beside the curb, and she was sitting in it with a lieutenant I had never seen before. They were so engrossed in each other that she didn't see me until I was five feet away.

"Hello, Jordan," she called unexpectedly. "Please come here."

I was flattered that she wanted to speak to me, because of all the older girls I admired her most. She asked me if I was going to the Red Cross and make bandages. I was. Well, then, would I tell them that she couldn't come that day? The officer looked at Daisy while she was speaking, in a way that every young girl wants to be looked at sometime, and because it seemed romantic to me I have remembered the incident ever since. His name was Jay Gatsby, and I didn't lay eyes on him again for over four years—even after I'd met him on Long Island I didn't realize it was the same man.

That was nineteen-seventeen. By the next year I had a few beaux myself, and I began to play in tournaments, so I didn't see Daisy very often. She went with a slightly older crowd—when she went with anyone at all. Wild rumors were circulating about her—how her mother had found her packing her bag one winter night to go to New York and say good-by to a soldier who was going overseas. She was effectually prevented, but she wasn't on speaking terms with her family for several weeks. After that she didn't play around with the soldiers any more, but only with a few flat-footed, short-sighted young men in town, who couldn't get into the army at all.

By the next autumn she was gay again, gay as ever. She had a début after the armistice, and in February she was presumably engaged to a man from New Orleans. In June she married Tom Buchanan of Chicago, with more pomp and circumstance than Louisville ever knew before. He came down with a hundred people in four private cars, and hired a whole floor of the Seelbach Hotel, and the day before the wedding he gave her a string of pearls valued at three hundred and fifty thousand dollars.

I was a bridesmaid. I came into her room half an hour before the bridal dinner, and found her lying on her bed as lovely as the June night in her flowered dress—and as drunk as a monkey. She had a bottle of Sauterne in one hand and a letter in the other.

"'Gratulate me," she muttered. "Never had a drink before, but oh how I do enjoy it."

"What's the matter, Daisy?"

I was scared, I can tell you; I'd never seen a girl like that before.

"Here, deares'." She groped around in a waste-basket she had with her on the bed and pulled out the string of pearls. "Take 'em downstairs and give 'em back to whoever they belong to. Tell 'em all Daisy's change' her mine. Say: 'Daisy's change' her mine!'"

She began to cry—she cried and cried. I rushed out and found her mother's maid, and we locked the door and got her into a cold bath. She wouldn't let go of the letter. She took it into the tub with her and squeezed it up into a wet ball, and only let me leave it in the soap dish when she saw that it was coming to pieces like snow.

But she didn't say another word. We gave her spirits of ammonia and put ice on her forehead and hooked her back into her dress, and half an hour later, when we walked out of the room, the pearls were around her neck and the incident was over. Next day at five o'clock she married Tom Buchanan without so much as a shiver, and started off on a three months' trip to the South Seas.

I saw them in Santa Barbara when they came back, and I thought I'd never seen a girl so mad about her husband. If he left the room for a minute she'd look around uneasily, and say: "Where's Tom gone?" and wear the most abstracted expression until she saw him coming in the door. She used to sit on the sand with his head in her lap by the hour, rubbing her fingers over his eyes and looking at him with unfathomable delight. It was touching to see them together—it made you laugh in a hushed, fascinated way. That was in August. A week after I left Santa Barbara Tom ran into a wagon on the Ventura road one night, and ripped a front wheel off his car. The girl who was with him got into the papers, too, because her arm was broken—she was one of the chambermaids in the Santa Barbara Hotel.

The next April Daisy had her little girl, and they went to France for a year. I saw them one spring in Cannes, and later in Deauville, and then they came back to Chicago to settle down. Daisy was popular in Chicago, as you know. They moved with a fast crowd, all of them young and rich and wild, but she came out with an absolutely perfect reputation. Perhaps because she doesn't drink. It's a great advantage not to drink among hard-drinking people. You can hold your tongue, and, moreover, you can time any little irregularity of your own so that everybody else is so blind that they don't see or care. Perhaps Daisy never went in for amour at all—and yet there's something in that voice of hers. . . .

Well, about six weeks ago, she heard the name Gatsby for the first time in years. It was when I asked you—do you remember?—if you knew Gatsby in West Egg. After you had gone home she came into my room and woke me up, and said: "What Gatsby?" and when I described him—I was half asleep—she said in the strangest voice that it must be the man she used to know. It wasn't until then that I connected this Gatsby with the officer in her white car.

When Jordan Baker had finished telling all this we had left the Plaza for half an hour and were driving in a Victoria through Central Park. The sun had gone down behind the tall apartments of the movie stars in the West Fifties, and the clear voices of children, already gathered like crickets on the grass, rose through the hot twilight:

> "I'm the Sheik of Araby.
> Your love belongs to me.
> At night when you're asleep
> Into your tent I'll creep——"

Chapter VI

ABOUT this time an ambitious young reporter from New York arrived one morning at Gatsby's door and asked him if he had anything to say.

"Anything to say about what?" inquired Gatsby politely.

"Why—any statement to give out."

It transpired after a confused five minutes that the man had heard Gatsby's name around his office in a connection which he either wouldn't reveal or didn't fully understand. This was his day off and with laudable initiative he had hurried out "to see."

It was a random shot, and yet the reporter's instinct was right. Gatsby's notoriety, spread about by the hundreds who had accepted his hospitality and so become authorities upon his past, had increased all summer until he fell just short of being news. Contemporary legends such as the "underground pipe-line to Canada" attached themselves to him, and there was one persistent story that he didn't live in a house at all, but in a boat that looked like a house and was moved secretly up and down the Long Island shore. Just why these inventions were a source of satisfaction to James Gatz of North Dakota isn't easy to say.

James Gatz—that was really, or at least legally, his name. He had changed it at the age of seventeen and at the specific moment that witnessed the beginning of his career—when he saw Dan Cody's yacht drop anchor over the most insidious flat on Lake Superior. It was James Gatz who had been loafing along the beach that afternoon in a torn green jersey and a pair of canvas pants, but it was already Jay Gatsby who borrowed a rowboat, pulled out to the *Tuolomee,* and informed Cody that a wind might catch him and break him up in half an hour.

I suppose he'd had the name ready for a long time, even then. His parents were shiftless and unsuccessful farm people—his imagination had never really accepted them as his parents at all. The truth was that Jay Gatsby of West Egg, Long Island, sprang from his Platonic conception of himself. He was a son of God—a phrase which, if it means anything, means just that—and he must be about His Father's business, the service of a vast, vulgar, and meretricious beauty. So he invented just the sort of Jay Gatsby that a seventeen-year-old boy would be likely to invent, and to this conception he was faithful to the end.

For over a year he had been beating his way along the south shore of Lake Superior as a clam-digger and a salmon-fisher or in any other capacity that brought him food and bed. His brown, hardening body lived naturally through the half fierce, half lazy work of the bracing days. He knew women early, and since they spoiled him he became contemptuous of them, of young virgins because they were ignorant, of the others because they were hysterical about things which in his overwhelming self-absorption he took for granted.

But his heart was in a constant, turbulent riot. The most grotesque and fantastic conceits haunted him in his bed at night. A universe of ineffable gaudiness spun itself out in his brain while the clock ticked on the wash-stand and the moon soaked with wet light his tangled clothes upon the floor. Each night he added to the pattern of his fancies until drowsiness closed down upon some vivid scene with an oblivious embrace. For a while these reveries provided an outlet for his imagination; they were a satisfactory hint of the unreality of reality, a promise that the rock of the world was founded securely on a fairy's wing.

An instinct toward his future glory had led him, some months before, to the small Lutheran college of St. Olaf's in southern Minnesota. He stayed there two weeks, dismayed at its ferocious indifference to the drums of his destiny, to destiny itself, and despising the janitor's work with which he was to pay his way through. Then he drifted back to Lake Superior, and he was still searching for something to do on the day that Dan Cody's yacht dropped anchor in the shallows alongshore.

Cody was fifty years old then, a product of the Nevada silver fields, of the Yukon, of every rush for metal since seventy-five. The transactions in Montana copper that made him many times a millionaire found him physically robust but on the verge of soft-mindedness, and, suspecting this, an infinite number of women tried to separate him from his money. The none too savory ramifications by which Ella Kaye, the newspaper woman, played Madame de Maintenon to his weakness and sent him to sea in a yacht, were common property of the turgid journalism of 1902. He had been coasting along all too hospitable shores for five years when he turned up as James Gatz's destiny in Little Girl Bay.

To young Gatz, resting on his oars and looking up at the railed deck, that yacht represented all the beauty and glamour in the world. I suppose he smiled at Cody—he had probably discovered that people liked him when he smiled. At any rate Cody asked him a few questions (one of them elicited the brand new name) and found that he was quick and extravagantly ambitious. A few days later he took him to Duluth and bought him a blue coat, six pair of white duck trousers, and a yachting cap. And when the *Tuolomee* left for the West Indies and the Barbary Coast, Gatsby left too.

He was employed in a vague personal capacity—while he remained with Cody he was in turn steward, mate, skipper, secretary, and even jailor, for Dan Cody sober knew what lavish doings Dan Cody drunk might soon be about, and he provided for such contingencies by reposing more and more trust in Gatsby. The arrangement lasted five years, during which the boat went three times around the Continent. It might have lasted indefinitely except for the fact that Ella Kaye came on board one night in Boston and a week later Dan Cody inhospitably died.

I remember the portrait of him up in Gatsby's bedroom, a gray, florid man with a hard, empty face—the pioneer debauchee, who during one phase of American life brought back to the Eastern seaboard the savage violence of the frontier brothel and saloon. It was indirectly due to Cody that Gatsby drank so little. Sometimes in the course of gay parties women used to rub champagne into his hair; for himself he formed the habit of letting liquor alone.

And it was from Cody that he inherited money—a legacy of twenty-five thousand dollars. He didn't get it. He never understood the legal device that was used against him, but what remained of the millions went intact to Ella Kaye. He was left with his singularly appropriate education; the vague contour of Jay Gatsby had filled out to the substantiality of a man.

He told me all this very much later, but I've put it down here with the idea of exploding those first wild rumors about his antecedents, which weren't even faintly true. Moreover he told it to me at a time of confusion, when I had reached the point of believing everything and nothing about him. So I take advantage of this short halt, while Gatsby, so to speak, caught his breath, to clear this set of misconceptions away.

It was a halt, too, in my association with his affairs. For several weeks I didn't see him or hear his voice on the phone—mostly I was in New York, trotting around with Jordan and trying to ingratiate myself with her senile aunt—but finally I went over to his house one Sunday afternoon. I hadn't been there two minutes when somebody brought Tom Buchanan in for a drink. I was startled, naturally, but the really surprising thing was that it hadn't happened before.

They were a party of three on horseback—Tom and a man named Sloane and a pretty woman in a brown riding habit, who had been there previously.

"I'm delighted to see you," said Gatsby, standing on his porch. "I'm delighted that you dropped in."

As though they cared!

"Sit right down. Have a cigarette or a cigar." He walked around the room quickly, ringing bells. "I'll have something to drink for you in just a minute."

He was profoundly affected by the fact that Tom was there. But he would be uneasy anyhow until he had given them something, realizing in a vague way that that was all they came for. Mr. Sloane wanted nothing. A lemonade? No, thanks. A little champagne? Nothing at all, thanks. . . . I'm sorry——

"Did you have a nice ride?"

"Very good roads around here."

"I suppose the automobiles——"

"Yeah."

Moved by an irresistible impulse, Gatsby turned to Tom, who had accepted the introduction as a stranger.

"I believe we've met somewhere before, Mr. Buchanan."

"Oh, yes," said Tom, gruffly polite, but obviously not remembering. "So we did. I remember very well."

"About two weeks ago."

"That's right. You were with Nick here."

"I know your wife," continued Gatsby, almost aggressively.

"That so?"

Tom turned to me.

"You live near here, Nick?"

"Next door."

"That so?"

Mr. Sloane didn't enter into the conversation, but lounged back haughtily in his chair; the woman said nothing either—until unexpectedly, after two highballs, she became cordial.

"We'll all come over to your next party, Mr. Gatsby," she suggested. "What do you say?"

"Certainly. I'd be delighted to have you."

"Be ver' nice," said Mr. Sloane, without gratitude. "Well—think ought to be starting home."

"Please don't hurry," Gatsby urged them. He had control of himself now, and he wanted to see more of Tom. "Why don't you—why don't you stay for supper? I wouldn't be surprised if some other people dropped in from New York."

"You come to supper with *me*," said the lady enthusiastically. "Both of you."

This included me. Mr. Sloane got to his feet.

"Come along," he said—but to her only.

"I mean it," she insisted. "I'd love to have you. Lots of room."

Gatsby looked at me questioningly. He wanted to go, and he didn't see that Mr. Sloane had determined he shouldn't.

"I'm afraid I won't be able to," I said.

"Well, you come," she urged, concentrating on Gatsby.

Mr. Sloane murmured something close to her ear.

"We won't be late if we start now," she insisted aloud.

"I haven't got a horse," said Gatsby. "I used to ride in the army, but I've never bought a horse. I'll have to follow you in my car. Excuse me for just a minute."

The rest of us walked out on the porch, where Sloane and the lady began an impassioned conversation aside.

"My God, I believe the man's coming," said Tom. "Doesn't he know she doesn't want him?"

"She says she does want him."

"She has a big dinner party and he won't know a soul there." He frowned. "I wonder where in the devil he met Daisy. By God, I may be old-fashioned in my ideas, but women run around too much these days to suit me. They meet all kinds of crazy fish."

Suddenly Mr. Sloane and the lady walked down the steps and mounted their horses.

"Come on," said Mr. Sloane to Tom. "We're late. We've got to go." And then to me: "Tell him we couldn't wait, will you?"

Tom and I shook hands, the rest of us exchanged a cool nod, and they trotted quickly down the drive, disappearing under the August foliage just as Gatsby, with hat and light overcoat in hand, came out the front door.

Tom was evidently perturbed at Daisy's running around alone, for on the following Saturday night he came with her to Gatsby's party. Perhaps his presence gave the evening its peculiar quality of oppressiveness—it stands out in my memory from Gatsby's other parties that summer. There were the same people, or at least the same sort of people, the same profusion of champagne, the same many-colored, many-keyed commotion, but I felt an unpleasantness in the air, a pervading harshness that hadn't been there before. Or perhaps I had merely grown used to it, grown to accept West Egg as a world complete in itself, with its own standards and its own great figures, second to nothing because it had no consciousness of being so, and now I was looking at it again, through Daisy's eyes. It is invariably saddening to look through new eyes at things upon which you have expended your own powers of adjustment.

They arrived at twilight, and, as we strolled out among the sparkling hundreds, Daisy's voice was playing murmurous tricks in her throat.

"These things excite me so," she whispered. "If you want to kiss me any time during the evening, Nick, just let me know and I'll be glad to arrange it for you. Just mention my name. Or present a green card. I'm giving out green——"

"Look around," suggested Gatsby.

"I'm looking around. I'm having a marvellous——"

"You must see the faces of many people you've heard about."

Tom's arrogant eyes roamed the crowd.

"We don't go around very much," he said. "In fact, I was just thinking I don't know a soul here."

"Perhaps you know that lady." Gatsby indicated a gorgeous, scarcely human orchid of a woman who sat in state under a white-plum tree. Tom and Daisy stared, with that peculiarly unreal feeling that accompanies the recognition of a hitherto ghostly celebrity of the movies.

"She's lovely," said Daisy.

"The man bending over her is her director."

He took them ceremoniously from group to group:

"Mrs. Buchanan . . . and Mr. Buchanan—" After an instant's hesitation he added: "the polo player."

"Oh no," objected Tom quickly, "not me."

But evidently the sound of it pleased Gatsby for Tom remained "the polo player" for the rest of the evening.

"I've never met so many celebrities," Daisy exclaimed. "I liked that man—what was his name?—with the sort of blue nose."

Gatsby identified him, adding that he was a small producer.

"Well, I liked him anyhow."

"I'd a little rather not be the polo player," said Tom pleasantly. "I'd rather look at all these famous people in—in oblivion."

Daisy and Gatsby danced. I remember being surprised by his graceful, conservative fox-trot—I had never seen him dance before. Then they sauntered over to my house and sat on the steps for half an hour, while at her request I remained watchfully in the garden. "In case there's a fire or a flood," she explained, "or any act of God."

Tom appeared from his oblivion as we were sitting down to supper together. "Do you mind if I eat with some people over here?" he said. "A fellow's getting off some funny stuff."

"Go ahead," answered Daisy genially, "and if you want to take down any addresses here's my little gold pencil." . . . She looked around after a moment and told me the girl was "common but pretty," and I knew that except for the half hour she'd been alone with Gatsby she wasn't having a good time.

We were at a particularly tipsy table. That was my fault—Gatsby had been called to the phone, and I'd enjoyed these same people only two weeks before. But what had amused me then turned septic on the air now.

"How do you feel, Miss Baedeker?"

The girl addressed was trying, unsuccessfully, to slump against my shoulder. At this inquiry she sat up and opened her eyes.

"Wha'?"

A massive and lethargic woman, who had been urging Daisy to play golf with her at the local club tomorrow, spoke in Miss Baedeker's defense:

"Oh, she's all right now. When she's had five or six cocktails she always starts screaming like that. I tell her she ought to leave it alone."

"I do leave it alone," affirmed the accused hollowly.

"We heard you yelling, so I said to Doc Civet here: 'There's somebody that needs your help, Doc.'"

"She's much obliged, I'm sure," said another friend, without gratitude, "but you got her dress all wet when you stuck her head in the pool."

"Anything I hate is to get my head stuck in a pool," mumbled Miss Baedeker. "They almost drowned me once over in New Jersey."

"Then you ought to leave it alone," countered Doctor Civet.

"Speak for yourself!" cried Miss Baedeker violently. "Your hand shakes. I wouldn't let you operate on me!"

It was like that. Almost the last thing I remember was standing with Daisy and watching the moving-picture director and his Star. They were still under the white-plum tree and their faces were touching except for a pale, thin ray of moonlight between. It occurred to me that he had been very slowly bending toward her all evening to attain this proximity, and even while I watched I saw him stoop one ultimate degree and kiss at her cheek.

"I like her," said Daisy. "I think she's lovely."

But the rest offended her—and inarguably, because it wasn't a gesture but an emotion. She was appalled by West Egg, this unprecedented "place" that Broadway had begotten upon a Long Island fishing village—appalled by its raw vigor that chafed under the old euphemisms and by the too obtrusive fate that herded its inhabitants along a short-cut from nothing to nothing. She saw something awful in the very simplicity she failed to understand.

I sat on the front steps with them while they waited for their car. It was dark here in front; only the bright door sent ten square feet of light volleying out into the soft black morning. Sometimes a shadow moved against a dressing-room blind above, gave way to another shadow, an indefinite procession of shadows, who rouged and powdered in an invisible glass.

"Who is this Gatsby anyhow?" demanded Tom suddenly. "Some big bootlegger?"

"Where'd you hear that?" I inquired.

"I didn't hear it. I imagined it. A lot of these newly rich people are just big bootleggers, you know."

"Not Gatsby," I said shortly.

He was silent for a moment. The pebbles of the drive crunched under his feet.

"Well, he certainly must have strained himself to get this menagerie together."

A breeze stirred the gray haze of Daisy's fur collar.

"At least they are more interesting than the people we know," she said with an effort.

"You didn't look so interested."

"Well, I was."

Tom laughed and turned to me.

"Did you notice Daisy's face when that girl asked her to put her under a cold shower?"

Daisy began to sing with the music in a husky, rhythmic whisper, bringing out a meaning in each word that it had never had before and would never have again. When the melody rose her voice broke up sweetly, following it, in a way contralto voices have, and each change tipped out a little of her warm human magic upon the air.

"Lots of people come who haven't been invited," she said suddenly. "That girl hadn't been invited. They simply force their way in and he's too polite to object."

"I'd like to know who he is and what he does," insisted Tom. "And I think I'll make a point of finding out."

"I can tell you right now," she answered. "He owned some drug-stores, a lot of drug-stores. He built them up himself."

The dilatory limousine came rolling up the drive.

"Good night, Nick," said Daisy.

Her glance left me and sought the lighted top of the steps, where "Three o'Clock in the Morning," a neat, sad little waltz of that year, was drifting out the open door. After all, in the very casualness of Gatsby's party there were romantic possibilities totally absent from her world. What was it up there in the song that seemed to be calling her back inside? What would happen now in the dim, incalculable hours? Perhaps some unbelievable guest would arrive, a person infinitely rare and to be marvelled at, some authentically radiant young girl who with one fresh glance at Gatsby, one moment of magical encounter, would blot out those five years of unwavering devotion.

I stayed late that night. Gatsby asked me to wait until he was free, and I lingered in the garden until the inevitable swimming party had run up, chilled and exalted, from the black beach, until the lights were extinguished in the guest-rooms overhead. When he came down the steps at last the tanned skin was drawn unusually tight on his face, and his eyes were bright and tired.

"She didn't like it," he said immediately.

"Of course she did."

"She didn't like it," he insisted. "She didn't have a good time."

He was silent, and I guessed at his unutterable depression.

"I feel far away from her," he said. "It's hard to make her understand."

"You mean about the dance?"

"The dance?" He dismissed all the dances he had given with a snap of his fingers. "Old sport, the dance is unimportant."

He wanted nothing less of Daisy than that she should go to Tom and say: "I never loved you." After she had obliterated four years with that sentence they could decide upon the more practical measures to be taken. One of them was that, after she was free, they were to go back to Louisville and be married from her house—just as if it were five years ago.

"And she doesn't understand," he said. "She used to be able to understand. We'd sit for hours——"

He broke off and began to walk up and down a desolate path of fruit rinds and discarded favors and crushed flowers.

"I wouldn't ask too much of her," I ventured. "You can't repeat the past."

"Can't repeat the past?" he cried incredulously. "Why of course you can!"

He looked around him wildly, as if the past were lurking here in the shadow of his house, just out of reach of his hand.

"I'm going to fix everything just the way it was before," he said, nodding determinedly. "She'll see."

He talked a lot about the past, and I gathered that he wanted to recover something, some idea of himself perhaps, that had gone into loving Daisy. His life had been confused and disordered since then, but if he could once return to a certain starting place and go over it all slowly, he could find out what that thing was. . . .

. . . One autumn night, five years before, they had been walking down the street when the leaves were falling, and they came to a place where there were no trees and the sidewalk was white with moonlight. They stopped here and turned toward each other. Now it was a cool night with that mysterious excitement in it which comes at the two changes of the year. The quiet lights in the houses were humming out into the darkness and there was a stir and bustle among the stars. Out of the corner of his eye Gatsby saw that the blocks of the sidewalks really formed a ladder and mounted to a secret place above the trees—he could climb to it, if he climbed alone, and once there he could suck on the pap of life, gulp down the incomparable milk of wonder.

His heart beat faster and faster as Daisy's white face came up to his own. He knew that when he kissed this girl, and forever wed his unutterable visions to her perishable breath, his mind would never romp again like the mind of God. So he waited, listening for a moment longer to the tuning-fork that had been struck upon a star. Then he kissed her. At his lips' touch she blossomed for him like a flower and the incarnation was complete.

Through all he said, even through his appalling sentimentality, I was reminded of something—an elusive rhythm, a fragment of lost words, that I had heard somewhere a long time ago. For a moment a phrase tried to take shape in my mouth and my lips parted like a dumb man's, as though there was more struggling upon them than a wisp of startled air. But they made no sound, and what I had almost remembered was uncommunicable forever.

Chapter VII

IT was when curiosity about Gatsby was at its highest that the lights in his house failed to go on one Saturday night—and, as obscurely as it had begun, his career as Trimalchio was over. Only gradually did I become aware that the automobiles which turned expectantly into his drive stayed for just a minute and then drove sulkily away. Wondering if he were sick I went over to find out—an unfamiliar butler with a villainous face squinted at me suspiciously from the door.

"Is Mr. Gatsby sick?"

"Nope." After a pause he added "sir" in a dilatory, grudging way.

"I hadn't seen him around, and I was rather worried. Tell him Mr. Carraway came over."

"Who?" he demanded rudely.

"Carraway."

"Carraway. All right, I'll tell him."

Abruptly he slammed the door.

My Finn informed me that Gatsby had dismissed every servant in his house a week ago and replaced them with half a dozen others, who never went into West Egg Village to be bribed by the tradesmen, but ordered moderate supplies over the telephone.

The grocery boy reported that the kitchen looked like a pigsty, and the general opinion in the village was that the new people weren't servants at all.

Next day Gatsby called me on the phone.

"Going away?" I inquired.

"No, old sport."

"I hear you fired all your servants."

"I wanted somebody who wouldn't gossip. Daisy comes over quite often—in the afternoons."

So the whole caravansary had fallen in like a card house at the disapproval in her eyes.

"They're some people Wolfshiem wanted to do something for. They're all brothers and sisters. They used to run a small hotel."

"I see."

He was calling up at Daisy's request—would I come to lunch at her house tomorrow? Miss Baker would be there. Half an hour later Daisy herself telephoned and seemed relieved to find that I was coming. Something was up. And yet I couldn't believe that they would choose this occasion for a scene—especially for the rather harrowing scene that Gatsby had outlined in the garden.

The next day was broiling, almost the last, certainly the warmest, of the summer. As my train emerged from the tunnel into sunlight, only the hot whistles of the National Biscuit Company broke the simmering hush at noon. The straw seats of the car hovered on the edge of combustion; the woman next to me perspired delicately for a while into her white shirtwaist, and then, as her newspaper dampened under her fingers, lapsed despairingly into deep heat with a desolate cry. Her pocket-book slapped to the floor.

"Oh, my!" she gasped.

I picked it up with a weary bend and handed it back to her, holding it at arm's length and by the extreme tip of the corners to indicate that I had no designs upon it—but everyone nearby, including the woman, suspected me just the same.

"Hot!" said the conductor to familiar faces. "Some weather! . . . Hot! . . . Hot! . . . Hot! . . . Is it hot enough for you? Is it hot? Is it . . . ?"

My commutation ticket came back to me with a dark stain from his hand. That anyone should care in this heat whose flushed lips he kissed, whose head made damp the pajama pocket over his heart!

. . . Through the hall of the Buchanans' house blew a faint wind, carrying the sound of the telephone bell out to Gatsby and me as we waited at the door.

"The master's body!" roared the butler into the mouthpiece. "I'm sorry, madame, but we can't furnish it—it's far too hot to touch this noon!"

What he really said was: "Yes . . . Yes . . . I'll see."

He set down the receiver and came toward us, glistening slightly, to take our stiff straw hats.

"Madame expects you in the salon!" he cried, needlessly indicating the direction. In this heat every extra gesture was an affront to the common store of life.

The room, shadowed well with awnings, was dark and cool. Daisy and Jordan lay upon an enormous couch, like silver idols weighing down their own white dresses against the singing breeze of the fans.

"We can't move," they said together.

Jordan's fingers, powdered white over their tan, rested for a moment in mine.

"And Mr. Thomas Buchanan, the athlete?" I inquired.

Simultaneously I heard his voice, gruff, muffled, husky, at the hall telephone.

Gatsby stood in the center of the crimson carpet and gazed around with fascinated eyes. Daisy watched him and laughed, her sweet, exciting laugh; a tiny gust of powder rose from her bosom into the air.

"The rumor is," whispered Jordan, "that that's Tom's girl on the telephone."

We were silent. The voice in the hall rose high with annoyance: "Very well, then, I won't sell you the car at all. . . . I'm under no obligations to you at all . . . and as for your bothering me about it at lunch-time, I won't stand that at all!"

"Holding down the receiver," said Daisy cynically.

"No, he's not," I assured her. "It's a bona-fide deal. I happen to know about it."

Tom flung open the door, blocked out its space for a moment with his thick body, and hurried into the room.

"Mr. Gatsby!" He put out his broad, flat hand with well-concealed dislike. "I'm glad to see you, sir . . . Nick. . . ."

"Make us a cold drink," cried Daisy.

As he left the room again she got up and went over to Gatsby and pulled his face down, kissing him on the mouth.

"You know I love you," she murmured.

"You forget there's a lady present," said Jordan.

Daisy looked around doubtfully.

"You kiss Nick too."

"What a low, vulgar girl!"

"I don't care!" cried Daisy, and began to clog on the brick fireplace. Then she remembered the heat and sat down guiltily on the couch just as a freshly laundered nurse leading a little girl came into the room.

"Bles-sed pre-cious," she crooned, holding out her arms. "Come to your own mother that loves you."

The child, relinquished by the nurse, rushed across the room and rooted shyly into her mother's dress.

"The bles-sed pre-cious! Did mother get powder on your old yellowy hair? Stand up now, and say—How-de-do."

Gatsby and I in turn leaned down and took the small reluctant hand. Afterward he kept looking at the child with surprise. I don't think he had ever really believed in its existence before.

"I got dressed before luncheon," said the child, turning eagerly to Daisy.

"That's because your mother wanted to show you off." Her face bent into the single wrinkle of the small white neck. "You dream, you. You absolute little dream."

"Yes," admitted the child calmly. "Aunt Jordan's got on a white dress too."

"How do you like mother's friends?" Daisy turned her around so that she faced Gatsby. "Do you think they're pretty?"

"Where's Daddy?"

"She doesn't look like her father," explained Daisy. "She looks like me. She's got my hair and shape of the face."

Daisy sat back upon the couch. The nurse took a step forward and held out her hand.

"Come, Pammy."

"Good-by, sweetheart!"

With a reluctant backward glance the well-disciplined child held to her nurse's hand and was pulled out the door, just as Tom came back, preceding four gin rickeys that clicked full of ice.

Gatsby took up his drink.

"They certainly look cool," he said, with visible tension.

We drank in long, greedy swallows.

"I read somewhere that the sun's getting hotter every year," said Tom genially. "It seems that pretty soon the earth's going to fall into the sun—or wait a minute—it's just the opposite—the sun's getting colder every year.

"Come outside," he suggested to Gatsby. "I'd like you to have a look at the place."

I went with them out to the veranda. On the green Sound, stagnant in the heat, one small sail crawled slowly toward the fresher sea. Gatsby's eyes followed it momentarily; he raised his hand and pointed across the bay.

"I'm right across from you."

"So you are."

Our eyes lifted over the rose-beds and the hot lawn and the weedy refuse of the dog-days alongshore. Slowly the white wings of the boat moved against the blue cool limit of the sky. Ahead lay the scalloped ocean and the abounding blessed isles.

"There's sport for you," said Tom, nodding. "I'd like to be out there with him for about an hour."

We had luncheon in the dining-room, darkened too against the heat, and drank down nervous gayety with the cold ale.

"What'll we do with ourselves this afternoon?" cried Daisy. "And the day after that, and the next thirty years?"

"Don't be morbid," Jordan said. "Life starts all over again when it gets crisp in the fall."

"But it's so hot," insisted Daisy, on the verge of tears, "and everything's so confused. Let's all go to town!"

Her voice struggled on through the heat, beating against it, molding its senselessness into forms.

"I've heard of making a garage out of a stable," Tom was saying to Gatsby, "but I'm the first man who ever made a stable out of a garage."

"Who wants to go to town?" demanded Daisy insistently. Gatsby's eyes floated toward her. "Ah," she cried, "you look so cool."

Their eyes met, and they stared together at each other, alone in space. With an effort she glanced down at the table.

"You always look so cool," she repeated.

She had told him that she loved him, and Tom Buchanan saw. He was astounded. His mouth opened a little, and he looked at Gatsby, and then back at Daisy as if he had just recognized her as someone he knew a long time ago.

"You resemble the advertisement of the man," she went on innocently. "You know the advertisement of the man——"

"All right," broke in Tom quickly, "I'm perfectly willing to go to town. Come on—we're all going to town."

He got up, his eyes still flashing between Gatsby and his wife. No one moved.

"Come on!" His temper cracked a little. "What's the matter, anyhow? If we're going to town, let's start."

His hand, trembling with his effort at self-control, bore to his lips the last of his glass of ale. Daisy's voice got us to our feet and out on to the blazing gravel drive.

"Are we just going to go?" she objected. "Like this? Aren't we going to let anyone smoke a cigarette first?"

"Everybody smoked all through lunch."

"Oh, let's have fun," she begged him. "It's too hot to fuss."

He didn't answer.

"Have it your own way," she said. "Come on, Jordan."

They went upstairs to get ready while we three men stood there shuffling the hot pebbles with our feet. A silver curve of the moon hovered already in the western sky. Gatsby started to speak, changed his mind, but not before Tom wheeled and faced him expectantly.

"Pardon me?"

"Have you got your stables here?" asked Gatsby with an effort.

"About a quarter of a mile down the road."

"Oh."

A pause.

"I don't see the idea of going to town," broke out Tom savagely. "Women get these notions in their heads——"

"Shall we take anything to drink?" called Daisy from an upper window.

"I'll get some whiskey," answered Tom. He went inside.

Gatsby turned to me rigidly:

"I can't say anything in his house, old sport."

"She's got an indiscreet voice," I remarked. "It's full of——" I hesitated.

"Her voice is full of money," he said suddenly.

That was it. I'd never understood before. It was full of money—that was the inexhaustible charm that rose and fell in it, the jingle of it, the cymbals' song of it. . . . High in a white palace the king's daughter, the golden girl. . . .

Tom came out of the house wrapping a quart bottle in a towel, followed by Daisy and Jordan wearing small tight hats of metallic cloth and carrying light capes over their arms.

"Shall we all go in my car?" suggested Gatsby. He felt the hot, green leather of the seat. "I ought to have left it in the shade."

"Is it standard shift?" demanded Tom.

"Yes."

"Well, you take my coupé and let me drive your car to town."

The suggestion was distasteful to Gatsby.

"I don't think there's much gas," he objected.

"Plenty of gas," said Tom boisterously. He looked at the gauge. "And if it runs out I can stop at a drug-store. You can buy anything at a drug-store nowadays."

A pause followed this apparently pointless remark. Daisy looked at Tom frowning, and an indefinable expression, at once definitely unfamiliar and vaguely recognizable, as if I had only heard it described in words, passed over Gatsby's face.

"Come on, Daisy," said Tom, pressing her with his hand toward Gatsby's car. "I'll take you in this circus wagon."

He opened the door, but she moved out from the circle of his arm.

"You take Nick and Jordan. We'll follow you in the coupé."

She walked close to Gatsby, touching his coat with her hand. Jordan and Tom and I got into the front seat of Gatsby's car, Tom pushed the unfamiliar gears tentatively, and we shot off into the oppressive heat, leaving them out of sight behind.

"Did you see that?" demanded Tom.

"See what?"

He looked at me keenly, realizing that Jordan and I must have known all along.

"You think I'm pretty dumb, don't you?" he suggested. "Perhaps I am, but I have a—almost a second sight, sometimes, that tells me what to do. Maybe you don't believe that, but science——"

He paused. The immediate contingency overtook him, pulled him back from the edge of the theoretical abyss.

"I've made a small investigation of this fellow," he continued. "I could have gone deeper if I'd known——"

"Do you mean you've been to a medium?" inquired Jordan humorously.

"What?" Confused, he stared at us as we laughed. "A medium?"

"About Gatsby."

"About Gatsby! No, I haven't. I said I'd been making a small investigation of his past."

"And you found he was an Oxford man," said Jordan helpfully.

"An Oxford man!" He was incredulous. "Like hell he is! He wears a pink suit."

"Nevertheless he's an Oxford man."

"Oxford, New Mexico," snorted Tom contemptuously, "or something like that."

"Listen, Tom. If you're such a snob, why did you invite him to lunch?" demanded Jordan crossly.

"Daisy invited him; she knew him before we were married—God knows where!"

We were all irritable now with the fading ale, and aware of it we drove for a while in silence. Then as Doctor T. J. Eckleburg's faded eyes came into sight down the road, I remembered Gatsby's caution about gasoline.

"We've got enough to get us to town," said Tom.

"But there's a garage right here," objected Jordan. "I don't want to get stalled in this baking heat."

Tom threw on both brakes impatiently, and we slid to an abrupt dusty stop under Wilson's sign. After a moment the proprietor emerged from the interior of his establishment and gazed hollow-eyed at the car.

"Let's have some gas!" cried Tom roughly. "What do you think we stopped for—to admire the view?"

"I'm sick," said Wilson without moving. "Been sick all day."

"What's the matter?"

"I'm all run down."

"Well, shall I help myself?" Tom demanded. "You sounded well enough on the phone."

With an effort Wilson left the shade and support of the doorway and, breathing hard, unscrewed the cap of the tank. In the sunlight his face was green.

"I didn't mean to interrupt your lunch," he said. "But I need money pretty bad, and I was wondering what you were going to do with your old car."

"How do you like this one?" inquired Tom. "I bought it last week."

"It's a nice yellow one," said Wilson, as he strained at the handle.

"Like to buy it?"

"Big chance," Wilson smiled faintly. "No, but I could make some money on the other."

"What do you want money for, all of a sudden?"

"I've been here too long. I want to get away. My wife and I want to go West."

"Your wife does!" exclaimed Tom, startled.

"She's been talking about it for ten years." He rested for a moment against the pump, shading his eyes. "And now she's going whether she wants to or not. I'm going to get her away."

The coupé flashed by us with a flurry of dust and the flash of a waving hand.

"What do I owe you?" demanded Tom harshly.

"I just got wised up to something funny the last two days," remarked Wilson. "That's why I want to get away. That's why I been bothering you about the car."

"What do I owe you?"

"Dollar twenty."

The relentless beating heat was beginning to confuse me and I had a bad moment there before I realized that so far his suspicions hadn't alighted on Tom. He had discovered that Myrtle had some sort of life apart from him in another world, and the shock had made him physically sick. I stared at him and then at Tom, who had made a parallel discovery less than an hour before—and it occurred to me that there was no difference between men, in intelligence or race, so profound as the difference between the sick and the well. Wilson was so sick that he looked guilty, unforgivably guilty—as if he had just got some poor girl with child.

"I'll let you have that car," said Tom. "I'll send it over tomorrow afternoon."

That locality was always vaguely disquieting, even in the broad glare of afternoon, and now I turned my head as though I had been warned of something behind. Over the ashheaps the giant eyes of Doctor T. J. Eckleburg kept their vigil, but I perceived, after a moment, that other eyes were regarding us with peculiar intensity from less than twenty feet away.

In one of the windows over the garage the curtains had been moved aside a little, and Myrtle Wilson was peering down at the car. So engrossed was she that she had no consciousness of being observed, and one emotion after another crept into her face like objects into a slowly developing picture. Her expression was curiously familiar—it was an expression I had often seen on women's faces, but on Myrtle Wilson's face it seemed purposeless and inexplicable until I realized that her eyes, wide with jealous terror, were fixed not on Tom, but on Jordan Baker, whom she took to be his wife.

There is no confusion like the confusion of a simple mind, and as we drove away Tom was feeling the hot whips of panic.

His wife and his mistress, until an hour ago secure and inviolate, were slipping precipitately from his control. Instinct made him step on the accelerator with the double purpose of overtaking Daisy and leaving Wilson behind, and we sped along toward Astoria at fifty miles an hour, until, among the spidery girders of the elevated, we came in sight of the easygoing blue coupé.

"Those big movies around Fiftieth Street are cool," suggested Jordan. "I love New York on summer afternoons when everyone's away. There's something very sensuous about it—overripe, as if all sorts of funny fruits were going to fall into your hands."

The word "sensuous" had the effect of further disquieting Tom, but before he could invent a protest the coupé came to a stop, and Daisy signalled us to draw up alongside.

"Where are we going?" she cried.

"How about the movies?"

"It's so hot," she complained. "You go. We'll ride around and meet you after." With an effort her wit rose faintly. "We'll meet you on some corner. I'll be the man smoking two cigarettes."

"We can't argue about it here," Tom said impatiently, as a truck gave out a cursing whistle behind us. "You follow me to the south side of Central Park, in front of the Plaza."

Several times he turned his head and looked back for their car, and if the traffic delayed them he slowed up until they came into sight. I think he was afraid they would dart down a side street and out of his life forever.

But they didn't. And we all took the less explicable step of engaging the parlor of a suite in the Plaza Hotel.

The prolonged and tumultuous argument that ended by herding us into that room eludes me, though I have a sharp physical memory that, in the course of it, my underwear kept climbing like a damp snake around my legs and intermittent beads of sweat raced cool across my back. The notion originated with Daisy's suggestion that we hire five bath-rooms and take cold baths, and then assumed more tangible form as "a place to have a mint julep." Each of us said over and over that it was a "crazy idea"—we all talked at once to a baffled clerk and thought, or pretended to think, that we were being very funny . . .

The room was large and stifling, and, though it was already four o'clock, opening the windows admitted only a gust of hot shrubbery from the Park. Daisy went to the mirror and stood with her back to us, fixing her hair.

"It's a swell suite," whispered Jordan respectfully, and everyone laughed.

"Open another window," commanded Daisy, without turning around.

"There aren't any more."

"Well, we'd better telephone for an axe——"

"The thing to do is to forget about the heat," said Tom impatiently. "You make it ten times worse by crabbing about it."

He unrolled the bottle of whiskey from the towel and put it on the table.

"Why not let her alone, old sport?" remarked Gatsby. "You're the one that wanted to come to town."

There was a moment of silence. The telephone book slipped from its nail and splashed to the floor, whereupon Jordan whispered, "Excuse me"—but this time no one laughed.

"I'll pick it up," I offered.

"I've got it." Gatsby examined the parted string, muttered "Hum!" in an interested way, and tossed the book on a chair.

"That's a great expression of yours, isn't it?" said Tom sharply.

"What is?"

"All this 'old sport' business. Where'd you pick that up?"

"Now see here, Tom," said Daisy, turning around from the mirror, "if you're going to make personal remarks I won't stay here a minute. Call up and order some ice for the mint julep."

As Tom took up the receiver the compressed heat exploded into sound and we were listening to the portentous chords of Mendelssohn's Wedding March from the ballroom below.

"Imagine marrying anybody in this heat!" cried Jordan dismally.

"Still—I was married in the middle of June," Daisy remembered. "Louisville in June! Somebody fainted. Who was it fainted, Tom?"

"Biloxi," he answered shortly.

"A man named Biloxi. 'Blocks' Biloxi, and he made boxes—that's a fact—and he was from Biloxi, Tennessee."

"They carried him into my house," appended Jordan, "because we lived just two doors from the church. And he stayed three weeks, until Daddy told him he had to get out. The day

after he left Daddy died." After a moment she added, as if she
might have sounded irreverent, "There wasn't any connection."

"I used to know a Bill Biloxi from Memphis," I remarked.

"That was his cousin. I knew his whole family history before
he left. He gave me an aluminum putter that I use today."

The music had died down as the ceremony began and now
a long cheer floated in at the window, followed by intermittent cries of "Yea—ea—ea!" and finally by a burst of jazz as the
dancing began.

"We're getting old," said Daisy. "If we were young we'd rise
and dance."

"Remember Biloxi," Jordan warned her. "Where'd you know
him, Tom?"

"Biloxi?" He concentrated with an effort. "I didn't know him.
He was a friend of Daisy's."

"He was not," she denied. "I'd never seen him before. He
came down in the private car."

"Well, he said he knew you. He said he was raised in Louisville. Asa Bird brought him around at the last minute and asked
if we had room for him."

Jordan smiled.

"He was probably bumming his way home. He told me he
was president of your class at Yale."

Tom and I looked at each other blankly.

"Biloxi?"

"First place, we didn't have any president——"

Gatsby's foot beat a short, restless tattoo and Tom eyed him
suddenly.

"By the way, Mr. Gatsby, I understand you're an Oxford
man."

"Not exactly."

"Oh, yes, I understand you went to Oxford."

"Yes—I went there."

A pause. Then Tom's voice, incredulous and insulting:

"You must have gone there about the time Biloxi went to
New Haven."

Another pause. A waiter knocked and came in with crushed
mint and ice but the silence was unbroken by his "thank you"
and the soft closing of the door. This tremendous detail was to
be cleared up at last.

"I told you I went there," said Gatsby.

"I heard you, but I'd like to know when."

"It was in nineteen-nineteen, I only stayed five months. That's why I can't really call myself an Oxford man."

Tom glanced around to see if we mirrored his unbelief. But we were all looking at Gatsby.

"It was an opportunity they gave to some of the officers after the armistice," he continued. "We could go to any of the universities in England or France."

I wanted to get up and slap him on the back. I had one of those renewals of complete faith in him that I'd experienced before.

Daisy rose, smiling faintly, and went to the table.

"Open the whiskey, Tom," she ordered, "and I'll make you a mint julep. Then you won't seem so stupid to yourself. . . . Look at the mint!"

"Wait a minute," snapped Tom. "I want to ask Mr. Gatsby one more question."

"Go on," Gatsby said politely.

"What kind of a row are you trying to cause in my house anyhow?"

They were out in the open at last and Gatsby was content.

"He isn't causing a row." Daisy looked desperately from one to the other. "You're causing a row. Please have a little self-control."

"Self-control!" repeated Tom incredulously. "I suppose the latest thing is to sit back and let Mr. Nobody from Nowhere make love to your wife. Well, if that's the idea you can count me out. . . . Nowadays people begin by sneering at family life and family institutions, and next they'll throw everything overboard and have intermarriage between black and white."

Flushed with his impassioned gibberish, he saw himself standing alone on the last barrier of civilization.

"We're all white here," murmured Jordan.

"I know I'm not very popular. I don't give big parties. I suppose you've got to make your house into a pigsty in order to have any friends—in the modern world."

Angry as I was, as we all were, I was tempted to laugh whenever he opened his mouth. The transition from libertine to prig was so complete.

"I've got something to tell *you*, old sport—" began Gatsby. But Daisy guessed at his intention.

"Please don't!" she interrupted helplessly. "Please let's all go home. Why don't we all go home?"

"That's a good idea." I got up. "Come on, Tom. Nobody wants a drink."

"I want to know what Mr. Gatsby has to tell me."

"Your wife doesn't love you," said Gatsby. "She's never loved you. She loves me."

"You must be crazy!" exclaimed Tom automatically.

Gatsby sprang to his feet, vivid with excitement.

"She never loved you, do you hear?" he cried. "She only married you because I was poor and she was tired of waiting for me. It was a terrible mistake, but in her heart she never loved anyone except me!"

At this point Jordan and I tried to go, but Tom and Gatsby insisted with competitive firmness that we remain—as though neither of them had anything to conceal and it would be a privilege to partake vicariously of their emotions.

"Sit down, Daisy." Tom's voice groped unsuccessfully for the paternal note. "What's been going on? I want to hear all about it."

"I told you what's been going on," said Gatsby. "Going on for five years—and you didn't know."

Tom turned to Daisy sharply.

"You've been seeing this fellow for five years?"

"Not seeing," said Gatsby. "No, we couldn't meet. But both of us loved each other all that time, old sport, and you didn't know. I used to laugh sometimes"—but there was no laughter in his eyes—"to think that you didn't know."

"Oh—that's all." Tom tapped his thick fingers together like a clergyman and leaned back in his chair.

"You're crazy!" he exploded. "I can't speak about what happened five years ago, because I didn't know Daisy then—and I'll be damned if I see how you got within a mile of her unless you brought the groceries to the back door. But all the rest of that's a God Damned lie. Daisy loved me when she married me and she loves me now."

"No," said Gatsby, shaking his head.

"She does, though. The trouble is that sometimes she gets foolish ideas in her head and doesn't know what she's doing." He nodded sagely. "And what's more, I love Daisy too. Once in a while I go off on a spree and make a fool of myself, but I always come back, and in my heart I love her all the time."

"You're revolting," said Daisy. She turned to me, and her voice, dropping an octave lower, filled the room with thrilling scorn: "Do you know why we left Chicago? I'm surprised that they didn't treat you to the story of that little spree."

Gatsby walked over and stood beside her.

"Daisy, that's all over now," he said earnestly. "It doesn't matter any more. Just tell him the truth—that you never loved him—and it's all wiped out forever."

She looked at him blindly. "Why—how could I love him—possibly?"

"You never loved him."

She hesitated. Her eyes fell on Jordan and me with a sort of appeal, as though she realized at last what she was doing—and as though she had never, all along, intended doing anything at all. But it was done now. It was too late.

"I never loved him," she said, with perceptible reluctance.

"Not at Kapiolani?" demanded Tom suddenly.

"No."

From the ballroom beneath, muffled and suffocating chords were drifting up on hot waves of air.

"Not that day I carried you down from the Punch Bowl to keep your shoes dry?" There was a husky tenderness in his tone. . . . "Daisy?"

"Please don't." Her voice was cold, but the rancor was gone from it. She looked at Gatsby. "There, Jay," she said—but her hand as she tried to light a cigarette was trembling. Suddenly she threw the cigarette and the burning match on the carpet.

"Oh, you want too much!" she cried to Gatsby. "I love you now—isn't that enough? I can't help what's past." She began to sob helplessly. "I did love him once—but I loved you too."

Gatsby's eyes opened and closed.

"You loved me *too?*" he repeated.

"Even that's a lie," said Tom savagely. "She didn't know you were alive. Why—there're things between Daisy and me that you'll never know, things that neither of us can ever forget."

The words seemed to bite physically into Gatsby.

"I want to speak to Daisy alone," he insisted. "She's all excited now——"

"Even alone I can't say I never loved Tom," she admitted in a pitiful voice. "It wouldn't be true."

"Of course it wouldn't," agreed Tom.

She turned to her husband.

"As if it mattered to you," she said.

"Of course it matters. I'm going to take better care of you from now on."

"You don't understand," said Gatsby, with a touch of panic. "You're not going to take care of her any more."

"I'm not?" Tom opened his eyes wide and laughed. He could afford to control himself now. "Why's that?"

"Daisy's leaving you."

"Nonsense."

"I am, though," she said with a visible effort.

"She's not leaving me!" Tom's words suddenly leaned down over Gatsby. "Certainly not for a common swindler who'd have to steal the ring he put on her finger."

"I won't stand this!" cried Daisy. "Oh, please let's get out."

"Who are you, anyhow?" broke out Tom. "You're one of that bunch that hangs around with Meyer Wolfshiem—that much I happen to know. I've made a little investigation into your affairs—and I'll carry it further tomorrow."

"You can suit yourself about that, old sport," said Gatsby steadily.

"I found out what your 'drug-stores' were." He turned to us and spoke rapidly. "He and this Wolfshiem bought up a lot of side-street drug-stores here and in Chicago and sold grain alcohol over the counter. That's one of his little stunts. I picked him for a bootlegger the first time I saw him, and I wasn't far wrong."

"What about it?" said Gatsby politely. "I guess your friend Walter Chase wasn't too proud to come in on it."

"And you left him in the lurch, didn't you? You let him go to jail for a month over in New Jersey. God! You ought to hear Walter on the subject of *you*."

"He came to us dead broke. He was very glad to pick up some money, old sport."

"Don't you call me 'old sport'!" cried Tom. Gatsby said nothing. "Walter could have you up on the betting laws too, but Wolfshiem scared him into shutting his mouth."

That unfamiliar yet recognizable look was back again in Gatsby's face.

"That drug-store business was just small change," continued Tom slowly, "but you've got something on now that Walter's afraid to tell me about."

I glanced at Daisy, who was staring terrified between Gatsby and her husband, and at Jordan, who had begun to balance an invisible but absorbing object on the tip of her chin. Then I turned back to Gatsby—and was startled at his expression. He looked—and this is said in all contempt for the babbled slander of his garden—as if he had "killed a man." For a moment the set of his face could be described in just that fantastic way.

It passed, and he began to talk excitedly to Daisy, denying everything, defending his name against accusations that had not been made. But with every word she was drawing further and further into herself, so he gave that up, and only the dead dream fought on as the afternoon slipped away, trying to touch what was no longer tangible, struggling unhappily, undespairingly, toward that lost voice across the room.

The voice begged again to go.

"*Please*, Tom! I can't stand this any more."

Her frightened eyes told that whatever intentions, whatever courage she had had, were definitely gone.

"You two start on home, Daisy," said Tom. "In Mr. Gatsby's car."

She looked at Tom, alarmed now, but he insisted with magnanimous scorn.

"Go on. He won't annoy you. I think he realizes that his presumptuous little flirtation is over."

They were gone, without a word, snapped out, made accidental, isolated, like ghosts, even from our pity.

After a moment Tom got up and began wrapping the unopened bottle of whiskey in the towel.

"Want any of this stuff? Jordan? . . . Nick?"

I didn't answer.

"Nick?" He asked again.

"What?"

"Want any?"

"No . . . I just remembered that today's my birthday."

I was thirty. Before me stretched the portentous, menacing road of a new decade.

It was seven o'clock when we got into the coupé with him and started for Long Island. Tom talked incessantly, exulting and laughing, but his voice was as remote from Jordan and me as the foreign clamor on the sidewalk or the tumult of the elevated overhead. Human sympathy has its limits, and we were content to let all their tragic arguments fade with the city lights behind. Thirty—the promise of a decade of loneliness, a thinning list of single men to know, a thinning brief-case of enthusiasm, thinning hair. But there was Jordan beside me, who, unlike Daisy, was too wise ever to carry well-forgotten dreams from age to age. As we passed over the dark bridge her wan face fell lazily against my coat's shoulder and the formidable stroke of thirty died away with the reassuring pressure of her hand.

So we drove on toward death through the cooling twilight.

The young Greek, Michaelis, who ran the coffee joint beside the ashheaps was the principal witness at the inquest. He had slept through the heat until after five, when he strolled over to the garage, and found George Wilson sick in his office—really sick, pale as his own pale hair and shaking all over. Michaelis advised him to go to bed, but Wilson refused, saying that he'd miss a lot of business if he did. While his neighbor was trying to persuade him a violent racket broke out overhead.

"I've got my wife locked in up there," explained Wilson calmly. "She's going to stay there till the day after tomorrow, and then we're going to move away."

Michaelis was astonished; they had been neighbors for four years, and Wilson had never seemed faintly capable of such a statement. Generally he was one of these worn-out men: when he wasn't working, he sat on a chair in the doorway and stared at the people and the cars that passed along the road. When anyone spoke to him he invariably laughed in an agreeable, colorless way. He was his wife's man and not his own.

So naturally Michaelis tried to find out what had happened, but Wilson wouldn't say a word—instead he began to throw curious, suspicious glances at his visitor and ask him what he'd been doing at certain times on certain days. Just as the latter was getting uneasy, some workmen came past the door bound for his restaurant, and Michaelis took the opportunity to get away, intending to come back later. But he didn't. He supposed he forgot to, that's all. When he came outside again, a little after seven, he was reminded of the conversation because he heard Mrs. Wilson's voice, loud and scolding, downstairs in the garage.

"Beat me!" he heard her cry. "Throw me down and beat me, you dirty little coward!"

A moment later she rushed out into the dusk, waving her hands and shouting—before he could move from his door the business was over.

The "death car," as the newspapers called it, didn't stop; it came out of the gathering darkness, wavered tragically for a moment, and then disappeared around the next bend. Michaelis wasn't even sure of its color—he told the first policeman that it was light green. The other car, the one going toward New York, came to rest a hundred yards beyond, and its driver hurried back to where Myrtle Wilson, her life violently extinguished, knelt in the road and mingled her thick dark blood with the dust.

Michaelis and this man reached her first, but when they had torn open her shirtwaist, still damp with perspiration, they saw that her left breast was swinging loose like a flap, and there was no need to listen for the heart beneath. The mouth was wide open and ripped at the corners, as though she had choked a little in giving up the tremendous vitality she had stored so long.

We saw the three of four automobiles and the crowd when we were still some distance away.

"Wreck!" said Tom. "That's good. Wilson'll have a little business at last."

He slowed down, but still without any intention of stopping, until, as we came nearer, the hushed, intent faces of the people at the garage door made him automatically put on the brakes.

"We'll take a look," he said doubtfully, "just a look."

I became aware now of a hollow, wailing sound which issued incessantly from the garage, a sound which as we got out of the coupé and walked toward the door resolved itself into the words "Oh, my God!" uttered over and over in a gasping moan.

"There's some bad trouble here," said Tom excitedly.

He reached up on tiptoes and peered over a circle of heads into the garage, which was lit only by a yellow light in a swinging wire basket overhead. Then he made a harsh sound in his throat, and with a violent thrusting movement of his powerful arms pushed his way through.

The circle closed up again with a running murmur of expostulation; it was a minute before I could see anything at all. Then new arrivals disarranged the line, and Jordan and I were pushed suddenly inside.

Myrtle Wilson's body, wrapped in a blanket, and then in another blanket, as though she suffered from a chill in the hot night, lay on a work table by the wall, and Tom, with his back to us, was bending over it, motionless. Next to him stood a motorcycle policeman taking down names with much sweat and correction in a little book. At first I couldn't find the source of the high, groaning words that echoed clamorously through the bare garage—then I saw Wilson standing on the raised threshold of his office, swaying back and forth and holding to the doorposts with both hands. Some man was talking to him in a low voice and attempting, from time to time, to lay a hand on his shoulder, but Wilson neither heard nor saw. His eyes would drop slowly from the swinging light to the laden table by the wall, and then jerk back to the light again, and he gave out incessantly his high, horrible call:

"Oh, my Ga-od! Oh, my Ga-od! Oh, Ga-od! Oh, my Ga-od!"

Presently Tom lifted his head with a jerk and, after staring around the garage with glazed eyes, addressed a mumbled incoherent remark to the policeman.

"M-a-v—" the policeman was saying, "—o——"

"No, r—" corrected the man, "M-a-v-r-o——"

"Listen to me!" muttered Tom fiercely.

"r—" said the policeman, "o——"

"g——"

"g—" He looked up as Tom's broad hand fell sharply on his shoulder. "What you want, fella?"

"What happened?—that's what I want to know."

"Auto hit her. Ins'antly killed."

"Instantly killed," repeated Tom, staring.

"She ran out ina road. Son-of-a-bitch didn't even stopus car."

"There was two cars," said Michaelis, "one comin', one goin', see?"

"Going where?" asked the policeman keenly.

"One goin' each way. Well, she"—his hand rose toward the blankets but stopped half way and fell to his side—"she ran out there an' the one comin' from N'York knock right into her, goin' thirty or forty miles an hour."

"What's the name of this place here?" demanded the officer.

"Hasn't got any name."

A pale well-dressed negro stepped near.

"It was a yellow car," he said, "big yellow car. New."

"See the accident?" asked the policeman.

"No, but the car passed me down the road, going faster'n forty. Going fifty, sixty."

"Come here and let's have your name. Look out now. I want to get his name."

Some words of this conversation must have reached Wilson, swaying in the office door, for suddenly a new theme found voice among his gasping cries:

"You don't have to tell me what kind of car it was! I know what kind of car it was!"

Watching Tom, I saw the wad of muscle back of his shoulder tighten under his coat. He walked quickly over to Wilson and, standing in front of him, seized him firmly by the upper arms.

"You've got to pull yourself together," he said with soothing gruffness.

Wilson's eyes fell upon Tom; he started up on his tiptoes and then would have collapsed to his knees had not Tom held him upright.

"Listen," said Tom, shaking him a little. "I just got here a minute ago, from New York. I was bringing you that coupé we've been talking about. That yellow car I was driving this afternoon wasn't mine—do you hear? I haven't seen it all afternoon."

Only the negro and I were near enough to hear what he said, but the policeman caught something in the tone and looked over with truculent eyes.

"What's all that?" he demanded.

"I'm a friend of his." Tom turned his head but kept his hands firm on Wilson's body. "He says he knows the car that did it. . . . It was a yellow car."

Some dim impulse moved the policeman to look suspiciously at Tom.

"And what color's your car?"

"It's a blue car, a coupé."

"We've come straight from New York," I said.

Someone who had been driving a little behind us confirmed this, and the policeman turned away.

"Now, if you'll let me have that name again correct——"

Picking up Wilson like a doll, Tom carried him into the office, set him down in a chair, and came back.

"If somebody'll come here and sit with him," he snapped authoritatively. He watched while the two men standing closest glanced at each other and went unwillingly into the room. Then Tom shut the door on them and came down the single step, his eyes avoiding the table. As he passed close to me he whispered: "Let's get out."

Self-consciously, with his authoritative arms breaking the way, we pushed through the still gathering crowd, passing a hurried doctor, case in hand, who had been sent for in wild hope half an hour ago.

Tom drove slowly until we were beyond the bend—then his foot came down hard, and the coupé raced along through the night. In a little while I heard a low husky sob, and saw that the tears were overflowing down his face.

"The God Damn coward!" he whimpered. "He didn't even stop his car."

The Buchanans' house floated suddenly toward us through the dark rustling trees. Tom stopped beside the porch and looked up at the second floor, where two windows bloomed with light among the vines.

"Daisy's home," he said. As we got out of the car he glanced at me and frowned slightly.

"I ought to have dropped you in West Egg, Nick. There's nothing we can do tonight."

A change had come over him, and he spoke gravely, and with decision. As we walked across the moonlit gravel to the porch he disposed of the situation in a few brisk phrases.

"I'll telephone for a taxi to take you home, and while you're waiting you and Jordan better go in the kitchen and have them get you some supper—if you want any." He opened the door. "Come in."

"No, thanks. But I'd be glad if you'd order me the taxi. I'll wait outside."

Jordan put her hand on my arm.

"Won't you come in, Nick?"

"No, thanks."

I was feeling a little sick and I wanted to be alone. But Jordan lingered for a moment more.

"It's only half past nine," she said.

I'd be damned if I'd go in; I'd had enough of all of them for one day, and suddenly that included Jordan too. She must have seen something of this in my expression, for she turned abruptly away and ran up the porch steps into the house. I sat down for a few minutes with my head in my hands, until I heard the phone taken up inside and the butler's voice calling a taxi. Then I walked slowly down the drive away from the house, intending to wait by the gate.

I hadn't gone twenty yards when I heard my name and Gatsby stepped from between two bushes into the path. I must have felt pretty weird by that time, because I could think of nothing except the luminosity of his pink suit under the moon.

"What are you doing?" I inquired.

"Just standing here, old sport."

Somehow, that seemed a despicable occupation. For all I knew he was going to rob the house in a moment; I wouldn't have been surprised to see sinister faces, the faces of "Wolfshiem's people," behind him in the dark shrubbery.

"Did you see any trouble on the road?" he asked after a minute.

"Yes."

He hesitated.

"Was she killed?"

"Yes."

"I thought so; I told Daisy I thought so. It's better that the shock should all come at once. She stood it pretty well."

He spoke as if Daisy's reaction was the only thing that mattered.

"I got to West Egg by a side road," he went on, "and left the car in my garage. I don't think anybody saw us, but of course I can't be sure."

I disliked him so much by this time that I didn't find it necessary to tell him he was wrong.

"Who was the woman?" he inquired.

"Her name was Wilson. Her husband owns the garage. How the devil did it happen?"

"Well, I tried to swing the wheel—" He broke off, and suddenly I guessed at the truth.

"Was Daisy driving?"

"Yes," he said after a moment, "but of course I'll say I was. You see, when we left New York she was very nervous and she thought it would steady her to drive—and this woman rushed out at us just as we were passing a car coming the other way. It all happened in a minute, but it seemed to me that she wanted to speak to us, thought we were somebody she knew. Well, first Daisy turned away from the woman toward the other car, and then she lost her nerve and turned back. The second my hand reached the wheel I felt the shock—it must have killed her instantly."

"It ripped her open——"

"Don't tell me, old sport." He winced. "Anyhow—Daisy stepped on it. I tried to make her stop, but she couldn't, so I pulled on the emergency brake. Then she fell over into my lap and I drove on.

"She'll be all right tomorrow," he said presently. "I'm just going to wait here and see if he tries to bother her about that unpleasantness this afternoon. She's locked herself into her room, and if he tries any brutality she's going to turn the light out and on again."

"He won't touch her," I said. "He's not thinking about her."

"I don't trust him, old sport."

"How long are you going to wait?"

"All night, if necessary. Anyhow, till they all go to bed."

A new point of view occurred to me. Suppose Tom found out that Daisy had been driving. He might think he saw a connection in it—he might think anything. I looked at the house; there were two or three bright windows downstairs and the pink glow from Daisy's room on the second floor.

"You wait here," I said. "I'll see if there's any sign of a commotion."

I walked back along the border of the lawn, traversed the gravel softly, and tiptoed up the veranda steps. The drawing-room curtains were open, and I saw that the room was empty. Crossing the porch where we had dined that June night three months before, I came to a small rectangle of light which I guessed was the pantry window. The blind was drawn, but I found a rift at the sill.

Daisy and Tom were sitting opposite each other at the kitchen table, with a plate of cold fried chicken between them, and two bottles of ale. He was talking intently across the table at her, and in his earnestness his hand had fallen upon and covered her own. Once in a while she looked up at him and nodded in agreement.

They weren't happy, and neither of them had touched the chicken or the ale—and yet they weren't unhappy either. There was an unmistakable air of natural intimacy about the picture, and anybody would have said that they were conspiring together.

As I tiptoed from the porch I heard my taxi feeling its way along the dark road toward the house. Gatsby was waiting where I had left him in the drive.

"Is it all quiet up there?" he asked anxiously.

"Yes, it's all quiet." I hesitated. "You'd better come home and get some sleep."

He shook his head.

"I want to wait here till Daisy goes to bed. Good night, old sport."

He put his hands in his coat pockets and turned back eagerly to his scrutiny of the house, as though my presence marred the sacredness of the vigil. So I walked away and left him standing there in the moonlight—watching over nothing.

Chapter VIII

I COULDN'T sleep all night; a fog-horn was groaning incessantly on the Sound, and I tossed half sick between grotesque reality and savage, frightening dreams. Toward dawn I heard a taxi go up Gatsby's drive, and immediately I jumped out of bed and began to dress—I felt that I had something to tell him, something to warn him about, and morning would be too late.

Crossing his lawn, I saw that his front door was still open and he was leaning against a table in the hall, heavy with dejection or sleep.

"Nothing happened," he said wanly. "I waited, and about four o'clock she came to the window and stood there for a minute and then turned out the light."

His house had never seemed so enormous to me as it did that night when we hunted through the great rooms for cigarettes. We pushed aside curtains that were like pavilions, and felt over innumerable feet of dark wall for electric light switches—once I tumbled with a sort of splash upon the keys of a ghostly piano. There was an inexplicable amount of dust everywhere, and the rooms were musty, as though they hadn't been aired for many days. I found the humidor on an unfamiliar table, with two stale, dry cigarettes inside. Throwing open the French windows of the drawing-room, we sat smoking out into the darkness.

"You ought to go away," I said. "It's pretty certain they'll trace your car."

"Go away *now*, old sport?"

"Go to Atlantic City for a week, or up to Montreal."

He wouldn't consider it. He couldn't possibly leave Daisy until he knew what she was going to do. He was clutching at some last hope and I couldn't bear to shake him free.

It was this night that he told me the strange story of his youth with Dan Cody—told it to me because "Jay Gatsby" had broken up like glass against Tom's hard malice, and the long secret extravaganza was played out. I think that he would have acknowledged anything now, without reserve, but he wanted to talk about Daisy.

She was the first "nice" girl he had ever known. In various unrevealed capacities he had come in contact with such people, but always with indiscernible barbed wire between. He found her excitingly desirable. He went to her house, at first with other officers from Camp Taylor, then alone. It amazed him—he had never been in such a beautiful house before. But what gave it an air of breathless intensity was that Daisy lived there—it was as casual a thing to her as his tent out at camp was to him. There was a ripe mystery about it, a hint of bedrooms upstairs more beautiful and cool than other bedrooms, of gay and radiant activities taking place through its corridors, and of romances that were not musty and laid away already in lavender but fresh and breathing and redolent of this year's shining motor-cars and of dances whose flowers were scarcely withered. It excited him, too, that many men had already loved Daisy—it increased her value in his eyes. He felt their presence all about the house, pervading the air with the shades and echoes of still vibrant emotions.

But he knew that he was in Daisy's house by a colossal accident. However glorious might be his future as Jay Gatsby, he was at present a penniless young man without a past, and at any moment the invisible cloak of his uniform might slip from his shoulders. So he made the most of his time. He took what he could get, ravenously and unscrupulously—eventually he took Daisy one still October night, took her because he had no real right to touch her hand.

He might have despised himself, for he had certainly taken her under false pretenses. I don't mean that he had traded on his phantom millions, but he had deliberately given Daisy a sense of security; he let her believe that he was a person from much the same strata as herself—that he was fully able to take care of her. As a matter of fact, he had no such facilities—he had no comfortable family standing behind him, and he was liable at the whim of an impersonal government to be blown anywhere about the world.

But he didn't despise himself and it didn't turn out as he had imagined. He had intended, probably, to take what he could and go—but now he found that he had committed himself to the following of a grail. He knew that Daisy was extraordinary, but he didn't realize just how extraordinary a "nice" girl could be.

She vanished into her rich house, into her rich, full life, leaving
Gatsby—nothing. He felt married to her, that was all.

When they met again, two days later, it was Gatsby who was
breathless, who was, somehow, betrayed. Her porch was bright
with the bought luxury of star-shine; the wicker of the settee
squeaked fashionably as she turned toward him and he kissed her
curious and lovely mouth. She had caught a cold, and it made
her voice huskier and more charming than ever, and Gatsby was
overwhelmingly aware of the youth and mystery that wealth
imprisons and preserves, of the freshness of many clothes, and of
Daisy, gleaming like silver, safe and proud above the hot struggles of the poor.

"I can't describe to you how surprised I was to find out I
loved her, old sport. I even hoped for a while that she'd throw
me over, but she didn't, because she was in love with me too.
She thought I knew a lot because I knew different things from
her . . . Well, there I was, way off my ambitions, getting deeper
in love every minute, and all of a sudden I didn't care. What was
the use of doing great things if I could have a better time telling
her what I was going to do?"

On the last afternoon before he went abroad, he sat with
Daisy in his arms for a long, silent time. It was a cold fall day,
with fire in the room and her cheeks flushed. Now and then she
moved and he changed his arm a little, and once he kissed her
dark shining hair. The afternoon had made them tranquil for a
while, as if to give them a deep memory for the long parting the
next day promised. They had never been closer in their month
of love, nor communicated more profoundly one with another,
than when she brushed silent lips against his coat's shoulder or
when he touched the end of her finger, gently, as though she
were asleep.

He did extraordinarily well in the war. He was a captain before
he went to the front, and following the Argonne battles he got
his majority and the command of the divisional machine-guns.
After the armistice he tried frantically to get home, but some
complication or misunderstanding sent him to Oxford instead.
He was worried now—there was a quality of nervous despair in
Daisy's letters. She didn't see why he couldn't come. She was

feeling the pressure of the world outside, and she wanted to see him and feel his presence beside her and be reassured that she was doing the right thing after all.

For Daisy was young and her artificial world was redolent of orchids and pleasant, cheerful snobbery and orchestras which set the rhythm of the year, summing up the sadness and suggestiveness of life in new tunes. All night the saxophones wailed the hopeless comment of the "Beale Street Blues" while a hundred pairs of golden and silver slippers shuffled the shining dust. At the gray tea hour there were always rooms that throbbed incessantly with this low, sweet fever, while fresh faces drifted here and there like rose petals blown by the sad horns around the floor.

Through this twilight universe Daisy began to move again with the season; suddenly she was again keeping half a dozen dates a day with half a dozen men, and drowsing asleep at dawn with the beads and chiffon of an evening dress tangled among dying orchids on the floor beside her bed. And all the time something within her was crying for a decision. She wanted her life shaped now, immediately—and the decision must be made by some force—of love, of money, of unquestionable practicality—that was close at hand.

That force took shape in the middle of spring with the arrival of Tom Buchanan. There was a wholesome bulkiness about his person and his position, and Daisy was flattered. Doubtless there was a certain struggle and a certain relief. The letter reached Gatsby while he was still at Oxford.

It was dawn now on Long Island and we went about opening the rest of the windows downstairs, filling the house with gray-turning, gold-turning light. The shadow of a tree fell abruptly across the dew and ghostly birds began to sing among the blue leaves. There was a slow, pleasant movement in the air, scarcely a wind, promising a cool, lovely day.

"I don't think she ever loved him." Gatsby turned around from a window and looked at me challengingly. "You must remember, old sport, she was very excited this afternoon. He told her those things in a way that frightened her—that made it look as if I was some kind of cheap sharper. And the result was she hardly knew what she was saying."

He sat down gloomily.

"Of course she might have loved him just for a minute, when they were first married—and loved me more even then, do you see?"

Suddenly he came out with a curious remark.

"In any case," he said, "it was just personal."

What could you make of that, except to suspect some intensity in his conception of the affair that couldn't be measured?

He came back from France when Tom and Daisy were still on their wedding trip, and made a miserable but irresistible journey to Louisville on the last of his army pay. He stayed there a week, walking the streets where their footsteps had clicked together through the November night and revisiting the out-of-the-way places to which they had driven in her white car. Just as Daisy's house had always seemed to him more mysterious and gay than other houses, so his idea of the city itself, even though she was gone from it, was pervaded with a melancholy beauty.

He left feeling that if he had searched harder, he might have found her—that he was leaving her behind. The day-coach—he was penniless now—was hot. He went out to the open vestibule and sat down on a folding chair, and the station slid away and the backs of unfamiliar buildings moved by. Then out into the spring fields, where a yellow trolley raced them for a minute with people in it who might once have seen the pale magic of her face along the casual street.

The track curved and now it was going away from the sun, which, as it sank lower, seemed to spread itself in benediction over the vanishing city where she had drawn her breath. He stretched out his hand desperately as if to snatch only a wisp of air, to save a fragment of the spot that she had made lovely for him. But it was all going by too fast now for his blurred eyes and he knew that he had lost that part of it, the freshest and the best, forever.

It was nine o'clock when we finished breakfast and went out on the porch. The night had made a sharp difference in the weather and there was an autumn flavor in the air. The gardener, the last one of Gatsby's former servants, came to the foot of the steps.

"I'm going to drain the pool today, Mr. Gatsby. Leaves'll start falling pretty soon, and then there's always trouble with the pipes."

"Don't do it today," Gatsby answered. He turned to me apologetically. "You know, old sport, I've never used that pool all summer?"

I looked at my watch and stood up.

"Twelve minutes to my train."

I didn't want to go to the city. I wasn't worth a decent stroke of work, but it was more than that—I didn't want to leave Gatsby. I missed that train, and then another, before I could get myself away.

"I'll call you up," I said finally.

"Do, old sport."

"I'll call you about noon."

We walked slowly down the steps.

"I suppose Daisy'll call too." He looked at me anxiously, as if he hoped I'd corroborate this.

"I suppose so."

"Well, good-by."

We shook hands and I started away. Just before I reached the hedge I remembered something and turned around.

"They're a rotten crowd," I shouted across the lawn. "You're worth the whole damn bunch put together."

I've always been glad I said that. It was the only compliment I ever gave him, because I disapproved of him from beginning to end. First he nodded politely, and then his face broke into that radiant and understanding smile, as if we'd been in ecstatic cahoots on that fact all the time. His gorgeous pink rag of a suit made a bright spot of color against the white steps, and I thought of the night when I first came to his ancestral home, three months before. The lawn and drive had been crowded with the faces of those who guessed at his corruption—and he had stood on those steps, concealing his incorruptible dream, as he waved them good-by.

I thanked him for his hospitality. We were always thanking him for that—I and the others.

"Good-by," I called. "I enjoyed breakfast, Gatsby."

Up in the city, I tried for a while to list the quotations on an interminable amount of stock, then I fell asleep in my swivel chair. Just before noon the phone woke me, and I started up with sweat breaking out on my forehead. It was Jordan Baker;

she often called me up at this hour because the uncertainty of her own movements between hotels and clubs and private houses made her hard to find in any other way. Usually her voice came over the wire as something fresh and cool, as if a divot from a green golf-links had come sailing in at the office window, but this morning it seemed harsh and dry.

"I've left Daisy's house," she said. "I'm at Hempstead, and I'm going down to Southampton this afternoon."

Probably it had been tactful to leave Daisy's house, but the act annoyed me, and her next remark made me rigid.

"You weren't so nice to me last night."

"How could it have mattered then?"

Silence for a moment. Then:

"However—I want to see you."

"I want to see you, too."

"Suppose I don't go to Southampton, and come into town this afternoon?"

"No—I don't think this afternoon."

"Very well."

"It's impossible this afternoon. Various——"

We talked like that for a while, and then abruptly we weren't talking any longer. I don't know which of us hung up with a sharp click, but I know I didn't care. I couldn't have talked to her across a tea-table that day if I never talked to her again in this world.

I called Gatsby's house a few minutes later, but the line was busy. I tried four times; finally an exasperated Central told me the wire was being kept open for Long Distance from Detroit. Taking out my time-table, I drew a small circle around the three-fifty train. Then I leaned back in my chair and tried to think. It was just noon.

When I passed the ashheaps on the train that morning I had crossed deliberately to the other side of the car. I supposed there'd be a curious crowd around there all day with little boys searching for dark spots in the dust, and some garrulous man telling over and over what had happened, until it became less and less real even to him and he could tell it no longer, and Myrtle Wilson's tragic achievement was forgotten. Now I want to go back a little and tell what happened at the garage after we left there the night before.

They had difficulty in locating the sister, Catherine. She must have broken her rule against drinking that night, for when she arrived she was stupid with liquor and unable to understand that the ambulance had already gone to Flushing. When they convinced her of this, she immediately fainted, as if that was the intolerable part of the affair. Someone, kind or curious, took her in his car and drove her in the wake of her sister's body.

Until long after midnight a changing crowd lapped up against the front of the garage, while George Wilson rocked himself back and forth on the couch inside. For a while the door of the office was open, and everyone who came into the garage glanced irresistibly through it. Finally someone said it was a shame, and closed the door. Michaelis and several other men were with him; first, four or five men, later two or three men. Still later Michaelis had to ask the last stranger to wait there fifteen minutes longer, while he went back to his own place and made a pot of coffee. After that, he stayed there alone with Wilson until dawn.

About three o'clock the quality of Wilson's incoherent muttering changed—he grew quieter and began to talk about the yellow car. He announced that he had a way of finding out whom the yellow car belonged to, and then he blurted out that a couple of months ago his wife had come from the city with her face bruised and her nose swollen.

But when he heard himself say this, he flinched and began to cry "Oh, my God!" again in his groaning voice. Michaelis made a clumsy attempt to distract him.

"How long have you been married, George? Come on there, try and sit still a minute and answer my question. How long have you been married?"

"Twelve years."

"Ever had any children? Come on, George, sit still—I asked you a question. Did you ever have any children?"

The hard brown beetles kept thudding against the dull light, and whenever Michaelis heard a car go tearing along the road outside it sounded to him like the car that hadn't stopped a few hours before. He didn't like to go into the garage, because the work bench was stained where the body had been lying, so he moved uncomfortably around the office—he knew every object in it before morning—and from time to time sat down beside Wilson trying to keep him more quiet.

"Have you got a church you go to sometimes, George? Maybe even if you haven't been there for a long time? Maybe I could call up the church and get a priest to come over and he could talk to you, see?"

"Don't belong to any."

"You ought to have a church, George, for times like this. You must have gone to church once. Didn't you get married in a church? Listen, George, listen to me. Didn't you get married in a church?"

"That was a long time ago."

The effort of answering broke the rhythm of his rocking—for a moment he was silent. Then the same half knowing, half bewildered look came back into his faded eyes.

"Look in the drawer there," he said, pointing at the desk.

"Which drawer?"

"That drawer—that one."

Michaelis opened the drawer nearest his hand. There was nothing in it but a small, expensive dog-leash, made of leather and braided silver. It was apparently new.

"This?" he inquired, holding it up.

Wilson stared and nodded.

"I found it yesterday afternoon. She tried to tell me about it, but I knew it was something funny."

"You mean your wife bought it?"

"She had it wrapped in tissue paper on her bureau."

Michaelis didn't see anything odd in that, and he gave Wilson a dozen reasons why his wife might have bought the dog-leash. But conceivably Wilson had heard some of these same explanations before, from Myrtle, because he began saying "Oh, my God!" again in a whisper—his comforter left several explanations in the air.

"Then he killed her," said Wilson. His mouth dropped open suddenly.

"Who did?"

"I have a way of finding out."

"You're morbid, George," said his friend. "This has been a strain to you and you don't know what you're saying. You'd better try and sit quiet till morning."

"He murdered her."

"It was an accident, George."

Wilson shook his head. His eyes narrowed and his mouth widened slightly with the ghost of a superior "Hm!"

"I know," he said definitely. "I'm one of these trusting fellas and I don't think any harm to *no*body, but when I get to know a thing I know it. It was the man in that car. She ran out to speak to him and he wouldn't stop."

Michaelis had seen this too, but it hadn't occurred to him that there was any special significance in it. He believed that Mrs. Wilson had been running away from her husband, rather than trying to stop any particular car.

"How could she of been like that?"

"She's a deep one," said Wilson, as if that answered the question. "Ah-h-h——"

He began to rock again, and Michaelis stood twisting the leash in his hand.

"Maybe you got some friend that I could telephone for, George?"

This was a forlorn hope—he was almost sure that Wilson had no friend: there was not enough of him for his wife. He was glad a little later when he noticed a change in the room, a blue quickening by the window, and realized that dawn wasn't far off. About five o'clock it was blue enough outside to snap off the light.

Wilson's glazed eyes turned out to the ashheaps, where small gray clouds took on fantastic shapes and scurried here and there in the faint dawn wind.

"I spoke to her," he muttered, after a long silence. "I told her she might fool me but she couldn't fool God. I took her to the window"—with an effort he got up and walked to the rear window and leaned with his face pressed against it—"and I said 'God knows what you've been doing, everything you've been doing. You may fool me, but you can't fool God!'"

Standing behind him, Michaelis saw with a shock that he was looking at the eyes of Doctor T. J. Eckleburg, which had just emerged, pale and enormous, from the dissolving night.

"God sees everything," repeated Wilson.

"That's an advertisement," Michaelis assured him. Something made him turn away from the window and look back into the room. But Wilson stood there a long time, his face close to the window pane, nodding into the twilight.

*

By six o'clock Michaelis was worn out, and grateful for the sound of a car stopping outside. It was one of the watchers of the night before who had promised to come back, so he cooked breakfast for three, which he and the other man ate together. Wilson was quieter now, and Michaelis went home to sleep; when he awoke four hours later and hurried back to the garage, Wilson was gone.

His movements—he was on foot all the time—were afterward traced to Port Roosevelt and then to Gad's Hill, where he bought a sandwich that he didn't eat, and a cup of coffee. He must have been tired and walking slowly, for he didn't reach Gad's Hill until noon. Thus far there was no difficulty in accounting for his time—there were boys who had seen a man "acting sort of crazy," and motorists at whom he stared oddly from the side of the road. Then for three hours he disappeared from view. The police, on the strength of what he said to Michaelis, that he "had a way of finding out," supposed that he spent that time going from garage to garage thereabouts, inquiring for a yellow car. On the other hand, no garage man who had seen him ever came forward, and perhaps he had an easier, surer way of finding out what he wanted to know. By half past two he was in West Egg, where he asked someone the way to Gatsby's house. So by that time he knew Gatsby's name.

At two o'clock Gatsby put on his bathing suit and left word with the butler that if anyone phoned word was to be brought to him at the pool. He stopped at the garage for a pneumatic mattress that had amused his guests during the summer, and the chauffeur helped him pump it up. Then he gave instructions that the open car wasn't to be taken out under any circumstances— and this was strange, because the front right fender needed repair.

Gatsby shouldered the mattress and started for the pool. Once he stopped and shifted it a little, and the chauffeur asked him if he needed help, but he shook his head and in a moment disappeared among the yellowing trees.

No telephone message arrived, but the butler went without his sleep and waited for it until four o'clock—until long after there was anyone to give it to if it came. I have an idea that Gatsby himself didn't believe it would come, and perhaps he no longer cared. If that was true he must have felt that he had lost the old warm world, paid a high price for living too long with a single dream. He must have looked up at an unfamiliar sky through frightening leaves and shivered as he found what a grotesque thing a rose is and how raw the sunlight was upon the scarcely created grass. A new world, material without being real, where poor ghosts, breathing dreams like air, drifted fortuitously about . . . like that ashen, fantastic figure gliding toward him through the amorphous trees.

The chauffeur—he was one of Wolfshiem's protégés—heard the shots—afterward he could only say that he hadn't thought anything much about them. I drove from the station directly to Gatsby's house and my rushing anxiously up the front steps was the first thing that alarmed anyone. But they knew then, I firmly believe. With scarcely a word said, four of us, the chauffeur, butler, gardener, and I, hurried down to the pool.

There was a faint, barely perceptible movement of the water as the fresh flow from one end urged its way toward the drain at the other. With little ripples that were hardly the shadows of waves, the laden mattress moved irregularly down the pool. A small gust of wind that scarcely corrugated the surface was enough to disturb its accidental course with its accidental burden. The touch of a cluster of leaves revolved it slowly, tracing, like the leg of a compass, a thin red circle in the water.

It was after we started with Gatsby toward the house that the gardener saw Wilson's body a little way off in the grass, and the holocaust was complete.

Chapter IX

Aᴠᴛᴇʀ two years I remember the rest of that day, and that night and the next day, only as an endless drill of police and photographers and newspaper men in and out of Gatsby's front door. A rope stretched across the main gate and a policeman by it kept out the curious, but little boys soon discovered that they could enter through my yard, and there were always a few of them clustered open-mouthed about the pool. Someone with a positive manner, perhaps a detective, used the expression "madman" as he bent over Wilson's body that afternoon, and the adventitious authority of his voice set the key for the newspaper reports next morning.

Most of those reports were a nightmare—grotesque, circumstantial, eager, and untrue. When Michaelis's testimony at the inquest brought to light Wilson's suspicions of his wife I thought the whole tale would shortly be served up in racy pasquinade—but Catherine, who might have said anything, didn't say a word. She showed a surprising amount of character about it too—looked at the coroner with determined eyes under that corrected brow of hers, and swore that her sister had never seen Gatsby, that her sister was completely happy with her husband, that her sister had been into no mischief whatever. She convinced herself of it, and cried into her handkerchief, as if the very suggestion was more than she could endure. So Wilson was reduced to a man "deranged by grief" in order that the case might remain in its simplest form. And it rested there.

But all this part of it seemed remote and unessential. I found myself on Gatsby's side, and alone. From the moment I telephoned news of the catastrophe to West Egg Village, every surmise about him, and every practical question, was referred to me. At first I was surprised and confused; then, as he lay in his house and didn't move or breathe or speak, hour upon hour, it grew upon me that I was responsible, because no one else was interested—interested, I mean, with that intense personal interest to which everyone has some vague right at the end.

I called up Daisy half an hour after we found him, called her instinctively and without hesitation. But she and Tom had gone away early that afternoon, and taken baggage with them.

"Left no address?"

"No."

"Say when they'd be back?"

"No."

"Any idea where they are? How I could reach them?"

"I don't know. Can't say."

I wanted to get somebody for him. I wanted to go into the room where he lay and reassure him: "I'll get somebody for you, Gatsby. Don't worry. Just trust me and I'll get somebody for you——"

Meyer Wolfshiem's name wasn't in the phone book. The butler gave me his office address on Broadway, and I called Information, but by the time I had the number it was long after five, and no one answered the phone.

"Will you ring again?"

"I've rung them three times."

"It's very important."

"Sorry. I'm afraid no one's there."

I went back to the drawing-room and thought for an instant that they were chance visitors, all these official people who suddenly filled it. But, as they drew back the sheet and looked at Gatsby with unmoved eyes, his protest continued in my brain:

"Look here, old sport, you've got to get somebody for me. You've got to try hard. I can't go through this alone."

Someone started to ask me questions, but I broke away and going upstairs looked hastily through the unlocked parts of his desk—he'd never told me definitely that his parents were dead. But there was nothing—only the picture of Dan Cody, a token of forgotten violence, staring down from the wall.

Next morning I sent the butler to New York with a letter to Wolfshiem, which asked for information and urged him to come out on the next train. That request seemed superfluous when I wrote it. I was sure he'd start when he saw the newspapers, just as I was sure there'd be a wire from Daisy before noon—but neither a wire nor Mr. Wolfshiem arrived; no one arrived except more police and photographers and newspaper men. When the butler brought back Wolfshiem's answer I began to have a feeling of defiance, of scornful solidarity between Gatsby and me against them all.

Dear Mr. Carraway. This has been one of the most terrible shocks of my life to me I hardly can believe it that it is true at all. Such a mad act as that man did should make us all think. I cannot come down now as I am tied up in some very important business and cannot get mixed up in this thing now. If there is anything I can do a little later let me know in a letter by Edgar. I hardly know where I am when I hear about a thing like this and am completely knocked down and out.

Yours truly

MEYER WOLFSHIEM

and then hasty addenda beneath:

Let me know about the funeral etc do not know his family at all.

When the phone rang that afternoon and Long Distance said Chicago was calling I thought this would be Daisy at last. But the connection came through as a man's voice, very thin and far away.

"This is Slagle speaking . . ."

"Yes?" The name was unfamiliar.

"Hell of a note, isn't it? Get my wire?"

"There haven't been any wires."

"Young Parke's in trouble," he said rapidly. "They picked him up when he handed the bonds over the counter. They got a circular from New York giving 'em the numbers just five minutes before. What d'you know about that, hey? You never can tell in these hick towns——"

"Hello!" I interrupted breathlessly. "Look here—this isn't Mr. Gatsby. Mr. Gatsby's dead."

There was a long silence on the other end of the wire, followed by an exclamation . . . then a quick squawk as the connection was broken.

I think it was on the third day that a telegram signed Henry C. Gatz arrived from a town in Minnesota. It said only that the sender was leaving immediately and to postpone the funeral until he came.

It was Gatsby's father, a solemn old man, very helpless and dismayed, bundled up in a long cheap ulster against the warm September day. His eyes leaked continuously with excitement, and when I took the bag and umbrella from his hands he began to pull so incessantly at his sparse gray beard that I had difficulty in getting off his coat. He was on the point of collapse, so I took him into the music-room and made him sit down while I sent for something to eat. But he wouldn't eat, and the glass of milk spilled from his trembling hand.

"I saw it in the Chicago newspaper," he said. "It was all in the Chicago newspaper. I started right away."

"I didn't know how to reach you."

His eyes, seeing nothing, moved ceaselessly about the room.

"It was a madman," he said. "He must have been mad."

"Wouldn't you like some coffee?" I urged him.

"I don't want anything. I'm all right now, Mr.———"

"Carraway."

"Well, I'm all right now. Where have they got Jimmy?"

I took him into the drawing-room, where his son lay, and left him there. Some little boys had come up on the steps and were looking into the hall; when I told them who had arrived, they went reluctantly away.

After a little while Mr. Gatz opened the door and came out, his mouth ajar, his face flushed slightly, his eyes leaking isolated and unpunctual tears. He had reached an age where death no longer has the quality of ghastly surprise, and when he looked around him now for the first time and saw the height and splendor of the hall and the great rooms opening out from it into other rooms, his grief began to be mixed with an awed pride. I helped him to a bedroom upstairs; while he took off his coat and vest I told him that all arrangements had been deferred until he came.

"I didn't know what you'd want, Mr. Gatsby———"

"Gatz is my name."

"—Mr. Gatz. I thought you might want to take the body West."

He shook his head.

"Jimmy always liked it better down East. He rose up to his position in the East. Were you a friend of my boy's, Mr.———?"

"We were close friends."

"He had a big future before him, you know. He was only a young man, but he had a lot of brain power here."

He touched his head impressively, and I nodded.

"If he'd of lived, he'd of been a great man. A man like James J. Hill. He'd of helped build up the country."

"That's true," I said, uncomfortably.

He fumbled at the embroidered coverlet, trying to take it from the bed, and lay down stiffly—was instantly asleep.

That night an obviously frightened person called up, and demanded to know who I was before he would give his name.

"This is Mr. Carraway," I said.

"Oh!" He sounded relieved. "This is Klipspringer."

I was relieved too, for that seemed to promise another friend at Gatsby's grave. I didn't want it to be in the papers and draw a sightseeing crowd, so I'd been calling up a few people myself. They were hard to find.

"The funeral's tomorrow," I said. "Three o'clock, here at the house. I wish you'd tell anybody who'd be interested."

"Oh, I will," he broke out hastily. "Of course I'm not likely to see anybody, but if I do."

His tone made me suspicious.

"Of course you'll be there yourself."

"Well, I'll certainly try. What I called up about is——"

"Wait a minute," I interrupted. "How about saying you'll come?"

"Well, the fact is—the truth of the matter is that I'm staying with some people up here in Greenwich, and they rather expect me to be with them tomorrow. In fact, there's a sort of picnic or something. Of course I'll do my very best to get away."

I ejaculated an unrestrained "Huh!" and he must have heard me, for he went on nervously:

"What I called up about was a pair of shoes I left there. I wonder if it'd be too much trouble to have the butler send them on. You see, they're tennis shoes, and I'm sort of helpless without them. My address is care of B. F.——"

I didn't hear the rest of the name, because I hung up the receiver.

After that I felt a certain shame for Gatsby—one gentleman to whom I telephoned implied that he had got what he deserved.

However, that was my fault, for he was one of those who used to sneer most bitterly at Gatsby on the courage of Gatsby's liquor, and I should have known better than to call him.

The morning of the funeral I went up to New York to see Meyer Wolfshiem; I couldn't seem to reach him any other way. The door that I pushed open, on the advice of an elevator boy, was marked "The Swastika Holding Company," and at first there didn't seem to be anyone inside. But when I'd shouted "hello" several times in vain, an argument broke out behind a partition, and presently a lovely Jewess appeared at an interior door and scrutinized me with black hostile eyes.

"Nobody's in," she said. "Mr. Wolfshiem's gone to Chicago."

The first part of this was obviously untrue, for someone had begun to whistle "The Rosary," tunelessly, inside.

"Please say that Mr. Carraway wants to see him."

"I can't get him back from Chicago, can I?"

At this moment a voice, unmistakably Wolfshiem's, called "Stella!" from the other side of the door.

"Leave your name on the desk," she said quickly. "I'll give it to him when he gets back."

"But I know he's there."

She took a step toward me and began to slide her hands indignantly up and down her hips.

"You young men think you can force your way in here any time," she scolded. "We're getting sickantired of it. When I say he's in Chicago, he's in Chi*ca*go."

I mentioned Gatsby.

"Oh-h!" She looked at me all over again. "Will you just— What was your name?"

She vanished. In a moment Meyer Wolfshiem stood solemnly in the doorway, holding out both hands. He drew me into his office, remarking in a reverent voice that it was a sad time for all of us, and offered me a cigar.

"My memory goes back to when first I met him," he said. "A young major just out of the army and covered over with medals he got in the war. He was so hard up he had to keep on wearing his uniform because he couldn't buy some regular clothes. First time I saw him was when he come into Winebrenner's poolroom at Forty-third Street and asked for a job. He hadn't eat anything for a couple of days. 'Come on have some lunch with me,' I sid. He ate more than four dollars' worth of food in half an hour."

"Did you start him in business?" I inquired.

"Start him! I made him."

"Oh."

"I raised him up out of nothing, right out of the gutter. I saw right away he was a fine-appearing, gentlemanly young man, and when he told me he was an Oggsford I knew I could use him good. I got him to join up in the American Legion and he used to stand high there. Right off he did some work for a client of mine up to Albany. We were so thick like that in everything"—he held up two bulbous fingers—"always together."

I wondered if this partnership had included the World's Series transaction in 1919.

"Now he's dead," I said after a moment. "You were his closest friend, so I know you'll want to come to his funeral this afternoon."

"I'd like to come."

"Well, come then."

The hair in his nostrils quivered slightly, and as he shook his head his eyes filled with tears.

"I can't do it—I can't get mixed up in it," he said.

"There's nothing to get mixed up in. It's all over now."

"When a man gets killed I never like to get mixed up in it in any way. I keep out. When I was a young man it was different—if a friend of mine died, no matter how, I stuck with them to the end. You may think that's sentimental, but I mean it—to the bitter end."

I saw that for some reason of his own he was determined not to come, so I stood up.

"Are you a college man?" he inquired suddenly.

For a moment I thought he was going to suggest a "gonnegtion," but he only nodded and shook my hand.

"Let us learn to show our friendship for a man when he is alive and not after he is dead," he suggested. "After that my own rule is to let everything alone."

When I left his office the sky had turned dark and I got back to West Egg in a drizzle. After changing my clothes I went next door and found Mr. Gatz walking up and down excitedly in the hall. His pride in his son and in his son's possessions was continually increasing and now he had something to show me.

"Jimmy sent me this picture." He took out his wallet with trembling fingers. "Look there."

It was a photograph of the house, cracked in the corners and dirty with many hands. He pointed out every detail to me eagerly. "Look there!" and then sought admiration from my eyes. He had shown it so often that I think it was more real to him now than the house itself.

"Jimmy sent it to me. I think it's a very pretty picture. It shows up well."

"Very well. Had you seen him lately?"

"He come out to see me two years ago and bought me the house I live in now. Of course we was broke up when he run off from home, but I see now there was a reason for it. He knew he had a big future in front of him. And ever since he made a success he was very generous with me."

He seemed reluctant to put away the picture, held it for another minute, lingeringly, before my eyes. Then he returned the wallet and pulled from his pocket a ragged old copy of a book called "Hopalong Cassidy."

"Look here, this is a book he had when he was a boy. It just shows you."

He opened it at the back cover and turned it around for me to see. On the last fly-leaf was printed the word SCHEDULE, and the date September 12, 1906. And underneath:

Rise from bed.. 6.00	A.M.
Dumbbell exercise and wall-scaling................. 6.15–6.30	"
Study electricity, etc.. 7.15–8.15	"
Work.. 8.30–4.30	P.M.
Baseball and sports 4.30–5.00	"
Practice elocution, poise and how to attain it 5.00–6.00	"
Study needed inventions................................. 7.00–9.00	"

GENERAL RESOLVES

No wasting time at Shafters or [a name, indecipherable]
No more smoking or chewing.

Bath every other day
Read one improving book or magazine per week
Save $5.00 [crossed out] $3.00 per week
Be better to parents

"I come across this book by accident," said the old man. "It just shows you, don't it?"

"It just shows you."

"Jimmy was bound to get ahead. He always had some resolves like this or something. Do you notice what he's got about improving his mind? He was always great for that. He told me I et like a hog once, and I beat him for it."

He was reluctant to close the book, reading each item aloud and then looking eagerly at me. I think he rather expected me to copy down the list for my own use.

A little before three the Lutheran minister arrived from Flushing, and I began to look involuntarily out the windows for other cars. So did Gatsby's father. And as the time passed and the servants came in and stood waiting in the hall, his eyes began to blink anxiously, and he spoke of the rain in a worried, uncertain way. The minister glanced several times at his watch, so I took him aside and asked him to wait for half an hour. But it wasn't any use. Nobody came.

About five o'clock our procession of three cars reached the cemetery and stopped in a thick drizzle beside the gate—first a motor-hearse, horribly black and wet, then Mr. Gatz and the minister and I in the limousine, and a little later four or five servants and the postman from West Egg, in Gatsby's station wagon, all wet to the skin. As we started through the gate into the cemetery I heard a car stop and then the sound of someone splashing after us over the soggy ground. I looked around. It was the man with owl-eyed glasses whom I had found marvelling over Gatsby's books in the library one night three months before.

I'd never seen him since then. I don't know how he knew about the funeral, or even his name. The rain poured down his thick glasses, and he took them off and wiped them to see the protecting canvas unrolled from Gatsby's grave.

I tried to think about Gatsby then for a moment, but he was already too far away, and I could only remember, without resentment, that Daisy hadn't sent a message or a flower. Dimly I heard someone murmur "Blessed are the dead that the rain falls on," and then the owl-eyed man said "Amen to that," in a brave voice.

We straggled down quickly through the rain to the cars. Owl Eyes spoke to me by the gate.

"I couldn't get to the house," he remarked.

"Neither could anybody else."

"Go on!" He started. "Why, my God! they used to go there by the hundreds."

He took off his glasses and wiped them again, outside and in.

"The poor son-of-a-bitch," he said.

One of my most vivid memories is of coming back West from prep school and later from college at Christmas time. Those who went farther than Chicago would gather in the old dim Union Station at six o'clock of a December evening, with a few Chicago friends, already caught up into their own holiday gayeties, to bid them a hasty good-by. I remember the fur coats of the girls returning from Miss This-or-That's and the chatter of frozen breath and the hands waving overhead as we caught sight of old acquaintances, and the matchings of invitations: "Are you going to the Ordways'? the Herseys'? the Schultzes'?" and the long green tickets clasped tight in our gloved hands. And last the murky yellow cars of the Chicago, Milwaukee & St. Paul railroad looking cheerful as Christmas itself on the tracks beside the gate.

When we pulled out into the winter night and the real snow, our snow, began to stretch out beside us and twinkle against the windows, and the dim lights of small Wisconsin stations moved by, a sharp wild brace came suddenly into the air. We drew in deep breaths of it as we walked back from dinner through the cold vestibules, unutterably aware of our identity with this country for one strange hour, before we melted indistinguishably into it again.

That's my Middle West—not the wheat or the prairies or the lost Swede towns, but the thrilling returning trains of my youth, and the street lamps and sleigh bells in the frosty dark and the shadows of holly wreaths thrown by lighted windows on the snow. I am part of that, a little solemn with the feel of those long winters, a little complacent from growing up in the Carraway house in a city where dwellings are still called through decades by a family's name. I see now that this has been a story of the West, after all—Tom and Gatsby, Daisy and Jordan and I, were all Westerners, and perhaps we possessed some deficiency in common which made us subtly unadaptable to Eastern life.

Even when the East excited me most, even when I was most keenly aware of its superiority to the bored, sprawling, swollen towns beyond the Ohio, with their interminable inquisitions which spared only the children and the very old—even then it had always for me a quality of distortion. West Egg, especially, still figures in my more fantastic dreams. I see it as a night scene by El Greco: a hundred houses, at once conventional and grotesque, crouching under a sullen, overhanging sky and a lustreless moon. In the foreground four solemn men in dress suits are walking along the sidewalk with a stretcher on which lies a drunken woman in a white evening dress. Her hand, which dangles over the side, sparkles cold with jewels. Gravely the men turn in at a house—the wrong house. But no one knows the woman's name, and no one cares.

After Gatsby's death the East was haunted for me like that, distorted beyond my eyes' power of correction. So when the blue smoke of brittle leaves was in the air and the wind blew the wet laundry stiff on the line I decided to come back home.

There was one thing to be done before I left, an awkward, unpleasant thing that perhaps had better have been let alone. But I wanted to leave things in order and not just trust that obliging and indifferent sea to sweep my refuse away. I saw Jordan Baker and talked over and around what had happened to us together, and what had happened afterward to me, and she lay perfectly still, listening, in a big chair.

She was dressed to play golf, and I remember thinking she looked like a good illustration, her chin raised a little jauntily, her hair the color of an autumn leaf, her face the same brown tint as the fingerless glove on her knee. When I had finished she told me without comment that she was engaged to another man. I doubted that, though there were several she could have married at a nod of her head, but I pretended to be surprised. For just a minute I wondered if I wasn't making a mistake, then I thought it all over again quickly and got up to say good-by.

"Nevertheless you did throw me over," said Jordan suddenly. "You threw me over on the telephone. I don't give a damn about you now, but it was a new experience for me, and I felt a little dizzy for a while."

We shook hands.

"Oh, and do you remember"—she added—"a conversation we had once about driving a car?"

"Why—not exactly."

"You said a bad driver was only safe until she met another bad driver? Well, I met another bad driver, didn't I? I mean it was careless of me to make such a wrong guess. I thought you were rather an honest, straightforward person. I thought it was your secret pride."

"I'm thirty," I said. "I'm five years too old to lie to myself and call it honor."

She didn't answer. Angry, and half in love with her, and tremendously sorry, I turned away.

One afternoon late in October I saw Tom Buchanan. He was walking ahead of me along Fifth Avenue in his alert, aggressive way, his hands out a little from his body as if to fight off interference, his head moving sharply here and there, adapting itself to his restless eyes. Just as I slowed up to avoid overtaking him he stopped and began frowning into the windows of a jewelry store. Suddenly he saw me and walked back, holding out his hand.

"What's the matter, Nick? Do you object to shaking hands with me?"

"Yes. You know what I think of you."

"You're crazy, Nick," he said quickly. "Crazy as hell. I don't know what's the matter with you."

"Tom," I inquired, "what did you say to Wilson that afternoon?"

He stared at me without a word, and I knew I had guessed right about those missing hours. I started to turn away, but he took a step after me and grabbed my arm.

"I told him the truth," he said. "He came to the door while we were getting ready to leave, and when I sent down word that we weren't in he tried to force his way upstairs. He was crazy enough to kill me if I hadn't told him who owned the car. His hand was on a revolver in his pocket every minute he was in the house—" He broke off defiantly. "What if I did tell him? That fellow had it coming to him. He threw dust into your eyes just like he did in Daisy's, but he was a tough one. He ran over Myrtle like you'd run over a dog and never even stopped his car."

There was nothing I could say, except the one unutterable fact that it wasn't true.

"And if you think I didn't have my share of suffering—look here, when I went to give up that flat and saw that damn box of dog biscuits sitting there on the sideboard, I sat down and cried like a baby. By God it was awful——"

I couldn't forgive him or like him, but I saw that what he had done was, to him, entirely justified. It was all very careless and confused. They were careless people, Tom and Daisy—they smashed up things and creatures and then retreated back into their money or their vast carelessness, or whatever it was that kept them together, and let other people clean up the mess they had made. . . .

I shook hands with him; it seemed silly not to, for I felt suddenly as though I were talking to a child. Then he went into the jewelry store to buy a pearl necklace—or perhaps only a pair of cuff buttons—rid of my provincial squeamishness forever.

Gatsby's house was still empty when I left—the grass on his lawn had grown as long as mine. One of the taxi drivers in the village never took a fare past the entrance gate without stopping for a minute and pointing inside; perhaps it was he who drove Daisy and Gatsby over to East Egg the night of the accident, and perhaps he had made a story about it all his own. I didn't want to hear it and I avoided him when I got off the train.

I spent my Saturday nights in New York because those gleaming, dazzling parties of his were with me so vividly that I could still hear the music and the laughter, faint and incessant, from his garden, and the cars going up and down his drive. One night I did hear a material car there, and saw its lights stop at his front steps. But I didn't investigate. Probably it was some final guest who had been away at the ends of the earth and didn't know that the party was over.

On the last night, with my trunk packed and my car sold to the grocer, I went over and looked at that huge incoherent failure of a house once more. On the white steps an obscene word, scrawled by some boy with a piece of brick, stood out clearly in the moonlight, and I erased it, drawing my shoe raspingly along the stone. Then I wandered down to the beach and sprawled out on the sand.

Most of the big shore places were closed now and there were hardly any lights except the shadowy, moving glow of a ferryboat across the Sound. And as the moon rose higher the inessential houses began to melt away until gradually I became aware of the old island here that flowered once for Dutch sailors' eyes—a fresh, green breast of the new world. Its vanished trees, the trees that had made way for Gatsby's house, had once pandered in whispers to the last and greatest of all human dreams; for a transitory enchanted moment man must have held his breath in the presence of this continent, compelled into an æsthetic contemplation he neither understood nor desired, face to face for the last time in history with something commensurate to his capacity for wonder.

And as I sat there brooding on the old, unknown world, I thought of Gatsby's wonder when he first picked out the green light at the end of Daisy's dock. He had come a long way to this blue lawn, and his dream must have seemed so close that he could hardly fail to grasp it. He did not know that it was already behind him, somewhere back in that vast obscurity beyond the city, where the dark fields of the republic rolled on under the night.

Gatsby believed in the green light, the orgastic future that year by year recedes before us. It eluded us then, but that's no matter—tomorrow we will run faster, stretch out our arms farther. . . . And one fine morning——

So we beat on, boats against the current, borne back ceaselessly into the past.

ALL THE SAD YOUNG MEN

TO
RING AND ELLIS LARDNER

The Rich Boy

BEGIN with an individual and before you know it you find that you have created a type; begin with a type, and you find that you have created—nothing. That is because we are all queer fish, queerer behind our faces and voices than we want anyone to know or than we know ourselves. When I hear a man proclaiming himself an "average, honest, open fellow" I feel pretty sure that he has some definite and perhaps terrible abnormality which he has agreed to conceal—and his protestation of being average and honest and open is his way of reminding himself of his misprision.

There are no types, no plurals. There is a rich boy, and this is his and not his brothers' story. All my life I have lived among his brothers but this one has been my friend. Besides, if I wrote about his brothers I should have to begin by attacking all the lies that the poor have told about the rich and the rich have told about themselves—such a wild structure they have erected that when we pick up a book about the rich, some instinct prepares us for unreality. Even the intelligent and impassioned reporters of life have made the country of the rich as unreal as fairyland.

Let me tell you about the very rich. They are different from you and me. They possess and enjoy early, and it does something to them, makes them soft where we are hard and cynical where we are trustful, in a way that, unless you were born rich, it is very difficult to understand. They think, deep in their hearts, that they are better than we are because we had to discover the compensations and refuges of life for ourselves. Even when they enter deep into our world or sink below us, they still think that they are better than we are. They are different. The only way I can describe young Anson Hunter is to approach him as if he were a foreigner and cling stubbornly to my point of view. If I accept his for a moment I am lost—I have nothing to show but a preposterous movie.

II

Anson was the eldest of six children who would some day divide a fortune of fifteen million dollars, and he reached the age of reason—is it seven?—at the beginning of the century when daring young women were already gliding along Fifth Avenue in electric "mobiles." In those days he and his brother had an English governess who spoke the language very clearly and crisply and well, so that the two boys grew to speak as she did—their words and sentences were all crisp and clear and not run together as ours are. They didn't talk exactly like English children but acquired an accent that is peculiar to fashionable people in the city of New York.

In the summer the six children were moved from the house on 71st Street to a big estate in northern Connecticut. It was not a fashionable locality—Anson's father wanted to delay as long as possible his children's knowledge of that side of life. He was a man somewhat superior to his class, which composed New York society, and to his period, which was the snobbish and formalized vulgarity of the Gilded Age, and he wanted his sons to learn habits of concentration and have sound constitutions and grow up into right-living and successful men. He and his wife kept an eye on them as well as they were able until the two older boys went away to school, but in huge establishments this is difficult—it was much simpler in the series of small and medium-sized houses in which my own youth was spent—I was never far out of the reach of my mother's voice, of the sense of her presence, her approval or disapproval.

Anson's first sense of his superiority came to him when he realized the half-grudging American deference that was paid to him in the Connecticut village. The parents of the boys he played with always inquired after his father and mother, and were vaguely excited when their own children were asked to the Hunters' house. He accepted this as the natural state of things, and a sort of impatience with all groups of which he was not the center—in money, in position, in authority—remained with him for the rest of his life. He disdained to struggle with other boys for precedence—he expected it to be given him freely and when it wasn't he withdrew into his family. His family was sufficient, for in the East money is still a somewhat feudal thing, a clan-forming thing. In the snobbish West, money separates families to form "sets."

At eighteen, when he went to New Haven, Anson was tall and thick-set with a clear complexion and a healthy color from the ordered life he had led in school. His hair was yellow and grew in a funny way on his head, his nose was beaked—these two things kept him from being handsome—but he had a confident charm and a certain brusque style, and the upper-class men who passed him on the street knew without being told that he was a rich boy and had gone to one of the best schools. Nevertheless his very superiority kept him from being a success in college—the independence was mistaken for egotism, and the refusal to accept Yale standards with the proper awe seemed to belittle all those who had. So, long before he graduated, he began to shift the center of his life to New York.

He was at home in New York—there was his own house with "the kind of servants you can't get anymore"—and his own family, of which, because of his good humor and a certain ability to make things go, he was rapidly becoming the center, and the debutante parties, and the correct manly world of the men's clubs, and the occasional wild spree with the gallant girls whom New Haven only knew from the fifth row. His aspirations were conventional enough—they included even the irreproachable shadow he would someday marry, but they differed from the aspirations of the majority of young men in that there was no mist over them, none of that quality which is variously known as "idealism" or "illusion." Anson accepted without reservation the world of high finance and high extravagance, of divorce and dissipation, of snobbery and of privilege. Most of our lives end as a compromise—it was as a compromise that his life began.

He and I first met in the late summer of 1917 when he was just out of Yale, and, like the rest of us, was swept up into the systematized hysteria of the war. In the blue-green uniform of the naval aviation he came down to Pensacola, where the hotel orchestras played "I'm Sorry, Dear" and we young officers danced with the girls. Everyone liked him, and though he ran with the drinkers and wasn't an especially good pilot, even the instructors treated him with a certain respect. He was always having long talks with them in his confident, logical voice—talks which ended by his getting himself, or more frequently another officer, out of some impending trouble. He was convivial, bawdy, robustly avid for pleasure, and we were all surprised when he fell in love with a conservative and rather proper girl.

Her name was Paula Legendre, a dark, serious beauty from somewhere in California. Her family kept a winter residence just outside of town, and in spite of her primness she was enormously popular; there is a large class of men whose egotism can't endure humor in a woman. But Anson wasn't that sort, and I couldn't understand the attraction of her "sincerity"— that was the thing to say about her—for his keen and somewhat sardonic mind.

Nevertheless, they fell in love—and on her terms. He no longer joined the twilight gathering at the De Soto bar, and whenever they were seen together they were engaged in a long, serious dialogue, which must have gone on several weeks. Long afterward he told me that it was not about anything in particular but was composed on both sides of immature and even meaningless statements—the emotional content that gradually came to fill it grew up not out of the words but out of its enormous seriousness. It was a sort of hypnosis. Often it was interrupted, giving way to that emasculated humor we call fun; when they were alone it was resumed again—solemn, low-keyed, and pitched so as to give each other a sense of unity in feeling and thought. They came to resent any interruptions of it, to be unresponsive to facetiousness about life, even to the mild cynicism of their contemporaries. They were only happy when the dialogue was going on and its seriousness bathed them like the amber glow of an open fire. Toward the end there came an interruption they did not resent—it began to be interrupted by passion.

Oddly enough Anson was as engrossed in the dialogue as she was and as profoundly affected by it, yet at the same time aware that, on his side, much was insincere and, on hers, much was merely simple. At first, too, he despised her emotional simplicity as well, but with his love her nature deepened and blossomed and he could despise it no longer. He felt that if he could enter into Paula's warm safe life he would be happy. The long preparation of the dialogue removed any constraint—he taught her some of what he had learned from more adventurous women and she responded with a rapt holy intensity. One evening after a dance they agreed to marry and he wrote a long letter about her to his mother. The next day Paula told him that she was rich, that she had a personal fortune of nearly a million dollars.

III

It was exactly as if they could say "Neither of us has anything: we shall be poor together"—just as delightful that they should be rich instead. It gave them the same communion of adventure. Yet when Anson got leave in April and Paula and her mother accompanied him north, she was impressed with the standing of his family in New York and with the scale on which they lived. Alone with Anson for the first time in the rooms where he had played as a boy, she was filled with a comfortable emotion, as though she were preeminently safe and taken care of. The pictures of Anson in a skull cap at his first school, of Anson on horseback with the sweetheart of a mysterious forgotten summer, of Anson in a gay group of ushers and bridesmaids at a wedding, made her jealous of his life apart from her in the past, and so completely did his authoritative person seem to sum up and typify these possessions of his that she was inspired with the idea of being married immediately and returning to Pensacola as his wife.

But an immediate marriage wasn't discussed—even the engagement was to be secret until after the war. When she realized that only two days of his leave remained, her dissatisfaction crystallized in the intention of making him as unwilling to wait as she was. They were driving to the country for dinner and she determined to force the issue that night.

Now a cousin of Paula's was staying with them at the Ritz, a severe bitter girl who loved Paula but was somewhat jealous of her impressive engagement, and as Paula was late in dressing, the cousin, who wasn't going to the party, received Anson in the parlor of the suite.

Anson had met friends at five o'clock and drunk freely and indiscreetly with them for an hour. He left the Yale Club at a proper time, and his mother's chauffeur drove him to the Ritz, but his usual capacity was not in evidence, and the impact of the steam-heated sitting-room made him suddenly dizzy. He knew it, and he was both amused and sorry.

Paula's cousin was twenty-five, but she was exceptionally naive, and at first failed to realize what was up. She had never met Anson before, and she was surprised when he mumbled strange information and nearly fell off his chair, but until Paula appeared it didn't occur to her that what she had taken for the odor of a dry-cleaned uniform was really whiskey. But Paula understood as soon as she appeared; her only thought was to get Anson away before her mother saw him, and at the look in her eyes the cousin understood too.

When Paula and Anson descended to the limousine they found two men inside, both asleep; they were the men with whom he had been drinking at the Yale Club, and they were also going to the party. He had entirely forgotten their presence in the car. On the way to Hempstead they awoke and sang. Some of the songs were rough, and though Paula tried to reconcile herself to the fact that Anson had few verbal inhibitions, her lips tightened with shame and distaste.

Back at the hotel the cousin, confused and agitated, considered the incident, and then walked into Mrs. Legendre's bedroom saying: "Isn't he funny?"

"Who is funny?"

"Why—Mr. Hunter. He seemed so funny."

Mrs. Legendre looked at her sharply.

"How is he funny?"

"Why, he said he was French. I didn't know he was French."

"That's absurd. You must have misunderstood." She smiled: "It was a joke."

The cousin shook her head stubbornly.

"No. He said he was brought up in France. He said he couldn't speak any English and that's why he couldn't talk to me. And he couldn't!"

Mrs. Legendre looked away with impatience just as the cousin added thoughtfully, "Perhaps it was because he was so drunk," and walked out of the room.

This curious report was true. Anson, finding his voice thick and uncontrollable, had taken the unusual refuge of announcing that he spoke no English. Years afterward he used to tell that part of the story, and he invariably communicated the uproarious laughter which the memory aroused in him.

Five times in the next hour Mrs. Legendre tried to get Hempstead on the phone. When she succeeded there was a ten-minute delay before she heard Paula's voice on the wire.

"Cousin Jo told me Anson was intoxicated."

"Oh, no. . . ."

"Oh, yes. Cousin Jo says he was intoxicated. He told her he was French and fell off his chair and behaved as if he was very intoxicated. I don't want you to come home with him."

"Mother, he's all right! Please don't worry about—"

"But I do worry. I think it's dreadful. I want you to promise me not to come home with him."

"I'll take care of it, Mother. . . ."

"I don't want you to come home with him."

"All right, Mother. Good-bye."

"Be sure now, Paula. Ask someone to bring you."

Deliberately Paula took the receiver from her ear and hung it up. Her face was flushed with helpless annoyance. Anson was stretched asleep out in a bedroom upstairs, while the dinner party below was proceeding lamely toward conclusion.

The hour's drive had sobered him somewhat—his arrival was merely hilarious—and Paula hoped that the evening was not spoiled after all, but two imprudent cocktails before dinner completed the disaster. He talked boisterously and somewhat offensively to the party at large for fifteen minutes and then slid silently under the table, like a man in an old print—but, unlike an old print, it was rather horrible without being at all quaint. None of the young girls present remarked upon the incident—it seemed to merit only silence. His uncle and two other men carried him upstairs, and it was just after this that Paula was called to the phone.

An hour later Anson awoke in a fog of nervous agony, through which he perceived after a moment the figure of his Uncle Robert standing by the door.

". . . I said are you better?"

"What?"

"Do you feel better, old man?"

"Terrible," said Anson.

"I'm going to try you on another bromo-seltzer. If you can hold it down, it'll do you good to sleep."

With an effort Anson slid his legs from the bed and stood up.

"I'm all right," he said dully.

"Take it easy."

"I thin' if you gave me a glassbrandy I could go downstairs."

"Oh, no—"

"Yes, that's the only thin'. I'm all right now. . . . I suppose I'm in Dutch dow' there."

"They know you're a little under the weather," said his uncle deprecatingly. "But don't worry about it. Schuyler didn't even get here. He passed away in the locker room over at the Links."

Indifferent to any opinion, except Paula's, Anson was nevertheless determined to save the debris of the evening, but when after a cold bath he made his appearance most of the party had already left. Paula got up immediately to go home.

In the limousine the old serious dialogue began. She had known that he drank, she admitted, but she had never expected anything like this—it seemed to her that perhaps they were not suited to each other, after all. Their ideas about life were too different, and so forth. When she finished speaking, Anson spoke in turn, very soberly. Then Paula said she'd have to think it over; she wouldn't decide tonight; she was not angry but she was terribly sorry. Nor would she let him come into the hotel with her, but just before she got out of the car she leaned and kissed him unhappily on the cheek.

The next afternoon Anson had a long talk with Mrs. Legendre while Paula sat listening in silence. It was agreed that Paula was to brood over the incident for a proper period and then, if mother and daughter thought it best, they would follow Anson to Pensacola. On his part he apologized with sincerity and dignity—that was all; with every card in her hand Mrs. Legendre was unable to establish any advantage over him. He made no promises, showed no humility, only delivered a few serious comments on life which brought him off with rather a moral superiority at the end. When they came south three weeks later, neither Anson in his satisfaction nor Paula in her relief at the reunion realized that the psychological moment had passed forever.

IV

He dominated and attracted her and at the same time filled her with anxiety. Confused by his mixture of solidity and self-indulgence, of sentiment and cynicism—incongruities which her gentle mind was unable to resolve—Paula grew to think of him as two alternating personalities. When she saw him alone, or at a formal party, or with his casual inferiors, she felt a tremendous pride in his strong attractive presence, the paternal, understanding stature of his mind. In other company she became uneasy when what had been a fine imperviousness to mere gentility showed its other face. The other face was gross, humorous, reckless of everything but pleasure. It startled her mind temporarily away from him, even led her into a short covert experiment with an old beau, but it was no use—after four months of Anson's enveloping vitality there was an anaemic pallor in all other men.

In July he was ordered abroad and their tenderness and desire reached a crescendo. Paula considered a last-minute marriage—decided against it only because there were always cocktails on his breath now, but the parting itself made her physically ill with grief. After his departure she wrote him long letters of regret for the days of love they had missed by waiting. In August Anson's plane slipped down into the North Sea. He was pulled onto a destroyer after a night in the water and sent to hospital with pneumonia; the armistice was signed before he was finally sent home.

Then, with every opportunity given back to them, with no material obstacle to overcome, the secret weavings of their temperaments came between them, drying up their kisses and their tears, making their voices less loud to one another, muffling the intimate chatter of their hearts until the old communication was only possible by letters from far away. One afternoon a society reporter waited for two hours in the Hunters' house for a confirmation of their engagement. Anson denied it; nevertheless an early issue carried the report as a leading paragraph—they were "constantly seen together at Southampton, Hot Springs, and Tuxedo Park." But the serious dialogue had turned a corner into a long, sustained quarrel, and the affair was almost played out. Anson got drunk flagrantly and missed an engagement with her, whereupon Paula made certain behavioristic demands. His despair was helpless before his pride and his knowledge of himself: the engagement was definitely broken.

"Dearest," said their letters now, "Dearest, Dearest, when I wake up in the middle of the night and realize that after all it was not to be, I feel that I want to die. I can't go on living anymore. Perhaps when we meet this summer we may talk things over and decide differently—we were so excited and sad that day and I don't feel that I can live all my life without you. You speak of other people. Don't you know there are no other people for me but only you. . . ."

But as Paula drifted here and there around the East she would sometimes mention her gaieties to make him wonder. Anson was too acute to wonder. When he saw a man's name in her letters he felt more sure of her and a little disdainful—he was always superior to such things. But he still hoped that they would some-day marry.

Meanwhile he plunged vigorously into all the movement and glitter of post-bellum New York, entering a brokerage house, joining half a dozen clubs, dancing late, and moving in three worlds—his own world, the world of young Yale graduates, and that section of the half-world which rests one end on Broadway. But there was always a thorough and infractible eight hours devoted to his work in Wall Street, where the combination of his influential family connection, his sharp intelligence, and his abundance of sheer physical energy brought him almost imme-diately forward. He had one of those invaluable minds with partitions in it; sometimes he appeared at his office refreshed by less than an hour's sleep, but such occurrences were rare. So early as 1920 his income in salary and commissions exceeded twelve thousand dollars.

As the Yale tradition slipped into the past he became more and more of a popular figure among his classmates in New York, more popular than he had ever been in college. He lived in a great house and had the means of introducing young men into other great houses. Moreover, his life already seemed secure, while theirs, for the most part, had arrived again at precarious beginnings. They commenced to turn to him for amusement and escape, and Anson responded readily, taking pleasure in helping people and arranging their affairs.

There were no men in Paula's letters now but a note of ten-derness ran through them that had not been there before. From several sources he heard that she had "a heavy beau," Lowell Thayer, a Bostonian of wealth and position, and though he was sure she still loved him, it made him uneasy to think that he might lose her after all. Save for one unsatisfactory day she had not been in New York for almost five months, and as the rumors multiplied he became increasingly anxious to see her. In February he took his vacation and went down to Florida.

Palm Beach sprawled plump and opulent between the sparkling sapphire of Lake Worth, flawed here and there by house-boats at anchor, and the great turquoise bar of the Atlantic Ocean. The huge bulks of the Breakers and the Royal Poinciana rose as twin paunches from the bright level of the sand and around them clustered the Dancing Glade, Bradley's House of Chance and a dozen modistes and milliners with goods at triple prices from New York. Upon the trellissed verandah of the Breakers two hundred women stepped right, stepped left, wheeled and slid in that then celebrated calisthenic known as the double-shuffle, while in half-time to the music two thousand bracelets clicked up and down on two hundred arms.

At the Everglades Club after dark Paula and Lowell Thayer and Anson and a casual fourth played bridge with hot cards. It seemed to Anson that her kind serious face was wan and tired—she had been around now for four, five years. He had known her for three.

"Two spades."

"Cigarette? . . . Oh, I beg your pardon. By me."

"By."

"I'll double three spades."

There were a dozen tables of bridge in the room, which was filling up with smoke. Anson's eyes met Paula's, held them persistently even when Thayer's glance fell between them. . . .

"What was bid?" he asked abstractedly.

"Rose of Washington Square"

sang the young people in the corners:

"I'm withering there
In basement air—"

The smoke banked like fog, and the opening of a door filled the room with blown swirls of ectoplasm. Little Bright Eyes streaked past the tables seeking Mr. Conan Doyle among the Englishmen who were posing as Englishmen about the lobby.

"You could cut it with a knife."

". . . cut it with a knife."

". . . a knife."

At the end of the rubber Paula suddenly got up and spoke to Anson in a tense, low voice. With scarcely a glance at Lowell

Thayer, they walked out the door and descended a long flight of stone steps—in a moment they were walking hand in hand along the moonlit beach.

"Darling, darling. . . ." They embraced recklessly, passionately, in a shadow. . . . Then Paula drew back her face to let his lips say what she wanted to hear—she could feel the words forming as they kissed again. . . . Again she broke away, listening, but as he pulled her close once more she realized that he had said nothing—only "*Darling! Darling!*" in that deep, sad whisper that always made her cry. Humbly, obediently, her emotions yielded to him and the tears streamed down her face, but her heart kept on crying: "Ask me—Oh, Anson, dearest, ask me!"

"Paula. . . . *Paula!*"

The words wrung her heart like hands and Anson feeling her tremble knew that emotion was enough. He need say no more, commit their destinies to no practical enigma. Why should he, when he might hold her so, biding his own time, for another year—forever? He was considering them both, her more than himself. For a moment, when she said suddenly that she must go back to her hotel, he hesitated, thinking first, "This is the moment after all," and then: "No, let it wait—she is mine. . . ."

He had forgotten that Paula too was worn away inside with the strain of three years. Her mood passed forever in the night.

He went back to New York next morning filled with a certain restless dissatisfaction. Late in April, without warning, he received a telegram from Bar Harbor in which Paula told him that she was engaged to Lowell Thayer and that they would be married immediately in Boston. What he never really believed could happen had happened at last.

Anson filled himself with whiskey that morning, and going to the office, carried on his work without a break—rather with a fear of what would happen if he stopped. In the evening he went out as usual, saying nothing of what had occurred; he was cordial, humorous, unabstracted. But one thing he could not help—for three days, in any place, in any company, he would suddenly bend his head into his hands and cry like a child.

V

In 1922 when Anson went abroad with the junior partner to investigate some London loans, the journey intimated that he was to be taken into the firm. He was twenty-seven now, a little heavy without being definitely stout, and with a manner older than his years. Old people and young people liked him and trusted him, and mothers felt safe when their daughters were in his charge, for he had a way, when he came into a room, of putting himself on a footing with the oldest and most conservative people there. "You and I," he seemed to say, "we're solid. We understand."

He had an instinctive and rather charitable knowledge of the weaknesses of men and women, and, like a priest, it made him the more concerned for the maintenance of outward forms. It was typical of him that every Sunday morning he taught in a fashionable Episcopal Sunday school—even though a cold shower and a quick change into a cutaway coat were all that separated him from the wild night before.

After his father's death he was the practical head of his family, and, in effect, guided the destinies of the younger children. Through a complication his authority did not extend to his father's estate, which was administrated by his Uncle Robert, who was the horsey member of the family, a good-natured, hard-drinking member of that set which centers about Wheatley Hills.

Uncle Robert and his wife, Edna, had been great friends of Anson's youth, and the former was disappointed when his nephew's superiority failed to take a horsey form. He backed him for a city club which was the most difficult in America to enter—one could only join if one's family had "helped to build up New York" (or, in other words, were rich before 1880)—and when Anson, after his election, neglected it for the Yale Club, Uncle Robert gave him a little talk on the subject. But when on top of that Anson declined to enter Robert Hunter's own conservative and somewhat neglected brokerage house, his manner grew cooler. Like a primary teacher who has taught all he knew, he slipped out of Anson's life.

There were so many friends in Anson's life—scarcely one for whom he had not done some unusual kindness and scarcely one whom he did not occasionally embarrass by his bursts of rough conversation or his habit of getting drunk whenever and however he liked. It annoyed him when anyone else blundered in that regard—about his own lapses he was always humorous. Odd things happened to him and he told them with infectious laughter.

I was working in New York that spring, and I used to lunch with him at the Yale Club, which my university was sharing until the completion of our own. I had read of Paula's marriage, and one afternoon, when I asked him about her, something moved him to tell me the story. After that he frequently invited me to family dinners at his house and behaved as though there was a special relation between us, as though with his confidence a little of that consuming memory had passed into me.

I found that despite the trusting mothers, his attitude toward girls was not indiscriminately protective. It was up to the girl—if she showed an inclination toward looseness, she must take care of herself, even with him.

"Life," he would explain sometimes, "has made a cynic of me."

By life he meant Paula. Sometimes, especially when he was drinking, it became a little twisted in his mind, and he thought that she had callously thrown him over.

This "cynicism," or rather his realization that naturally fast girls were not worth sparing, led to his affair with Dolly Karger. It wasn't his only affair in those years, but it came nearest to touching him deeply, and it had a profound effect upon his attitude toward life.

Dolly was the daughter of a notorious "publicist" who had married into society. She herself grew up into the Junior League, came out at the Plaza, and went to the Assembly; and only a few old families like the Hunters could question whether or not she "belonged," for her picture was often in the papers, and she had more enviable attention than many girls who undoubtedly did. She was dark-haired with carmine lips and a high lovely color which she concealed under pinkish-grey powder all through the first year out, because high color was unfashionable—Victorian-pale was the thing to be. She wore black, severe suits and stood with her hands in her pockets, leaning a little forward, with a humorous restraint on her face. She

danced exquisitely—better than anything she liked to dance—
better than anything except making love. Since she was ten she
had always been in love, and, usually, with some boy who didn't
respond to her. Those who did—and there were many—bored
her after a brief encounter, but for her failures she reserved the
warmest spot in her heart. When she met them she would always
try once more—sometimes she succeeded, more often she failed.

It never occurred to this gypsy of the unattainable that there
was a certain resemblance in those who refused to love her—
they shared a hard intuition that saw through to her weakness,
not a weakness of emotion but a weakness of rudder. Anson perceived this when he first met her, less than a month after Paula's
marriage. He was drinking rather heavily, and he pretended for
a week that he was falling in love with her. Then he dropped her
abruptly and forgot—immediately he took up the commanding
position in her heart.

Like so many girls of that day Dolly was slackly and indiscreetly wild. The unconventionality of a slightly older generation
had been simply one facet of a post-war movement to discredit
obsolete manners—Dolly's was both older and shabbier, and she
saw in Anson the two extremes which the emotionally shiftless
woman seeks, an abandon to indulgence alternating with a protective strength. In his character she felt both the sybarite and
the solid rock, and these two satisfied every need of her nature.

She felt that it was going to be difficult, but she mistook
the reason—she thought that Anson and his family expected a
more spectacular marriage, but she guessed immediately that
her advantage lay in his tendency to drink.

They met at the large debutante dances, but as her infatuation
increased they managed to be more and more together. Like
most mothers Mrs. Karger believed that Anson was exceptionally
reliable, so she allowed Dolly to go with him to distant country
clubs and suburban houses without inquiring closely into their
activities or questioning her explanations when they came in
late. At first these explanations might have been accurate, but
Dolly's worldly ideas of capturing Anson were soon engulfed in
the rising sweep of her emotion. Kisses in the back of taxis and
motor cars were no longer enough; they did a curious thing:

They dropped out of their world for awhile and made another
world just beneath it where Anson's tippling and Dolly's

irregular hours would be less noticed and commented on. It was composed, this world, of varying elements—several of Anson's Yale friends and their wives, two or three young brokers and bond salesmen and a handful of unattached men, fresh from college, with money and a propensity to dissipation. What this world lacked in spaciousness and scale it made up for by allowing them a liberty that it scarcely permitted itself. Moreover it centered around them and permitted Dolly the pleasure of a faint condescension—a pleasure which Anson, whose whole life was a condescension from the certitudes of his childhood, was unable to share.

He was not in love with her and in the long feverish winter of their affair he frequently told her so. In the spring he was weary—he wanted to renew his life at some other source—moreover, he saw that either he must break with her now or accept the responsibility of a definite seduction. Her family's encouraging attitude precipitated his decision—one evening when Mr. Karger knocked discreetly at the library door to announce that he had left a bottle of old brandy in the dining room, Anson felt that life was hemming him in. That night he wrote her a short letter in which he told her that he was going on his vacation and that in view of all the circumstances they had better meet no more.

It was June. His family had closed up the house and gone to the country, so he was living temporarily at the Yale Club. I had heard about his affair with Dolly as it developed—accounts salted with humor, for he despised unstable women, and granted them no place in the social edifice in which he believed—and when he told me that night that he was definitely breaking with her I was glad. I had seen Dolly here and there and each time with a feeling of pity at the hopelessness of her struggle, and of shame at knowing so much about her that I had no right to know. She was what is known as "a pretty little thing," but there was a certain recklessness which rather fascinated me. Her dedication to the goddess of waste would have been less obvious had she been less spirited—she would most certainly throw herself away, but I was glad when I heard that the sacrifice would not be consummated in my sight.

Anson was going to leave the letter of farewell at her house next morning. It was one of the few houses left open in the

Fifth Avenue district, and he knew that the Kargers, acting upon erroneous information from Dolly, had foregone a trip abroad to give their daughter her chance. As he stepped out the door of the Yale Club into Vanderbilt Avenue the postman passed him, and he followed back inside. The first letter that caught his eye was in Dolly's hand.

He knew what it would be—a lonely and tragic monologue, full of the reproaches he knew, the invoked memories, the "I wonder if's"—all the immemorial intimacies that he had communicated to Paula Legendre in what seemed another age. Thumbing over some bills, he brought it on top again and opened it. To his surprise it was a short, somewhat formal note, which said that Dolly would be unable to go to the country with him for the week-end, because Perry Hull from Chicago had unexpectedly come to town. It added that Anson had brought this on himself: "—if I felt that you loved me as I love you I would go with you at any time any place, but Perry is *so* nice, and he so much wants me to marry him—"

Anson smiled contemptuously—he had had experience with such decoy epistles. Moreover, he knew how Dolly had labored over this plan, probably sent for the faithful Perry and calculated the time of his arrival—even labored over the note so that it would make him jealous without driving him away. Like most compromises it had neither force nor vitality but only a timorous despair.

Suddenly he was angry. He sat down in the lobby and read it again. Then he went to the phone, called Dolly and told her in his clear, compelling voice that he had received her note and would call for her at five o'clock as they had previously planned. Scarcely waiting for the pretended uncertainty of her "Perhaps I can see you for an hour," he hung up the receiver and went down to his office. On the way he tore his own letter into bits and dropped it in the street.

He was not jealous—she meant nothing to him—but at her pathetic ruse everything stubborn and self-indulgent in him came to the surface. It was a presumption from a mental inferior and it could not be overlooked. If she wanted to know to whom she belonged she would see.

He was on the doorstep at quarter past five. Dolly was dressed for the street, and he listened in silence to the paragraph of "I can only see you for an hour," which she had begun on the phone.

"Put on your hat, Dolly," he said, "we'll take a walk."

They strolled up Madison Avenue and over to Fifth while Anson's shirt dampened upon his portly body in the deep heat. He talked little, scolding her, making no love to her, but before they had walked six blocks she was his again, apologizing for the note, offering not to see Perry at all as an atonement, offering anything. She thought that he had come because he was beginning to love her.

"I'm hot," he said when they reached 71st Street. "This is a winter suit. If I stop by the house and change, would you mind waiting for me downstairs? I'll only be a minute."

She was happy; the intimacy of his being hot, of any physical fact about him, thrilled her. When they came to the iron-grated door and Anson took out his key she experienced a sort of delight.

Downstairs it was dark, and after he ascended in the lift Dolly raised a curtain and looked out through opaque lace at the houses over the way. She heard the lift machinery stop and, with the notion of teasing him, pressed the button that brought it down. Then on what was more than an impulse she got into it and sent it up to what she guessed was his floor.

"Anson," she called, laughing a little.

"Just a minute," he answered from his bedroom . . . then after a brief delay: "Now you can come in."

He had changed and was buttoning his vest.

"This is my room," he said lightly. "How do you like it?"

She caught sight of Paula's picture on the wall and stared at it in fascination, just as Paula had stared at the pictures of Anson's childish sweethearts five years before. She knew something about Paula—sometimes she tortured herself with fragments of the story.

Suddenly she came close to Anson, raising her arms. They embraced. Outside the area window a soft artificial twilight already hovered, though the sun was still bright on a back roof across the way. In half an hour the room would be quite dark. The uncalculated opportunity overwhelmed them, made them both breathless, and they clung more closely. It was imminent, inevitable. Still holding one another, they raised their heads—their eyes fell together upon Paula's picture, staring down at them from the wall.

Suddenly Anson dropped his arms, and sitting down at his desk tried the drawer with a bunch of keys.

"Like a drink?" he asked in a gruff voice.

"No, Anson."

He poured himself half a tumbler of whiskey, swallowed it and then opened the door into the hall.

"Come on," he said.

Dolly hesitated.

"Anson—I'm going to the country with you tonight, after all. You understand that, don't you?"

"Of course," he answered brusquely.

In Dolly's car they rode out to Long Island, closer in their emotions than they had ever been before. They knew what would happen—not with Paula's face to remind them that something was lacking, but when they were alone in the still hot Long Island night that did not care.

The estate in Port Washington where they were to spend the week-end belonged to a cousin of Anson's who had married a Montana copper operator. An interminable drive began at the lodge and twisted under imported poplar saplings toward a huge, pink, Spanish house. Anson had often visited there before.

After dinner they danced at the Linx Club. About midnight Anson assured himself that his cousins would not leave before two—then he explained that Dolly was tired; he would take her home and return to the dance later. Trembling a little with excitement they got into a borrowed car together and drove to Port Washington. As they reached the lodge he stopped and spoke to the night-watchman.

"When are you making a round, Carl?"

"Right away."

"Then you'll be here till everybody's in?"

"Yes, sir."

"All right. Listen: if any automobile, no matter whose it is, turns in at this gate, I want you to phone the house immediately." He put a five-dollar bill into Carl's hand. "Is that clear?"

"Yes, Mr. Anson." Being of the Old World, he neither winked nor smiled. Yet Dolly sat with her face turned slightly away.

Anson had a key. Once inside he poured a drink for both of them—Dolly left hers untouched—then he ascertained definitely the location of the phone, and found that it was within easy hearing distance of their rooms, both of which were on the first floor.

Five minutes later he knocked at the door of Dolly's room.

"Anson?" He went in, closing the door behind him. She was in bed, leaning up anxiously with elbows on the pillow; sitting beside her he took her in his arms.

"Anson, darling."

He didn't answer.

"Anson. . . . Anson! I love you. . . . Say you love me. Say it now—can't you say it now? Even if you don't mean it?"

He did not listen. Over her head he perceived that the picture of Paula was hanging here upon this wall.

He got up and went close to it. The frame gleamed faintly with thrice-reflected moonlight—within was a blurred shadow of a face that he saw he did not know. Almost sobbing, he turned around and stared with abomination at the little figure on the bed.

"This is all foolishness," he said thickly. "I don't know what I was thinking about. I don't love you and you'd better wait for somebody that loves you. I don't love you a bit, can't you understand?"

His voice broke and he went hurriedly out. Back in the salon he was pouring himself a drink with uneasy fingers, when the front door opened suddenly, and his cousin came in.

"Why, Anson, I hear Dolly's sick," she began solicitously. "I hear she's sick. . . ."

"It was nothing," he interrupted, raising his voice so that it would carry into Dolly's room. "She was a little tired. She went to bed."

For a long time afterwards Anson believed that a protective God sometimes interfered in human affairs. But Dolly Karger, lying awake and staring at the ceiling, never again believed in anything at all.

VI

When Dolly married during the following autumn, Anson was in London on business. Like Paula's marriage, it was sudden, but it affected him in a different way. At first he felt that it was funny and had an inclination to laugh when he thought of it. Later it depressed him—it made him feel old.

There was something repetitive about it—why, Paula and Dolly had belonged to different generations. He had a foretaste of the sensation of a man of forty who hears that the daughter of an old flame has married. He wired congratulations and, as was not the case with Paula, they were sincere—he had never really hoped that Paula would be happy.

When he returned to New York, he was made a partner in the firm, and as his responsibilities increased he had less time on his hands. The refusal of a life-insurance company to issue him a policy made such an impression on him that he stopped drinking for a year and claimed that he felt better physically, though I think he missed the convivial recounting of those Celliniesque adventures which, in his early twenties, had played such a part in his life. But he never abandoned the Yale Club. He was a figure there, a personality, and the tendency of his class, who were now seven years out of college, to drift away to more sober haunts was checked by his presence.

His day was never too full nor his mind too weary to give any sort of aid to anyone who asked it. What had been done at first through pride and superiority had become a habit and a passion. And there was always something—a younger brother in trouble at New Haven, a quarrel to be patched up between a friend and his wife, a position to be found for this man, an investment for that. But his specialty was the solving of problems for young married people. Young married people fascinated him and their apartments were almost sacred to him—he knew the story of their love affair, advised them where to live and how, and remembered their babies' names. Toward young wives his attitude was circumspect: he never abused the trust which their husbands—strangely enough in view of his unconcealed irregularities—invariably reposed in him.

He came to take a vicarious pleasure in happy marriages and to be inspired to an almost equally pleasant melancholy by those that went astray. Not a season passed that he did not witness the collapse of an affair that perhaps he himself had fathered. When Paula was divorced and almost immediately remarried to another Bostonian, he talked about her to me all one afternoon. He would never love anyone as he had loved Paula, but he insisted that he no longer cared.

"I'll never marry," he came to say; "I've seen too much of it, and I know a happy marriage is a very rare thing. Besides, I'm too old."

But he did believe in marriage. Like all men who spring from a happy and successful marriage, he believed in it passionately— nothing he had seen would change his belief, his cynicism dissolved upon it like air. But he did really believe he was too old. At twenty-eight he began to accept with equanimity the prospect of marrying without romantic love; he resolutely chose a New York girl of his own class, pretty, intelligent, congenial, above reproach—and set about falling in love with her. The things he had said to Paula with sincerity, to other girls with grace, he could no longer say at all without smiling, or with the force necessary to convince.

"When I'm forty," he told his friends, "I'll be ripe. I'll fall for some chorus girl like the rest."

Nevertheless he persisted in his attempt. His mother wanted to see him married, and he could now well afford it—he had a seat on the stock exchange, and his earned income came to twenty-five thousand a year. The idea was agreeable: when his friends—he spent most of his time with the set he and Dolly had evolved—closed themselves in behind domestic doors at night, he no longer rejoiced in his freedom. He even wondered if he should have married Dolly. Not even Paula had loved him more, and he was learning the rarity, in a single life, of encountering true emotion.

Just as this mood began to creep over him a disquieting story reached his ear. His Aunt Edna, a woman just this side of forty, was carrying on an open intrigue with a dissolute, hard-drinking young man named Cary Sloane. Everyone knew of it except Anson's Uncle Robert, who for fifteen years had talked long in clubs and taken his wife for granted.

Anson heard the story again and again with increasing annoyance. Something of his old feeling for his uncle came back to him, a feeling that was more than personal, a reversion toward that family solidarity on which he had based his pride. His intuition singled out the essential point of the affair, which was that his uncle shouldn't be hurt. It was his first experiment in unsolicited meddling, but with his knowledge of Edna's character he felt that he could handle the matter better than a district judge, or his uncle.

His uncle was in Hot Springs. Anson traced down the sources of the scandal so that there should be no possibility of mistake and then he called Edna and asked her to lunch with him at the Plaza next day. Something in his tone must have frightened her, for she was reluctant, but he insisted, putting off the date until she had no excuse for refusing.

She met him at the appointed time in the Plaza lobby, a lovely, faded, grey-eyed blonde in a coat of Russian sable. Five great rings, cold with diamonds and emeralds, sparkled on her slender hands. It occurred to Anson that it was his father's intelligence and not his uncle's that had earned the fur and the stones, the rich brilliance that buoyed up her passing beauty.

Though Edna scented his hostility, she was unprepared for the directness of his approach.

"Edna, I'm astonished at the way you've been acting," he said in a strong frank voice. "At first I couldn't believe it."

"Believe what?" she demanded sharply.

"You needn't pretend with me, Edna. I'm talking about Cary Sloane. Aside from any other consideration, I didn't think you could treat Uncle Robert—"

"Now look here, Anson—" she began angrily, but his peremptory voice broke through hers:

"—and your children in such a way. You've been married eighteen years, and you're old enough to know better."

"You can't talk to me like that! You—"

"Yes I can. Uncle Robert has always been my best friend." He was tremendously moved. He felt a real distress about his uncle, about his three young cousins.

Edna stood up, leaving her crab-flake cocktail untasted.

"This is the silliest thing—"

"Very well, if you won't listen to me I'll go to Uncle Robert and tell him the whole story—he's bound to hear it sooner or later. And afterwards I'll go to old Moses Sloane."

Edna faltered back into her chair.

"Don't talk so loud," she begged him. Her eyes blurred with tears. "You have no idea how your voice carries. You might have chosen a less public place to make all these crazy accusations."

He didn't answer.

"Oh, you never liked me, I know," she went on. "You're just taking advantage of some silly gossip to try and break up the only interesting friendship I've ever had. What did I ever do to make you hate me so?"

Still Anson waited. There would be the appeal to his chivalry, then to his pity, finally to his superior sophistication—when he had shouldered his way through all these there would be admissions, and he could come to grips with her. By being silent, by being impervious, by returning constantly to his main weapon, which was his own true emotion, he bullied her into frantic despair as the luncheon hour slipped away. At two o'clock she took out a mirror and a handkerchief, shined away the marks of her tears and powdered the slight hollows where they had lain. She had agreed to meet him at her own house at five.

When he arrived she was stretched on a chaise-longue which was covered with cretonne for the summer, and the tears he had called up at luncheon seemed still to be standing in her eyes. Then he was aware of Cary Sloane's dark anxious presence upon the cold hearth.

"What's this idea of yours?" broke out Sloane immediately. "I understand you invited Edna to lunch and then threatened her on the basis of some cheap scandal."

Anson sat down.

"I have no reason to think it's only scandal."

"I hear you're going to take it to Robert Hunter and to my father."

Anson nodded.

"Either you break it off—or I will," he said.

"What God damned business is it of yours, Hunter?"

"Don't lose your temper, Cary," said Edna nervously. "It's only a question of showing him how absurd—"

"For one thing, it's my name that's being handed around," interrupted Anson. "That's all that concerns you, Cary."

"Edna isn't a member of your family."

"She most certainly is!" His anger mounted. "Why—she owes this house and the rings on her fingers to my father's brains. When Uncle Robert married her she didn't have a penny."

They all looked at the rings as if they had a significant bearing on the situation. Edna made a gesture to take them from her hand.

"I guess they're not the only rings in the world," said Sloane.

"Oh, this is absurd," cried Edna. "Anson, will you listen to me? I've found out how the silly story started. It was a maid I discharged who went right to the Chilicheffs—all these Russians pump things out of their servants and then put a false meaning on them." She brought down her fist angrily on the table: "And after Tom lent them the limousine for a whole month when we were south last winter—"

"Do you see?" demanded Sloane eagerly. "This maid got hold of the wrong end of the thing. She knew that Edna and I were friends, and she carried it to the Chilicheffs. In Russia they assume that if a man and a woman—"

He enlarged the theme to a disquisition upon social relations in the Caucasus.

"If that's the case it better be explained to Uncle Robert," said Anson dryly, "so that when the rumors do reach him he'll know they're not true."

Adopting the method he had followed with Edna at luncheon he let them explain it all away. He knew that they were guilty and that presently they would cross the line from explanation into justification and convict themselves more definitely than he could ever do. By seven they had taken the desperate step of telling him the truth—Robert Hunter's neglect, Edna's empty life, the casual dalliance that had flamed up into passion—but like so many true stories it had the misfortune of being old, and its enfeebled body beat helplessly against the armor of Anson's will. The threat to go to Sloane's father sealed their helplessness, for the latter, a retired cotton broker out of Alabama, was a notorious fundamentalist who controlled his son by a rigid allowance and the promise that at his next vagary the allowance would stop forever.

They dined at a small French restaurant and the discussion continued—at one time Sloane resorted to physical threats, a little later they were both imploring him to give them time. But

Anson was obdurate. He saw that Edna was breaking up and that her spirit must not be refreshed by any renewal of their passion.

At two o'clock in a small night-club on 53d Street, Edna's nerves suddenly collapsed and she cried to go home. Sloane had been drinking heavily all evening, and he was faintly maudlin, leaning on the table and weeping a little with his face in his hands. Quickly Anson gave them his terms. Sloane was to leave town for six months, and he must be gone within forty-eight hours. When he returned there was to be no resumption of the affair, but at the end of a year Edna might, if she wished, tell Robert Hunter that she wanted a divorce and go about it in the usual way.

He paused, gaining confidence from their faces for his final word.

"Or there's another thing you can do," he said slowly. "If Edna wants to leave her children, there's nothing I can do to prevent your running off together."

"I want to go home!" cried Edna again. "Oh, haven't you done enough to us for one day?"

Outside it was dark, save for a blurred glow from Sixth Avenue down the street. In that light those two who had been lovers looked for the last time into each other's tragic faces, realizing that between them there was not enough youth and strength to avert their eternal parting. Sloane walked suddenly off down the street and Anson tapped a dozing taxi-driver on the arm.

It was almost four: there was a patient flow of cleaning water along the ghostly pavement of Fifth Avenue, and the shadows of two night women flitted over the dark façade of St. Thomas's church. Then the desolate shrubbery of Central Park where Anson had often played as a child, and the mounting numbers, significant as names, of the marching streets. This was his city, he thought, where his name had flourished through five generations. No change could alter the permanence of its place here, for change itself was the essential substratum by which he and those of his name identified themselves with the spirit of New York. Resourcefulness and a powerful will—for his threats in weaker hands would have been less than nothing—had beaten the gathering dust from his uncle's name, from the name of his family, from even this shivering figure that sat beside him in the car.

Cary Sloane's body was found next morning on the lower shelf of a pillar of Queensboro Bridge. In the darkness and in his excitement he had thought that it was the water flowing black beneath him, but in less than a second it made no possible difference—unless he had planned to think one last thought of Edna, and call out her name as he struggled feebly in the water.

VII

Anson never blamed himself for his part in this affair—the situation which brought it about had not been of his making. But the just suffer with the unjust, and he found that his oldest and somehow his most precious friendship was over. He never knew what distorted story Edna told, but he was welcome in his uncle's house no longer.

Just before Christmas Mrs. Hunter retired to a select Episcopal heaven, and Anson became the responsible head of his family. An unmarried aunt who had lived with them for years ran the house and attempted with helpless inefficiency to chaperone the younger girls. All the children were less self-reliant than Anson, more conventional both in their virtues and in their shortcomings. Mrs. Hunter's death had postponed the debut of one daughter and the wedding of another. Also it had taken something deeply material from all of them, for with her passing the quiet, expensive superiority of the Hunters came to an end.

For one thing, the estate, considerably diminished by two inheritance taxes and soon to be divided among six children, was not a notable fortune anymore. Anson saw a tendency in his youngest sisters to speak rather respectfully of families that hadn't "existed" twenty years ago. His own feeling of precedence was not echoed in them—sometimes they were conventionally snobbish, that was all. For another thing, this was the last summer they would spend on the Connecticut estate; the clamor against it was too loud: "Who wants to waste the best months of the year shut up in that dead old town?" Reluctantly he yielded—the house would go into the market in the fall, and next summer they would rent a smaller place in Westchester County. It was a step down from the expensive simplicity of his father's idea, and, while he sympathized with the revolt, it also annoyed him; during his mother's lifetime he had gone up there at least every other week-end—even in the gayest summers.

Yet he himself was part of this change, and his strong instinct for life had turned him in his twenties from the hollow obsequies of that abortive leisure class. He did not see this clearly—he still felt that there was a norm, a standard of society. But there was no norm, it was doubtful if there had ever been a true norm in New York. The few who still paid and fought to enter a particular set succeeded only to find that as a society it scarcely functioned—or, what was more alarming, that the Bohemia from which they fled sat above them at table.

At twenty-nine Anson's chief concern was his own growing loneliness. He was sure now that he would never marry. The number of weddings at which he had officiated as best man or usher was past all counting—there was a drawer at home that bulged with the official neckties of this or that wedding-party, neckties standing for romances that had not endured a year, for couples who had passed completely from his life. Scarf-pins, gold pencils, cuff-buttons, presents from a generation of grooms had passed through his jewel-box and been lost—and with every ceremony he was less and less able to imagine himself in the groom's place. Under his hearty good-will toward all those marriages there was despair about his own.

And as he neared thirty he became not a little depressed at the inroads that marriage, especially lately, had made upon his friendships. Groups of people had a disconcerting tendency to dissolve and disappear. The men from his own college—and it was upon them he had expended the most time and affection—were the most elusive of all. Most of them were drawn deep into domesticity, two were dead, one lived abroad, one was in Hollywood writing continuities for pictures that Anson went faithfully to see.

Most of them, however, were permanent commuters with an intricate family life centering around some suburban country club, and it was from these that he felt his estrangement most keenly.

In the early days of their married life they had all needed him; he gave them advice about their slim finances, he exorcised their doubts about the advisability of bringing a baby into two rooms and a bath, especially he stood for the great world outside. But now their financial troubles were in the past and the fearfully expected child had evolved into an absorbing family. They were always glad to see old Anson, but they dressed up for him and tried to impress him with their present importance, and kept their troubles to themselves. They needed him no longer.

A few weeks before his thirtieth birthday the last of his early and intimate friends was married. Anson acted in his usual role of best man, gave his usual silver tea-service, and went down to the usual Homeric to say good-bye. It was a hot Friday afternoon in May, and as he walked from the pier he realized that Saturday closing had begun and he was free until Monday morning.

"Go where?" he asked himself.

The Yale Club, of course; bridge until dinner, then four or five raw cocktails in somebody's room and a pleasant confused evening. He regretted that this afternoon's groom wouldn't be along—they had always been able to cram so much into such nights: they knew how to attach women and how to get rid of them, how much consideration any girl deserved from their intelligent hedonism. A party was an adjusted thing—you took certain girls to certain places and spent just so much on their amusement; you drank a little, not much more than you ought to drink, and at a certain time in the morning you stood up and said you were going home. You avoided college boys, sponges, future engagements, fights, sentiment and indiscretions. That was the way it was done. All the rest was dissipation.

In the morning you were never violently sorry—you made no resolutions, but if you had overdone it and your heart was slightly out of order, you went on the wagon for a few days without saying anything about it, and waited until an accumulation of nervous boredom projected you into another party.

The lobby of the Yale Club was unpopulated. In the bar three very young alumni looked up at him, momentarily and without curiosity.

"Hello there, Oscar," he said to the bartender. "Mr. Cahill been around this afternoon?"

"Mr. Cahill's gone to New Haven."

"Oh . . . that so?"

"Gone to the ball game. Lot of men gone up."

Anson looked once again into the lobby, considered for a moment and then walked out and over to Fifth Avenue. From the broad window of one of his clubs—one that he had scarcely visited in five years—a grey man with watery eyes stared down at him. Anson looked quickly away—that figure sitting in vacant resignation, in supercilious solitude, depressed him. He stopped and, retracing his steps, started over 47th Street toward Teak Warden's apartment. Teak and his wife had once been his most familiar friends—it was a household where he and Dolly Karger had been used to go in the days of their affair. But Teak had taken to drink, and his wife had remarked publicly that Anson was a bad influence on him. The remark reached Anson in an exaggerated form—when it was finally cleared up, the delicate spell of intimacy was broken, never to be renewed.

"Is Mr. Warden at home?" he inquired.

"They've gone to the country."

The fact unexpectedly cut at him. They were gone to the country and he hadn't known. Two years before he would have known the date, the hour, come up at the last moment for a final drink and planned his first visit to them. Now they had gone without a word.

Anson looked at his watch and considered a week-end with his family, but the only train was a local that would jolt through the aggressive heat for three hours. And tomorrow in the country, and Sunday—he was in no mood for porch-bridge with polite undergraduates, and dancing after dinner at a rural road-house, a diminutive of gaiety which his father had estimated too well.

"Oh no," he said to himself. . . . "No."

He was a dignified, impressive young man, rather stout now, but otherwise unmarked by dissipation. He could have been cast for a pillar of something—at times you were sure it was not society, at others nothing else—for the law, for the church. He stood for a few minutes motionless on the sidewalk in front of a 47th Street apartment-house; for almost the first time in his life he had nothing whatever to do.

Then he began to walk briskly up Fifth Avenue, as if he had just been reminded of an important engagement there. The necessity of dissimulation is one of the few characteristics that we share with dogs, and I think of Anson on that day as some well-bred specimen who had been disappointed at a familiar back door. He was going to see Nick, once a fashionable bartender in demand at all private dances, and now employed in cooling non-alcoholic champagne among the labyrinthine cellars of the Plaza Hotel.

"Nick," he said, "what's happened to everything?"

"Dead," Nick said.

"Make me a whiskey sour." Anson handed a pint bottle over the counter. "Nick, the girls are different; I had a little girl in Brooklyn and she got married last week without letting me know."

"That a fact? Ha-ha-ha," responded Nick diplomatically. "Slipped it over on you."

"Absolutely," said Anson. "And I was out with her the night before."

"Ha-ha-ha," said Nick, "ha-ha-ha!"

"Do you remember the wedding, Nick, in Hot Springs where I had the waiters and the musicians singing 'God Save the King'?"

"Now where was that, Mr. Hunter?" Nick concentrated doubtfully. "Seems to me that was—"

"Next time they were back for more, and I began to wonder how much I'd paid them," continued Anson.

"—seems to me that was at Mr. Trenholm's wedding."

"Don't know him," said Anson decisively. He was offended that a strange name should intrude upon his reminiscences; Nick perceived this.

"Naw—aw—" he admitted, "I ought to know that. It was one of *your* crowd—Brakins . . . Baker—"

"Bicker Baker," said Anson responsively. "They put me in a hearse after it was over and covered me up with flowers and drove me away."

"Ha-ha-ha," said Nick. "Ha-ha-ha."

Nick's simulation of the old family servant paled presently and Anson went upstairs to the lobby. He looked around—his eyes met the glance of an unfamiliar clerk at the desk, then fell upon a flower from the morning's marriage hesitating in the mouth of a brass cuspidor. He went out and walked slowly toward the blood-red sun over Columbus Circle. Suddenly he turned around and, retracing his steps to the Plaza, immured himself in a telephone-booth.

Later he said that he tried to get me three times that afternoon, that he tried everyone who might be in New York—men and girls he had not seen for years, an artist's model of his college days whose faded number was still in his address book—Central told him that even the exchange existed no longer. At length his quest roved into the country, and he held brief disappointing conversations with emphatic butlers and maids. So-and-so was out, riding, swimming, playing golf, sailed to Europe last week. Who shall I say phoned?

It was intolerable that he should pass the evening alone—the private reckonings, which one plans for a moment of leisure, lose every charm when the solitude is enforced. There were always women of a sort, but the ones he knew had temporarily vanished, and to pass a New York evening in the hired company of a stranger never occurred to him—he would have considered that that was something shameful and secret, the diversion of a traveling salesman in a strange town.

Anson paid the telephone bill—the girl tried unsuccessfully to joke with him about its size—and for the second time that afternoon started to leave the Plaza and go he knew not where. Near the revolving door the figure of a woman, obviously with child, stood sideways to the light—a sheer beige cape fluttered at her shoulders when the door turned and, each time, she looked impatiently toward it as if she were weary of waiting. At the first sight of her a strong nervous thrill of familiarity went over him, but not until he was within five feet of her did he realize that it was Paula.

"Why, Anson Hunter!"

His heart turned over.

"Why, Paula—"

"Why, this is wonderful. I can't believe it, *Anson!*"

She took both his hands and he saw in the freedom of the gesture that the memory of him had lost poignancy to her. But not to him—he felt that old mood that she evoked in him stealing over his brain, that gentleness with which he had always met her optimism as if afraid to mar its surface.

"We're at Rye for the summer. Pete had to come east on business—you know of course I'm Mrs. Peter Hagerty now—so we brought the children and took a house. You've got to come out and see us."

"Can I?" he asked directly. "When?"

"When you like. Here's Pete." The revolving door functioned, giving up a fine tall man of thirty with a tanned face and a trim mustache. His immaculate fitness made a sharp contrast with Anson's increasing bulk, which was obvious under the faintly tight cutaway coat.

"You oughtn't to be standing," said Hagerty to his wife. "Let's sir down here." He indicated lobby chairs but Paula hesitated.

"I've got to go right home," she said. "Anson, why don't you—why don't you come out and have dinner with us tonight? We're just getting settled, but if you can stand that—"

Hagerty confirmed the invitation cordially.

"Come out for the night."

Their car waited in front of the hotel, and Paula with a tired gesture sank back against silk cushions in the corner.

"There's so much I want to talk to you about," she said. "It seems hopeless."

"I want to hear about you."

"Well"—she smiled at Hagerty—"that would take a long time too. I have three children—by my first marriage. The oldest is five, then four, then three." She smiled again. "I didn't waste much time having them, did I?"

"Boys?"

"A boy and two girls. Then—oh, a lot of things happened, and I got a divorce in Paris a year ago and married Pete. That's all—except that I'm awfully happy."

In Rye they drove up to a large house near the beach club, from which there issued presently three dark slim children who broke from an English governess and approached them with an esoteric cry. Abstractedly and with difficulty Paula took each one into her arms, a caress which they accepted stiffly, as they had evidently been told not to bump into Mummy. Even against their fresh faces Paula's skin showed scarcely any weariness—for all her physical languor she seemed younger than when he had last seen her at Palm Beach seven years ago.

At dinner she was preoccupied, and afterwards, during the homage to the radio, she lay with closed eyes on the sofa, until Anson wondered if his presence at this time were not an intrusion. But at nine o'clock, when Hagerty rose and said pleasantly that he was going to leave them by themselves for awhile, she began to talk slowly about herself and the past.

"My first baby," she said—"the one we call Darling, the biggest little girl—I wanted to die when I knew I was going to have her, because Lowell was like a stranger to me. It didn't seem as though she could be my own. I wrote you a letter and tore it up. Oh, you were *so* bad to me, Anson."

It was the dialogue again, rising and falling. Anson felt a sudden quickening of memory.

"Weren't you engaged once?" she asked—"a girl named Dolly something?"

"I wasn't ever engaged. I tried to be engaged, but I never loved anybody but you, Paula."

"Oh," she said. Then after a moment: "This baby is the first one I ever really wanted. You see, I'm in love now—at last."

He didn't answer, shocked at the treachery of her remembrance. She must have seen that the "at last" bruised him, for she continued:

"I was infatuated with you, Anson—you could make me do anything you liked. But we wouldn't have been happy. I'm not smart enough for you. I don't like things to be complicated like you do." She paused. "You'll never settle down," she said.

The phrase struck at him from behind—it was an accusation that of all accusations he had never merited.

"I could settle down if women were different," he said. "If I didn't understand so much about them, if women didn't spoil you for other women, if they had only a little pride. If I could go to sleep for awhile and wake up into a home that was really mine—why, that's what I'm made for, Paula, that's what women have seen in me and liked in me. It's only that I can't get through the preliminaries anymore."

Hagerty came in a little before eleven; after a whiskey Paula stood up and announced that she was going to bed. She went over and stood by her husband.

"Where did you go, dearest?" she demanded.

"I had a drink with Ed Saunders."

"I was worried. I thought maybe you'd run away."

She rested her head against his coat.

"He's sweet, isn't he, Anson?" she demanded.

"Absolutely," said Anson, laughing.

She raised her face to her husband.

"Well, I'm ready," she said. She turned to Anson: "Do you want to see our family gymnastic stunt?"

"Yes," he said in an interested voice.

"All right. Here we go!"

Hagerty picked her up easily in his arms.

"This is called the family acrobatic stunt," said Paula. "He carries me upstairs. Isn't it sweet of him?"

"Yes," said Anson.

Hagerty bent his head slightly until his face touched Paula's.

"And I love him," she said. "I've just been telling you, haven't I, Anson?"

"Yes," he said.

"He's the dearest thing that ever lived in this world, aren't you, darling? . . . Well, good-night. Here we go. Isn't he strong?"

"Yes," Anson said.

"You'll find a pair of Pete's pajamas laid out for you. Sweet dreams—see you at breakfast."

"Yes," Anson said.

VIII

The older members of the firm insisted that Anson should go abroad for the summer. He had scarcely had a vacation in seven years, they said. He was stale and needed a change. Anson resisted.

"If I go," he declared, "I won't come back anymore."

"That's absurd, old man. You'll be back in three months with all this depression gone. Fit as ever."

"No." He shook his head stubbornly. "If I stop, I won't go back to work. If I stop, that means I've given up—I'm through."

"We'll take a chance on that. Stay six months if you like—we're not afraid you'll leave us. Why, you'd be miserable if you didn't work."

They arranged his passage for him. They liked Anson—everyone liked Anson—and the change that had been coming over him cast a sort of pall over the office. The enthusiasm that had invariably signalled up business, the consideration toward his equals and his inferiors, the lift of his vital presence—within the past four months his intense nervousness had melted down these qualities into the fussy pessimism of a man of forty. On every transaction in which he was involved he acted as a drag and a strain.

"If I go I'll never come back," he said.

Three days before he sailed Paula Legendre Hagerty died in childbirth. I was with him a great deal then, for we were crossing together, but for the first time in our friendship he told me not a word of how he felt, nor did I see the slightest sign of emotion. His chief preoccupation was with the fact that he was thirty years old—he would turn the conversation to the point where he could remind you of it and then fall silent, as if he assumed that the statement would start a chain of thought sufficient to itself. Like his partners I was amazed at the change in him, and I was glad when the *Paris* moved off into the wet space between the worlds, leaving his principality behind.

"How about a drink?" he suggested.

We walked into the bar with that defiant feeling that characterizes the day of departure and ordered four martinis. After one cocktail a change came over him—he suddenly reached across and slapped my knee with the first joviality I had seen him exhibit for months.

"Did you see that girl in the red tam?" he demanded, "the one with the high color who had the two police dogs down to bid her good-bye."

"She's pretty," I agreed.

"I looked her up in the purser's office and found out that she's alone. I'm going down to see the steward in a few minutes. We'll have dinner with her tonight."

After awhile he left me and within an hour he was walking up and down the deck with her, talking to her in his strong, clear voice. Her red tam was a bright spot of color against the steel-green sea, and from time to time she looked up with a flashing bob of her head, and smiled with amusement and interest, and anticipation. At dinner we had champagne, and were very joyous—afterwards Anson ran the pool with infectious gusto, and several people who had seen me with him asked me his name. He and the girl were talking and laughing together on a lounge in the bar when I went to bed.

I saw less of him on the trip than I had hoped. He wanted to arrange a foursome, but there was no one available, so I saw him only at meals. Sometimes, though, he would have a cocktail in the bar, and he told me about the girl in the red tam, and his adventures with her, making them all bizarre and amusing, as he had a way of doing, and I was glad that he was himself again, or at least the self that I knew, and with which I felt at home. I don't think he was ever happy unless someone was in love with

him, responding to him like filings to a magnet, helping him
to explain himself, promising him something. What it was I do
not know. Perhaps they promised that there would always be
women in the world who would spend their brightest, freshest,
rarest hours to nurse and protect that superiority he cherished
in his heart.

Winter Dreams

SOME of the caddies were poor as sin and lived in one-room
houses with a neurasthenic cow in the front yard, but Dexter Green's father owned the second best grocery store in
Black Bear—the best one was "The Hub," patronized by the
wealthy people from Sherry Island—and Dexter caddied only
for pocket-money.

In the fall when the days became crisp and grey and the long
Minnesota winter shut down like the white lid of a box, Dexter's skis moved over the snow that hid the fairways of the golf
course. At these times the country gave him a feeling of profound melancholy—it offended him that the links should lie in
enforced fallowness, haunted by ragged sparrows for the long
season. It was dreary, too, that on the tees where the gay colors
fluttered in summer there were now only the desolate sand boxes
knee-deep in crusted ice. When he crossed the hills the wind
blew cold as misery, and if the sun was out he tramped with his
eyes squinted up against the hard dimensionless glare.

In April the winter ceased abruptly. The snow ran down into
Black Bear Lake scarcely tarrying for the early golfers to brave
the season with red and black balls. Without elation, without an
interval of moist glory, the cold was gone.

Dexter knew that there was something dismal about this
northern spring, just as he knew there was something gorgeous about the fall. Fall made him clench his hands and
tremble and repeat idiotic sentences to himself and make
brisk abrupt gestures of command to imaginary audiences
and armies. October filled him with hope which November raised to a sort of ecstatic triumph, and in this mood
the fleeting brilliant impressions of the summer at Sherry
Island were ready grist to his mill. He became a golf champion and defeated Mr. T. A. Hedrick in a marvelous match
played a hundred times over the fairways of his imagination,
a match each detail of which he changed about untiringly—
sometimes he won with almost laughable ease, sometimes he
came up magnificently from behind. Again, stepping from

When he was twenty-three Mr. Hart—one of the grey-haired men who liked to say "Now there's a boy"—gave him a guest card to the Sherry Island Golf Club for a week-end. So he signed his name one day on the register, and that afternoon played golf in a foursome with Mr. Hart and Mr. Sandwood and Mr. T. A. Hedrick. He did not consider it necessary to remark that he had once carried Mr. Hart's bag over these same links and that he knew every trap and gully with his eyes shut—but he found himself glancing at the four caddies who trailed them, trying to catch a gleam or gesture that would remind him of himself, that would lessen the gap which lay between his present and his past.

It was a curious day, slashed abruptly with fleeting, familiar impressions. One minute he had the sense of being a trespasser—in the next he was impressed by the tremendous superiority he felt toward Mr. T. A. Hedrick, who was a bore and not even a good golfer anymore.

Then, because of a ball Mr. Hart lost near the fifteenth green, an enormous thing happened. While they were searching the stiff grasses of the rough there was a clear call of "Fore!" from behind a hill in their rear. And as they all turned abruptly from their search a bright new ball sliced abruptly over the hill and caught Mr. T. A. Hedrick in the abdomen.

"By Gad!" cried Mr. T. A. Hedrick, "they ought to put some of these crazy women off the course. It's getting to be outrageous."

A head and a voice came up together over the hill:

"Do you mind if we go through?"

"You hit me in the stomach!" declared Mr. Hedrick wildly.

"Did I?" The girl approached the group of men. "I'm sorry. I yelled 'Fore!'"

Her glance fell casually on each of the men—then scanned the fairway for her ball.

"Did I bounce into the rough?"

It was impossible to determine whether this question was ingenuous or malicious. In a moment, however, she left no doubt, for as her partner came up over the hill she called cheerfully:

"Here I am! I'd have gone on the green except that I hit something."

As she took her stance for a short mashie shot, Dexter looked at her closely. She wore a blue gingham dress, rimmed at throat and shoulders with a white edging that accentuated her tan. The quality of exaggeration, of thinness, which had made her passionate eyes and down-turning mouth absurd at eleven, was gone now. She was arrestingly beautiful. The color in her cheeks was centered like the color in a picture—it was not a "high" color, but a sort of fluctuating and feverish warmth, so shaded that it seemed at any moment it would recede and disappear. This color and the mobility of her mouth gave a continual impression of flux, of intense life, of passionate vitality—balanced only partially by the sad luxury of her eyes.

She swung her mashie impatiently and without interest, pitching the ball into a sandpit on the other side of the green. With a quick insincere smile and a careless "Thank you!" she went on after it.

"That Judy Jones!" remarked Mr. Hedrick on the next tee, as they waited—some moments—for her to play on ahead. "All she needs is to be turned up and spanked for six months and then to be married off to an old-fashioned cavalry captain."

"My God, she's good-looking!" said Mr. Sandwood, who was just over thirty.

"Good-looking!" cried Mr. Hedrick contemptuously. "She always looks as if she wanted to be kissed! Turning those big cow-eyes on every calf in town!"

It was doubtful if Mr. Hedrick intended a reference to the maternal instinct.

"She'd play pretty good golf if she'd try," said Mr. Sandwood.

"She has no form," said Mr. Hedrick solemnly.

"She has a nice figure," said Mr. Sandwood.

"Better thank the Lord she doesn't drive a swifter ball," said Mr. Hart, winking at Dexter.

Later in the afternoon the sun went down with a riotous swirl of gold and varying blues and scarlets, and left the dry rustling night of western summer. Dexter watched from the verandah of the golf club, watched the even overlap of the waters in the little wind, silver molasses under the harvest moon. Then the moon held a finger to her lips and the lake became a clear pool, pale and quiet. Dexter put on his bathing suit and swam out to the farthest raft, where he stretched dripping on the wet canvas of the springboard.

There was a fish jumping and a star shining and the lights around the lake were gleaming. Over on a dark peninsula a piano was playing the songs of last summer and of summers before that—songs from "Chin-Chin" and "The Count of Luxembourg" and "The Chocolate Soldier"—and because the sound of a piano over a stretch of water had always seemed beautiful to Dexter he lay perfectly quiet and listened.

The tune the piano was playing at that moment had been gay and new five years before when Dexter was a sophomore at college. They had played it at a prom once when he could not afford the luxury of proms, and he had stood outside the gymnasium and listened. The sound of the tune precipitated in him a sort of ecstasy and it was with that ecstasy he viewed what happened to him now. It was a mood of intense appreciation, a sense that, for once, he was magnificently attuned to life and that everything about him was radiating a brightness and a glamour he might never know again.

A low pale oblong detached itself suddenly from the darkness of the island, spitting forth the reverberate sound of a racing motorboat. Two white streamers of cleft water rolled themselves out behind it and almost immediately the boat was beside him, drowning out the hot tinkle of the piano in the drone of its spray. Dexter, raising himself on his arms, was aware of a figure standing at the wheel, of two dark eyes regarding him over the lengthening space of water—then the boat had gone by and was sweeping in an immense and purposeless circle of spray round and round in the middle of the lake. With equal eccentricity one of the circles flattened out and headed back toward the raft.

"Who's that?" she called, shutting off her motor. She was so near now that Dexter could see her bathing suit, which consisted apparently of pink rompers.

The nose of the boat bumped the raft, and as the latter tilted rakishly he was precipitated toward her. With different degrees of interest they recognized each other.

"Aren't you one of those men we played through this afternoon?" she demanded.

He was.

"Well, do you know how to drive a motorboat? Because if you do I wish you'd drive this one so I can ride on the surf-board behind. My name is Judy Jones"—she favored him with an absurd smirk—rather, what tried to be a smirk, for, twist her mouth as she might, it was not grotesque, it was merely beautiful—"and I live in a house over there on the island, and in that house there is a man waiting for me. When he drove up at the door I drove out of the dock because he says I'm his ideal."

There was a fish jumping and a star shining and the lights around the lake were gleaming. Dexter sat beside Judy Jones and she explained how her boat was driven. Then she was in the water, swimming to the floating surf-board with a sinuous crawl. Watching her was without effort to the eye, watching a branch waving or a sea-gull flying. Her arms, burned to butter-nut, moved sinuously among the dull platinum ripples, elbow appearing first, casting the forearm back with a cadence of falling water, then reaching out and down, stabbing a path ahead.

They moved out into the lake; turning, Dexter saw that she was kneeling on the low rear of the now up-tilted surf-board.

"Go faster," she called, "fast as it'll go."

Obediently he jammed the lever forward and the white spray mounted at the bow. When he looked around again the girl was standing up on the rushing board, her arms spread wide, her eyes lifted toward the moon.

"It's awful cold," she shouted. "What's your name?"

He told her.

"Well, why don't you come to dinner tomorrow night?"

His heart turned over like the fly-wheel of the boat, and, for the second time, her casual whim gave a new direction to his life.

III

Next evening while he waited for her to come downstairs, Dexter peopled the soft deep summer room and the sun-porch that opened from it with the men who had already loved Judy Jones. He knew the sort of men they were—the men who when he first went to college had entered from the great prep schools with graceful clothes and the deep tan of healthy sum-mers. He had seen that, in one sense, he was better than these men. He was newer and stronger. Yet in acknowledging to himself that he wished his children to be like them he was admitting that he was but the rough, strong stuff from which they eternally sprang.

When the time had come for him to wear good clothes, he had known who were the best tailors in America, and the best tailors in America had made him the suit he wore this evening. He had acquired that particular reserve peculiar to his university, that set it off from other universities. He recognized the value to him of such a mannerism and he had adopted it; he knew that to be careless in dress and manner required more confidence than to be careful. But carelessness was for his children. His mother's name had been Krimslich. She was a Bohemian of the peasant class and she had talked broken English to the end of her days. Her son must keep to the set patterns.

At a little after seven Judy Jones came downstairs. She wore a blue silk afternoon dress, and he was disappointed at first that she had not put on something more elaborate. This feeling was accentuated when, after a brief greeting, she went to the door of a butler's pantry and pushing it open called: "You can serve dinner, Martha." He had rather expected that a butler would announce dinner, that there would be a cocktail. Then he put these thoughts behind him as they sat down side by side on a lounge and looked at each other.

"Father and Mother won't be here," she said thoughtfully.

He remembered the last time he had seen her father, and he was glad the parents were not to be here tonight—they might wonder who he was. He had been born in Keeble, a Minnesota village fifty miles farther north, and he always gave Keeble as his home instead of Black Bear Village. Country towns were well enough to come from if they weren't inconveniently in sight and used as foot-stools by fashionable lakes.

They talked of his university, which she had visited frequently during the past two years, and of the nearby city which supplied Sherry Island with its patrons, and whither Dexter would return next day to his prospering laundries.

During dinner she slipped into a moody depression which gave Dexter a feeling of uneasiness. Whatever petulance she uttered in her throaty voice worried him. Whatever she smiled at—at him, at a chicken liver, at nothing—it disturbed him that her smile could have no root in mirth, or even in amusement.

When the scarlet corners of her lips curved down, it was less a smile than an invitation to a kiss.

Then, after dinner, she led him out on the dark sun-porch and deliberately changed the atmosphere.

"Do you mind if I weep a little?" she said.

"I'm afraid I'm boring you," he responded quickly.

"You're not. I like you. But I've just had a terrible afternoon. There was a man I cared about, and this afternoon he told me out of a clear sky that he was poor as a church-mouse. He'd never even hinted it before. Does this sound horribly mundane?"

"Perhaps he was afraid to tell you."

"Suppose he was," she answered. "He didn't start right. You see, if I'd thought of him as poor—well, I've been mad about loads of poor men, and fully intended to marry them all. But in this case, I hadn't thought of him that way and my interest in him wasn't strong enough to survive the shock. As if a girl calmly informed her fiancé that she was a widow. He might not object to widows, but—

"Let's start right," she interrupted herself suddenly. "Who are you, anyhow?"

For a moment Dexter hesitated. Then:

"I'm nobody," he announced. "My career is largely a matter of futures."

"Are you poor?"

"No," he said frankly, "I'm probably making more money than any man my age in the Northwest. I know that's an obnoxious remark, but you advised me to start right."

There was a pause. Then she smiled and the corners of her mouth drooped and an almost imperceptible sway brought her closer to him, looking up into his eyes. A lump rose in Dexter's throat, and he waited breathless for the experiment, facing the unpredictable compound that would form mysteriously from the elements of their lips. Then he saw—she communicated her excitement to him, lavishly, deeply, with kisses that were not a promise but a fulfilment. They aroused in him not hunger demanding renewal but surfeit that would demand more surfeit . . . kisses that were like charity, creating want by holding back nothing at all.

It did not take him many hours to decide that he had wanted Judy Jones ever since he was a proud, desirous little boy.

IV

It began like that—and continued, with varying shades of intensity, on such a note right up to the dénouement. Dexter surrendered a part of himself to the most direct and unprincipled personality with which he had ever come in contact. Whatever Judy wanted, she went after with the full pressure of her charm. There was no divergence of method, no jockeying for position or premeditation of effects—there was a very little mental side to any of her affairs. She simply made men conscious to the highest degree of her physical loveliness. Dexter had no desire to change her. Her deficiencies were knit up with a passionate energy that transcended and justified them.

When, as Judy's head lay against his shoulder that first night, she whispered, "I don't know what's the matter with me. Last night I thought I was in love with a man and tonight I think I'm in love with you—" —it seemed to him a beautiful and romantic thing to say. It was the exquisite excitability that for the moment he controlled and owned. But a week later he was compelled to view this same quality in a different light. She took him in her roadster to a picnic supper and after supper she disappeared, likewise in her roadster, with another man. Dexter became enormously upset and was scarcely able to be decently civil to the other people present. When she assured him that she had not kissed the other man, he knew she was lying—yet he was glad that she had taken the trouble to lie to him.

He was, as he found before the summer ended, one of a varying dozen who circulated about her. Each of them had at one time been favored above all others—about half of them still basked in the solace of occasional sentimental revivals. Whenever one showed signs of dropping out through long neglect, she granted him a brief honeyed hour, which encouraged him to tag along for a year or so longer. Judy made these forays upon the helpless and defeated without malice, indeed half unconscious that there was anything mischievous in what she did.

When a new man came to town everyone dropped out—dates were automatically cancelled.

The helpless part of trying to do anything about it was that she did it all herself. She was not a girl who could be "won" in the kinetic sense—she was proof against cleverness, she was proof against charm; if any of these assailed her too strongly she would immediately resolve the affair to a physical basis, and under the magic of her physical splendor the strong as well as the brilliant played her game and not their own. She was entertained only by the gratification of her desires and by the direct exercise of her own charm. Perhaps from so much youthful love, so many youthful lovers, she had come, in self-defense, to nourish herself wholly from within.

Succeeding Dexter's first exhilaration came restlessness and dissatisfaction. The helpless ecstasy of losing himself in her was opiate rather than tonic. It was fortunate for his work during the winter that those moments of ecstasy came infrequently. Early in their acquaintance it had seemed for awhile that there was a deep and spontaneous mutual attraction—that first August, for example—three days of long evenings on her dusky verandah, of strange wan kisses through the late afternoon, in shadowy alcoves or behind the protecting trellises of the garden arbors, of mornings when she was fresh as a dream and almost shy at meeting him in the clarity of the rising day. There was all the ecstasy of an engagement about it, sharpened by his realization that there was no engagement. It was during those three days that, for the first time, he had asked her to marry him. She said "maybe someday," she said "kiss me," she said "I'd like to marry you," she said "I love you"—she said—nothing.

The three days were interrupted by the arrival of a New York man who visited at her house for half September. To Dexter's agony, rumor engaged them. The man was the son of the president of a great trust company. But at the end of a month it was reported that Judy was yawning. At a dance one night she sat all evening in a motorboat with a local beau, while the New Yorker searched the club for her frantically. She told the local beau that she was bored with her visitor and two days later he left. She was seen with him at the station and it was reported that he looked very mournful indeed.

On this note the summer ended. Dexter was twenty-four and he found himself increasingly in a position to do as he wished. He joined two clubs in the city and lived at one of them. Though he was by no means an integral part of the stag-lines at these clubs, he managed to be on hand at dances where Judy Jones was likely to appear. He could have gone out socially as much as he liked—he was an eligible young man, now, and popular with downtown fathers. His confessed devotion to Judy Jones had rather solidified his position. But he had no social aspirations and rather despised the dancing men who were always on tap for the Thursday or Saturday parties and who filled in at dinners with the younger married set. Already he was playing with the idea of going east to New York. He wanted to take Judy Jones with him. No disillusion as to the world in which she had grown up could cure his illusion as to her desirability.

Remember that—for only in the light of it can what he did for her be understood.

Eighteen months after he first met Judy Jones he became engaged to another girl. Her name was Irene Scheerer, and her father was one of the men who had always believed in Dexter. Irene was light-haired and sweet and honorable, and a little stout, and she had two suitors whom she pleasantly relinquished when Dexter formally asked her to marry him.

Summer, fall, winter, spring, another summer, another fall—so much he had given of his active life to the incorrigible lips of Judy Jones. She had treated him with interest, with encouragement, with malice, with indifference, with contempt. She had inflicted on him the innumerable little slights and indignities possible in such a case—as if in revenge for having ever cared for him at all. She had beckoned him and yawned at him and beckoned him again and he had responded often with bitterness and narrowed eyes. She had brought him ecstatic happiness and intolerable agony of spirit. She had caused him untold inconvenience and not a little trouble. She had insulted him and she had ridden over him and she had played his interest in her against his interest in his work—for fun. She had done everything to him except to criticize him—this she had not done—it seemed to him only because it might have sullied the utter indifference she manifested and sincerely felt toward him.

When autumn had come and gone again it occurred to him that he could not have Judy Jones. He had to beat this into his mind but he convinced himself at last. He lay awake at night for awhile and argued it over. He told himself the trouble and the pain she had caused him, he enumerated her glaring deficiencies as a wife. Then he said to himself that he loved her, and after awhile he fell asleep. For a week, lest he imagined her husky voice over the telephone or her eyes opposite him at lunch, he worked hard and late and at night he went to his office and plotted out his years.

At the end of a week he went to a dance and cut in on her once. For almost the first time since they had met he did not ask her to sit out with him or tell her that she was lovely. It hurt him that she did not miss these things—that was all. He was not jealous when he saw that there was a new man tonight. He had been hardened against jealousy long before.

He stayed late at the dance. He sat for an hour with Irene Scheerer and talked about books and about music. He knew very little about either. But he was beginning to be master of his own time now, and he had a rather priggish notion that he—the young and already fabulously successful Dexter Green—should know more about such things.

That was in October when he was twenty-five. In January, Dexter and Irene became engaged. It was to be announced in June and they were to be married three months later.

The Minnesota winter prolonged itself interminably, and it was almost May when the winds came soft and the snow ran down into Black Bear Lake at last. For the first time in over a year Dexter was enjoying a certain tranquillity of spirit. Judy Jones had been in Florida and afterwards in Hot Springs and somewhere she had been engaged and somewhere she had broken it off. At first, when Dexter had definitely given her up, it had made him sad that people still linked them together and asked for news of her, but when he began to be placed at dinner next to Irene Scheerer people didn't ask him about her anymore—they told him about her. He ceased to be an authority on her.

May at last. Dexter walked the streets at night when the darkness was damp as rain, wondering that so soon, with so little done, so much of ecstasy had gone from him. May one year back had been marked by Judy's poignant, unforgivable, yet forgiven turbulence—it had been one of those rare times when he fancied she had grown to care for him. That old penny's worth of happiness he had spent for this bushel of content. He knew that Irene would be no more than a curtain spread behind him, a hand moving among gleaming tea cups, a voice calling to children . . . fire and loveliness were gone, the magic of nights and the wonder of the varying hours and seasons . . . slender lips, down-turning, dropping to his lips and bearing him up into a heaven of eyes. . . . The thing was deep in him. He was too strong and alive for it to die lightly.

In the middle of May when the weather balanced for a few days on the thin bridge that led to deep summer he turned in one night at Irene's house. Their engagement was to be announced in a week now—no one would be surprised at it. And tonight they would sit together on the lounge at the University Club and look on for an hour at the dancers. It gave him a sense of solidity to go with her—she was so sturdily popular, so intensely "great."

He mounted the steps of the brownstone house and stepped inside.

"Irene," he called.

Mrs. Scheerer came out of the living room to meet him.

"Dexter," she said, "Irene's gone upstairs with a splitting headache. She wanted to go with you but I made her go to bed."

"Nothing serious, I—"

"Oh, no. She's going to play golf with you in the morning. You can spare her for just one night, can't you, Dexter?"

Her smile was kind. She and Dexter liked each other. In the living room he talked for a moment before he said good-night.

Returning to the University Club, where he had rooms, he stood in the doorway for a moment and watched the dancers. He leaned against the doorpost, nodded at a man or two—yawned.

"Hello, darling."

The familiar voice at his elbow startled him. Judy Jones had left a man and crossed the room to him—Judy Jones, a slender enamelled doll in cloth of gold: gold in a band at her head, gold in two slipper points at her dress's hem. The fragile glow of her face seemed to blossom as she smiled at him. A breeze of warmth and light blew through the room. His hands in the pockets of his dinner jacket tightened spasmodically. He was filled with a sudden excitement.

"When did you get back?" he asked casually.

"Come here and I'll tell you about it."

She turned and he followed her. She had been away—he could have wept at the wonder of her return. She had passed through enchanted streets, doing things that were like provocative music. All mysterious happenings, all fresh and quickening hopes, had gone away with her, come back with her now.

She turned in the doorway.

"Have you a car here? If you haven't, I have."

"I have a coupé."

In then, with a rustle of golden cloth. He slammed the door. Into so many cars she had stepped—like this—like that—her back against the leather, so—her elbow resting on the door— waiting. She would have been soiled long since had there been anything to soil her—except herself—but this was her own self outpouring.

With an effort he forced himself to start the car and back into the street. This was nothing, he must remember. She had done this before and he had put her behind him, as he would have crossed a bad account from his books.

He drove slowly downtown and, affecting abstraction, traversed the deserted streets of the business section, peopled here and there where a movie was giving out its crowd or where consumptive or pugilistic youth lounged in front of pool halls. The clink of glasses and the slap of hands on the bars issued from saloons, cloisters of glazed glass and dirty yellow light.

She was watching him closely and the silence was embarrassing, yet in this crisis he could find no casual word with which to profane the hour. At a convenient turning he began to zig-zag back toward the University Club.

"Have you missed me?" she asked suddenly.

"Everybody missed you."

He wondered if she knew of Irene Scheerer. She had been back only a day—her absence had been almost contemporaneous with his engagement.

"What a remark!" Judy laughed sadly—without sadness. She looked at him searchingly. He became absorbed in the dashboard.

"You're handsomer than you used to be," she said thoughtfully. "Dexter, you have the most rememberable eyes."

He could have laughed at this, but he did not laugh. It was the sort of thing that was said to sophomores. Yet it stabbed at him.

"I'm awfully tired of everything, darling." She called everyone darling, endowing the endearment with careless, individual camaraderie. "I wish you'd marry me."

The directness of this confused him. He should have told her now that he was going to marry another girl, but he could not tell her. He could as easily have sworn that he had never loved her.

"I think we'd get along," she continued, on the same note, "unless probably you've forgotten me and fallen in love with another girl."

Her confidence was obviously enormous. She had said, in effect, that she found such a thing impossible to believe, that if it were true he had merely committed a childish indiscretion—and probably to show off. She would forgive him, because it was not a matter of any moment but rather something to be brushed aside lightly.

"Of course you could never love anybody but me," she continued. "I like the way you love me. Oh, Dexter, have you forgotten last year?"

"No, I haven't forgotten."

"Neither have I!"

Was she sincerely moved—or was she carried along by the wave of her own acting?

"I wish we could be like that again," she said, and he forced himself to answer:

"I don't think we can."

"I suppose not. . . . I hear you're giving Irene Scheerer a violent rush."

There was not the faintest emphasis on the name, yet Dexter was suddenly ashamed.

"Oh, take me home," cried Judy suddenly; "I don't want to go back to that idiotic dance—with those children."

Then, as he turned up the street that led to the residence district, Judy began to cry quietly to herself. He had never seen her cry before.

The dark street lightened, the dwellings of the rich loomed up around them, he stopped his coupé in front of the great white bulk of the Mortimer Jones house, somnolent, gorgeous, drenched with the splendor of the damp moonlight. Its solidity startled him. The strong walls, the steel of the girders, the breadth and beam and pomp of it were there only to bring out the contrast with the young beauty beside him. It was sturdy to accentuate her slightness—as if to show what a breeze could be generated by a butterfly's wing.

He sat perfectly quiet, his nerves in wild clamor, afraid that if he moved he would find her irresistibly in his arms. Two tears had rolled down her wet face and trembled on her upper lip.

"I'm more beautiful than anybody else," she said brokenly. "Why can't I be happy?" Her moist eyes tore at his stability—her mouth turned slowly downward with an exquisite sadness: "I'd like to marry you if you'll have me, Dexter. I suppose you think I'm not worth having, but I'll be so beautiful for you, Dexter."

A million phrases of anger, pride, passion, hatred, tenderness fought on his lips. Then a perfect wave of emotion washed over him, carrying off with it a sediment of wisdom, of convention, of doubt, of honor. This was his girl who was speaking, his own, his beautiful, his pride.

"Won't you come in?" He heard her draw in her breath sharply.

Waiting.

"All right," his voice was trembling, "I'll come in."

V

It was strange that neither when it was over nor a long time afterward did he regret that night. Looking at it from the perspective of ten years, the fact that Judy's flare for him endured just one month seemed of little importance. Nor did it matter that by his yielding he subjected himself to a deeper agony in the end and gave serious hurt to Irene Scheerer and to Irene's parents, who had befriended him. There was nothing sufficiently pictorial about Irene's grief to stamp itself on his mind.

Dexter was at bottom hard-minded. The attitude of the city on his action was of no importance to him, not because he was going to leave the city, but because any outside attitude on the situation seemed superficial. He was completely indifferent to popular opinion. Nor, when he had seen that it was no use, that he did not possess in himself the power to move fundamentally or to hold Judy Jones, did he bear any malice toward her. He loved her and he would love her until the day he was too old for loving—but he could not have her. So he tasted the deep pain that is reserved only for the strong, just as he had tasted for a little while the deep happiness.

Even the ultimate falsity of the grounds upon which Judy terminated the engagement, that she did not want to "take him away" from Irene—Judy, who had wanted nothing else—did not revolt him. He was beyond any revulsion or any amusement.

He went east in February with the intention of selling out his laundries and settling in New York—but the war came to America in March and changed his plans. He returned to the West, handed over the management of the business to his partner, and went into the first officers' training-camp in late April. He was one of those young thousands who greeted the war with a certain amount of relief, welcoming the liberation from webs of tangled emotion.

VI

This story is not his biography, remember, although things creep into it which have nothing to do with those dreams he had when he was young. We are almost done with them and with him now. There is only one more incident to be related here, and it happens seven years farther on.

It took place in New York, where he had done well—so well that there were no barriers too high for him. He was thirty-two years old, and, except for one flying trip immediately after the war, he had not been west in seven years. A man named Devlin from Detroit came into his office to see him in a business way, and then and there this incident occurred, and closed out, so to speak, this particular side of his life.

"So you're from the Middle West," said the man Devlin with careless curiosity. "That's funny—I thought men like you were probably born and raised on Wall Street. You know—wife of one of my best friends in Detroit came from your city. I was an usher at the wedding."

Dexter waited with no apprehension of what was coming.

"Judy Simms," said Devlin with no particular interest; "Judy Jones she was once."

"Yes, I knew her." A dull impatience spread over him. He had heard, of course, that she was married—perhaps deliberately he had heard no more.

"Awfully nice girl," brooded Devlin meaninglessly. "I'm sort of sorry for her."

"Why?" Something in Dexter was alert, receptive, at once.

"Oh, Lud Simms has gone to pieces in a way. I don't mean he ill-uses her, but he drinks and runs around—"

"Doesn't she run around?"

"No. Stays at home with her kids."

"Oh."

"She's a little too old for him," said Devlin.

"Too old!" cried Dexter. "Why, man, she's only twenty-seven."

He was possessed with a wild notion of rushing out into the streets and taking a train to Detroit. He rose to his feet spasmodically.

"I guess you're busy," Devlin apologized quickly. "I didn't realize—"

"No, I'm not busy," said Dexter, steadying his voice. "I'm not busy at all. Not busy at all. Did you say she was—twenty-seven? No, I said she was twenty-seven."

"Yes, you did," agreed Devlin dryly.

"Go on, then. Go on."

"What do you mean?"

"About Judy Jones."

Devlin looked at him helplessly.

"Well, that's—I told you all there is to it. He treats her like the devil. Oh, they're not going to get divorced or anything. When he's particularly outrageous she forgives him. In fact, I'm inclined to think she loves him. She was a pretty girl when she first came to Detroit."

A pretty girl! The phrase struck Dexter as ludicrous.

"Isn't she—a pretty girl, anymore?"

"Oh, she's all right."

"Look here," said Dexter, sitting down suddenly, "I don't understand. You say she was a 'pretty girl' and now you say she's 'all right.' I don't understand what you mean—Judy Jones wasn't a pretty girl, at all. She was a great beauty. Why, I knew her, I knew her. She was—"

Devlin laughed pleasantly.

"I'm not trying to start a row," he said. "I think Judy's a nice girl and I like her. I can't understand how a man like Lud Simms could fall madly in love with her, but he did." Then he added: "Most of the women like her."

Dexter looked closely at Devlin, thinking wildly that there must be a reason for this, some insensitivity in the man or some private malice.

"Lots of women fade just like *that*," Devlin snapped his fingers. "You must have seen it happen. Perhaps I've forgotten how pretty she was at her wedding. I've seen her so much since then, you see. She has nice eyes."

A sort of dullness settled down upon Dexter. For the first time in his life he felt like getting very drunk. He knew that he was laughing loudly at something Devlin had said, but he did not know what it was or why it was funny. When, in a few minutes, Devlin went he lay down on his lounge and looked out the window at the New York skyline into which the sun was sinking in dull lovely shades of pink and gold.

He had thought that having nothing else to lose he was invulnerable at last—but he knew that he had just lost something more, as surely as if he had married Judy Jones and seen her fade away before his eyes.

The dream was gone. Something had been taken from him. In a sort of panic he pushed the palms of his hands into his eyes and tried to bring up a picture of the waters lapping on Sherry Island and the moonlit verandah, and gingham on the golf links and the dry sun and the gold color of her neck's soft down. And her mouth damp to his kisses and her eyes plaintive with melancholy and her freshness like new fine linen in the morning. Why, these things were no longer in the world! They had existed and they existed no longer.

For the first time in years the tears were streaming down his face. But they were for himself now. He did not care about mouth and eyes and moving hands. He wanted to care and he could not care. For he had gone away and he could never go back anymore. The gates were closed, the sun was gone down and there was no beauty but the grey beauty of steel that withstands all time. Even the grief he could have borne was left behind in the country of illusion, of youth, of the richness of life, where his winter dreams had flourished.

"Long ago," he said, "long ago, there was something in me, but now that thing is gone. Now that thing is gone, that thing is gone. I cannot cry. I cannot care. That thing will come back no more."

The Baby Party

WHEN John Andros felt old he found solace in the thought of life continuing through his child. The dark trumpets of oblivion were less loud at the patter of his child's feet or at the sound of his child's voice babbling mad non sequiturs to him over the telephone. The latter incident occurred every afternoon at three when his wife called the office from the country, and he came to look forward to it as one of the vivid minutes of his day.

He was not physically old, but his life had been a series of struggles up a series of rugged hills, and here at thirty-eight having won his battles against ill health and poverty he cherished less than the usual number of illusions. Even his feeling about his little girl was qualified. She had interrupted his rather intense love affair with his wife, and she was the reason for their living in a suburban town, where they paid for country air with endless servant troubles and the weary merry-go-round of the commuting train.

It was little Ede as a definite piece of youth that chiefly interested him. He liked to take her on his lap and examine minutely her fragrant, downy scalp and her eyes with their irises of morning blue. Having paid this homage John was content that the nurse should take her away. After ten minutes the very vitality of the child irritated him; he was inclined to lose his temper when things were broken, and one Sunday afternoon when she had disrupted a bridge game by permanently hiding the ace of spades, he had made a scene that had reduced his wife to tears.

This was absurd and John was ashamed of himself. It was inevitable that such things would happen, and it was impossible that little Ede should spend all her indoor hours in the nursery upstairs when she was becoming, as her mother said, more nearly a "real person" every day.

She was two and a half and this afternoon, for instance, she was going to a baby party. Grown-up Edith, her mother, had telephoned the information to the office, and little Ede had confirmed the business by shouting "I yam going to a *pantry!*" into John's unsuspecting left ear.

"Drop in at the Markeys' when you get home, won't you, dear?" resumed her mother. "It'll be funny. Ede's going to be all dressed up in her new pink dress—"

The conversation terminated abruptly with a squawk which indicated that the telephone had been pulled violently to the floor. John laughed and decided to get an early train out; the prospect of a baby party in someone else's house amused him.

"What a peach of a mess!" he thought humorously. "A dozen mothers and each one looking at nothing but her own child. All the babies breaking things and grabbing at the cake, and each mama going home thinking about the subtle superiority of her own child to every other child there."

He was in a good humor today—all the things in his life were going better than they had ever gone before. When he got off the train at his station he shook his head at an importunate taxi-man and began to walk up the long hill toward his house through the crisp December twilight. It was only six o'clock but the moon was out, shining with proud brilliance on the thin sugary snow that lay over the lawns.

As he walked along drawing his lungs full of cold air his happiness increased, and the idea of a baby party appealed to him more and more. He began to wonder how Ede compared to other children of her own age and if the pink dress she was to wear was something radical and mature. Increasing his gait he came in sight of his own house, where the lights of a defunct Christmas tree still blossomed in the window, but he continued on past the walk. The party was at the Markeys' next door.

As he mounted the brick step and rang the bell he became aware of voices inside, and he was glad he was not too late. Then he raised his head and listened—the voices were not children's voices, but they were loud and pitched high with anger; there were at least three of them and one, which rose as he listened to a hysterical sob, he recognized immediately as his wife's.

"There's been some trouble," he thought quickly.

Trying the door he found it unlocked and pushed it open.

The baby party began at half past four, but Edith Andros, calculating shrewdly that the new dress would stand out more sensationally against vestments already rumpled, planned the arrival of herself and little Ede for five. When they appeared it was already a flourishing affair. Four baby girls and nine baby boys, each one curled and washed and dressed with all the care of a proud and jealous heart, were dancing to the music of a phonograph. Never more than two or three were dancing at once, but as all were continually in motion running to and from their mothers for encouragement, the general effect was the same.

As Edith and her daughter entered, the music was temporarily drowned out by a sustained chorus, consisting largely of the word *cute* and directed toward little Ede, who stood looking timidly about and fingering the edges of her pink dress. She was not kissed—this is the sanitary age—but she was passed along a row of mamas each one of whom said "cu-u-ute" to her and held her pink little hand before passing her on to the next. After some encouragement and a few mild pushes she was absorbed into the dance and became an active member of the party.

Edith stood near the door talking to Mrs. Markey and keeping one eye on the tiny figure in the pink dress. She did not care for Mrs. Markey; she considered her both snippy and common, but John and Joe Markey were congenial and went in together on the commuting train every morning, so the two women kept up an elaborate pretense of warm amity. They were always reproaching each other for "not coming to see me," and they were always planning the kind of parties that began with "You'll have to come to dinner with us soon, and we'll go in to the theatre," but never matured further.

"Little Ede looks perfectly darling," said Mrs. Markey, smiling and moistening her lips in a way that Edith found particularly repulsive. "So *grown-up*—I can't *believe* it!"

Edith wondered if "little Ede" referred to the fact that Billy Markey, though several months younger, weighed almost five pounds more. Accepting a cup of tea she took a seat with two other ladies on a divan and launched into the real business of the afternoon, which of course lay in relating the recent accomplishments and insouciances of her child.

An hour passed. Dancing palled and the babies took to sterner sport. They ran into the dining room, rounded the big table and essayed the kitchen door, from which they were rescued by an expeditionary force of mothers. Having been rounded up they immediately broke loose, and rushing back to the dining room tried the familiar swinging door again. The word "overheated" began to be used, and small white brows were dried with small white handkerchiefs. A general attempt to make the babies sit down began, but the babies squirmed off laps with peremptory cries of "Down! Down!" and the rush into the fascinating dining room began anew.

This phase of the party came to an end with the arrival of refreshments, a large cake with two candles, and saucers of vanilla ice cream. Billy Markey, a stout laughing baby with red hair and legs somewhat bowed, blew out the candles and placed an experimental thumb on the white frosting. The refreshments were distributed, and the children ate greedily but without confusion—they had behaved remarkably well all afternoon. They were modern babies who ate and slept at regular hours, so their dispositions were good and their faces healthy and pink—such a peaceful party would not have been possible thirty years ago.

After the refreshments a gradual exodus began. Edith glanced anxiously at her watch—it was almost six and John had not arrived. She wanted him to see Ede with the other children—to see how dignified and polite and intelligent she was and how the only ice-cream spot on her dress was some that had dropped from her chin when she was joggled from behind.

"You're a darling," she whispered to her child, drawing her suddenly against her knee. "Do you know you're a darling? Do you *know* you're a darling?"

Ede laughed. "Bow-wow," she said suddenly.

"Bow-wow?" Edith looked around. "There isn't any bow-wow."

"Bow-wow," repeated Ede. "I want a bow-wow."

Edith followed the small pointing finger.

"That isn't a bow-wow, dearest, that's a teddy-bear."

"Bear?"

"Yes, that's a teddy-bear, and it belongs to Billy Markey. You don't want Billy Markey's teddy-bear, do you?"

Ede did want it.

She broke away from her mother and approached Billy Markey, who held the toy closely in his arms. Ede stood regarding him with inscrutable eyes and Billy laughed.

Grown-up Edith looked at her watch again, this time impatiently.

The party had dwindled until, besides Ede and Billy, there were only two babies remaining—and one of the two remained only by virtue of having hidden himself under the dining-room table. It was selfish of John not to come. It showed so little pride in the child. Other fathers had come, half a dozen of them, to call for their wives, and they had stayed for awhile and looked on.

There was a sudden wail. Ede had obtained Billy's teddy-bear by pulling it forcibly from his arms, and on Billy's attempt to recover it, she had pushed him casually to the floor.

"Why, Ede!" cried her mother, repressing an inclination to laugh.

Joe Markey, a handsome, broad-shouldered man of thirty-five, picked up his son and set him on his feet. "You're a fine fellow," he said jovially. "Let a girl knock you over! You're a fine fellow."

"Did he bump his head?" Mrs. Markey returned anxiously from bowing the next to last remaining mother out the door.

"No-o-o-o," exclaimed Markey. "He bumped something else, didn't you, Billy? He bumped something else."

Billy had so far forgotten the bump that he was already making an attempt to recover his property. He seized a leg of the bear which projected from Ede's enveloping arms and tugged at it but without success.

"No," said Ede emphatically.

Suddenly, encouraged by the success of her former half accidental maneuver, Ede dropped the teddy-bear, placed her hands on Billy's shoulders and pushed him backward off his feet.

This time he landed less harmlessly; his head hit the bare floor just off the rug with a dull hollow sound, whereupon he drew in his breath and delivered an agonized yell.

Immediately the room was in confusion. With an exclamation Markey hurried to his son, but his wife was first to reach the injured baby and catch him up into her arms.

"Oh, *Billy*," she cried, "what a terrible bump! She ought to be spanked."

Edith, who had rushed immediately to her daughter, heard this remark and her lips came sharply together.

"Why, Ede," she whispered perfunctorily, "you bad girl!"

Ede put back her little head suddenly and laughed. It was a loud laugh, a triumphant laugh with victory in it and challenge and contempt. Unfortunately it was also an infectious laugh. Before her mother realized the delicacy of the situation, she too had laughed, an audible, distinct laugh not unlike the baby's and partaking of the same overtones.

Then, as suddenly, she stopped.

Mrs. Markey's face had grown red with anger and Markey, who had been feeling the back of the baby's head with one finger, looked at her, frowning.

"It's swollen already," he said with a note of reproof in his voice. "I'll get some witch-hazel."

But Mrs. Markey had lost her temper. "I don't see anything funny about a child being hurt!" she said in a trembling voice.

Little Ede meanwhile had been looking at her mother curiously. She noted that her own laugh had produced her mother's, and she wondered if the same cause would always produce the same effect. So she chose this moment to throw back her head and laugh again.

To her mother the additional mirth added the final touch of hysteria to the situation. Pressing her handkerchief to her mouth she giggled irrepressibly. It was more than nervousness—she felt that in a peculiar way she was laughing with her child—they were laughing together.

It was in a way a defiance—those two against the world.

While Markey rushed upstairs to the bathroom for ointment, his wife was walking up and down rocking the yelling boy in her arms.

"Please go home!" she broke out suddenly. "The child's badly hurt, and if you haven't the decency to be quiet, you'd better go home."

"Very well," said Edith, her own temper rising. "I've never seen anyone make such a mountain out of—"

"Get out!" cried Mrs. Markey frantically. "There's the door, get out—I never want to see you in our house again. You or your brat either!"

Edith had taken her daughter's hand and was moving quickly toward the door, but at this remark she stopped and turned around, her face contracting with indignation.

"Don't you dare call her that!"

Mrs. Markey did not answer but continued walking up and down, muttering to herself and to Billy in an inaudible voice.

Edith began to cry.

"I will get out!" she sobbed. "I've never heard anybody so rude and c-common in my life. I'm glad your baby did get pushed down—he's nothing but a f-fat little fool anyhow."

Joe Markey reached the foot of the stairs just in time to hear this remark.

"Why, Mrs. Andros," he said sharply, "can't you see the child's hurt? You really ought to control yourself."

"Control m-myself!" exclaimed Edith brokenly. "You better ask her to c-control herself. I've never heard anybody so c-common in my life."

"She's insulting me!" Mrs. Markey was now livid with rage. "Did you hear what she said, Joe? I wish you'd put her out. If she won't go, just take her by the shoulders and put her out!"

"Don't you dare touch me!" cried Edith. "I'm going just as quick as I can find my c-coat!"

Blind with tears she took a step toward the hall. It was just at this moment that the door opened and John Andros walked anxiously in.

"John!" cried Edith and fled to him wildly.

"What's the matter? Why, what's the matter?"

"They're—they're putting me out!" she wailed, collapsing against him. "He'd just started to take me by the shoulders and put me out. I want my coat!"

"That's not true," objected Markey hurriedly. "Nobody's going to put you out." He turned to John. "Nobody's going to put her out," he repeated. "She's—"

"What do you mean 'put her out'?" demanded John abruptly. "What's all this talk, anyhow?"

"Oh, let's go!" cried Edith. "I want to go. They're so *common*, John!"

"Look here!" Markey's face darkened. "You've said that about enough. You're acting sort of crazy."

"They called Ede a brat!"

For the second time that afternoon little Ede expressed emotion at an inopportune moment. Confused and frightened at the shouting voices, she began to cry, and her tears had the effect of conveying that she felt the insult in her heart.

"What's the idea of this?" broke out John. "Do you insult your guests in your own house?"

"It seems to me it's your wife that's done the insulting!" answered Markey crisply. "In fact, your baby there started all the trouble."

John gave a contemptuous snort. "Are you calling names at a little baby?" he inquired. "That's a fine manly business!"

"Don't talk to him, John," insisted Edith. "Find my coat!"

"You must be in a bad way," went on John angrily, "if you have to take out your temper on a helpless little baby."

"I never heard anything so damn twisted in my life," shouted Markey. "If that wife of yours would shut her mouth for a minute—"

"Wait a minute! You're not talking to a woman and child now—"

There was an incidental interruption. Edith had been fumbling on a chair for her coat, and Mrs. Markey had been watching her with hot angry eyes. Suddenly she laid Billy down on the sofa, where he immediately stopped crying and pulled himself upright, and coming into the hall she quickly found Edith's coat and handed it to her without a word. Then she went back to the sofa, picked up Billy, and rocking him in her arms looked again at Edith with hot angry eyes. The interruption had taken less than half a minute.

"Your wife comes in here and begins shouting around about how common we are!" burst out Markey violently. "Well, if we're so damn common you'd better stay away! And what's more you'd better get out now!"

Again John gave a short, contemptuous laugh.

"You're not only common," he returned. "You're evidently an awful bully—when there's any helpless women and children around." He felt for the knob and swung the door open. "Come on, Edith."

Taking up her daughter in her arms, his wife stepped outside and John, still looking contemptuously at Markey, started to follow.

"Wait a minute!" Markey took a step forward; he was trembling slightly, and two large veins on his temple were suddenly full of blood. "You don't think you can get away with that, do you? With me?"

Without a word John walked out the door, leaving it open.

Edith, still weeping, had started for home. After following her with his eyes until she reached her own walk, John turned back toward the lighted doorway where Markey was slowly coming down the slippery steps. He took off his overcoat and hat, tossed them off the path onto the snow. Then, sliding a little on the iced walk, he took a step forward.

At the first blow, they both slipped and fell heavily to the sidewalk, half rising then, and again pulling each other to the ground. They found a better foothold in the thin snow to the side of the walk and rushed at each other, both swinging wildly and pressing out the snow into a pasty mud underfoot.

The street was deserted, and except for their short tired gasps and the padded sound as one or the other slipped down into the slushy mud, they fought in silence, clearly defined to each other by the full moonlight as well as by the amber glow that shone out of the open door. Several times they both slipped down together, and then for awhile the conflict threshed about wildly on the lawn.

For ten, fifteen, twenty minutes they fought there senselessly in the moonlight. They had both taken off coats and vests at some silently agreed upon interval and now their shirts dripped from their backs in wet pulpy shreds. Both were torn and bleeding and so exhausted that they could stand only when by their position they mutually supported each other—the impact, the mere effort of a blow, would send them both to their hands and knees.

But it was not weariness that ended the business, and the very meaninglessness of the fight was a reason for not stopping. They stopped because once when they were straining at each other on the ground, they heard a man's footsteps coming along the sidewalk. They had rolled somehow into the shadow, and when they heard these footsteps they stopped fighting, stopped moving, stopped breathing, lay huddled together like two boys playing Indian until the footsteps had passed. Then, staggering to their feet, they looked at each other like two drunken men.

"I'll be damned if I'm going on with this thing anymore," cried Markey thickly.

"I'm not going on anymore either," said John Andros. "I've had enough of this thing."

Again they looked at each other, sulkily this time, as if each suspected the other of urging him to a renewal of the fight. Markey spat out a mouthful of blood from a cut lip; then he cursed softly, and picking up his coat and vest, shook off the snow from them in a surprised way, as if their comparative dampness was his only worry in the world.

"Want to come in and wash up?" he asked suddenly.

"No thanks," said John. "I ought to be going home—my wife'll be worried."

He too picked up his coat and vest and then his overcoat and hat. Soaking wet and dripping with perspiration, it seemed absurd that less than half an hour ago he had been wearing all these clothes.

"Well—good-night," he said hesitantly.

Suddenly they both walked toward each other and shook hands. It was no perfunctory hand-shake: John Andros's arm went around Markey's shoulder, and he patted him softly on the back for a little while.

"No harm done," he said brokenly.

"No—you?"

"No, no harm done."

"Well," said John Andros after a minute, "I guess I'll say good-night."

"Good-night."

Limping slightly and with his clothes over his arm, John Andros turned away. The moonlight was still bright as he left the dark patch of trampled ground and walked over the intervening lawn. Down at the station, half a mile away, he could hear the rumble of the seven o'clock train.

"But you must have been crazy," cried Edith brokenly. "I thought you were going to fix it all up there and shake hands. That's why I went away."

"Did you want us to fix it up?"

"Of course not, I never want to see them again. But I thought of course that was what you were going to do." She was touching the bruises on his neck and back with iodine as he sat placidly in a hot bath. "I'm going to get the doctor," she said insistently. "You may be hurt internally."

He shook his head. "Not a chance," he answered. "I don't want this to get all over town."

"I don't understand yet how it all happened."

"Neither do I." He smiled grimly. "I guess these baby parties are pretty rough affairs."

"Well, one thing—" suggested Edith hopefully, "I'm certainly glad we have beefsteak in the house for tomorrow's dinner."

"Why?"

"For your eye, of course. Do you know I came within an ace of ordering veal? Wasn't that the luckiest thing?"

Half an hour later, dressed except that his neck would accommodate no collar, John moved his limbs experimentally before the glass. "I believe I'll get myself in better shape," he said thoughtfully. "I must be getting old."

"You mean so that next time you can beat him?"

"I did beat him," he announced. "At least, I beat him as much as he beat me. And there isn't going to be any next time. Don't you go calling people common anymore. If you get in any trouble, you just take your coat and go home. Understand?"

"Yes, dear," she said meekly. "I was very foolish and now I understand."

Out in the hall, he paused abruptly by the baby's door.

"Is she asleep?"

"Sound asleep. But you can go in and peek at her—just to say good-night."

They tiptoed in and bent together over the bed. Little Ede, her cheeks flushed with health, her pink hands clasped tight together, was sleeping soundly in the cool dark room. John reached over the railing of the bed and passed his hand lightly over the silken hair.

"She's asleep," he murmured in a puzzled way.

"Naturally, after such an afternoon."

"Miz Andros," the colored maid's stage whisper floated in from the hall, "Mr. and Miz Markey downstairs an' want to see you. Mr. Markey he's all cut up in pieces, mam'n. His face look like a roast beef. An' Miz Markey she 'pear mighty mad."

"Why, what incomparable nerve!" exclaimed Edith. "Just tell them we're not home. I wouldn't go down for anything in the world."

"You most certainly will." John's voice was hard and set.

"What?"

"You'll go down right now, and what's more, whatever that other woman does, you'll apologize for what you said this afternoon. After that you don't ever have to see her again."

"Why—John, I can't."

"You've got to. And just remember that she probably hated to come over here just twice as much as you hate to go downstairs."

"Aren't you coming? Do I have to go alone?"

"I'll be down—in just a minute."

John Andros waited until she had closed the door behind her; then he reached over into the bed, and picking up his daughter, blankets and all, sat down in the rocking-chair holding her tightly in his arms. She moved a little and he held his breath, but she was sleeping soundly and in a moment she was resting quietly in the hollow of his elbow. Slowly he bent his head until his cheek was against her bright hair. "Dear little girl," he whispered. "Dear little girl, dear little girl."

John Andros knew at length what it was he had fought for so savagely that evening. He had it now, he possessed it forever, and for some time he sat there rocking very slowly to and fro in the darkness.

Absolution

T HERE was once a priest with cold, watery eyes, who, in the still of the night, wept cold tears. He wept because the afternoons were warm and long, and he was unable to attain a complete mystical union with our Lord. Sometimes, near four o'clock, was a rustle of Swede girls along the path by his window, and in their shrill laughter he found a terrible dissonance that made him pray aloud for the twilight to come. At twilight the laughter and the voices were quieter, but several times he had walked past Romberg's Drug Store when it was dusk and the yellow lights shone inside and the nickel taps of the soda fountain were gleaming, and he had found the scent of cheap toilet soap desperately sweet upon the air. He passed that way when he returned from hearing confessions on Saturday nights, and he grew careful to walk on the other side of the street so that the smell of the soap would float upward before it reached his nostrils as it drifted, rather like incense, toward the summer moon.

But there was no escape from the hot madness of four o'clock. From his window, as far as he could see, the Dakota wheat thronged the valley of the Red River. The wheat was terrible to look upon and the carpet pattern to which in agony he bent his eyes sent his thoughts brooding through grotesque labyrinths, open always to the unavoidable sun.

One afternoon when he had reached the point where the mind runs down like an old clock, his housekeeper brought into his study a beautiful, intense little boy of eleven named Rudolph Miller. The little boy sat down in a patch of sunshine and the priest, at his walnut desk, pretended to be very busy. This was to conceal his relief that someone had come into his haunted room.

Presently he turned around and found himself staring into two enormous, staccato eyes, lit with gleaming points of cobalt light. For a moment their expression startled him—then he saw that his visitor was in a state of abject fear.

"Your mouth is trembling," said Father Schwartz, in a haggard voice.

The little boy covered his quivering mouth with his hand.

"Are you in trouble?" asked Father Schwartz, sharply. "Take your hand away from your mouth and tell me what's the matter."

The boy—Father Schwartz recognized him now as the son of a parishioner, Mr. Miller, the freight agent—moved his hand reluctantly off his mouth and became articulate in a despairing whisper.

"Father Schwartz—I've committed a terrible sin."

"A sin against purity?"

"No, Father . . . worse."

Father Schwartz's body jerked sharply.

"Have you killed somebody?"

"No—but I'm afraid—" the voice rose to a shrill whimper.

"Do you want to go to confession?"

The little boy shook his head miserably. Father Schwartz cleared his throat so that he could make his voice soft and say some quiet, kind thing. In this moment he should forget his own agony and try to act like God. He repeated to himself a devotional phrase, hoping that in return God would help him to act correctly.

"Tell me what you've done," said his new soft voice.

The little boy looked at him through his tears and was reassured by the impression of moral resiliency which the distraught priest had created. Abandoning as much of himself as he was able to this man, Rudolph Miller began to tell his story.

"On Saturday, three days ago, my father he said I had to go to confession, because I hadn't been for a month, and the family they go every week, and I hadn't been. So I just as leave go, I didn't care. So I put it off till after supper because I was playing with a bunch of kids and Father asked me if I went and I said 'no,' and he took me by the neck and he said 'You go now,' so I said 'All right,' so I went over to church. And he yelled after me: 'Don't come back till you go.' . . ."

II
"On Saturday, Three Days Ago"

The plush curtain of the confessional rearranged its dismal creases, leaving exposed only the bottom of an old man's old shoe. Behind the curtain an immortal soul was alone with God and the Reverend Adolphus Schwartz, priest of the parish.

Sound began, a labored whispering, sibilant and discreet, broken at intervals by the voice of the priest in audible question.

Rudolph Miller knelt in the pew beside the confessional and waited, straining nervously to hear and yet not to hear what was being said within. The fact that the priest was audible alarmed him. His own turn came next, and the three or four others who waited might listen unscrupulously while he admitted his violations of the Sixth and Ninth Commandments.

Rudolph had never committed adultery, not even coveted his neighbor's wife—but it was the confession of the associate sins that was particularly hard to contemplate. In comparison he relished the less shameful fallings away—they formed a greyish background which relieved the ebony mark of sexual offenses upon his soul.

He had been covering his ears with his hands, hoping that his refusal to hear would be noticed, and a like courtesy rendered to him in turn, when a sharp movement of the penitent in the confessional made him sink his face precipitately into the crook of his elbow. Fear assumed solid form and pressed out a lodging between his heart and his lungs. He must try now with all his might to be sorry for his sins—not because he was afraid, but because he had offended God. He must convince God that he was sorry and to do so he must first convince himself. After a tense emotional struggle he achieved a tremulous self-pity, and decided that he was now ready. If, by allowing no other thought to enter his head, he could preserve this state of emotion unimpaired until he went into that large coffin set on end, he would have survived another crisis in his religious life.

For some time, however, a demoniac notion had partially possessed him. He could go home now, before his turn came, and tell his mother that he had arrived too late and found the priest gone. This, unfortunately, involved the risk of being caught in a lie. As an alternative he could say that he *had* gone to confession, but this meant that he must avoid communion next day, for communion taken upon an uncleansed soul would turn to poison in his mouth, and he would crumple limp and damned from the altar rail.

Again Father Schwartz's voice became audible.

"And for your—"

The words blurred to a husky mumble and Rudolph got excitedly to his feet. He felt that it was impossible for him to go to confession this afternoon. He hesitated tensely. Then from the confessional came a tap, a creak and a sustained rustle. The slide had fallen and the plush curtain trembled. Temptation had come to him too late. . . .

"Bless me, Father, for I have sinned. . . . I confess to Almighty God and to you, Father, that I have sinned. . . . Since my last confession it has been one month and three days. . . . I accuse myself of—taking the Name of the Lord in vain. . . ."

This was an easy sin. His curses had been but bravado—telling of them was little less than a brag.

". . . of being mean to an old lady."

The wan shadow moved a little on the latticed slat.

"How, my child?"

"Old lady Swenson," Rudolph's murmur soared jubilantly. "She got our baseball that we knocked in her window, and she wouldn't give it back, so we yelled 'Twenty-three Skidoo' at her all afternoon. Then about five o'clock she had a fit and they had to have the doctor."

"Go on, my child."

"Of—of not believing I was the son of my parents."

"What?" The interrogator was distinctly startled.

"Of not believing that I was the son of my parents."

"Why not?"

"Oh, just pride," answered the penitent airily.

"You mean you thought you were too good to be the son of your parents?"

"Yes, Father." On a less jubilant note.

"Go on."

"Of being disobedient and calling my mother names. Of slandering people behind my back. Of smoking—"

Rudolph had now exhausted the minor offenses and was approaching the sins it was agony to tell. He held his fingers against his face like bars as if to press out between them the shame in his heart.

"Of dirty words and immodest thoughts and desires," he whispered very low.

"How often?"

"I don't know."

"Once a week? Twice a week?"

"Twice a week."

"Did you yield to these desires?"

"No, Father."

"Were you alone when you had them?"

"No, Father. I was with two boys and a girl."

"Don't you know, my child, that you should avoid the occasions of sin as well as the sin itself? Evil companionship leads to evil desires and evil desires to evil actions. Where were you when this happened?"

"In a barn in back of—"

"I don't want to hear any names," interrupted the priest sharply.

"Well, it was up in the loft of this barn and this girl and—a fella, they were saying things—saying immodest things, and I stayed."

"You should have gone—you should have told the girl to go."

He should have gone! He could not tell Father Schwartz how his pulse had bumped in his wrist, how a strange, romantic excitement had possessed him when those curious things had been said. Perhaps in the houses of delinquency among the dull and hard-eyed incorrigible girls can be found those for whom has burned the whitest fire.

"Have you anything else to tell me?"

"I don't think so, Father."

Rudolph felt a great relief. Perspiration had broken out under his tight-pressed fingers.

"Have you told any lies?"

The question startled him. Like all those who habitually and instinctively lie, he had an enormous respect and awe for the truth. Something almost exterior to himself dictated a quick, hurt answer.

"Oh, no, Father, I never tell lies."

For a moment, like the commoner in the king's chair, he tasted the pride of the situation. Then as the priest began to murmur conventional admonitions he realized that in heroically denying he had told lies, he had committed a terrible sin—he had told a lie in confession.

In automatic response to Father Schwartz's "Make an act of contrition," he began to repeat aloud meaninglessly:

"Oh, my God, I am heartily sorry for having offended Thee. . . ."

He must fix this now—it was a bad mistake—but as his teeth shut on the last words of his prayer there was a sharp sound, and the slat was closed.

A minute later when he emerged into the twilight the relief in coming from the muggy church into an open world of wheat and sky postponed the full realization of what he had done. Instead of worrying he took a deep breath of the crisp air and began to say over and over to himself the words "Blatchford Sarnemington, Blatchford Sarnemington!"

Blatchford Sarnemington was himself, and these words were in effect a lyric. When he became Blatchford Sarnemington a suave nobility flowed from him. Blatchford Sarnemington lived in great sweeping triumphs. When Rudolph half closed his eyes it meant that Blatchford had established dominance over him and, as he went by, there were envious mutters in the air: "Blatchford Sarnemington! There goes Blatchford Sarnemington."

He was Blatchford now for awhile as he strutted homeward along the staggering road, but when the road braced itself in macadam in order to become the main street of Ludwig, Rudolph's exhilaration faded out and his mind cooled and he felt the horror of his lie. God, of course, already knew of it—but Rudolph reserved a corner of his mind where he was safe from God, where he prepared the subterfuges with which he often tricked God. Hiding now in this corner he considered how he could best avoid the consequences of his misstatement.

At all costs he must avoid communion next day. The risk of angering God to such an extent was too great. He would have to drink water "by accident" in the morning and thus, in accordance with a church law, render himself unfit to receive communion that day. In spite of its flimsiness this subterfuge was the most feasible that occurred to him. He accepted its risks and was concentrating on how best to put it into effect, as he turned the corner by Romberg's Drug Store and came in sight of his father's house.

III

Rudolph's father, the local freight agent, had floated with the second wave of German and Irish stock to the Minnesota-Dakota country. Theoretically, great opportunities lay ahead of a young man of energy in that day and place, but Carl Miller had been incapable of establishing either with his superiors or his subordinates the reputation for approximate immutability which is essential to success in a hierarchic industry. Somewhat gross, he was, nevertheless, insufficiently hard-headed and unable to take fundamental relationships for granted, and this inability made him suspicious, unrestful and continually dismayed.

His two bonds with the colorful life were his faith in the Roman Catholic Church and his mystical worship of the Empire Builder, James J. Hill. Hill was the apotheosis of that quality in which Miller himself was deficient—the sense of things, the feel of things, the hint of rain in the wind on the cheek. Miller's mind worked late on the old decisions of other men, and he had never in his life felt the balance of any single thing in his hands. His weary, sprightly, undersized body was growing old in Hill's gigantic shadow. For twenty years he had lived alone with Hill's name and God.

On Sunday morning Carl Miller awoke in the dustless quiet of six o'clock. Kneeling by the side of the bed he bent his yellow-grey hair and the full dapple bangs of his mustache into the pillow, and prayed for several minutes. Then he drew off his night-shirt—like the rest of his generation he had never been able to endure pajamas—and clothed his thin, white, hairless body in woollen underwear.

He shaved. Silence in the other bedroom where his wife lay nervously asleep. Silence from the screened-off corner of the hall where his son's cot stood, and his son slept among his Alger books, his collection of cigar-bands, his mothy pennants—"Cornell," "Hamline," and "Greetings from Pueblo, New Mexico"—and the other possessions of his private life. From outside Miller could hear the shrill birds and the whirring movement of the poultry and, as an undertone, the low, swelling click-a-tick of the six-fifteen through-train for Montana and the green coast beyond. Then as the cold water dripped from the washrag in his hand he raised his head suddenly—he had heard a furtive sound from the kitchen below.

He dried his razor hastily, slipped his dangling suspenders to his shoulders, and listened. Someone was walking in the kitchen, and he knew by the light foot-fall that it was not his wife. With his mouth faintly ajar he ran quickly down the stairs and opened the kitchen door.

Standing by the sink, with one hand on the still dripping faucet and the other clutching a full glass of water, stood his son. The boy's eyes, still heavy with sleep, met his father's with a frightened, reproachful beauty. He was barefooted and his pajamas were rolled up at the knees and sleeves.

For a moment they both remained motionless—Carl Miller's brow went down and his son's went up, as though they were striking a balance between the extremes of emotion which filled them. Then the bangs of the parent's mustache descended portentously until they obscured his mouth, and he gave a short glance around to see if anything had been disturbed.

The kitchen was garnished with sunlight which beat on the pans and made the smooth boards of the floor and table yellow and clean as wheat. It was the center of the house where the fire burned and the tins fitted into tins like toys, and the steam whistled all day on a thin pastel note. Nothing was moved, nothing touched—except the faucet where beads of water still formed and dripped with a white flash into the sink below.

"What are you doing?"

"I got awful thirsty, so I thought I'd just come down and get—"

"I thought you were going to communion."

A look of vehement astonishment spread over his son's face.

"I forgot all about it."

"Have you drunk any water?"

"No—"

As the word left his mouth Rudolph knew it was the wrong answer, but the faded indignant eyes facing him had signalled up the truth before the boy's will could act. He realized, too, that he should never have come downstairs; some vague necessity for verisimilitude had made him want to leave a wet glass as evidence by the sink; the honesty of his imagination had betrayed him.

"Pour it out," commanded his father, "that water!"

Rudolph despairingly inverted the tumbler.

"What's the matter with you, anyways?" demanded Miller angrily.

"Nothing."

"Did you go to confession yesterday?"

"Yes."

"Then why were you going to drink water?"

"I don't know—I forgot."

"Maybe you care more about being a little bit thirsty than you do about your religion."

"I forgot." Rudolph could feel the tears straining in his eyes.

"That's no answer."

"Well, I did."

"You better look out!" His father held to a high, persistent, inquisitory note: "If you're so forgetful that you can't remember your religion something better be done about it."

Rudolph filled a sharp pause with:

"I can remember it all right."

"First you begin to neglect your religion," cried his father, fanning his own fierceness, "the next thing you'll begin to lie and steal, and the *next* thing is the *reform* school!"

Not even this familiar threat could deepen the abyss that Rudolph saw before him. He must either tell all now, offering his body for what he knew would be a ferocious beating, or else tempt the thunderbolts by receiving the Body and Blood of Christ with sacrilege upon his soul. And of the two the former seemed more terrible—it was not so much the beating he dreaded as the savage ferocity, outlet of the ineffectual man, which would lie behind it.

"Put down that glass and go upstairs and dress!" his father ordered. "And when we get to church, before you go to communion, you better kneel down and ask God to forgive you for your carelessness."

Some accidental emphasis in the phrasing of this command acted like a catalytic agent on the confusion and terror of Rudolph's mind. A wild, proud anger rose in him, and he dashed the tumbler passionately into the sink.

His father uttered a strained, husky sound, and sprang for him. Rudolph dodged to the side, tipped over a chair, and tried to get beyond the kitchen table. He cried out sharply when a hand grasped his pajama shoulder, then he felt the dull impact of a fist against the side of his head and glancing blows on the upper part of his body. As he slipped here and there in his father's grasp, dragged or lifted when he clung instinctively to an arm, aware of sharp smarts and strains, he made no sound except that he laughed hysterically several times. Then in less than a minute the blows abruptly ceased. After a lull during which Rudolph was tightly held and during which they both trembled violently and uttered strange, truncated words, Carl Miller half dragged, half threatened his son upstairs.

"Put on your clothes!"

Rudolph was now both hysterical and cold. His head hurt him, and there was a long, shallow scratch on his neck from his father's fingernail, and he sobbed and trembled as he dressed. He was aware of his mother standing at the doorway in a wrapper, her wrinkled face compressing and squeezing and opening out into a new series of wrinkles which floated and eddied from neck to brow. Despising her nervous ineffectuality and avoiding her rudely when she tried to touch his neck with witch-hazel, he made a hasty, choking toilet. Then he followed his father out of the house and along the road toward the Catholic church.

IV

They walked without speaking except when Carl Miller acknowledged automatically the existence of passers-by. Rudolph's uneven breathing alone ruffled the hot Sunday silence.

His father stopped decisively at the door of the church.

"I've decided you'd better go to confession again. Go in and tell Father Schwartz what you did and ask God's pardon."

"You lost your temper, too!" said Rudolph quickly.

Carl Miller took a step toward his son, who moved cautiously backward.

"All right, I'll go."

"Are you going to do what I say?" cried his father in a hoarse whisper.

"All right."

Rudolph walked into the church and for the second time in two days entered the confessional and knelt down. The slat went up almost at once.

"I accuse myself of missing my morning prayers."

"Is that all?"

"That's all."

A maudlin exultation filled him. Not easily ever again would he be able to put an abstraction before the necessities of his ease and pride. An invisible line had been crossed and he had become aware of his isolation—aware that it applied not only to those moments when he was Blatchford Sarnemington but that it applied to all his inner life. Hitherto such phenomena as "crazy" ambitions and petty shames and fears had been but private reservations, unacknowledged before the throne of his official soul. Now he realized unconsciously that his private reservations were himself—and all the rest a garnished front and a conventional flag. The pressure of his environment had driven him into the lonely secret road of adolescence.

He knelt in the pew beside his father. Mass began. Rudolph knelt up—when he was alone he slumped his posterior back against the seat—and tasted the consciousness of a sharp, subtle revenge. Beside him his father prayed that God would forgive Rudolph, and asked also that his own outbreak of temper would be pardoned. He glanced sidewise at this son and was relieved to see that the strained, wild look had gone from his face and that he had ceased sobbing. The Grace of God, inherent in the Sacrament, would do the rest, and perhaps after Mass everything would be better. He was proud of Rudolph in his heart and beginning to be truly as well as formally sorry for what he had done.

Usually, the passing of the collection box was a significant point for Rudolph in the services. If, as was often the case, he had no money to drop in he would be furiously ashamed and bow his head and pretend not to see the box, lest Jeanne Brady in the pew behind should take notice and suspect an acute family poverty. But today he glanced coldly into it as it skimmed under his eyes, noting with casual interest the large number of pennies it contained.

When the bell rang for communion, however, he quivered. There was no reason why God should not stop his heart. During the past twelve hours he had committed a series of mortal sins increasing in gravity, and he was now to crown them all with a blasphemous sacrilege.

"*Dómini, non sum dignus, ut intres sub tectum meum: sed tantum dic verbo, et sánábitur ánima mea. . . .*"

There was a rustle in the pews and the communicants worked their ways into the aisle with downcast eyes and joined hands. Those of larger piety pressed together their fingertips to form steeples. Among these latter was Carl Miller. Rudolph followed him toward the altar rail and knelt down, automatically taking up the napkin under his chin. The bell rang sharply, and the priest turned from the altar with the white Host held above the chalice:

"*Corpus Dómini nostri Jesu Christi custódiat ánimam meam in vitam ætérnam.*"

A cold sweat broke out on Rudolph's forehead as the communion began. Along the line Father Schwartz moved, and with gathering nausea Rudolph felt his heart-valves weakening at the will of God. It seemed to him that the church was darker and that a great quiet had fallen, broken only by the inarticulate mumble which announced the approach of the Creator of Heaven and Earth. He dropped his head down between his shoulders and waited for the blow.

Then he felt a sharp nudge in his side. His father was poking him to sit up, not to slump against the rail; the priest was only two places away.

"*Corpus Dómini nostri Jesu Christi custódiat ánimam meam in vitam ætérnam.*"

Rudolph opened his mouth. He felt the sticky wax taste of the wafer on his tongue. He remained motionless for what seemed an interminable period of time, his head still raised, the wafer undissolved in his mouth. Then again he started at the pressure of his father's elbow, and saw that the people were falling away from the altar like leaves and turning with blind downcast eyes to their pews, alone with God.

Rudolph was alone with himself, drenched with perspiration and deep in mortal sin. As he walked back to his pew the sharp taps of his cloven hoofs were loud upon the floor, and he knew that it was a dark poison he carried in his heart.

V

"Sagitta Volante in Die"

The beautiful little boy with eyes like blue stones, and lashes that sprayed open from them like flower-petals, had finished telling his sin to Father Schwartz—and the square of sunshine in which he sat had moved forward half an hour into the room. Rudolph had become less frightened now; once eased of the story a reaction had set in. He knew that as long as he was in the room with this priest God would not stop his heart, so he sighed and sat quietly, waiting for the priest to speak.

Father Schwartz's cold watery eyes were fixed upon the carpet pattern on which the sun had brought out the swastikas and the flat bloomless vines and the pale echoes of flowers. The hall clock ticked insistently toward sunset, and from the ugly room and from the afternoon outside the window arose a stiff monotony, shattered now and then by the reverberate clapping of a far-away hammer on the dry air. The priest's nerves were strung thin and the beads of his rosary were crawling and squirming like snakes upon the green felt of his table top. He could not remember now what it was he should say.

Of all the things in this lost Swede town he was most aware of this little boy's eyes—the beautiful eyes, with lashes that left them reluctantly and curved back as though to meet them once more.

For a moment longer the silence persisted while Rudolph waited, and the priest struggled to remember something that was slipping farther and farther away from him, and the clock ticked in the broken house. Then Father Schwartz stared hard at the little boy and remarked in a peculiar voice—

"When a lot of people get together in the best places things go glimmering."

Rudolph started and looked quickly at Father Schwartz's face.

"I said—" began the priest, and paused, listening. "Do you hear the hammer and the clock ticking and the bees? Well, that's no good. The thing is to have a lot of people in the center of the world, wherever that happens to be. Then"—his watery eyes widened knowingly—"things go glimmering."

"Yes, Father," agreed Rudolph, feeling a little frightened.

"What are you going to be when you grow up?"

"Well, I was going to be a baseball player for awhile," answered Rudolph nervously, "but I don't think that's a very good ambition, so I think I'll be an actor or a navy officer."

Again the priest stared at him.

"I see *exactly* what you mean," he said, with a fierce air.

Rudolph had not meant anything in particular, and at the implication that he had, he became more uneasy.

"This man is crazy," he thought, "and I'm scared of him. He wants me to help him out some way, and I don't want to."

"You look as if things went glimmering," cried Father Schwartz wildly. "Did you ever go to a party?"

"Yes, Father."

"And did you notice that everybody was properly dressed? That's what I mean. Just as you went into the party there was a moment when everybody was properly dressed. Maybe two little girls were standing by the door and some boys were leaning over the banisters, and there were bowls around full of flowers."

"I've been to a lot of parties," said Rudolph, rather relieved that the conversation had taken this turn.

"Of course," continued Father Schwartz triumphantly, "I knew you'd agree with me. But my theory is that when a whole lot of people get together in the best places things go glimmering all the time."

Rudolph found himself thinking of Blatchford Sarnemington.

"Please listen to me!" commanded the priest impatiently. "Stop worrying about last Saturday. Apostasy implies an absolute damnation only on the supposition of a previous perfect faith. Does that fix it?"

Rudolph had not the faintest idea what Father Schwartz was talking about, but he nodded and the priest nodded back at him and returned to his mysterious preoccupation.

"Why," he cried, "they have lights now as big as stars—do you realize that? I heard of one light they had in Paris or somewhere that was as big as a star. A lot of people had it—a lot of gay people. They have all sorts of things now that you never dreamed of.

"Look here—" He came nearer to Rudolph, but the boy drew away, so Father Schwartz went back and sat down in his chair, his eyes dried out and hot.

"Did you ever see an amusement park?"

"No, Father."

"Well, go and see an amusement park." The priest waved his hand vaguely. "It's a thing like a fair, only much more glittering. Go to one at night and stand a little way off from it in a dark place—under dark trees. You'll see a big wheel made of lights turning in the air and a long slide shooting boats down into the water. A band playing somewhere and a smell of peanuts—and everything will twinkle. But it won't remind you of anything, you see. It will all just hang out there in the night like a colored balloon—like a big yellow lantern on a pole."

Father Schwartz frowned as he suddenly thought of something.

"But don't get up close," he warned Rudolph, "because if you do you'll only feel the heat and the sweat and the life."

All this talking seemed particularly strange and awful to Rudolph, because this man was a priest. He sat there, half terrified, his beautiful eyes open wide and staring at Father Schwartz. But underneath his terror he felt that his own inner convictions were confirmed. There was something ineffably gorgeous somewhere that had nothing to do with God. He no longer thought that God was angry at him about the original lie, because He must have understood that Rudolph had done it to make things finer in the confessional, brightening up the dinginess of his admissions by saying a thing radiant and proud. At the moment when he had affirmed immaculate honor a silver pennon had flapped out into the breeze somewhere and there had been the crunch of leather and the shine of silver spurs and a troop of horsemen waiting for dawn on a low green hill. The sun had made stars of light on their breastplates like the picture at home of the German cuirassiers at Sedan.

But now the priest was muttering inarticulate and heart-broken words, and the boy became wildly afraid. Horror entered suddenly in at the open window, and the atmosphere of the room changed. Father Schwartz collapsed precipitously down on his knees and let his body settle back against a chair.

"Oh, my God!" he cried out, in a strange voice, and wilted to the floor.

Then a human oppression rose from the priest's worn clothes and mingled with the faint smell of old food in the corners. Rudolph gave a sharp cry and ran in a panic from the house—while the collapsed man lay there quite still, filling his room, filling it with voices and faces until it was crowded with echolalia, and rang loud with a steady, shrill note of laughter.

*

Outside the window the blue sirocco trembled over the wheat, and girls with yellow hair walked sensuously along roads that bounded the fields, calling innocent, exciting things to the young men who were working in the lines between the grain. Legs were shaped under starchless gingham, and rims of the necks of dresses were warm and damp. For five hours now hot fertile life had burned in the afternoon. It would be night in three hours, and all along the land there would be these blonde northern girls and the tall young men from the farms lying out beside the wheat, under the moon.

Rags Martin-Jones and the Pr-nce of W-les

THE *Majestic* came gliding into New York harbor on an
April morning. She sniffed at the tug-boats and turtle-
gaited ferries, winked at a gaudy young yacht, and ordered
a cattle-boat out of her way with a snarling whistle of steam.
Then she parked at her private dock with all the fuss of a stout
lady sitting down, and announced complacently that she had
just come from Cherbourg and Southampton with a cargo of
the very best people in the world.

The very best people in the world stood on the deck and
waved idiotically to their poor relations who were waiting on
the dock for gloves from Paris. Before long a great toboggan
had connected the *Majestic* with the North American continent and the ship began to disgorge these very best people in
the world—who turned out to be Gloria Swanson, two buyers
from Lord & Taylor, the financial minister from Graustark
with a proposal for funding the debt, and an African king who
had been trying to land somewhere all winter and was feeling
violently seasick.

The photographers worked passionately as the stream of
passengers flowed onto the dock. There was a burst of cheer-
ing at the appearance of a pair of stretchers laden with two
middle-westerners who had drunk themselves delirious on the
last night out.

The deck gradually emptied but when the last bottle of Bene-
dictine had reached shore the photographers still remained at
their posts. And the officer in charge of debarkation still stood
at the foot of the gang-way, glancing first at his watch and
then at the deck as if some important part of the cargo was
still on board. At last from the watchers on the pier there arose
a long-drawn "Ah-h-h!" as a final entourage began to stream
down from deck B.

First came two French maids, carrying small, purple dogs, and
followed by a squad of porters, blind and invisible under innumerable bunches and bouquets of fresh flowers. Another maid
followed, leading a sad-eyed orphan child of a French flavor, and

close upon its heels walked the second officer pulling along three neurasthenic wolfhounds, much to their reluctance and his own.

A pause. Then the captain, Sir Howard George Witchcraft, appeared at the rail, with something that might have been a pile of gorgeous silver fox fur standing by his side—

Rags Martin-Jones, after five years in the capitals of Europe, was returning to her native land!

Rags Martin-Jones was not a dog. She was half a girl and half a flower and as she shook hands with Captain Sir Howard George Witchcraft she smiled as if someone had told her the newest, freshest joke in the world. All the people who had not already left the pier felt that smile trembling on the April air and turned around to see.

She came slowly down the gang-way. Her hat, an expensive, inscrutable experiment, was crushed under her arm so that her scant boy's hair, convict's hair, tried unsuccessfully to toss and flop a little in the harbor wind. Her face was like seven o'clock on a wedding morning save where she had slipped a preposterous monocle into an eye of clear childish blue. At every few steps her long lashes would tilt out the monocle and she would laugh, a bored, happy laugh, and replace the supercilious spectacle in the other eye.

Tap! Her one hundred and five pounds reached the pier and it seemed to sway and bend from the shock of her beauty. A few porters fainted. A large, sentimental shark which had followed the ship across made a despairing leap to see her once more, and then dove, broken-hearted, back into the deep sea. Rags Martin-Jones had come home.

There was no member of her family there to meet her for the simple reason that she was the only member of her family left alive. In 1912 her parents had gone down on the *Titanic* together rather be separated in this world, and so the Martin-Jones fortune of seventy-five millions had been inherited by a very little girl on her tenth birthday. It was what the consumer always refers to as a "shame."

Rags Martin-Jones (everybody had forgotten her real name long ago) was now photographed from all sides. The monocle persistently fell out and she kept laughing and yawning and replacing it, so no very clear picture of her was taken—except by the motion-picture camera. All the photographs, however,

included a flustered, handsome young man, with an almost ferocious love-light burning in his eyes, who had met her on the
dock. His name was John M. Chestnut, he had already written
the story of his success for the "American Magazine" and he had
been hopelessly in love with Rags ever since the time when she,
like the tides, had come under the influence of the summer moon.

When Rags became really aware of his presence they were
walking down the pier, and she looked at him blankly as though
she had never seen him before in this world.

"Rags," he began, "Rags—"

"John M. Chestnut?" she inquired, inspecting him with great
interest.

"Of course!" he exclaimed angrily. "Are you trying to pretend
you don't know me? That you didn't write me to meet you here?"

She laughed. A chauffeur appeared at her elbow and she
twisted out of her coat, revealing a dress made in great splashy
checks of sea-blue and grey. She shook herself like a wet bird.

"I've got a lot of junk to declare," she remarked absently.

"So have I," said Chestnut anxiously, "and the first thing I
want to declare is that I've loved you, Rags, every minute since
you've been away."

She stopped him with a groan.

"Please! There were some young Americans on the boat. The
subject has become a bore."

"My God!" cried Chestnut. "Do you mean to say that you
class *my* love with what was said to you on a *boat?*"

His voice had risen and several people in the vicinity turned
to hear.

"Sh!" she warned him. "I'm not giving a circus. If you want
me to even see you while I'm here you'll have to be less violent."

But John M. Chestnut seemed unable to control his voice.

"Do you mean to say"—it trembled to a carrying pitch—"that
you've forgotten what you said on this very pier five years ago
last Thursday?"

Half the passengers from the ship were now watching the
scene on the dock and another little eddy drifted out of the
customs house to see.

"John"—her displeasure was increasing—"if you raise your
voice again I'll arrange it so you'll have plenty of chance to cool
off. I'm going to the Ritz. Come and see me there this afternoon."

"But, Rags—!" he protested hoarsely. "Listen to me. Five years ago—"

Then the watchers on the dock were treated to a curious sight. A beautiful lady in a checkered dress of sea-blue and grey took a brisk step forward so that her hands came into contact with an excited young man by her side. The young man retreating instinctively reached back with his foot, but, finding nothing, relapsed gently off the thirty-foot dock and plopped, after a not ungraceful revolution, into the Hudson River.

A shout of alarm went up and there was a rush to the edge just as his head appeared above water. He was swimming easily and, perceiving this, the young lady who had apparently been the cause of the accident leaned over the pier and made a megaphone of her hands.

"I'll be in at half past four," she cried.

And with a cheerful wave of her hand, which the engulfed gentleman was unable to return, she adjusted her monocle, threw one haughty glance at the gathered crowd and walked leisurely from the scene.

II

The five dogs, the three maids and the French orphan were installed in the largest suite at the Ritz and Rags tumbled lazily into a steaming path, fragrant with herbs, where she dozed for the greater part of an hour. At the end of that time she received business calls from a masseuse, a manicure and finally a Parisian hair-dresser, who restored her hair-cut to criminal's length. When John M. Chestnut arrived at four he found half a dozen lawyers and bankers, the administrators of the Martin-Jones trust fund, waiting in the hall. They had been there since half past one and were now in a state of considerable agitation.

After one of the maids had subjected him to a severe scrutiny, possibly to be sure that he was thoroughly dry, John was conducted immediately into the presence of M'selle. M'selle was in her bedroom reclining on the chaise longue among two dozen silk pillows that had accompanied her from the other side. John came into the room somewhat stiffly and greeted her with a formal bow.

"You look better," she said, raising herself from her pillows and staring at him appraisingly. "It gave you a color."

He thanked her coldly for the compliment.

"You ought to go in every morning." And then she added irrelevantly, "I'm going back to Paris tomorrow."

John Chestnut gasped.

"I wrote you that I didn't intend to stay more than a week anyhow," she added.

"But, Rags—"

"Why should I? There isn't an amusing man in New York."

"But listen, Rags, won't you give me a chance? Won't you stay for, say, ten days and get to know me a little?"

"Know you!" Her tone implied that he was already a far too open book. "I want a man who's capable of a gallant gesture."

"Do you mean you want me to express myself entirely in pantomime?"

Rags uttered a disgusted sigh.

"I mean you haven't any imagination," she explained patiently. "No Americans have any imagination. Paris is the only large city where a civilized woman can breathe."

"Don't you care for me at all anymore?"

"I wouldn't have crossed the Atlantic to see you if I didn't. But as soon as I looked over the Americans on the boat I knew I couldn't marry one. I'd just hate you, John, and the only fun I'd have out of it would be the fun of breaking your heart."

She began to twist herself down among the cushions until she almost disappeared from view.

"I've lost my monocle," she explained.

After an unsuccessful search in the silken depths she discovered the elusive glass hanging down the back of her neck.

"I'd love to be in love," she went on, replacing the monocle in her childish eye. "Last spring in Sorrento I almost eloped with an Indian rajah, but he was half a shade too dark, and I took an intense dislike to one of his other wives."

"Don't talk that rubbish!" cried John, sinking his face into his hands.

"Well, I didn't marry him," she protested. "But in one way he had a lot to offer. He was the third richest subject of the British Empire. That's another thing—are you rich?"

"Not as rich as you."

"There you are. What have you to offer me?"

"Love."

"Love!" She disappeared again among the cushions. "Listen, John. Life to me is a series of glistening bazaars with a merchant in front of each one rubbing his hands together and saying 'Patronize this place here. Best bazaar in the world.' So I go in with my purse full of beauty and money and youth, all prepared to buy. 'What have you got for sale?' I ask him, and he rubs his hands together and says: 'Well, Mademoiselle, today we have some perfectly be-*oo*-tiful love.' Sometimes he hasn't even got that in stock but he sends out for it when he finds I have so much money to spend. Oh, he always gives me love before I go—and for nothing. That's the one revenge I have."

John Chestnut rose despairingly to his feet and took a step toward the window.

"Don't throw yourself out," Rags exclaimed quickly.

"All right." He tossed his cigarette down into Madison Avenue.

"It isn't just you," she said in a softer voice. "Dull and uninspired as you are, I care for you more than I can say. But life's so endless here. Nothing ever comes off."

"Loads of things come off," he insisted. "Why, today there was an intellectual murder in Hoboken and a suicide by proxy in Maine. A bill to sterilize agnostics is before Congress—"

"I have no interest in humor," she objected, "but I have an almost archaic predilection for romance. Why, John, last month I sat at a dinner table while two men flipped a coin for the kingdom of Schwartzberg-Rhineminster. In Paris I knew a man named Blutchdak who really started the war, and has a new one planned for year after next."

"Well, just for a rest you come out with me tonight," he said doggedly.

"Where to?" demanded Rags with scorn. "Do you think I still thrill at a night-club and a bottle of sugary mousseux? I prefer my own gaudy dreams."

"I'll take you to the most highly strung place in the city."

"What'll happen? You've got to tell me what'll happen."

John Chestnut suddenly drew a long breath and looked cautiously around as if he were afraid of being overheard.

"Well, to tell you the truth," he said in a low worried tone, "if everything was known, something pretty awful would be liable to happen to *me*."

She sat upright and the pillows tumbled about her like leaves.

"Do you mean to imply that there's anything shady in your life?" she cried, with laughter in her voice. "Do you expect me to believe that? No, John, you'll have your fun by plugging ahead on the beaten path—just plugging ahead."

Her mouth, a small insolent rose, dropped the words on him like thorns. John took his hat and coat from the chair and picked up his cane.

"For the last time—will you come along with me tonight and see what you will see?"

"See what? See who? Is there anything in this country worth seeing?"

"Well," he said, in a matter-of-fact tone, "for one thing you'll see the Prince of Wales."

"What?" She left the chaise longue at a bound. "Is he back in New York?"

"He will be tonight. Would you care to see him?"

"Would I? I've never seen him. I've missed him everywhere. I'd give a year of my life to see him for an hour." Her voice trembled with excitement.

"He's been in Canada. He's down here incognito for the big prize fight this afternoon. And I happen to know where he's going to be tonight."

Rags gave a sharp ecstatic cry:

"Dominic! Louise! Germaine!"

The three maids came running. The room filled suddenly with vibrations of wild, startled light.

"Dominic, the car!" cried Rags in French. "St. Raphael, my gold dress and the slippers with the real gold heels. The big pearls too—all the pearls, and the egg diamond and the stockings with the sapphire clocks. Germaine—send for a beauty-parlor on the run. My bath again—ice cold and half full of almond cream. Dominic—Tiffany's, like lightning, before they close! Find me a brooch, a pendant, a tiara, anything—it doesn't matter—with the arms of the House of Windsor."

She was fumbling at the buttons of her dress—and as John turned quickly to go it was already sliding from her shoulders.

"Orchids!" she called after him, "orchids, for the love of heaven! Four dozen, so I can choose four."

And then maids flew here and there about the room like frightened birds. "Perfume, St. Raphael, open the perfume trunk, and my rose-colored sables, and my diamond garters, and the sweet-oil for my hands! Here, take these things! This too—and this—Ouch!—and this!"

With becoming modesty John Chestnut closed the outside door. The six trustees in various postures of fatigue, of ennui, of resignation, of despair, were still cluttering up the outer hall.

"Gentlemen," announced John Chestnut, "I fear that Miss Martin-Jones is much too weary from her trip to talk to you this afternoon."

III

"This place, for no particular reason, is called the Hole in the Sky."

Rags looked around her. They were on a roof garden wide open to the April night. Overhead the true stars winked cold and there was a lunar sliver of ice in the dark west. But where they stood it was warm as June, and the couples dining or dancing on the opaque glass floor were unconcerned with the forbidding sky.

"What makes it so warm?" she whispered as they moved toward a table.

"It's some new invention that keeps the warm air from rising. I don't know the principle of the thing, but I know that they can keep it open like this even in the middle of winter—"

"Where's the Prince of Wales?" she demanded tensely.

John looked around.

"He hasn't arrived yet. He won't be here for about half an hour."

She sighed profoundly.

"It's the first time I've been excited in four years."

Four years—one year less than he had loved her. He wondered if when she was sixteen, a wild lovely child, sitting up all night in restaurants with officers who were to leave for Brest next day, losing the glamour of life too soon in the old, sad, poignant days of the war, she had ever been so lovely as under these amber lights and this dark sky. From her excited eyes to her tiny slipper heels, which were striped with layers of real silver and gold, she was like one of those amazing ships that are carved complete in a bottle. She was finished with that delicacy, with that care, as though the long lifetime of some worker in fragility had been used to make her so. John Chestnut wanted to take her up in his hands, turn her this way and that, examine the tip of a slipper or the tip of an ear or squint closely at the fairy stuff from which her lashes were made.

"Who's that?" She pointed suddenly to a handsome Latin at a table over the way.

"That's Roderigo Minerlino, the movie and face-cream star. Perhaps he'll dance after while."

Rags became suddenly aware of the sound of violins and drums but the music seemed to come from far away, seemed to float over the crisp night and on to the floor with the added remoteness of a dream.

"The orchestra's on another roof," explained John. "It's a new idea— Look, the entertainment's beginning."

A negro girl, thin as a reed, emerged suddenly from a masked entrance into a circle of harsh barbaric light, startled the music to a wild minor and commenced to sing a rhythmic, tragic song. The pipe of her body broke abruptly and she began a slow incessant step, without progress and without hope, like the failure of a savage insufficient dream. She had lost Papa Jack, she cried over and over with a hysterical monotony at once despairing and unreconciled. One by one the loud horns tried to force her from the steady beat of madness but she listened only to the mutter of the drums which were isolating her in some lost place in time, among many thousand forgotten years. After the failure of the piccolo, she made herself again into a thin brown line, wailed once with a sharp and terrible intensity, then vanished into sudden darkness.

"If you lived in New York you wouldn't need to be told who she is," said John when the amber light flashed on. "The next fella is Sheik B. Smith, a comedian of the fatuous, garrulous sort—"

He broke off. Just as the lights went down for the second number Rags had given a long sigh and leaned forward tensely in her chair. Her eyes were rigid like the eyes of a pointer dog, and John saw that they were fixed on a party that had come through a side entrance and were arranging themselves around a table in the half darkness.

The table was shielded with palms and Rags at first made out only three dim forms. Then she distinguished a fourth who seemed to be placed well behind the other three—a pale oval of a face topped with a glimmer of dark yellow hair.

"Hello!" ejaculated John. "There's his majesty now."

Her breath seemed to die murmurously in her throat. She was dimly aware that the comedian was now standing in a glow of white light on the dancing floor, that he had been talking for some moments, and that there was a constant ripple of laughter in the air. But her eyes remained motionless, enchanted. She saw one of the party bend and whisper to another, and, after the low glitter of a match, the bright button of a cigarette end gleamed in the background. How long it was before she moved she did not know. Then something seemed to happen to her eyes, something white, something terribly urgent, and she wrenched about sharply to find herself full in the center of a baby spotlight from above. She became aware that words were being said to her from somewhere and that a quick trail of laughter was circling the roof, but the light blinded her and instinctively she made a half movement from her chair.

"Sit still!" John was whispering across the table. "He picks somebody out for this every night."

Then she realized—it was the comedian, Sheik B. Smith. He was talking to her, arguing with her—about something that seemed incredibly funny to everyone else, but came to her ears only as a blur of muddled sound. Instinctively she had composed her face at the first shock of the light and now she smiled. It was a gesture of rare self-possession. Into this smile she insinuated a vast impersonality, as if she were unconscious of the light, unconscious of his attempt to play upon her loveliness—but amused at an infinitely removed *him*, whose darts might have been thrown just as successfully at the moon. She was no longer a "lady"—a lady would have been harsh or pitiful or absurd; Rags stripped her attitude to a sheer consciousness of her own impervious beauty, sat there glittering until the comedian began to feel alone as he had never felt alone before. At a signal from him the spotlight was switched suddenly out. The moment was over.

The moment was over, the comedian left the floor and the faraway music began. John leaned toward her.

"I'm sorry. There really wasn't anything to do. You were wonderful."

She dismissed the incident with a casual laugh—then she started, there were now only two men sitting at the table across the floor.

"He's gone!" she exclaimed in quick distress.

"Don't worry—he'll be back. He's got to be awfully careful, you see, so he's probably waiting outside with one of his aides until it gets dark again."

"Why has he got to be careful?"

"Because he's not supposed to be in New York. He's even under one of his second-string names."

The lights dimmed again and almost immediately a tall man appeared out of the darkness and approached their table.

"May I introduce myself?" he said rapidly to John in a supercilious British voice. "Lord Charles Este, of Baron Marchbanks' party." He glanced at John closely as if to be sure that he appreciated the significance of the name.

John nodded.

"That is between ourselves, you understand."

"Of course."

Rags groped on the table for her untouched champagne and tipped the glassful down her throat.

"Baron Marchbanks requests that your companion will join his party during this number."

Both men looked at Rags. There was a moment's pause.

"Very well," she said, and glanced back again interrogatively at John. Again he nodded. She rose and with her heart beating wildly threaded the tables, making the half circuit of the room; then melted, a slim figure in shimmering gold, into the table set in half darkness.

IV

The number drew to a close and John Chestnut sat alone at his table, stirring auxiliary bubbles in his glass of champagne. Just before the lights went on there was a soft rasp of gold cloth and Rags, flushed and breathing quickly, sank into her chair. Her eyes were shining with tears.

John looked at her moodily.

"Well, what did he say?"

"He was very quiet."

"Didn't he say a word?"

Her hand trembled as she took up her glass of champagne.

"He just looked at me while it was dark. And he said a few conventional things. He was like his pictures, only he looks very bored and tired. He didn't even ask my name."

"Is he leaving New York tonight?"

"In half an hour. He and his aides have a car outside, and they expect to be over the border before dawn."

"Did you find him—fascinating?"

She hesitated and then slowly nodded her head.

"That's what everybody says," admitted John glumly. "Do they expect you back there?"

"I don't know." She looked uncertainly across the floor but the celebrated personage had again withdrawn from his table to some retreat outside. As she turned back an utterly strange young man who had been standing for a moment in the main entrance came toward them hurriedly. He was a deathly pale person in a dishevelled and inappropriate business suit, and he laid a trembling hand on John Chestnut's shoulder.

"Monte!" exclaimed John, starting up so suddenly that he upset his champagne. "What is it? What's the matter?"

"They've picked up the trail!" said the young man in a shaken whisper. He looked around. "I've got to speak to you alone."

John Chestnut jumped to his feet, and Rags noticed that his face too had become white as the napkin in his hand. He excused himself and they retreated to an unoccupied table a few feet away. Rags watched them curiously for a moment, then she resumed her scrutiny of the table across the floor. Would she be asked to come back? The prince had simply risen and bowed and gone outside. Perhaps she should have waited until he returned, but though she was still tense with excitement she had, to some extent, become Rags Martin-Jones again. Her curiosity was satisfied—any new urge must come from him. She wondered if she had really felt an intrinsic charm—she wondered especially if he had in any marked way responded to her beauty.

The pale person called Monte disappeared and John returned to the table. Rags was startled to find that a tremendous change had come over him. He lurched into his chair like a drunken man.

"John! What's the matter?"

Instead of answering he reached for the champagne bottle, but his fingers were trembling so that the splattered wine made a wet yellow ring around his glass.

"Are you sick?"

"Rags," he said unsteadily, "I'm all through."

"What do you mean?"

"I'm all through, I tell you." He managed a sickly smile. "There's been a warrant out for me for over an hour."

"What have you done?" she demanded in a frightened voice. "What's the warrant for?"

The lights went out for the next number and he collapsed suddenly over the table.

"What is it?" she insisted, with rising apprehension. She leaned forward—his answer was barely audible.

"Murder?" She could feel her body grow cold as ice.

He nodded. She took hold of both arms and tried to shake him upright, as one shakes a coat into place. His eyes were rolling in his head.

"Is it true? Have they got proof?"

Again he nodded drunkenly.

"Then you've got to get out of the country now! Do you understand, John? You've got to get out *now*, before they come looking for you here!"

He loosed a wild glance of terror toward the entrance.

"Oh, God!" cried Rags, "why don't you do something?" Her eyes strayed here and there in desperation, became suddenly fixed. She drew in her breath sharply, hesitated and then whispered fiercely into his ear.

"If I arrange it, will you go to Canada tonight?"

"How?"

"I'll arrange it—if you'll pull yourself together a little. This is Rags talking to you, don't you understand, John? I want you to sit here and not move until I come back!"

A minute later she had crossed the room under cover of the darkness.

"Baron Marchbanks," she whispered softly, standing just behind his chair.

He motioned her to sit down.

"Have you room in your car for two more passengers tonight?"

One of the aides turned around abruptly.

"His lordship's car is full," he said shortly.

"It's terribly urgent." Her voice was trembling.

"Well," said the prince hesitantly, "I don't know."

Lord Charles Este looked at the prince and shook his head.

"I don't think it's advisable. This is a ticklish business anyhow with contrary orders from home. You know we agreed there'd be no complications."

The prince frowned.

"This isn't a complication," he objected.

Este turned frankly to Rags.

"Why is it urgent?"

Rags hesitated.

"Why"—she flushed suddenly—"it's a runaway marriage."

The prince laughed.

"Good!" he exclaimed. "That settles it. Este is just being official. Bring him over right away. We're leaving shortly, what?"

Este looked at his watch.

"Right now!"

Rags rushed away. She wanted to move the whole party from the roof while the lights were still down.

"Hurry!" she cried in John's ear. "We're going over the border—with the Prince of Wales. You'll be safe by morning."

He looked up at her with dazed eyes. She hurriedly paid the check, and seizing his arm piloted him as inconspicuously as possible to the other table, where she introduced him with a word. The prince acknowledged his presence by shaking hands—the aides nodded, only faintly concealing their displeasure.

"We'd better start," said Este, looking impatiently at his watch.

They were on their feet when suddenly an exclamation broke from all of them—two policemen and a redhaired man in plain clothes had come in at the main door.

"Out we go," breathed Este, impelling the party toward the side entrance. "There's going to be some kind of riot here." He swore—two more bluecoats barred the exit there. They paused uncertainly. The plain-clothes man was beginning a careful inspection of the people at the tables.

Este looked sharply at Rags and then at John, who shrank back behind the palms.

"Is that one of your revenue fellas out there?" demanded Este.

"No," whispered Rags. "There's going to be trouble. Can't we get out this entrance?"

The prince with rising impatience sat down again in his chair.

"Let me know when you chaps are ready to go." He smiled at Rags. "Now just suppose we all get in trouble just for that jolly face of yours."

Then suddenly the lights went up. The plain-clothes man whirled around quickly and sprang to the middle of the cabaret floor.

"Nobody try to leave this room!" he shouted. "Sit down, that party behind the palms! Is John M. Chestnut in this room?"

Rags gave a short involuntary cry.

"Here!" cried the detective to the policeman behind him. "Take a look at that funny bunch over there. Hands up, you men!"

"My God!" whispered Este, "we've got to get out of here!" He turned to the prince. "This won't do, Ted. You can't be seen here. I'll stall them off while you get down to the car."

He took a step toward the side entrance.

"Hands up, there!" shouted the plain-clothes man. "And when I say hands up I mean it! Which one of you's Chestnut?"

"You're mad!" cried Este. "We're British subjects. We're not involved in this affair in any way!"

A woman screamed somewhere and there was a general movement toward the elevator, a movement which stopped short before the muzzles of two automatic pistols. A girl next to Rags collapsed in a dead faint to the floor, and at the same moment the music on the other roof began to play.

"Stop that music!" bellowed the plain-clothes man. "And get some earrings on that whole bunch—quick!"

Two policemen advanced toward the party, and simultaneously Este and the other aides drew their revolvers, and, shielding the prince as they best could, began to edge toward the side. A shot rang out and then another, followed by a crash of silver and china as half a dozen diners overturned their tables and dropped quickly behind.

The panic became general. There were three shots in quick succession and then a fusillade. Rags saw Este firing coolly at the eight amber lights above, and a thick fume of grey smoke began to fill the air. As a strange undertone to the shouting and screaming came the incessant clamor of the distant jazz band.

Then in a moment it was all over. A shrill whistle rang out over the roof, and through the smoke Rags saw John Chestnut advancing toward the plain-clothes man, his hands held out in a gesture of surrender. There was a last nervous cry, a chill clatter as someone inadvertently stepped into a pile of dishes, and then a heavy silence fell on the roof—even the band seemed to have died away.

"It's all over!" John Chestnut's voice rang out wildly on the night air. "The party's over. Everybody who wants to can go home!"

Still there was silence—Rags knew it was the silence of awe—the strain of guilt had driven John Chestnut insane.

"It was a great performance," he was shouting. "I want to thank you one and all. If you can find any tables still standing, champagne will be served as long as you care to stay."

It seemed to Rags that the roof and the high stars suddenly began to swim round and round. She saw John take the detective's hand and shake it heartily, and she watched the detective grin and pocket his gun. The music had recommenced, and the girl who had fainted was suddenly dancing with Lord Charles Este in the corner. John was running here and there patting people on the back, and laughing and shaking hands. Then he was coming toward her, fresh and innocent as a child.

"Wasn't it wonderful?" he cried.

Rags felt a faintness stealing over her. She groped backward with her hand toward a chair.

"What was it?" she cried dazedly. "Am I dreaming?"

"Of course not! You're wide awake. I made it up, Rags, don't you see? I made up the whole thing for you. I had it invented! The only thing real about it was my name!"

She collapsed suddenly against his coat, clung to his lapels and would have wilted to the floor if he had not caught her quickly in his arms.

"Some champagne—quick!" he called, and then he shouted at the Prince of Wales, who stood nearby. "Order my car quick, you! Miss Martin-Jones has fainted from excitement."

v

The skyscraper rose bulkily through thirty tiers of windows before it attenuated itself to a graceful sugar-loaf of shining white. Then it darted up again another hundred feet, thinned to a mere oblong tower in its last fragile aspiration toward the sky. At the highest of its high windows Rags Martin-Jones stood full in the stiff breeze, gazing down at the city.

"Mr. Chestnut wants to know if you'll come right in to his private office."

Obediently her slim feet moved along the carpet into a high cool chamber overlooking the harbor and the wide sea.

John Chestnut sat at his desk, waiting, and Rags walked to him and put her arms around his shoulder.

"Are you sure *you*'re real?" she asked anxiously. "Are you absolutely *sure*?"

"You only wrote me a week before you came," he protested modestly, "or I could have arranged a revolution."

"Was the whole thing just *mine*?" she demanded. "Was it a perfectly useless, gorgeous thing, just for me?"

"Useless?" He considered. "Well, it started out to be. At the last minute I invited a big restaurant man to be there, and while you were at the other table I sold him the whole idea of the night-club."

He looked at his watch.

"I've got one more thing to do—and then we've got just time to be married before lunch." He picked up his telephone. "Jackson? . . . Send a triplicated cable to Paris, Berlin and Budapest and have those two bogus dukes who tossed up for Schwartzberg-Rhineminster chased over the Polish border. If the Duchy won't act, lower the rate of exchange to point triple zero naught two. Also, that idiot Blutchdak is in the Balkans again, trying to start a new war. Put him on the first boat for New York or else throw him in a Greek jail."

He rang off, turned to the startled cosmopolite with a laugh.

"The next stop is the City Hall. Then if you like we'll run over to Paris."

"John," she asked him intently, "who was the Prince of Wales?"

He waited till they were in the elevator, dropping twenty floors at a swoop. Then he leaned forward and tapped the lift boy on the shoulder.

"Not so fast, Cedric. This lady isn't used to falls from high places."

The elevator boy turned around, smiled. His face was pale, oval, framed in yellow hair. Rags blushed like fire.

"Cedric's from Wessex," explained John. "The resemblance is, to say the least, amazing. Princes are not particularly discreet, and I suspect Cedric of being a Guelph in some left-handed way."

Rags took the monocle from around her neck and threw the ribbon over Cedric's head.

"Thank you," she said simply, "for the second greatest thrill of my life."

John Chestnut began rubbing his hands together in a commercial gesture.

"Patronize this place, lady," he besought her. "Best bazaar in the city!"

"What have you got for sale?"

"Well, M'selle, today we have some perfectly bee-*oo*-tiful love."

"Wrap it up, Mr. Merchant," cried Rags Martin-Jones. "It looks like a bargain to me."

The Adjuster

A T five o'clock the somber egg-shaped room at the Ritz ripens to a subtle melody—the light *clat-clat* of one lump, two lumps, into the cup and the *ding* of the shining teapots and cream pots as they kiss elegantly in transit upon a silver tray. There are those who cherish that amber hour above all other hours, for now the pale pleasant toil of the lilies who inhabit the Ritz is over—the singing decorative part of the day remains.

Moving your eyes around the slightly raised horseshoe balcony you might, one spring afternoon, have seen young Mrs. Alphonse Karr and young Mrs. Charles Hemple at a table for two. The one in the dress was Mrs. Hemple—when I say "the dress" I refer to that black immaculate affair with the big buttons and the red ghost of a cape at the shoulders, a gown suggesting with faint and fashionable irreverence the garb of a French cardinal, as it was meant to do when it was invented in the Rue de la Paix. Mrs. Karr and Mrs. Hemple were twenty-three years old and their enemies said that they had done very well for themselves. Either might have had her limousine waiting at the hotel door, but both of them much preferred to walk home (up Park Avenue) through the April twilight.

Luella Hemple was tall with the sort of flaxen hair that English country girls should have, but seldom do. Her skin was radiant and there was no need of putting anything on it at all, but in deference to an antiquated fashion—this was the year 1920—she had powdered out its high roses and drawn on it a new mouth and new eyebrows—which were no more successful than such meddling deserves. This, of course, is said from the vantage-point of 1925. In those days the effect she gave was exactly right.

"I've been married three years," she was saying as she squashed out a cigarette in an exhausted lemon. "The baby will be two years old tomorrow. I must remember to get—"

She took a gold pencil from her case and wrote "Candles" and "Things you pull, with paper caps" on an ivory date pad. Then, raising her eyes, she looked at Mrs. Karr and hesitated.

"Shall I tell you something outrageous?"

"Try," said Mrs. Karr cheerfully.

"Even my baby bores me. That sounds unnatural, Ede, but it's true. He doesn't *begin* to fill my life. I love him with all my heart, but when I have him to take care of for an afternoon I get so nervous that I want to scream. After two hours I begin praying for the moment the nurse'll walk in the door."

When she had made this confession Luella breathed quickly and looked closely at her friend. She didn't really feel unnatural at all. This was the truth. There couldn't be anything vicious in the truth.

"It may be because you don't love Charles," ventured Mrs. Karr, unmoved.

"But I do! I hope I haven't given you that impression with all this talk." She decided that Ede Karr was stupid. "It's the very fact that I do love Charles that complicates matters. I cried myself to sleep last night because I know we're drifting slowly but surely toward a divorce. It's the baby that keeps us together."

Ede Karr, who had been married five years, looked at her critically to see if this was a pose, but Luella's lovely eyes were grave and sad.

"And what is the trouble?" Ede inquired.

"It's plural," said Luella, frowning. "First there's food. I'm a vile housekeeper and I have no intention of turning into a good one. I hate to order groceries, and I hate to go into the kitchen and poke around to see if the ice box is clean, and I hate to pretend to the servants that I'm interested in their work, when really I never want to hear about food until it comes on the table. You see, I never learned to cook, and consequently a kitchen is about as interesting to me as a—as a boiler room. It's simply a machine that I don't understand. It's easy to say, 'Go to cooking school,' the way people do in books—but, Ede, in real life does anybody ever change into a model *Hausfrau*—unless they have to?"

"Go on," said Ede noncommittally. "Tell me more."

"Well, as a result the house is always in a riot. The servants leave every week. If they're young and incompetent I can't train them, so we have to let them go. If they're experienced, they hate a house where a woman doesn't take an intense interest in the price of asparagus. So they leave—and half the time we eat at restaurants and hotels."

"I don't suppose Charles likes that."

"Hates it. In fact he hates about everything that I like. He's lukewarm about the theatre, hates the opera, hates dancing, hates cocktail parties—sometimes I think he hates everything pleasant in the world. I sat home for a year or so. While Chuck was on the way, and while I was nursing him, I didn't mind. But this year I told Charles frankly that I was still young enough to want some fun. And since then we've been going out whether he wants to or not." She paused, brooding. "I'm so sorry for him I don't know what to do, Ede—but if we sat home I'd just be sorry for myself. And to tell you another true thing, I'd rather that he'd be unhappy than me."

Luella was not so much stating a case as thinking aloud. She considered that she was being very fair. Before her marriage men had always told her that she was "a good sport" and she had tried to carry this fairness into her married life. So she always saw Charley's point of view as clearly as she saw her own.

If she had been a pioneer wife she would probably have fought the fight side by side with her husband. But here in New York there wasn't any fight. They weren't struggling together to obtain a far-off peace and leisure—she had more of either than she could use. Luella, like several thousand other young wives in New York, honestly wanted something to do. If she had had a little more money and a little less love, she could have gone in for horses or for vagarious amour. Or if they had had a little less money, her surplus energy would have been absorbed by hope and even by effort. But the Charles Hemples were in between. They were of that enormous American class who wander over Europe every summer, sneering rather pathetically and wistfully at the customs and traditions and pastimes of other countries, because they have no customs or traditions or pastimes of their own. It is a class sprung yesterday from fathers and mothers who might just as well have lived two hundred years ago.

The tea-hour had turned abruptly into the before-dinner hour. Most of the tables had emptied until the room was dotted rather than crowded with shrill isolated voices and remote, surprising laughter—in one corner the waiters were already covering the tables with white for dinner.

"Charles and I are on each other's nerves." In the new silence Luella's voice rang out with startling clearness, and she lowered it precipitately. "Little things. He keeps rubbing his face with his hand—all the time, at table, at the theatre—even when he's in bed. It drives me wild, and when things like that begin to irritate you, it's nearly over." She broke off and, reaching backward, drew up a light fur around her neck. "I hope I haven't bored you, Ede. It's on my mind because tonight tells the story. I made an engagement for tonight—an interesting engagement, a supper after the theatre to meet some Russians, singers or dancers or something, and Charles says he won't go. If he doesn't—then I'm going alone. And that's the end."

She put her elbows on the table suddenly and, bending her eyes down into her smooth gloves, began to cry, stubbornly and quietly. There was no one near to see, but Ede Karr wished that she had taken her gloves off. She would have reached out consolingly and touched her bare hand. But the gloves were a symbol of the difficulty of sympathizing with a woman to whom life had given so much. Ede wanted to say that it would "come out all right," that it wasn't "so bad as it seemed," but she said nothing. Her only reaction was impatience and distaste.

A waiter stepped near and laid a folded paper on the table, and Mrs. Karr reached for it.

"No, you mustn't," murmured Luella brokenly. "No, I invited *you!* I've got the money right here."

II

The Hemples' apartment—they owned it—was in one of those impersonal white palaces that are known by number instead of name. They had furnished it on their honeymoon, gone to England for the big pieces, to Florence for the bric-à-brac and to Venice for the lace and sheer linen of the curtains and for the glass of many colors which littered the table when they entertained. Luella enjoyed choosing things on her honeymoon. It gave a purposeful air to the trip and saved it from ever turning into the rather dismal wandering among big hotels and desolate ruins which European honeymoons are apt to be.

They returned and life began. On the grand scale. Luella found herself a lady of substance. It amazed her sometimes that the specially created apartment and the specially created limousine were hers, just as indisputably as the mortgaged suburban bungalow out of the "Ladies' Home Journal" and the last year's car that fate might have given her instead. She was even more amazed when it all began to bore her. But it did. . . .

The evening was at seven when she turned out of the April dusk, let herself into the hall and saw her husband waiting in the living room before an open fire. She came in without a sound, closed the door noiselessly behind her and stood watching him for a moment through the pleasant effective vista of the small salon which intervened. Charles Hemple was in the middle thirties, with a young serious face and distinguished iron-grey hair which would be white in ten years more. That and his deep-set, dark-grey eyes were his most noticeable features—women always thought his hair was romantic; most of the time Luella thought so too.

At this moment she found herself hating him a little, for she saw that he had raised his hand to his face and was rubbing it nervously over his chin and mouth. It gave him an air of unflattering abstraction and sometimes even obscured his words so that she was continually saying "What?" She had spoken about it several times, and he had apologized in a surprised way. But obviously he didn't realize how noticeable and how irritating it was, for he continued to do it. Things had now reached such a precarious state that Luella dreaded speaking of such matters anymore—a certain sort of word might precipitate the imminent scene.

Luella tossed her gloves and purse abruptly on the table. Hearing the faint sound her husband looked out toward the hall.

"Is that you, dear?"

"Yes, dear."

She went into the living room, and walked into his arms and kissed him tensely. Charles Hemple responded with unusual formality and then turned her slowly around so that she faced across the room.

"I've brought someone home to dinner."

She saw then that they were not alone, and her first feeling was of strong relief; the rigid expression on her face softened into a shy charming smile as she held out her hand.

"This is Doctor Moon—this is my wife."

A man a little older than her husband, with a round, pale, slightly lined face, came forward to meet her.

"Good evening, Mrs. Hemple," he said. "I hope I'm not interfering with any arrangement of yours."

has an irresistible appeal to many men. Luella's selfishness existed side by side with a childish beauty and, in consequence, Charles Hemple had begun to take the blame upon himself for situations which she had obviously brought about. It was an unhealthy attitude and his mind had sickened, at length, with his attempts to put himself in the wrong.

After the first shock and the momentary flush of pity that followed it, Luella looked at the situation with impatience. She was "a good sport"—she couldn't take advantage of Charles when he was sick. The question of her liberties had to be postponed until he was on his feet. Just when she had determined to be a wife no longer, Luella was compelled to be a nurse as well. She sat beside his bed while he talked about her in his delirium—about the days of their engagement, and how some friend had told him then that he was making a mistake, and about his happiness in the early months of their marriage, and his growing disquiet as the gap appeared. Evidently he had been more aware of it than she had thought—more than he ever said.

"Luella!" He would lurch up in bed. "Luella! Where *are* you?"

"I'm right here, Charles, beside you." She tried to make her voice cheerful and warm.

"If you want to go, Luella, you'd better go. I don't seem to be enough for you anymore."

She denied this soothingly.

"I've thought it over, Luella, and I can't ruin my health on account of you—" Then quickly, and passionately: "Don't go, Luella, for God's sake, don't go away and leave me! Promise me you won't! I'll do anything you say if you won't go."

His humility annoyed her most; he was a reserved man, and she had never guessed at the extent of his devotion before.

"I'm only going for a minute. It's Doctor Moon, your friend, Charles. He came today to see how you were, don't you remember? And he wants to talk to me before he goes."

"You'll come back?" he persisted.

"In just a little while. There—lie quiet."

She raised his head and plumped his pillow into freshness. A new trained nurse would arrive tomorrow.

In the living room Doctor Moon was waiting—his suit more worn and shabby in the afternoon light. She disliked him inordinately, with an illogical conviction that he was in some way to blame for her misfortune, but he was so deeply interested that she couldn't refuse to see him. She hadn't asked him to consult with the specialists, though—a doctor who was so down at the heel. . . .

"Mrs. Hemple." He came forward, holding out his hand, and Luella touched it, lightly and uneasily.

"You seem well," he said.

"I am well, thank you."

"I congratulate you on the way you've taken hold of things."

"But I haven't taken hold of things at all," she said coldly. "I do what I have to—"

"That's just it."

Her impatience mounted rapidly.

"I do what I have to, and nothing more," she continued. "And with no particular good-will."

Suddenly she opened up to him again, as she had the night of the catastrophe—realizing that she was putting herself on a footing of intimacy with him, yet unable to restrain her words.

"The house isn't going," she broke out bitterly. "I had to discharge the servants, and now I've got a woman in by the day. And the baby has a cold, and I've found out that his nurse doesn't know her business, and everything's just as messy and terrible as it can be!"

"Would you mind telling me how you found out the nurse didn't know her business?"

"You find out various unpleasant things when you're forced to stay around the house."

He nodded, his weary face turning here and there about the room.

"I feel somewhat encouraged," he said slowly. "As I told you, I promise nothing. I only do the best I can."

Luella looked up at him, startled.

"What do you mean?" she protested. "You've done nothing for me—nothing at all!"

"Nothing much—yet," he said heavily. "It takes time, Mrs. Hemple."

The words were said in a dry monotone that was somehow without offense, but Luella felt that he had gone too far. She got to her feet.

"I've met your type before," she said coldly. "For some reason you seem to think that you have a standing here as 'the old friend of the family.' But I don't make friends quickly, and I haven't given you the privilege of being so"—she wanted to say "insolent," but the word eluded her—"so personal with me."

When the front door had closed behind him, Luella went into the kitchen to see if the woman understood about the three different dinners—one for Charles, one for the baby and one for herself. It was hard to do with only a single servant when things were so complicated. She must try another employment agency—this one had begun to sound bored.

To her surprise, she found the cook with hat and coat on, reading a newspaper at the kitchen table.

"Why"—Luella tried to think of the name—"why, what's the matter, Mrs.—"

"Mrs. Danski is my name."

"What's the matter?"

"I'm afraid I won't be able to accommodate you," said Mrs. Danski. "You see, I'm only a plain cook, and I'm not used to preparing invalid's food."

"But I've counted on you."

"I'm very sorry." She shook her head stubbornly. "I've got my own health to think of. I'm sure they didn't tell me what kind of a job it was when I came. And when you asked me to clean out your husband's room, I knew it was way beyond my powers."

"I won't ask you to clean anything," said Luella desperately. "If you'll just stay until tomorrow. I can't possibly get anybody else tonight."

Mrs. Danski smiled politely.

"I got my own children to think of, just like you."

It was on Luella's tongue to offer her more money, but suddenly her temper gave way.

"I've never heard of anything so selfish in my life!" she broke out. "To leave me at a time like this! You're an old fool!"

"If you'd pay me for my time, I'd go," said Mrs. Danski calmly.

"I won't pay you a cent unless you'll stay!"

She was immediately sorry she had said this, but she was too proud to withdraw the threat.

"You will so pay me!"

"You go out that door!"

"I'll go when I get my money," asserted Mrs. Danski indignantly. "I got my children to think of."

Luella drew in her breath sharply and took a step forward. Intimidated by her intensity, Mrs. Danski turned and flounced, muttering, out of the door.

Luella went to the phone and, calling up the agency, explained that the woman had left.

"Can you send me someone right away? My husband is sick and the baby's sick—"

"I'm sorry, Mrs. Hemple. There's no one in the office now. It's after four o'clock."

Luella argued for awhile. Finally she obtained a promise that they would telephone to an emergency woman they knew. That was the best they could do until tomorrow.

She called several other agencies, but the servant industry had apparently ceased to function for the day. After giving Charles his medicine she tiptoed softly into the nursery.

"How's baby?" she asked abstractedly.

"Ninety-nine one," whispered the nurse, holding the thermometer to the light. "I just took it."

"Is that much?" asked Luella, frowning.

"It's just three-fifths of a degree. That isn't so much for the afternoon. They often run up a little with a cold."

Luella went over to the cot and laid her hand on her son's flushed cheek, thinking, in the midst of her anxiety, how much he resembled the incredible cherub of the "Lux" advertisement in the bus.

She turned to the nurse.

"Do you know how to cook?"

"Why—I'm not a good cook."

"Well, can you do the baby's food tonight? That old fool has left and I can't get anyone and I don't know what to do."

"Oh yes, I can do the baby's food."

"That's all right, then. I'll try to fix something for Mr. Hemple. Please have your door open so you can hear the bell when the doctor comes. And let me know."

So many doctors! There had scarcely been an hour all day when there wasn't a doctor in the house. The specialist and their family physician every morning, then the baby doctor—and this afternoon there had been Doctor Moon, placid, persistent, unwelcome, in the parlor. Luella went into the kitchen. She could cook bacon and eggs for herself—she had often done that after the theatre. But the vegetables for Charles were a different matter—they must be left to boil or stew or something, and the stove had so many doors and ovens that she couldn't decide which to use. She chose a blue pan that looked new, sliced carrots into it and covered them with a little water. As she put it on the stove and tried to remember what to do next, the phone rang. It was the agency.

"Yes, this is Mrs. Hemple speaking."

"Why, the woman we sent to you has returned here with the claim that you refused to pay her for her time."

"I explained to you that she refused to stay," said Luella hotly. "She didn't keep her agreement and I didn't feel I was under any obligation—"

"We have to see that our people are paid," the agency informed her. "Otherwise we wouldn't be helping them at all, would we? I'm sorry, Mrs. Hemple, but we won't be able to furnish you with anyone else until this little matter is arranged."

"Oh, I'll pay, I'll pay!" she cried.

"Of course we like to keep on good terms with our clients—"

"Yes—yes!"

"So if you'll send her money around tomorrow? It's seventy-five cents an hour."

"But how about tonight?" she exclaimed. "I've got to have someone tonight."

"Why—it's pretty late now. I was just going home myself."

"But I'm Mrs. Charles Hemple! Don't you understand? I'm perfectly good for what I say I'll do. I'm the wife of Charles Hemple, of 14 Broadway—"

Simultaneously she realized that Charles Hemple of 14 Broadway was a helpless invalid—he was neither a reference nor a refuge anymore. In despair at the sudden callousness of the world, she hung up the receiver.

After another ten minutes of frantic muddling in the kitchen she went to the baby's nurse, whom she disliked, and confessed that she was unable to cook her husband's dinner. The nurse announced that she had a splitting headache, and that with a sick child her hands were full already, but she consented, without enthusiasm, to show Luella what to do.

Swallowing her humiliation, Luella obeyed orders while the nurse experimented, grumbling, with the unfamiliar stove.

Dinner was started after a fashion. Then it was time for the nurse to bathe Chuck, and Luella sat down alone at the kitchen table, and listened to the bubbling perfume that escaped from the pans.

"And women do this every day," she thought. "Thousands of women. Cook and take care of sick people—and go out to work too."

But she didn't think of those women as being like her, except in the superficial aspect of having two feet and two hands. She said it as she might have said "South Sea Islanders wear nose-rings." She was merely slumming today in her own home and she wasn't enjoying it. For her, it was merely a ridiculous exception.

Suddenly she became aware of slow approaching steps in the dining room and then in the butler's pantry. Half afraid that it was Doctor Moon coming to pay another call, she looked up—and saw the nurse coming through the pantry door. It flashed through Luella's mind that the nurse was going to be sick too. And she was right—the nurse had hardly reached the kitchen door when she lurched and clutched at the handle as a winged bird clings to a branch. Then she receded wordlessly to the floor. Simultaneously, the doorbell rang and Luella, getting to her feet, gasped with relief that the baby doctor had come.

"Fainted, that's all," he said, taking the girl's head into his lap. The eyes fluttered. "Yep, she fainted, that's all."

"Everybody's sick!" cried Luella with a sort of despairing humor. "Everybody's sick but me, doctor."

"This one's not sick," he said after a moment. "Her heart is normal already. She just fainted."

When she had helped the doctor raise the quickening body to a chair, Luella hurried into the nursery and bent over the baby's bed. She let down one of the iron sides quietly. The fever seemed to be gone now—the flush had faded away. She bent over to touch the small cheek.

Suddenly Luella began to scream.

IV

Even after her baby's funeral, Luella still couldn't believe that she had lost him. She came back to the apartment and walked around the nursery in a circle, saying his name. Then, frightened by grief, she sat down and stared at his white rocker with the red chicken painted on the side.

"What will become of me now?" she whispered to herself. "Something awful is going to happen to me when I realize that I'll never see Chuck anymore!"

She wasn't sure yet. If she waited here till twilight, the nurse might still bring him in from his walk. She remembered a tragic confusion in the midst of which someone had told her that Chuck was dead, but if that was so, then why was his room waiting, with his small brush and comb still on the bureau, and why was she here at all?

"Mrs. Hemple."

She looked up. The weary, shabby figure of Doctor Moon stood in the door.

"You go away," Luella said dully.

"Your husband needs you."

"I don't care."

Doctor Moon came a little way into the room.

"I don't think you understand, Mrs. Hemple. He's been call-ing for you. You haven't anyone now except him."

"I hate you," she said suddenly.

"If you like. I promised nothing, you know. I do the best I can. You'll be better when you realize that your baby is gone, that you're not going to see him anymore."

Luella sprang to her feet.

"My baby isn't dead!" she cried. "You lie! You always lie!" Her flashing eyes looked into his and caught something there, at once brutal and kind, that awed her and made her impotent and acquiescent. She lowered her own eyes in tired despair.

"All right," she said wearily. "My baby is gone. What shall I do now?"

"Your husband is much better. All he needs is rest and kind-ness. But you must go to him and tell him what's happened."

"I suppose you think you made him better," said Luella bitterly.

"Perhaps. He's nearly well."

Nearly well—then the last link that held her to her home was broken. This part of her life was over—she could cut it off here, with its grief and oppression, and be off now, free as the wind.

"I'll go to him in a minute," Luella said in a far-away voice. "Please leave me alone."

Doctor Moon's unwelcome shadow melted into the darkness of the hall.

"I can go away," Luella whispered to herself. "Life has given me back freedom, in place of what it took away from me."

But she mustn't linger even a minute, or Life would bind her again and make her suffer once more. She called the apartment porter and asked that her trunk be brought up from the storeroom. Then she began taking things from the bureau and wardrobe, trying to approximate as nearly as possible the possessions that she had brought to her married life. She even found two old dresses that had formed part of her trousseau—out of style now, and a little tight in the hips—which she threw in with the rest. A new life. Charles was well again, and her baby, whom she had worshipped, and who had bored her a little, was dead.

When she had packed her trunk, she went into the kitchen automatically, to see about the preparations for dinner. She spoke to the cook about the special things for Charles and said that she herself was dining out. The sight of one of the small pans that had been used to cook Chuck's food caught her attention for a moment—but she stared at it unmoved. She looked into the ice box and saw it was clean and fresh inside. Then she went into Charles's room. He was sitting up in bed and the nurse was reading to him. His hair was almost white now, silvery white, and underneath it his eyes were huge and dark in his thin young face.

"The baby is sick?" he asked in his own natural voice.

She nodded.

He hesitated, closing his eyes for a moment. Then he asked:

"The baby is dead?"

"Yes."

For a long time he didn't speak. The nurse came over and put her hand on his forehead. Two large, strange tears welled from his eyes.

"I knew the baby was dead."

After another long wait, the nurse spoke.

"The doctor said he could be taken out for a drive today while there was still sunshine. He needs a little change."

"Yes."

"I thought"—the nurse hesitated. "I thought perhaps it would do you both good, Mrs. Hemple, if you took him instead of me."

Luella shook her head hastily.

"Oh no," she said. "I don't feel able to, today."

The nurse looked at her oddly. With a sudden feeling of pity for Charles, Luella bent down gently and kissed his cheek. Then, without a word, she went to her own room, put on her hat and coat, and with her suitcase started for the front door.

Immediately she saw that there was a shadow in the hall. If she could get past that shadow, she was free. If she could go to the right or left of it, or order it out of her way! But stubbornly, it refused to move, and with a little cry she sank down into a hall chair.

"I thought you'd gone," she wailed. "I told you to go away."

"I'm going soon," said Doctor Moon, "but I don't want you to make an old mistake."

"I'm not making a mistake—I'm leaving my mistakes behind."

"You're trying to leave yourself behind but you can't. The more you try to run away from yourself, the more you'll have yourself with you."

"But I've got to go away," she insisted wildly. "Out of this house of death and failure!"

"You haven't failed yet. You've only begun."

She stood up.

"Let me pass."

"No."

Abruptly she gave way, as she always did when he talked to her. She covered her face with her hands and burst into tears.

"Go back into that room and tell the nurse you'll take your husband for a drive," he suggested.

"I can't."

"Oh, yes."

Once more Luella looked at him and knew that she would obey. With the conviction that her spirit was broken at last, she took up her suitcase and walked back through the hall.

V

The nature of the curious influence that Doctor Moon exerted upon her Luella could not guess. But as the days passed, she found herself doing many things that had been repugnant to her before. She stayed at home with Charles, and when he grew better she went out with him sometimes to dinner, or the theatre, but only when he expressed a wish. She visited the kitchen every day, and kept an unwilling eye on the house, at first with a horror that it would go wrong again, then from habit. And she felt that it was all somehow mixed up with Doctor Moon—it was something he kept telling her about life, or almost telling her, and yet concealing from her as though he were afraid to have her know.

With the resumption of their normal life, she found that Charles was less nervous. His habit of rubbing his face had left him, and if the world seemed less gay and happy to her than it had before she experienced a certain peace, sometimes, that she had never known.

Then, one afternoon, Doctor Moon told her suddenly that he was going away.

"Do you mean for good?" she demanded with a touch of panic.

"For good."

For a strange moment she wasn't sure whether she was glad or sorry.

"You don't need me anymore," he said quietly. "You don't realize it, but you've grown up."

He came over and, sitting on the couch beside her, took her hand.

Luella sat silent and tense—listening.

"We make an agreement with children that they can sit in the audience without helping to make the play," he said, "but if they still sit in the audience after they're grown, somebody's got to work double time for them, so that they can enjoy the light and glitter of the world."

"But I want the light and glitter," she protested. "That's all there is in life. There can't be anything wrong in wanting to have things warm."

"Things will still be warm."

"How?"

"Things will warm themselves from you."

Luella looked at him, startled.

"It's your turn to be the center, to give others what was given to you for so long. You've got to give security to young people and peace to your husband, and a sort of charity to the old. You've got to let the people who work for you depend on you. You've got to cover up a few more troubles than you show, and be a little more patient than the average person, and do a little more instead of a little less than your share. The light and glitter of the world is in your hands."

He broke off suddenly.

"Get up," he said, "and go to that mirror and tell me what you see."

Obediently Luella got up and went close to a purchase of her honeymoon, a Venetian pier-glass on the wall.

"I see new lines in my face here," she said, raising her finger and placing it between her eyes, "and a few shadows at the sides that might be—that are little wrinkles."

"Do you care?"

She turned quickly. "No," she said.

"Do you realize that Chuck is gone? That you'll never see him anymore?"

"Yes." She passed her hands slowly over her eyes. "But that all seems so vague and far away."

"Vague and far away," he repeated; and then: "And are you afraid of me now?"

"Not any longer," she said, and she added frankly, "now that you're going away."

He moved toward the door. He seemed particularly weary tonight, as though he could hardly move about at all.

"The household here is in your keeping," he said in a tired whisper. "If there is any light and warmth in it, it will be your light and warmth; if it is happy, it will be because you've made it so. Happy things may come to you in life, but you must never go seeking them anymore. It is your turn to make the fire."

"Won't you sit down a moment longer?" Luella ventured.

"There isn't time." His voice was so low now that she could scarcely hear the words. "But remember that whatever suffering comes to you, I can always help you—if it is something that can be helped. I promise nothing."

He opened the door. She must find out now what she most wanted to know, before it was too late.

"What have you done to me?" she cried. "Why have I no sorrow left for Chuck—for anything at all? Tell me; I almost see, yet I can't see. Before you go—tell me who you are!"

"Who am I?—" His worn suit paused in the doorway. His round, pale face seemed to dissolve into two faces, a dozen faces, a score, each one different yet the same—sad, happy, tragic, indifferent, resigned—until threescore Doctor Moons were ranged like an infinite series of reflections, like months stretching into the vista of the past.

"Who am I?" he repeated. "I am five years."

The door closed.

At six o'clock Charles Hemple came home, and as usual Luella met him in the hall. Except that now his hair was dead white, his long illness of two years had left no mark upon him. Luella herself was more noticeably changed—she was a little stouter, and there were those lines around her eyes that had come when Chuck died one evening back in 1921. But she was still lovely, and there was a mature kindness about her face at twenty-eight, as if suffering had touched her only reluctantly and then hurried away.

"Ede and her husband are coming to dinner," she said. "I've got theatre tickets, but if you're tired, I don't care whether we go or not."

"I'd like to go."

She looked at him.

"You wouldn't."

"I really would."

"We'll see how you feel after dinner."

He put his arm around her waist. Together they walked into the nursery where the two children were waiting up to say good-night.

Hot and Cold Blood

ONE day when the young Mathers had been married for about a year, Jaqueline walked into the rooms of the hardware brokerage which her husband carried on with more than average success. At the open door of the inner office she stopped and said: "Oh, excuse me—" She had interrupted an apparently trivial yet somehow intriguing scene. A young man named Bronson whom she knew slightly was standing with her husband; the latter had risen from his desk. Bronson seized her husband's hand and shook it earnestly—something more than earnestly. When they heard Jaqueline's step in the doorway both men turned and Jaqueline saw that Bronson's eyes were red.

A moment later he came out, passing her with a somewhat embarrassed "How do you do?" She walked into her husband's office.

"What was Ed Bronson doing here?" she demanded curiously, and at once.

Jim Mather smiled at her, half shutting his grey eyes, and drew her quietly to a sitting position on his desk.

"He just dropped in for a minute," he answered easily. "How's everything at home?"

"All right." She looked at him with curiosity. "What did he want?" she insisted.

"Oh, he just wanted to see me about something."

"What?"

"Oh, just something. Business."

"Why were his eyes red?"

"Were they?" He looked at her innocently—and then suddenly they both began to laugh. Jaqueline rose and walked around the desk and plumped down into his swivel chair.

"You might as well tell me," she announced cheerfully, "because I'm going to stay right here till you do."

"Well,—" he hesitated, frowning. "He wanted me to do him a little favor."

Then Jaqueline understood—or rather her mind leaped half accidentally to the truth.

"Oh." Her voice tightened a little. "You've been lending him some money."

"Only a little."

"How much?"

"Only three hundred."

"*Only* three hundred." The voice was of the texture of Bessemer cooled. "How much do we spend a month, Jim?"

"Why,—why, about five or six hundred, I guess." He shifted uneasily. "Listen, Jack. Bronson'll pay that back. He's in a little trouble. He's made a mistake about a girl out in Woodmere—"

"And he knows you're famous for being an easy mark, so he comes to you," interrupted Jaqueline.

"No." He denied this formally.

"Don't you suppose I could use that three hundred dollars?" she demanded. "How about that trip to New York we couldn't afford last November?"

The lingering smile faded from Mather's face. He went over and shut the door to the outer office.

"Listen, Jack," he began, "you don't understand this. Bronson's one of the men I eat lunch with almost every day. We used to play together when we were kids—we went to school together. Don't you see that I'm just the person he'd be right to come to in trouble? And that's just why I couldn't refuse."

Jaqueline gave her shoulders a twist as if to shake off this reasoning.

"Well," she answered decidedly, "all I know is that he's no good. He's always lit and if he doesn't choose to work he has no business living off the work you do."

They were sitting now on either side of the desk, each having adopted the attitude of one talking to a child. They began their sentences with "Listen!" and their faces wore expressions of rather tried patience.

"If you can't understand, I can't tell you," Mather concluded, at the end of fifteen minutes, on what was, for him, an irritated key. "Such obligations do happen to exist sometimes among men and they have to be met. It's more complicated than just refusing to lend money—especially in a business like mine where so much depends on the good will of men downtown."

Mather was putting on his coat as he said this. He was going home with her on the street car to lunch. They were between automobiles—they had sold their old one and were going to get a new one in the spring.

Now the street car, on this particular day, was distinctly unfortunate. The argument in the office might have been forgotten under other circumstances, but what followed irritated the scratch until it became a serious temperamental infection.

They found a seat near the front of the car. It was late February and an eager, unpunctilious sun was turning the scrawny street snow into dirty cheerful rivulets that echoed in the gutters. Because of this the car was less full than usual—there was no one standing. The motorman had even opened his window and a yellow breeze was blowing the late breath of winter from the car.

It occurred pleasurably to Jaqueline that her husband sitting beside her was handsome and kind above other men. It was silly to try to change him. Perhaps Bronson might return the money after all, and anyhow three hundred dollars wasn't a fortune. Of course he had no business doing it—but then—

Her musings were interrupted as an eddy of passengers pushed up the aisle. Jaqueline wished they'd put their hands over their mouths when they coughed, and she hoped that Jim would get a new machine pretty soon. You couldn't tell what disease you'd run into in these trolleys.

She turned to Jim to discuss the subject—but Jim had stood up and was offering his seat to a woman who had been standing beside him in the aisle. The woman, without so much as a grunt, sat down. Jaqueline frowned.

The woman was about fifty and enormous. When she first sat down she was content merely to fill the unoccupied part of the seat, but after a moment she began to expand and to spread her great rolls of fat over a larger and larger area until the process took on the aspect of violent trespassing. When the car rocked in Jacqueline's direction the woman slid with it, but when it rocked back she managed by some exercise of ingenuity to dig in and hold the ground won.

Jaqueline caught her husband's eye—he was swaying on a strap—and in an angry glance conveyed to him her entire disapproval of his action. He apologized mutely and became urgently engrossed in a row of car cards. The fat woman moved once more against Jaqueline—she was now practically overlapping her. Then she turned puffy, disagreeable eyes full on Mrs. James Mather, and coughed rousingly in her face.

With a smothered exclamation Jaqueline got to her feet, squeezed with brisk violence past the fleshy knees and made her way, pink with rage, toward the rear of the car. There she seized a strap, and there she was presently joined by her husband in a state of considerable alarm.

They exchanged no word but stood silently side by side for ten minutes while a row of men sitting in front of them crackled their newspapers and kept their eyes fixed virtuously upon the day's cartoons.

When they left the car at last Jaqueline exploded.

"You big *fool!*" she cried wildly. "Did you see that horrible woman you gave your seat to? Why don't you consider *me* occasionally instead of every fat selfish washwoman you meet?"

"How should I know——"

But Jaqueline was as angry at him as she had ever been—it was unusual for anyone to get angry at him.

"You didn't see any of those men getting up for *me*, did you? No wonder you were too tired to go out last Monday night. You'd probably given your seat to some—to some horrible, Polish *wash*woman that's strong as an ox and *likes* to stand up!"

They were walking along the slushy street stepping wildly into great pools of water. Confused and distressed, Mather could utter neither apology nor defense.

Jaqueline broke off and then turned to him with a curious light in her eyes. The words in which she couched her summary of the situation were probably the most disagreeable that had ever been addressed to him in his life.

"The trouble with you, Jim, the reason you're such an easy mark, is that you've got the ideas of a college freshman—you're a professional nice fellow."

II

The incident and the unpleasantness were forgotten. Mather's vast good nature had smoothed over the roughness within an hour. References to it fell with a dying cadence throughout several days—then ceased and tumbled into the limbo of oblivion. I say "limbo," for oblivion is, unfortunately, never quite oblivious. The subject was drowned out by the fact that Jaqueline with her customary spirit and coolness began the long, arduous, uphill business of bearing a child. Her natural traits and prejudices became intensified and she was less inclined to let things pass.

It was April now, and as yet they had not bought a car. Mather had discovered that he was saving practically nothing and that in another half-year he would have a family on his hands. It worried him. A wrinkle—small, tentative, undisturbing—appeared for the first time as a shadow around his honest, friendly eyes. He worked far into the spring twilight now and frequently brought home with him the overflow from his office day. The new car would have to be postponed for awhile.

April afternoon, and all the city shopping on Washington Street. Jaqueline walked slowly past the shops, brooding without fear or depression on the shape into which her life was now being arbitrarily forced. Dry summer dust was in the wind; the sun bounded cheerily from the plate-glass windows and made radiant gasoline rainbows where automobile drippings had formed pools on the street.

Jaqueline stopped. Not six feet from her a bright new sport roadster was parked at the curb. Beside it stood two men in conversation, and at the moment when she identified one of them as young Bronson she heard him say to the other in a casual tone:

"What do you think of it? Just got it this morning."

Jaqueline turned abruptly and walked with quick tapping steps to her husband's office. With her usual curt nod to the stenographer she strode by her to the inner room. Mather looked up from his desk in surprise at her brusque entry.

"Jim," she began breathlessly, "did Bronson ever pay you that three hundred?"

"Why—no," he answered hesitantly, "not yet. He was in here last week and he explained that he was a little bit hard up."

Her eyes gleamed with angry triumph.

"Oh, he did?" she snapped. "Well, he's just bought a new sport roadster that must have cost anyhow twenty-five hundred dollars."

He shook his head, unbelieving.

"I saw it," she insisted. "I heard him say he'd just bought it."

"He *told* me he was hard up," repeated Mather helplessly.

Jaqueline audibly gave up by heaving a profound noise, a sort of groanish sigh.

"He was *us*ing you! He knew you were easy and he was *us*ing you. Can't you see? He wanted *you* to buy him the car and you *did!*" She laughed bitterly. "He's probably roaring his sides out to think how easily he worked you."

"Oh, no," protested Mather with a shocked expression, "you must have mistaken somebody for him—"

"We walk—and he rides on our money," she interrupted excitedly. "Oh, it's rich—it's rich. If it wasn't so maddening, it'd be just absurd. Look here—!" Her voice grew sharper, more restrained—there was a touch of contempt in it now. "You spend half your time doing things for people who don't give a damn about you or what becomes of you. You give up your seat on the street car to *hogs*, and come home too dead tired to even *move*. You're on all sorts of committees that take at least an hour a day out of your business and you don't get a cent out of them. You're—eternally—being *used!* I won't stand it! I thought I married a man—not a professional samaritan who's going to fetch and carry for the world!"

As she finished her invective Jaqueline reeled suddenly and sank into a chair—nervously exhausted.

"Just at this time," she went on brokenly, "I need you. I need your strength and your health and your arms around me. And if you—if you just give it to *every*one, it's spread *so* thin when it reaches me—"

He knelt by her side, moving her tired young head until it lay against his shoulder.

"I'm sorry, Jaqueline," he said humbly. "I'll be more careful. I didn't realize what I was doing."

"You're the dearest person in the world," murmured Jaqueline huskily, "but I want all of you and the best of you for me."

He smoothed her hair over and over. For a few minutes they rested there silently, having attained a sort of Nirvana of peace and understanding. Then Jaqueline reluctantly raised her head as they were interrupted by the voice of Miss Clancy in the doorway.

"Oh, I beg your pardon."

"What is it?"

"A boy's here with some boxes. It's C.O.D."

Mather rose and followed Miss Clancy into the outer office. "It's fifty dollars."

He searched his wallet—he had omitted to go to the bank that morning.

"Just a minute," he said abstractedly. His mind was on Jaqueline, Jaqueline who seemed forlorn in her trouble, waiting for him in the other room. He walked into the corridor, and opening the door of "Clayton and Drake, Brokers" across the way, swung wide a low gate and went up to a man seated at a desk.

"Morning, Fred," said Mather.

Drake, a little man of thirty with pince-nez and bald head, rose and shook hands.

"Morning, Jim. What can I do for you?"

"Why, a boy's in my office with some stuff C.O.D. and I haven't a cent. Can you let me have fifty till this afternoon?"

Drake looked closely at Mather. Then, slowly and startlingly, he shook his head—not up and down but from side to side.

"Sorry, Jim," he answered stiffly, "I've made a rule never to make a personal loan to anybody on any conditions. I've seen it break up too many friendships."

"What?"

Mather had come out of his abstraction now, and the monosyllable held an undisguised quality of shock. Then his natural tact acted automatically, springing to his aid and dictating his words though his brain was suddenly numb. His immediate instinct was to put Drake at ease in his refusal.

"Oh, I see." He nodded his head as if in full agreement, as if he himself had often considered adopting just such a rule. "Oh, I see how you feel. Well—I just—I wouldn't have you break a rule like that for anything. It's probably a good thing."

They talked for a minute longer. Drake justified his position easily; he had evidently rehearsed the part a great deal. He treated Mather to an exquisitely frank smile.

Mather went politely back to his office leaving Drake under the impression that the latter was the most tactful man in the city. Mather knew how to leave people with that impression. But when he entered his own office and saw his wife staring dismally out the window into the sunshine he clenched his hands, and his mouth moved in an unfamiliar shape.

"All right, Jack," he said slowly, "I guess you're right about most things, and I'm wrong as hell."

III

During the next three months Mather thought back through many years. He had had an unusually happy life. Those frictions between man and man, between man and society, which harden most of us into a rough and cynical quarrelling trim, had been conspicuous by their infrequency in his life. It had never occurred to him before that he had paid a price for this immunity, but now he perceived how here and there, and constantly, he had taken the rough side of the road to avoid enmity or argument, or even question.

There was, for instance, much money that he had lent privately, about thirteen hundred dollars in all, which he realized, in his new enlightenment, he would never see again. It had taken Jaqueline's harder, feminine intelligence to know this. It was only now when he owed it to Jaqueline to have money in the bank that he missed these loans at all.

He realized too the truth of her assertions that he was continually doing favors—a little something here, a little something there; the sum total, in time and energy expended, was appalling. It had pleased him to do the favors. He reacted warmly to being thought well of, but he wondered now if he had not been merely indulging a selfish vanity of his own. In suspecting this, he was, as usual, not quite fair to himself. The truth was that Mather was essentially and enormously romantic.

He decided that these expenditures of himself made him tired at night, less efficient in his work and less of a prop to Jaqueline, who, as the months passed, grew more heavy and bored, and sat through the long summer afternoons on the screened verandah waiting for his step at the end of the walk.

Lest that step falter, Mather gave up many things—among them the presidency of his college alumni association. He let slip other labors less prized. When he was put on a committee, men had a habit of electing him chairman and retiring into a dim background, where they were inconveniently hard to find. He was done with such things now. Also he avoided those who were prone to ask favors—fleeing a certain eager look that would be turned on him from some group at his club.

The change in him came slowly. He was not exceptionally unworldly—under other circumstances Drake's refusal of money would not have surprised him. Had it come to him as a story he would scarcely have given it a thought. But it had broken in with harsh abruptness upon a situation existing in his own mind, and the shock had given it a powerful and literal significance.

It was mid-August now and the last of a baking week. The curtains of his wide-open office windows had scarcely rippled all the day, but lay like sails becalmed in warm juxtaposition with the smothering screens. Mather was worried—Jaqueline had overtired herself and was paying for it by violent sick headaches, and business seemed to have come to an apathetic standstill. That morning he had been so irritable with Miss Clancy that she had looked at him in surprise. He had immediately apologized, wishing afterwards that he hadn't. He was working at high speed through this heat—why shouldn't she?

She came to his door now, and he looked up faintly frowning.

"Mr. Edward Lacy."

"All right," he answered listlessly. Old man Lacy—he knew him slightly. A melancholy figure—a brilliant start back in the eighties, and now one of the city's failures. He couldn't imagine what Lacy wanted unless he were soliciting.

"Good afternoon, Mr. Mather."

A little, solemn, grey-haired man stood on the threshold. Mather rose and greeted him politely.

"Are you busy, Mr. Mather?"

"Well, not so *very*." He stressed the qualifying word slightly.

Mr. Lacy sat down, obviously ill at ease. He kept his hat in his hands and clung to it tightly as he began to speak.

"Mr. Mather, if you've got five minutes to spare, I'm going to tell you something that—that I find at present it's necessary for me to tell you."

Mather nodded. His instinct warned him that there was a favor to be asked, but he was tired, and with a sort of lassitude he let his chin sink into his hand, welcoming any distraction from his more immediate cares.

"You see," went on Mr. Lacy—Mather noticed that the hands which fingered at the hat were trembling—"back in eighty-four your father and I were very good friends. You've heard him speak of me no doubt."

Mather nodded.

"I was asked to be one of the pallbearers. Once we were—very close. It's because of that that I come to you now. Never before in my life have I ever had to come to anyone as I've come to you now, Mr. Mather—come to a stranger. But as you grow older your friends die or move away or some misunderstanding separates you. And your children die unless you're fortunate enough to go first—and pretty soon you get to be alone, so that you don't have any friends at all. You're isolated." He smiled faintly. His hands were trembling violently now.

"Once upon a time almost forty years ago your father came to me and asked me for a thousand dollars. I was a few years older than he was, and though I knew him only slightly, I had a high opinion of him. That was a lot of money in those days, and he had no security—he had nothing but a plan in his head—but I liked the way he had of looking out of his eyes—you'll pardon me if I say you look not unlike him—so I gave it to him without security."

Mr. Lacy paused.

"Without security," he repeated. "I could afford it then. I didn't lose by it. He paid it back with interest at six per-cent before the year was up."

Mather was looking down at his blotter, tapping out a series of triangles with his pencil. He knew what was coming now, and his muscles physically tightened as he mustered his forces for the refusal he would have to make.

"I'm now an old man, Mr. Mather," the cracked voice went on. "I've made a failure—I *am* a failure—only we needn't go into that now. I have a daughter, an unmarried daughter who lives with me. She does stenographic work and has been very kind to me. We live together, you know, on Selby Avenue—we have an apartment, quite a nice apartment."

The old man sighed quaveringly. He was trying—and at the same time was afraid—to get to his request. It was insurance, it seemed. He had a ten-thousand-dollar policy, he had borrowed on it up to the limit, and he stood to lose the whole amount unless he could raise four hundred and fifty dollars. He and his daughter had about seventy-five dollars between them. They had no friends—he had explained that—and they had found it impossible to raise the money. . . .

Mather could stand the miserable story no longer. He could not spare the money, but he could at least relieve the old man of the blistered agony of asking for it.

"I'm sorry, Mr. Lacy," he interrupted as gently as possible, "but I can't lend you that money."

"No?" The old man looked at him with faded, blinking eyes that were beyond all shock, almost, it seemed, beyond any human emotion except ceaseless care. The only change in his expression was that his mouth dropped slowly ajar.

Mather fixed his eyes determinately upon his blotter.

"We're going to have a baby in a few months, and I've been saving for that. It wouldn't be fair to my wife to take anything from her—or the child—right now."

His voice sank to a sort of mumble. He found himself saying platitudinously that business was bad—saying it with revolting facility.

Mr. Lacy made no argument. He rose without visible signs of disappointment. Only his hands were still trembling and they worried Mather. The old man was apologetic—he was sorry to have bothered him at a time like this. Perhaps something would turn up. He had thought that if Mr. Mather did happen to have a good deal extra—why, he might be the person to go to because he was the son of an old friend.

As he left the office he had trouble opening the outer door. Miss Clancy helped him. He went shabbily and unhappily down the corridor with his faded eyes blinking and his mouth still faintly ajar.

Jim Mather stood by his desk and put his hand over his face and shivered suddenly as if he were cold. But the five-o'clock air outside was hot as a tropic noon.

IV

The twilight was hotter still an hour later as he stood at the corner waiting for his car. The trolley-ride to his house was twenty-five minutes, and he bought a pink-jacketed newspaper to appetize his listless mind. Life had seemed less happy, less glamorous of late. Perhaps he had learned more of the world's ways—perhaps its glamor was evaporating little by little with the hurried years.

Nothing like this afternoon, for instance, had ever happened to him before. He could not dismiss the old man from his mind. He pictured him plodding home in the weary heat—on foot, probably, to save carfare—opening the door of a hot little flat, and confessing to his daughter that the son of his friend had not been able to help him out. All evening they would plan helplessly until they said good night to each other—father and daughter, isolated by chance in this world—and went to lie awake with a pathetic loneliness in their two beds.

Mather's street car came along, and he found a seat near the front, next to an old lady who looked at him grudgingly as she moved over. At the next block a crowd of girls from the department-store district flowed up the aisle, and Mather unfolded his paper. Of late he had not indulged his habit of giving up his seat. Jaqueline was right—the average young girl was able to stand as well as he was. Giving up his seat was silly, a mere gesture. Nowadays not one woman in a dozen even bothered to thank him.

It was stifling hot in the car, and he wiped the heavy damp from his forehead. The aisle was thickly packed now, and a woman standing beside his seat was thrown momentarily against his shoulder as the car turned a corner. Mather took a long breath of the hot foul air, which persistently refused to circulate, and tried to center his mind on a cartoon at the top of the sporting page.

"Move for'ard ina car, please!" The conductor's voice pierced the opaque column of humanity with raucous irritation. "Plen'y of room for'ard!"

The crowd made a feeble attempt to shove forward, but the unfortunate fact that there was no space into which to move precluded any marked success. The car turned another corner, and again the woman next to Mather swayed against his shoulder. Ordinarily he would have given up his seat if only to avoid this reminder that she was there. It made him feel unpleasantly cold-blooded. And the car was horrible—horrible. They ought to put more of them on the line these sweltering days.

For the fifth time he looked at the pictures in the comic strip. There was a beggar in the second picture, and the wavering image of Mr. Lacy persistently inserted itself in the beggar's place. God! Suppose the old man really did starve to death—suppose he threw himself into the river.

"Once," thought Mather, "he helped my father. Perhaps if he hadn't my own life would have been different than it has been. But Lacy could afford it then—and I can't."

To force out the picture of Mr. Lacy, Mather tried to think of Jaqueline. He said to himself over and over that he would have been sacrificing Jaqueline to a played-out man who had had his chance and failed. Jaqueline needed her chance now as never before.

Mather looked at his watch. He had been on the car ten minutes. Fifteen minutes still to ride, and the heat increasing with breathless intensity. The woman swayed against him once more, and looking out the window he saw that they were turning the last downtown corner.

It occurred to him that perhaps he ought, after all, to give the woman his seat—her last sway toward him had been a particularly tired sway. If he were sure she was an older woman—but the texture of her dress as it brushed his hand gave somehow the impression that she was a young girl. He did not dare look up to see. He was afraid of the appeal that might look out of her eyes if they were old eyes or the sharp contempt if they were young.

For the next five minutes his mind worked in a vague suffocated way on what now seemed to him the enormous problem of whether or not to give her the seat. He felt dimly that doing so would partially atone for his refusal to Mr. Lacy that afternoon. It would be rather terrible to have done those two cold-blooded things in succession—and on such a day.

He tried the cartoon again, but in vain. He must concentrate on Jaqueline. He was dead tired now, and if he stood up he would be more tired. Jaqueline would be waiting for him, needing him. She would be depressed and she would want him to hold her quietly in his arms for an hour after dinner. When he was tired this was rather a strain. And afterwards when they went to bed she would ask him from time to time to get her her medicine or a glass of ice-water. He hated to show any weariness in doing these things. She might notice and, needing something, refrain from asking for it.

The girl in the aisle swayed against him once more—this time it was more like a sag. She was tired, too. Well, it was weary to work. The ends of many proverbs that had to do with toil and the long day floated fragmentarily through his mind. Everybody in the world was tired—this woman, for instance, whose body was sagging so wearily, so strangely against his. But his home came first and his girl that he loved was waiting for him there. He must keep his strength for her, and he said to himself over and over that he would not give up his seat.

Then he heard a long sigh, followed by a sudden exclamation, and he realized that the girl was no longer leaning against him. The exclamation multiplied into a clatter of voices—then came a pause—then a renewed clatter that travelled down the car in calls and little staccato cries to the conductor. The bell clanged violently, and the hot car jolted to a sudden stop.

"Girl fainted up here!"

"Too hot for her!"

"Just keeled right over!"

"Get back there! Gangway, you!"

The crowd eddied apart. The passengers in front squeezed back and those on the rear platform temporarily disembarked. Curiosity and pity bubbled out of suddenly conversing groups. People tried to help, got in the way. Then the bell rang and voices rose stridently again.

"Get her out all right?"

"Say, did you see that?"

"This damn company ought to—"

"Did you see the man that carried her out? He was pale as a ghost, too."

"Yes, but did you hear—"

"What?"

"That fella. That pale fella that carried her out. He was sittin' beside her—he says she's his wife!"

The house was quiet. A breeze pressed back the dark vine leaves of the verandah, letting in thin yellow rods of moonlight on the wicker chairs. Jaqueline rested placidly on the long settee with her head in his arms. After awhile she stirred lazily; her hand reaching up patted his check.

"I think I'll go to bed now. I'm so tired. Will you help me up?"

He lifted her and then laid her back among the pillows.

"I'll be with you in a minute," he said gently. "Can you wait for just a minute?"

He passed into the lighted living room, and she heard him thumbing the pages of a telephone directory; then she listened as he called a number.

"Hello, is Mr. Lacy there? Why—yes, it *is* pretty important—if he hasn't gone to sleep."

A pause. Jaqueline could hear restless sparrows splattering through the leaves of the magnolia over the way. Then her husband at the telephone:

"Is this Mr. Lacy? Oh, this is Mather. Why—why, in regard to that matter we talked about this afternoon, I think I'll be able to fix that up after all." He raised his voice a little as though someone at the other end found it difficult to hear. "James Mather's son, I said— About that little matter this afternoon—"

"The Sensible Thing"

A T the Great American Lunch Hour young George O'Kelly straightened his desk deliberately and with an assumed air of interest. No one in the office must know that he was in a hurry, for success is a matter of atmosphere, and it is not well to advertise the fact that your mind is separated from your work by a distance of seven hundred miles.

But once out of the building he set his teeth and began to run, glancing now and then at the gay noon of early spring which filled Times Square and loitered less than twenty feet over the heads of the crowd. The crowd all looked slightly upward and took deep March breaths, and the sun dazzled their eyes so that scarcely anyone saw anyone else but only their own reflection on the sky.

George O'Kelly, whose mind was over seven hundred miles away, thought that all outdoors was horrible. He rushed into the subway and for ninety-five blocks bent a frenzied glance on a car-card which showed vividly how he had only one chance in five of keeping his teeth for ten years. At 137th Street he broke off his study of commercial art, left the subway and began to run again, a tireless, anxious run that brought him this time to his home—one room in a high, horrible apartment-house in the middle of nowhere.

There it was on the bureau, the letter—in sacred ink, on blessed paper—all over the city, people, if they listened, could hear the beating of George O'Kelly's heart. He read the commas, the blots, and the thumb-smudge on the margin—then he threw himself hopelessly upon his bed.

He was in a mess, one of those terrific messes which are ordinary incidents in the life of the poor, which follow poverty like birds of prey. The poor go under or go up or go wrong or even go on, somehow, in a way the poor have—but George O'Kelly was so new to poverty that had any one denied the uniqueness of his case he would have been astounded.

Less than two years ago he had been graduated with honors from the Massachusetts Institute of Technology and had taken a position with a firm of construction engineers in southern Tennessee. All his life he had thought in terms of tunnels and skyscrapers and great squat dams and tall, three-towered bridges that were like dancers holding hands in a row, with heads as tall as cities and skirts of cable strand. It had seemed romantic to George O'Kelly to change the sweep of rivers and the shape of mountains so that life could flourish in the old bad lands of the world where it had never taken root before. He loved steel, and there was always steel near him in his dreams, liquid steel, steel in bars and blocks and beams and formless plastic masses, waiting for him, as paint and canvas to his hand. Steel inexhaustible, to be made lovely and austere in his imaginative fire. . . .

At present he was an insurance clerk at forty dollars a week with his dream slipping fast behind him. The dark little girl who had made this mess, this terrible and intolerable mess, was waiting to be sent for in a town in Tennessee.

In fifteen minutes the woman from whom he sublet his room knocked and asked him with maddening kindness if, since he was home, he would have some lunch. He shook his head, but the interruption aroused him, and getting up from the bed he wrote a telegram.

"Letter depressed me have you lost your nerve you are foolish and just upset to think of breaking off why not marry me immediately sure we can make it all right—"

He hesitated for a wild minute and then added in a hand that could scarcely be recognized as his own: "In any case I will arrive tomorrow at six o'clock."

When he finished he ran out of the apartment and down to the telegraph office near the subway stop. He possessed in this world not quite one hundred dollars, but the letter showed that she was "nervous" and this left him no choice. He knew what "nervous" meant—that she was emotionally depressed, that the prospect of marrying into a life of poverty and struggle was putting too much strain upon her love.

George O'Kelly reached the insurance company at his usual run, the run that had become almost second nature to him, that seemed best to express the tension under which he lived. He went straight to the manager's office.

"I want to see you, Mr. Chambers," he announced breathlessly.

"Well?" Two eyes, eyes like winter windows, glared at him with ruthless impersonality.

"I want to get four days' vacation."

"Why, you had a vacation just two weeks ago!" said Mr. Chambers in surprise.

"That's true," admitted the distraught young man, "but now I've got to have another."

"Where'd you go last time? To your home?"

"No, I went to—a place in Tennessee."

"Well, where do you want to go this time?"

"Well, this time I want to go to—a place in Tennessee."

"You're consistent, anyhow," said the manager dryly. "But I didn't realize you were employed here as a traveling salesman."

"I'm not," cried George desperately, "but I've got to go."

"All right," agreed Mr. Chambers, "but you don't have to come back. So don't!"

"I won't." And to his own astonishment as well as Mr. Chambers' George's face grew pink with pleasure. He felt happy, exultant—for the first time in six months he was absolutely free. Tears of gratitude stood in his eyes, and he seized Mr. Chambers warmly by the hand.

"I want to thank you," he said with a rush of emotion. "I don't want to come back. I think I'd have gone crazy if you'd said that I could come back. Only I couldn't quit myself, you see, and I want to thank you for—for quitting for me."

He waved his hand magnanimously, shouted aloud, "You owe me three days' salary but you can keep it!" and rushed from the office. Mr. Chambers rang for his stenographer to ask if O'Kelly had seemed queer lately. He had fired many men in the course of his career, and they had taken it in many different ways, but none of them had thanked him—ever before.

II

Jonquil Cary was her name, and to George O'Kelly nothing had ever looked so fresh and pale as her face when she saw him and fled to him eagerly along the station platform. Her arms were raised to him, her mouth was half parted for his kiss, when she held him off suddenly and lightly and, with a touch of embarrassment, looked around. Two boys, somewhat younger than George, were standing in the background.

"This is Mr. Craddock and Mr. Holt," she announced cheerfully. "You met them when you were here before."

Disturbed by the transition of a kiss into an introduction and suspecting some hidden significance, George was more confused when he found that the automobile which was to carry them to Jonquil's house belonged to one of the two young men. It seemed to put him at a disadvantage. On the way Jonquil chattered between the front and back seats, and when he tried to slip his arm around her under cover of the twilight she compelled him with a quick movement to take her hand instead.

"Is this street on the way to your house?" he whispered. "I don't recognize it."

"It's the new boulevard. Jerry just got this car today, and he wants to show it to me before he takes us home."

When, after twenty minutes, they were deposited at Jonquil's house, George felt that the first happiness of the meeting, the joy he had recognized so surely in her eyes back in the station, had been dissipated by the intrusion of the ride. Something that he had looked forward to had been rather casually lost, and he was brooding on this as he said good-night stiffly to the two young men. Then his ill humor faded as Jonquil drew him into a familiar embrace under the dim light of the front hall and told him in a dozen ways, of which the best was without words, how she had missed him. Her emotion reassured him, promised his anxious heart that everything would be all right.

They sat together on the sofa, overcome by each other's presence, beyond all except fragmentary endearments. At the supper hour Jonquil's father and mother appeared and were glad to see George. They liked him, and had been interested in his engineering career when he had first come to Tennessee over a year before. They had been sorry when he had given it up and gone to New York to look for something more immediately profitable, but while they deplored the curtailment of his career they sympathized with him and were ready to recognize the engagement. During dinner they asked about his progress in New York.

"Everything's going fine," he told them with enthusiasm. "I've been promoted—better salary."

He was miserable as he said this—but they were all *so* glad.

"They must like you," said Mrs. Cary, "that's certain—or they wouldn't let you off twice in three weeks to come down here."

"I told them they had to," explained George hastily; "I told them if they didn't I wouldn't work for them anymore."

"But you ought to save your money," Mrs. Cary reproached him gently. "Not spend it all on this expensive trip."

Dinner was over—he and Jonquil were alone and she came back into his arms.

"So glad you're here," she sighed. "Wish you never were going away again, darling."

"Do you miss me?"

"Oh, so much, so much."

"Do you—do other men come to see you often? Like those two kids?"

The question surprised her. The dark velvet eyes stared at him.

"Why, of course they do. All the time. Why—I've told you in letters that they did, dearest."

This was true—when he had first come to the city there had been already a dozen boys around her, responding to her picturesque fragility with adolescent worship, and a few of them perceiving that her beautiful eyes were also sane and kind.

"Do you expect me never to go anywhere"—Jonquil demanded, leaning back against the sofa-pillows until she seemed to look at him from many miles away—"and just fold my hands and sit still—forever?"

"What do you mean?" he blurted out in a panic. "Do you mean you think I'll never have enough money to marry you?"

"Oh, don't jump at conclusions so, George."

"I'm not jumping at conclusions. That's what you said."

George decided suddenly that he was on dangerous ground. He had not intended to let anything spoil this night. He tried to take her again in his arms, but she resisted unexpectedly, saying:

"It's hot. I'm going to get the electric fan."

When the fan was adjusted they sat down again, but he was in a supersensitive mood and involuntarily he plunged into the specific world he had intended to avoid.

"When will you marry me?"

"Are you ready for me to marry you?"

All at once his nerves gave way, and he sprang to his feet.

"Let's shut off that damned fan," he cried. "It drives me wild. It's like a clock ticking away all the time I'll be with you. I came here to be happy and forget everything about New York and time—"

He sank down on the sofa as suddenly as he had risen. Jonquil turned off the fan, and drawing his head down into her lap began stroking his hair.

"Let's sit like this," she said softly. "Just sit quiet like this, and I'll put you to sleep. You're all tired and nervous and your sweetheart'll take care of you."

"But I don't want to sit like this," he complained, jerking up suddenly. "I don't want to sit like this at all. I want you to kiss me. That's the only thing that makes me rest. And anyway I'm not nervous—it's you that's nervous. I'm not nervous at all."

To prove that he wasn't nervous he left the couch and plumped himself into a rocking-chair across the room.

"Just when I'm ready to marry you you write me the most nervous letters, as if you're going to back out, and I have to come rushing down here—"

"You don't have to come if you don't want to."

"But I *do* want to!" insisted George.

It seemed to him that he was being very cool and logical and that she was putting him deliberately in the wrong. With every word they were drawing farther and farther apart—and he was unable to stop himself or to keep worry and pain out of his voice.

But in a minute Jonquil began to cry sorrowfully and he came back to the sofa and put his arm around her. He was the comforter now, drawing her head close to his shoulder, murmuring old familiar things until she grew calmer and only trembled a little, spasmodically, in his arms. For over an hour they sat there, while the evening pianos thumped their last cadences into the street outside. George did not move, or think, or hope, lulled into numbness by the premonition of disaster. The clock would tick on, past eleven, past twelve, and then Mrs. Cary would call down gently over the banister—beyond that he saw only tomorrow and despair.

III

In the heat of the next day the breaking-point came. They had each guessed the truth about the other, but of the two she was the more ready to admit the situation.

"There's no use going on," she said miserably. "You know you hate the insurance business, and you'll never do well in it."

"That's not it," he insisted stubbornly. "I hate going on alone. If you'll marry me and come with me and take a chance with me, I can make good at anything, but not while I'm worrying about you down here."

She was silent a long time before she answered, not thinking—for she had seen the end—but only waiting, because she knew that every word would seem more cruel than the last. Finally she spoke:

"George, I love you with all my heart, and I don't see how I can ever love anyone else but you. If you'd been ready for me two months ago I'd have married you—now I can't because it doesn't seem to be the sensible thing."

He made wild accusations—there was someone else—she was keeping something from him!

"No, there's no one else."

This was true. But reacting from the strain of this affair she had found relief in the company of young boys like Jerry Holt, who had the merit of meaning absolutely nothing in her life.

George didn't take the situation well, at all. He seized her in his arms and tried literally to kiss her into marrying him at once. When this failed he broke into a long monologue of self-pity and ceased only when he saw that he was making himself despicable in her sight. He threatened to leave when he had no intention of leaving, and refused to go when she told him that, after all, it was best that he should.

For awhile she was sorry, then for another while she was merely kind.

"You'd better go now!" she cried at last, so loud that Mrs. Cary came downstairs in alarm.

"Is something the matter?"

"I'm going away, Mrs. Cary," said George brokenly. Jonquil had left the room.

"Don't feel so badly, George." Mrs. Cary blinked at him in helpless sympathy—sorry and, in the same breath, glad that the little tragedy was almost done. "If I were you I'd go home to your mother for a week or so. Perhaps after all this is the sensible thing—"

"Please don't talk!" he cried. "Please don't say anything to me now!"

Jonquil came into the room again, her sorrow and her nervousness alike tucked under powder and rouge and hat.

"I've ordered a taxi-cab," she said impersonally. "We can drive around until your train leaves."

She walked out on the front porch. George put on his coat and hat and stood for a minute exhausted in the hall—he had eaten scarcely a bite since he had left New York. Mrs. Cary came over, drew his head down and kissed him on the cheek, and he felt very ridiculous and weak in his knowledge that the scene had been ridiculous and weak at the end. If he had only gone the night before—left her for the last time with a decent pride.

The taxi had come, and for an hour these two that had been lovers rode along the less-frequented streets. He held her hand and grew calmer in the sunshine, seeing too late that there had been nothing all along to do or say.

"I'll come back," he told her.

"I know you will," she answered, trying to put a cheery faith into her voice. "And we'll write each other—sometimes."

"No," he said, "we won't write. I couldn't stand that. Someday I'll come back."

"I'll never forget you, George."

They reached the station, and she went with him while he bought his ticket. . . .

"Why, George O'Kelly and Jonquil Cary!"

It was a man and a girl whom George had known when he had worked in town, and Jonquil seemed to greet their presence with relief. For an interminable five minutes they all stood there talking; then the train roared into the station, and with ill-concealed agony in his face George held out his arms toward Jonquil. She took an uncertain step toward him, faltered, and then pressed his hand quickly as if she were taking leave of a chance friend.

"Good-bye, George," she was saying, "I hope you have a pleasant trip."

"Good-bye, George. Come back and see us all again."

Dumb, almost blind with pain, he seized his suitcase, and in some dazed way got himself aboard the train.

Past clanging street-crossings, gathering speed through wide suburban spaces toward the sunset. Perhaps she too would see the sunset and pause for a moment, turning, remembering, before he faded with her sleep into the past. This night's dusk would cover up forever the sun and the trees and the flowers and laughter of his young world.

IV

On a damp afternoon in September of the following year a young man with his face burned to a deep copper glow got off a train at a city in Tennessee. He looked around anxiously, and seemed relieved when he found that there was no one in the station to meet him. He taxied to the best hotel in the city where he registered with some satisfaction as George O'Kelly, Cuzco, Peru.

Up in his room he sat for a few minutes at the window looking down into the familiar street below. Then with his hand trembling faintly he took off the telephone receiver and called a number.

"Is Miss Jonquil in?"

"This is she."

"Oh—" His voice after overcoming a faint tendency to waver went on with friendly formality.

"This is George O'Kelly. Did you get my letter?"

"Yes. I thought you'd be in today."

Her voice, cool and unmoved, disturbed him, but not as he had expected. This was the voice of a stranger, unexcited, pleasantly glad to see him—that was all. He wanted to put down the telephone and catch his breath.

"I haven't seen you for—a long time." He succeeded in making this sound offhand. "Over a year."

He knew how long it had been—to the day.

"It'll be awfully nice to talk to you again."

"I'll be there in about an hour."

He hung up. For four long seasons every minute of his leisure had been crowded with anticipation of this hour, and now this hour was here. He had thought of finding her married, engaged, in love—he had not thought she would be unstirred at his return.

There would never again in his life, he felt, be another ten months like these he had just gone through. He had made an admittedly remarkable showing for a young engineer—stumbled into two unusual opportunities, one in Peru, whence he had just returned, and another, consequent upon it, in New York, whither he was bound. In this short time he had risen from poverty into a position of unlimited opportunity.

He looked at himself in the dressing-table mirror. He was almost black with tan, but it was a romantic black, and in the last week, since he had had time to think about it, it had given him considerable pleasure. The hardiness of his frame, too, he appraised with a sort of fascination. He had lost part of an eyebrow somewhere, and he still wore an elastic bandage on his knee, but he was too young not to realize that on the steamer many women had looked at him with unusual tributary interest.

His clothes, of course, were frightful. They had been made for him by a Greek tailor in Lima—in two days. He was young enough, too, to have explained this sartorial deficiency to Jonquil in his otherwise laconic note. The only further detail it contained was a request that he should *not* be met at the station.

George O'Kelly, of Cuzco, Peru, waited an hour and a half in the hotel, until, to be exact, the sun had reached a midway position in the sky. Then, freshly shaven and talcum-powdered toward a somewhat more Caucasian hue, for vanity at the last minute had overcome romance, he engaged a taxi-cab and set out for the house he knew so well.

He was breathing hard—he noticed this but he told himself that it was excitement, not emotion. He was here; she was not married—that was enough. He was not even sure what he had to say to her. But this was the moment of his life that he felt he could least easily have dispensed with. There was no triumph, after all, without a girl concerned, and if he did not lay his spoils at her feet he could at least hold them for a passing moment before her eyes.

The house loomed up suddenly beside him, and his first thought was that it had assumed a strange unreality. There was nothing changed—only everything was changed. It was smaller and it seemed shabbier than before—there was no cloud of magic hovering over its roof and issuing from the windows of the upper floor. He rang the doorbell and an unfamiliar colored maid appeared. Miss Jonquil would be down in a moment. He wet his lips nervously and walked into the sitting room—and the feeling of unreality increased. After all, he saw, this was only a room, and not the enchanted chamber where he had passed those poignant hours. He sat in a chair, amazed to find it a chair, realizing that his imagination had distorted and colored all these simple familiar things.

Then the door opened and Jonquil came into the room—and it was as though everything in it suddenly blurred before his eyes. He had not remembered how beautiful she was, and he felt his face grow pale and his voice diminish to a poor sigh in his throat.

She was dressed in pale green, and a gold ribbon bound back her dark, straight hair like a crown. The familiar velvet eyes caught his as she came through the door, and a spasm of fright went through him at her beauty's power of inflicting pain.

He said "Hello," and they each took a few steps forward and shook hands. Then they sat in chairs quite far apart and gazed at each other across the room.

"You've come back," she said, and he answered just as tritely: "I wanted to stop in and see you as I came through."

He tried to neutralize the tremor in his voice by looking anywhere but at her face. The obligation to speak was on him, but, unless he immediately began to boast, it seemed that there was nothing to say. There had never been anything casual in their previous relations—it didn't seem possible that people in this position would talk about the weather.

"This is ridiculous," he broke out in sudden embarrassment. "I don't know exactly what to do. Does my being here bother you?"

"No." The answer was both reticent and impersonally sad. It depressed him.

"Are you engaged?" he demanded.

"No."

"Are you in love with someone?"

She shook her head.

"Oh." He leaned back in his chair. Another subject seemed exhausted—the interview was not taking the course he had intended.

"Jonquil," he began, this time on a softer key, "after all that's happened between us, I wanted to come back and see you. Whatever I do in the future I'll never love another girl as I've loved you."

This was one of the speeches he had rehearsed. On the steamer it had seemed to have just the right note—a reference to the tenderness he would always feel for her combined with a non-committal attitude toward his present state of mind. Here with the past around him, beside him, growing minute by minute more heavy on the air, it seemed theatrical and stale.

She made no comment, sat without moving, her eyes fixed on him with an expression that might have meant everything or nothing.

"You don't love me anymore, do you?" he asked her in a level voice.

"No."

When Mrs. Cary came in a minute later, and spoke to him about his success—there had been a half-column about him in the local paper—he was a mixture of emotions. He knew now that he still wanted this girl, and he knew that the past sometimes comes back—that was all. For the rest he must be strong and watchful and he would see.

"And now," Mrs. Cary was saying, "I want you two to go and see the lady who has the chrysanthemums. She particularly told me she wanted to see you because she'd read about you in the paper."

They went to see the lady with the chrysanthemums. They walked along the street, and he recognized with a sort of excitement just how her shorter footsteps always fell in between his own. The lady turned out to be nice, and the chrysanthemums were enormous and extraordinarily beautiful. The lady's gardens were full of them, white and pink and yellow, so that to be among them was a trip back into the heart of summer. There were two gardens full, and a gate between them; when they strolled toward the second garden the lady went first through the gate.

And then a curious thing happened. George stepped aside to let Jonquil pass, but instead of going through she stood still and stared at him for a minute. It was not so much the look, which was not a smile, as it was the moment of silence. They saw each other's eyes, and both took a short, faintly accelerated breath, and then they went on into the second garden. That was all.

The afternoon waned. They thanked the lady and walked home slowly, thoughtfully, side by side. Through dinner too they were silent. George told Mr. Cary something of what had happened in South America and managed to let it be known that everything would be plain sailing for him in the future.

Then dinner was over, and he and Jonquil were alone in the room which had seen the beginning of their love affair and the end. It seemed to him long ago and inexpressibly sad. On that sofa he had felt agony and grief such as he would never feel again. He would never be so weak or so tired and miserable and poor. Yet he knew that that boy of fifteen months before had had something, a trust, a warmth that was gone forever. The sensible thing—they had done the sensible thing. He had traded his first youth for strength and carved success out of despair. But with his youth, life had carried away the freshness of his love.

"You won't marry me, will you?" he said quietly.

Jonquil shook her dark head.

"I'm never going to marry," she answered.

He nodded.

"I'm going on to Washington in the morning," he said.

"Oh—"

"I have to go. I've got to be in New York by the first, and meanwhile I want to stop off in Washington."

"Business?"

"No-o," he said as if reluctantly. "There's someone there I must see who was very kind to me when I was so—down and out."

This was invented. There was no one in Washington for him to see—but he was watching Jonquil narrowly, and he was sure that she winced a little, that her eyes closed and then opened wide again.

"But before I go I want to tell you the things that happened to me since I saw you, and, as maybe we won't meet again, I wonder if—if just this once you'd sit in my lap like you used to. I wouldn't ask except since there's no one else—yet—perhaps it doesn't matter."

She nodded, and in a moment was sitting in his lap as she had sat so often in that vanished spring. The feel of her head against his shoulder, of her familiar body, sent a shock of emotion over him. His arms holding her had a tendency to tighten around her, so he leaned back and began to talk thoughtfully into the air.

He told her of a despairing two weeks in New York which had terminated with an attractive if not very profitable job in a construction plant in Jersey City. When the Peru business had first presented itself it had not seemed an extraordinary opportunity. He was to be third assistant engineer on the expedition, but only ten of the American party, including eight rodmen and surveyors, had ever reached Cuzco. Ten days later the chief of the expedition was dead of yellow fever. That had been his chance, a chance for anybody but a fool, a marvelous chance—

"A chance for anybody but a fool?" she interrupted innocently.

"Even for a fool," he continued. "It was wonderful. Well, I wired New York—"

"And so," she interrupted again, "they wired that you ought to take a chance?"

"Ought to!" he exclaimed, still leaning back. "That I *had* to. There was no time to lose—"

"Not a minute?"

"Not a minute."

"Not even time for—" she paused.

"For what?"

"Look."

He bent his head forward suddenly, and she drew herself to him in the same moment, her lips half open like a flower.

"Yes," he whispered into her lips. "There's all the time in the world. . . ."

All the time in the world—his life and hers. But for an instant as he kissed her he knew that though he search through eternity he could never recapture those lost April hours. He might press her close now till the muscles knotted on his arms—she was something desirable and rare that he had fought for and made his own—but never again an intangible whisper in the dusk or on the breeze of night. . . .

Well, let it pass, he thought; April is over, April is over. There are all kinds of love in the world, but never the same love twice.

Gretchen's Forty Winks

T HE sidewalks were scratched with brittle leaves, and the bad little boy next door froze his tongue to the iron mail-box. Snow before night, sure. Autumn was over. This, of course, raised the coal question and the Christmas question; but Roger Halsey, standing on his own front porch, assured the dead suburban sky that he hadn't time for worrying about the weather. Then he let himself hurriedly into the house, and shut the subject out into the cold twilight.

The hall was dark but from above he heard the voices of his wife and the nursemaid and the baby in one of their interminable conversations—which consisted chiefly of "Don't!" and "Look out, Maxy!" and "Oh, there he *goes!*" punctuated by wild threats and vague bumpings and the recurrent sound of small, venturing feet.

Roger turned on the hall light and walked into the living room and turned on the red silk lamp. He put his bulging port- folio on the table, and sitting down rested his intense young face in his hand for a few minutes, shading his eyes carefully from the light. Then he lit a cigarette, squashed it out, and going to the foot of the stairs called for his wife.

"Gretchen!"

"Hello, dear." Her voice was full of laughter. "Come see baby."

He swore softly.

"I can't see baby now," he said aloud. "How long 'fore you'll be down?"

There was a mysterious pause and then a succession of "Don'ts" and "Look outs, Maxy" evidently meant to avert some threatened catastrophe.

"How long 'fore you'll be down?" repeated Roger, slightly irritated.

"Oh, I'll be right down."

"How soon?" he shouted.

He had trouble every day at this hour in adapting his voice from the urgent key of the city to the proper casualness for a model home. But tonight he was deliberately impatient. It almost disappointed him when Gretchen came running down the stairs, three at a time, crying "What is it?" in a rather surprised voice.

They kissed—lingered over it some moments. They had been married three years, and they were much more in love than that implies. It was seldom that they hated each other with that violent hate of which only young couples are capable, for Roger was still actively sensitive to her beauty.

"Come in here," he said abruptly. "I want to talk to you."

His wife, a bright-colored, Titian-haired girl, vivid as a French rag-doll, followed him into the living room.

"Listen, Gretchen"—he sat down at the end of the sofa—"beginning with tonight I'm going to— What's the matter?"

"Nothing. I'm just looking for a cigarette. Go on."

She tiptoed breathlessly back to the sofa and settled at the other end.

"Gretchen—" Again he broke off. Her hand, palm upward, was extended toward him. "Well, what is it?" he asked wildly.

"Matches."

"What?"

In his impatience it seemed incredible that she should ask for matches, but he fumbled automatically in his pocket.

"Thank you," she whispered. "I didn't mean to interrupt you. Go on."

"Gretch—"

Scratch! The match flared. They exchanged a tense look.

Her fawn's eyes apologized mutely this time and he laughed. After all she had done no more than light a cigarette; but when he was in this mood her slightest positive action irritated him beyond measure.

"When you've got time to listen," he said crossly, "you might be interested in discussing the poorhouse question with me."

"What poorhouse?" Her eyes were wide, startled; she sat quiet as a mouse.

"That was just to get your attention. But beginning tonight I start on what'll probably be the most important six weeks of my life—the six weeks that'll decide whether we're going on forever in this rotten little house in this rotten little suburban town."

Boredom replaced alarm in Gretchen's black eyes. She was a southern girl, and any question that had to do with getting ahead in the world always tended to give her a headache.

"Six months ago I left the New York Lithographic Company," announced Roger, "and went in the advertising business for myself."

"I know," interrupted Gretchen resentfully; "and now instead of getting six hundred a month sure, we're living on a risky five hundred."

"Gretchen," said Roger sharply, "if you'll just believe in me as hard as you can for six weeks more, we'll be rich. I've got a chance now to get some of the biggest accounts in the country." He hesitated. "And for these six weeks we won't go out at all, and we won't have anyone here. I'm going to bring home work every night, and we'll pull down all the blinds and if anyone rings the doorbell we won't answer."

He smiled airily as if it were a new game they were going to play. Then, as Gretchen was silent, his smile faded, and he looked at her uncertainly.

"Well, what's the matter?" she broke out finally. "Do you expect me to jump up and sing? You do enough work as it is. If you try to do any more you'll end up with a nervous breakdown. I read about a—"

"Don't worry about me," he interrupted; "I'm all right. But you're going to be bored to death sitting here every evening."

"No, I won't," she said without conviction—"except tonight."

"What about tonight?"

"George Tompkins asked us to dinner."

"Did you accept?"

"Of course I did," she said impatiently. "Why not? You're always talking about what a terrible neighborhood this is, and I thought maybe you'd like to go to a nicer one for a change."

"When I go to a nicer neighborhood I want to go for good," he said grimly.

"Well, can we go?"

"I suppose we'll have to if you've accepted."

Somewhat to his annoyance the conversation abruptly ended. Gretchen jumped up and kissed him sketchily and rushed into the kitchen to light the hot water for a bath. With a sigh he carefully deposited his portfolio behind the bookcase—it contained only sketches and layouts for display advertising, but it seemed to him the first thing a burglar would look for. Then he went abstractedly upstairs, dropped into the baby's room for a casual moist kiss and began dressing for dinner.

They had no automobile, so George Tompkins called for them at six-thirty. Tompkins was a successful interior decorator, a broad, rosy man with a handsome mustache and a strong odor of jasmine. He and Roger had once roomed side by side in a boarding house in New York, but they had met only intermittently in the past five years.

"We ought to see each other more," he told Roger tonight. "You ought to go out more often, old boy. Cocktail?"

"No thanks."

"No? Well, your fair wife will—won't you, Gretchen?"

"I love this house," she exclaimed, taking the glass and looking admiringly at ship models, Colonial whiskey bottles, and other fashionable débris of 1925.

"*I* like it," said Tompkins with satisfaction. "I did it to please myself, and I succeeded."

Roger stared moodily around the stiff, plain room, wondering if they could have blundered into the kitchen by mistake.

"You look like the devil, Roger," said his host. "Have a cocktail and cheer up."

"Have one," urged Gretchen.

"What?" Roger turned around absently. "Oh, no thanks. I've got to work after I get home."

"Work!" Tompkins smiled. "Listen, Roger, you'll kill yourself with work. Why don't you bring a little balance into your life—work a little, then play a little?"

"That's what I tell him," said Gretchen.

"Do you know an average business man's day?" demanded Tompkins as they went in to dinner. "Coffee in the morning, eight hours' work interrupted by a bolted luncheon, and then home again with dyspepsia and a bad temper to give the wife a pleasant evening."

Roger laughed shortly.

"You've been going to the movies too much," he said dryly.

"What?" Tompkins looked at him with some irritation. "Movies? I've hardly ever been to the movies in my life. I think the movies are atrocious. My opinions on life are drawn from my own observations. I believe in a balanced life."

"What's that?" demanded Roger.

"Well"—he hesitated—"probably the best way to tell you would be to describe my own day. Would that seem horribly egotistic?"

"Oh, no!" Gretchen looked at him with interest. "I'd love to hear about it."

"Well, in the morning I get up and go through a series of exercises. I've got one room fitted up as a little gymnasium, and I punch the bag and do shadow-boxing and weight-pulling for an hour. Then after a cold bath— There's a thing now! Do you take a daily cold bath?"

"No," admitted Roger, "I take a hot bath in the evening three or four times a week."

A horrified silence fell. Tompkins and Gretchen exchanged a glance as if something obscene had been said.

"What's the matter?" broke out Roger, glancing from one to the other in some irritation. "You know I don't take a bath every day—I haven't got the time."

Tompkins gave a prolonged sigh.

"After my bath," he continued, drawing a merciful veil of silence over the matter, "I have breakfast and drive to my office in New York, where I work until four. Then I lay off, and if it's summer I hurry out here for nine holes of golf, or if it's winter I play squash for an hour at my club. Then a good snappy game of bridge until dinner. Dinner is liable to have something to do with business—but in a pleasant way. Perhaps I've just finished a house for some customer, and he wants me to be on hand for his first party to see that the lighting is soft enough and all that sort of thing. Or maybe I sit down with a good book of poetry and spend the evening alone. At any rate I do something every night to get me out of myself."

"It must be wonderful," said Gretchen enthusiastically. "I wish we lived like that."

Tompkins bent forward earnestly over the table.

"You can," he said impressively. "There's no reason why you shouldn't. Look here, if Roger'll play nine holes of golf every day it'll do wonders for him. He won't know himself. He'll do his work better, never get that tired nervous feeling— What's the matter?"

He broke off. Roger had perceptibly yawned.

"Roger," cried Gretchen sharply, "there's no need to be so rude. If you did what George said, you'd be a lot better off." She turned indignantly to their host. "The latest is that he's going to work at *night* for the next six weeks. He says he's going to pull down the blinds and shut us up like hermits in a cave. He's been doing it every Sunday for the last year; now he's going to do it *every night* for *six weeks*."

Tompkins shook his head sadly.

"At the end of six weeks," he remarked, "he'll be starting for the sanitarium. Let me tell you, every private hospital in New York is full of cases like yours. You just strain the human nervous system a little too far, and *bang!*—you've broken something. And in order to save sixty hours you're laid up sixty weeks for repairs." He broke off, changed his tone and turned to Gretchen with a smile. "Not to mention what happens to you. It seems to me it's the wife rather than the husband who bears the brunt of these insane periods of overwork."

"I don't mind," protested Gretchen loyally.

"Yes, she does," said Roger grimly; "she minds like the devil. She's a shortsighted little egg, and she thinks it's going to be forever until I get started and she can have some new clothes. But it can't be helped. The saddest thing about women is that, after all, their best trick is to sit down and fold their hands."

"Your ideas on women are about twenty years out of date," said Tompkins pityingly. "Women won't sit down and wait anymore."

"Then they'd better marry men of forty," insisted Roger stubbornly. "If a girl marries a young man for love she ought to be willing to make any sacrifice within reason, so long as her husband keeps going ahead."

"Let's not talk about it," said Gretchen impatiently. "Please, Roger, let's have a good time just this once."

When Tompkins dropped them in front of their house at eleven Roger and Gretchen stood for a moment on the sidewalk looking at the winter moon. There was a fine damp dusty snow in the air, and Roger drew a long breath of it and put his arm around Gretchen exultantly.

"I can make more money than he can," he said tensely. "And I'll be doing it in just forty days."

"Forty days," she sighed. "It seems such a long time—when everybody else is always having fun. If I could only sleep for forty days."

"Why don't you, honey? Just take forty winks, and when you wake up everything'll be fine."

She was silent for a moment.

"Roger," she asked thoughtfully, "do you think George meant what he said about taking me horseback riding on Sunday?"

Roger frowned.

"I don't know. Probably not—I hope to Heaven he didn't." He hesitated. "As a matter of fact, he made me sort of sore tonight—all that junk about his cold bath."

With their arms about each other they started up the walk to the house.

"I'll bet he doesn't take a cold bath every morning," continued Roger ruminatively, "or three times a week either." He fumbled in his pocket for the key and inserted it in the lock with savage precision. Then he turned around defiantly. "I'll bet he hasn't had a bath for a month."

II

After a fortnight of intensive work, Roger Halsey's days blurred into each other and passed by in blocks of twos and threes and fours. From eight until five-thirty he was in his office. Then a half-hour on the commuting train, where he scrawled notes on the backs of envelopes under the dull yellow light. By seven-thirty his crayons, shears and sheets of white cardboard were spread over the living-room table, and he labored there with much grunting and sighing until midnight, while Gretchen lay on the sofa with a book, and the doorbell tinkled occasionally behind the drawn blinds. At twelve there was always an argument as to whether he would come to bed. He would agree to come after he had cleared up everything; but as he was invariably sidetracked by half a dozen new ideas, he usually found Gretchen sound asleep when he tiptoed upstairs.

Sometimes it was three o'clock before Roger squashed his last cigarette into the overloaded ash-tray, and he would undress in the darkness, disembodied with fatigue, but with a sense of triumph that he had lasted out another day.

Christmas came and went and he scarcely noticed that it was gone. He remembered it afterwards as the day he completed the window-cards for Garrod's shoes. This was one of the eight large accounts for which he was pointing in January—if he got half of them he was assured a quarter of a million dollars' worth of business during the year.

But the world outside his business became a chaotic dream. He was aware that on two cool December Sundays George Tompkins had taken Gretchen horseback riding, and that another time she had gone out with him in his automobile to spend the afternoon skiing on the country-club hill. A picture of Tompkins, in an expensive frame, had appeared one morning on their bedroom wall. And one night he was shocked into a startled protest when Gretchen went to the theatre with Tompkins in town.

But his work was almost done. Daily now his layouts arrived from the printers until seven of them were piled and docketed in his office safe. He knew how good they were. Money alone couldn't buy such work; more than he realized himself, it had been a labor of love.

December tumbled like a dead leaf from the calendar. There was an agonizing week when he had to give up coffee because it made his heart pound so. If he could hold on now for four days—three days—

On Thursday afternoon H. G. Garrod was to arrive in New York. On Wednesday evening Roger came home at seven to find Gretchen poring over the December bills with a strange expression in her eyes.

"What's the matter?"

She nodded at the bills. He ran through them, his brow wrinkling in a frown.

"Gosh!"

"I can't help it," she burst out suddenly. "They're terrible."

"Well, I didn't marry you because you were a wonderful housekeeper. I'll manage about the bills some way. Don't worry your little head over it."

She regarded him coldly.

"You talk as if I were a child."

"I have to," he said with sudden irritation.

"Well, at least I'm not a piece of bric-à-brac that you can just put somewhere and forget."

He knelt down by her quickly and took her arms in his hands.

"Gretchen, listen!" he said breathlessly. "For God's sake don't go to pieces now! We're both all stored up with malice and reproach, and if we had a quarrel it'd be terrible. I love you, Gretchen. Say you love me—quick!"

"You know I love you."

The quarrel was averted but there was an unnatural tenseness all through dinner. It came to a climax afterwards when he began to spread his working materials on the table.

"Oh, Roger," she protested, "I thought you didn't have to work tonight."

"I didn't think I'd have to, but something came up."

"I've invited George Tompkins over."

"Oh, gosh!" he exclaimed. "Well, I'm sorry, honey, but you'll have to phone him not to come."

"He's left," she said. "He's coming straight from town. He'll be here any minute now."

Roger groaned. It occurred to him to send them both to the movies, but somehow the suggestion stuck on his lips. He did not want her at the movies—he wanted her here, where he could look up and know she was by his side.

George Tompkins arrived breezily at eight o'clock.

"Aha!" he cried reprovingly, coming into the room. "Still at it." Roger agreed coolly that he was.

"Better quit—better quit before you have to." He sat down with a long sigh of physical comfort and lit a cigarette. "Take it from a fellow who's looked into the question scientifically. We can stand so much, and then—Bang!"

"If you'll excuse me"—Roger made his voice as polite as possible—"I'm going upstairs and finish this work."

"Just as you like, Roger." George waved his hand carelessly. "It isn't that *I* mind. I'm the friend of the family and I'd just as soon see the Missus as the Mister." He smiled playfully. "But if I were you, old boy, I'd put away my work and get a good night's sleep."

When Roger had spread out his materials on the bed upstairs he found that he could still hear the rumble and murmur of their voices through the thin floor. He began wondering what they found to talk about. As he plunged deeper into his work his mind had a tendency to revert sharply to his question, and several times he arose and paced nervously up and down the room.

The bed was ill adapted to his work. Several times the paper slipped from the board on which it rested and the pencil punched through. Everything was wrong tonight. Letters and figures blurred before his eyes, and as an accompaniment to the beating of his temples came those persistent murmuring voices.

At ten he realized that he had done nothing for more than an hour, and with a sudden exclamation he gathered together his papers, replaced them in his portfolio and went downstairs. They were sitting together on the sofa when he came in.

"Oh, hello!" cried Gretchen, rather unnecessarily, he thought. "We were just discussing you."

"Thank you," he answered ironically. "What particular part of my anatomy was under the scalpel?"

"Your health," said Tompkins jovially.

"My health's all right," answered Roger shortly.

"But you look at it so selfishly, old fella," cried Tompkins. "You only consider yourself in the matter. Don't you think Gretchen has any rights? If you were working on a wonderful sonnet or a—a portrait of some madonna or something"—he glanced at Gretchen's Titian hair—"why, then I'd say go ahead. But you're not. It's just some silly advertisement about how to sell Nobald's hair tonic, and if all the hair tonic ever made was dumped into the ocean tomorrow the world wouldn't be one bit the worse for it."

"Wait a minute," said Roger angrily; "that's not quite fair. I'm not kidding myself about the importance of my work—it's just as useless as the stuff you do. But to Gretchen and me it's just about the most important thing in the world."

"Are you implying that *my* work is useless?" demanded Tompkins incredulously.

"No. Not if it brings happiness to some poor sucker of a pants manufacturer who doesn't know how to spend his money."

Tompkins and Gretchen exchanged a glance.

"Oh-h-h!" exclaimed Tompkins ironically. "I didn't realize that all these years I've just been wasting my time."

"You're a loafer," said Roger rudely.

"Me?" cried Tompkins angrily. "You call me a loafer because I have a little balance in my life and find time to do interesting things? Because I play hard as well as work hard and don't let myself get to be a dull, tiresome drudge?"

Both men were angry now and their voices had risen, though on Tompkins's face there still remained the semblance of a smile.

"What I object to," said Roger steadily, "is that for the last six weeks you seem to have done all your playing around here."

"Roger!" cried Gretchen. "What do you mean by talking like that?"

"Just what I said."

"You've just lost your temper." Tompkins lit a cigarette with ostentatious coolness. "You're so nervous from overwork you don't know what you're saying. You're on the verge of a nervous break—"

"You get out of here!" cried Roger fiercely. "You get out of here right now—before I throw you out!"

Tompkins got angrily to his feet.

"You—*you* throw me out?" he cried incredulously.

They were actually moving toward each other when Gretchen stepped between them, and grabbing Tompkins's arm urged him toward the door.

"He's acting like a fool, George, but you better get out," she cried, groping in the hall for his hat.

"He insulted me!" shouted Tompkins. "He threatened to throw me out!"

"Never mind, George," pleaded Gretchen. "He doesn't know what he's saying. Please go! I'll see you at ten o'clock tomorrow."

She opened the door.

"You won't see him at ten o'clock tomorrow," said Roger steadily. "He's not coming to this house anymore."

Tompkins turned to Gretchen.

"It's his house," he suggested. "Perhaps we'd better meet at mine."

Then he was gone and Gretchen had shut the door behind him. Her eyes were full of angry tears.

"See what you've done!" she sobbed. "The only friend I had, the only person in the world who liked me enough to treat me decently, is insulted by my husband in my own house."

She threw herself on the sofa and began to cry passionately into the pillows.

"He brought it on himself," said Roger stubbornly. "I've stood as much as my self-respect will allow. I don't want you going out with him anymore."

"I will go out with him!" cried Gretchen wildly. "I'll go out with him all I want! Do you think it's any fun living here with you?"

"Gretchen," he said coldly, "get up and put on your hat and coat and go out that door and never come back!"

Her mouth fell slightly ajar.

"But I don't want to get out," she said dazedly.

"Well then, behave yourself." And he added in a gentler voice: "I thought you were going to sleep for this forty days."

"Oh yes," she cried bitterly, "easy enough to say! But I'm tired of sleeping." She got up, faced him defiantly. "And what's more I'm going riding with George Tompkins tomorrow."

"You won't go out with him if I have to take you to New York and sit you down in my office until I get through."

She looked at him with rage in her eyes.

"I hate you," she said slowly. "And I'd like to take all the work you've done and tear it up and throw it in the fire. And just to give you something to worry about tomorrow, I probably won't be here when you get back."

She got up from the sofa and very deliberately looked at her flushed, tear-stained face in the mirror. Then she ran upstairs and slammed herself into the bedroom.

Automatically Roger spread out his work on the living-room table. The bright colors of the designs, the vivid ladies— Gretchen had posed for one of them—holding orange ginger ale or glistening silk hosiery, dazzled his mind into a sort of coma. His restless crayon moved here and there over the pictures, shifting a block of letters half an inch to the right, trying a dozen blues for a cool blue, and eliminating the word that made a phrase anaemic and pale. Half an hour passed—he was deep in the work now; there was no sound in the room but the velvety scratch of the crayon over the glossy board.

After a long while he looked at his watch—it was after three. The wind had come up outside and was rushing by the house corners in loud alarming swoops, like a heavy body falling through space. He stopped his work and listened. He was not tired now, but his head felt as if it was covered with bulging veins like those pictures that hang in doctors' offices showing a body stripped of decent skin. He put his hands to his head and felt it all over. It seemed to him that on his temple the veins were knotty and brittle around an old scar.

Suddenly he began to be afraid. A hundred warnings he had heard swept into his mind. People did wreck themselves with overwork, and his body and brain were of the same vulnerable and perishable stuff. For the first time he found himself envying George Tompkins' calm nerves and healthy routine. He arose and began pacing the room in a panic.

"I've got to sleep," he whispered to himself tensely. "Otherwise I'm going crazy."

He rubbed his hand over his eyes and returned to the table to put up his work, but his fingers were shaking so that he could scarcely grasp the board. The sway of a bare branch against the window made him start and cry out. He sat down on the sofa and tried to think.

"Stop! Stop! Stop!" the clock said: "Stop! Stop! Stop!"

"I can't stop," he answered aloud. "I can't afford to stop."

Listen! Why, there was the wolf at the door now! He could hear its sharp claws scrape along the varnished woodwork. He jumped up, and running to the front door flung it open—then started back with a ghastly cry. An enormous wolf was standing on the porch, glaring at him with red, malignant eyes. As he watched it the hair bristled on its neck; it gave a low growl and disappeared in the darkness. Then Roger realized with a silent, mirthless laugh that it was the police dog from over the way.

Dragging his limbs wearily into the kitchen, he brought the alarm-clock into the living room and set it for seven. Then he wrapped himself in his overcoat, lay down on the sofa and fell immediately into a heavy, dreamless sleep.

When he awoke the light was still shining feebly, but the room was the grey color of a winter morning. He got up, and looking anxiously at his hands found to his relief that they no longer trembled. He felt much better. Then he began to remember in detail the events of the night before, and his brow drew up again in three shallow wrinkles. There was work ahead of him, twenty-four hours of work; and Gretchen, whether she wanted to or not, must sleep for one more day.

Roger's mind glowed suddenly as if he had just thought of a new advertising idea. A few minutes later he was hurrying through the sharp morning air to Kingsley's drug store.

"Is Mr. Kingsley down yet?"

The druggist's head appeared around the corner of the prescription room.

"I wonder if I can talk to you alone."

At seven-thirty, back home again, Roger walked into his own kitchen. The general housework girl had just arrived and was taking off her hat.

"Bebé"—he was not on familiar terms with her; this was her name—"I want you to cook Mrs. Halsey's breakfast right away. I'll take it up myself."

It struck Bebé that this was an unusual service for so busy a man to render his wife, but if she had seen his conduct when he had carried the tray from the kitchen she would have been even more surprised. For he set it down on the dining-room table and put into the coffee half a teaspoonful of a white substance that was *not* powdered sugar. Then he mounted the stairs and opened the door of the bedroom.

Gretchen woke up with a start, glanced at the twin bed which had not been slept in and bent on Roger a glance of astonishment—which changed to contempt when she saw the breakfast in his hand. She thought he was bringing it as a capitulation.

"I don't want any breakfast," she said coldly, and his heart sank, "except some coffee."

"No breakfast?" Roger's voice expressed disappointment.

"I said I'd take some coffee."

Roger discreetly deposited the tray on a table beside the bed and returned quickly to the kitchen.

"We're going away until tomorrow afternoon," he told Bebé, "and I want to close up the house right now. So you just put on your hat and go home."

He looked at his watch. It was ten minutes to eight and he wanted to catch the eight-ten train. He waited five minutes and then tiptoed softly upstairs and into Gretchen's room. She was sound asleep. The coffee cup was empty save for black dregs and a film of thin brown paste on the bottom. He looked at her rather anxiously but her breathing was regular and clear.

From the closet he took a suitcase and very quickly began filling it with her shoes—street shoes, evening slippers, rubber-soled oxfords—he had not realized that she owned so many pairs. When he closed the suitcase it was bulging.

He hesitated a minute, took a pair of sewing scissors from a box and, following the telephone wire until it went out of sight behind the dresser, severed it in one neat clip. He jumped as there was a soft knock at the door. It was the nursemaid. He had forgotten her existence.

"Mrs. Halsey and I are going up to the city till tomorrow," he said glibly. "Take Maxy to the beach and have lunch there. Stay all day."

Back in the room, a wave of pity passed over him. Gretchen seemed suddenly lovely and helpless, sleeping there. It was somehow terrible to rob her young life of a day. He touched her hair with his fingers and as she murmured something in her dream he leaned over and kissed her bright cheek. Then he picked up the suitcase full of shoes, locked the door and ran briskly down the stairs.

III

By five o'clock that afternoon the last package of cards for Garrod's shoes had been sent by messenger to H. G. Garrod at the Biltmore Hotel. He was to give a decision next morning. At five-thirty Roger's stenographer tapped him on the shoulder.

"Mr. Golden, the superintendent of the building, to see you."

Roger turned around dazedly.

"Oh, how-do?"

Mr. Golden came directly to the point. If Mr. Halsey intended to keep the office any longer, the little oversight about the rent had better be remedied right away.

"Mr. Golden," said Roger wearily, "everything'll be all right tomorrow. If you worry me now maybe you'll never get your money. After tomorrow nothing'll matter."

Mr. Golden looked at the tenant uneasily. Young men sometimes did away with themselves when business went wrong. Then his eye fell unpleasantly on the initialled suitcase beside the desk.

"Going on a trip?" he asked pointedly.

"What? Oh, no. That's just some clothes."

"Clothes, eh? Well, Mr. Halsey, just to prove that you mean what you say, suppose you let me keep that suitcase until tomorrow noon."

"Help yourself."

Mr. Golden picked it up with a deprecatory gesture.

"Just a matter of form," he remarked.

"I understand," said Roger, swinging around to his desk. "Good afternoon."

Mr. Golden seemed to feel that the conversation should close on a softer key.

"And don't work too hard, Mr. Halsey. You don't want to have a nervous break—"

"No," shouted Roger, "I don't. But I will if you don't leave me alone!"

As the door closed behind Mr. Golden, Roger's stenographer turned sympathetically around.

"You shouldn't have let him get away with that," she said. "What's in there? Clothes?"

"No," answered Roger absently. "Just all my wife's shoes."

He slept in the office that night on a sofa beside his desk. At dawn he awoke with a nervous start, rushed out into the street for coffee and returned in ten minutes in a panic—afraid that he might have missed Mr. Garrod's telephone call. It was then six-thirty.

By eight o'clock his whole body seemed to be on fire. When his two artists arrived he was stretched on the couch in almost physical pain. The phone rang imperatively at nine-thirty, and he picked up the receiver with trembling hands.

"Hello."

"Is this the Halsey agency?"

"Yes, this is Mr. Halsey speaking."

"This is Mr. H. G. Garrod."

Roger's heart stopped beating.

"I called up, young fellow, to say that this is wonderful work you've given us here. We want all of it and as much more as your office can do."

"Oh God!" cried Roger into the transmitter.

"What?" Mr. H. G. Garrod was considerably startled. "Say, wait a minute there!"

But he was talking to nobody. The phone had clattered to the floor, and Roger, stretched full length on the couch, was sobbing as if his heart would break.

IV

Three hours later, his face somewhat pale but his eyes calm as a
child's, Roger opened the door of his wife's bedroom with the
morning paper under his arm. At the sound of his footsteps she
started awake.

"What time is it?" she demanded.

He looked at his watch.

"Twelve o'clock."

Suddenly she began to cry.

"Roger," she said brokenly, "I'm sorry I was so bad last night."

He nodded coolly.

"Everything's all right now," he answered. Then, after a pause:
"I've got the account—the biggest one."

She turned toward him quickly.

"You have?" Then, after a minute's silence: "Can I get a new
dress?"

"Dress?" He laughed shortly. "You can get a dozen. This
account alone will bring us in forty thousand a year. It's one of
the biggest in the West."

She looked at him, startled.

"Forty thousand a year!"

"Yes."

"Gosh"—and then faintly—"I didn't know it'd really be anything like that." Again she thought a minute. "We can have a
house like George Tompkins'."

"I don't want an interior-decoration shop."

"Forty thousand a year!" she repeated again, and then added
softly: "Oh, Roger—"

"Yes?"

"I'm not going out with George Tompkins."

"I wouldn't let you, even if you wanted to," he said shortly.

She made a show of indignation.

"Why, I've had a date with him for this Thursday for weeks."

"It isn't Thursday."

"It is."

"It's Friday."

"Why, Roger, you must be crazy! Don't you think I know
what day it is?"

"It isn't Thursday," he said stubbornly. "Look!" And he held
out the morning paper.

"Friday!" she exclaimed. "Why, this is a mistake! This must be last week's paper. Today's Thursday."

She closed her eyes and thought for a moment.

"Yesterday was Wednesday," she said decisively. "The laundress came yesterday. I guess I *know*."

"Well," he said smugly, "look at the paper. There isn't any question about it."

With a bewildered look on her face she got out of bed and began searching for her clothes. Roger went into the bathroom to shave. A minute later he heard the springs creak again. Gretchen was getting back into bed.

"What's the matter?" he inquired, putting his head around the corner of the bathroom.

"I'm scared," she said in a trembling voice. "I think my nerves are giving away. I can't find any of my shoes."

"Your shoes? Why, the closet's full of them."

"I know, but I can't see one." Her face was pale with fear. "Oh, Roger!"

Roger came to her bedside and put his arm around her.

"Oh, Roger," she cried, "what's the matter with me? First that newspaper and now all my shoes. Take care of me, Roger."

"I'll get the doctor," he said.

He walked remorselessly to the telephone and took up the receiver.

"Phone seems to be out of order," he remarked after a minute; "I'll send Bebé."

The doctor arrived in ten minutes.

"I think I'm on the verge of a collapse," Gretchen told him in a strained voice.

Doctor Gregory sat down on the edge of the bed and took her wrist in his hand.

"It seems to be in the air this morning."

"I got up," said Gretchen in an awed voice, "and I found that I'd lost a whole day. I had an engagement to go riding with George Tompkins—"

"What?" exclaimed the doctor in surprise. Then he laughed.

"George Tompkins won't go riding with anyone for many days to come."

"Has he gone away?" asked Gretchen curiously.

"He's going west."

"Why?" demanded Roger. "Is he running away with some-body's wife?"

"No," said Doctor Gregory. "He's had a nervous breakdown."

"What?" they exclaimed in unison.

"He just collapsed like an opera-hat in his cold shower."

"But he was always talking about his—his balanced life," gasped Gretchen. "He had it on his mind."

"I know," said the doctor. "He's been babbling about it all morning. I think it's driven him a little mad. He worked pretty hard at it, you know."

"At what?" demanded Roger in bewilderment.

"At keeping his life balanced." He turned to Gretchen. "Now all I'll prescribe for this lady here is a good rest. If she'll just stay around the house for a few days and take forty winks of sleep she'll be as fit as ever. She's been under some strain."

"Doctor," exclaimed Roger hoarsely, "don't you think I'd better have a rest or something? I've been working pretty hard lately."

"You!" Doctor Gregory laughed, slapped him violently on the back. "My boy, I never saw you looking better in your life."

Roger turned away quickly to conceal his smile—winked forty times, or almost forty times, at the autographed picture of Mr. George Tompkins, which hung slightly askew on the bedroom wall.

UNCOLLECTED STORIES
1920–1926

Myra Meets His Family

P ROBABLY every boy who has attended an Eastern college in the last ten years has met Myra half a dozen times, for the Myras live on the Eastern colleges, as kittens live on warm milk. When Myra is young, seventeen or so, they call her a "wonderful kid"; in her prime—say, at nineteen—she is tendered the subtle compliment of being referred to by her name alone; and after that she is a "prom-trotter" or "the famous coast-to-coast Myra."

You can see her practically any winter afternoon if you stroll through the Biltmore lobby. She will be standing in a group of sophomores just in from Princeton or New Haven, trying to decide whether to dance away the mellow hours at the Club de Vingt or the Plaza Rose Room. Afterward one of the sophomores will take her to the theatre and ask her down to the February prom—and then dive for a taxi to catch the last train back to college.

Invariably she has a somnolent mother sharing a suite with her on one of the floors above.

When Myra is about twenty-four she thinks over all the nice boys she might have married at one time or other, sighs a little and does the best she can. But no remarks, please! She has given her youth to you; she has blown fragrantly through many ball-rooms to the tender tribute of many eyes; she has roused strange surges of romance in a hundred pagan young breasts; and who shall say she hasn't counted?

The particular Myra whom this story concerns will have to have a paragraph of history. I will get it over with as swiftly as possible.

When she was sixteen she lived in a big house in Cleveland and attended Derby School in Connecticut, and it was while she was still there that she started going to prep-school dances and college proms. She decided to spend the war at Smith College, but in January of her freshman year falling violently in love with a young infantry officer she failed all her midyear examinations and retired to Cleveland in disgrace. The young infantry officer arrived about a week later.

Just as she had about decided that she didn't love him after all he was ordered abroad, and in a great revival of sentiment she rushed down to the port of embarkation with her mother to bid him good-bye. She wrote him daily for two months, and then weekly for two months, and then once more. This last letter he never got, for a machine-gun bullet ripped through his head one rainy July morning. Perhaps this was just as well, for the letter informed him that it had all been a mistake, and that something told her they would never be happy together, and so on.

The "something" wore boots and silver wings and was tall and dark. Myra was quite sure that it was the real thing at last, but as an engine went through his chest at Kelly Field in mid-August she never had a chance to find out.

Instead she came East again, a little slimmer, with a becoming pallor and new shadows under her eyes, and throughout armistice year she left the ends of cigarettes all over New York on little china trays marked "Midnight Frolic" and "Cocoanut Grove" and "Palais Royal." She was twenty-one now, and Cleveland people said that her mother ought to take her back home—that New York was spoiling her.

You will have to do your best with that. The story should have started long ago.

It was an afternoon in September when she broke a theatre date in order to have tea with young Mrs. Arthur Elkins, once her roommate at school.

"I wish," began Myra as they sat down exquisitely, "that I'd been a señorita or a mademoiselle or something. Good grief! What is there to do over here once you're out, except marry and retire!"

Lilah Elkins had seen this form of ennui before.

"Nothing," she replied coolly; "do it."

"I can't seem to get interested, Lilah," said Myra, bending forward earnestly. "I've played round so much that even while I'm kissing the man I just wonder how soon I'll get tired of him. I never get carried away like I used to."

"How old are you, Myra?"

"Twenty-one last spring."

"Well," said Lilah complacently, "take it from me, don't get married unless you're absolutely through playing round. It means giving up an awful lot, you know."

"Through! I'm sick and tired of my whole pointless existence. Funny, Lilah, but I do feel ancient. Up at New Haven
last spring men danced with me that seemed like little boys
and once I overheard a girl say in the dressing room, 'There's
Myra Harper! She's been coming up here for eight years.' Of
course she was about three years off, but it did give me the
calendar blues."

"You and I went to our first prom when we were sixteen, five
years ago."

"Heavens!" sighed Myra. "And now some men are afraid of
me. Isn't that odd? Some of the nicest boys. One man dropped
me like a hotcake after coming down from Morristown for three
straight week-ends. Some kind friend told him I was husband
hunting this year, and he was afraid of getting in too deep."

"Well, you are husband hunting, aren't you?"

"I suppose so—after a fashion." Myra paused and looked
about her rather cautiously. "Have you ever met Knowleton
Whitney? You know what a wiz he is on looks, and his father's
worth a fortune, they say. Well, I noticed that the first time he
met me he started when he heard my name and fought shy—
and, Lilah darling, I'm not so ancient and homely as all that,
am I?"

"You certainly are not!" laughed Lilah. "And here's my advice:
Pick out the best thing in sight—the man who has all the mental,
physical, social and financial qualities you want, and then go after
him hammer and tongs—the way we used to. After you've got
him don't say to yourself 'Well, he can't sing like Billy,' or 'I wish
he played better golf.' You can't have everything. Shut your eyes
and turn off your sense of humor, and then after you're married
it'll be very different and you'll be mighty glad."

"Yes," said Myra absently; "I've had that advice before."

"Drifting into romance is easy when you're eighteen," continued Lilah emphatically; "but after five years of it your capacity
for it simply burns out."

"I've had such nice times," sighed Myra, "and such sweet
men. To tell you the truth I have decided to go after someone."

"Who?"

"Knowleton Whitney. Believe me, I may be a bit blasé, but I
can still get any man I want."

"You really want him?"

"Yes—as much as I'll ever want anyone. He's smart as a whip, and shy—rather sweetly shy—and they say his family have the best-looking place in Westchester County."

Lilah sipped the last of her tea and glanced at her wrist watch.

"I've got to tear, dear."

They rose together and, sauntering out on Park Avenue, hailed taxi-cabs.

"I'm awfully glad, Myra; and I know you'll be glad too."

Myra skipped a little pool of water and, reaching her taxi, balanced on the running board like a ballet dancer.

"Bye, Lilah. See you soon."

"Good-bye, Myra. Good luck!"

And knowing Myra as she did, Lilah felt that her last remark was distinctly superfluous.

II

That was essentially the reason that one Friday night six weeks later Knowlton Whitney paid a taxi bill of seven dollars and ten cents and with a mixture of emotions paused beside Myra on the Biltmore steps.

The outer surface of his mind was deliriously happy, but just below that was a slowly hardening fright at what he had done. He, protected since his freshman year at Harvard from the snares of fascinating fortune hunters, dragged away from several sweet young things by the acquiescent nape of his neck, had taken advantage of his family's absence in the West to become so enmeshed in the toils that it was hard to say which was toils and which was he.

The afternoon had been like a dream: November twilight along Fifth Avenue after the matinée, and he and Myra looking out at the swarming crowds from the romantic privacy of a hansom cab—quaint device—then tea at the Ritz and her white hand gleaming on the arm of a chair beside him; and suddenly quick broken words. After that had come the trip to the jeweler's and a mad dinner in some little Italian restaurant where he had written "Do you?" on the back of the bill of fare and pushed it over for her to add the ever-miraculous "You know I do!" And now at the day's end they paused on the Biltmore steps.

"Say it," breathed Myra close to his ear.

He said it. Ah, Myra, how many ghosts must have flitted across your memory then!

"You've made me so happy, dear," she said softly.

"No—you've made me happy. Don't you know—Myra——"

"I know."

"For good?"

"For good. I've got this, you see." And she raised the diamond solitaire to her lips. She knew how to do things, did Myra.

"Good-night."

"Good-night. Good-night."

Like a gossamer fairy in shimmering rose she ran up the wide stairs and her cheeks were glowing wildly as she rang the elevator bell.

At the end of a fortnight she got a telegram from him saying that his family had returned from the West and expected her up in Westchester County for a week's visit. Myra wired her train time, bought three new evening dresses and packed her trunk.

It was a cool November evening when she arrived, and stepping from the train in the late twilight she shivered slightly and looked eagerly round for Knowleton. The station platform swarmed for a moment with men returning from the city; there was a shouting medley of wives and chauffeurs, and a great snorting of automobiles as they backed and turned and slid away. Then before she realized it the platform was quite deserted and not a single one of the luxurious cars remained. Knowleton must have expected her on another train.

With an almost inaudible "Damn!" she started toward the Elizabethan station to telephone, when suddenly she was accosted by a very dirty, dilapidated man who touched his ancient cap to her and addressed her in a cracked, querulous voice.

"You Miss Harper?"

"Yes," she confessed, rather startled. Was this unmentionable person by any wild chance the chauffeur?

"The chauffeur's sick," he continued in a high whine. "I'm his son."

Myra gasped.

"You mean Mr. Whitney's chauffeur?"

"Yes; he only keeps just one since the war. Great on economizin'—regelar Hoover." He stamped his feet nervously and smacked enormous gauntlets together. "Well, no use waitin' here gabbin' in the cold. Le's have your grip."

Too amazed for words and not a little dismayed, Myra followed her guide to the edge of the platform, where she looked in vain for a car. But she was not left to wonder long, for the person led her steps to a battered old flivver, wherein was deposited her grip.

"Big car's broke," he explained. "Have to use this or walk."

He opened the front door for her and nodded.

"Step in."

"I b'lieve I'll sit in back if you don't mind."

"Surest thing you know," he cackled, opening the back door. "I thought the trunk bumpin' round back there might make you nervous."

"What trunk?"

"Yourn."

"Oh, didn't Mr. Whitney—can't you make two trips?"

He shook his head obstinately.

"Wouldn't allow it. Not since the war. Up to rich people to set 'n example; that's what Mr. Whitney says. Le's have your check, please."

As he disappeared Myra tried in vain to conjure up a picture of the chauffeur if this was his son. After a mysterious argument with the station agent he returned, gasping violently, with the trunk on his back. He deposited it in the rear seat and climbed up in front beside her.

It was quite dark when they swerved out of the road and up a long dusky driveway to the Whitney place, whence lighted windows flung great blots of cheerful, yellow light over the gravel and grass and trees. Even now she could see that it was very beautiful, that its blurred outline was Georgian Colonial and that great shadowy garden parks were flung out at both sides. The car plumped to a full stop before a square stone doorway and the chauffeur's son climbed out after her and pushed open the outer door.

"Just go right in," he cackled; and as she passed the threshold she heard him softly shut the door, closing out himself and the dark.

Myra looked round her. She was in a large somber hall paneled in old English oak and lit by dim shaded lights clinging like luminous yellow turtles at intervals along the wall. Ahead of her was a broad staircase and on both sides there were several doors, but there was no sight or sound of life, and an intense stillness seemed to rise ceaselessly from the deep crimson carpet.

She must have waited there a full minute before she began to have that unmistakable sense of someone looking at her. She forced herself to turn casually round.

A sallow little man, bald and clean shaven, trimly dressed in a frock coat and white spats, was standing a few yards away regarding her quizzically. He must have been fifty at the least, but even before he moved she had noticed a curious alertness about him—something in his pose which promised that it had been instantaneously assumed and would be instantaneously changed in a moment. His tiny hands and feet and the odd twist to his eyebrows gave him a faintly elfish expression, and she had one of those vague transient convictions that she had seen him before, many years ago.

For a minute they stared at each other in silence and then she flushed slightly and discovered a desire to swallow.

"I suppose you're Mr. Whitney." She smiled faintly and advanced a step toward him. "I'm Myra Harper."

For an instant longer he remained silent and motionless, and it flashed across Myra that he might be deaf; then suddenly he jerked into spirited life exactly like a mechanical toy started by the pressure of a button.

"Why, of course—why, naturally. I know—ah!" he exclaimed excitedly in a high-pitched elfin voice. Then raising himself on his toes in a sort of attenuated ecstasy of enthusiasm and smiling a wizened smile, he minced toward her across the dark carpet.

She blushed appropriately.

"That's awfully nice of——"

"Ah!" he went on. "You must be tired; a rickety, cindery, ghastly trip, I know. Tired and hungry and thirsty, no doubt, no doubt!" He looked round him indignantly. "The servants are frightfully inefficient in this house!"

Myra did not know what to say to this, so she made no answer. After an instant's abstraction Mr. Whitney crossed over with his furious energy and pressed a button; then almost as if he were dancing he was by her side again, making thin, disparaging gestures with his hands.

"A little minute," he assured her, "sixty seconds, scarcely more. Here!"

He rushed suddenly to the wall and with some effort lifted a great carved Louis Fourteenth chair and set it down carefully in the geometrical center of the carpet.

"Sit down—won't you? Sit down! I'll go get you something. Sixty seconds at the outside."

She demurred faintly, but he kept on repeating "Sit down!" in such an aggrieved yet hopeful tone that Myra sat down. Instantly her host disappeared.

She sat there for five minutes and a feeling of oppression fell over her. Of all the receptions she had ever received this was decidedly the oddest—for though she had read somewhere that Ludlow Whitney was considered one of the most eccentric figures in the financial world, to find a sallow, elfin little man who, when he walked, danced was rather a blow to her sense of form. Had he gone to get Knowleton? She revolved her thumbs in interminable concentric circles.

Then she started nervously at a quick cough at her elbow. It was Mr. Whitney again. In one hand he held a glass of milk and in the other a blue kitchen bowl full of those hard cubical crackers used in soup.

"Hungry from your trip!" he exclaimed compassionately. "Poor girl, poor little girl, starving!" He brought out this last word with such emphasis that some of the milk plopped gently over the side of the glass.

Myra took the refreshments submissively. She was not hungry, but it had taken him ten minutes to get them so it seemed ungracious to refuse. She sipped gingerly at the milk and ate a cracker, wondering vaguely what to say. Mr. Whitney, however, solved the problem for her by disappearing again—this time by way of the wide stairs—four steps at a hop—the back of his bald head gleaming oddly for a moment in the half dark.

Minutes passed. Myra was torn between resentment and bewilderment that she should be sitting on a high comfortless chair in the middle of this big hall munching crackers. By what code was a visiting fiancée ever thus received!

Her heart gave a jump of relief as she heard a familiar whistle on the stairs. It was Knowleton at last, and when he came in sight he gasped with astonishment.

"Myra!"

She carefully placed the bowl and glass on the carpet and rose, smiling.

"Why," he exclaimed, "they didn't tell me you were here!"

"Your father—welcomed me."

"Lordy! He must have gone upstairs and forgotten all about it. Did he insist on your eating this stuff? Why didn't you just tell him you didn't want any?"

"Why—I don't know."

"You mustn't mind Father, dear. He's forgetful and a little unconventional in some ways, but you'll get used to him."

He pressed a button and a butler appeared.

"Show Miss Harper to her room and have her bag carried up—and her trunk if it isn't there already." He turned to Myra. "Dear, I'm awfully sorry I didn't know you were here. How long have you been waiting?"

"Oh, only a few minutes."

It had been twenty at the least, but she saw no advantage in stressing it. Nevertheless it had given her an oddly uncomfortable feeling.

Half an hour later as she was hooking the last eye on her dinner dress there was a knock on the door.

"It's Knowleton, Myra; if you're about ready we'll go in and see Mother for a minute before dinner."

She threw a final approving glance at her reflection in the mirror and turning out the light joined him in the hall. He led her down a central passage which crossed to the other wing of the house, and stopping before a closed door he pushed it open and ushered Myra into the weirdest room upon which her young eyes had ever rested.

It was a large luxurious boudoir, paneled, like the lower hall, in dark English oak and bathed by several lamps in a mellow orange glow that blurred its every outline into misty amber. In a great armchair piled high with cushions and draped with a curiously figured cloth of silk reclined a very sturdy old lady with bright white hair, heavy features, and an air about her of having been there for many years. She lay somnolently against the cushions, her eyes half-closed, her great bust rising and falling under her black negligee.

But it was something else that made the room remarkable, and Myra's eyes scarcely rested on the woman, so engrossed was she in another feature of her surroundings. On the carpet, on the chairs and sofas, on the great canopied bed and on the soft Angora rug in front of the fire sat and sprawled and slept a great army of white poodle dogs. There must have been almost two dozen of them, with curly hair twisting in front of their wistful eyes and wide yellow bows flaunting from their necks. As Myra and Knowleton entered a stir went over the dogs; they raised one-and-twenty cold black noses in the air and from one-and-twenty little throats went up a great clatter of staccato barks until the room was filled with such an uproar that Myra stepped back in alarm.

But at the din the somnolent fat lady's eyes trembled open and in a low husky voice that was in itself oddly like a bark she snapped out: "Hush that racket!" and the clatter instantly ceased. The two or three poodles round the fire turned their silky eyes on each other reproachfully, and lying down with little sighs faded out on the white Angora rug; the tousled ball on the lady's lap dug his nose into the crook of an elbow and went back to sleep, and except for the patches of white wool scattered about the room Myra would have thought it all a dream.

"Mother," said Knowleton after an instant's pause, "this is Myra."

From the lady's lips flooded one low husky word: "Myra?"

"She's visiting us, I told you."

Mrs. Whitney raised a large arm and passed her hand across her forehead wearily.

"Child!" she said—and Myra started, for again the voice was like a low sort of growl— "you want to marry my son Knowleton?"

Myra felt that this was putting the tonneau before the radiator, but she nodded. "Yes, Mrs. Whitney."

"How old are you?" This very suddenly.

"I'm twenty-one, Mrs. Whitney."

"Ah—and you're from Cleveland?"

This was in what was surely a series of articulate barks.

"Yes, Mrs. Whitney."

"Ah——"

Myra was not certain whether this last ejaculation was conversation or merely a groan, so she did not answer.

"You'll excuse me if I don't appear downstairs," continued Mrs. Whitney; "but when we're in the East I seldom leave this room and my dear little doggies."

Myra nodded and a conventional health question was trembling on her lips when she caught Knowleton's warning glance and checked it.

"Well," said Mrs. Whitney with an air of finality, "you seem like a very nice girl. Come in again."

"Good-night, Mother," said Knowleton.

"'Night!" barked Mrs. Whitney drowsily, and her eyes sealed gradually up as her head receded back again into the cushions.

Knowleton held open the door and Myra feeling a bit blank left the room. As they walked down the corridor she heard a burst of furious sound behind them; the noise of the closing door had again roused the poodle dogs.

When they went downstairs they found Mr. Whitney already seated at the dinner table.

"Utterly charming, completely delightful!" he exclaimed, beaming nervously. "One big family, and you the jewel of it, my dear."

Myra smiled, Knowleton frowned and Mr. Whitney tittered.

"It's been lonely here," he continued; "desolate, with only us three. We expect you to bring sunlight and warmth, the peculiar radiance and efflorescence of youth. It will be quite delightful. Do you sing?"

"Why—I have. I mean, I do, some."

He clapped his hands enthusiastically.

"Splendid! Magnificent! What do you sing? Opera? Ballads? Popular music?"

"Well, mostly popular music."

"Good; personally I prefer popular music. By the way, there's a dance tonight."

"Father," demanded Knowleton sulkily, "did you go and invite a crowd here?"

"I had Monroe call up a few people—just some of the neighbors," he explained to Myra. "We're all very friendly hereabouts; give informal things continually. Oh, it's quite delightful."

Myra caught Knowleton's eye and gave him a sympathetic glance. It was obvious that he had wanted to be alone with her this first evening and was quite put out.

"I want them to meet Myra," continued his father. "I want them to know this delightful jewel we've added to our little household."

"Father," said Knowleton suddenly, "eventually of course Myra and I will want to live here with you and Mother, but for the first two or three years I think an apartment in New York would be more the thing for us."

Crash! Mr. Whitney had raked across the tablecloth with his fingers and swept his silver to a jangling heap on the floor.

"Nonsense!" he cried furiously, pointing a tiny finger at his son. "Don't talk that utter nonsense! You'll live here, do you understand me? Here! What's a home without children?"

"But, Father——"

In his excitement Mr. Whitney rose and a faint unnatural color crept into his sallow face.

"Silence!" he shrieked. "If you expect one bit of help from me you can have it under my roof—nowhere else! Is that clear? As for you, my exquisite young lady," he continued, turning his wavering finger on Myra, "you'd better understand that the best thing you can do is to decide to settle down right here. This is my home, and I mean to keep it so!"

He stood then for a moment on his tiptoes, bending furiously indignant glances first on one, then on the other, and then suddenly he turned and skipped from the room.

"Well," gasped Myra, turning to Knowleton in amazement, "what do you know about that!"

III

Some hours later she crept into bed in a great state of restless discontent. One thing she knew—she was not going to live in this house. Knowleton would have to make his father see reason to the extent of giving them an apartment in the city. The sallow little man made her nervous; she was sure Mrs. Whitney's dogs would haunt her dreams; and there was a general casualness in the chauffeur, the butler, the maids and even the guests she had met that night, that did not in the least coincide with her ideas on the conduct of a big estate.

She had lain there an hour perhaps when she was startled from a slow reverie by a sharp cry which seemed to proceed from the adjoining room. She sat up in bed and listened, and in a minute it was repeated. It sounded exactly like the plaint of a weary child stopped summarily by the placing of a hand over its mouth. In the dark silence her bewilderment shaded gradually off into uneasiness. She waited for the cry to recur, but straining her ears she heard only the intense crowded stillness of three o'clock. She wondered where Knowleton slept, remembered that his bedroom was over in the other wing just beyond his mother's. She was alone over here—or was she?

With a little gasp she slid down into bed again and lay listening. Not since childhood had she been afraid of the dark, but the unforeseen presence of someone next door startled her and sent her imagination racing through a host of mystery stories that at one time or another had whiled away a long afternoon.

She heard the clock strike four and found she was very tired. A curtain drifted slowly down in front of her imagination, and changing her position she fell suddenly to sleep.

Next morning, walking with Knowleton under starry frosted bushes in one of the bare gardens, she grew quite light-hearted and wondered at her depression of the night before. Probably all families seemed odd when one visited them for the first time in such an intimate capacity. Yet her determination that she and Knowleton were going to live elsewhere than with the white dogs and the jumpy little man was not abated. And if the nearby Westchester County society was typified by the chilly crowd she had met at the dance——

"The family," said Knowleton, "must seem rather unusual. I've been brought up in an odd atmosphere, I suppose, but Mother is really quite normal outside of her penchant for poodles in great quantities, and father in spite of his eccentricities seems to hold a secure position in Wall Street."

"Knowleton," she demanded suddenly, "who lives in the room next door to me?"

Did he start and flush slightly—or was that her imagination?

"Because," she went on deliberately, "I'm almost sure I heard someone crying in there during the night. It sounded like a child, Knowleton."

"There's no one in there," he said decidedly. "It was either your imagination or something you ate. Or possibly one of the maids was sick."

Seeming to dismiss the matter without effort he changed the subject.

The day passed quickly. At lunch Mr. Whitney seemed to have forgotten his temper of the previous night; he was as nervously enthusiastic as ever; and watching him Myra again had that impression that she had seen him somewhere before. She and Knowleton paid another visit to Mrs. Whitney—and again the poodles stirred uneasily and set up a barking, to be summarily silenced by the harsh throaty voice. The conversation was short and of inquisitional flavor. It was terminated as before by the lady's drowsy eyelids and a pæan of farewell from the dogs.

In the evening she found that Mr. Whitney had insisted on organizing an informal neighborhood vaudeville. A stage had been erected in the ballroom and Myra sat beside Knowleton in the front row and watched proceedings curiously. Two slim and haughty ladies sang, a man performed some ancient card tricks, a girl gave impersonations, and then to Myra's astonishment Mr. Whitney appeared and did a rather effective buck-and-wing dance. There was something inexpressibly weird in the motion of the well-known financier flitting solemnly back and forth across the stage on his tiny feet. Yet he danced well, with an effortless grace and an unexpected suppleness, and he was rewarded with a storm of applause.

In the half-dark the lady on her left suddenly spoke to her.

"Mr. Whitney is passing the word along that he wants to see you behind the scenes."

Puzzled, Myra rose and ascended the side flight of stairs that led to the raised platform. Her host was waiting for her anxiously.

"Ah," he chuckled, "splendid!"

He held out his hand, and wonderingly she took it. Before she realized his intention he had half led, half drawn her out onto the stage. The spotlight's glare bathed them, and the ripple of conversation washing the audience ceased. The faces before her were pallid splotches on the gloom and she felt her ears burning as she waited for Mr. Whitney to speak.

"Ladies and gentlemen," he began, "most of you know Miss Myra Harper. You had the honor of meeting her last night. She is a delicious girl, I assure you. I am in a position to know. She intends to become the wife of my son."

He paused and nodded and began clapping his hands. The audience immediately took up the clapping and Myra stood there in motionless horror, overcome by the most violent confusion of her life.

The piping voice went on: "Miss Harper is not only beautiful but talented. Last night she confided to me that she sang. I asked whether she preferred the opera, the ballad or the popular song, and she confessed that her taste ran to the latter. Miss Harper will now favor us with a popular song."

And then Myra was standing alone on the stage, rigid with embarrassment. She fancied that on the faces in front of her she saw critical expectation, boredom, ironic disapproval. Surely this was the height of bad form—to drop a guest unprepared into such a situation.

In the first hush she considered a word or two explaining that Mr. Whitney had been under a misapprehension—then anger came to her assistance. She tossed her head and those in front saw her lips close together sharply.

Advancing to the platform's edge she said succinctly to the orchestra leader: "Have you got 'Wave That Wishbone'?"

"Lemme see. Yes, we got it."

"All right. Let's go!"

She hurriedly reviewed the words, which she had learned quite by accident at a dull house party the previous summer. It was perhaps not the song she would have chosen for her first public appearance, but it would have to do. She smiled radiantly, nodded at the orchestra leader and began the verse in a light clear alto.

As she sang a spirit of ironic humor slowly took possession of her—a desire to give them all a run for their money. And she did. She injected an East Side snarl into every word of slang; she ragged; she shimmied; she did a tickle-toe step she had learned once in an amateur musical comedy; and in a burst of inspiration finished up in an Al Jolson position, on her knees with her arms stretched out to her audience in syncopated appeal.

Then she rose, bowed and left the stage.

For an instant there was silence, the silence of a cold tomb; then perhaps half a dozen hands joined in a faint, perfunctory applause that in a second had died completely away.

"Heavens!" thought Myra. "Was it as bad as all that? Or did I shock 'em?"

Mr. Whitney, however, seemed delighted. He was waiting for her in the wings and seizing her hand shook it enthusiastically.

"Quite wonderful!" he chuckled. "You are a delightful little actress—and you'll be a valuable addition to our little plays. Would you like to give an encore?"

"No!" said Myra shortly, and turned away.

In a shadowy corner she waited until the crowd had filed out, with an angry unwillingness to face them immediately after their rejection of her effort.

When the ballroom was quite empty she walked slowly up the stairs, and there she came upon Knowleton and Mr. Whitney alone in the dark hall, evidently engaged in a heated argument.

They ceased when she appeared and looked toward her eagerly.

"Myra," said Mr. Whitney, "Knowleton wants to talk to you."

"Father," said Knowleton intensely, "I ask you——"

"Silence!" cried his father, his voice ascending testily. "You'll do your duty—now."

Knowleton cast one more appealing glance at him, but Mr. Whitney only shook his head excitedly and, turning, disappeared phantomlike up the stairs.

Knowleton stood silent a moment and finally with a look of dogged determination took her hand and led her toward a room that opened off the hall at the back. The yellow light fell through the door after them and she found herself in a dark wide chamber where she could just distinguish on the walls great square shapes which she took to be frames. Knowleton pressed a button, and immediately forty portraits sprang into life—old gallants from colonial days, ladies with floppity Gainsborough hats, fat women with ruffs and placid clasped hands.

She turned to Knowleton inquiringly, but he led her forward to a row of pictures on the side.

"Myra," he said slowly and painfully, "there's something I have to tell you. These"—he indicated the pictures with his hand—"are family portraits."

There were seven of them, three men and three women, all of them of the period just before the Civil War. The one in the middle, however, was hidden by crimson velvet curtains.

"Ironic as it may seem," continued Knowleton steadily, "that frame contains a picture of my great-grandmother."

Reaching out, he pulled a little silken cord and the curtains parted, to expose a portrait of a lady dressed as a European but with the unmistakable features of a Chinese.

"My great-grandfather, you see, was an Australian tea importer. He met his future wife in Hong-Kong."

Myra's brain was whirling. She had a sudden vision of Mr. Whitney's yellowish face, peculiar eyebrows and tiny hands and feet—she remembered ghastly tales she had heard of reversions to type—of Chinese babies—and then with a final surge of horror she thought of that sudden hushed cry in the night. She gasped, her knees seemed to crumple up and she sank slowly to the floor.

In a second Knowleton's arms were round her.

"Dearest, dearest!" he cried. "I shouldn't have told you! I shouldn't have told you!"

As he said this Myra knew definitely and unmistakably that she could never marry him, and when she realized it she cast at him a wild pitiful look, and for the first time in her life fainted dead away.

IV

When she next recovered full consciousness she was in bed. She imagined a maid had undressed her, for on turning up the reading lamp she saw that her clothes had been neatly put away. For a minute she lay there, listening idly while the hall clock struck two, and then her overwrought nerves jumped in terror as she heard again that child's cry from the room next door. The morning seemed suddenly infinitely far away. There was some shadowy secret near her—her feverish imagination pictured a Chinese child brought up there in the half-dark.

In a quick panic she crept into a negligee and, throwing open the door, slipped down the corridor toward Knowleton's room. It was very dark in the other wing, but when she pushed open his door she could see by the faint hall light that his bed was empty and had not been slept in. Her terror increased. What could take him out at this hour of the night? She started for Mrs. Whitney's room, but at the thought of the dogs and her bare ankles she gave a little discouraged cry and passed by the door.

Then she suddenly heard the sound of Knowleton's voice issuing from a faint crack of light far down the corridor, and with a glow of joy she fled toward it. When she was within a foot of the door she found she could see through the crack—and after one glance all thought of entering left her.

Before an open fire, his head bowed in an attitude of great dejection, stood Knowleton, and in the corner, feet perched on the table, sat Mr. Whitney in his shirt sleeves, very quiet and calm, and pulling contentedly on a huge black pipe. Seated on the table was a part of Mrs. Whitney—that is, Mrs. Whitney without any hair. Out of the familiar great bust projected Mrs. Whitney's head, but she was bald; on her cheeks was the faint stubble of a beard, and in her mouth was a large black cigar, which she was puffing with obvious enjoyment.

"A thousand," groaned Knowleton as if in answer to a question. "Say twenty-five hundred and you'll be nearer the truth. I got a bill from the Graham Kennels today for those poodle dogs. They're soaking me two hundred and saying that they've got to have 'em back tomorrow."

"Well," said Mrs. Whitney in a low barytone voice, "send 'em back. We're through with 'em."

"That's a mere item," continued Knowleton glumly. "Including your salary, and Appleton's here, and that fellow who did the chauffeur, and seventy supes for two nights, and an orchestra—that's nearly twelve hundred, and then there's the rent on the costumes and that darn Chinese portrait and the bribes to the servants. Lord! There'll probably be bills for one thing or another coming in for the next month."

"Well, then," said Appleton, "for pity's sake pull yourself together and carry it through to the end. Take my word for it, that girl will be out of the house by twelve noon."

Knowleton sank into a chair and covered his face with his hands.

"Oh——"

"Brace up! It's all over. I thought for a minute there in the hall that you were going to balk at that Chinese business."

"It was the vaudeville that knocked the spots out of me," groaned Knowleton. "It was about the meanest trick ever pulled on any girl, and she was so darned game about it!"

"She had to be," said Mrs. Whitney cynically.

"Oh, Kelly, if you could have seen the girl look at me tonight just before she fainted in front of that picture. Lord, I believe she loves me! Oh, if you could have seen her!"

Outside Myra flushed crimson. She leaned closer to the door, biting her lip until she could taste the faintly bitter savor of blood.

"If there was anything I could do now," continued Knowleton—"anything in the world that would smooth it over I believe I'd do it."

Kelly crossed ponderously over, his bald shiny head ludicrous above his feminine negligee, and put his hand on Knowleton's shoulder.

"See here, my boy—your trouble is just nerves. Look at it this way: You undertook somep'n to get yourself out of an awful mess. It's a cinch the girl was after your money—now you've beat her at her own game an' saved yourself an unhappy marriage and your family a lot of suffering. Ain't that so, Appleton?"

"Absolutely!" said Appleton emphatically. "Go through with it."

"Well," said Knowleton with a dismal attempt to be righteous, "if she really loved me she wouldn't have let it all affect her this much. She's not marrying my family."

Appleton laughed.

"I thought we'd tried to make it pretty obvious that she is."

"Oh, shut up!" cried Knowleton miserably.

Myra saw Appleton wink at Kelly.

"'At's right," he said; "she's shown she was after your money. Well, now then, there's no reason for not going through with it. See here. On one side you've proved she didn't love you and you're rid of her and free as air. She'll creep away and never say a word about it—and your family never the wiser. On the other side twenty-five hundred thrown to the bow-wows, miserable marriage, girl sure to hate you as soon as she finds out, and your family all broken up and probably disownin' you for marryin' her. One big mess, I'll tell the world."

"You're right," admitted Knowleton gloomily. "You're right, I suppose—but oh, the look in that girl's face! She's probably in there now lying awake, listening to the Chinese baby——"

Appleton rose and yawned.

"Well——" he began.

But Myra waited to hear no more. Pulling her silk kimono close about her she sped like lightning down the soft corridor, to dive headlong and breathless into her room.

"My heavens!" she cried, clenching her hands in the darkness. "My heavens!"

V

Just before dawn Myra drowsed into a jumbled dream that seemed to act on through interminable hours. She awoke about seven and lay listlessly with one blue-veined arm hanging over the side of the bed. She who had danced in the dawn at many proms was very tired.

A clock outside her door struck the hour, and with her nervous start something seemed to collapse within her—she turned over and began to weep furiously into her pillow, her tangled hair spreading like a dark aura round her head. To her, Myra Harper, had been done this cheap vulgar trick by a man she had thought shy and kind.

Lacking the courage to come to her and tell her the truth he had gone into the highways and hired men to frighten her.

Between her fevered broken sobs she tried in vain to comprehend the workings of a mind which could have conceived this in all its subtlety. Her pride refused to let her think of it as a deliberate plan of Knowleton's. It was probably an idea fostered by this little actor Appleton or by the fat Kelly with his horrible poodles. But it was all unspeakable—unthinkable. It gave her an intense sense of shame.

But when she emerged from her room at eight o'clock and, disdaining breakfast, walked into the garden she was a very self-possessed young beauty, with dry cool eyes only faintly shadowed. The ground was firm and frosty with the promise of winter, and she found grey sky and dull air vaguely comforting and one with her mood. It was a day for thinking and she needed to think.

And then turning a corner suddenly she saw Knowleton seated on a stone bench, his head in his hands, in an attitude of profound dejection. He wore his clothes of the night before and it was quite evident that he had not been to bed.

He did not hear her until she was quite close to him, and then as a dry twig snapped under her heel he looked up wearily.

She saw that the night had played havoc with him—his face was deathly pale and his eyes were pink and puffed and tired. He jumped up with a look that was very like dread.

"Good morning," said Myra quietly.

"Sit down," he began nervously. "Sit down; I want to talk to you! I've got to talk to you."

Myra nodded and taking a seat beside him on the bench clasped her knees with her hands and half closed her eyes.

"Myra, for heaven's sake have pity on me!"

She turned wondering eyes on him.

"What do you mean?"

He groaned.

"Myra, I've done a ghastly thing—to you, to me, to us. I haven't a word to say in favor of myself—I've been just rotten. I think it was a sort of madness that came over me."

"You'll have to give me a clue to what you're talking about."

"Myra—Myra"—like all large bodies his confession seemed difficult to imbue with momentum—"Myra—Mr. Whitney is not my father."

"You mean you were adopted?"

"No; I mean—Ludlow Whitney is my father, but this man you've met isn't Ludlow Whitney."

"I know," said Myra coolly. "He's Warren Appleton, the actor."

Knowleton leaped to his feet.

"How on earth——"

"Oh," lied Myra easily, "I recognized him the first night. I saw him five years ago in 'The Swiss Grapefruit.'"

At this Knowleton seemed to collapse utterly. He sank down limply onto the bench.

"You knew?"

"Of course! How could I help it? It simply made me wonder what it was all about."

With a great effort he tried to pull himself together.

"I'm going to tell you the whole story, Myra."

"I'm all ears."

"Well, it starts with my mother—my real one, not the woman with those idiotic dogs; she's an invalid and I'm her only child. Her one idea in life has always been for me to make a fitting match, and her idea of a fitting match centers round social position in England. Her greatest disappointment was that I wasn't a girl so I could marry a title; instead she wanted to drag me to England—marry me off to the sister of an earl or the daughter of a duke. Why, before she'd let me stay up here alone this fall she made me promise I wouldn't go to see any girl more than twice. And then I met you."

He paused for a second and continued earnestly: "You were the first girl in my life whom I ever thought of marrying. You intoxicated me, Myra. It was just as though you were making me love you by some invisible force."

"I was," murmured Myra.

"Well, that first intoxication lasted a week, and then one day a letter came from mother saying she was bringing home some wonderful English girl, Lady Helena Something-or-Other. And the same day a man told me that he'd heard I'd been caught by the most famous husband hunter in New York. Well, between these two things I went half-crazy. I came into town to see you and call it off—got as far as the Biltmore entrance and didn't dare. I started wandering down Fifth Avenue like a wild man, and then I met Kelly. I told him the whole story—and within an hour we'd hatched up this ghastly plan. It was his plan—all the details. His histrionic instinct got the better of him and he had me thinking it was the kindest way out."

"Finish," commanded Myra crisply.

"Well, it went splendidly, we thought. Everything—the station meeting, the dinner scene, the scream in the night, the vaudeville—though I thought that was a little too much until—until——— Oh, Myra, when you fainted under that picture and I held you there in my arms, helpless as a baby, I knew I loved you. I was sorry then, Myra."

There was a long pause while she sat motionless, her hands still clasping her knees—then he burst out with a wild plea of passionate sincerity.

"Myra!" he cried. "If by any possible chance you can bring yourself to forgive and forget I'll marry you when you say, let my family go to the devil, and love you all my life."

For a long while she considered, and Knowleton rose and began pacing nervously up and down the aisle of bare bushes, his hands in his pockets, his tired eyes pathetic now, and full of dull appeal. And then she came to a decision.

"You're perfectly sure?" she asked calmly.

"Yes."

"Very well, I'll marry you today."

With her words the atmosphere cleared and his troubles seemed to fall from him like a ragged cloak. An Indian summer sun drifted out from behind the grey clouds and the dry bushes rustled gently in the breeze.

"It was a bad mistake," she continued, "but if you're sure you love me now, that's the main thing. We'll go to town this morning, get a license, and I'll call up my cousin, who's a minister in the First Presbyterian Church. We can go West tonight."

"Myra!" he cried jubilantly. "You're a marvel and I'm not fit to tie your shoe strings. I'm going to make up to you for this, darling girl."

And taking her supple body in his arms he covered her face with kisses.

The next two hours passed in a whirl. Myra went to the telephone and called her cousin, and then rushed upstairs to pack. When she came down a shining roadster was waiting miraculously in the drive and by ten o'clock they were bowling happily toward the city.

They stopped for a few minutes at the City Hall and again at the jeweler's, and then they were in the house of the Reverend Walter Gregory on 69th Street, where a sanctimonious gentleman with twinkling eyes and a slight stutter received them cordially and urged them to a breakfast of bacon and eggs before the ceremony.

On the way to the station they stopped only long enough to wire Knowleton's father, and then they were sitting in their compartment on the Broadway Limited.

"Darn!" exclaimed Myra. "I forgot my bag. Left it at Cousin Walter's in the excitement."

"Never mind. We can get a whole new outfit in Chicago."

She glanced at her wrist watch.

"I've got time to telephone him to send it on."

She rose.

"Don't be long, dear."

She leaned down and kissed his forehead.

"You know I couldn't. Two minutes, honey."

Outside Myra ran swiftly along the platform and up the steel stairs to the great waiting room, where a man met her—a twinkly-eyed man with a slight stutter.

"How d-did it go, M-myra?"

"Fine! Oh, Walter, you were splendid! I almost wish you'd join the ministry so you could officiate when I do get married."

"Well—I r-rehearsed for half an hour after I g-got your tele-phone call."

"Wish we'd had more time. I'd have had him lease an apart-ment and buy furniture."

"H'm," chuckled Walter. "Wonder how far he'll go on his honeymoon."

"Oh, he'll think I'm on the train till he gets to Elizabeth." She shook her little fist at the great contour of the marble dome. "Oh, he's getting off too easy—far too easy!"

"I haven't f-figured out what the f-fellow did to you, M-myra."

"You never will, I hope."

They had reached the side drive and he hailed her a taxi-cab.

"You're an angel!" beamed Myra. "And I can't thank you enough."

"Well, anytime I can be of use t-to you—— By the way, what are you going to do with all the rings?"

Myra looked laughingly at her hand.

"That's the question," she said. "I may send them to Lady Helena Something-or-Other—and—well, I've always had a strong penchant for souvenirs. Tell the driver 'Biltmore,' Walter."

The Smilers

W̌E all have that exasperated moment!
   There are times when you almost tell the harmless old
lady next door what you really think of her face—that it ought
to be on a night-nurse in a house for the blind; when you'd like
to ask the man you've been waiting ten minutes for if he isn't all
overheated from racing the postman down the block; when you
nearly say to the waiter that if they deducted a cent from the bill
for every degree the soup was below tepid the hotel would owe
you half a dollar; when—and this is the infallible earmark of true
exasperation—a smile affects you as an oil-baron's undershirt
affects a cow's husband.

But the moment passes. Scars may remain on your dog or
your collar or your telephone receiver, but your soul has slid
gently back into its place between the lower edge of your heart
and the upper edge of your stomach, and all is at peace.

But the imp who turns on the shower-bath of exasperation
apparently made it so hot one time in Sylvester Stockton's early
youth that he never dared dash in and turn it off—in consequence no first old man in an amateur production of a Victorian
comedy was ever more pricked and prodded by the daily phenomena of life than was Sylvester at thirty.

Accusing eyes behind spectacles—suggestion of a stiff neck—
this will have to do for his description, since he is not the hero
of this story. He is the plot. He is the factor that makes it one
story instead of three stories. He makes remarks at the beginning
and end.

The late afternoon sun was loitering pleasantly along Fifth
Avenue when Sylvester, who had just come out of that hideous
public library where he had been consulting some ghastly book,
told his impossible chauffeur (it is true that I am following his
movements through his own spectacles) that he wouldn't need
his stupid, incompetent services any longer. Swinging his cane
(which he found too short) in his left hand (which he should
have cut off long ago since it was constantly offending him), he
began walking slowly down the Avenue.

When Sylvester walked at night he frequently glanced behind and on both sides to see if anyone was sneaking up on him. This had become a constant mannerism. For this reason he was unable to pretend that he didn't see Betty Tearle sitting in her machine in front of Tiffany's.

Back in his early twenties he had been in love with Betty Tearle. But he had depressed her. He had misanthropically dissected every meal, motor trip and musical comedy that they attended together, and on the few occasions when she had tried to be especially nice to him—from a mother's point of view he had been rather desirable—he had suspected hidden motives and fallen into a deeper gloom than ever. Then one day she told him that she would go mad if he ever again parked his pessimism in her sun-parlor.

And ever since then she had seemed to be smiling—uselessly, insultingly, charmingly smiling.

"Hello, Sylvo," she called.

"Why—how do Betty." He wished she wouldn't call him Sylvo—it sounded like a—like a darn monkey or something.

"How goes it?" she asked cheerfully. "Not very well, I suppose."

"Oh, yes," he answered stiffly, "I manage."

"Taking in the happy crowd?"

"Heavens, yes." He looked around him. "Betty, why are they happy? What are they smiling at? What do they find to smile at?"

Betty flashed at him a glance of radiant amusement.

"The women may smile because they have pretty teeth, Sylvo."

"You smile," continued Sylvester cynically, "because you're comfortably married and have two children. You imagine you're happy, so you suppose everyone else is."

Betty nodded.

"You may have hit it, Sylvo——" The chauffeur glanced around and she nodded at him. "Good-bye."

Sylvo watched with a pang of envy which turned suddenly to exasperation as he saw she had turned and smiled at him once more. Then her car was out of sight in the traffic, and with a voluminous sigh he galvanized his cane into life and continued his stroll.

At the next corner he stopped in at a cigar store and there he ran into Waldron Crosby. Back in the days when Sylvester had been a prize pigeon in the eyes of debutantes he had also been a game partridge from the point of view of promoters. Crosby, then a young bond salesman, had given him much safe and sane advice and saved him many dollars. Sylvester liked Crosby as much as he could like anyone. Most people did like Crosby.

"Hello, you old bag of 'nerves,'" cried Crosby genially, "come and have a big gloom-dispelling Corona."

Sylvester regarded the cases anxiously. He knew he wasn't going to like what he bought.

"Still out at Larchmont, Waldron?" he asked.

"Right-o."

"How's your wife?"

"Never better."

"Well," said Sylvester suspiciously, "you brokers always look as if you're smiling at something up your sleeve. It must be a hilarious profession."

Crosby considered.

"Well," he admitted, "it varies—like the moon and the price of soft drinks—but it has its moments."

"Waldron," said Sylvester earnestly, "you're a friend of mine—please do me the favor of not smiling when I leave you. It seems like a—like a mockery."

A broad grin suffused Crosby's countenance.

"Why, you crabbed old son-of-a-gun!"

But Sylvester with an irate grunt had turned on his heel and disappeared.

He strolled on. The sun finished its promenade and began calling in the few stray beams it had left among the westward streets. The Avenue darkened with black bees from the department stores; the traffic swelled into an interlaced jam; the busses were packed four deep like platforms above the thick crowd; but Sylvester, to whom the daily shift and change of the city was a matter only of sordid monotony, walked on, taking only quick sideward glances through his frowning spectacles.

He reached his hotel and was elevated to his four-room suite on the twelfth floor.

"If I dine downstairs," he thought, "the orchestra will play either 'Smile, Smile, Smile' or 'The Smiles that You Gave to Me.' But then if I go to the Club I'll meet all the cheerful people I know, and if I go somewhere else where there's no music, I won't get anything fit to eat."

He decided to have dinner in his rooms.

An hour later, after disparaging some broth, a squab and a salad, he tossed fifty cents to the room waiter, and then held up his hand warningly.

"Just oblige me by not smiling when you say thanks?"

He was too late. The waiter had grinned.

"Now, will you please tell me," asked Sylvester peevishly, "what on earth you have to smile about?"

The waiter considered. Not being a reader of the magazines he was not sure what was characteristic of waiters, yet he supposed something characteristic was expected of him.

"Well, Mister," he answered, glancing at the ceiling with all the ingenuousness he could muster in his narrow, sallow countenance, "it's just something my face does when it sees four bits comin'."

Sylvester waved him away.

"Waiters are happy because they've never had anything better," he thought. "They haven't enough imagination to want anything."

At nine o'clock from sheer boredom he sought his expressionless bed.

II

As Sylvester left the cigar store, Waldron Crosby followed him out, and turning off Fifth Avenue down a cross street entered a brokerage office. A plump man with nervous hands rose and hailed him.

"Hello, Waldron."

"Hello, Potter—I just dropped in to hear the worst."

The plump man frowned.

"We've just got the news," he said.

"Well, what is it. Another drop?"

"Closed at seventy-eight. Sorry, old boy."

"Whew!"

"Hit pretty hard?"

"Cleaned out!"

The plump man shook his head, indicating that life was too much for him, and turned away.

Crosby sat there for a moment without moving. Then he rose, walked into Potter's private office and picked up the phone.

"Gi'me Larchmont 838."

In a moment he had his connection.

"Mrs. Crosby there?"

A man's voice answered him.

"Yes; this you, Crosby? This is Doctor Shipman."

"Dr. Shipman?" Crosby's voice showed sudden anxiety.

"Yes—I've been trying to reach you all afternoon. The situation's changed and we expect the child tonight."

"Tonight?"

"Yes. Everything's O.K. But you'd better come right out."

"I will. Good-bye."

He hung up the receiver and started out the door, but paused as an idea struck him. He returned, and this time called a Manhattan number.

"Hello, Donny, this is Crosby."

"Hello, there, old boy. You just caught me; I was going——"

"Say, Donny, I want a job right away, quick."

"For whom?"

"For me."

"Why, what's the——"

"Never mind. Tell you later. Got one for me?"

"Why, Waldron, there's not a blessed thing here except a clerkship. Perhaps next——"

"What salary goes with the clerkship?"

"Forty—say forty-five a week."

"I've got you. I start tomorrow."

"All right. But say, old man——"

"Sorry, Donny, but I've got to run."

Crosby hurried from the brokerage office with a wave and a smile at Potter. In the street he took out a handful of small change and after surveying it critically hailed a taxi.

"Grand Central—quick!" he told the driver.

III

At six o'clock Betty Tearle signed the letter, put it into an envelope and wrote her husband's name upon it. She went into his room and after a moment's hesitation set a black cushion on the bed and laid the white letter on it so that it could not fail to attract his attention when he came in. Then with a quick glance around the room she walked into the hall and upstairs to the nursery.

"Clare," she called softly.

"Oh, Mummy!" Clare left her doll's house and scurried to her mother.

"Where's Billy, Clare?"

Billy appeared eagerly from under the bed.

"Got anything for me?" he inquired politely.

His mother's laugh ended in a little catch and she caught both her children to her and kissed them passionately. She found that she was crying quietly and their flushed little faces seemed cool against the sudden fever racing through her blood.

"Take care of Clare—always—Billy darling——"

Billy was puzzled and rather awed.

"You're crying," he accused gravely.

"I know—I know I am——"

Clare gave a few tentative sniffles, hesitated, and then clung to her mother in a storm of weeping.

"I d-don't feel good, Mummy—I don't feel good."

Betty soothed her quietly.

"We won't cry any more, Clare dear—either of us."

But as she rose to leave the room her glance at Billy bore a mute appeal, too vain, she knew, to be registered on his childish consciousness.

Half an hour later as she carried her traveling bag to a taxi-cab at the door she raised her hand to her face in mute admission that a veil served no longer to hide her from the world.

"But I've chosen," she thought dully.

As the car turned the corner she wept again, resisting a temptation to give up and go back.

"Oh, my God!" she whispered. "What am I doing? What have I done? What have I done?"

IV

When Jerry, the sallow, narrow-faced waiter, left Sylvester's rooms he reported to the head-waiter, and then checked out for the day.

He took the subway south and alighting at Williams Street walked a few blocks and entered a billiard parlor.

An hour later he emerged with a cigarette drooping from his bloodless lips, and stood on the sidewalk as if hesitating before making a decision. He set off eastward.

As he reached a certain corner his gait suddenly increased and then quite as suddenly slackened. He seemed to want to pass by, yet some magnetic attraction was apparently exerted on him, for with a sudden face-about he turned in at the door of a cheap restaurant—half-cabaret, half chop-suey parlor—where a miscellaneous assortment gathered nightly.

Jerry found his way to a table situated in the darkest and most obscure corner. Seating himself with a contempt for his surroundings that betokened familiarity rather than superiority he ordered a glass of claret.

The evening had begun. A fat woman at the piano was expelling the last jauntiness from a hackneyed fox-trot, and a lean, dispirited male was assisting her with lean, dispirited notes from a violin. The attention of the patrons was directed at a dancer wearing soiled stockings and done largely in peroxide and rouge who was about to step upon a small platform, meanwhile exchanging pleasantries with a fat, eager person at the table beside her who was trying to capture her hand.

Over in the corner Jerry watched the two by the platform and, as he gazed, the ceiling seemed to fade out, the walls growing into tall buildings and the platform becoming the top of a Fifth Avenue bus on a breezy spring night three years ago. The fat, eager person disappeared, the short skirt of the dancer rolled down and the rouge faded from her cheeks—and he was beside her again in an old delirious ride, with the lights blinking kindly at them from the tall buildings beside and the voices of the street merging into a pleasant somnolent murmur around them.

"Jerry," said the girl on top of the bus, "I've said that when you were gettin' seventy-five I'd take a chance with you. But, Jerry, I can't wait forever."

Jerry watched several street numbers sail by before he answered.

"I don't know what's the matter," he said helplessly, "they won't raise me. If I can locate a new job——"

"You better hurry, Jerry," said the girl; "I'm gettin' sick of just livin' along. If I can't get married I got a couple of chances to work in a cabaret—get on the stage maybe."

"You keep out of that," said Jerry quickly. "There ain't no need, if you just wait about another month or two."

"I can't wait forever, Jerry," repeated the girl. "I'm tired of stayin' poor alone."

"It won't be so long," said Jerry clenching his free hand. "I can make it somewhere, if you'll just wait."

But the bus was fading out and the ceiling was taking shape and the murmur of the April streets was fading into the rasping whine of the violin—for that was all three years before and now he was sitting here.

The girl glanced up on the platform and exchanged a metallic impersonal smile with the dispirited violinist, and Jerry shrank farther back in his corner watching her with burning intensity.

"Your hands belong to anybody that wants them now," he cried silently and bitterly. "I wasn't man enough to keep you out of that—not man enough, by God, by God!"

But the girl by the door still toyed with the fat man's clutching fingers as she waited for her time to dance.

V

Sylvester Stockton tossed restlessly upon his bed. The room, big as it was, smothered him, and a breeze drifting in and bearing with it a rift of moon seemed laden only with the cares of the world he would have to face next day.

"They don't understand," he thought. "They don't see, as I do, the underlying misery of the whole damn thing. They're hollow optimists. They smile because they think they're always going to be happy.

"Oh, well," he mused drowsily, "I'll run up to Rye tomorrow and endure more smiles and more heat. That's all life is—just smiles and heat, smiles and heat."

The Popular Girl

A LONG about half past ten every Saturday night Yanci Bowman eluded her partner by some graceful subterfuge and from the dancing floor went to a point of vantage overlooking the country-club bar. When she saw her father she would either beckon to him, if he chanced to be looking in her direction, or else she would dispatch a waiter to call attention to her impendent presence. If it were no later than half past ten—that is, if he had had no more than an hour of synthetic gin rickeys—he would get up from his chair and suffer himself to be persuaded into the ballroom.

"Ballroom," for want of a better word. It was that room, filled by day with wicker furniture, which was always connotated in the phrase "Let's go in and dance." It was referred to as "inside" or "downstairs." It was that nameless chamber wherein occur the principal transactions of all the country clubs in America.

Yanci knew that if she could keep her father there for an hour, talking, watching her dance, or even on rare occasions dancing himself, she could safely release him at the end of that time. In the period that would elapse before midnight ended the dance, he could scarcely become sufficiently stimulated to annoy anyone.

All this entailed considerable exertion on Yanci's part, and it was less for her father's sake than for her own that she went through with it. Several rather unpleasant experiences were scattered through this past summer. One night when she had been detained by the impassioned and impossible-to-interrupt speech of a young man from Chicago her father had appeared swaying gently in the ballroom doorway; in his ruddy handsome face two faded blue eyes were squinted half-shut as he tried to focus them on the dancers, and he was obviously preparing to offer himself to the first dowager who caught his eye. He was ludicrously injured when Yanci insisted upon an immediate withdrawal.

After that night Yanci went through her Fabian maneuver to the minute.

Yanci and her father were the handsomest two people in the Middle Western city where they lived. Tom Bowman's complexion was hearty from twenty years spent in the service of good whisky and bad golf. He kept an office downtown, where he was thought to transact some vague real-estate business; but in point of fact his chief concern in life was the exhibition of a handsome profile and an easy well-bred manner at the country club, where he had spent the greater part of the ten years that had elapsed since his wife's death.

Yanci was twenty, with a vague die-away manner which was partly the setting for her languid disposition and partly the effect of a visit she had paid to some Eastern relatives at an impressionable age. She was intelligent, in a flitting way, romantic under the moon and unable to decide whether to marry for sentiment or for comfort, the latter of these two abstractions being well enough personified by one of the most ardent among her admirers. Meanwhile she kept house, not without efficiency, for her father, and tried in a placid unruffled tempo to regulate his constant tippling to the sober side of inebriety.

She admired her father. She admired him for his fine appearance and for his charming manner. He had never quite lost the air of having been a popular Bones man at Yale. This charm of his was a standard by which her susceptible temperament unconsciously judged the men she knew. Nevertheless, father and daughter were far from that sentimental family relationship which is a stock plant in fiction, but in life usually exists in the mind of only the older party to it. Yanci Bowman had decided to leave her home by marriage within the year. She was heartily bored.

Scott Kimberly, who saw her for the first time this November evening at the country club, agreed with the lady whose house guest he was that Yanci was an exquisite little beauty. With a sort of conscious sensuality surprising in such a young man—Scott was only twenty-five—he avoided an introduction that he might watch her undisturbed for a fanciful hour, and sip the pleasure or the disillusion of her conversation at the drowsy end of the evening.

"She never got over the disappointment of not meeting the Prince of Wales when he was in this country," remarked Mrs. Orrin Rogers, following his gaze. "She said so, anyhow; whether she was serious or not I don't know. I hear that she has her walls simply plastered with pictures of him."

"Who?" asked Scott suddenly.

"Why, the Prince of Wales."

"Who has plaster pictures of him?"

"Why, Yanci Bowman, the girl you said you thought was so pretty."

"After a certain degree of prettiness, one pretty girl is as pretty as another," said Scott argumentatively.

"Yes, I suppose so."

Mrs. Rogers' voice drifted off on an indefinite note. She had never in her life compassed a generality until it had fallen familiarly on her ear from constant repetition.

"Let's talk her over," Scott suggested.

With a mock reproachful smile Mrs. Rogers lent herself agreeably to slander. An encore was just beginning. The orchestra trickled a light overflow of music into the pleasant green-latticed room and the two score couples who for the evening comprised the local younger set moved placidly into time with its beat. Only a few apathetic stags gathered one by one in the doorways, and to a close observer it was apparent that the scene did not attain the gayety which was its aspiration. These girls and men had known each other from childhood; and though there were marriages incipient upon the floor tonight, they were marriages of environment, of resignation, or even of boredom.

Their trappings lacked the sparkle of the seventeen-year-old affairs that took place through the short and radiant holidays. On such occasions as this, thought Scott as his eyes still sought casually for Yanci, occurred the matings of the left-overs, the plainer, the duller, the poorer of the social world; matings actuated by the same urge toward perhaps a more glamorous destiny, yet, for all that, less beautiful and less young. Scott himself was feeling very old.

But there was one face in the crowd to which his generalization did not apply. When his eyes found Yanci Bowman among the dancers he felt much younger. She was the incarnation of all in which the dance failed—graceful youth, arrogant, languid freshness and beauty that was sad and perishable as a memory in a dream. Her partner, a young man with one of those fresh red complexions ribbed with white streaks, as though he had been slapped on a cold day, did not appear to be holding her interest, and her glance fell here and there upon a group, a face, a garment, with a far-away and oblivious melancholy.

"Dark-blue eyes," said Scott to Mrs. Rogers. "I don't know that they mean anything except that they're beautiful, but that nose and upper lip and chin are certainly aristocratic—if there is any such thing," he added apologetically.

"Oh, she's very aristocratic," agreed Mrs. Rogers. "Her grand-father was a senator or governor or something in one of the Southern states. Her father's very aristocratic-looking too. Oh, yes, they're very aristocratic; they're aristocratic people."

"She looks lazy."

Scott was watching the yellow gown drift and submerge among the dancers.

"She doesn't like to move. It's a wonder she dances so well. Is she engaged? Who is the man who keeps cutting in on her, the one who tucks his tie under his collar so rakishly and affects the remarkable slanting pockets?"

He was annoyed at the young man's persistence, and his sarcasm lacked the ring of detachment.

"Oh, that's"—Mrs. Rogers bent forward, the tip of her tongue just visible between her lips—"that's the O'Rourke boy. He's quite devoted, I believe."

"I believe," Scott said suddenly, "that I'll get you to introduce me if she's near when the music stops."

They arose and stood looking for Yanci—Mrs. Rogers, small, stoutening, nervous, and Scott Kimberly, her husband's cousin, dark and just below medium height. Scott was an orphan with half a million of his own, and he was in this city for no more reason than that he had missed a train. They looked for several minutes, and in vain. Yanci, in her yellow dress, no longer moved with slow loveliness among the dancers.

The clock stood at half past ten.

II

"Good evening," her father was saying to her at that moment in syllables faintly slurred. "This seems to be getting to be a habit."

They were standing near a side stairs, and over his shoulder through a glass door Yanci could see a party of half a dozen men sitting in familiar joviality about a round table.

"Don't you want to come out and watch for awhile?" she suggested, smiling and affecting a casualness she did not feel.

"Not tonight, thanks."

Her father's dignity was a bit too emphasized to be convincing.

"Just come out and take a look," she urged him. "Everybody's here, and I want to ask you what you think of somebody."

This was not so good, but it was the best that occurred to her.

"I doubt very strongly if I'd find anything to interest me out there," said Tom Bowman emphatically. "I observe that f'some insane reason I'm always taken out and aged on the wood for half an hour as though I was irresponsible."

"I only ask you to stay a little while."

"Very considerate, I'm sure. But tonight I happ'n be interested in a discussion that's taking place in here."

"Come on, Father."

Yanci put her arm through his ingratiatingly; but he released it by the simple expedient of raising his own arm and letting hers drop.

"I'm afraid not."

"I'll tell you," she suggested lightly, concealing her annoyance at this unusually protracted argument, "you come in and look, just once, and then if it bores you you can go right back."

He shook his head.

"No thanks."

Then without another word he turned suddenly and reentered the bar. Yanci went back to the ballroom. She glanced easily at the stag line as she passed, and making a quick selection murmured to a man near her, "Dance with me, will you, Carty? I've lost my partner."

"Glad to," answered Carty truthfully.

"Awfully sweet of you."

"Sweet of me? Of you, you mean."

She looked up at him absently. She was furiously annoyed at her father. Next morning at breakfast she would radiate a consuming chill, but for tonight she could only wait, hoping that if the worst happened he would at least remain in the bar until the dance was over.

Mrs. Rogers, who lived next door to the Bowmans, appeared suddenly at her elbow with a strange young man.

"Yanci," Mrs. Rogers was saying with a social smile. "I want to introduce Mr. Kimberly. Mr. Kimberly's spending the week-end with us, and I particularly wanted him to meet you."

"How perfectly slick!" drawled Yanci with lazy formality.

Mr. Kimberly suggested to Miss Bowman that they dance, to which proposal Miss Bowman dispassionately acquiesced. They mingled their arms in the gesture prevalent and stepped into time with the beat of the drum. Simultaneously it seemed to Scott that the room and the couples who danced up and down upon it converted themselves into a background behind her. The commonplace lamps, the rhythm of the music playing some paraphrase of a paraphrase, the faces of many girls, pretty, undistinguished or absurd, assumed a certain solidity as though they had grouped themselves in a retinue for Yanci's languid eyes and dancing feet.

"I've been watching you," said Scott simply. "You look rather bored this evening."

"Do I?" Her dark-blue eyes exposed a borderland of fragile iris as they opened in a delicate burlesque of interest. "How perfectly kill-ing!" she added.

Scott laughed. She had used the exaggerated phrase without smiling, indeed without any attempt to give it verisimilitude. He had heard the adjectives of the year—"hectic," "marvelous" and "slick"—delivered casually, but never before without the faintest meaning. In this lackadaisical young beauty it was inexpressibly charming.

The dance ended. Yanci and Scott strolled toward a lounge set against the wall, but before they could take possession there was a shriek of laughter and a brawny damsel dragging an embarrassed boy in her wake skidded by them and plumped down upon it.

"How rude!" observed Yanci.

"I suppose it's her privilege."

"A girl with ankles like that has no privileges."

They seated themselves uncomfortably on two stiff chairs.

"Where do you come from?" she asked of Scott with polite disinterest.

"New York."

This having transpired, Yanci deigned to fix her eyes on him for the best part of ten seconds.

"Who was the gentleman with the invisible tie," Scott asked rudely, in order to make her look at him again, "who was giving you such a rush? I found it impossible to keep my eyes off him. Is his personality as diverting as his haberdashery?"

"I don't know," she drawled; "I've only been engaged to him for a week."

"My Lord!" exclaimed Scott, perspiring suddenly under his eyes. "I beg your pardon. I didn't——"

"I was only joking," she interrupted with a sighing laugh. "I thought I'd see what you'd say to that."

Then they both laughed, and Yanci continued, "I'm not engaged to anyone. I'm too horribly unpopular." Still the same key, her languorous voice humorously contradicting the content of her remark. "No one'll ever marry me."

"How pathetic!"

"Really," she murmured; "because I have to have compliments all the time, in order to live, and no one thinks I'm attractive anymore, so no one ever gives them to me."

Seldom had Scott been so amused.

"Why, you beautiful child," he cried, "I'll bet you never hear anything else from morning till night!"

"Oh, yes I do," she responded, obviously pleased. "I never get compliments unless I fish for them."

"Everything's the same," she was thinking as she gazed around her in a peculiar mood of pessimism. Same boys sober and same boys tight; same old women sitting by the walls—and one or two girls sitting with them who were dancing this time last year.

Yanci had reached the stage where these country-club dances seemed little more than a display of sheer idiocy. From being an enchanted carnival where jeweled and immaculate maidens rouged to the pinkest propriety displayed themselves to strange and fascinating men, the picture had faded to a medium-sized hall where was an almost indecent display of unclothed motives and obvious failures. So much for several years! And the dance had changed scarcely by a ruffle in the fashions or a new flip in a figure of speech.

Yanci was ready to be married.

Meanwhile the dozen remarks rushing to Scott Kimberly's lips were interrupted by the apologetic appearance of Mrs. Rogers.

"Yanci," the older woman was saying, "the chauffeur's just telephoned to say that the car's broken down. I wonder if you and your father have room for us going home. If it's the slightest inconvenience don't hesitate to tell——"

"I know he'll be terribly glad to. He's got loads of room, because I came out with someone else."

She was wondering if her father would be presentable at twelve.

He could always drive at any rate—and, besides, people who asked for a lift could take what they got.

"That'll be lovely. Thank you so much," said Mrs. Rogers.

Then, as she had just passed the kittenish late thirties when women still think they are *persona grata* with the young and entered upon the early forties when their children convey to them tactfully that they no longer are, Mrs. Rogers obliterated herself from the scene. At that moment the music started and the unfortunate young man with white streaks in his red complexion appeared in front of Yanci.

Just before the end of the next dance Scott Kimberly cut in on her again.

"I've come back," he began, "to tell you how beautiful you are."

"I'm not, really," she answered. "And, besides, you tell everyone that."

The music gathered gusto for its finale, and they sat down upon the comfortable lounge.

"I've told no one that for three years," said Scott.

There was no reason why he should have made it three years, yet somehow it sounded convincing to both of them. Her curiosity was stirred. She began finding out about him. She put him to a lazy questionnaire which began with his relationship to the Rogerses and ended, he knew not by what steps, with a detailed description of his apartment in New York.

"I want to live in New York," she told him; "on Park Avenue, in one of those beautiful white buildings that have twelve big rooms in each apartment and cost a fortune to rent."

"That's what I'd want, too, if I were married. Park Avenue—it's one of the most beautiful streets in the world, I think, perhaps chiefly because it hasn't any leprous park trying to give it an artificial suburbanity."

"Whatever that is," agreed Yanci. "Anyway, Father and I go to New York about three times a year. We always go to the Ritz."

This was not precisely true. Once a year she generally pried her father from his placid and not unbeneficent existence that she might spend a week lolling by the Fifth Avenue shop windows, lunching or having tea with some former school friend from Farmover, and occasionally going to dinner and the theatre with boys who came up from Yale or Princeton for the occasion. These had been pleasant adventures—not one but was filled to the brim with colorful hours—dancing at Montmartre, dining at the Ritz, with some movie star or supereminent society woman at the next table, or else dreaming of what she might buy at Hempel's or Waxe's or Thrumble's if her father's income had but one additional naught on the happy side of the decimal. She adored New York with a great impersonal affection—adored it as only a Middle Western or Southern girl can. In its gaudy bazaars she felt her soul transported with turbulent delight, for to her eyes it held nothing ugly, nothing sordid, nothing plain.

She had stayed once at the Ritz—once only. The Manhattan, where they usually registered, had been torn down. She knew that she could never induce her father to afford the Ritz again.

After a moment she borrowed a pencil and paper and scribbled a notification "To Mr. Bowman in the grill" that he was expected to drive Mrs. Rogers and her guest home, "by request"—this last underlined. She hoped that he would be able to do so with dignity. This note she sent by a waiter to her father. Before the next dance began it was returned to her with a scrawled O.K. and her father's initials.

The remainder of the evening passed quickly. Scott Kimberly cut in on her as often as time permitted, giving her those comforting assurances of her enduring beauty which not without a whimsical pathos she craved. He laughed at her also, and she was not so sure that she liked that. In common with all vague people, she was unaware that she was vague. She did not entirely comprehend when Scott Kimberly told her that her personality would endure long after she was too old to care whether it endured or not.

She liked best to talk about New York, and each of their interrupted conversations gave her a picture or a memory of the metropolis on which she speculated as she looked over the

shoulder of Jerry O'Rourke or Carty Braden or some other
beau, to whom, as to all of them, she was comfortably anesthetic. At midnight she sent another note to her father, saying
that Mrs. Rogers and Mrs. Rogers' guest would meet him immediately on the porch by the main driveway. Then, hoping for the
best, she walked out into the starry night and was assisted by
Jerry O'Rourke into his roadster.

III

"Good night, Yanci." With her late escort she was standing
on the curbstone in front of the rented stucco house where
she lived. Mr. O'Rourke was attempting to put significance
into his lingering rendition of her name. For weeks he had
been straining to boost their relations almost forcibly onto
a sentimental plane; but Yanci, with her vague impassivity,
which was a defense against almost anything, had brought
to naught his efforts. Jerry O'Rourke was an old story. His
family had money; but he—he worked in a brokerage house
along with most of the rest of his young generation. He sold
bonds—bonds were now the thing; real estate was once the
thing—in the days of the boom; then automobiles were the
thing. Bonds were the thing now. Young men sold them who
had nothing else to go into.

"Don't bother to come up, please." Then as he put his car into
gear, "Call me up soon!"

A minute later he turned the corner of the moonlit street and
disappeared, his cut-out resounding voluminously through the
night as it declared that the rest of two dozen weary inhabitants
was of no concern to his gay meanderings.

Yanci sat down thoughtfully upon the porch steps. She had
no key and must wait for her father's arrival. Five minutes later
a roadster turned into the street, and approaching with an exaggerated caution stopped in front of the Rogers' large house next
door. Relieved, Yanci arose and strolled slowly down the walk.
The door of the car had swung open and Mrs. Rogers, assisted
by Scott Kimberly, had alighted safely upon the sidewalk; but to
Yanci's surprise Scott Kimberly, after escorting Mrs. Rogers to
her steps, returned to the car. Yanci was close enough to notice
that he took the driver's seat. As he drew up at the Bowmans'

curbstone Yanci saw that her father was occupying the far corner, fighting with ludicrous dignity against a sleep that had come upon him. She groaned. The fatal last hour had done its work— Tom Bowman was once more *hors de combat.*

"Hello," cried Yanci as she reached the curb.

"Yanci," muttered her parent, simulating, unsuccessfully, a brisk welcome. His lips were curved in an ingratiating grin.

"Your father wasn't feeling quite fit, so he let me drive home," explained Scott cheerfully as he got himself out and came up to her.

"Nice little car. Had it long?"

Yanci laughed, but without humor.

"Is he paralyzed?"

"Is who paralyze'?" demanded the figure in the car with an offended sigh.

Scott was standing by the car.

"Can I help you out, sir?"

"I c'n get out. I c'n get out," insisted Mr. Bowman. "Just step a li'l' out my way. Someone must have given me some stremely bad wisk'."

"You mean a lot of people must have given you some," retorted Yanci in cold unsympathy.

Mr. Bowman reached the curb with astonishing ease; but this was a deceitful success, for almost immediately he clutched at a handle of air perceptible only to himself, and was saved by Scott's quickly proffered arm. Followed by the two men, Yanci walked toward the house in a furor of embarrassment. Would the young man think that such scenes went on every night? It was chiefly her own presence that made it humiliating for Yanci. Had her father been carried to bed by two butlers each evening she might even have been proud of the fact that he could afford such dissipation; but to have it thought that she assisted, that she was burdened with the worry and the care! And finally she was annoyed with Scott Kimberly for being there, and for his officiousness in helping to bring her father into the house.

Reaching the low porch of tapestry brick, Yanci searched in Tom Bowman's vest for the key and unlocked the front door. A minute later the master of the house was deposited in an easy-chair.

"Thanks very much," he said, recovering for a moment. "Sit down. Like a drink? Yanci, get some crackers and cheese, if there's any, won't you, dear?"

At the unconscious coolness of this Scott and Yanci laughed.

"It's your bedtime, Father," she said, her anger struggling with diplomacy.

"Give me my guitar," he suggested, "and I'll play you tune."

Except on such occasions as this, he had not touched his guitar for twenty years. Yanci turned to Scott.

"He'll be fine now. Thanks a lot. He'll fall asleep in a minute and when I wake him he'll go to bed like a lamb."

"Well——"

They strolled together out the door.

"Sleepy?" he asked.

"No, not a bit."

"Then perhaps you'd better let me stay here with you a few minutes until you see if he's all right. Mrs. Rogers gave me a key so I can get in without disturbing her."

"It's quite all right," protested Yanci. "I don't mind a bit, and he won't be any trouble. He must have taken a glass too much, and this whisky we have out here—you know! This has happened once before—last year," she added.

Her words satisfied her; as an explanation it seemed to have a convincing ring.

"Can I sit down for a moment, anyway?" They sat side by side upon a wicker porch settee.

"I'm thinking of staying over a few days," Scott said.

"How lovely!" Her voice had resumed its die-away note.

"Cousin Pete Rogers wasn't well today, but tomorrow he's going duck shooting, and he wants me to go with him."

"Oh, how thrill-ing! I've always been mad to go, and Father's always promised to take me, but he never has."

"We're going to be gone about three days, and then I thought I'd come back here and stay over the next week-end——" He broke off suddenly and bent forward in a listening attitude.

"Now what on earth is that?"

The sounds of music were proceeding brokenly from the room they had lately left—a ragged chord on a guitar and half a dozen feeble starts.

"It's father!" cried Yanci.

And now a voice drifted out to them, drunken and murmurous, taking the long notes with attempted melancholy:

> *Sing a song of cities,*
> *Ridin' on a rail,*
> *A niggah's ne'er so happy*
> *As when he's out-a jail.*

"How terrible!" exclaimed Yanci. "He'll wake up everybody in the block."

The chorus ended, the guitar jangled again, then gave out a last harsh spang! and was still. A moment later these disturbances were followed by a low but quite definite snore. Mr. Bowman, having indulged his musical proclivity, had dropped off to sleep.

"Let's go to ride," suggested Yanci impatiently. "This is too hectic for me."

Scott arose with alacrity and they walked down to the car.

"Where'll we go?" she wondered.

"I don't care."

"We might go up half a block to Crest Avenue—that's our show street—and then ride out to the river boulevard."

IV

As they turned into Crest Avenue the new cathedral, immense and unfinished, in imitation of a cathedral left unfinished by accident in some little Flemish town, squatted just across the way like a plump white bulldog on its haunches. The ghosts of four moonlit apostles looked down at them wanly from wall niches still littered with the white, dusty trash of the builders. The cathedral inaugurated Crest Avenue. After it came the great brownstone mass built by R. R. Comerford, the flour king, followed by a half mile of pretentious stone houses put up in the gloomy 90's. These were adorned with monstrous driveways and porte-cochères which had once echoed to the hoofs of good horses and with huge circular windows that corseted the second stories.

The continuity of these mausoleums was broken by a small park, a triangle of grass where Nathan Hale stood ten feet tall with his hands bound behind his back by stone cord and stared over a great bluff at the slow Mississippi. Crest Avenue ran along the bluff, but neither faced it nor seemed aware of it, for all the houses fronted inward toward the street. Beyond the first half mile it became newer, essayed ventures in terraced lawns, in concoctions of stucco or in granite mansions which imitated through a variety of gradual refinements the marble contours of the Petit Trianon. The houses of this phase rushed by the roadster for a succession of minutes; then the way turned and the car was headed directly into the moonlight which swept toward it like the lamp of some gigantic motorcycle far up the avenue.

Past the low Corinthian lines of the Christian Science Temple, past a block of dark frame horrors, a deserted row of grim red brick—an unfortunate experiment of the late 90's—then new houses again, bright-red brick now, with trimmings of white, black iron fences and hedges binding flowery lawns. These swept by, faded, passed, enjoying their moment of grandeur; then waiting there in the moonlight to be outmoded as had the frame, cupolaed mansions of lower town and the brownstone piles of older Crest Avenue in their turn.

The roofs lowered suddenly, the lots narrowed, the houses shrank up in size and shaded off into bungalows. These held the street for the last mile, to the bend in the river which terminated the prideful avenue at the statue of Chelsea Arbuthnot. Arbuthnot was the first governor—and almost the last of Anglo-Saxon blood.

All the way thus far Yanci had not spoken, absorbed still in the annoyance of the evening, yet soothed somehow by the fresh air of Northern November that rushed by them. She must take her fur coat out of storage next day, she thought.

"Where are we now?"

As they slowed down Scott looked up curiously at the pompous stone figure, clear in the crisp moonlight, with one hand on a book and the forefinger of the other pointing, as though with reproachful symbolism, directly at some construction work going on in the street.

"This is the end of Crest Avenue," said Yanci, turning to him. "This is our show street."

"A museum of American architectural failures."

"What?"

"Nothing," he murmured.

"I should have explained it to you. I forgot. We can go along the river boulevard if you'd like—or are you tired?"

Scott assured her that he was not tired—not in the least.

Entering the boulevard, the cement road twisted under darkling trees.

"The Mississippi—how little it means to you now!" said Scott suddenly.

"What?" Yanci looked around. "Oh, the river."

"I guess it was once pretty important to your ancestors up here."

"My ancestors weren't up here then," said Yanci with some dignity. "My ancestors were from Maryland. My father came out here when he left Yale."

"Oh!" Scott was politely impressed.

"My mother was from here. My father came out here from Baltimore because of his health."

"Oh!"

"Of course we belong here now, I suppose"—this with faint condescension—"as much as anywhere else."

"Of course."

"Except that I want to live in the East and I can't persuade Father to," she finished.

It was after one o'clock and the boulevard was almost deserted. Occasionally two yellow disks would top a rise ahead of them and take shape as a late-returning automobile. Except for that they were alone in a continual rushing dark. The moon had gone down.

"Next time the road goes near the river let's stop and watch it," he suggested.

Yanci smiled inwardly. This remark was obviously what one boy of her acquaintance had named an international petting cue, by which was meant a suggestion that aimed to create naturally a situation for a kiss. She considered the matter. As yet the man had made no particular impression on her. He was good-looking, apparently well-to-do and from New York. She had begun to like him during the dance, increasingly as the evening had drawn to a close; then the incident of her father's appalling arrival had thrown cold water upon this tentative warmth; and now—it was November, and the night was cold. Still——

"All right," she agreed suddenly.

The road divided; she swerved around and brought the car to a stop in an open place high above the river.

"Well?" she demanded in the deep quiet that followed the shutting off of the engine.

"Thanks."

"Are you satisfied here?"

"Almost. Not quite."

"Why not?"

"I'll tell you in a minute," he answered. "Why is your name Yanci?"

"It's a family name."

"It's very pretty." He repeated it several times caressingly. "Yanci—it has all the grace of Nancy, and yet it isn't prim."

"What's your name?" she inquired.

"Scott."

"Scott what?"

"Kimberly. Didn't you know?"

"I wasn't sure. Mrs. Rogers introduced you in such a mumble."

There was a slight pause.

"Yanci," he repeated; "beautiful Yanci, with her dark-blue eyes and her lazy soul. Do you know why I'm not quite satisfied, Yanci?"

"Why?"

Imperceptibly she had moved her face nearer until as she waited for an answer with her lips faintly apart he knew that in asking she had granted.

Without haste he bent his head forward and touched her lips.

He sighed, and both of them felt a sort of relief—relief from the embarrassment of playing up to what conventions of this sort of thing remained.

"Thanks," he said as he had when she first stopped the car.

"Now are you satisfied?"

Her blue eyes regarded him unsmilingly in the darkness.

"After a fashion; of course, you can never say—definitely."

Again he bent toward her, but she stooped and started the motor. It was late and Yanci was beginning to be tired. What purpose there was in the experiment was accomplished. He had had what he asked. If he liked it he would want more, and that put her one move ahead in the game which she felt she was beginning.

"I'm hungry," she complained. "Let's go down and eat."

"Very well," he acquiesced sadly. "Just when I was so enjoying—the Mississippi."

"Do you think I'm beautiful?" she inquired almost plaintively as they backed out.

"What an absurd question!"

"But I like to hear people say so."

"I was just about to—when you started the engine."

Downtown in a deserted all-night lunch room they ate bacon and eggs. She was pale as ivory now. The night had drawn the lazy vitality and languid color out of her face. She encouraged him to talk to her of New York until he was beginning every sentence with, "Well, now, let's see——"

The repast over, they drove home. Scott helped her put the car in the little garage, and just outside the front door she lent him her lips again for the faint brush of a kiss. Then she went in.

The long living room which ran the width of the small stucco house was reddened by a dying fire which had been high when Yanci left and now was faded to a steady undancing glow. She took a log from the fire box and threw it on the embers, then started as a voice came out of the half-darkness at the other end of the room.

"Back so soon?"

It was her father's voice, not yet quite sober, but alert and intelligent.

"Yes. Went riding," she answered shortly, sitting down in a wicker chair before the fire. "Then went down and had something to eat."

"Oh!"

Her father left his place and moved to a chair nearer the fire, where he stretched himself out with a sigh. Glancing at him from the corner of her eye, for she was going to show an appropriate coldness, Yanci was fascinated by his complete recovery of dignity in the space of two hours. His greying hair was scarcely rumpled; his handsome face was ruddy as ever. Only his eyes, crisscrossed with tiny red lines, were evidence of his late dissipation.

"Have a good time?"

"Why should you care?" she answered rudely.

"Why shouldn't I?"

"You didn't seem to care earlier in the evening. I asked you to take two people home for me, and you weren't able to drive your own car."

"The deuce I wasn't!" he protested. "I could have driven in—in a race in an arana, areaena. That Mrs. Rogers insisted that her young admirer should drive, so what could I do?"

"That isn't her young admirer," retorted Yanci crisply. There was no drawl in her voice now. "She's as old as you are. That's her niece—I mean her nephew."

"Excuse me!"

"I think you owe me an apology." She found suddenly that she bore him no resentment. She was rather sorry for him, and it occurred to her that in asking him to take Mrs. Rogers home she had somehow imposed on his liberty. Nevertheless, discipline was necessary—there would be other Saturday nights. "Don't you?" she concluded.

"I apologize, Yanci."

"Very well, I accept your apology," she answered stiffly.

"What's more, I'll make it up to you."

Her blue eyes contracted. She hoped—she hardly dared to hope that he might take her to New York.

"Let's see," he said. "November, isn't it? What date?"

"The twenty-third."

"Well, I'll tell you what I'll do." He knocked the tips of his fingers together tentatively. "I'll give you a present. I've been meaning to let you have a trip all fall, but business has been bad." She almost smiled—as though business was of any consequence in his life. "But then you need a trip. I'll make you a present of it."

He rose again, and crossing over to his desk sat down.

"I've got a little money in a New York bank that's been lying there quite a while," he said as he fumbled in a drawer for a check book. "I've been intending to close out the account. Let—me—see. There's just——" His pen scratched. "Where the devil's the blotter? Uh!"

He came back to the fire and a pink oblong paper fluttered into her lap.

"Why, Father!"

It was a check for three hundred dollars.

"But can you afford this?" she demanded.

"It's all right," he reassured her, nodding. "That can be a Christmas present, too, and you'll probably need a dress or a hat or something before you go."

"Why," she began uncertainly, "I hardly know whether I ought to take this much or not! I've got two hundred of my own downtown, you know. Are you sure——"

"Oh, yes!" He waved his hand with magnificent carelessness. "You need a holiday. You've been talking about New York, and I want you to go down there. Tell some of your friends at Yale and the other colleges and they'll ask you to the prom or something. That'll be nice. You'll have a good time."

He sat down abruptly in his chair and gave vent to a long sigh. Yanci folded up the check and tucked it into the low bosom of her dress.

"Well," she drawled softly with a return to her usual manner, "you're a perfect lamb to be so sweet about it, but I don't want to be horribly extravagant."

Her father did not answer. He gave another little sigh and relaxed sleepily into his chair.

"Of course I do want to go," went on Yanci.

Still her father was silent. She wondered if he were asleep.

"Are you asleep?" she demanded, cheerfully now. She bent toward him; then she stood up and looked at him.

"Father," she said uncertainly.

Her father remained motionless; the ruddy color had melted suddenly out of his face.

"Father!"

It occurred to her—and at the thought she grew cold, and a brassière of iron clutched at her breast—that she was alone in the room. After a frantic instant she said to herself that her father was dead.

V

Yanci judged herself with inevitable gentleness—judged herself very much as a mother might judge a wild, spoiled child. She was not hard-minded, nor did she live by any ordered and considered philosophy of her own. To such a catastrophe as the death of her father her immediate reaction was a hysterical self-pity. The first three days were something of a nightmare; but sentimental civilization, being as infallible as Nature in healing the wounds of its more fortunate children, had inspired a certain Mrs. Oral, whom Yanci had always loathed, with a passionate interest in all such crises. To all intents and purposes Mrs. Oral buried Tom Bowman. The morning after his death Yanci had wired her maternal aunt in Chicago, but as yet that undemonstrative and well-to-do lady had sent no answer.

All day long, for four days, Yanci sat in her room upstairs, hearing steps come and go on the porch, and it merely increased her nervousness that the doorbell had been disconnected. This by order of Mrs. Oral! Doorbells were always disconnected! After the burial of the dead the strain relaxed. Yanci, dressed in her new black, regarded herself in the pier glass, and then wept because she seemed to herself very sad and beautiful. She went downstairs and tried to read a moving-picture magazine, hoping that she would not be alone in the house when the winter dark came down just after four.

This afternoon Mrs. Oral had said *carpe diem* to the maid, and Yanci was just starting for the kitchen to see whether she had yet gone when the reconnected bell rang suddenly through the house. Yanci started. She waited a minute, then went to the door. It was Scott Kimberly.

"I was just going to inquire for you," he said.

"Oh! I'm much better, thank you," she responded with the quiet dignity that seemed suited to her role.

They stood there in the hall awkwardly, each reconstructing the half-facetious, half-sentimental occasion on which they had last met. It seemed such an irreverent prelude to such a somber disaster. There was no common ground for them now, no gap that could be bridged by a slight reference to their mutual past, and there was no foundation on which he could adequately pretend to share her sorrow.

"Won't you come in?" she said, biting her lip nervously. He followed her to the sitting room and sat beside her on the lounge. In another minute, simply because he was there and alive and friendly, she was crying on his shoulder.

"There, there!" he said, putting his arm behind her and patting her shoulder idiotically. "There, there, there!"

He was wise enough to attribute no ulterior significance to her action. She was overstrained with grief and loneliness and sentiment; almost any shoulder would have done as well. For all the biological thrill to either of them he might have been a hundred years old. In a minute she sat up.

"I beg your pardon," she murmured brokenly. "But it's—it's so dismal in this house today."

"I know just how you feel, Yanci."

"Did I—did I—get—tears on your coat?"

In tribute to the tenseness of the incident they both laughed hysterically, and with the laughter she momentarily recovered her propriety.

"I don't know why I should have chosen you to collapse on," she wailed. "I really don't just go round doing it in-indiscriminately on anyone who comes in."

"I consider it a—a compliment," he responded soberly, "and I can understand the state you're in." Then, after a pause, "Have you any plans?"

She shook her head.

"Va-vague ones," she muttered between little gasps. "I tho-ought I'd go down and stay with my aunt in Chicago awhile."

"I should think that'd be best—much the best thing." Then, because he could think of nothing else to say, he added, "Yes, very much the best thing."

"What are you doing—here in town?" she inquired, taking in her breath in minute gasps and dabbing at her eyes with a handkerchief.

"Oh, I'm here with—with the Rogerses. I've been here."

"Hunting?"

"No, I've just been here."

He did not tell her that he had stayed over on her account. She might think it fresh.

"I see," she said. She didn't see.

"I want to know if there's any possible thing I can do for you, Yanci. Perhaps go downtown for you, or do some errands— anything. Maybe you'd like to bundle up and get a bit of air. I could take you out to drive in your car some night, and no one would see you."

He clipped his last word short as the inadvertency of this suggestion dawned on him. They stared at each other with horror in their eyes.

"Oh, no, thank you!" she cried. "I really don't want to drive."

To his relief the outer door opened and an elderly lady came in. It was Mrs. Oral. Scott rose immediately and moved backward toward the door.

"If you're sure there isn't anything I can do——"

Yanci introduced him to Mrs. Oral; then leaving the elder woman by the fire walked with him to the door. An idea had suddenly occurred to her.

"Wait a minute."

She ran up the front stairs and returned immediately with a slip of pink paper in her hand.

"Here's something I wish you'd do," she said. "Take this to the First National Bank and have it cashed for me. You can leave the money here for me any time."

Scott took out his wallet and opened it.

"Suppose I cash it for you now," he suggested.

"Oh, there's no hurry."

"But I may as well." He drew out three new one-hundred-dollar bills and gave them to her.

"That's awfully sweet of you," said Yanci.

"Not at all. May I come in and see you next time I come West?"

"I wish you would."

"Then I will. I'm going East tonight."

The door shut him out into the snowy dusk and Yanci returned to Mrs. Oral. Mrs. Oral had come to discuss plans.

"And now, my dear, just what do you plan to do? We ought to have some plan to go by, and I thought I'd find out if you had any definite plan in your mind."

Yanci tried to think. She seemed to herself to be horribly alone in the world.

"I haven't heard from my aunt. I wired her again this morning. She may be in Florida."

"In that case you'd go there?"

"I suppose so."

"Would you close this house?"

"I suppose so."

Mrs. Oral glanced around with placid practicality. It occurred to her that if Yanci gave the house up she might like it for herself.

"And now," she continued, "do you know where you stand financially?"

"All right, I guess," answered Yanci indifferently. And then with a rush of sentiment, "There was enough for t-two; there ought to be enough for o-one."

"I didn't mean that," said Mrs. Oral. "I mean, do you know the details?"

"No."

"Well, I thought you didn't know the details. And I thought you ought to know all the details—have a detailed account of what and where your money is. So I called up Mr. Haedge, who knew your father very well personally, to come up this afternoon and glance through his papers. He was going to stop in your father's bank, too, by the way, and get all the details there. I don't believe your father left any will."

Details! Details! Details!

"Thank you," said Yanci. "That'll be—nice."

Mrs. Oral gave three or four vigorous nods that were like heavy periods. Then she got up.

"And now if Hilma's gone out I'll make you some tea. Would you like some tea?"

"Sort of."

"All right, I'll make you some ni-ice tea."

Tea! Tea! Tea!

Mr. Haedge, who came from one of the best Swedish families in town, arrived to see Yanci at five o'clock. He greeted her funereally; said that he had been several times to inquire for her; had organized the pallbearers and would now find out how she stood in no time. Did she have any idea whether or not there was a will? No? Well, there probably wasn't one.

There was one. He found it almost at once in Mr. Bowman's desk—but he worked there until eleven o'clock that night before he found much else. Next morning he arrived at eight, went down to the bank at ten, then to a certain brokerage firm, and came back to Yanci's house at noon. He had known Tom Bowman for some years, but he was utterly astounded when he discovered the condition in which that handsome gallant had left his affairs.

He consulted Mrs. Oral, and that afternoon he informed a frightened Yanci in measured language that she was practically penniless. In the midst of the conversation a telegram from Chicago told her that her aunt had sailed the week previous for a trip through the Orient and was not expected back until late spring.

The beautiful Yanci, so profuse, so debonair, so careless with her gorgeous adjectives, had no adjectives for this calamity. She crept upstairs like a hurt child and sat before a mirror, brushing her luxurious hair to comfort herself. One hundred and fifty strokes she gave it, as it said in the treatment, and then a hundred and fifty more—she was too distraught to stop the nervous motion. She brushed it until her arm ached, then she changed arms and went on brushing.

The maid found her next morning, asleep, sprawled across the toilet things on the dresser in a room that was heavy and sweet with the scent of spilled perfume.

VI

To be precise, as Mr. Haedge was to a depressing degree, Tom Bowman left a bank balance that was more than ample—that is to say, more than ample to supply the post-mortem requirements of his own person. There was also twenty years' worth of furniture, a temperamental roadster with asthmatic cylinders and two one-thousand-dollar bonds of a chain of jewelry stores which yielded 7.5 per cent interest. Unfortunately these were not known in the bond market.

When the car and the furniture had been sold and the stucco bungalow sublet, Yanci contemplated her resources with dismay. She had a bank balance of almost a thousand dollars. If she invested this she would increase her total income to about fifteen dollars a month. This, as Mrs. Oral cheerfully observed, would pay for the boarding-house room she had taken for Yanci as long as Yanci lived. Yanci was so encouraged by this news that she burst into tears.

So she acted as any beautiful girl would have acted in this emergency. With rare decision she told Mr. Haedge that she would leave her thousand dollars in a checking account, and then she walked out of his office and across the street to a beauty parlor to have her hair waved. This raised her morale astonishingly. Indeed, she moved that very day out of the boarding house and into a small room at the best hotel in town. If she must sink into poverty she would at least do so in the grand manner.

Sewed into the lining of her best mourning hat were the three new one-hundred-dollar bills, her father's last present. What she expected of them, why she kept them in such a way, she did not know, unless perhaps because they had come to her under cheerful auspices and might through some gayety inherent in their crisp and virgin paper buy happier things than solitary meals and narrow hotel beds. They were hope and youth and luck and beauty; they began, somehow, to stand for all the things she had lost in that November night when Tom Bowman, having led her recklessly into space, had plunged off himself, leaving her to find the way back alone.

Yanci remained at the Hiawatha Hotel for three months, and she found that after the first visits of condolence her friends had happier things to do with their time than to spend it in her company. Jerry O'Rourke came to see her one day with a wild Celtic look in his eyes, and demanded that she marry him immediately. When she asked for time to consider he walked out in a rage. She heard later that he had been offered a position in Chicago and had left the same night.

She considered, frightened and uncertain. She had heard of people sinking out of place, out of life. Her father had once told her of a man in his class at college who had become a worker around saloons, polishing brass rails for the price of a can of beer; and she knew also that there were girls in this city with whose mothers her own mother had played as a little girl, but who were poor now and had grown common; who worked in stores and had married into the proletariat. But that such a fate should threaten her—how absurd! Why, she knew everyone! She had been invited everywhere; her great-grandfather had been governor of one of the Southern states!

She had written to her aunt in India and again in China, receiving no answer. She concluded that her aunt's itinerary had changed, and this was confirmed when a post card arrived from Honolulu which showed no knowledge of Tom Bowman's death, but announced that she was going with a party to the east coast of Africa. This was a last straw. The languorous and lackadaisical Yanci was on her own at last.

"Why not go to work for awhile?" suggested Mr. Haedge with some irritation. "Lots of nice girls do nowadays, just for something to occupy themselves with. There's Elsie Prendergast, who does society news on the 'Bulletin,' and that Semple girl——"

"I can't," said Yanci shortly with a glitter of tears in her eyes. "I'm going East in February."

"East? Oh, you're going to visit someone?"

She nodded.

"Yes, I'm going to visit," she lied, "so it'd hardly be worth while to go to work." She could have wept, but she managed a haughty look. "I'd like to try reporting sometime, though, just for the fun of it."

"Yes, it's quite a lot of fun," agreed Mr. Haedge with some irony. "Still, I suppose there's no hurry about it. You must have plenty of that thousand dollars left."

"Oh, plenty!"

There were a few hundred, she knew.

"Well, then I suppose a good rest, a change of scene would be the best thing for you."

"Yes," answered Yanci. Her lips were trembling and she rose, scarcely able to control herself. Mr. Haedge seemed so impersonally cold. "That's why I'm going. A good rest is what I need."

"I think you're wise."

What Mr. Haedge would have thought had he seen the dozen drafts she wrote that night of a certain letter is problematical. Here are two of the earlier ones. The bracketed words are proposed substitutions:

> *Dear Scott:* Not having seen you since that day I was such a silly ass and wept on your coat, I thought I'd write and tell you that I'm coming East pretty soon and would like you to have lunch [dinner] with me or something. I have been living in a room [suite] at the Hiawatha Hotel, intending to meet my aunt, with whom I am going to live [stay], and who is coming back from China this month [spring]. Meanwhile I have a lot of invitations to visit, etc., in the East, and I thought I would do it now. So I'd like to see you——

This draft ended here and went into the wastebasket. After an hour's work she produced the following:

> *My dear Mr. Kimberly:* I have often [sometimes] wondered how you've been since I saw you. I am coming East next month

before going to visit my aunt in Chicago, and you must come
and see me. I have been going out very little, but my physician
advises me that I need a change, so I expect to shock the pro-
prieties by some very gay visits in the East——

Finally in despondent abandon she wrote a simple note without explanation or subterfuge, tore it up and went to bed. Next
morning she identified it in the wastebasket, decided it was the
best one after all and sent him a fair copy. It ran:

Dear Scott: Just a line to tell you I will be at the Ritz-Carlton
Hotel from February seventh, probably for ten days. If you'll
phone me some rainy afternoon I'll invite you to tea.

Sincerely,
YANCI BOWMAN.

VII

Yanci was going to the Ritz for no more reason than that she
had once told Scott Kimberly that she always went there. When
she reached New York—a cold New York, a strangely menacing New York, quite different from the gay city of theatres
and hotel-corridor rendezvous that she had known—there was
exactly two hundred dollars in her purse.

It had taken a large part of her bank account to live, and
she had at last broken into her sacred three hundred dollars to
substitute pretty and delicate quarter-mourning clothes for the
heavy black she had laid away.

Walking into the hotel at the moment when its exquisitely
dressed patrons were assembling for luncheon, it drained at
her confidence to appear bored and at ease. Surely the clerks
at the desk knew the contents of her pocketbook. She fancied
even that the bell boys were snickering at the foreign labels she
had steamed from an old trunk of her father's and pasted on
her suitcase. This last thought horrified her. Perhaps the very
hotels and steamers so grandly named had long since been out
of commission!

As she stood drumming her fingers on the desk she was
wondering whether if she were refused admittance she could
muster a casual smile and stroll out coolly enough to deceive

two richly dressed women standing near. It had not taken long for the confidence of twenty years to evaporate. Three months without security had made an ineffaceable mark on Yanci's soul.

"Twenty-four sixty-two," said the clerk callously.

Her heart settled back into place as she followed the bell-boy to the elevator, meanwhile casting a nonchalant glance at the two fashionable women as she passed them. Were their skirts long or short?—longer, she noticed.

She wondered how much the skirt of her new walking suit could be let out.

At luncheon her spirits soared. The head-waiter bowed to her. The light rattle of conversation, the subdued hum of the music soothed her. She ordered supreme of melon, eggs Susette and an artichoke, and signed her room number to the check with scarcely a glance at it as it lay beside her plate. Up in her room, with the telephone directory open on the bed before her, she tried to locate her scattered metropolitan acquaintances. Yet even as the phone numbers, with their supercilious tags, Plaza, Circle and Rhinelander, stared out at her, she could feel a cold wind blow at her unstable confidence. These girls, acquaintances of school, of a summer, of a house party, even of a week-end at a college prom—what claim or attraction could she, poor and friendless, exercise over them? They had their loves, their dates, their week's gayety planned in advance. They would almost resent her inconvenient memory.

Nevertheless, she called four girls. One of them was out, one at Palm Beach, one in California. The only one to whom she talked said in a hearty voice that she was in bed with grippe, but would phone Yanci as soon as she felt well enough to go out. Then Yanci gave up the girls. She would have to create the illusion of a good time in some other manner. The illusion must be created—that was part of her plan.

She looked at her watch and found that it was three o'clock. Scott Kimberly should have phoned before this, or at least left some word. Still, he was probably busy—at a club, she thought vaguely, or else buying some neckties. He would probably call at four.

Yanci was well aware that she must work quickly. She had figured to a nicety that one hundred and fifty dollars carefully expended would carry her through two weeks, no more. The idea of failure, the fear that at the end of that time she would be friendless and penniless had not begun to bother her.

It was not the first time that for amusement, for a coveted invitation or for curiosity she had deliberately set out to capture a man; but it was the first time she had laid her plans with necessity and desperation pressing in on her.

One of her strongest cards had always been her background, the impression she gave that she was popular and desired and happy. This she must create now, and apparently out of nothing. Scott must somehow be brought to think that a fair portion of New York was at her feet.

At four she went over to Park Avenue, where the sun was out walking and the February day was fresh and odorous of spring and the high apartments of her desire lined the street with radiant whiteness. Here she would live on a gay schedule of pleasure. In these smart not-to-be-entered-without-a-card women's shops she would spend the morning hours acquiring and acquiring, ceaselessly and without thought of expense; in these restaurants she would lunch at noon in company with other fashionable women, orchid-adorned always, and perhaps bearing an absurdly dwarfed Pomeranian in her sleek arms.

In the summer—well, she would go to Tuxedo, perhaps to an immaculate house perched high on a fashionable eminence, where she would emerge to visit a world of teas and balls, of horse shows and polo. Between the halves of the polo game the players would cluster around her in their white suits and helmets, admiringly, and when she swept away, bound for some new delight, she would be followed by the eyes of many envious but intimidated women.

Every other summer they would, of course, go abroad. She began to plan a typical year, distributing a few months here and a few months there until she—and Scott Kimberly, by implication—would become the very auguries of the season, shifting with the slightest stirring of the social barometer from rusticity to urbanity, from palm to pine.

She had two weeks, no more, in which to attain to this position. In an ecstasy of determined emotion she lifted up her head toward the tallest of the tall white apartments.

"It will be too marvelous!" she said to herself.

For almost the first time in her life her words were not too exaggerated to express the wonder shining in her eyes.

VIII

About five o'clock she hurried back to the hotel, demanding feverishly at the desk if there had been a telephone message for her. To her profound disappointment there was nothing. A minute after she had entered her room the phone rang.

"This is Scott Kimberly."

At the words a call to battle echoed in her heart.

"Oh, how do you do?"

Her tone implied that she had almost forgotten him. It was not frigid—it was merely casual.

As she answered the inevitable question as to the hour when she had arrived, a warm glow spread over her. Now that, from a personification of all the riches and pleasure she craved, he had materialized as merely a male voice over the telephone, her confidence became strengthened. Male voices were male voices. They could be managed; they could be made to intone syllables of which the minds behind them had no approval. Male voices could be made sad or tender or despairing at her will. She rejoiced. The soft clay was ready to her hand.

"Won't you take dinner with me tonight?" Scott was suggesting.

"Why"—perhaps not, she thought; let him think of her tonight—"I don't believe I'll be able to," she said. "I've got an engagement for dinner and the theatre. I'm terribly sorry."

Her voice did not sound sorry—it sounded polite. Then as though a happy thought had occurred to her as to a time and place where she could work him into her list of dates, "I'll tell you: Why don't you come around here this afternoon and have tea with me?"

He would be there immediately. He had been playing squash and as soon as he took a plunge he would arrive. Yanci hung up the phone and turned with a quiet efficiency to the mirror, too tense to smile.

She regarded her lustrous eyes and dusky hair in critical approval. Then she took a lavender tea gown from her trunk and began to dress.

She let him wait seven minutes in the lobby before she appeared; then she approached him with a friendly, lazy smile.

"How do you do?" she murmured. "It's marvelous to see you again. How are you?" And, with a long sigh, "I'm frightfully tired. I've been on the go ever since I got here this morning; shopping and then tearing off to luncheon and a matinée. I've bought everything I saw. I don't know how I'm going to pay for it all."

She remembered vividly that when they had first met she had told him, without expecting to be believed, how unpopular she was. She could not risk such a remark now, even in jest. He must think that she had been on the go every minute of the day.

They took a table and were served with olive sandwiches and tea. He was so good-looking, she thought, and marvelously dressed. His grey eyes regarded her with interest from under immaculate ash-blond hair. She wondered how he passed his days, how he liked her costume, what he was thinking of at that moment.

"How long will you be here?" he asked.

"Well, two weeks, off and on. I'm going down to Princeton for the February prom and then up to a house party in Westchester County for a few days. Are you shocked at me for going out so soon? Father would have wanted me to, you know. He was very modern in all his ideas."

She had debated this remark on the train. She was not going to a house party. She was not invited to the Princeton prom. Such things, nevertheless, were necessary to create the illusion. That was everything—the illusion.

"And then," she continued, smiling, "two of my old beaus are in town, which makes it nice for me."

She saw Scott blink and she knew that he appreciated the significance of this.

"What are your plans for this winter?" he demanded. "Are you going back West?"

"No. You see, my aunt returns from India this week. She's going to open her Florida house, and we'll stay there until the middle of March. Then we'll come up to Hot Springs and we may go to Europe for the summer."

This was all the sheerest fiction. Her first letter to her aunt, which had given the bare details of Tom Bowman's death, had at last reached its destination. Her aunt had replied with a note of conventional sympathy and the announcement that she would be back in America within two years if she didn't decide to live in Italy.

"But you'll let me see something of you while you're here," urged Scott, after attending to this impressive program. "If you can't take dinner with me tonight, how about Wednesday—that's the day after tomorrow?"

"Wednesday? Let's see." Yanci's brow was knit with imitation thought. "I think I have a date for Wednesday, but I don't know for certain. How about phoning me tomorrow, and I'll let you know? Because I want to go with you, only I think I've made an engagement."

"Very well, I'll phone you."

"Do—about ten."

"Try to be able to—then or any time."

"I'll tell you—if I can't go to dinner with you Wednesday I can go to lunch surely."

"All right," he agreed. "And we'll go to a matinée."

They danced several times. Never by word or sign did Yanci betray more than the most cursory interest in him until just at the end, when she offered him her hand to say good-bye.

"Good-bye, Scott."

For just the fraction of a second—not long enough for him to be sure it had happened at all, but just enough so that he would be reminded, however faintly, of that night on the Mississippi boulevard—she looked into his eyes. Then she turned quickly and hurried away.

She took her dinner in a little tea room around the corner. It was an economical dinner which cost a dollar and a half. There was no date concerned in it at all, and no man except an elderly person in spats who tried to speak to her as she came out the door.

IX

Sitting alone in one of the magnificent moving-picture theatres—a luxury which she thought she could afford—Yanci watched Mae Murray swirl through splendidly imagined vistas, and meanwhile considered the progress of the first day. In retrospect it was a distinct success. She had given the correct impression both as to her material prosperity and as to her attitude toward Scott himself. It seemed best to avoid evening dates.

Let him have the evenings to himself, to think of her, to imagine her with other men, even to spend a few lonely hours in his apartment, considering how much more cheerful it might be if—— Let time and absence work for her.

Engrossed for awhile in the moving picture, she calculated the cost of the apartment in which its heroine endured her movie wrongs. She admired its slender Italian table, occupying only one side of the large dining room and flanked by a long bench which gave it an air of medieval luxury. She rejoiced in the beauty of Mae Murray's clothes and furs, her gorgeous hats, her short-seeming French shoes. Then after a moment her mind returned to her own drama; she wondered if Scott were already engaged, and her heart dipped at the thought. Yet it was unlikely. He had been too quick to phone her on her arrival, too lavish with his time, too responsive that afternoon.

After the picture she returned to the Ritz, where she slept deeply and happily for almost the first time in three months. The atmosphere around her no longer seemed cold. Even the floor clerk had smiled kindly and admiringly when Yanci asked for her key.

Next morning at ten Scott phoned. Yanci, who had been up for hours, pretended to be drowsy from her dissipation of the night before.

No, she could not take dinner with him on Wednesday. She was terribly sorry; she had an engagement, as she had feared. But she could have luncheon and go to a matinée if he would get her back in time for tea.

She spent the day roving the streets. On top of a bus, though not on the front seat, where Scott might possibly spy her, she sailed out Riverside Drive and back along Fifth Avenue just at the winter twilight, and her feeling for New York and its gorgeous splendors deepened and redoubled. Here she must live and be rich, be nodded to by the traffic policemen at the corners as she sat in her limousine—with a small dog—and here she must stroll on Sunday to and from a stylish church, with Scott, handsome in his cutaway and tall hat, walking devotedly at her side.

At luncheon on Wednesday she described for Scott's benefit a fanciful two days. She told of a motoring trip up the Hudson and gave him her opinion of two plays she had seen with—it was implied—adoring gentlemen beside her. She had read up very carefully on the plays in the morning paper and chosen two concerning which she could garner the most information.

"Oh," he said in dismay, "you've seen 'Dulcy'? I have two seats for it—but you won't want to go again."

"Oh, no, I don't mind," she protested truthfully. "You see, we went late, and anyway I adored it."

But he wouldn't hear of her sitting through it again—besides, he had seen it himself. It was a play Yanci was mad to see, but she was compelled to watch him while he exchanged the tickets for others, and for the poor seats available at the last moment. The game seemed difficult at times.

"By the way," he said afterwards as they drove back to the hotel in a taxi, "you'll be going down to the Princeton prom tomorrow, won't you?"

She started. She had not realized that it would be so soon or that he would know of it.

"Yes," she answered coolly. "I'm going down tomorrow afternoon."

"On the 2:20, I suppose," Scott commented. And then, "Are you going to meet the boy who's taking you down—at Princeton?"

For an instant she was off her guard.

"Yes, he'll meet the train."

"Then I'll take you to the station," proposed Scott. "There'll be a crowd, and you may have trouble getting a porter."

She could think of nothing to say, no valid objection to make. She wished she had said that she was going by automobile, but she could conceive of no graceful and plausible way of amending her first admission.

"That's mighty sweet of you."

"You'll be at the Ritz when you come back?"

"Oh, yes," she answered. "I'm going to keep my rooms."

Her bedroom was the smallest and least expensive in the hotel.

She concluded to let him put her on the train for Princeton; in fact, she saw no alternative. Next day as she packed her suitcase after luncheon the situation had taken such hold of her imagination that she filled it with the very things she would have chosen had she really been going to the prom. Her intention was to get out at the first stop and take the train back to New York.

Scott called for her at half past one and they took a taxi to the Pennsylvania Station. The train was crowded as he had expected, but he found her a seat and stowed her grip in the rack overhead.

"I'll call you Friday to see how you've behaved," he said.

"All right. I'll be good."

Their eyes met and in an instant, with an inexplicable, only half-conscious rush of emotion, they were in perfect communion. When Yanci came back, the glance seemed to say, ah, then——

A voice startled her ear:

"Why, Yanci!"

Yanci looked around. To her horror she recognized a girl named Ellen Harley, one of those to whom she had phoned upon her arrival.

"Well, Yanci Bowman! You're the last person I ever expected to see. How are you?"

Yanci introduced Scott. Her heart was beating violently.

"Are you coming to the prom? How perfectly slick!" cried Ellen. "Can I sit here with you? I've been wanting to see you. Who are you going with?"

"No one you know."

"Maybe I do."

Her words, falling like sharp claws on Yanci's sensitive soul, were interrupted by an unintelligible outburst from the conductor. Scott bowed to Ellen, cast at Yanci one level glance and then hurried off.

The train started. As Ellen arranged her grip and threw off her fur coat Yanci looked around her. The car was gay with girls whose excited chatter filled the damp, rubbery air like smoke. Here and there sat a chaperon, a mass of decaying rock in a field of flowers, predicting with a mute and somber fatality the end of all gayety and all youth. How many times had Yanci herself been one of such a crowd, careless and happy, dreaming of the men she would meet, of the battered hacks waiting at the station, the snow-covered campus, the big open fires in the clubhouses, and the imported orchestra beating out defiant melody against the approach of morning.

And now—she was an intruder, uninvited, undesired. As at the Ritz on the day of her arrival, she felt that at any instant her mask would be torn from her and she would be exposed as a pretender to the gaze of all the car.

"Tell me everything!" Ellen was saying. "Tell me what you've been doing. I didn't see you at any of the football games last fall."

This was by way of letting Yanci know that she had attended them herself.

The conductor was bellowing from the rear of the car, "Manhattan Transfer next stop!"

Yanci's cheeks burned with shame. She wondered what she had best do—meditating a confession, deciding against it, answering Ellen's chatter in frightened monosyllables—then, as with an ominous thunder of brakes the speed of the train began to slacken, she sprang on a despairing impulse to her feet.

"My heavens!" she cried. "I've forgotten my shoes! I've got to go back and get them."

Ellen reacted to this with annoying efficiency.

"I'll take your suitcase," she said quickly, "and you can call for it. I'll be at the Charter Club."

"No!" Yanci almost shrieked. "It's got my dress in it!"

Ignoring the lack of logic in her own remark, she swung the suitcase off the rack with what seemed to her a superhuman effort and went reeling down the aisle, stared at curiously by the arrogant eyes of many girls. When she reached the platform just as the train came to a stop she felt weak and shaken. She stood on the hard cement which marks the quaint old village of Manhattan Transfer and tears were streaming down her cheeks as she watched the unfeeling cars speed off to Princeton with their burden of happy youth.

After half an hour's wait Yanci got on a train and returned to New York. In thirty minutes she had lost the confidence that a week had gained for her. She came back to her little room and lay down quietly upon the bed.

X

By Friday Yanci's spirits had partly recovered from their chill depression. Scott's voice over the telephone in mid-morning was like a tonic, and she told him of the delights of Princeton with convincing enthusiasm, drawing vicariously upon a prom she had attended there two years before. He was anxious to see her, he said. Would she come to dinner and the theatre that night? Yanci considered, greatly tempted. Dinner—she had been economizing on meals, and a gorgeous dinner in some extravagant show place followed by a musical comedy appealed to her starved fancy, indeed; but instinct told her that the time was not yet right. Let him wait. Let him dream a little more, a little longer.

"I'm too tired, Scott," she said with an air of extreme frankness; "that's the whole truth of the matter. I've been out every night since I've been here, and I'm really half-dead. I'll rest up on this house party over the weekend and then I'll go to dinner with you any day you want me."

There was a minute's silence while she held the phone expectantly.

"Lot of resting up you'll do on a house party," he replied; "and, anyway, next week is so far off. I'm awfully anxious to see you, Yanci."

"So am I, Scott."

She allowed the faintest caress to linger on his name. When she had hung up she felt happy again. Despite her humiliation on the train her plan had been a success. The illusion was still intact; it was nearly complete. And in three meetings and half a dozen telephone calls she had managed to create a tenser atmosphere between them than if he had seen her constantly in the moods and avowals and beguilements of an out-and-out flirtation.

When Monday came she paid her first week's hotel bill. The size of it did not alarm her—she was prepared for that—but the shock of seeing so much money go, of realizing that there remained only one hundred and twenty dollars of her father's present, gave her a peculiar sinking sensation in the pit of her stomach. She decided to bring guile to bear immediately, to tantalize Scott by a carefully planned incident, and then at the end of the week to show him simply and definitely that she loved him.

As a decoy for Scott's tantalization she located by telephone a certain Jimmy Long, a handsome boy with whom she had played as a little girl and who had recently come to New York to work. Jimmy Long was deftly maneuvered into asking her to go to a matinée with him on Wednesday afternoon. He was to meet her in the lobby at two.

On Wednesday she lunched with Scott. His eyes followed her every motion, and knowing this she felt a great rush of tenderness toward him. Desiring at first only what he represented, she had begun half-unconsciously to desire him also. Nevertheless, she did not permit herself the slightest relaxation on that account. The time was too short and the odds too great. That she was beginning to love him only fortified her resolve.

"Where are you going this afternoon?" he demanded.

"To a matinée—with an annoying man."

"Why is he annoying?"

"Because he wants me to marry him and I don't believe I want to."

There was just the faintest emphasis on the word "believe." The implication was that she was not sure—that is, not quite.

"Don't marry him."

"I won't—probably."

"Yanci," he said in a low voice, "do you remember a night on that boulevard——"

She changed the subject. It was noon and the room was full of sunlight. It was not quite the place, the time. When he spoke she must have every aspect of the situation in control. He must say only what she wanted said; nothing else would do.

"It's five minutes to two," she told him, looking at her wrist watch. "We'd better go. I've got to keep my date."

"Do you want to go?"

"No," she answered simply.

This seemed to satisfy him, and they walked out to the lobby. Then Yanci caught sight of a man waiting there, obviously ill at ease and dressed as no habitué of the Ritz ever was. The man was Jimmy Long, not long since a favored beau of his Western city. And now—his hat was green, actually! His coat, seasons old, was quite evidently the product of a well-known ready-made concern. His shoes, long and narrow, turned up at the toes. From head to foot everything that could possibly be wrong about him was wrong. He was embarrassed by instinct only, unconscious of his *gaucherie*, an obscene specter, a Nemesis, a horror.

"Hello, Yanci!" he cried, starting toward her with evident relief.

With a heroic effort Yanci turned to Scott, trying to hold his glance to herself. In the very act of turning she noticed the impeccability of Scott's coat, his tie.

"Thanks for luncheon," she said with a radiant smile. "See you tomorrow."

Then she dived rather than ran for Jimmy Long, disposed of his outstretched hand and bundled him bumping through the revolving door with only a quick "Let's hurry!" to appease his somewhat sulky astonishment.

The incident worried her. She consoled herself by remembering that Scott had had only a momentary glance at the man, and that he had probably been looking at her anyhow. Nevertheless, she was horrified, and it is to be doubted whether Jimmy Long enjoyed her company enough to compensate him for the cut-price, twentieth-row tickets he had obtained at Black's Drug Store.

But if Jimmy as a decoy had proved a lamentable failure, an occurrence of Thursday offered her considerable satisfaction and paid tribute to her quickness of mind. She had invented an engagement for luncheon, and Scott was going to meet her at two o'clock to take her to the Hippodrome. She lunched alone somewhat imprudently in the Ritz dining room and sauntered out almost side by side with a good-looking young man who had been at the table next to her. She expected to meet Scott in the outer lobby, but as she reached the entrance to the restaurant she saw him standing not far away.

On a lightning impulse she turned to the good-looking man abreast of her, bowed sweetly and said in an audible, friendly voice, "Well, I'll see you later."

Then before he could even register astonishment she faced about quickly and joined Scott.

"Who was that?" he asked, frowning.

"Isn't he darling-looking?"

"If you like that sort of looks."

Scott's tone implied that the gentleman referred to was effete and overdressed. Yanci laughed, impersonally admiring the skill-fulness of her ruse.

It was in preparation for that all-important Saturday night that on Thursday she went into a shop on 42nd Street to buy some long gloves. She made her purchase and handed the clerk a fifty-dollar bill so that her lightened pocketbook would feel heavier with the change she could put in. To her surprise the clerk tendered her the package and a twenty-five-cent piece.

"Is there anything else?"

"The rest of my change."

"You've got it. You gave me five dollars. Four-seventy-five for the gloves leaves twenty-five cents."

"I gave you fifty dollars."

"You must be mistaken."

Yanci searched her purse.

"I gave you fifty!" she repeated frantically.

"No, ma'am, I saw it myself."

They glared at each other in hot irritation. A cash girl was called to testify, then the floor-manager; a small crowd gathered.

"Why, I'm perfectly sure!" cried Yanci, two angry tears trembling in her eyes. "I'm positive!"

The floor-manager was sorry, but the lady really must have left it at home. There was no fifty-dollar bill in the cash drawer. The bottom was creaking out of Yanci's rickety world.

"If you'll leave your address," said the floor manager, "I'll let you know if anything turns up."

"Oh, you damn fools!" cried Yanci, losing control. "I'll get the police!"

And weeping like a child she left the shop. Outside, helplessness overpowered her. How could she prove anything? It was after six and the store was closing even as she left it. Whichever employee had the fifty-dollar bill would be on her way home now before the police could arrive, and why should the New York police believe her, or even give her fair play?

In despair she returned to the Ritz, where she searched through her trunk for the bill with hopeless and mechanical gestures. It was not there. She had known it would not be there. She gathered every penny together and found that she had fifty-one dollars and thirty cents. Telephoning the office, she asked that her bill be made out up to the following noon—she was too dispirited to think of leaving before then.

She waited in her room, not daring even to send for ice water. Then the phone rang and she heard the room clerk's voice, cheerful and metallic.

"Miss Bowman?"

"Yes."

"Your bill, including tonight, is ex-act-ly fifty-one twenty."

"Fifty-one twenty?" Her voice was trembling.

"Yes, ma'am."

"Thank you very much."

Breathless, she sat there beside the telephone, too frightened now to cry. She had ten cents left in the world!

XI

Friday. She had scarcely slept. There were dark rings under her eyes, and even a hot bath followed by a cold one failed to arouse her from a despairing lethargy. She had never fully realized what it would mean to be without money in New York; her determination and vitality seemed to have vanished at last with her fifty-dollar bill. There was no help for it now—she must attain her desire today or never.

She was to meet Scott at the Plaza for tea. She wondered—was it her imagination, or had his manner been consciously cool the afternoon before? For the first time in several days she had needed to make no effort to keep the conversation from growing sentimental. Suppose he had decided that it must come to nothing—that she was too extravagant, too frivolous. A hundred eventualities presented themselves to her during the morning—a dreary morning, broken only by her purchase of a ten-cent bun at a grocery store.

It was her first food in twenty hours, but she self-consciously pretended to the grocer to be having an amusing and facetious time in buying one bun. She even asked to see his grapes, but told him, after looking at them appraisingly—and hungrily—that she didn't think she'd buy any. They didn't look ripe to her, she said. The store was full of prosperous women who, with thumb and first finger joined and held high in front of them, were inspecting food. Yanci would have liked to ask one of them for a bunch of grapes. Instead she went up to her room in the hotel and ate her bun.

When four o'clock came she found that she was thinking more about the sandwiches she would have for tea than of what else must occur there, and as she walked slowly up Fifth Avenue toward the Plaza she felt a sudden faintness which she took several deep breaths of air to overcome. She wondered vaguely where the bread line was. That was where people in her condition should go—but where was it? How did one find out? She imagined fantastically that it was in the phone book under *B*, or perhaps under *N*, for New York Bread Line.

She reached the Plaza. Scott's figure, as he stood waiting for her in the crowded lobby, was a personification of solidity and hope.

"Let's hurry!" she cried with a tortured smile. "I feel rather punk and I want some tea."

She ate a club sandwich, some chocolate ice cream and six tea biscuits. She could have eaten much more, but she dared not. The eventuality of her hunger having been disposed of, she must turn at bay now and face this business of life, represented by the handsome young man who sat opposite watching her with some emotion whose import she could not determine just behind his level eyes.

But the words, the glance, subtle, pervasive and sweet, that she had planned, failed somehow to come.

"Oh, Scott," she said in a low voice, "I'm so tired."

"Tired of what?" he asked coolly.

"Of—everything."

There was a silence.

"I'm afraid," she said uncertainly—"I'm afraid I won't be able to keep that date with you tomorrow."

There was no pretense in her voice now. The emotion was apparent in the waver of each word, without intention or control.

"I'm going away."

"Are you? Where?"

His tone showed a strong interest, but she winced as she saw that that was all.

"My aunt's come back. She wants me to join her in Florida right away."

"Isn't this rather unexpected?"

"Yes."

"You'll be coming back soon?" he said after a moment.

"I don't think so. I think we'll go to Europe from—from New Orleans."

"Oh!"

Again there was a pause. It lengthened. In the shadow of a moment it would become awkward, she knew. She had lost—well? Yet, she would go on to the end.

"Will you miss me?"

"Yes."

One word. She caught his eyes, wondered for a moment if she saw more there than that kindly interest; then she dropped her own again.

"I like it—here at the Plaza," she heard herself saying.

They spoke of things like that. Afterwards she could never remember what they said. They spoke—even of the tea, of the thaw that was ended and the cold coming down outside. She was sick at heart and she seemed to herself very old. She rose at last.

"I've got to tear," she said. "I'm going out to dinner."

To the last she would keep on—the illusion, that was the important thing. To hold her proud lies inviolate—there was only a moment now. They walked toward the door.

"Put me in a taxi," she said quietly. "I don't feel equal to walking."

He helped her in. They shook hands.

"Good-bye, Scott," she said.

"Good-bye, Yanci," he answered slowly.

"You've been awfully nice to me. I'll always remember what a good time you helped to give me this two weeks."

"The pleasure was mine. Shall I tell the driver the Ritz?"

"No. Just tell him to drive out Fifth. I'll tap on the glass when I want him to stop."

Out Fifth! He would think, perhaps, that she was dining on Fifth. What an appropriate finish that would be! She wondered if he were impressed. She could not see his face clearly, because the air was dark with the snow and her own eyes were blurred by tears.

"Good-bye," he said simply.

He seemed to realize that any pretense of sorrow on his part would be transparent. She knew that he did not want her.

The door slammed, the car started, skidding in the snowy street.

Yanci leaned back dismally in the corner. Try as she might, she could not see where she had failed or what it was that had changed his attitude toward her. For the first time in her life she had ostensibly offered herself to a man—and he had not wanted her. The precariousness of her position paled beside the tragedy of her defeat.

She let the car go on—the cold air was what she needed, of course. Ten minutes had slipped away drearily before she realized that she had not a penny with which to pay the driver.

"It doesn't matter," she thought. "They'll just send me to jail, and that's a place to sleep."

She began thinking of the taxi driver.

"He'll be mad when he finds out, poor man. Maybe he's very poor, and he'll have to pay the fare himself." With a vague sentimentality she began to cry.

"Poor taxi man," she was saying half aloud. "Oh, people have such a hard time—such a hard time!"

She rapped on the window and when the car drew up at a curb she got out. She was at the end of Fifth Avenue and it was dark and cold.

"Send for the police!" she cried in a quick low voice. "I haven't any money!"

The taxi man scowled down at her.

"Then what'd you get in for?"

She had not noticed that another car had stopped about twenty-five feet behind them. She heard running footsteps in the snow and then a voice at her elbow.

"It's all right," someone was saying to the taxi man. "I've got it right here."

A bill was passed up. Yanci slumped sideways against Scott's overcoat.

Scott knew—he knew because he had gone to Princeton to surprise her, because the stranger she had spoken to in the Ritz had been his best friend, because the check of her father's for three hundred dollars had been returned to him marked "No funds." Scott knew—he had known for days.

But he said nothing; only stood there holding her with one arm as her taxi drove away.

"Oh, it's you," said Yanci faintly. "Lucky you came along. I left my purse back at the Ritz, like an awful fool. I do such ridiculous things——"

Scott laughed with some enjoyment. There was a light snow falling, and lest she should slip in the damp he picked her up and carried her back toward his waiting taxi.

"Such ridiculous things," she repeated.

"Go to the Ritz first," he said to the driver. "I want to get a trunk."

Dice, Brassknuckles and Guitar

PARTS of New Jersey are underwater, and other parts are under continual surveillance by the authorities. But here and there lie patches of garden country dotted with old-fashioned frame mansions, which have wide shady porches and a red swing on the lawn; and perhaps, on the widest and shadiest of the porches there is even a hammock left over from the hammock days, stirring gently in a mid-Victorian wind.

When tourists come to such last-century landmarks they stop their cars and gaze for awhile and say: "Well, of course, that house is mostly halls and has a thousand rats and one bathroom, but there's a sort of atmosphere about it——"

The tourist doesn't stay long. He drives on to his Elizabethan villa of pressed cardboard or his early Norman meat-market or his medieval Italian pigeon-coop—because this is the twentieth century and Victorian houses are as unfashionable as the works of Mrs. Humphry Ward. He can't see the hammock from the road—but sometimes there's a girl in the hammock. There was this afternoon. She was asleep in it and apparently unaware of the aesthetic horrors which surrounded her, the stone statue of Diana, for example, which grinned idiotically under the sunlight on the lawn.

There was something enormously yellow about the whole scene—there was this sunlight, for instance, that was yellow, and the hammock was of the particularly hideous yellow peculiar to hammocks, and the girl's yellow hair was spread out upon the hammock in a sort of invidious comparison. She slept with her lips closed and her hands clasped behind her head, as it is proper for young girls to sleep. Her breast rose and fell slightly with no more emphasis than the sway of the hammock's fringe. Her name, Amanthis, was as old-fashioned as the house she lived in. I regret to say that her mid-Victorian connections ceased abruptly at this point.

Now if this were a moving picture (as, of course, I hope it will someday be) I would take as many thousand feet of her as I was allowed—then I would move the camera up close and show the yellow down on the back of her neck where her hair stopped and the warm color of her cheeks and arms, because I like to think of her sleeping there, as you yourself might have slept, back in your young days. Then I would hire a man named Israel Glucose to write some idiotic line of transition, and switch thereby to another scene that was taking place at no particular spot far down the road.

In a moving automobile sat a southern gentleman accompanied by his body-servant. He was on his way, after a fashion, to New York but he was somewhat hampered by the fact that the upper and lower portions of his automobile were no longer in exact juxtaposition. In fact from time to time the two riders would dismount, shove the body onto the chassis, corner to corner, and then continue onward, vibrating slightly in involuntary unison with the motor. Except that it had no door in back the car might have been built early in the mechanical age. It was covered with the mud of eight states and adorned in front by an enormous defunct motometer and behind by a mangy pennant bearing the legend "Tarleton, Ga." In the dim past someone had begun to paint the hood yellow but unfortunately had been called away when but half through the task.

As the gentleman and his body-servant were passing the house where Amanthis lay asleep in the hammock, something happened—the body fell off the car. My only apology for stating this so suddenly is that it happened very suddenly indeed. When the noise had died down and the dust had drifted away master and man arose and inspected the two halves.

"Look-a-there," said the gentleman in disgust, "the doggone thing got all separated that time."

"She bust in two," agreed the body-servant.

"Hugo," said the gentleman, after some consideration, "we got to get a hammer an' nails an' *tack* it on."

They glanced up at the Victorian house. On all sides faintly irregular fields stretched away to a faintly irregular unpopulated horizon. There was no choice, so the black Hugo opened the gate and followed his master up a gravel walk, casting only the blasé glances of a confirmed traveler at the red swing and the stone statue of Diana which turned on them a storm-crazed stare.

At the exact moment when they reached the porch Amanthis awoke, sat up suddenly and looked them over.

The gentleman was young, perhaps twenty-four, and his name was Jim Powell. He was dressed in a tight and dusty suit, the coat of which was evidently expected to take flight at a moment's notice, for it was secured to his body by a line of eight preposterous buttons.

There were supernumerary buttons upon the coat-sleeves also and Amanthis could not resist a glance to determine whether or not more buttons ran up the side of his trouser leg. In his green hat a feather from some dejected bird fluttered in the warm wind. He bowed formally, dusting his knees with the hat. Simultaneously he smiled, half-shutting his faded blue eyes and displaying white and beautifully symmetrical teeth.

"Good-evenin'," he said in abandoned Georgian. "My automobile has met with an accident out yonder by your gate. I wondered if it wouldn't be too much to ask you if I could have the use of a hammer and some tacks for a little while."

Amanthis laughed. For a moment she laughed uncontrollably. Mr. Jim Powell laughed, politely and appreciatively, with her. His body-servant, deep in the throes of colored adolescence, alone preserved a dignified gravity.

"I better introduce who I am, maybe," said the visitor. "My name's Powell. I'm a resident of Tarleton, Georgia. This here nigger's my boy Hugo."

"Your *son!*" The girl stared from one to the other in wild fascination.

"No, he's my body-servant, I guess you'd call it. We call a nigger a boy down yonder."

At this reference to the finer customs of his native soil the boy Hugo put his hands behind his back and looked darkly and superciliously down the lawn.

"Yas'm," he muttered, "I'm a body-servant."

"Where you going in your automobile," demanded Amanthis.

"Goin' north for the summer."

"Where to?"

The tourist waved his hand with a careless gesture as if to indicate the Adirondacks, the Thousand Islands, Newport—but he said:

"We're tryin' New York."

"Have you ever been there before?"

"Never have. But I been to Atlanta lots of times. An' we passed through all kinds of cities this trip. Man!"

He whistled to express the enormous spectacularity of his recent travels.

"Listen," said Amanthis intently, "you better have something to eat. Tell your—your body-servant to go round in back and ask the cook to send us out some sandwiches and lemonade. Or maybe you don't drink lemonade—very few people do anymore."

Mr. Powell by a circular motion of his finger sped Hugo on the designated mission. Then he seated himself gingerly in a rocking-chair and began fanning himself formally with the feathers of his hat.

"You cer'nly are mighty kind," he told her. "An' if I wanted anything stronger than lemonade I got a bottle of good old corn out in the car. I brought it along because I thought maybe I wouldn't be able to drink the whiskey they got up here."

"Listen," she said, "my name's Powell too. Amanthis Powell."

"Say, is that right?" He laughed ecstatically. "Maybe we're kin to each other. I come from mighty good people," he went on. "Pore though. But I did right well this last year so I thought I'd come north for the summer."

At this point Hugo reappeared on the veranda steps and became audible.

"White lady back there she asked me don't I want eat some too. What I tell her?"

"You tell her yes mamm if she be so kind," directed his master. And as Hugo retired he confided to Amanthis: "That boy's got no sense at all. He don't want to do nothing without I tell him he can. I brought him up," he added, not without pride.

When the sandwiches arrived Mr. Powell stood up. Unaccustomed to white servants he obviously expected an introduction.

"Are you a married lady?" he inquired of Amanthis, when the servant was gone.

"No," she answered, and added from the security of eighteen, "I'm an old maid."

Again he laughed politely.

"You mean you're a society girl."

She shook her head. Mr. Powell noted with embarrassed enthusiasm the particular yellowness of her yellow hair.

"Does this old place look like it?" she said cheerfully. "No, you perceive in me a daughter of the countryside. My suitors are

farmers—or else, promising young barbers from the next village
with somebody's late hair still clinging to their coat-sleeves."

"Your daddy oughtn't to let you go with a barber," said the
tourist disapprovingly. He considered—"You ought to be a
society girl."

He began to tap his foot rhythmically on the porch and in a
moment Amanthis discovered that she was unconsciously doing
the same thing.

"Stop!" she commanded. "Don't make me do that."

He looked down at his foot.

"Excuse me," he said humbly. "I don't know—it's just something I do."

This intense discussion was now interrupted by Hugo who
appeared on the steps bearing a hammer and a handful of nails.

Mr. Powell arose unwillingly and looked at his watch.

"We got to go, daggone it," he said, frowning heavily. "See
here. Wouldn't you *like* to be a New York society girl and go to
those dances an' all, like you read about, where they throw gold
pieces away?"

She looked at him and nodded, smiling. Then she got herself
by some means from the hammock and they went down toward
the road, side by side.

"I'll keep my eyes open for you and let you know," he persisted. "A pretty girl like you ought to go around in society. We
may be kin to each other, you see, and us Powells ought to stick
together."

"What are you going to do in New York?"

They were now almost at the gate and the tourist pointed to
the two depressing sectors of his automobile.

"I'm goin' to drive a taxi. This one right here. Only it's got so
it busts in two all the time."

"You're going to drive *that* in New York?"

Jim looked at her uncertainly. Such a pretty girl should certainly control the habit of shaking all over upon no provocation
at all.

"Yes mamm," he said with dignity.

Amanthis watched while they placed the upper half of the car
upon the lower half and nailed it severely into place. Then Mr.
Powell took the wheel and his body-servant climbed in beside
him.

"I'm cer'nly very much obliged to you indeed for your hospitality. Convey my respects to your father."

"I will," she assured him. "Come back and see me, if you don't mind barbers in the room."

He dismissed this unpleasant thought with a gesture.

"Your company would always be charming." He put the car into gear as though to drown out the temerity of his parting speech. "You're the prettiest girl I've seen up north—by far."

Then with a groan and a rattle Mr. Powell of Georgia with his own car and his own body-servant and his own ambitions and his own private cloud of dust continued on north for the summer.

II

She thought she would never see him again. She lay in her hammock, slim and beautiful, opened her left eye slightly to see June come in and then closed it and retired contentedly back into her dreams.

But one day when the midsummer vines had climbed the precarious sides of the red swing in the lawn, Mr. Jim Powell of Tarleton, Georgia, came vibrating back into her life. They sat on the wide porch as before.

"I've got a great scheme," he told her.

"Did you drive your taxi like you said?"

"Yes mamm, but the business was right bad. I waited around in front of all those hotels and theatres an' nobody ever got in."

"*No*body?"

"Well, one night there was some drunk fellas they got in— only just as I was gettin' started my automobile came apart. And another night it was rainin' and there wasn't no other taxis and a lady got in because she said she had to go a long ways. But before we got there she made me stop and she got out. She seemed kinda mad and went walkin' off in the rain. Mighty proud lot of people they got up in New York."

"And so you're going home?" asked Amanthis sympathetically.

"No *mamm*. I got an idea." His blue eyes looked closely at her. "Has that barber been around here—with hair on his sleeves?"

"No. He's—he's gone away."

"Well, then, first thing is I want to leave this car of mine here with you. It ain't the right color for a taxi. To pay for its keep I'd like to have you drive it just as much as you want. Long as you got a hammer an' nails with you there ain't much bad that can happen——"

"I'll take care of it," interrupted Amanthis, "but where are *you* going?"

"Southampton. It's one of the swellest places they got up here, so that's where I'm going."

She sat up in amazement.

"What are you going to do there?"

"Listen." He leaned toward her confidentially. "Were you serious about wanting to be a New York society girl?"

"Deadly serious."

"That's all I wanted to know," he said inscrutably. "You just wait here on this porch a couple of weeks and—and sleep. And if any barbers come to see you with hair on their sleeves you tell 'em you're too sleepy to see 'em."

"What then?"

"Then you'll hear from me, mamm," he continued decisively. "You talk about society! Before one month I'm goin' to have you in more society than there is."

Further than this he would say nothing. His manner conveyed that she was going to be suspended over a pool of gaiety and periodically immersed: "Is it gay enough for you, mamm? Shall I let in a little more excitement, mamm?"

"Well," answered Amanthis, lazily considering, "there are few things for which I'd forego the luxury of sleeping through July and August—but if you'll write me a letter I'll run up to Southampton."

Three days later a young man wearing a yellow feather in his hat rang the doorbell of the enormous and astounding Madison Harlan house at Southampton. He asked the butler if there were any people in the house between the ages of sixteen and twenty. He was informed that Miss Genevieve Harlan and Mr. Ronald Harlan answered that description and thereupon he handed in a most peculiar card and requested in fetching Georgian that it be brought to their attention.

As a result he was closeted for almost an hour with Mr. Ronald Harlan (who was a student at the Hillkiss School) and Miss

Genevieve Harlan (who was not uncelebrated at Southampton dances). When he left he bore a short note in Miss Harlan's handwriting which he presented together with his peculiar card at the next large estate. It happened to be that of the Clifton Garneaus. Here, as if by magic, the same audience was granted him.

He went on—it was a hot day, and men who could not afford to do so were carrying their coats on the public highway, but Jim, a native of southernmost Georgia, was as fresh and cool at the last house as at the first. He visited ten houses that day. Anyone following him in his course might have taken him to be some gifted bootlegger.

There was something in his unexpected demand for the adolescent members of the family which made hardened butlers lose their critical acumen. As he left each house a close observer might have seen that fascinated eyes followed him to the door and excited voices whispered something which hinted at a future meeting.

The second day he visited twelve houses. He might have kept on his round for a week and never seen the same butler twice but it was only the palatial, the amazing houses which intrigued him.

On the third day he did a thing that many people have been told to do and few have done—he hired a hall. Exactly one week later he sent a wire to Miss Amanthis Powell saying that if she still aspired to the gaiety of the highest society she should set out for Southampton by the earliest possible train. He himself would meet her at the station.

Jim Powell was no longer a man of leisure, so when she failed to arrive at the time her wire had promised he grew restless. He supposed she was coming on a later train, turned to go back to his project—and met her entering the station from the street side.

"Why, how did you——"

"Well," said Amanthis, "I arrived this morning instead, and I didn't want to bother you so I found a respectable boarding house on the Ocean Road."

She was quite different from the indolent Amanthis of the porch hammock, he thought. She wore a suit of robin's-egg blue and a rakish young hat with a curling feather—she was attired not unlike those young ladies between sixteen and twenty who of late were absorbing his attention. Yes, she would do very well.

He bowed her profoundly into a taxi-cab and got in beside her.

"Isn't it about time you told me your scheme?" she suggested.

"Well, it's about these society girls up here." He waved his hand airily. "I know 'em all."

"Where are they?"

"Right now they're with Hugo. You remember—that's my body-servant."

"With Hugo!" Her eyes widened. "Why? What's it all about?"

"Well, I got—I got sort of a school, I guess you'd call it."

"A school?"

"It's a sort of academy. And I'm the head of it. I invented it."

He flipped a card from his case as though he were shaking down a thermometer.

"Look."

She took the card. In large lettering it bore the legend

JAMES POWELL; J. M.
"Dice, Brassknuckles and Guitar"

She stared in amazement.

"Dice, Brassknuckles and Guitar?" she repeated in awe.

"Yes mamm."

"What does it mean? What——do you *sell* 'em?"

"No mamm, I teach 'em. It's a profession."

"Dice, Brassknuckles and Guitar? What's the J. M.?"

"That stands for Jazz Master."

"But what *is* it? What's it about?"

"Well, you see, it's like this. One night when I was in New York I got talkin' to a young fella who'd been drinking some. He was one of my fares. And he'd taken some society girl somewhere and lost her."

"*Lost* her?"

"Yes mamm. He forgot her, I guess. And he was right worried. Well, I got to thinkin' that these girls nowadays—these society girls—they lead a sort of dangerous life and my course of study offers a means of protection against these dangers."

"You teach 'em to use brassknuckles?"

"Yes mamm, if necessary. Look here, you take a girl and she goes into some café where she's got no business to go. Well then, her escort he gets a little too much to drink an' he goes to sleep an' then some other fella comes up and says 'Hello, sweet mamma' or whatever one of those mashers says up here. What does she do? She can't scream, on account of no real lady'll scream nowadays. She just reaches down in her pocket and slips her fingers into a pair of Powell's Defensive Brassknuckles, debutante's size, executes what I call the Society Hook, and *Wham!* that big fella's on his way to the cellar."

"Well—what's the guitar for?" whispered the awed Amanthis. "Do they have to knock somebody over with the guitar?"

"No, *mamm!*" exclaimed Jim in horror. "No mamm! In my course no lady would be taught to raise a guitar against anybody. I teach 'em to play. Shucks! you ought to hear 'em. Why, when I've given 'em two lessons you'd think some of 'em was colored."

"And the dice?"

"Dice? I'm related to a dice. My grandfather was a dice. I teach 'em how to make those dice perform. I protect pocketbook as well as person."

"Did you—— Have you got any pupils?"

"Mamm I got all the really nice, rich people in the place. What I told you ain't all. I teach lots of things. I teach 'em the Boodlin' Bend—and the Mississippi Sunrise. Why, there was one girl she came to me and said she wanted to learn to snap her fingers. I mean *really* snap 'em—like they do. She said she never could snap her fingers since she was little. I gave her two lessons and now *Wham!* Her daddy says he's goin' to leave home."

"When do you have it?" demanded the weak and shaken Amanthis.

"Three times a week. You'll just be one of the pupils. I got it fixed up that you come from very high-tone people down in New Jersey. I told 'em your daddy was the man that had the original patent on lump sugar."

She gasped.

"So all you got to do," he went on, "is to pretend you never saw any barber."

They were now at the south end of the village and Amanthis saw a row of cars parked in front of a two-story building. The cars were all low, long, rakish and of a brilliant hue. Then she was ascending a narrow stairs to the second story. Here, painted on a door from which came the sounds of music and voices were the words:

JAMES POWELL; J. M.
"Dice, Brassknuckles and Guitar"
Mon.—Wed.—Fri.
Hours 3–5 P.M.

"Now if you'll just step this way——" said the Principal, pushing open the door.

Amanthis found herself in a long, bright room, populated with girls and men of about her own age. The scene presented itself to her at first as a sort of animated afternoon tea but after a moment she began to see, here and there, a motive and a pattern to the proceedings.

The students were scattered into groups, sitting, kneeling, standing, but all rapaciously intent on the subjects which engrossed them. From six young ladies gathered in a ring around some indistinguishable objects came a medley of cries and exclamations—plaintive, pleading, supplicating, exhorting, imploring and lamenting—their voices serving as tenor to an undertone of mysterious clatters.

Next to this group, four young men were surrounding an adolescent black, who proved to be none other than Mr. Powell's late body-servant. The young men were roaring at Hugo apparently unrelated phrases, expressing a wide gamut of emotion. Now their voices rose to a sort of clamor, now they spoke softly and gently, with mellow implication. Every little while Hugo would answer them with words of approbation, correction or disapproval.

"What are they doing?" whispered Amanthis to Jim.

"That there's a course in southern accent. Lot of young men up here want to learn southern accent—so we teach it—Georgia, Florida, Alabama, Eastern Shore, Ole Virginian. Some of 'em even want straight nigger—for song purposes."

They walked around among the groups. Some girls with metal knuckles were furiously insulting two punching bags on each of which was painted the leering, winking face of a masher. A mixed group, led by a banjo tom-tom, were rolling harmonic syllables from their guitars; there were couples dancing flat-footed in the corner to a record made by Rastus Muldoon's Savannah Band. "Now, Miss Powell, if you're ready I'll ask you to take off your hat and go over and join Miss Genevieve Harlan at that punching bag in the corner." He raised his voice. "Hugo," he called, "there's a new student here. Equip her with a pair of Powell's Defensive Brassknuckles—debutante size."

III

I regret to say that I never saw Jim Powell's famous school in action nor followed his personally conducted tours into the mysteries of Dice, Brassknuckles and Guitar. So I can give you only such details as were later reported to me by one of his admiring pupils. During all the discussion of it afterwards no one ever denied that it was an enormous success, and no pupil ever regretted having received its degree—Bachelor of Jazz.

"If I could keep it dark," Jim confided to Amanthis, "I'd have up Rastus Muldoon's Band from Savannah. That's the band I've always wanted to lead."

He was making money. His charges were not exorbitant—as a rule his pupils were not particularly flush—but he moved from his boarding house to the Casino Hotel where he took a suite and had Hugo serve him his breakfast in bed.

The establishing of Amanthis as a member of Southampton's younger set was easier than he had expected. Within a week she was known to everyone in the school by her first name. Jim saw less of her than he would have liked. Not that her manner toward him changed—she walked with him often, she was always willing to listen to his plans—but after she was taken up by the fashionable her evenings seemed to be monopolized. Several times Jim arrived at her boarding house to find her out of breath, as if she had just come in at a run, presumably from some festivity in which he had no share.

So as the summer waned he found that one thing was lacking to complete the triumph of his enterprise. Despite the hospitality shown to Amanthis, the doors of Southampton were closed to him. Polite to, or rather, fascinated by him as his pupils were from three to five, after that hour they moved in another world.

His was the position of a golf professional who, though he may fraternize, and even command, on the links, loses his privileges at sundown. He may look in the club window but he cannot dance. And, likewise, it was not given to Jim to see his teachings put into effect. He could hear the gossip of the morning after—that was all.

But while the golf professional, being English, holds himself proudly below his patrons, Jim Powell, who "came from a right good family down there—pore though," lay awake many nights in his hotel bed and heard the music drifting into his window from the Katzbys' house or the Beach Club, and turned over restlessly and wondered what was the matter. In the early days of his success he had bought himself a dress-suit, thinking that he would soon have a chance to wear it—but it still lay untouched in the box in which it had come from the tailor's. Perhaps, he thought, there was some real gap which separated him from the rest. It worried him.

Late in September came the Harlan dance, which was to be the last and biggest of the season for this younger crowd. His academy would close the day before because of the general departure of his pupils for more conventional schools. Jim, as usual, was not invited to the dance. He had hoped that he would be. The two young Harlans, Ronald and Genevieve, had been his first patrons when he arrived at Southampton—and it was Genevieve who had taken such a fancy to Amanthis. To have been at their dance—the most magnificent dance of all—would have crowned and justified the success of the waning summer.

His class, gathering for the afternoon, was loudly anticipating the next day's revel and he was relieved when closing time came.

"Good-bye," he told them. He was wistful because his idea was played out and because, after all, they were not sorry to go. Outside, the sound of their starting motors, the triumphant putt-putt of their cut-outs cutting the warm September air, was a jubilant sound—a sound of youth and hopes high as the sun.

They were gone—he was alone with Hugo in the room. He sat down suddenly with his face in his hands.

"Hugo," he said huskily. "They don't want us up here."

"Don't you care," said a voice.

He looked up to see Amanthis standing beside him.

"You better go with them," he told her.

"Why?"

"Because you're in society now and I'm no better to those people than a servant. You're in society—I fixed that up. You better go or they won't invite you to any of their dances."

"They won't anyhow, Jim," she said gently. "They didn't invite me to the one tomorrow night."

He looked up indignantly.

"They *did*n't?"

She shook her head.

"I'll *make* 'em!" he said wildly. "I'll tell 'em they got to. I'll—I'll——"

She came close to him with shining eyes.

"Don't you mind, Jim," she soothed him. "Don't you mind. They don't matter. We'll have a party of our own tomorrow—just you and I."

"I come from right good folks," he said, defiantly. "Pore though."

She laid her hand softly on his shoulder.

"I understand. You're nicer than any of them, Jim."

He got up and went to the window and stared out mournfully into the late afternoon.

"I reckon I should have let you sleep in that hammock."

She laughed.

"I'm awfully glad you didn't."

He turned and faced the room, and his face was dark.

"Sweep up and lock up, Hugo," he said, his voice trembling. "The summer's over and we're going down home."

Autumn had come early. Jim Powell woke next morning to find his room cool, and the phenomenon of frosted breath in September absorbed him for a moment to the exclusion of the day before. Then the lines of his face drooped with unhappiness as he remembered the humiliation which had washed the cheery glitter from the summer. There was nothing left for him except to go back where he was known.

After breakfast a measure of his customary light-heartedness returned. He was a child of the South—brooding was alien to his nature. He could conjure up an injury only a certain number of times before it faded into the great vacancy of the past.

But when, from force of habit, he strolled over to his defunct establishment, melancholy again dwelt in his heart. Hugo was there, a specter of gloom, deep in the lugubrious blues.

Usually a few words from Jim were enough to raise him to an inarticulate ecstasy, but this morning there were no words to utter. For two months Hugo had lived on a pinnacle of which he had never dreamed. He had enjoyed his work simply and passionately, arriving before school hours and lingering long after Mr. Powell's pupils had gone.

The day dragged toward a not-too-promising night. Amanthis did not appear and Jim wondered forlornly if she had not changed her mind about dining with him that night. Perhaps it would be better if she were not seen with them. But then, he reflected dismally, no one would see them anyhow—everybody was going to the big dance at the Harlans' house.

When twilight threw unbearable shadows into the hall he locked it up for the last time, took down the sign "James Powell; J. M., Dice, Brassknuckles and Guitar," and went back to his hotel. Looking over his scrawled accounts he saw that there was another month's rent to pay on the hall and some bills for windows broken and new equipment that had hardly been used. Jim had lived in state, and he realized that financially he would have nothing to show for the summer after all.

When he had finished he took his new dress-suit out of its box and inspected it, running his hand over the satin of the lapels and lining. This, at least, he owned and perhaps in Tarleton somebody would ask him to a party where he could wear it.

"Shucks!" he said scoffingly. "It was just a no account old academy, anyhow. Some of those boys round the garage down home could of beat it all hollow."

Whistling "Jeanne of Jelly-bean Town" to a not-dispirited rhythm Jim encased himself in his first dress-suit and walked downtown.

"Orchids," he said to the clerk. He surveyed his purchase with some pride. He knew that no girl at the Harlan dance would wear anything lovelier than these exotic blossoms that leaned languorously backward against green ferns.

In a taxi-cab, carefully selected to look like a private car, he drove to Amanthis's boarding house. She came down wearing a rose-colored evening dress into which the orchids melted like colors into a sunset.

"I reckon we'll go to the Casino Hotel," he suggested, "unless you got some other place——"

At their table, looking out over the dark ocean, his mood became a contented sadness. The windows were shut against the cool but the orchestra played "All Alone" and "Tea for Two" and for awhile, with her young loveliness opposite him, he felt himself to be a romantic participant in the life around him. They did not dance, and he was glad—it would have reminded him of that other brighter and more radiant dance to which they could not go.

After dinner they took a taxi and followed the sandy roads for an hour, glimpsing the now starry ocean through the casual trees.

"I want to thank you," she said, "for all you've done for me, Jim."

"That's all right—we Powells ought to stick together."

"What are you going to do?"

"I'm going to Tarleton tomorrow."

"I'm sorry," she said softly. "Are you going to drive down?"

"I got to. I got to get the car south because I couldn't get what she was worth by sellin' it. You don't suppose anybody's stole my car out of your barn?" he asked in sudden alarm.

She repressed a smile.

"No."

"I'm sorry about this—about you," he went on huskily, "and—and I would like to have gone to just one of their dances. You shouldn't of stayed with me yesterday. Maybe it kept 'em from asking you."

"Jim," she suggested eagerly, "let's go and stand outside and listen to their old music. We don't care."

"They'll be coming out," he objected.

"No, it's too cold."

She gave the chauffeur a direction and a few minutes later they stopped in front of the heavy Georgian beauty of the Madison Harlan house whence the windows cast their gaiety in bright patches on the lawn. There was laughter inside and the plaintive wind of fashionable horns, and now and again the slow, mysterious shuffle of dancing feet.

"Let's go up close," whispered Amanthis in an ecstatic trance. "I want to hear."

They walked toward the house, keeping in the shadow of the great trees. Jim proceeded with awe—suddenly he stopped and seized Amanthis's arm.

"Man!" he cried in an excited whisper. "Do you know what that is?"

"A night watchman?" Amanthis cast a startled look around.

"It's Rastus Muldoon's Band from Savannah! I heard 'em once, and I *know*. It's Rastus Muldoon's Band!"

They moved closer till they could see first pompadours, then slicked male heads, and high coiffures and finally even bobbed hair pressed under black ties. They could distinguish chatter below the ceaseless laughter. Two figures appeared on the porch, gulped something quickly from flasks and returned inside. But the music had bewitched Jim Powell. His eyes were fixed and he moved his feet like a blind man.

Pressed in close behind some dark bushes they listened. The number ended. A breeze from the ocean blew over them and Jim shivered slightly. Then, in a wistful whisper:

"I've always wanted to lead that band. Just once." His voice grew listless. "Come on. Let's go. I reckon I don't belong around here."

He held out his arm to her but instead of taking it she stepped suddenly out of the bushes and into a bright patch of light.

"Come on, Jim," she said startlingly. "Let's go inside."

"What——?"

She seized his arm and though he drew back in a sort of stupefied horror at her boldness she urged him persistently toward the great front door.

"Watch out!" he gasped. "Somebody's coming out of that house and see us."

"No, Jim," she said firmly. "Nobody's coming out of that house—but two people are going in."

"Why?" he demanded wildly, standing in full glare of the porte-cochère lamps. "Why?"

"Why?" she mocked him. "Why, just because this dance happens to be given for me."

He thought she was mad.

"Come home before they see us," he begged her.

The great doors swung open and a gentleman stepped out on the porch. In horror Jim recognized Mr. Madison Harlan. He made a movement as though to break away and run. But the man walked down the steps holding out both hands to Amanthis.

"Hello at last," he cried. "Where on earth have you two been? Cousin Amanthis——" He kissed her, and turned cordially to Jim. "And for you, Mr. Powell," he went on, "to make up for being late you've got to promise that for just one number you're going to lead that band."

IV

New Jersey was warm, all except that part that was underwater, and that mattered only to the fishes. All the tourists who rode through the long green miles stopped their cars in front of a spreading old-fashioned country house and looked at the red swing on the lawn and the wide, shady porch, and sighed and drove on—swerving a little to avoid a jet-black body-servant in the road. The body-servant was applying a hammer and nails to a decayed flivver which flaunted from its rear the legend, "Tarleton, Ga."

A girl with yellow hair and a warm color to her face was lying in the hammock looking as though she could fall asleep any moment. Near her sat a gentleman in an extraordinarily tight suit. They had come down together the day before from the fashionable resort at Southampton.

"When you first appeared," she was explaining, "I never thought I'd see you again so I made that up about the barber and all. As a matter of fact, I've been around quite a bit—with or without brassknuckles. I'm coming out this autumn."

"I reckon I had a lot to learn," said Jim.

"And you see," went on Amanthis, looking at him rather anxiously, "I'd been invited up to Southampton to visit my cousins—and when you said you were going, I wanted to see what you'd do. I always slept at the Harlans' but I kept a room at the boarding house so you wouldn't know. The reason I didn't get there on the right train was because I had to come early and warn a lot of people to pretend not to know me."

Jim got up, nodding his head in comprehension.

"I reckon I and Hugo had better be movin' along. We got to make Baltimore by night."

"That's a long way."

"I want to sleep south tonight," he said.

Together they walked down the path and past the idiotic statue of Diana on the lawn.

"You see," added Amanthis gently, "you don't have to be rich up here in order to go around, any more than you do in Georgia——" She broke off abruptly. "Won't you come back next year and start another academy?"

"No mamm, not me. That Mr. Harlan told me I could go on with the one I had but I told him no."

"Haven't you——didn't you make money?"

"No mamm," he answered. "I got enough of my own income to just get me home. One time I was ahead but I was livin' high and there was my rent an' apparatus and those musicians."

He didn't consider it necessary to mention that Mr. Harlan had tried to present him with a check.

They reached the automobile just as Hugo drove in his last nail. Jim opened a pocket of the door and took from it an unlabeled bottle containing a whitish-yellow liquid.

"I intended to get you a present," he told her awkwardly, "but my money got away before I could, so I thought I'd send you something from Georgia. This here's just a personal remembrance. It won't do for you to drink but maybe after you come out into society you might want to show some of those young fellas what good old corn tastes like."

She took the bottle.

"Thank you, Jim."

"That's all right." He turned to Hugo. "I reckon we'll go along now. Give the lady the hammer."

"Oh, you can have the hammer," said Amanthis tearfully. "Won't you promise to come back?"

"Someday—maybe."

He looked for a moment at her yellow hair and her blue eyes misty with sleep and tears. Then he got into his car and as his foot found the clutch his whole manner underwent a change.

"I'll say good-bye mamm," he announced with impressive dignity. "We're goin' south for the winter."

The gesture of his straw hat indicated Palm Beach, St. Augustine, Miami. His body-servant spun the crank, gained his seat and became part of the intense vibration into which the automobile was thrown.

"South for the winter," repeated Jim. And then he added softly, "You're the prettiest girl I ever knew. You go back up there and lie down in that hammock, and sleep—sle-eep——"

It was almost a lullaby, as he said it. He bowed to her, magnificently, profoundly, including the whole North in the splendor of his obeisance——

Then they were gone down the road in quite a preposterous cloud of dust. Just before they reached the first bend Amanthis saw them come to a full stop, dismount and shove the top part of the car onto the bottom part. They took their seats again without looking around. Then the bend—and they were out of sight, leaving only a faint brown mist to show that they had passed.

Diamond Dick

WHEN Diana Dickey came back from France in the spring of 1919, her parents considered that she had atoned for her nefarious past. She had served a year in the Red Cross and she was presumably engaged to a young American ace of position and charm. They could ask no more; of Diana's former sins only her nickname survived——

Diamond Dick!—she had selected it herself, of all the names in the world, when she was a thin, black-eyed child of ten.

"Diamond Dick," she would insist, "that's my name. Anybody that won't call me that's a double darn fool."

"But that's not a nice name for a little lady," objected her governess. "If you want to have a boy's name why don't you call yourself George Washington?"

"Be-cause my name's Diamond Dick," explained Diana patiently. "Can't you understand? I got to be named that be-cause if I don't I'll have a fit and upset the family, see?"

She ended by having the fit—a fine frenzy that brought a disgusted nerve specialist out from New York—and the nickname too. And once in possession she set about modeling her facial expression on that of a butcher boy who delivered meats at Greenwich back doors. She stuck out her lower jaw and parted her lips on one side, exposing sections of her first teeth—and from this alarming aperture there issued the harsh voice of one far gone in crime.

"Miss Caruthers," she would sneer crisply, "what's the idea of no jam? Do you wanta whack the side of the head?"

"*Diana!* I'm going to call your mother *this minute!*"

"Look at here!" threatened Diana darkly. "If you call her you're liable to get a bullet the side of the head."

Miss Caruthers raised her hand uneasily to her bangs. She was somewhat awed.

"Very well," she said uncertainly, "if you want to act like a little ragamuffin——"

Diana did want to. The evolutions which she practiced daily on the sidewalk and which were thought by the neighbors to be some new form of hop-scotch were in reality the preliminary work on an Apache slouch. When it was perfected, Diana lurched forth into the streets of Greenwich, her face violently distorted and half-obliterated by her father's slouch hat, her body reeling from side to side, jerked hither and yon by the shoulders, until to look at her long was to feel a faint dizziness rising to the brain.

At first it was merely absurd, but when Diana's conversation commenced to glow with weird rococo phrases, which she imagined to be the dialect of the underworld, it became alarming. And a few years later she further complicated the problem by turning into a beauty—a dark little beauty with tragedy eyes and a rich voice stirring in her throat.

Then America entered the war and Diana on her eighteenth birthday sailed with a canteen unit to France.

The past was over; all was forgotten. Just before the armistice was signed, she was cited in orders for coolness under fire. And—this was the part that particularly pleased her mother—it was rumored that she was engaged to be married to Mr. Charley Abbot of Boston and Bar Harbor, "a young aviator of position and charm."

But Mrs. Dickey was scarcely prepared for the changed Diana who landed in New York. Seated in the limousine bound for Greenwich, she turned to her daughter with astonishment in her eyes.

"Why, everybody's proud of you, Diana," she cried. "The house is simply bursting with flowers. Think of all you've seen and done, at *nineteen!*"

Diana's face, under an incomparable saffron hat, stared out into Fifth Avenue, gay with banners for the returning divisions.

"The war's over," she said in a curious voice, as if it had just occurred to her this minute.

"Yes," agreed her mother cheerfully, "and we won. I knew we would all the time."

She wondered how to best introduce the subject of Mr. Abbot.

"You're quieter," she began tentatively. "You look as if you were more ready to settle down."

"I want to come out this fall."

"But I thought——" Mrs. Dickey stopped and coughed —"Rumors had led me to believe——"

"Well, go on, Mother. What did you hear?"

"It came to my ears that you were engaged to that young Charles Abbot."

Diana did not answer and her mother licked nervously at her veil. The silence in the car became oppressive. Mrs. Dickey had always stood somewhat in awe of Diana—and she began to wonder if she had gone too far.

"The Abbots are such nice people in Boston," she ventured uneasily. "I've met his mother several times—she told me how devoted——"

"Mother!" Diana's voice, cold as ice, broke in upon her loquacious dream. "I don't care what you heard or where you heard it, but I'm not engaged to Charley Abbot. And please don't ever mention the subject to me again."

In November Diana made her debut in the ballroom of the Ritz. There was a touch of irony in this "introduction to life"—for at nineteen Diana had seen more of reality, of courage and terror and pain, than all the pompous dowagers who peopled the artificial world.

But she was young and the artificial world was redolent of orchids and pleasant, cheerful snobbery and orchestras which set the rhythm of the year, summing up the sadness and suggestiveness of life in new tunes. All night the saxophones wailed the hopeless comment of the "Beale Street Blues," while five hundred pairs of gold and silver slippers shuffled the shining dust. At the grey tea hour there were always rooms that throbbed incessantly with this low sweet fever, while fresh faces drifted here and there like rose petals blown by the sad horns around the floor.

In the center of this twilight universe Diana moved with the season, keeping half a dozen dates a day with half a dozen men, drowsing asleep at dawn with the beads and chiffon of an evening dress tangled among dying orchids on the floor beside her bed.

The year melted into summer. The flapper craze startled New York, and skirts went absurdly high and the sad orchestras played new tunes. For a while Diana's beauty seemed to embody this new fashion as once it had seemed to embody the higher excitement of the war; but it was noticeable that she encouraged no lovers, that for all her popularity her name never became identified with that of any one man. She had had a hundred "chances," but when she felt that an interest was becoming an infatuation she was at pains to end it once and for all.

A second year dissolved into long dancing nights and swimming trips to the warm South. The flapper movement scattered to the winds and was forgotten; skirts tumbled precipitously to the floor and there were fresh songs from the saxophones for a new crop of girls. Most of those with whom she had come out were married now—some of them had babies. But Diana, in a changing world, danced on to newer tunes.

With a third year it was hard to look at her fresh and lovely face and realize that she had once been in the war. To the young generation it was already a shadowy event that had absorbed their older brothers in the dim past—ages ago. And Diana felt that when its last echoes had finally died away her youth, too, would be over. It was only occasionally now that anyone called her "Diamond Dick." When it happened, as it did sometimes, a curious, puzzled expression would come into her eyes as though she could never connect the two pieces of her life that were broken sharply asunder.

Then, when five years had passed, a brokerage house failed in Boston and Charley Abbot, the war hero, came back from Paris, wrecked and broken by drink and with scarcely a penny to his name.

Diana saw him first at the Restaurant Mont Mihiel, sitting at a side table with a plump, indiscriminate blonde from the half-world. She excused herself unceremoniously to her escort and made her way toward him. He looked up as she approached and she felt a sudden faintness, for he was worn to a shadow and his eyes, large and dark like her own, were burning in red rims of fire.

"Why, Charley——"

He got drunkenly to his feet and they shook hands in a dazed way. He murmured an introduction, but the girl at the table evinced her displeasure at the meeting by glaring at Diana with cold blue eyes.

"Why, Charley——" said Diana again, "you've come home, haven't you."

"I'm here for good."

"I want to see you, Charley. I—I want to see you as soon as possible. Will you come out to the country tomorrow?"

"Tomorrow?" He glanced with an apologetic expression at the blonde girl. "I've got a date. Don't know about tomorrow. Maybe later in the week——"

"Break your date."

His companion had been drumming with her fingers on the cloth and looking restlessly around the room. At this remark she wheeled sharply back to the table.

"Charley," she ejaculated, with a significant frown.

"Yes, I know," he said to her cheerfully, and turned to Diana. "I can't make it tomorrow. I've got a date."

"It's absolutely necessary that I see you tomorrow," went on Diana ruthlessly. "Stop looking at me in that idiotic way and say you'll come out to Greenwich."

"What's the idea?" cried the other girl in a slightly raised voice. "Why don't you stay at your own table? You must be tight."

"Now Elaine!" said Charley, turning to her reprovingly.

"I'll meet the train that gets to Greenwich at six," Diana went on coolly. "If you can't get rid of this—this woman——" she indicated his companion with a careless wave of her hand— "send her to the movies."

With an exclamation the other girl got to her feet and for a moment a scene was imminent. But nodding to Charley, Diana turned from the table, beckoned to her escort across the room and left the café.

"I don't like her," cried Elaine querulously when Diana was out of hearing. "Who is she anyhow? Some old girl of yours?"

"That's right," he answered, frowning. "Old girl of mine. In fact, my only old girl."

"Oh, you've known her all your life."

"No." He shook his head. "When I first met her she was a canteen worker in the war."

"*She* was!" Elaine raised her brows in surprise. "Why she doesn't look——"

"Oh, she's not nineteen anymore—she's nearly twenty-five." He laughed. "I saw her sitting on a box at an ammunition dump near Soissons one day with enough lieutenants around her to officer a regiment. Three weeks after that we were engaged!"

"Then what?" demanded Elaine sharply.

"Usual thing," he answered with a touch of bitterness. "She broke it off. Only unusual part of it was that I never knew why.

Said good-bye to her one day and left for my squadron. I must have said something or done something then that started the big fuss. I'll never know. In fact I don't remember anything about it very clearly because a few hours later I had a crash and what happened just before has always been damn dim in my head. As soon as I was well enough to care about anything I saw that the situation was changed. Thought at first that there must be another man."

"Did she break the engagement?"

"She cern'ly did. While I was getting better she used to sit by my bed for hours looking at me with the funniest expression in her eyes. Finally I asked for a mirror—I thought I must be all cut up or something. But I wasn't. Then one day she began to cry. She said she'd been thinking it over and perhaps it was a mistake and all that sort of thing. Seemed to be referring to some quarrel we'd had when we said good-bye just before I got hurt. But I was still a pretty sick man and the whole thing didn't seem to make any sense unless there was another man in it somewhere. She said that we both wanted our freedom, and then she looked at me as if she expected me to make some explanation or apology—and I couldn't think what I'd done. I remember leaning back in the bed and wishing I could die right then and there. Two months later I heard she'd sailed for home."

Elaine leaned anxiously over the table.

"Don't go to the country with her, Charley," she said. "Please don't go. She wants you back—I can tell by looking at her."

He shook his head and laughed.

"Yes she does," insisted Elaine. "I can tell. I hate her. She had you once and now she wants you back. I can see it in her eyes. I wish you'd stay in New York with me."

"No," he said stubbornly. "Going out and look her over. Diamond Dick's an old girl of mine."

Diana was standing on the station platform in the late afternoon, drenched with golden light. In the face of her immaculate freshness Charley Abbot felt ragged and old. He was only twenty-nine, but four wild years had left many lines around his dark, handsome eyes. Even his walk was tired—it was no longer a demonstration of fitness and physical grace. It was a way of getting somewhere, failing other forms of locomotion; that was all.

"Charley," Diana cried, "where's your bag?"

"I only came out to dinner—I can't possibly spend the night."

He was sober, she saw, but he looked as if he needed a drink badly. She took his arm and guided him to a red-wheeled coupé parked in the street.

"Get in and sit down," she commanded. "You walk as if you were about to fall down anyhow."

"Never felt better in my life."

She laughed scornfully.

"Why do you have to get back tonight?" she demanded.

"I promised—you see I had an engagement——"

"Oh, let her wait!" exclaimed Diana impatiently. "She didn't look as if she had much else to do. Who is she anyhow?"

"I don't see how that could possibly interest you, Diamond Dick."

She flushed at the familiar name.

"Everything about you interests me. Who is that girl?"

"Elaine Russel. She's in the movies—sort of."

"She looked pulpy," said Diana thoughtfully. "I keep thinking of her. You look pulpy too. What are you doing with yourself—waiting for another war?"

They turned into the drive of a big rambling house on the Sound. Canvas was being stretched for dancing on the lawn.

"Look!" She was pointing at a figure in knickerbockers on a side veranda. "That's my brother Breck. You've never met him. He's home from New Haven for the Easter holidays and he's having a dance tonight."

A handsome boy of eighteen came down the veranda steps toward them.

"He thinks you're the greatest man in the world," whispered Diana. "Pretend you're wonderful."

There was an embarrassed introduction.

"Done any flying lately?" asked Breck immediately.

"Not for some years," admitted Charley.

"I was too young for the war myself," said Breck regretfully, "but I'm going to try for a pilot's license this summer. It's the only thing, isn't it—flying I mean."

"Why, I suppose so," said Charley somewhat puzzled. "I hear you're having a dance tonight."

Breck waved his hand carelessly.

"Oh, just a lot of people from around here. I should think anything like that'd bore you to death—after all you've seen."

Charley turned helplessly to Diana.

"Come on," she said, laughing, "we'll go inside."

Mrs. Dickey met them in the hall and subjected Charley to a polite but somewhat breathless scrutiny. The whole household seemed to treat him with unusual respect, and the subject had a tendency to drift immediately to the war.

"What are you doing now?" asked Mr. Dickey. "Going into your father's business?"

"There isn't any business left," said Charley frankly. "I'm just about on my own."

Mr. Dickey considered for a moment.

"If you haven't made any plans why don't you come down and see me at my office some day this week. I've got a little proposition that may interest you."

It annoyed Charley to think that Diana had probably arranged all this. He needed no charity. He had not been crippled, and the war was over five years. People did not talk like this anymore.

The whole first floor had been set with tables for the supper that would follow the dance, so Charley and Diana had dinner with Mr. and Mrs. Dickey in the library upstairs. It was an uncomfortable meal at which Mr. Dickey did the talking and Diana covered up the gaps with nervous gaiety. He was glad when it was over and he was standing with Diana on the veranda in the gathering darkness.

"Charley——" She leaned close to him and touched his arm gently. "Don't go to New York tonight. Spend a few days down here with me. I want to talk to you and I don't feel that I can talk tonight with this party going on."

"I'll come out again—later in the week," he said evasively.

"Why not stay tonight?"

"I promised I'd be back at eleven."

"At eleven?" She looked at him reproachfully. "Do you have to account to that girl for your evenings?"

"I like her," he said defiantly. "I'm not a child, Diamond Dick, and I rather resent your attitude. I thought you closed out your interest in my life five years ago."

"You won't stay?"

"No."

"All right—then we only have an hour. Let's walk out and sit on the wall by the Sound."

Side by side they started through the deep twilight where the air was heavy with salt and roses.

"Do you remember the last time we walked somewhere together?" she whispered.

"Why—no. I don't think I do. Where was it?"

"It doesn't matter—if you've forgotten."

When they reached the shore she swung herself up on the low wall that skirted the water.

"It's spring, Charley."

"Another spring."

"No—just spring. If you say 'another spring' it means you're getting old." She hesitated. "Charley——"

"Yes, Diamond Dick."

"I've been waiting to talk to you like this for five years."

Looking at him out of the corner of her eye she saw he was frowning and changed her tone.

"What kind of work are you going into, Charley?"

"I don't know. I've got a little money left and I won't have to do anything for awhile. I don't seem to fit into business very well."

"You mean like you fitted into the war."

"Yes." He turned to her with a spark of interest. "I belonged to the war. It seems a funny thing to say but I think I'll always look back to those days as the happiest in my life."

"I know what you mean," she said slowly. "Nothing quite so intense or so dramatic will ever happen to our generation again."

They were silent for a moment. When he spoke again his voice was trembling a little.

"There are things lost in it—parts of me—that I can look for and never find. It was my war in a way, you see, and you can't quite hate what was your own." He turned to her suddenly. "Let's be frank, Diamond Dick—we loved each other once and it seems—seems rather silly to be stalling this way with you."

She caught her breath.

"Yes," she said faintly, "let's be frank."

"I know what you're up to and I know you're doing it to be kind. But life doesn't start all over again when a man talks to an old love on a spring night."

"I'm not doing it to be kind."

He looked at her closely.

"You lie, Diamond Dick. But—even if you loved me now it wouldn't matter. I'm not like I was five years ago—I'm a different person, can't you see? I'd rather have a drink this minute than all the moonlight in the world. I don't even think I could love a girl like you anymore."

She nodded.

"I see."

"Why wouldn't you marry me five years ago, Diamond Dick?"

"I don't know," she said after a minute's hesitation. "I was wrong."

"Wrong!" he exclaimed bitterly. "You talk as if it had been guesswork, like betting on white or red."

"No, it wasn't guesswork."

There was a silence for a minute—then she turned to him with shining eyes.

"Won't you kiss me, Charley?" she asked simply.

He started.

"Would it be so hard to do?" she went on. "I've never asked a man to kiss me before."

With an exclamation he jumped off the wall.

"I'm going to the city," he said.

"Am I—such bad company as all that?"

"Diana." He came close to her and put his arms around her knees and looked into her eyes. "You know that if I kiss you I'll have to stay. I'm afraid of you—afraid of your kindness, afraid to remember anything about you at all. And I couldn't go from a kiss of yours to—another girl."

"Good-bye," she said suddenly.

He hesitated for a moment; then he protested helplessly.

"You put me in a terrible position."

"Good-bye."

"Listen Diana——"

"Please go away."

He turned and walked quickly toward the house.

Diana sat without moving while the night breeze made cool puffs and ruffles on her chiffon dress. The moon had risen higher now, and floating in the Sound was a triangle of silver scales, trembling a little to the stiff, tinny drip of the banjos on the lawn.

Alone at last—she was alone at last. There was not even a ghost left now to drift with through the years. She might stretch out her arms as far as they could reach into the night without fear that they would brush friendly cloth. The thin silver had worn off from all the stars.

She sat there for almost an hour, her eyes fixed upon the points of light on the other shore. Then the wind ran cold fingers along her silk stockings so she jumped off the wall, landing softly among the bright pebbles of the sand.

"Diana!"

Breck was coming toward her, flushed with the excitement of his party.

"Diana! I want you to meet a man in my class at New Haven. His brother took you to a prom three years ago."

She shook her head.

"I've got a headache; I'm going upstairs."

Coming closer Breck saw that her eyes were glittering with tears.

"Diana, what's the matter?"

"Nothing."

"Something's the matter."

"Nothing, Breck. But oh, take care, take care! Be careful who you love."

"Are you in love with—Charley Abbot?"

She gave a strange, hard little laugh.

"Me? Oh, God, no, Breck! I don't love anybody. I wasn't made for anything like love. I don't even love myself anymore. It was you I was talking about. That was advice, don't you understand?"

She ran suddenly toward the house, holding her skirts high out of the dew. Reaching her own room she kicked off her slippers and threw herself on the bed in the darkness.

"I should have been careful," she whispered to herself. "All my life I'll be punished for not being more careful. I wrapped all my love up like a box of candy and gave it away."

Her window was open and outside on the lawn the sad, dissonant horns were telling a melancholy story. A blackamoor was two-timing the lady to whom he had pledged faith. The lady warned him, in so many words, to stop fooling 'round Sweet Jelly-Roll, even though Sweet Jelly-Roll was the color of pale cinnamon——

The phone on the table by her bed rang imperatively. Diana took up the receiver.

"Yes."

"One minute please, New York calling."

It flashed through Diana's head that it was Charley—but that was impossible. He must be still on the train.

"Hello." A woman was speaking. "Is this the Dickey residence?"

"Yes."

"Well, is Mr. Charles Abbot there?"

Diana's heart seemed to stop beating as she recognized the voice—it was the blonde girl of the café.

"What?" she asked dazedly.

"I would like to speak to Mr. Abbot at once please."

"You—you can't speak to him. He's gone."

There was a pause. Then the girl's voice, suspiciously:

"He isn't gone."

Diana's hands tightened on the telephone.

"I know who's talking," went on the voice, rising to a hysterical note, "and I want to speak to Mr. Abbot. If you're not telling the truth, and he finds out, there'll be trouble."

"Be quiet!"

"If he's gone, where did he go?"

"I don't know."

"If he isn't at my apartment in half an hour I'll know you're lying and I'll——"

Diana hung up the receiver and tumbled back on the bed—too weary of life to think or care. Out on the lawn the orchestra was singing and the words drifted in her window on the breeze.

> *"Lis-sen while I—get you tole:*
> *Stop foolin' 'roun' sweet—Jelly-Roll——"*

She listened. The negro voices were wild and loud—life was in that key, so harsh a key. How abominably helpless she was! Her appeal was ghostly, impotent, absurd, before the barbaric urgency of this other girl's desire.

> *"Just treat me pretty, just treat me sweet*
> *Cause I possess a fo'ty-fo' that don't repeat."*

The music sank to a weird, threatening minor. It reminded her of something—some mood in her own childhood—and a new atmosphere seemed to open up around her. It was not so much a definite memory as it was a current, a tide setting through her whole body.

Diana jumped suddenly to her feet and groped for her slippers in the darkness. The song was beating in her head and her little teeth set together in a click. She could feel the tense golf-muscles rippling and tightening along her arms.

Running into the hall she opened the door to her father's room, closed it cautiously behind her and went to the bureau. It was in the top drawer—black and shining among the pale anemic collars. Her hand closed around the grip and she drew out the bullet clip with steady fingers. There were five shots in it.

Back in her room she called the garage.

"I want my roadster at the side entrance right away!"

Wriggling hurriedly out of her evening dress to the sound of breaking snaps she let it drop in a soft pile on the floor, replacing it with a golf sweater, a checked sport-skirt and an old blue-and-white blazer which she pinned at the collar with a diamond bar. Then she pulled a tam-o'-shanter over her dark hair and looked once in the mirror before turning out the light.

"Come on, Diamond Dick!" she whispered aloud.

With a short exclamation she plunged the automatic into her blazer pocket and hurried from the room.

Diamond Dick! The name had jumped out at her once from a lurid cover, symbolizing her childish revolt against the softness of life. Diamond Dick was a law unto himself, making his own judgments with his back against the wall. If justice was slow he vaulted into his saddle and was off for the foothills, for in the unvarying rightness of his instincts he was higher and harder than the law. She had seen in him a sort of deity, infinitely resourceful, infinitely just. And the commandment he laid down for himself in the cheap, ill-written pages was first and foremost to keep what was his own.

An hour and a half from the time when she had left Greenwich, Diana pulled up her roadster in front of the Restaurant Mont Mihiel. The theaters were already dumping their crowds into Broadway and half a dozen couples in evening dress looked at her curiously as she slouched through the door. A moment later she was talking to the head-waiter.

"Do you know a girl named Elaine Russel?"

"Yes, Miss Dickey. She comes here quite often."

"I wonder if you can tell me where she lives."

The head-waiter considered.

"Find out," she said sharply. "I'm in a hurry."

He bowed. Diana had come here many times with many men. She had never asked him a favor before.

His eyes roved hurriedly around the room.

"Sit down," he said.

"I'm all right. You hurry."

He crossed the room and whispered to a man at a table—in a minute he was back with the address, an apartment on 49th Street.

In her car again she looked at her wrist watch—it was almost midnight, the appropriate hour. A feeling of romance, of desperate and dangerous adventure thrilled her, seemed to flow out of the electric signs and the rushing cabs and the high stars. Perhaps she was only one out of a hundred people bound on such an adventure tonight—for her there had been nothing like this since the war.

Skidding the corner into East 49th Street she scanned the apartments on both sides. There it was—"The Elkson"—a wide mouth of forbidding yellow light. In the hall a negro elevator boy asked her name.

"Tell her it's a girl with a package from the moving-picture company."

He worked a plug noisily.

"Miss Russel? There's a lady here says she's got a package from the moving-picture company."

A pause.

"That's what she says. . . . All right." He turned to Diana. "She wasn't expecting no package but you can bring it up." He looked at her, frowned suddenly. "You ain't got no package."

Without answering she walked into the elevator and he followed, shoving the gate closed with maddening languor. . . .

"First door to your right."

She waited until the elevator had started down again. Then she knocked, her fingers tightening on the automatic in her blazer pocket.

Running foot-steps, a laugh; the door swung open and Diana stepped quickly into the room.

It was a small apartment, bedroom, bath and kitchenette, furnished in pink and white and heavy with last week's smoke. Elaine Russel had opened the door herself. She was dressed to go out and a green evening cape was over her arm. Charley Abbot sipping at a highball was stretched out in the room's only easy chair.

"What is it?" cried Elaine quickly.

With a sharp movement Diana slammed the door behind her and Elaine stepped back, her mouth falling ajar.

"Good evening," said Diana coldly, and then a line from a forgotten nickel novel flashed into her head. "I hope I don't intrude."

"What do you want?" demanded Elaine. "You've got your nerve to come butting in here!"

Charley who had not said a word set down his glass heavily on the arm of the chair. The two girls looked at each other with unwavering eyes.

"Excuse me," said Diana slowly, "but I think you've got my man."

"I thought you were supposed to be a lady!" cried Elaine in rising anger. "What do you mean by forcing your way into this room?"

"I mean business. I've come for Charley Abbot."

Elaine gasped.

"Why, you must be crazy!"

"On the contrary, I've never been so sane in my life. I came here to get something that belongs to me."

Charley uttered an exclamation but with a simultaneous gesture the two women waved him silent.

"All right," cried Elaine, "we'll settle this right now."

"I'll settle it myself," said Diana sharply. "There's no question or argument about it. Under other circumstances I might feel a certain pity for you—in this case you happen to be in my way. What is there between you two? Has he promised to marry you?"

"That's none of your business!"

"You'd better answer," Diana warned her.

"I won't answer."

Diana took a sudden step forward, drew back her arm and with all the strength in her slim hard muscles, hit Elaine a smashing blow in the cheek with her open hand.

Elaine staggered up against the wall. Charley uttered an exclamation and sprang forward to find himself looking into the muzzle of a forty-four held in a small determined hand.

"Help!" cried Elaine wildly. "Oh, she's hurt me! She's hurt me!"

"Shut up!" Diana's voice was hard as steel. "You're not hurt. You're just pulpy and soft. But if you start to raise a row I'll pump you full of tin as sure as you're alive. Sit down! Both of you. Sit *down!*"

Elaine sat down quickly, her face pale under her rouge. After an instant's hesitation Charley sank down again into his chair.

"Now," went on Diana, waving the gun in a constant arc that included them both. "I guess you know I'm in a serious mood. Understand this first of all. As far as I'm concerned neither of you have any rights whatsoever and I'd kill you both rather than leave this room without getting what I came for. I asked if he'd promised to marry you."

"Yes," said Elaine sullenly.

The gun moved toward Charley.

"Is that so?"

He licked his lips, nodded.

"My God!" said Diana in contempt. "And you admit it. Oh, it's funny, it's absurd—if I didn't care so much I'd laugh."

"Look here!" muttered Charley, "I'm not going to stand much of this, you know."

"Yes you are! You're soft enough to stand anything now." She turned to the girl, who was trembling. "Have you any letters of his?"

Elaine shook her head.

"You lie," said Diana. "Go and get them! I'll give you three. One——"

Elaine rose nervously and went into the other room. Diana edged along the table, keeping her constantly in sight.

"Hurry!"

Elaine returned with a small package in her hand which Diana took and slipped into her blazer pocket.

"Thanks. You had 'em all carefully preserved I see. Sit down again and we'll have a little talk."

Elaine sat down. Charley drained off his whiskey and soda and leaned back stupidly in his chair.

"Now," said Diana, "I'm going to tell you a little story. It's about a girl who went to a war once and met a man who she thought was the finest and bravest man she had ever known. She fell in love with him and he with her and all the other men she had ever known became like pale shadows compared with this man that she loved. But one day he was shot down out of the air, and when he woke up into the world he'd changed. He didn't know it himself but he'd forgotten things and become a different man. The girl felt sad about this—she saw that she wasn't necessary to him anymore, so there was nothing to do but say good-bye.

"So she went away and every night for awhile she cried herself to sleep but he never came back to her and five years went by. Finally word came to her that this same injury that had come between them was ruining his life. He didn't remember anything important anymore—how proud and fine he had once been, and what dreams he had once had. And then the girl knew that she had the right to try and save what was left of his life because she was the only one who knew all the things he'd forgotten. But it was too late. She couldn't approach him anymore—she wasn't coarse enough and gross enough to reach him now—he'd forgotten so much.

"So she took a revolver, very much like this one here, and she came after this man to the apartment of a poor, weak, harmless rat of a girl who had him in tow. She was going to either bring him to himself—or go back to the dust with him where nothing would matter anymore."

She paused. Elaine shifted uneasily in her chair. Charley was leaning forward with his face in his hands.

"Charley!"

The word, sharp and distinct, startled him. He dropped his hands and looked up at her.

"Charley!" she repeated in a thin clear voice. "Do you remember Fontenay in the late fall?"

A bewildered look passed over his face.

"Listen, Charley. Pay attention. Listen to every word I say. Do you remember the poplar trees at twilight, and a long column of French infantry going through the town? You had on your blue uniform, Charley, with the little numbers on the tabs and you were going to the front in an hour. Try and remember, Charley!"

He passed his hand over his eyes and gave a funny little sigh. Elaine sat bolt upright in her chair and gazed from one to the other of them with wide eyes.

"Do you remember the poplar trees?" went on Diana. "The sun was going down and the leaves were silver and there was a bell ringing. Do you remember, Charley? Do you remember?"

Again silence. Charley gave a curious little groan and lifted his head.

"I can't—understand," he muttered hoarsely. "There's something funny here."

"Can't you remember?" cried Diana. The tears were streaming from her eyes. "Oh God! Can't you remember? The brown road and the poplar trees and the yellow sky." She sprang suddenly to her feet. "Can't you remember?" she cried wildly. "Think, think—there's time. The bells are ringing—the bells are ringing, Charley! And there's just one hour!"

Then he too was on his feet, reeling and swaying.

"Oh-h-h-h!" he cried.

"Charley," sobbed Diana, "remember, remember, remember!"

"I see!" he said wildly. "I can see now—I remember, oh I remember!"

With a choking sob his whole body seemed to wilt under him and he pitched back senseless into his chair.

In a minute the two girls were beside him.

"He's fainted!" Diana cried—"get some water quick."

"You devil!" screamed Elaine, her face distorted. "Look what's happened! What right have you to do this? What right? What right?"

"What right?" Diana turned to her with black, shining eyes. "Every right in the world. I've been married to Charley Abbot for five years."

Charley and Diana were married again in Greenwich early in June. After the wedding her oldest friends stopped calling her Diamond Dick—it had been a most inappropriate name for some years, they said, and it was thought that the effect on her children might be unsettling, if not distinctly pernicious.

Yet perhaps if the occasion should arise Diamond Dick would come to life again from the colored cover and, with spurs shining and buckskin fringes fluttering in the breeze, ride into the lawless hills to protect her own. For under all her softness Diamond Dick was always hard as steel—so hard that the years knew it and stood still for her and the clouds rolled apart and a sick man, hearing those untiring hoof-beats in the night, rose up and shook off the dark burden of the war.

The Third Casket

W HEN you come into Cyrus Girard's office suite on the thirty-second floor you think at first that there has been a mistake, that the elevator instead of bringing you upstairs has brought you uptown, and that you are walking into an apartment on Fifth Avenue where you have no business at all. What you take to be the sound of a stock ticker is only a businesslike canary swinging in a silver cage overhead, and while the languid debutante at the mahogany table gets ready to ask you your name you can feast your eyes on etchings, tapestries, carved panels and fresh flowers.

Cyrus Girard does not, however, run an interior-decorating establishment, though he has, on occasion, run almost everything else. The lounging aspect of his ante-room is merely an elaborate camouflage for the wild clamor of affairs that goes on ceaselessly within. It is merely the padded glove over the mailed fist, the smile on the face of the prizefighter.

No one was more intensely aware of this than the three young men who were waiting there one April morning to see Mr. Girard. Whenever the door marked Private trembled with the pressure of enormous affairs they started nervously in unconscious unison. All three of them were on the hopeful side of thirty, each of them had just got off the train, and they had never seen one another before. They had been waiting side by side on a Circassian leather lounge for the best part of an hour.

Once the young man with the pitch-black eyes and hair had pulled out a package of cigarettes and offered it hesitantly to the two others. But the two others had refused in such a politely alarmed way that the dark young man, after a quick look around, had returned the package unsampled to his pocket. Following this disrespectful incident a long silence had fallen, broken only by the clatter of the canary as it ticked off the bond market in bird land.

When the Louis XIII clock stood at noon the door marked Private swung open in a tense, embarrassed way, and a frantic

430

secretary demanded that the three callers step inside. They stood up as one man.

"Do you mean—all together?" asked the tallest one in some embarrassment.

"All together."

Falling unwillingly into a sort of lockstep and glancing neither to left nor right, they passed through a series of embattled rooms and marched into the private office of Cyrus Girard, who filled the position of Telamonian Ajax among the Homeric characters of Wall Street.

He was a thin, quiet-mannered man of sixty, with a fine, restless face and the clear, fresh, trusting eyes of a child. When the procession of young men walked in he stood up behind his desk with an expectant smile.

"Parrish?" he said eagerly.

The tall young man said "Yes, sir," and was shaken by the hand. "Jones?"

This was the young man with the black eyes and hair. He smiled back at Cyrus Girard and announced in a slightly southern accent that he was mighty glad to meet him.

"And so you must be Van Buren," said Girard, turning to the third. Van Buren acknowledged as much. He was obviously from a large city—unflustered and very spick-and-span.

"Sit down," said Girard, looking eagerly from one to the other. "I can't tell you the pleasure of this minute."

They all smiled nervously and sat down.

"Yes, sir," went on the older man, "if I'd had any boys of my own I don't know but what I'd have wanted them to look just like you three." He saw that they were all growing pink, and he broke off with a laugh. "All right, I won't embarrass you anymore. Tell me about the health of your respective fathers and we'll get down to business."

Their fathers, it seemed, were very well; they had all sent congratulatory messages by their sons for Mr. Girard's sixtieth birthday.

"Thanks. Thanks. Now that's over." He leaned back suddenly in his chair. "Well, boys, here's what I have to say. I'm retiring from business next year. I've always intended to retire at sixty, and my wife's always counted on it, and the time's come. I can't put it off any longer. I haven't any sons and I haven't any nephews and I haven't any cousins and I have a brother who's fifty years old and in the same boat I am. He'll perhaps hang on for ten years more down here; after that it looks as if the house, Cyrus Girard, Incorporated, would change its name.

"A month ago I wrote to the three best friends I had in college, the three best friends I ever had in my life, and asked them if they had any sons between twenty-five and thirty years old. I told them I had room for just one young man here in my business, but he had to be about the best in the market. And as all three of you arrived here this morning I guess your fathers think you are. There's nothing complicated about my proposition. It'll take me three months to find out what I want to know, and at the end of that time two of you'll be disappointed; the other one can have about everything they used to give away in the fairy tales, half my kingdom and, if she wants him, my daughter's hand." He raised his head slightly. "Correct me, Lola, if I've said anything wrong."

At these words the three young men started violently, looked behind them, and then jumped precipitately to their feet. Reclining lazily in an armchair not two yards away sat a gold-and-ivory little beauty with dark eyes and a moving, childish smile that was like all the lost youth in the world. When she saw the startled expressions on their faces she gave vent to a suppressed chuckle in which the victims after a moment joined.

"This is my daughter," said Cyrus Girard, smiling innocently. "Don't be so alarmed. She has many suitors come from far and near—and all that sort of thing. Stop making these young men feel silly, Lola, and ask them if they'll come to dinner with us tonight."

Lola got to her feet gravely and her grey eyes fell on them one after another.

"I only know part of your names," she said.

"Easily arranged," said Van Buren. "Mine's George."

The tall young man bowed.

"I respond to John Hardwick Parrish," he confessed, "or anything of that general sound."

She turned to the dark-haired southerner, who had volunteered no information. "How about Mr. Jones?"

"Oh, just—Jones," he answered uneasily.

She looked at him in surprise.

"Why, how partial!" she exclaimed, laughing. "How—I might even say how fragmentary."

Mr. Jones looked around him in a frightened way.

"Well, I tell you," he said finally, "I don't guess my first name is much suited to this sort of thing."

"What is it?"

"It's Rip."

"Rip!"

Eight eyes turned reproachfully upon him.

"Young man," exclaimed Girard, "you don't mean that my old friend in his senses named his son that!"

Jones shifted defiantly on his feet.

"No, he didn't," he admitted. "He named me Oswald."

There was a ripple of sympathetic laughter.

"Now you four go along," said Girard, sitting down at his desk. "Tomorrow at nine o'clock sharp you report to my general manager, Mr. Galt, and the tournament begins. Meanwhile if Lola has her coupé-sport-limousine-roadster-landaulet, or whatever she drives now, she'll probably take you to your respective hotels."

After they had gone Girard's face grew restless again and he stared at nothing for a long time before he pressed the button that started the long-delayed stream of traffic through his mind.

"One of them's sure to be all right," he muttered, "but suppose it turned out to be the dark one. Rip Jones, Incorporated!"

II

As the three months drew to an end it began to appear that not one, but all of the young men were going to turn out all right. They were all industrious, they were all possessed of that mysterious ease known as personality and, moreover, they all had brains. If Parrish, the tall young man from the West, was a little the quicker in sizing up the market; if Jones, the southerner, was a bit the most impressive in his relations with customers, then Van Buren made up for it by spending his nights in the study of investment securities. Cyrus Girard's mind was no sooner drawn to one of them by some exhibition of shrewdness or resourcefulness than a parallel talent appeared in one of the others. Instead of having to enforce upon himself a strict neutrality he found himself trying to concentrate upon the individual merits of first one and then another—but so far without success.

Every week-end they all came out to the Girard place at Tuxedo Park, where they fraternized a little self-consciously with the young and lovely Lola, and on Sunday mornings tactlessly defeated her father at golf. On the last tense week-end before the decision was to be made Cyrus Girard asked them to meet him in his study after dinner. On their respective merits as future partners in Cyrus Girard, Inc., he had been unable to decide, but his despair had evoked another plan, on which he intended to base his decision.

"Gentlemen," he said, when they had convoked in his study at the appointed hour, "I have brought you here to tell you that you're all fired."

Immediately the three young men were on their feet, with shocked, reproachful expressions in their eyes.

"Temporarily," he added, smiling good-humoredly. "So spare a decrepit old man your violence and sit down."

They sat down, with short relieved smiles.

"I like you all," he went on, "and I don't know which one I like better than the others. In fact—this thing hasn't come out right at all. So I'm going to extend the competition for two more weeks—but in an entirely different way."

They all sat forward eagerly in their chairs.

"Now my generation," he went on, "have made a failure of our leisure hours. We grew up in the most hard-boiled commercial age any country ever knew, and when we retire we never know what to do with the rest of our lives. Here I am, getting out at sixty, and miserable about it. I haven't any resources—I've never been much of a reader, I can't stand golf except once a week, and I haven't got a hobby in the world. Now someday you're going to be sixty too. You'll see other men taking it easy and having a good time, and you'll want to do the same. I want to find out which one of you will be the best sort of man after his business days are over."

He looked from one to the other of them eagerly. Parrish and Van Buren nodded at him comprehendingly. Jones after a puzzled half-moment nodded too.

"I want you each to take two weeks and spend them as you think you'll spend your time when you're too old to work. I want you to solve my problem for me. And whichever one I think has got the most out of his leisure—he'll be the man to carry on my business. I'll know it won't swamp him like it's swamped me."

"You mean you want us to enjoy ourselves?" inquired Rip Jones politely. "Just go out and have a big time?"

Cyrus Girard nodded.

"Anything you want to do."

"I take it Mr. Girard doesn't include dissipation," remarked Van Buren.

"Anything you want to do," repeated the older man. "I don't bar anything. When it's all done I'm going to judge of its merits."

"Two weeks of travel for me," said Parrish dreamily. "That's what I've always wanted to do. I'll——"

"Travel!" interrupted Van Buren contemptuously. "When there's so much to do here at home? Travel, perhaps, if you had a year; but for two weeks—— I'm going to try and see how the retired business man can be of some use in the world."

"I said travel," repeated Parrish sharply. "I believe we're all to employ our leisure in the best——"

"Wait a minute," interrupted Cyrus Girard. "Don't fight this out in talk. Meet me in the office at ten-thirty on the morning of August first—that's two weeks from tomorrow—and then let's see what you've done." He turned to Rip Jones. "I suppose you've got a plan too."

"No, sir," admitted Rip Jones with a puzzled look; "I'll have to think this over."

But though he thought it over for the rest of the evening Rip Jones went to bed still uninspired. At midnight he got up, found a pencil and wrote out a list of all the good times he had ever had. But all his holidays now seemed unprofitable and stale, and when he fell asleep at five his mind still threshed disconsolately on the prospect of hollow useless hours.

Next morning as Lola Girard was backing her car out of the garage she saw him hurrying toward her over the lawn.

"Ride in town, Rip?" she asked cheerfully.

"I reckon so."

"Why do you only reckon so? Father and the others left on the nine-o'clock train."

He explained to her briefly that they had all temporarily lost their jobs and there was no necessity of getting to the office today.

"I'm kind of worried about it," he said gravely. "I sure hate to leave my work. I'm going to run in this afternoon and see if they'll let me finish up a few things I had started."

"But you better be thinking how you're going to amuse yourself."

He looked at her helplessly.

"All I can think of doing is maybe take to drink," he confessed. "I come from a little town, and when they say leisure they mean hanging round the corner store." He shook his head. "I don't want any leisure. This is the first chance I ever had, and I want to make good."

"Listen, Rip," said Lola on a sudden impulse. "After you finish up at the office this afternoon you meet me and we'll fix up something together."

He met her, as she suggested, at five o'clock, but the melancholy had deepened in his dark eyes.

"They wouldn't let me in," he said. "I met your father in there, and he told me I had to find some way to amuse myself or I'd be just a bored old man like him."

"Never mind. We'll go to a show," she said consolingly; "and after that we'll run up on some roof and dance."

It was the first of a week of evenings they spent together. Sometimes they went to the theatre, sometimes to a cabaret; once they spent most of an afternoon strolling in Central Park. But she saw that from having been the most light-hearted and gay of the three young men, he was now the most moody and depressed. Everything whispered to him of the work he was missing.

Even when they danced at teatime, the click of bracelets on a hundred women's arms only reminded him of the busy office sound on Monday morning. He seemed incapable of inaction.

"This is mighty sweet of you," he said to her one afternoon, "and if it was after business hours I can't tell you how I'd enjoy it. But my mind is on all the things I ought to be doing. I'm—I'm right sad."

He saw then that he had hurt her, that by his frankness he had rejected all she was trying to do for him. But he was incapable of feeling differently.

"Lola, I'm mighty sorry," he said softly, "and maybe someday it'll be after hours again, and I can come to you——"

"I won't be interested," she said coldly. "And I see I was foolish ever to be interested at all."

He was standing beside her car when this conversation took place, and before he could reply she had thrown it into gear and started away.

He stood there looking after her sadly, thinking that perhaps he would never see her anymore and that she would remember him always as ungrateful and unkind. But there was nothing he could have said. Something dynamic in him was incapable of any except a well-earned rest.

"If it was only after hours," he muttered to himself as he walked slowly away. "If it was only after hours."

III

At ten o'clock on the morning of August first a tall, bronzed young man presented himself at the office of Cyrus Girard, Inc., and sent in his card to the president. Less than five minutes later another young man arrived, less blatantly healthy, perhaps, but with the light of triumphant achievement blazing in his eyes. Word came out through the palpitating inner door that they were both to wait.

"Well, Parrish," said Van Buren condescendingly, "how did you like Niagara Falls?"

"I couldn't tell you," answered Parrish haughtily. "You can determine that on your honeymoon."

"My honeymoon!" Van Buren started. "How—what made you think I was contemplating a honeymoon?"

"I merely meant that when you do contemplate it you will probably choose Niagara Falls."

They sat for a few minutes in stony silence.

"I suppose," remarked Parrish coolly, "that you've been making a serious study of the deserving poor."

"On the contrary, I have done nothing of the kind." Van Buren looked at his watch. "I'm afraid that our competitor with the rakish name is going to be late. The time set was ten-thirty; it now lacks three minutes of the half-hour."

The private door opened, and at a command from the frantic secretary they both arose eagerly and went inside. Cyrus Girard was standing behind his desk waiting for them, watch in hand.

"Hello!" he exclaimed in surprise. "Where's Jones?"

Parrish and Van Buren exchanged a smile. If Jones were snagged somewhere so much the better.

"I beg your pardon, sir," spoke up the secretary, who had been lingering near the door; "Mr. Jones is in Chicago."

"What's he doing there?" demanded Cyrus Girard in astonishment.

"He went out to handle the matter of those silver shipments. There wasn't anyone else who knew much about it, and Mr. Galt thought——"

"Never mind what Mr. Galt thought," broke in Girard impatiently. "Mr. Jones is no longer employed by this concern. When he gets back from Chicago pay him off and let him go." He nodded curtly. "That's all."

The secretary bowed and went out. Girard turned to Parrish and Van Buren with an angry light in his eyes.

"Well, that finishes him," he said determinedly. "Any young man who won't even attempt to obey my orders doesn't deserve a good chance." He sat down and began drumming with his fingers on the arm of his chair.

"All right, Parrish, let's hear what you've been doing with your leisure hours."

Parrish smiled ingratiatingly.

"Mr. Girard," he began, "I've had a bully time. I've been traveling."

"Traveling where? The Adirondacks? Canada?"

"No, sir. I've been to Europe."

Cyrus Girard sat up.

"I spent five days going over and five days coming back. That left me two days in London and a run over to Paris by aeroplane to spend the night. I saw Westminster Abbey, the Tower of London and the Louvre, and spent an afternoon at Versailles. On the boat I kept in wonderful condition—swam, played deck tennis, walked five miles every day, met some interesting people and found time to read. I came back after the greatest two weeks of my life, feeling fine and knowing more about my own country since I had something to compare it with. That, sir, is how I spent my leisure time and that's how I intend to spend my leisure time after I'm retired."

Girard leaned back thoughtfully in his chair.

"Well, Parrish, that isn't half-bad," he said. "I don't know but what the idea appeals to me—take a run over there for the sea voyage and a glimpse of the London Stock Ex—— I mean the Tower of London. Yes, sir, you've put an idea in my head." He turned to the other young man, who during this recital had been shifting uneasily in his chair. "Now, Van Buren, let's hear how you took your ease."

"I thought over the travel idea," burst out Van Buren excitedly, "and I decided against it. A man of sixty doesn't want to spend his time running back and forth between the capitals of Europe. It might fill up a year or so, but that's all. No, sir, the main thing is to have some strong interest—and especially one that'll be for the public good, because when a man gets along in years he wants to feel that he's leaving the world better for having lived in it. So I worked out a plan—it's for a historical and archeological endowment center, a thing that'd change the whole face of public education, a thing that any man would be interested in giving his time and money to. I've spent my whole two weeks working out the plan in detail, and let me tell you it'd be nothing but play work—just suited to the last years of an active man's life. It's been fascinating, Mr. Girard. I've learned more from doing it than I ever knew before—and I don't think I ever had a happier two weeks in my life."

When he had finished, Cyrus Girard nodded his head up and down many times in an approving and yet somehow dissatisfied way.

"Found an institute, eh?" he muttered aloud. "Well, I've always thought that maybe I'd do that someday—but I never figured on running it myself. My talents aren't much in that line. Still, it's certainly worth thinking over."

He got restlessly to his feet and began walking up and down the carpet, the dissatisfied expression deepening on his face. Several times he took out his watch and looked at it as if hoping that perhaps Jones had not gone to Chicago after all, but would appear in a few moments with a plan nearer his heart.

"What's the matter with me?" he said to himself unhappily. "When I say a thing I'm used to going through with it. I must be getting old."

Try as he might, however, he found himself unable to decide. Several times he stopped in his walk and fixed his glance first on one and then on the other of the two young men, trying to pick out some attractive characteristic to which he could cling and make his choice. But after several of these glances their faces seemed to blur together and he couldn't tell one from the other. They were twins who had told him the same story—of carrying the stock exchange by aeroplane to London and making it into a moving-picture show.

"I'm sorry, boys," he said haltingly. "I promised I'd decide this morning, and I will, but it means a whole lot to me and you'll have to give me a little time."

They both nodded, fixing their glances on the carpet to avoid encountering his distraught eyes.

Suddenly he stopped by the table and picking up the telephone called the general manager's office.

"Say, Galt," he shouted into the mouthpiece, "you sure you sent Jones to Chicago?"

"Positive," said a voice on the other end. "He came in here couple of days ago and said he was half-crazy for something to do. I told him it was against orders, but he said he was out of the competition anyhow—and we needed somebody who was competent to handle that silver. So I——"

"Well, you shouldn't have done it, see? I wanted to talk to him about something, and you shouldn't have done it."

Clack! He hung up the receiver and resumed his endless pacing up and down the floor. Confound Jones, he thought. Most ungrateful thing he ever heard of after he'd gone to all this trouble for his father's sake. Outrageous! His mind went off on a tangent and he began to wonder whether Jones would handle that business out in Chicago. It was a complicated situation—but then, Jones was a trustworthy fellow. They were all trustworthy fellows. That was the whole trouble.

Again he picked up the telephone. He would call Lola; he felt vaguely that if she wanted to she could help him. The personal element had eluded him here; her opinion would be better than his own.

"I have to ask your pardon, boys," he said unhappily; "I didn't mean there to be all this fuss and delay. But it almost breaks my heart when I think of handing this shop over to anybody at all, and when I try to decide, it all gets dark in my mind." He hesitated. "Have either one of you asked my daughter to marry him?"

"I did," said Parrish, "three weeks ago."

"So did I," confessed Van Buren; "and I still have hopes that she'll change her mind."

Girard wondered if Jones had asked her also. Probably not; he never did anything he was expected to do. He even had the wrong name.

The phone in his hand rang shrilly and with an automatic gesture he picked up the receiver.

"Chicago calling, Mr. Girard."

"I don't want to talk to anybody."

"It's personal. It's Mr. Jones."

"All right," he said, his eyes narrowing. "Put him on."

A series of clicks—then Jones' faintly southern voice over the wire.

"Mr. Girard?"

"Yeah."

"I've been trying to get you since ten o'clock in order to apologize."

"I should think you would!" exploded Girard. "Maybe you know you're fired."

"I knew I would be," said Jones gloomily. "I guess I must be pretty dumb, Mr. Girard, but I'll tell you the truth—I can't have a good time when I quit work."

"Of course you can't!" snapped Girard. "Nobody can——" He corrected himself. "What I mean is, it isn't an easy matter."

There was a pause at the other end of the line.

"That's exactly the way I feel," came Jones' voice regretfully. "I guess we understand each other, and there's no use my saying anymore."

"What do you mean—we understand each other?" shouted Girard. "That's an impertinent remark, young man. We don't understand each other at all."

"That's what I meant," amended Jones; "I don't understand you and you don't understand me. I don't want to quit working, and you—you do."

"Me quit work!" cried Girard, his face reddening. "Say, what are you talking about? Did you say I wanted to quit work?" He shook the telephone up and down violently. "Don't talk back to me, young man! Don't tell me I want to quit! Why—why, I'm not going to quit work at all! Do you hear that? I'm not going to quit work at all!"

The transmitter slipped from his grasp and bounced from the table to the floor. In a minute he was on his knees, groping for it wildly.

"Hello!" he cried. "Hello—hello! Say, get Chicago back! I wasn't through!"

The two young men were on their feet. He hung up the receiver and turned to them, his voice husky with emotion.

"I've been an idiot," he said brokenly. "Quit work at sixty! Why—I must have been an idiot! I'm a young man still—I've got twenty good years in front of me! I'd like to see anybody send me home to die!"

The phone rang again and he took up the receiver with fire blazing in his eyes.

"Is this Jones? No, I want Mr. Jones; Rip Jones. He's—he's my partner." There was a pause. "No, Chicago, that must be another party. I don't know any Mrs. Jones—I want Mr.——"

He broke off and the expression on his face changed slowly. When he spoke again his husky voice had grown suddenly quiet.

"Why—why, Lola——"

The Unspeakable Egg

WHEN Fifi visited her Long Island aunts the first time she was only ten years old, but after she went back to New York the man who worked around the place said that the sand dunes would never be the same again. She had spoiled them. When she left, everything on Montauk Point seemed sad and futile and broken and old. Even the gulls wheeled about less enthusiastically, as if they missed the brown, hardy little girl with big eyes who played barefoot in the sand.

The years bleached out Fifi's tan and turned her a pale pink color, but she still managed to spoil many places and plans for many hopeful men. So when at last it was announced in the best newspapers that she had concentrated on a gentleman named Van Tyne everyone was rather glad that all the sadness and longing that followed in her wake should become the responsibility of one self-sacrificing individual; not better for the individual, but for Fifi's little world very much better indeed.

The engagement was not announced on the sporting page, or even in the help-wanted column, because Fifi's family belonged to the Society for the Preservation of Large Fortunes; and Mr. Van Tyne was descended from the man who accidentally founded that society, back before the Civil War. It appeared on the page of great names and was illustrated by a picture of a cross-eyed young lady holding the hand of a savage gentleman with four rows of teeth. That was how their pictures came out, anyhow, and the public was pleased to know that they were ugly monsters for all their money, and everyone was satisfied all around. The society editor set up a column telling how Mrs. Van Tyne started off in the *Aquitania* wearing a blue traveling dress of starched felt with a round square hat to match; and so far as human events can be prophesied, Fifi was as good as married; or, as not a few young men considered, as bad as married.

"An exceptionally brilliant match," remarked Aunt Cal on the eve of the wedding, as she sat in her house on Montauk Point and clipped the notice for the cousins in Scotland, and then she added abstractedly, "All is forgiven."

443

"Why, Cal!" cried Aunt Josephine. "What do you mean when you say all is forgiven? Fifi has never injured you in any way."

"In the past nine years she has not seen fit to visit us here at Montauk Point, though we have invited her over and over again."

"But I don't blame her," said Aunt Josephine, who was only thirty-one herself. "What would a young pretty girl do down here with all this sand?"

"We like the sand, Jo."

"But we're old maids, Cal, with no vices except cigarettes and double-dummy mah-jongg. Now Fifi, being young, naturally likes exciting, vicious things—late hours, dice playing, all the diversions we read about in these books."

She waved her hand vaguely.

"I don't blame her for not coming down here. If I were in her place——"

What unnatural ambitions lurked in Aunt Jo's head were never disclosed, for the sentence remained unfinished. The front door of the house opened in an abrupt, startled way, and a young lady walked into the room in a dress marked "Paris, France."

"Good-evening, dear ladies," she cried, smiling radiantly from one to the other. "I've come down here for an indefinite time in order to play in the sand."

"Fifi!"

"Fifi!"

"Aunts!"

"But, my dear child," cried Aunt Jo, "I thought this was the night of the bridal dinner."

"It is," admitted Fifi cheerfully. "But I didn't go. I'm not going to the wedding either. I sent in my regrets today."

It was all very vague; but it seemed, as far as her aunts could gather, that young Van Tyne was too perfect—whatever that meant. After much urging Fifi finally explained that he reminded her of an advertisement for a new car.

"A new car?" inquired Aunt Cal, wide eyed. "What new car?"

"Any new car."

"Do you mean——"

Aunt Cal blushed.

"I don't understand this new slang, but isn't there some part of a car that's called the—the clutch?"

"Oh, I like him physically," remarked Fifi coolly. Her aunts started in unison. "But he was just—— Oh, too perfect, too new; as if they'd fooled over him at the factory for a long time and put special curtains on him——"

Aunt Jo had visions of a black-leather sheik.

"——and balloon tires and a permanent shave. He was too civilized for me, Aunt Cal." She sighed. "I must be one of the rougher girls, after all."

She was as immaculate and dainty sitting there as though she were the portrait of a young lady and about to be hung on the wall. But underneath her cheerfulness her aunts saw that she was in a state of hysterical excitement, and they persisted in suspecting that something more definite and shameful was the matter.

"But it isn't," insisted Fifi. "Our engagement was announced three months ago, and not a single chorus girl has sued George for breach of promise. Not one! He doesn't use alcohol in any form except as hair tonic. Why, we've never even quarreled until today!"

"You've made a serious mistake," said Aunt Cal.

Fifi nodded.

"I'm afraid I've broken the heart of the nicest man I ever met in my life, but it can't be helped. Immaculate! Why, what's the use of being immaculate when, no matter how hard you try, you can't be half so immaculate as your husband? And tactful? George could introduce Mr. Trotzky to Mr. Rockefeller and there wouldn't be a single blow. But after a certain point, I want to have all the tact in my family, and I told him so. I've never left a man practically at the church door before, so I'm going to stay here until everyone has had a chance to forget."

And stay she did—rather to the surprise of her aunts, who expected that next morning she would rush wildly and remorsefully back to New York. She appeared at breakfast very calm and fresh and cool, and as though she had slept soundly all night, and spent the day reclining under a red parasol beside the sunny dunes, watching the Atlantic roll in from the east. Her aunts intercepted the evening paper and burnt it unseen in the open fire, under the impression that Fifi's flight would be recorded in red headlines across the front page. They accepted the fact that Fifi was here, and except that Aunt Jo was inclined to go mah-jongg without a pair when she speculated on the too perfect man, their lives went along very much the same. But not quite the same.

"What's the matter with that niece of yourn?" demanded the yardman gloomily of Aunt Josephine. "What's a young pretty girl want to come and hide herself down here for?"

"My niece is resting," declared Aunt Josephine stiffly.

"Them dunes ain't good for wore-out people," objected the yardman, soothing his head with his fingers. "There's a mono-toness about them. I seen her yesterday take her parasol and like to beat one down, she got so mad at it. Someday she's going to notice how many of them there are, and all of a sudden go loony." He sniffed. "And then what kind of a proposition we going to have on our hands?"

"That will do, Percy," snapped Aunt Jo. "Go about your busi-ness. I want ten pounds of broken-up shells rolled into the front walk."

"What'll I do with that parasol?" he demanded. "I picked up the pieces."

"It's not my parasol," said Aunt Jo tartly. "You can take the pieces and roll them into the front walk too."

And so the June of Fifi's abandoned honeymoon drifted away, and every morning her rubber shoes left wet footprints along a desolate shore at the end of nowhere. For a while she seemed to thrive on the isolation, and the sea wind blew her cheeks scarlet with health; but after a week had passed, her aunts saw that she was noticeably restless and less cheerful even than when she came.

"I'm afraid it's getting on your nerves, my dear," said Aunt Cal one particularly wild and windy afternoon. "We love to have you here, but we hate to see you looking so sad. Why don't you ask your mother to take you to Europe for the summer?"

"Europe's too dressed up," objected Fifi wearily. "I like it here where everything's rugged and harsh and rude, like the end of the world. If you don't mind, I'd like to stay longer."

She stayed longer, and seemed to grow more and more mel-ancholy as the days slipped by to the raucous calls of the gulls and the flashing tumult of the waves along the shore. Then one afternoon she returned at twilight from the longest of her long walks with a strange derelict of a man. And after one look at him her aunts thought that the gardener's prophecy had come true and that solitude had driven Fifi mad at last.

II

He was a very ragged wreck of a man as he stood in the doorway on that summer evening, blinking into Aunt Cal's eyes; rather like a beachcomber who had wandered accidentally out of a movie of the South Seas. In his hands he carried a knotted stick of a brutal, treacherous shape. It was a murderous-looking stick, and the sight of it caused Aunt Cal to shrink back a little into the room.

Fifi shut the door behind them and turned to her aunts as if this were the most natural occasion in the world.

"This is Mr. Hopkins," she announced, and then turned to her companion for corroboration. "Or is it Hopwood?"

"Hopkins," said the man hoarsely. "Hopkins."

Fifi nodded cheerfully.

"I've asked Mr. Hopkins to dinner," she said.

There was some dignity which Aunt Cal and Aunt Josephine had acquired, living here beside the proud sea, that would not let them show surprise. The man was a guest now; that was enough. But in their hearts all was turmoil and confusion. They would have been no more surprised had Fifi brought in a many-headed monster out of the Atlantic.

"Won't you—won't you sit down, Mr. Hopkins?" said Aunt Cal nervously.

Mr. Hopkins looked at her blankly for a moment, and then made a loud clicking sound in the back of his mouth. He took a step toward a chair and sank down on its gilt frailty as though he meant to annihilate it immediately. Aunt Cal and Aunt Josephine collapsed rather weakly on the sofa.

"Mr. Hopkins and I struck up an acquaintance on the beach," explained Fifi. "He's been spending the summer down here for his health."

Mr. Hopkins fixed his eyes glassily on the two aunts.

"I come down for my health," he said.

Aunt Cal made some small sound; but recovering herself quickly, joined Aunt Jo in nodding eagerly at the visitor, as if they deeply sympathized.

"Yeah," he repeated cheerfully.

"He thought the sea air would make him well and strong again," said Fifi eagerly. "That's why he came down here. Isn't that it, Mr. Hopkins?"

"You said it, sister," agreed Mr. Hopkins, nodding.

"So you see, Aunt Cal," smiled Fifi, "you and Aunt Jo aren't the only two people who believe in the medicinal quality of this location."

"No," agreed Aunt Cal faintly. "There are—there are three of us now."

Dinner was announced.

"Would you—would you"—Aunt Cal braced herself and looked Mr. Hopkins in the eye—"would you like to wash your hands before dinner?"

"Don't mention it." Mr. Hopkins waved his fingers at her carelessly.

They went in to dinner, and after some furtive backing and bumping due to the two aunts trying to keep as far as possible from Mr. Hopkins, sat down at table.

"Mr. Hopkins lives in the woods," said Fifi. "He has a little house all by himself, where he cooks his own meals and does his own washing week in and week out."

"How fascinating!" said Aunt Jo, looking searchingly at their guest for some signs of the scholarly recluse. "Have you been living near here for some time?"

"Not so long," he answered with a leer. "But I'm stuck on it, see? I'll maybe stay here till I rot."

"Are you—do you live far away?" Aunt Cal was wondering what price she could get for the house at a forced sale, and how she and her sister could ever bear to move.

"Just a mile down the line. . . . This is a pretty gal you got here," he added, indicating their niece with his spoon.

"Why—yes." The two ladies glanced uneasily at Fifi.

"Someday I'm going to pick her up and run away with her," he added pleasantly.

Aunt Cal, with a heroic effort, switched the subject away from their niece. They discussed Mr. Hopkins' shack in the woods. Mr. Hopkins liked it well enough, he confessed, except for the presence of minute animal life, a small fault in an otherwise excellent habitat.

After dinner Fifi and Mr. Hopkins went out to the porch, while her aunts sat side by side on the sofa turning over the pages of magazines and from time to time glancing at each other with stricken eyes. That a savage had a few minutes since been sitting at their dinner table, that he was now alone with their niece on the dark veranda—no such terrible adventure had ever been allotted to their prim, quiet lives before.

Aunt Cal determined that at nine, whatever the consequences, she would call Fifi inside; but she was saved this necessity, for after half an hour the young lady strolled in calmly and announced that Mr. Hopkins had gone home. They looked at her, speechless.

"Fifi!" groaned Aunt Cal. "My poor child! Sorrow and loneliness have driven you insane!"

"We understand, my dear," said Aunt Jo, touching her handkerchief to her eyes. "It's our fault for letting you stay. A few weeks in one of those rest-cure places, or perhaps even a good cabaret, will——"

"What do you mean?" Fifi looked from one to the other in surprise. "Do you mean you object to my bringing Mr. Hopkins here?"

Aunt Cal flushed a dull red and her lips shut tight together.

"'Object' is not the word. You find some horrible, brutal roustabout along the beach——"

She broke off and gave a little cry. The door had swung open suddenly and a hairy face was peering into the room.

"I left my stick."

Mr. Hopkins discovered the unpleasant weapon leaning in the corner and withdrew as unceremoniously as he had come, banging the door shut behind him. Fifi's aunt sat motionless until his footsteps left the porch. Then Aunt Cal went swiftly to the door and pulled down the latch.

"I don't suppose he'll try to rob us tonight," she said grimly, "because he must know we'll be prepared. But I'll warn Percy to go around the yard several times during the night."

"Rob you!" cried Fifi incredulously.

"Don't excite yourself, Fifi," commanded Aunt Cal. "Just rest quietly in that chair while I call up your mother."

"I don't want you to call up my mother."

"Sit calmly and close your eyes and try to—try to count sheep jumping over a fence."

"Am I never to see another man unless he has a cutaway coat on?" exclaimed Fifi with flashing eyes. "Is this the Dark Ages, or the century of—of illumination? Mr. Hopkins is one of the most attractive eggs I've ever met in my life."

"Mr. Hopkins is a savage!" said Aunt Cal succinctly.

"Mr. Hopkins is a very attractive egg."

"A very attractive what?"

"A very attractive egg."

"Mr. Hopkins is a—a—an unspeakable egg," proclaimed Aunt Cal, adopting Fifi's locution.

"Just because he's natural," cried Fifi impatiently. "All right, I don't care; he's good enough for me."

The situation, it seemed, was even worse than they thought. This was no temporary aberration; evidently Fifi, in the reaction from her recent fiancé, was interested in this outrageous man. She had met him several days ago, she confessed, and she intended to see him tomorrow. They had a date to go walking.

The worst of it was that after Fifi had gone scornfully to bed, Aunt Cal called up her mother—and found that her mother was not at home; her mother had gone to White Sulphur Springs and wouldn't be home for a week. It left the situation definitely in the hands of Aunt Cal and Aunt Jo, and the situation came to a head the next afternoon at teatime, when Percy rushed in upon them excitedly through the kitchen door.

"Miss Marsden," he exclaimed in a shocked, offended voice, "I want to give up my position!"

"Why, Percy!"

"I can't help it. I lived here on the Point for more'n forty-five years, and I never seen such a sight as I seen just now."

"What's the matter?" cried the two ladies, springing up in wild alarm.

"Go to the window and look for yourself. Miss Fifi is kissing a tramp in broad daylight, down on the beach!"

III

Five minutes later two maiden ladies were making their way across the sand toward a couple who stood close together on the shore, sharply outlined against the bright afternoon sky. As they came closer Fifi and Mr. Hopkins, absorbed in the contemplation of each other, perceived them and drew lingeringly apart. Aunt Cal began to speak when they were still thirty yards away.

"Go into the house, Fifi!" she cried.

Fifi looked at Mr. Hopkins, who touched her hand reassuringly and nodded. As if under the influence of a charm, Fifi turned away from him, and with her head lowered walked with slender grace toward the house.

"Now, my man," said Aunt Cal, folding her arms, "what are your intentions?"

Mr. Hopkins returned her glare rudely. Then he gave a low hoarse laugh.

"What's that to you?" he demanded.

"It's everything to us. Miss Marsden is our niece, and your attentions are unwelcome—not to say obnoxious."

Mr. Hopkins turned half away.

"Aw, go on and blab your mouth out!" he advised her.

Aunt Cal tried a new approach.

"What if I were to tell you that Miss Marsden were mentally deranged?"

"What's that?"

"She's—she's a little crazy."

He smiled contemptuously.

"What's the idea? Crazy 'cause she likes me?"

"That merely indicates it," answered Aunt Cal bravely. "She's had an unfortunate love affair and it's affected her mind. Look here!" She opened the purse that swung at her waist. "If I give you fifty—a hundred dollars right now in cash, will you promise to move yourself ten miles up the beach?"

"Ah-h-h-h!" he exclaimed, so venomously that the two ladies swayed together.

"Two hundred!" cried Aunt Cal, with a catch in her voice.

He shook his finger at them.

"You can't buy me!" he growled. "I'm as good as anybody. There's chauffeurs and such that marry millionaires' daughters every day in the week. This is Umerica, a free country, see?"

"You won't give her up?" Aunt Cal swallowed hard on the words. "You won't stop bothering her and go away?"

He bent over suddenly and scooped up a large double handful of sand, which he threw in a high parabola so that it scattered down upon the horrified ladies, enveloping them for a moment in a thick mist. Then laughing once again in his hoarse, boorish way, he turned and set off at a loping run along the sand.

In a daze the two women brushed the casual sand from their shoulders and walked stiffly toward the house.

"I'm younger than you are," said Aunt Jo firmly when they reached the living room. "I want a chance now to see what I can do."

She went to the telephone and called a New York number.

"Doctor Roswell Gallup's office? Is Doctor Gallup there?" Aunt Cal sat down on the sofa and gazed tragically at the ceiling. "Doctor Gallup? This is Miss Josephine Marsden, of Montauk Point. . . . Doctor Gallup, a very curious state of affairs has arisen concerning my niece. She has become entangled with a—a—an unspeakable egg." She gasped as she said this, and went on to explain in a few words the uncanny nature of the situation.

"And I think that perhaps psychoanalysis might clear up what my sister and I have been unable to handle."

Doctor Gallup was interested. It appeared to be exactly his sort of a case.

"There's a train in half an hour that will get you here at nine o'clock," said Aunt Jo. "We can give you dinner and accommodate you overnight."

She hung up the receiver.

"There! Except for our change from bridge to mah-jongg, this will be the first really modern step we've ever taken in our lives."

The hours passed slowly. At seven Fifi came down to dinner, as unperturbed as though nothing had happened; and her aunts played up bravely to her calmness, determined to say nothing until the doctor had actually arrived. After dinner Aunt Jo suggested mah-jongg, but Fifi declared that she would rather read, and settled on the sofa with a volume of the encyclopedia. Looking over her shoulder, Aunt Cal noted with alarm that she had turned to the article on the Australian bush.

It was very quiet in the room. Several times Fifi raised her head as if listening, and once she got up and went to the door and stared out for a long time into the night. Her aunts were both poised in their chairs to rush after her if she showed signs of bolting, but after a moment she closed the door with a sigh and returned to her chair. It was with relief that a little after nine they heard the sound of automobile wheels on the shell drive and knew that Doctor Gallup had arrived at last.

He was a short, stoutish man, with alert black eyes and an intense manner. He came in, glancing eagerly about him, and his eye brightened as it fell on Fifi like the eye of a hungry man when he sees prospective food. Fifi returned his gaze curiously, evidently unaware that his arrival had anything to do with herself.

"Is this the lady?" he cried, dismissing her aunts with a perfunctory handshake and approaching Fifi at a lively hop.

"This gentleman is Doctor Gallup, dear," beamed Aunt Jo, expectant and reassured. "He's an old friend of mine who's going to help you."

"Of course I am!" insisted Doctor Gallup, jumping around her cordially. "I'm going to fix her up just fine."

"He understands everything about the human mind," said Aunt Jo.

"Not everything," admitted Doctor Gallup, smiling modestly. "But we often make the regular doctors wonder." He turned roguishly to Fifi. "Yes, young lady, we often make the regular doctors wonder."

Clapping his hands together decisively, he drew up a chair in front of Fifi.

"Come," he cried, "let us see what can be the matter. We'll start by having you tell me the whole story in your own way. Begin."

"The story," remarked Fifi, with a slight yawn, "happens to be none of your business."

"None of my business!" he exclaimed incredulously. "Why, my girl, I'm trying to help you! Come now, tell old Doctor Gallup the whole story."

"Let my aunts tell you," said Fifi coldly. "They seem to know more about it than I do."

Doctor Gallup frowned.

"They've already outlined the situation. Perhaps I'd better begin by asking you questions."

"You'll answer the doctor's questions, won't you, dear?" coaxed Aunt Jo. "Doctor Gallup is one of the most modern doctors in New York."

"I'm an old-fashioned girl," objected Fifi maliciously. "And I think it's immoral to pry into people's affairs. But go ahead and I'll try to think up a comeback for everything you say."

Doctor Gallup overlooked the unnecessary rudeness of this remark and mustered a professional smile.

"Now, Miss Marsden, I understand that about a month ago you came out here for a rest."

Fifi shook her head.

"No, I came out to hide my face."

"You were ashamed because you had broken your engagement?"

"Terribly. If you desert a man at the altar you brand him for the rest of his life."

"Why?" he demanded sharply.

"Why not?"

"You're not asking me. I'm asking you. . . . However, let that pass. Now, when you arrived here, how did you pass your time?"

"I walked mostly—walked along the beach."

"It was on one of these walks that you met the—ah—person your aunt told me of over the telephone?"

Fifi pinkened slightly.

"Yes."

"What was he doing when you first saw him?"

"He was looking down at me out of a tree."

There was a general exclamation from her aunts, in which the word "monkey" figured.

"Did he attract you immediately?" demanded Doctor Gallup.

"Why, not especially. At first I only laughed."

"I see. Now, as I understand, this man was very—ah—very originally clad."

"Yes," agreed Fifi.

"He was unshaven?"

"Yes."

"Ah!" Doctor Gallup seemed to go through a sort of convolution like a medium coming out of a trance. "Miss Fifi," he cried out triumphantly, "did you ever read 'The Sheik'?"

"Never heard of it."

"Did you ever read any book in which a girl was wooed by a so-called sheik or cave man?"

"Not that I remember."

"What, then, was your favorite book when you were a girl?"

"'Little Lord Fauntleroy.'"

Doctor Gallup was considerably disappointed. He decided to approach the case from a new angle.

"Miss Fifi, won't you admit that there's nothing behind this but some fancy in your head?"

"On the contrary," said Fifi startlingly, "there's a great deal more behind it than any of you suspect. He's changed my entire attitude on life."

"What do you mean?"

She seemed on the point of making some declaration, but after a moment her lovely eyes narrowed obstinately and she remained silent.

"Miss Fifi"—Doctor Gallup raised his voice sharply—"the daughter of C. T. J. Calhoun, the biscuit man, ran away with a taxi-driver. Do you know what she's doing now?"

"No."

"She's working in a laundry on the East Side, trying to keep her child's body and soul together."

He looked at her keenly; there were signs of agitation in her face.

"Estelle Holliday ran away in 1920 with her father's second man!" he cried. "Shall I tell you where I heard of her last? She stumbled into a charity hospital, bruised from head to foot, because her drunken husband had beaten her to within an inch of her life!"

Fifi was breathing hard. Her aunts leaned forward. Doctor Gallup sprang suddenly to his feet.

"But they were playing safe compared to you!" he shouted. "They didn't woo an ex-convict with blood on his hands."

And now Fifi was on her feet, too, her eyes flashing fire.

"Be careful!" she cried. "Don't go too far!"

"I can't go too far!" He reached in his pocket, plucked out a folded evening paper and slapped it down on the table.

"Read that, Miss Fifi!" he shouted. "It'll tell you how four man-killers entered a bank in West Crampton three weeks ago. It'll tell you how they shot down the cashier in cold blood, and how one of them, the most brutal, the most ferocious, the most inhuman, got away. And it will tell you that that human gorilla is now supposed to be hiding in the neighborhood of Montauk Point!"

There was a short stifled sound as Aunt Jo and Aunt Cal, who had always done everything in complete unison, fainted away together. At the same moment there was loud, violent knocking, like the knocking of a heavy club, upon the barred front door.

IV

"Who's there?" cried Doctor Gallup, starting. "Who's there—or I'll shoot!"

His eyes roved quickly about the room, looking for a possible weapon.

"Who are you?" shouted a voice from the porch. "You better open up or I'll blow a hole through the door."

"What'll we do?" exclaimed Doctor Gallup, perspiring freely.

Fifi, who had been sprinkling water impartially upon her aunts, turned around with a scornful smile.

"It's just Percy, the yardman," she explained. "He probably thinks that you're a burglar."

She went to the door and lifted the latch. Percy, gun in hand, peered cautiously into the room.

"It's all right, Percy. This is just an insane specialist from New York."

"Everything's a little insane tonight," announced Percy in a frightened voice. "For the last hour I've been hearing the sound of oars."

The eyes of Aunt Jo and Aunt Cal fluttered open simultaneously.

"There's a fog all over the Point," went on Percy dazedly, "and it's got voices in it. I couldn't see a foot before my face, but I could swear there was boats offshore, and I heard a dozen people talkin' and callin' to each other, just as if a lot of ghosts was havin' a picnic supper on the beach."

"What was that noise?" cried Aunt Jo, sitting upright.

"The door was locked," explained Percy, "so I knocked on it with my gun."

"No, I mean now!"

They listened. Through the open door came a low, groaning sound, issuing out of the dark mist which covered shore and sea alike.

"We'll go right down and find out!" cried Doctor Gallup, who had recovered his shattered equilibrium; and, as the moaning sound drifted in again, like the last agony of some monster from the deep, he added, "I think you needed more than a psychoanalyst here tonight. Is there another gun in the house?"

Aunt Cal got up and took a small pearl-mounted revolver from the desk drawer.

"You can't leave us in this house alone," she declared emphatically. "Wherever you go we're going too!"

Keeping close together, the four of them, for Fifi had suddenly disappeared, made their way outdoors and down the porch steps, where they hesitated a moment, peering into the impenetrable haze, more mysterious than darkness upon their eyes.

"It's out there," whispered Percy, facing the sea.

"Forward we go!" muttered Doctor Gallup tensely. "I'm inclined to think this is all a question of nerves."

They moved slowly and silently along the sand, until suddenly Percy caught hold of the doctor's arm.

"Listen!" he whispered sharply.

They all became motionless. Out of the neighboring darkness a dim, indistinguishable figure had materialized, walking with unnatural rigidity along the shore. Pressed against his body he carried some long, dark drape that hung almost to the sand. Immediately he disappeared into the mist, to be succeeded by another phantom walking at the same military gait, this one with something white and faintly terrible dangling from his arm. A moment later, not ten yards away from them, in the direction in which the figure had gone, a faint dull glow sprang into life, proceeding apparently from behind the largest of the dunes.

Huddled together, they advanced toward the dune, hesitated, and then, following Doctor Gallup's example, dropped to their knees and began to crawl cautiously up its shoreward side. The glow became stronger as they reached the top, and at the same moment their heads popped up over the crest. This is what they saw:

In the light of four strong pocket flashlights, borne by four sailors in spotless white, a gentleman was shaving himself, standing clad only in athletic underwear upon the sand. Before his eyes an irreproachable valet held a silver mirror which gave back the soapy reflection of his face. To right and left stood two additional men-servants, one with a dinner coat and trousers hanging from his arm and the other bearing a white stiff shirt whose studs glistened in the glow of the electric lamps. There was not a sound except the dull scrape of the razor along its wielder's face and the intermittent groaning sound that blew in out of the sea.

But it was not the bizarre nature of the ceremony, with its dim, weird surroundings under the unsteady light, that drew from the two women a short, involuntary sigh. It was the fact that the face in the mirror, the unshaven half of it, was terribly familiar, and in a moment they knew to whom that half-face belonged—it was the countenance of their niece's savage wooer who had lately prowled half-naked along the beach.

Even as they looked he completed one side of his face, whereupon a valet stepped forward and with a scissors sheared off the exterior growth on the other, disclosing, in its entirety now, the symmetrical visage of a young, somewhat haggard but not unhandsome man. He lathered the bearded side, pulled the razor quickly over it and then applied a lotion to the whole surface, and inspected himself with considerable interest in the mirror. The sight seemed to please him, for he smiled. At a word one of the valets held forth the trousers in which he now incased his likely legs. Diving into his open shirt, he procured the collar, flipped a proper black bow with a practiced hand and slipped into the waiting dinner coat. After a transformation which had taken place before their very eyes, Aunt Cal and Aunt Jo found themselves gazing upon as immaculate and impeccable a young man as they had ever seen.

"Walters!" he said suddenly, in a clear, cultured voice.

One of the white-clad sailors stepped forward and saluted.

"You can take the boats back to the yacht. You ought to be able to find it all right by the foghorn."

"Yes, sir."

"When the fog lifts you'd better stand out to sea. Meanwhile, wireless New York to send down my car. It's to call for me at the Marsden house on Montauk Point."

As the sailor turned away, his torch flashed upward accidentally wavering upon the four amazed faces which were peering down at the curious scene.

"Look there, sir!" he exclaimed.

The four torches picked out the eavesdropping party at the top of the hill.

"Hands up, there!" cried Percy, pointing his rifle down into the glare of light.

"Miss Marsden!" called the young man eagerly. "I was just coming to call."

"Don't move!" shouted Percy. And then to the doctor, "Had I better fire?"

"Certainly not!" cried Doctor Gallup. "Young man, does your name happen to be what I think it is?"

The young man bowed politely.

"My name is George Van Tyne."

A few minutes later the immaculate young man and two completely bewildered ladies were shaking hands. "I owe you more apologies than I can ever make," he confessed, "for having sacrificed you to the strange whim of a young girl."

"What whim?" demanded Aunt Cal.

"Why"—he hesitated—"you see, all my life I have devoted much attention to the so-called niceties of conduct; niceties of dress, of manners, of behavior———"

He broke off apologetically.

"Go on," commanded Aunt Cal.

"And your niece has too. She always considered herself rather a model of—of civilized behavior"—he flushed—"until she met me."

"I see," Doctor Gallup nodded. "She couldn't bear to marry anyone who was more of a—shall we say, a dandy?—than herself."

"Exactly," said George Van Tyne, with a perfect eighteenth-century bow. "It was necessary to show her what a—what an———"

"———unspeakable egg," supplied Aunt Josephine.

"———what an unspeakable egg I could be. It was difficult, but not impossible. If you know what's correct, you must necessarily know what's incorrect; and my aim was to be as ferociously incorrect as possible. My one hope is that someday you'll be able to forgive me for throwing the sand—I'm afraid that my impersonation ran away with me."

A moment later they were all walking toward the house.

"But I still can't believe that a gentleman could be so—so unspeakable," gasped Aunt Jo. "And what will Fifi say?"

"Nothing," answered Van Tyne cheerfully. "You see, Fifi knew about it all along. She even recognized me in the tree that first day. She begged me to—to desist until this afternoon; but I refused until she had kissed me tenderly, beard and all."

Aunt Cal stopped suddenly.

"This is all very well, young man," she said sternly; "but since you have so many sides to you, how do we know that in one of your off moments you aren't the murderer who's hiding on the Point?"

"The murderer?" asked Van Tyne blankly. "What murderer?"

"Ah, I can explain that, Miss Marsden." Doctor Gallup smiled apologetically. "As a matter of fact, there wasn't any murderer."

"No murderer?" Aunt Cal looked at him sharply.

"No, I invented the bank robbery and the escaped murderer and all. I was merely applying a form of strong medicine to your niece."

Aunt Cal looked at him scornfully and turned to her sister. "All your modern ideas are not so successful as mah-jongg," she remarked significantly.

The fog had blown back to sea, and as they came in sight of the house the lamps were glowing out into the darkness. On the porch waited an immaculate girl in a gleaming white dress, strung with beads which glistened in the new moonlight.

"The perfect man," murmured Aunt Jo, flushing, "is, of course, he who will make any sacrifice."

Van Tyne did not answer; he was engaged in removing some imperceptible flaw, less visible than a hair, from his elbow, and when he had finished he smiled. There was now not the faintest imperfection anywhere about him, except where the strong beating of his heart disturbed faintly the satin facing of his coat.

John Jackson's Arcady

THE first letter, crumpled into an emotional ball, lay at his elbow, and it did not matter faintly now what this second letter contained. For a long time after he had stripped off the envelope, he still gazed up at the oil painting of slain grouse over the sideboard, just as though he had not faced it every morning at breakfast for the past twelve years. Finally he lowered his eyes and began to read:

"*Dear Mr. Jackson:* This is just a reminder that you have consented to speak at our annual meeting Thursday. We don't want to dictate your choice of a topic, but it has occurred to me that it would be interesting to hear from you on What Have I Got Out of Life. Coming from you this should be an inspiration to everyone.

"We are delighted to have you anyhow, and we appreciate the honor that you confer on us by coming at all.

"Most cordially yours,
"ANTHONY ROREBACK,
"Sec. Civic Welfare League."

"What have I got out of life?" repeated John Jackson aloud, raising up his head.

He wanted no more breakfast, so he picked up both letters and went out on his wide front porch to smoke a cigar and lie about for a lazy half-hour before he went downtown. He had done this each morning for ten years—ever since his wife ran off one windy night and gave him back the custody of his leisure hours. He loved to rest on this porch in the fresh warm mornings and through a porthole in the green vines watch the automobiles pass along the street, the widest, shadiest, pleasantest street in town.

"What have I got out of life?" he said again, sitting down on a creaking wicker chair; and then, after a long pause, he whispered, "Nothing."

The word frightened him. In all his forty-five years he had never said such a thing before. His greatest tragedies had not embittered

461

him, only made him sad. But here beside the warm friendly rain that tumbled from his eaves onto the familiar lawn, he knew at last that life had stripped him clean of all happiness and all illusion.

He knew this because of the crumpled ball which closed out his hope in his only son. It told him what a hundred hints and indications had told him before; that his son was weak and vicious, and the language in which it was conveyed was no less emphatic for being polite. The letter was from the dean of the college at New Haven, a gentleman who said exactly what he meant in every word:

> "*Dear Mr. Jackson:* It is with much regret that I write to tell you that your son, Ellery Hamil Jackson, has been requested to withdraw from the university. Last year largely, I am afraid, out of personal feeling toward you, I yielded to your request that he be allowed another chance. I see now that this was a mistake, and I should be failing in my duty if I did not tell you that he is not the sort of boy we want here. His conduct at the sophomore dance was such that several undergraduates took it upon themselves to administer violent correction.
>
> "It grieves me to write you this, but I see no advantage in presenting the case otherwise than as it is. I have requested that he leave New Haven by the day after tomorrow. I am, sir,
>
> > "Yours very sincerely,
> > "Austin Schemmerhorn
> > "Dean of the College."

What particularly disgraceful thing his son had done John Jackson did not care to imagine. He knew without any question that what the dean said was true. Why, there were houses already in this town where his son, John Jackson's son, was no longer welcome! For a while Ellery had been forgiven because of his father, and he had been more than forgiven at home, because John Jackson was one of those rare men who can forgive even their own families. But he would never be forgiven anymore. Sitting on his porch this morning beside the gentle April rain, something had happened in his father's heart.

"What have I had out of life?" John Jackson shook his head from side to side with quiet, tired despair. "Nothing!"

He picked up the second letter, the civic-welfare letter, and read it over; and then helpless, dazed laughter shook him physically until he trembled in his chair. On Wednesday, at the hour when his delinquent boy would arrive at the motherless home, John Jackson would be standing on a platform downtown, delivering one hundred resounding platitudes of inspiration and cheer. "Members of the association"—their faces, eager, optimistic, impressed, would look up at him like hollow moons—"I have been requested to try to tell you in a few words what I have had from life——"

Many people would be there to hear, for the clever young secretary had hit upon a topic with the personal note—what John Jackson, successful, able and popular, had found for himself in the tumultuous grab bag. They would listen with wistful attention, hoping that he would disclose some secret formula that would make their lives as popular and successful and happy as his own. They believed in rules; all the young men in the city believed in hard-and-fast rules, and many of them clipped coupons and sent away for little booklets that promised them the riches and good fortune they desired.

"Members of the association, to begin with, let me say that there is so much in life that if we don't find it, it is not the fault of life, but of ourselves."

The ring of the stale, dull words mingled with the patter of the rain went on and on endlessly, but John Jackson knew that he would never make that speech, or any speeches ever again. He had dreamed his last dream too long, but he was awake at last.

"I shall not go on flattering a world that I have found unkind," he whispered to the rain. "Instead, I shall go out of this house and out of this town and somewhere find again the happiness that I possessed when I was young."

Nodding his head, he tore both letters into small fragments and dropped them on the table beside him. For half an hour longer he sat there, rocking a little and smoking his cigar slowly and blowing the blue smoke out into the rain.

II

Down at his office, his chief clerk, Mr. Fowler, approached him with his morning smile.

"Looking fine, Mr. Jackson. Nice day if it hadn't rained."

"Yeah," agreed John Jackson cheerfully. "Clear up in an hour. Anybody outside?"

"A lady named Mrs. Ralston."

Mr. Fowler raised his grizzled eyebrows in facetious mournfulness.

"Tell her I can't see her," said John Jackson, rather to his clerk's surprise. "And let me have a pencil memorandum of the money I've given away through her these twenty years."

"Why—yes, sir."

Mr. Fowler had always urged John Jackson to look more closely into his promiscuous charities; but now, after these two decades, it rather alarmed him.

When the list arrived—its preparation took an hour of burrowing through old ledgers and check stubs—John Jackson studied it for a long time in silence.

"That woman's got more money than you have," grumbled Fowler at his elbow. "Every time she comes in she's wearing a new hat. I bet she never hands out a cent herself—just goes around asking other people."

John Jackson did not answer. He was thinking that Mrs. Ralston had been one of the first women in town to bar Ellery Jackson from her house. She did quite right, of course; and yet perhaps back there when Ellery was sixteen, if he had cared for some nice girl——

"Thomas J. MacDowell's outside. Do you want to see him? I said I didn't think you were in, because on second thoughts, Mr. Jackson, you look tired this morning——"

"I'll see him," interrupted John Jackson.

He watched Fowler's retreating figure with an unfamiliar expression in his eyes. All that cordial diffuseness of Fowler's— he wondered what it covered in the man's heart. Several times, without Fowler's knowledge, Jackson had seen him giving imitations of the boss for the benefit of the other employees; imitations with a touch of malice in them that John Jackson had smiled at then, but that now crept insinuatingly into his mind.

"Doubtless he considers me a good deal of a fool," murmured John Jackson thoughtfully, "because I've kept him long after his usefulness was over. It's a way men have, I suppose, to despise anyone they can impose on."

Thomas J. MacDowell, a big barn door of a man with huge white hands, came boisterously into the office. If John Jackson had gone in for enemies he must have started with Tom

MacDowell. For twenty years they had fought over every question of municipal affairs, and back in 1908 they had once stood facing each other with clenched hands on a public platform, because Jackson had said in print what everyone knew—that MacDowell was the worst political influence that the town had ever known. That was forgotten now; all that was remembered of it went into a peculiar flash of the eye that passed between them when they met.

"Hello, Mr. Jackson," said MacDowell with full, elaborate cordiality. "We need your help and we need your money."

"How so?"

"Tomorrow morning, in the 'Eagle,' you'll see the plan for the new Union Station. The only thing that'll stand in the way is the question of location. We want your land."

"My land?"

"The railroad wants to build on the twenty acres just this side of the river, where your warehouse stands. If you'll let them have it cheap we get our station; if not, we can just whistle into the air."

Jackson nodded.

"I see."

"What price?" asked MacDowell mildly.

"No price."

His visitor's mouth dropped open in surprise.

"That from you?" he demanded.

John Jackson got to his feet.

"I've decided not to be the local goat anymore," he announced steadily. "You threw out the only fair, decent plan because it interfered with some private reservations of your own. And now that there's a snag, you'd like the punishment to fall on me. I tear down my warehouse and hand over some of the best property in the city for a song because you made a little 'mistake' last year!"

"But last year's over now," protested MacDowell. "Whatever happened then doesn't change the situation now. The city needs the station, and so"—there was a faint touch of irony in his voice—"and so naturally I come to its leading citizen, counting on his well-known public spirit."

"Go out of my office, MacDowell," said John Jackson suddenly. "I'm tired."

MacDowell scrutinized him severely.

"What's come over you today?"

Jackson closed his eyes.

"I don't want to argue," he said after awhile.

MacDowell slapped his fat upper leg and got to his feet.

"This is a funny attitude from you," he remarked. "You better think it over."

"Good-bye."

Perceiving, to his astonishment, that John Jackson meant what he said, MacDowell took his monstrous body to the door.

"Well, well," he said, turning and shaking his finger at Jackson as if he were a bad boy, "who'd have thought it from you after all?"

When he had gone Jackson rang again for his clerk.

"I'm going away," he remarked casually. "I may be gone for some time—perhaps a week, perhaps longer. I want you to cancel every engagement I have and pay off my servants at home and close up my house."

Mr. Fowler could hardly believe his ears.

"Close up your house?"

Jackson nodded.

"But why—why is it?" demanded Fowler in amazement.

Jackson looked out the high window upon the grey little city drenched now by slanting, slapping rain—his city, he had felt sometimes, in those rare moments when life had lent him time to be happy. That flash of green trees running up the main boulevard—he had made that possible, and Children's Park, and the white dripping buildings around Courthouse Square over the way.

"I don't know," he answered, "but I think I ought to get a breath of spring."

When Fowler had gone he put on his hat and raincoat and, to avoid anyone who might be waiting, went through an unused filing room that gave access to the elevator. The filing room was actively inhabited this morning, however; and, rather to his surprise, by a young boy about nine years old, who was laboriously writing his initials in chalk on the steel files.

"Hello!" exclaimed John Jackson.

He was accustomed to speak to children in a tone of interested equality.

"I didn't know this office was occupied this morning."

The little boy looked at him steadily.

"My name's John Jackson Fowler," he announced.

"What?"

"My name's John Jackson Fowler."

"Oh, I see. You're—you're Mr. Fowler's son?"

"Yeah, he's my father."

"I see." John Jackson's eyes narrowed a little. "Well, I bid you good-morning."

He passed on out the door, wondering cynically what particular axe Fowler hoped to grind by this unwarranted compliment. John Jackson Fowler! It was one of his few sources of relief that his own son did not bear his name.

A few minutes later he was writing on a yellow blank in the telegraph office below:

"ELLERY JACKSON, CHAPEL STREET, NEW HAVEN, CONNECTICUT.

"THERE IS NOT THE SLIGHTEST REASON FOR COMING HOME, BECAUSE YOU HAVE NO HOME TO COME TO ANYMORE. THE MAMMOTH TRUST COMPANY OF NEW YORK WILL PAY YOU FIFTY DOLLARS A MONTH FOR THE REST OF YOUR LIFE, OR FOR AS LONG AS YOU CAN KEEP YOURSELF OUT OF JAIL.

"JOHN JACKSON."

"That's—that's a long message, sir," gasped the dispatcher, startled. "Do you want it to go straight?"

"Straight," said John Jackson, nodding.

III

He rode seventy miles that afternoon, while the rain dried up into rills of dust on the windows of the train and the country became green with vivid spring. When the sun was growing definitely crimson in the west he disembarked at a little lost town named Florence, just over the border of the next state. John Jackson had been born in this town; he had not been back here for twenty years.

The taxi-driver, whom he recognized, silently, as a certain George Stirling, playmate of his youth, drove him to a battered hotel, where, to the surprise of the delighted landlord, he engaged a room. Leaving his raincoat on the sagging bed, he strolled out through a deserted lobby into the street.

It was a bright, warm afternoon, and the silver sliver of a moon riding already in the east promised a clear, brilliant night. John Jackson walked along a somnolent Main Street, where every shop and hitching post and horse fountain made some strange thing happen inside him, because he had known these things for more than inanimate objects as a little boy. At one shop, catching a glimpse of a familiar face through the glass, he hesitated; but changing his mind, continued along the street, turning off at a wide road at the corner. The road was lined sparsely by a row of battered houses, some of them repainted a pale unhealthy blue and all of them set far back in large plots of shaggy and unkempt land.

He walked along the road for a sunny half-mile—a half-mile shrunk up now into a short green aisle crowded with memories. Here, for example, a careless mule had stamped permanently on his thigh the mark of an iron shoe. In that cottage had lived two gentle old maids, who gave brown raisin cakes every Thursday to John Jackson and his little brother—the brother who had died as a child.

As he neared the end of his pilgrimage his breath came faster and the house where he was born seemed to run up to him on living feet. It was a collapsed house, a retired house, set far back from the road and sunned and washed to the dull color of old wood.

One glance told him it was no longer a dwelling. The shutters that remained were closed tight, and from the tangled vines arose, as a single chord, a rich shrill sound of a hundred birds. John Jackson left the road and stalked across the yard knee-deep in abandoned grass. When he came near, something choked up his throat. He paused and sat down on a stone in a patch of welcome shade.

This was his own house, as no other house would ever be; within these plain walls he had been incomparably happy. Here he had known and learned that kindness which he had carried into life. Here he had found the secret of those few simple decencies, so often invoked, so inimitable and so rare, which in the turmoil of competitive industry had made him to coarser men a source of half-scoffing, half-admiring surprise. This was his house, because his honor had been born and nourished here; he had known every hardship of the country poor, but no preventable regret.

And yet another memory, a memory more haunting than any other, and grown strong at this crisis in his life, had really drawn him back. In this yard, on this battered porch, in the very tree over his head, he seemed still to catch the glint of yellow hair and the glow of bright childish eyes that had belonged to his first love, the girl who had lived in the long-vanished house across the way. It was her ghost who was most alive here, after all.

He got up suddenly, stumbling through the shrubbery, and followed an almost obliterated path to the house, starting at the whirring sound of a blackbird which rose out of the grass close by. The front porch sagged dangerously at his step as he pushed open the door. There was no sound inside, except the steady slow throb of silence; but as he stepped in a word came to him, involuntary as his breath, and he uttered it aloud, as if he were calling to someone in the empty house.

"Alice," he cried; and then louder, "Alice!"

From a room at the left came a short, small, frightened cry. Startled, John Jackson paused in the door, convinced that his own imagination had evoked the reality of the cry.

"Alice!" he called doubtfully.

"Who's there?"

There was no mistake this time. The voice, frightened, strange, and yet familiar, came from what had once been the parlor, and as he listened John Jackson was aware of a nervous step within. Trembling a little, he pushed open the parlor door.

A woman with alarmed bright eyes and reddish-gold hair was standing in the center of the bare room. She was of that age that trembles between the enduring youth of a fine, unworried life and the imperative call of forty years, and there was that indefinable loveliness in her face that youth gives sometimes just before it leaves a dwelling it has possessed for long. Her figure, just outside of slenderness, leaned with dignified grace against the old mantel on which her white hand rested, and through a rift in the shutter a shaft of late sunshine fell through upon her gleaming hair.

When John Jackson came in the doorway her large grey eyes closed and then opened again, and she gave another little cry. Then a curious thing happened; they stared at each other for a moment without a word, her hand dropped from the mantel and she took a swaying step toward him. And, as if it were the most natural thing in the world, John Jackson came forward, too, and took her into his arms and kissed her as if she were a little child.

"Alice!" he said huskily.

She drew a long breath and pushed herself away from him.

"I've come back here," he muttered unsteadily, "and find you waiting in this room where we used to sit, just as if I'd never been away."

"I only dropped in for a minute," she said, as if that was the most important thing in the world. "And now, naturally, I'm going to cry."

"Don't cry."

"I've got to cry. You don't think"—she smiled through wet eyes—"you don't think that things like this hap—happen to a person every day."

John Jackson walked in wild excitement to the window and threw it open to the afternoon.

"What were you doing here?" he cried, turning around. "Did you just come by accident today?"

"I come every week. I bring the children sometimes, but usually I come alone."

"The children!" he exclaimed. "Have you got children?"

She nodded.

"I've been married for years and years."

They stood there looking at each other for a moment; then they both laughed and glanced away.

"I kissed you," she said.

"Are you sorry?"

She shook her head.

"And the last time I kissed you was down by that gate ten thousand years ago."

He took her hand, and they went out and sat side by side on the broken stoop. The sun was painting the west with sweeping bands of peach bloom and pigeon blood and golden yellow.

"You're married," she said. "I saw in the paper—years ago."

He nodded.

"Yes, I've been married," he answered gravely. "My wife went away with someone she cared for many years ago."

"Ah, I'm sorry." And after another long silence—"It's a gorgeous evening, John Jackson."

"It's a long time since I've been so happy."

*

There was so much to say and to tell that neither of them tried to talk, but only sat there holding hands, like two children who had wandered for a long time through a wood and now came upon each other with unimaginable happiness in an accidental glade. Her husband was poor, she said; he knew that from the worn, unfashionable dress which she wore with such an air. He was George Harland—he kept a garage in the village.

"George Harland—a red-headed boy?" he asked wonderingly. She nodded.

"We were engaged for years. Sometimes I thought we'd never marry. Twice I postponed it, but it was getting late to just be a girl—I was twenty-five, and so finally we did. After that I was in love with him for over a year."

When the sunset fell together in a jumbled heap of color in the bottom of the sky, they strolled back along the quiet road, still hand in hand.

"Will you come to dinner? I want you to see the children. My oldest boy is just fifteen."

She lived in a plain frame house two doors from the garage, where two little girls were playing around a battered and ancient but occupied baby carriage in the yard.

"Mother! Oh Mother!" they cried.

Small brown arms swirled around her neck as she knelt beside them on the walk.

"Sister says Anna didn't come, so we can't have any dinner."

"Mother'll cook dinner. What's the matter with Anna?"

"Anna's father's sick. She couldn't come."

A tall, tired man of fifty, who was reading a paper on the porch, rose and slipped a coat over his suspenders as they mounted the steps.

"Anna didn't come," he said in a noncommittal voice.

"I know. I'm going to cook dinner. Who do you suppose this is here?"

The two men shook hands in a friendly way, and with a certain deference to John Jackson's clothes and his prosperous manner, Harland went inside for another chair.

"We've heard about you a great deal, Mr. Jackson," he said as Alice disappeared into the kitchen. "We heard about a lot of ways you made them sit up and take notice over yonder."

John nodded politely, but at the mention of the city he had just left a wave of distaste went over him.

"I'm sorry I ever left here," he answered frankly. "And I'm not just saying that either. Tell me what the years have done for you, Harland. I hear you've got a garage."

"Yeah—down the road a ways. I'm doing right well, matter of fact. Nothing you'd call well in the city," he added in hasty depreciation.

"You know, Harland," said John Jackson, after a moment, "I'm very much in love with your wife."

"Yeah?" Harland laughed. "Well, she's a pretty nice lady, I find."

"I think I always have been in love with her, all these years."

"Yeah?" Harland laughed again. That someone should be in love with his wife seemed the most casual pleasantry. "You better tell her about it. She don't get so many nice compliments as she used to in her young days."

Six of them sat down at table, including an awkward boy of fifteen, who looked like his father, and two little girls whose faces shone from a hasty toilet. Many things had happened in the town, John discovered; the factitious prosperity which had promised to descend upon it in the late nineties had vanished when two factories had closed up and moved away, and the population was smaller now by a few hundred than it had been a quarter of a century ago.

After a plentiful plain dinner they all went to the porch, where the children silhouetted themselves in silent balance on the railing and unrecognizable people called greeting as they passed along the dark, dusty street. After awhile the younger children went to bed, and the boy and his father arose and put on their coats.

"I guess I'll run up to the garage," said Harland. "I always go up about this time every night. You two just sit here and talk about old times."

As father and son moved out of sight along the dim street John Jackson turned to Alice and slipped his arm about her shoulder and looked into her eyes.

"I love you, Alice."

"I love you."

Never since his marriage had he said that to any woman except his wife. But this was a new world tonight, with spring all about him in the air, and he felt as if he were holding his own lost youth in his arms.

"I've always loved you," she murmured. "Just before I go to sleep every night, I've always been able to see your face. Why didn't you come back?"

Tenderly he smoothed her hair. He had never known such happiness before. He felt that he had established dominance over time itself, so that it rolled away for him, yielding up one vanished springtime after another to the mastery of his overwhelming emotion.

"We're still young, we two people," he said exultantly. "We made a silly mistake a long, long time ago, but we found out in time."

"Tell me about it," she whispered.

"This morning, in the rain, I heard your voice."

"What did my voice say?"

"It said, 'Come home.'"

"And here you are, my dear."

"Here I am."

Suddenly he got to his feet.

"You and I are going away," he said. "Do you understand that?"

"I always knew that when you came for me I'd go."

Later, when the moon had risen, she walked with him to the gate.

"Tomorrow!" he whispered.

"Tomorrow!"

His heart was going like mad, and he stood carefully away from her to let foot-steps across the way approach, pass and fade out down the dim street. With a sort of wild innocence he kissed her once more and held her close to his heart under the April moon.

IV

When he awoke it was eleven o'clock, and he drew himself a cool bath, splashing around in it with much of the exultation of the night before.

"I have thought too much these twenty years," he said to himself. "It's thinking that makes people old."

It was hotter than it had been the day before, and as he looked out the window the dust in the street seemed more tangible than on the night before. He breakfasted alone downstairs, wondering with the incessant wonder of the city man why fresh cream is almost unobtainable in the country. Word had spread already that he was home, and several men rose to greet him as he came into the lobby. Asked if he had a wife and children, he said no, in a careless way, and after he had said it he had a vague feeling of discomfort.

"I'm all alone," he went on, with forced jocularity. "I wanted to come back and see the old town again."

"Stay long?" They looked at him curiously.

"Just a day or so."

He wondered what they would think tomorrow. There would be excited little groups of them here and there along the street with the startling and audacious news.

"See here," he wanted to say, "you think I've had a wonderful life over there in the city, but I haven't. I came down here because life had beaten me, and if there's any brightness in my eyes this morning it's because last night I found a part of my lost youth tucked away in this little town."

At noon, as he walked toward Alice's house, the heat increased and several times he stopped to wipe the sweat from his forehead. When he turned in at the gate he saw her waiting on the porch, wearing what was apparently a Sunday dress and moving herself gently back and forth in a rocking-chair in a way that he remembered her doing as a girl.

"Alice!" he exclaimed happily.

Her finger rose swiftly and touched her lips.

"Look out!" she said in a low voice.

He sat down beside her and took her hand, but she replaced it on the arm of her chair and resumed her gentle rocking.

"Be careful. The children are inside."

"But I can't be careful. Now that life's begun all over again, I've forgotten all the caution that I learned in the other life, the one that's past."

"Sh-h-h!"

Somewhat irritated, he glanced at her closely. Her face, unmoved and unresponsive, seemed vaguely older than it had yesterday; she was white and tired. But he dismissed the impression with a low, exultant laugh.

"Alice, I haven't slept as I slept last night since I was a little boy, except that several times I woke up just for the joy of seeing the same moon we once knew together. I'd got it back."

"I didn't sleep at all."

"I'm sorry."

"I realized about two o'clock or three o'clock that I could never go away from my children—even with you."

He was struck dumb. He looked at her blankly for a moment, and then he laughed—a short, incredulous laugh.

"Never, never!" she went on, shaking her head passionately. "Never, never, never! When I thought of it I began to tremble all over, right in my bed." She hesitated. "I don't know what came over me yesterday evening, John. When I'm with you, you can always make me do or feel or think just exactly what you like. But this is too late, I guess. It doesn't seem real at all; it just seems sort of crazy to me, as if I'd dreamed it, that's all."

John Jackson laughed again, not incredulously this time, but on a menacing note.

"What do you mean?" he demanded.

She began to cry and hid her eyes behind her hand because some people were passing along the road.

"You've got to tell me more than that," cried John Jackson, his voice rising a little. "I can't just take that and go away."

"Please don't talk so loud," she implored him. "It's so hot and I'm so confused. I guess I'm just a small-town woman, after all. It seems somehow awful to be talking here with you, when my husband's working all day in the dust and heat."

"Awful to be talking here?" he repeated.

"Don't look that way!" she cried miserably. "I can't bear to hurt you so. You have children, too, to think of—you said you had a son."

"A son." The fact seemed so far away that he looked at her, startled. "Oh, yes, I have a son."

A sort of craziness, a wild illogic in the situation had communicated itself to him; and yet he fought blindly against it as he felt his own mood of ecstasy slipping away. For twenty hours he had recaptured the power of seeing things through a mist of hope—hope in some vague, happy destiny that lay just over the hill—and now with every word she uttered the mist was passing, the hope, the town, the memory, the very face of this woman before his eyes.

"Never again in this world," he cried with a last despairing effort, "will you and I have a chance at happiness!"

But he knew, even as he said this, that it had never been a chance; simply a wild, desperate sortie from two long-beleaguered fortresses by night.

He looked up to see that George Harland had turned in at the gate.

"Lunch is ready," called Alice, raising her head with an expression of relief. "John's going to be with us too."

"I can't," said John Jackson quickly. "You're both very kind."

"Better stay." Harland, in oily overalls, sank down wearily on the steps and with a large handkerchief polished the hot space beneath his thin grey hair. "We can give you some iced tea." He looked up at John. "I don't know whether these hot days make you feel your age like I feel mine."

"I guess—it affects all of us alike," said John Jackson with an effort. "The awful part of it is that I've got to go back to the city this afternoon."

"Really?" Harland nodded with polite regret.

"Why, yes. The fact is I promised to make a speech."

"Is that so? Speak on some city problem, I suppose."

"No; the fact is"—the words, forming in his mind to a senseless rhythm, pushed themselves out—"I'm going to speak on What Have I Got Out of Life."

Then he became conscious of the heat indeed; and still wearing that smile he knew so well how to muster, he felt himself sway dizzily against the porch rail. After a minute they were walking with him toward the gate.

"I'm sorry you're leaving," said Alice, with frightened eyes. "Come back and visit your old town again."

"I will."

Blind with unhappiness, he set off up the street at what he felt must be a stumble; but some dim necessity made him turn after he had gone a little way and smile back at them and wave his hand. They were still standing there, and they waved at him and he saw them turn and walk together into their house.

"I must go back and make my speech," he said to himself as he walked on, swaying slightly, down the street. "I shall get up and ask aloud 'What have I got out of life?' And there before them all I shall answer, 'Nothing.' I shall tell them the truth; that life has beaten me at every turning and used me for its own obscure purposes over and over; that everything I have loved has turned to ashes, and that every time I have stooped to pat a dog I have felt his teeth in my hand. And so at last they will learn the truth about one man's heart."

V

The meeting was at four, but it was nearly five when he dismounted from the sweltering train and walked toward the Civic Club hall. Numerous cars were parked along the surrounding streets, promising an unusually large crowd. He was surprised to find that even the rear of the hall was thronged with standing people, and that there were recurrent outbursts of applause at some speech which was being delivered upon the platform.

"Can you find me a seat near the rear?" he whispered to an attendant. "I'm going to speak later, but I don't—I don't want to go up on the platform just now."

"Certainly, Mr. Jackson."

The only vacant chair was half behind a pillar in a far corner of the hall, but he welcomed its privacy with relief; and settling himself, looked curiously around him. Yes, the gathering was large, and apparently enthusiastic. Catching a glimpse of a face here and there, he saw that he knew most of them, even by name; faces of men he had lived beside and worked with for twenty years. All the better. These were the ones he must reach now, as soon as that figure on the platform there ceased mouthing his hollow cheer.

His eyes swung back to the platform, and as there was another ripple of applause he leaned his face around the corner to see. Then he uttered a low exclamation—the speaker was Thomas MacDowell. They had not been asked to speak together in several years.

"I've had many enemies in my life," boomed the loud voice over the hall, "and don't think I've had a change of heart, now that I'm fifty and a little grey. I'll go on making enemies to the end. This is just a little lull when I want to take off my armor and pay a tribute to an enemy—because that enemy happens to be the finest man I ever knew."

John Jackson wondered what candidate or protégé of Mac-Dowell's was in question. It was typical of the man to seize any opportunity to make his own hay.

"Perhaps I wouldn't have said what I've said," went on the booming voice, "were he here today. But if all the young men in this city came up to me and asked me 'What is being honorable?' I'd answer them, 'Go up to that man and look into his eyes.' They're not happy eyes. I've often sat and looked at him and wondered what went on back of them that made those eyes so sad. Perhaps the fine, simple hearts that spend their hours smoothing other people's troubles never find time for happiness of their own. It's like the man at the soda fountain who never makes an ice-cream soda for himself."

There was a faint ripple of laughter here, but John Jackson saw wonderingly that a woman he knew just across the aisle was dabbing with a handkerchief at her eyes.

His curiosity increased.

"He's gone away now," said the man on the platform, bending his head and staring down for a minute at the floor; "gone away suddenly, I understand. He seemed a little strange when I saw him yesterday; perhaps he gave in at last under the strain of trying to do many things for many men. Perhaps this meeting we're holding here comes a little too late now. But we'll all feel better for having said our say about him.

"I'm almost through. A lot of you will think it's funny that I feel this way about a man who, in fairness to him, I must call an enemy. But I'm going to say one thing more"—his voice rose defiantly—"and it's a stranger thing still. Here, at fifty, there's one honor I'd like to have more than any honor this city ever gave me, or ever had it in its power to give. I'd like to be able to stand up here before you and call John Jackson my friend."

He turned away and a storm of applause rose like thunder through the hall. John Jackson half rose to his feet, and then sank back again in a stupefied way, shrinking behind the pillar. The applause continued until a young man arose on the platform and waved them silent.

"Mrs. Ralston," he called, and sat down.

A woman rose from the line of chairs and came forward to the edge of the stage and began to speak in a quiet voice. She told a story about a man whom—so it seemed to John Jackson—he had known once, but whose actions, repeated here, seemed utterly unreal, like something that had happened in a dream. It appeared that every year many hundreds of babies in the city owed their lives to something this man had done five years before; he had put a mortgage upon his own house to assure the children's hospital on the edge of town. It told how this had been kept secret at the man's own request, because he wanted the city to take pride in the hospital as a community affair, when but for the man's effort, made after the community attempt had failed, the hospital would never have existed at all.

Then Mrs. Ralston began to talk about the parks; how the town had baked for many years under the midland heat; and how this man, not a very rich man, had given up land and time and money for many months that a green line of shade might skirt the boulevards, and that the poor children could leave the streets and play in fresh grass in the center of town.

That was only the beginning, she said; and she went on to tell how, when any such plan tottered, or the public interest lagged, word was brought to John Jackson, and somehow he made it go and seemed to give it life out of his own body, until there was scarcely anything in this city that didn't have a little of John Jackson's heart in it, just as there were few people in this city that didn't have a little of their hearts for John Jackson.

Mrs. Ralston's speech stopped abruptly at this point. She had been crying a little for several moments, but there must have been many people there in the audience who understood what she meant—a mother or a child here and there who had been the recipients of some of that kindness—because the applause seemed to fill the whole room like an ocean, and echoed back and forth from wall to wall.

Only a few people recognized the short grizzled man who now got up from his chair in the rear of the platform, but when he began to speak silence settled gradually over the house.

"You didn't hear my name," he said in a voice which trembled a little, "and when they first planned this surprise meeting I wasn't expected to speak at all. I'm John Jackson's head clerk. Fowler's my name, and when they decided they were going to hold the meeting, anyhow, even though John Jackson had gone away, I thought perhaps I'd like to say a few words"—those who were closest saw his hands clench tighter—"say a few words that I couldn't say if John Jackson was here.

"I've been with him twenty years. That's a long time. Neither of us had grey hair when I walked into his office one day just fired from somewhere and asked him for a job. Since then I can't tell you, gentlemen, I can't tell you what his—his presence on this earth has meant to me. When he told me yesterday, suddenly, that he was going away, I thought to myself that if he never came back I didn't—I didn't want to go on living. That man makes everything in the world seem all right. If you knew how we felt around the office——" He paused and shook his head wordlessly. "Why, there's three of us there—the janitor and one of the other clerks and me—that have sons named after John Jackson. Yes, sir. Because none of us could think of anything better than for a boy to have that name or that example before him through life. But would we tell him? Not a chance. He wouldn't even know what it was all about. Why"—he sank his voice to a hushed whisper—"he'd just look at you in a puzzled way and say, 'What did you wish that on the poor kid for?'"

He broke off, for there was a sudden and growing interruption. An epidemic of head turning had broken out and was spreading rapidly from one corner of the hall until it had affected the whole assemblage. Someone had discovered John Jackson behind the post in the corner, and first an exclamation and then a growing mumble that mounted to a cheer swept over the auditorium.

Suddenly two men had taken him by the arms and set him on his feet, and then he was pushed and pulled and carried toward the platform, arriving somehow in a standing position after having been lifted over many heads.

They were all standing now, arms waving wildly, voices filling the hall with tumultuous clamor. Someone in the back of the hall began to sing "For he's a jolly good fellow," and five hundred voices took up the air and sang it with such feeling, with such swelling emotion, that all eyes were wet and the song assumed a significance far beyond the spoken words.

This was John Jackson's chance now to say to these people that he had got so little out of life. He stretched out his arms in a sudden gesture and they were quiet, listening, every man and woman and child.

"I have been asked——" His voice faltered. "My dear friends, I have been asked to—to tell you what I have got out of life——"

Five hundred faces, touched and smiling, every one of them full of encouragement and love and faith, turned up to him.

"What have I got out of life?"

He stretched out his arms wide, as if to include them all, as if to take to his breast all the men and women and children of this city. His voice rang in the hushed silence.

"Everything!"

At six o'clock, when he walked up his street alone, the air was already cool with evening. Approaching his house, he raised his head and saw that someone was sitting on the outer doorstep, resting his face in his hands. When John Jackson came up the walk, the caller—he was a young man with dark, frightened eyes—saw him and sprang to his feet.

"Father," he said quickly, "I got your telegram, but I—I came home."

John Jackson looked at him and nodded.

"The house was locked," said the young man in an uneasy way.

"I've got the key."

John Jackson unlocked the front door and preceded his son inside.

"Father," cried Ellery Jackson quickly, "I haven't any excuse to make—anything to say. I'll tell you all about it if you're still interested—if you can stand to hear——"

John Jackson rested his hand on the young man's shoulder.

"Don't feel too badly," he said in his kind voice. "I guess I can always stand anything my son does."

This was an understatement. For John Jackson could stand anything now forever—anything that came, anything at all.

The Pusher-in-the-Face

THE last prisoner was a man—his masculinity was not much in evidence, it is true; he would perhaps better be described as a "person," but he undoubtedly came under that general heading and was so classified in the court record. He was a small, somewhat shriveled, somewhat wrinkled American who had been living along for probably thirty-five years.

His body looked as if it had been left by accident in his suit the last time it went to the tailor's and pressed out with hot, heavy irons to its present sharpness. His face was merely a face. It was the kind of face that makes up crowds, grey in color with ears that shrank back against the head as if fearing the clamor of the city, and with the tired, tired eyes of one whose forebears have been underdogs for five thousand years.

Brought into the dock between two towering Celts in executive blue he seemed like the representative of a long-extinct race, a very fagged-out and shriveled elf who had been caught poaching on a buttercup in Central Park.

"What's your name?"

"Stuart."

"Stuart what?"

"Charles David Stuart."

The clerk recorded it without comment in the book of little crimes and great mistakes.

"Age?"

"Thirty."

"Occupation?"

"Night cashier."

The clerk paused and looked at the judge. The judge yawned.

"Wha's charge?" he asked.

"The charge is"—the clerk looked down at the notation in his hand—"the charge is that he pushed a lady in the face."

"Pleads guilty?"

"Yes."

482

The preliminaries were now disposed of. Charles David Stuart, looking very harmless and uneasy, was on trial for assault and battery.

The evidence disclosed, rather to the judge's surprise, that the lady whose face had been pushed was not the defendant's wife.

On the contrary the victim was an absolute stranger—the prisoner had never seen her before in his life. His reasons for the assault had been two: first, that she talked during a theatrical performance; and, second, that she kept joggling the back of his chair with her knees. When this had gone on for some time he had turned around and without any warning pushed her severely in the face.

"Call the plaintiff," said the judge, sitting up a little in his chair. "Let's hear what she has to say."

The courtroom, sparsely crowded and unusually languid in the hot afternoon, had become suddenly alert. Several men in the back of the room moved into benches near the desk and a young reporter leaned over the clerk's shoulder and copied the defendant's name on the back of an envelope.

The plaintiff arose. She was a woman just this side of fifty with a determined, rather overbearing face under yellowish-white hair. Her dress was a dignified black and she gave the impression of wearing glasses; indeed the young reporter, who believed in observation, had so described her in his mind before he realized that no such adornment sat upon her thin, beaked nose.

It developed that she was Mrs. George D. Robinson of 1219 Riverside Drive. She had always been fond of the theatre and sometimes she went to the matinee. There had been two ladies with her yesterday, her cousin, who lived with her, and a Miss Ingles—both ladies were in court.

This is what had occurred:

As the curtain went up for the first act a woman sitting behind had asked her to remove her hat. Mrs. Robinson had been about to do so anyhow, and so she was a little annoyed at the request and had remarked as much to Miss Ingles and her cousin. At this point she had first noticed the defendant who was sitting directly in front, for he had turned around and looked at her quickly in a most insolent way. Then she had forgotten his existence until just before the end of the act when she made some remark to

Miss Ingles—when suddenly he had stood up, turned around and pushed her in the face.

"Was it a hard blow?" asked the judge at this point.

"A hard blow!" said Mrs. Robinson indignantly, "I should say it was. I had hot and cold applications on my nose all night."

—"on her nose all night."

This echo came from the witness bench where two faded ladies were leaning forward eagerly and nodding their heads in corroboration.

"Were the lights on?" asked the judge.

No, but everyone around had seen the incident and some people had taken hold of the man right then and there.

This concluded the case for the plaintiff. Her two companions gave similar evidence and in the minds of everyone in the courtroom the incident defined itself as one of unprovoked and inexcusable brutality.

The one element which did not fit in with this interpretation was the physiognomy of the prisoner himself. Of any one of a number of minor offenses he might have appeared guilty—pickpockets were notoriously mild-mannered, for example—but of this particular assault in a crowded theatre he seemed physically incapable. He did not have the kind of voice or the kind of clothes or the kind of mustache that went with such an attack.

"Charles David Stuart," said the judge, "you've heard the evidence against you?"

"Yes."

"And you plead guilty?"

"Yes."

"Have you anything to say before I sentence you?"

"No." The prisoner shook his head hopelessly. His small hands were trembling.

"Not one word in extenuation of this unwarranted assault?"

The prisoner appeared to hesitate.

"Go on," said the judge. "Speak up—it's your last chance."

"Well," said Stuart with an effort, "she began talking about the plumber's stomach."

There was a stir in the courtroom. The judge leaned forward.

"What do you mean?"

"Why, at first she was only talking about her own stomach to—to those two ladies there"—he indicated the cousin and

Miss Ingles—"and that wasn't so bad. But when she began talking about the plumber's stomach it got different."

"How do you mean—different."

Charles Stuart looked around helplessly.

"I can't explain," he said, his mustache wavering a little, "but when she began talking about the plumber's stomach you—you had to listen."

A snicker ran about the courtroom. Mrs. Robinson and her attendant ladies on the bench were visibly horrified. The guard took a step nearer as if at a nod from the judge he would whisk off this criminal to the dingiest dungeon in Manhattan.

But much to his surprise the judge settled himself comfortably in his chair.

"Tell us about it, Stuart," he said not unkindly. "Tell us the whole story from the beginning."

This request was a shock to the prisoner and for a moment he looked as though he would have preferred the order of condemnation. Then after one nervous look around the room he put his hands on the edge of the desk, like the paws of a fox-terrier just being trained to sit up, and began to speak in a quivering voice.

"Well, I'm a night cashier, your honor, in T. Cushmael's restaurant on Third Avenue. I'm not married"—he smiled a little, as if he knew they had all guessed *that*—"and so on Wednesday and Saturday afternoons I usually go to the matinee. It helps to pass the time till dinner. There's a drug store, maybe you know, where you can get tickets for a dollar sixty-five to some of the shows and I usually go there and pick out something. They got awful prices at the box office now." He gave out a long silent whistle and looked feelingly at the judge. "Four or five dollars for one seat—"

The judge nodded his head.

"Well," continued Charles Stuart, "when I pay even a dollar sixty-five I expect to see my money's worth. About two weeks ago I went to one of these here mystery plays where they have one fella that did the crime and nobody knows who it was. Well, the fun at a thing like that is to guess who did it. And there was a lady behind me that'd been there before and she gave it all away to the fella with her. Gee"—his face fell and he shook his head from side to side—"I like to died right there. When I got home to my room I was so mad that they had to come and ask me to stop walking up and down. Dollar sixty-five of my money gone for nothing.

"Well, Wednesday came around again, and this show was one show I wanted to see. I'd been wanting to see it for months, and every time I went into the drug store I asked them if they had any tickets. But they never did." He hesitated. "So Tuesday I took a chance and went over to the box office and got a seat. Two seventy-five it cost me." He nodded impressively. "Two seventy-five. Like throwing money away. But I wanted to see that show."

Mrs. Robinson in the front row rose suddenly to her feet.

"I don't see what all this story has to do with it," she broke out a little shrilly. "I'm sure I don't care—"

The judge brought his gavel sharply down on the desk.

"Sit down, please," he said. "This is a court of law, not a matinee."

Mrs. Robinson sat down, drawing herself up into a thin line and sniffing a little as if to say she'd see about this after awhile. The judge pulled out his watch.

"Go on," he said to Stuart. "Take all the time you want."

"I got there first," continued Stuart in a flustered voice. "There wasn't anybody in there but me and the fella that was cleaning up. After awhile the audience came in, and it got dark and the play started, but just as I was all settled in my seat and ready to have a good time I heard an awful row directly behind me. Somebody had asked this lady"—he pointed to Mrs. Robinson—"to remove her hat like she should of done anyhow and she was sore about it. She kept telling the two ladies that was with her how she'd been at the theatre before and knew enough to take off her hat. She kept that up for a long time, five minutes maybe, and then every once in a while she'd think of something new and say it in a loud voice. So finally I turned around and looked at her because I wanted to see what a lady looked like that could be so inconsiderate as that. Soon as I turned back she began on me. She said I was insolent and then she said 'Tchk! Tchk! Tchk!' a lot with her tongue and the two ladies that was with her said 'Tchk! Tchk! Tchk!' until you could hardly hear yourself think, much less listen to the play. You'd have thought I'd done something terrible.

"By and by, after they calmed down and I began to catch up with what was doing on the stage, I felt my seat sort of creak forward and then creak back again and I knew the lady had her feet on it and I was in for a good rock. Gosh!" he wiped his pale, narrow brow on which the sweat had gathered thinly, "it was awful. I hope to tell you I wished I'd never come at all. Once I got excited at a show and rocked a man's chair without knowing it and I was glad when he asked me to stop. But I knew this lady wouldn't be glad if I asked her. She'd of just rocked harder than ever."

Some time before, the population of the courtroom had begun stealing glances at the middle-aged lady with yellowish-white hair. She was of a deep, life-like lobster color with rage.

"It got to be near the end of the act," went on the little pale man, "and I was enjoying it as well as I could, seeing that sometimes she'd push me toward the stage and sometimes she'd let go, and the seat and me would fall back into place. Then all of a sudden she began to talk. She said she had an operation or something—I remember she said she told the doctor that she guessed she knew more about her own stomach than he did. The play was getting good just then—the people next to me had their handkerchiefs out and was weeping—and I was feeling sort of that way myself. And all of a sudden this lady began to tell her friends what she told the plumber about his indigestion. Gosh!" Again he shook his head from side to side; his pale eyes fell involuntarily on Mrs. Robinson—then looked quickly away. "You couldn't help but hear some and I begun missing things and then missing more things and then everybody began laughing and I didn't know what they were laughing at and, as soon as they'd leave off, her voice would begin again. Then there was a great big laugh that lasted for a long time and everybody bent over double and kept laughing and laughing, and I hadn't heard a word. First thing I knew the curtain came down and then I don't know what happened. I must of been a little crazy or something because I got up and closed my seat, and reached back and pushed the lady in the face."

As he concluded there was a long sigh in the courtroom as though everyone had been holding in his breath waiting for the climax. Even the judge gasped a little and the three ladies on the witness bench burst into a shrill chatter and grew louder and louder and shriller and shriller until the judge's gavel rang out again upon his desk.

"Charles Stuart," said the judge in a slightly raised voice, "is this the only extenuation you can make for raising your hand against a woman of the plaintiff's age?"

Charles Stuart's head sank a little between his shoulders, seeming to withdraw as far as it was able into the poor shelter of his body.

"Yes, sir," he said faintly.

Mrs. Robinson sprang to her feet.

"Yes, judge," she cried shrilly, "and there's more than that. He's a liar too, a dirty little liar. He's just proclaimed himself a dirty little—"

"Silence!" cried the judge in a terrible voice. "I'm running this court, and I'm capable of making my own decisions!" He paused. "I will now pronounce sentence upon Charles Stuart," he referred to the register, "upon Charles David Stuart of 212½ West 22nd Street."

The courtroom was silent. The reporter drew nearer—he hoped the sentence would be light—just a few days on the Island in lieu of a fine.

The judge leaned back in his chair and hid his thumbs somewhere under his black robe.

"Assault justified," he said. "Case dismissed."

The little man Charles Stuart came blinking out into the sunshine, pausing for a moment at the door of the court and looking furtively behind him as if he half-expected that it was a judicial error. Then, sniffing once or twice, not because he had a cold but for those dim psychological reasons that make people sniff, he moved slowly south with an eye out for a subway station.

He stopped at a news-stand to buy a morning paper; then entering the subway was borne south to 18th Street where he disembarked and walked east to Third Avenue. Here he was employed in an all-night restaurant built of glass and plaster white tile. Here he sat at a desk from curfew until dawn, taking in money and balancing the books of T. Cushmael, the proprietor. And here, through the interminable nights, his eyes, by turning a little to right or left, could rest upon the starched linen uniform of Miss Edna Schaeffer.

Miss Edna Schaeffer was twenty-three, with a sweet mild face and hair that was a living example of how henna should not be applied. She was unaware of this latter fact, because all the girls she knew used henna just this way, so perhaps the odd vermilion tint of her coiffure did not matter.

Charles Stuart had forgotten about the color of her hair long ago—if he had ever noticed its strangeness at all. He was much more interested in her eyes, and in her white hands which, as they moved deftly among piles of plates and cups, always looked as if they should be playing the piano. He had almost asked her to go to a matinee with him once, but when she had faced him her lips half-parted in a weary, cheerful smile, she had seemed so beautiful that he had lost courage and mumbled something else instead.

It was not to see Edna Schaeffer, however, that he had come to the restaurant so early in the afternoon. It was to consult with T. Cushmael, his employer, and discover if he had lost his job during his night in jail. T. Cushmael was standing in the front of the restaurant looking gloomily out the plate-glass window, and Charles Stuart approached him with ominous forebodings.

"Where've you been?" demanded T. Cushmael.

"Nowhere," answered Charles Stuart discreetly.

"Well, you're fired."

Stuart winced.

"Right now?"

Cushmael waved his hands apathetically.

"Stay two or three days if you want to, till I find somebody. Then"—he made a gesture of expulsion—"outside for you."

Charles Stuart assented with a weary little nod. He assented to everything. At nine o'clock, after a depressed interval during which he brooded upon the penalty of spending a night among the police, he reported for work.

"Hello, Mr. Stuart," said Edna Schaeffer, sauntering curiously toward him as he took his place behind the desk. "What become of you last night? Get pinched?"

She laughed, cheerfully, huskily, charmingly he thought, at her joke.

"Yes," he answered on a sudden impulse, "I was in the 35th Street jail."

"Yes, you were," she scoffed.

"That's the truth," he insisted. "I was arrested."

Her face grew serious at once.

"Go *on*. What did you do?"

He hesitated.

"I pushed somebody in the face."

Suddenly she began to laugh, at first with amusement and then immoderately.

"It's a fact," mumbled Stuart. "I almost got sent to prison account of it."

Setting her hand firmly over her mouth Edna turned away from him and retired to the refuge of the kitchen. A little later, when he was pretending to be busy at the accounts, he saw her retailing the story to the two other girls.

The night wore on. The little man in the greyish suit with the greyish face attracted no more attention from the customers than the whirring electric fan over his head. They gave him their money and his hand slid their change into a little hollow in the marble counter. But to Charles Stuart the hours of this night, this last night, began to assume a quality of romance. The slow routine of a hundred other nights unrolled with a new enchantment before his eyes. Midnight was always a sort of a dividing point—after that the intimate part of the evening began. Fewer people came in, and the ones that did seemed depressed and tired: a casual ragged man for coffee, the beggar from the street corner who ate a heavy meal of cakes and a beefsteak, a few nightbound street-women and a watchman with a red face who exchanged warning phrases with him about his health.

Midnight seemed to come early tonight and business was brisk until after one. When Edna began to fold napkins at a nearby table he was tempted to ask her if she too had not found the night unusually short. Vainly he wished that he might impress himself on her in some way, make some remark to her, some sign of his devotion that she would remember forever.

She finished folding the vast pile of napkins, loaded it onto the stand and bore it away, humming to herself. A few minutes later the door opened and two customers came in. He recognized them immediately, and as he did so a flush of jealousy went over him. One of them, a young man in a handsome brown suit, cut away rakishly from his abdomen, had been a frequent visitor for the last ten days. He came in always at about this hour, sat down at one of Edna's tables, and drank two cups of coffee with lingering ease. On his last two visits he had been accompanied by his present companion, a swarthy Greek with sour eyes who ordered in a loud voice and gave vent to noisy sarcasm when anything was not to his taste.

It was chiefly the young man, though, who annoyed Charles Stuart. The young man's eyes followed Edna wherever she went, and on his last two visits he had made unnecessary requests in order to bring her more often to his table.

"Good-evening, girlie," Stuart heard him say tonight. "How's tricks?"

"O.K.," answered Edna formally. "What'll it be?"

"What have you?" smiled the young man. "Everything, eh? Well, what'd you recommend?"

Edna did not answer. Her eyes were staring straight over his head into some invisible distance.

He ordered finally at the urging of his companion. Edna withdrew and Stuart saw the young man turn and whisper to his friend, indicating Edna with his head.

Stuart shifted uncomfortably in his seat. He hated that young man and wished passionately that he would go away. It seemed as if his last night here, his last chance to watch Edna, and perhaps even in some blessed moment to talk to her a little, was marred by every moment this man stayed.

Half a dozen more people had drifted into the restaurant—two or three workmen, the newsdealer from over the way—and Edna was too busy for a few minutes to be bothered with attentions. Suddenly Charles Stuart became aware that the sour-eyed Greek had raised his hand and was beckoning him. Somewhat puzzled he left his desk and approached the table.

"Say, fella," said the Greek, "what time does the boss come in?"

"Why—two o'clock. Just a few minutes now."

"All right. That's all. I just wanted to speak to him about something."

Stuart realized that Edna was standing beside the table; both men turned toward her.

"Say, girlie," said the young man, "I want to talk to you. Sit down."

"I can't."

"Sure you can. The boss don't mind." He turned menacingly to Stuart. "She can sit down, can't she?"

Stuart did not answer.

"I say she can sit down, can't she?" said the young man more intently, and added, "Speak up, you little dummy."

Still Stuart did not answer. Strange blood currents were flowing all over his body. He was frightened; anything said determinedly had a way of frightening him. But he could not move.

"Sh!" said the Greek to his companion.

But the younger man was angered.

"Say," he broke out, "sometime somebody's going to take a paste at you when you don't answer what they say. Go on back to your desk!"

Still Stuart did not move.

"Go on away!" repeated the young man in a dangerous voice. "Hurry up! *Run!*"

Then Stuart ran. He ran as hard as he was able. But instead of running away from the young man he ran *toward* him, stretching out his hands as he came near in a sort of straight arm that brought his two palms, with all the force of his hundred and thirty pounds, against his victim's face. With a crash of china the young man went over backward in his chair and, his head striking the edge of the next table, lay motionless on the floor.

The restaurant was in a small uproar. There was a terrified scream from Edna, an indignant protest from the Greek, and the customers arose with exclamations from their tables. Just at this moment the door opened and Mr. Cushmael came in.

"Why, you little fool!" cried Edna wrathfully. "What are you trying to do! Lose me my job?"

"What's this?" demanded Mr. Cushmael, hurrying over. "What's the idea?"

"Mr. Stuart pushed a customer in the face!" cried a waitress, taking Edna's cue. "For no reason at all!"

The population of the restaurant had now gathered around the prostrate victim. He was doused thoroughly with water and a folded tablecloth was placed under his head.

"Oh, he did, did he?" shouted Mr. Cushmael in a terrible voice, seizing Stuart by the lapels of his coat.

"He's raving crazy!" sobbed Edna. "He was in jail last night for pushing a lady in the face. He told me so himself!"

A large laborer reached over and grasped Stuart's small trembling arm. Stuart gazed around dumbly. His mouth was quivering.

"Look what you done!" shouted Mr. Cushmael. "You like to kill a man."

Stuart shivered violently. His mouth opened and he fought the air for a moment. Then he uttered a half-articulate sentence:

"Only meant to push him in the face."

"Push him in the face?" ejaculated Cushmael in a frenzy. "So you got to be a pusher-in-the-face, eh? Well, we'll push your face right into jail!"

"I—I couldn't help it," gasped Stuart. "Sometimes I can't help it." His voice rose unevenly. "I guess I'm a dangerous man and you better take me and lock me up!" He turned wildly to Cushmael, "I'd push you in the face if he'd let go my arm. Yes, I would! I'd push you—right-in-the-*face!*"

For a moment an astonished silence fell, broken by the voice of one of the waitresses who had been groping under the table.

"Some stuff dropped out of this fella's back pocket when he tipped over," she explained, getting to her feet. "It's—why, it's a revolver and——"

She had been about to say handkerchief, but as she looked at what she was holding her mouth fell open and she dropped the thing quickly on the table. It was a small black mask about the size of her hand.

Simultaneously the Greek, who had been shifting uneasily upon his feet ever since the accident, seemed to remember an important engagement that had slipped his mind. He dashed suddenly around the table and made for the front door, but it opened just at that moment to admit several customers who, at the cry of "Stop him!" obligingly spread out their arms. Barred in that direction, he jumped an overturned chair, vaulted over the delicatessen counter, and set out for the kitchen, collapsing precipitately in the firm grasp of the chef in the doorway.

"Hold him! Hold him!" screamed Mr. Cushmael, realizing the turn of the situation. "They're after my cash drawer!"

Willing hands assisted the Greek over the counter, where he stood panting and gasping under two dozen excited eyes.

"After my money, hey?" shouted the proprietor, shaking his fist under the captive's nose.

The stout man nodded, panting.

"We'd of got it too!" he gasped, "if it hadn't been for that little pusher-in-the-face."

Two dozen eyes looked around eagerly. The little pusher-in-the-face had disappeared.

The beggar on the corner had just decided to tip the policeman and shut up shop for the night when he suddenly felt a small, somewhat excited hand fall on his shoulder.

"Help a poor man get a place to sleep—" he was beginning automatically when he recognized the little cashier from the restaurant. "Hello, brother," he added, leering up at him and changing his tone.

"You know what?" cried the little cashier in a strangely ominous tone. "I'm going to push you in the face!"

"What do you mean?" snarled the beggar. "Why, you Ga——"

He got no farther. The little man seemed to run at him suddenly, holding out his hands, and there was a sharp, smacking sound as the beggar came in contact with the sidewalk.

"You're a fakir!" shouted Charles Stuart wildly. "I gave you a dollar when I first came here, before I found out you had ten times as much as I had. And you never gave it back!"

A stout, faintly intoxicated gentleman who was strutting expansively along the other sidewalk had seen the incident and came running benevolently across the street.

"What does this mean!" he exclaimed in a hearty, shocked voice. "Why, poor fellow—" He turned indignant eyes on Charles Stuart and knelt unsteadily to raise the beggar.

The beggar stopped cursing and assumed a piteous whine.

"I'm a poor man, Cap'n—"

"This is—this is *horrible!*" cried the Samaritan, with tears in his eyes. "It's a disgrace! Police! *Pol——!*"

He got no farther. His hands, which he was raising for a megaphone, never reached his face—other hands reached his face, however, hands held stiffly out from a one-hundred-and-thirty-pound body! He sank down suddenly upon the beggar's abdomen, forcing out a sharp curse which faded into a groan.

"This beggar'll take you home in his car!" shouted the little man who stood over him. "He's got it parked around the corner."

Turning his face toward the hot strip of sky which lowered over the city the little man began to laugh, with amusement at first, then loudly and triumphantly until his high laughter rang out in the quiet street with a weird, elfish sound, echoing up the sides of the tall buildings, growing shriller and shriller until people blocks away heard its eerie cadence on the air and stopped to listen.

Still laughing the little man divested himself of his coat and then of his vest and hurriedly freed his neck of tie and collar. Then he spat upon his hands and with a wild, shrill, exultant cry began to run down the dark street.

He was going to clean up New York, and his first objective was the disagreeable policeman on the corner!

They caught him at two o'clock, and the crowd which had joined in the chase were flabbergasted when they found that the ruffian was only a weeping little man in his shirt-sleeves. Someone at the station house was wise enough to give him an opiate instead of a padded cell, and in the morning he felt much better.

Mr. Cushmael, accompanied by an anxious young lady with crimson hair, called at the jail before noon.

"I'll get you out," cried Mr. Cushmael, shaking hands excitedly through the bars. "One policeman, he'll explain it all to the other."

"And there's a surprise for you too," added Edna softly, taking his other hand. "Mr. Cushmael's got a big heart and he's going to make you his day man now."

"All right," agreed Charles Stuart calmly. "But I can't start till tomorrow."

"Why not?"

"Because this afternoon I got to go to a matinee—with a friend."

He relinquished his employer's hand but kept Edna's white fingers twined firmly in his.

"One more thing," he went on in a strong, confident voice that was new to him, "if you want to get me off don't have the case come up in the 35th Street court."

"Why not?"

"Because," he answered with a touch of swagger in his voice, "that's the judge I had when I was arrested last time."

"Charles," whispered Edna suddenly, "what would you do if I refused to go with you this afternoon?"

He bristled. Color came into his checks and he rose defiantly from his bench.

"Why, I'd—I'd——"

"Never mind," she said, flushing slightly. "You'd do nothing of the kind."

Love in the Night

THE words thrilled Val. They had come into his mind sometime during the fresh gold April afternoon and he kept
repeating them to himself over and over: "Love in the night;
love in the night." He tried them in three languages—Russian,
French and English—and decided that they were best in English. In each language they meant a different sort of love and
a different sort of night—the English night seemed the warmest and softest with a thinnest and most crystalline sprinkling
of stars. The English love seemed the most fragile and romantic—a white dress and a dim face above it and eyes that were
pools of light. And when I add that it was a French night he was
thinking about, after all, I see I must go back and begin over.

Val was half-Russian and half-American. His mother was the
daughter of that Morris Hasylton who helped finance the Chicago World's Fair in 1892, and his father was—see the Alma-
nach de Gotha, issue of 1910—Prince Paul Serge Boris Rostoff,
son of Prince Vladimir Rostoff, grandson of a grand duke—
"Jimber-jawed Serge"—and third-cousin-once-removed to the
czar. It was all very impressive, you see, on that side—house in
St. Petersburg, shooting lodge near Riga, and swollen villa, more
like a palace, overlooking the Mediterranean. It was at this villa
in Cannes that the Rostoffs passed the winter—and it wasn't at
all the thing to remind Princess Rostoff that this Riviera villa,
from the marble fountain—after Bernini—to the gold cordial
glasses—after dinner—was paid for with American gold.

The Russians, of course, were gay people on the Continent in
the gala days before the war. Of the three races that used southern France for a pleasure ground they were easily the most adept
at the grand manner. The English were too practical, and the
Americans, though they spent freely, had no tradition of romantic
conduct. But the Russians—there was a people as gallant as the
Latins, and rich besides! When the Rostoffs arrived at Cannes late
in January the restaurateurs telegraphed north for the Prince's
favorite labels to paste on their champagne, and the jewelers put
incredibly gorgeous articles aside to show to him—but not to the

princess—and the Russian Church was swept and garnished for the season that the Prince might beg orthodox forgiveness for his sins. Even the Mediterranean turned obligingly to a deep wine color in the spring evenings, and fishing boats with robin-breasted sails loitered exquisitely offshore.

In a vague way young Val realized that this was all for the benefit of him and his family. It was a privileged paradise, this white little city on the water, in which he was free to do what he liked because he was rich and young and the blood of Peter the Great ran indigo in his veins. He was only seventeen in 1914, when this history begins, but he had already fought a duel with a young man four years his senior, and he had a small hairless scar to show for it on top of his handsome head.

But the question of love in the night was the thing nearest his heart. It was a vague pleasant dream he had, something that was going to happen to him someday that would be unique and incomparable. He could have told no more about it than that there was a lovely unknown girl concerned in it, and that it ought to take place beneath the Riviera moon.

The odd thing about all this was not that he had this excited and yet almost spiritual hope of romance, for all boys of any imagination have just such hopes, but that it actually came true. And when it happened, it happened so unexpectedly; it was such a jumble of impressions and emotions, of curious phrases that sprang to his lips, of sights and sounds and moments that were here, were lost, were past, that he scarcely understood it at all. Perhaps its very vagueness preserved it in his heart and made him forever unable to forget.

There was an atmosphere of love all about him that spring—his father's loves, for instance, which were many and indiscreet, and which Val became aware of gradually from overhearing the gossip of servants, and definitely from coming on his American mother unexpectedly one afternoon, to find her storming hysterically at his father's picture on the salon wall. In the picture his father wore a white uniform with a furred dolman and looked back impassively at his wife as if to say "Were you under the impression, my dear, that you were marrying into a family of clergymen?"

Val tiptoed away, surprised, confused—and excited. It didn't shock him as it would have shocked an American boy of his age. He had known for years what life was among the Continental rich, and he condemned his father only for making his mother cry.

Love went on around him—reproachless love and illicit love alike. As he strolled along the seaside promenade at nine o'clock, when the stars were bright enough to compete with the bright lamps, he was aware of love on every side. From the open-air cafés, vivid with dresses just down from Paris, came a sweet pungent odor of flowers and chartreuse and fresh black coffee and cigarettes—and mingled with them all he caught another scent, the mysterious thrilling scent of love. Hands touched jewel-sparkling hands upon the white tables. Gay dresses and white shirt fronts swayed together, and matches were held, trembling a little, for slow-lighting cigarettes. On the other side of the boulevard lovers less fashionable, young Frenchmen who worked in the stores of Cannes, sauntered with their fiancées under the dim trees, but Val's young eyes seldom turned that way. The luxury of music and bright colors and low voices—they were all part of his dream. They were the essential trappings of love in the night.

But assume as he might the rather fierce expression that was expected from a young Russian gentleman who walked the streets alone, Val was beginning to be unhappy. April twilight had succeeded March twilight, the season was almost over, and he had found no use to make of the warm spring evenings. The girls of sixteen and seventeen whom he knew, were chaperoned with care between dusk and bedtime—this, remember, was before the war—and the others who might gladly have walked beside him were an affront to his romantic desire. So April passed by—one week, two weeks, three weeks——

He had played tennis until seven and loitered at the courts for another hour, so it was half past eight when a tired cab horse accomplished the hill on which gleamed the façade of the Rostoff villa. The lights of his mother's limousine were yellow in the drive, and the princess, buttoning her gloves, was just coming out the glowing door. Val tossed two francs to the cabman and went to kiss her on the cheek.

"Don't touch me," she said quickly. "You've been handling money."

"But not in my mouth, Mother," he protested humorously.

The princess looked at him impatiently.

"I'm angry," she said. "Why must you be so late tonight? We're dining on a yacht and you were to have come along too."

"What yacht?"

"Americans." There was always a faint irony in her voice when she mentioned the land of her nativity. Her America was the Chicago of the nineties which she still thought of as the vast upstairs to a butcher shop. Even the irregularities of Prince Paul were not too high a price to have paid for her escape.

"Two yachts," she continued; "in fact we don't know which one. The note was very indefinite. Very careless indeed."

Americans. Val's mother had taught him to look down on Americans, but she hadn't succeeded in making him dislike them. American men noticed you, even if you were seventeen. He liked Americans. Although he was thoroughly Russian he wasn't immaculately so—the exact proportion, like that of a celebrated soap, was about ninety-nine and three-quarters per cent.

"I want to come," he said. "I'll hurry up, Mother. I'll——"

"We're late now." The princess turned as her husband appeared in the door. "Now Val says he wants to come."

"He can't," said Prince Paul shortly. "He's too outrageously late."

Val nodded. Russian aristocrats, however indulgent about themselves, were always admirably Spartan with their children. There were no arguments.

"I'm sorry," he said.

Prince Paul grunted. The footman, in red-and-silver livery, opened the limousine door. But the grunt decided the matter for Val, because Princess Rostoff at that day and hour had certain grievances against her husband which gave her command of the domestic situation.

"On second thought you'd better come, Val," she announced coolly. "It's too late now, but come after dinner. The yacht is either the Minnehaha or the Privateer." She got into the limousine. "The one to come to will be the gayer one, I suppose—the Jacksons' yacht——"

"Find got sense," muttered the Prince cryptically, conveying that Val would find it if he had any sense. "Have my man take a look at you 'fore you start. Wear tie of mine 'stead of that outrageous string you affected in Vienna. Grow up. High time."

As the limousine crawled crackling down the pebbled drive Val's face was burning.

II

It was dark in Cannes harbor; rather it seemed dark after the brightness of the promenade that Val had just left behind. Three frail dock lights glittered dimly upon innumerable fishing boats heaped like shells along the beach. Farther out in the water there were other lights where a fleet of slender yachts rode the tide with slow dignity, and farther still a full ripe moon made the water bosom into a polished dancing floor. Occasionally there was a swish! creak! drip! as a rowboat moved about in the shallows, and its blurred shape threaded the labyrinth of hobbled fishing skiffs and launches. Val, descending the velvet slope of sand, stumbled over a sleeping boatman and caught the rank savor of garlic and plain wine. Taking the man by the shoulders he shook open his startled eyes.

"Do you know where the Minnehaha is anchored, and the Privateer?"

As they slid out into the bay he lay back in the stern and stared with vague discontent at the Riviera moon. That was the right moon, all right. Frequently, five nights out of seven, there was the right moon. And here was the soft air, aching with enchantment, and here was the music, many strains of music from many orchestras, drifting out from the shore. Eastward lay the dark Cape of Antibes, and then Nice, and beyond that Monte Carlo, where the night rang chinking full of gold. Someday he would enjoy all that, too, know its every pleasure and success—when he was too old and wise to care.

But tonight—tonight, that stream of silver that waved like a wide strand of curly hair toward the moon; those soft romantic lights of Cannes behind him, the irresistible ineffable love in this air—that was to be wasted forever.

"Which one?" asked the boatman suddenly.

"Which what?" demanded Val, sitting up.

"Which boat?"

He pointed. Val turned; above hovered the grey, sword-like prow of a yacht. During the sustained longing of his wish they had covered half a mile.

He read the brass letters over his head. It was the Privateer, but there were only dim lights on board, and no music and no voices, only a murmurous k-plash at intervals as the small waves leaped at the sides.

"The other one," said Val; "the Minnehaha."

"Don't go yet."

Val started. The voice, low and soft, had dropped down from the darkness overhead.

"What's the hurry?" said the soft voice. "Thought maybe somebody was coming to see me, and have suffered terrible disappointment."

The boatman lifted his oars and looked hesitatingly at Val. But Val was silent, so the man let the blades fall into the water and swept the boat out into the moonlight.

"Wait a minute!" cried Val sharply.

"Good-bye," said the voice. "Come again when you can stay longer."

"But I am going to stay now," he answered breathlessly.

He gave the necessary order and the rowboat swung back to the foot of the small companionway. Someone young, someone in a misty white dress, someone with a lovely low voice, had actually called to him out of the velvet dark. "If she has eyes!" Val murmured to himself. He liked the romantic sound of it and repeated it under his breath—"If she has eyes."

"What are you?" She was directly above him now; she was looking down and he was looking up as he climbed the ladder, and as their eyes met they both began to laugh.

She was very young, slim, almost frail, with a dress that accentuated her youth by its blanched simplicity. Two wan dark spots on her cheeks marked where the color was by day.

"What are you?" she repeated, moving back and laughing again as his head appeared on the level of the deck. "I'm frightened now and I want to know."

"I am a gentleman," said Val, bowing.

"What sort of a gentleman? There are all sorts of gentlemen. There was a—there was a colored gentleman at the table next to ours in Paris, and so——" She broke off. "You're not American, are you?"

"I'm Russian," he said, as he might have announced himself to be an archangel. He thought quickly and then added, "And

I am the most fortunate of Russians. All this day, all this spring I have dreamed of falling in love on such a night, and now I see that heaven has sent me to you."

"Just one moment!" she said, with a little gasp. "I'm sure now that this visit is a mistake. I don't go in for anything like that. Please!"

"I beg your pardon." He looked at her in bewilderment, unaware that he had taken too much for granted. Then he drew himself up formally.

"I have made an error. If you will excuse me I will say good-night."

He turned away. His hand was on the rail.

"Don't go," she said, pushing a strand of indefinite hair out of her eyes. "On second thought you can talk any nonsense you like if you'll only not go. I'm miserable and I don't want to be left alone."

Val hesitated; there was some element in this that he failed to understand. He had taken it for granted that a girl who called to a strange man at night, even from the deck of a yacht, was certainly in a mood for romance. And he wanted intensely to stay. Then he remembered that this was one of the two yachts he had been seeking.

"I imagine that the dinner's on the other boat," he said.

"The dinner? Oh, yes, it's on the Minnehaha. Were you going there?"

"I was going there—a long time ago."

"What's your name?"

He was on the point of telling her when something made him ask a question instead.

"And you? Why are you not at the party?"

"Because I preferred to stay here. Mrs. Jackson said there would be some Russians there—I suppose that's you." She looked at him with interest. "You're a very young man, aren't you?"

"I am much older than I look," said Val stiffly. "People always comment on it. It's considered rather a remarkable thing."

"How old are you?"

"Twenty-one," he lied.

She laughed.

"What nonsense! You're not more than nineteen."

His annoyance was so perceptible that she hastened to reassure him. "Cheer up! I'm only seventeen myself. I might have gone to the party if I'd thought there'd be anyone under fifty there."

He welcomed the change of subject.

"You preferred to sit and dream here beneath the moon."

"I've been thinking of mistakes." They sat down side by side in two canvas deck chairs. "It's a most engrossing subject—the subject of mistakes. Women very seldom brood about mistakes—they're much more willing to forget than men are. But when they do brood——"

"You have made a mistake?" inquired Val.

She nodded.

"Is it something that cannot be repaired?"

"I think so," she answered. "I can't be sure. That's what I was considering when you came along."

"Perhaps I can help in some way," said Val. "Perhaps your mistake is not irreparable, after all."

"You can't," she said unhappily. "So let's not think about it. I'm very tired of my mistake and I'd much rather you'd tell me about all the gay, cheerful things that are going on in Cannes tonight."

They glanced shoreward at the line of mysterious and alluring lights, the big toy banks with candles inside that were really the great fashionable hotels, the lighted clock in the old town, the blurred glow of the Café de Paris, the pricked-out points of villa windows rising on slow hills toward the dark sky.

"What is everyone doing there?" she whispered. "It looks as though something gorgeous was going on, but what it is I can't quite tell."

"Everyone there is making love," said Val quietly.

"Is that it?" She looked for a long time, with a strange expression in her eyes. "Then I want to go home to America," she said. "There is too much love here. I want to go home tomorrow."

"You are afraid of being in love then?"

She shook her head.

"It isn't that. It's just because—there is no love here for me."

"Or for me either," added Val quietly. "It is sad that we two should be at such a lovely place on such a lovely night and have—nothing."

He was leaning toward her intently, with a sort of inspired and chaste romance in his eyes—and she drew back.

"Tell me more about yourself," she inquired quickly. "If you are Russian where did you learn to speak such excellent English?"

"My mother was American," he admitted. "My grandfather was American also, so she had no choice in the matter."

"Then you're American too!"

"I am Russian," said Val with dignity.

She looked at him closely, smiled and decided not to argue. "Well then," she said diplomatically, "I suppose you must have a Russian name."

But he had no intention now of telling her his name. A name, even the Rostoff name, would be a desecration of the night. They were their own low voices, their two white faces—and that was enough. He was sure, without any reason for being sure but with a sort of instinct that sang triumphantly through his mind, that in a little while, a minute or an hour, he was going to undergo an initiation into the life of romance. His name had no reality beside what was stirring in his heart.

"You are beautiful," he said suddenly.

"How do you know?"

"Because for women moonlight is the hardest light of all."

"Am I nice in the moonlight?"

"You are the loveliest thing that I have ever known."

"Oh." She thought this over. "Of course I had no business to let you come on board. I might have known what we'd talk about—in this moon. But I can't sit here and look at the shore—forever. I'm too young for that. Don't you think I'm too young for that?"

"Much too young," he agreed solemnly.

Suddenly they both became aware of new music that was close at hand, music that seemed to come out of the water not a hundred yards away.

"Listen!" she cried. "It's from the Minnehaha. They've finished dinner."

For a moment they listened in silence.

"Thank you," said Val suddenly.

"For what?"

He hardly knew he had spoken. He was thanking the deep low horns for singing in the breeze, the sea for its warm murmurous complaint against the bow, the milk of the stars for washing over them until he felt buoyed up in a substance more taut than air.

"So lovely," she whispered.

"What are we going to do about it?"

"Do we have to do something about it? I thought we could just sit and enjoy——"

"You didn't think that," he interrupted quietly. "You know that we must do something about it. I am going to make love to you—and you are going to be glad."

"I can't," she said very low. She wanted to laugh now, to make some light cool remark that would bring the situation back into the safe waters of a casual flirtation. But it was too late now. Val knew that the music had completed what the moon had begun.

"I will tell you the truth," he said. "You are my first love. I am seventeen—the same age as you, no more."

There was something utterly disarming about the fact that they were the same age. It made her helpless before the fate that had thrown them together. The deck chairs creaked and he was conscious of a faint illusive perfume as they swayed suddenly and childishly together.

III

Whether he kissed her once or several times he could not afterward remember, though it must have been an hour that they sat there close together and he held her hand. What surprised him most about making love was that it seemed to have no element of wild passion—regret, desire, despair—but a delirious promise of such happiness in the world, in living, as he had never known. First love—this was only first love! What must love itself in its fullness, its perfection be. He did not know that what he was experiencing then, that unreal, undesirous medley of ecstasy and peace, would be unrecapturable forever.

The music had ceased for some time when presently the murmurous silence was broken by the sound of a rowboat disturbing the quiet waves. She sprang suddenly to her feet and her eyes strained out over the bay.

"Listen!" she said quickly. "I want you to tell me your name."

"No."

"Please," she begged him. "I'm going away tomorrow."

He didn't answer.

"I don't want you to forget me," she said. "My name is——"

"I won't forget you. I will promise to remember you always. Whoever I may love I will always compare her to you, my first love. So long as I live you will always have that much freshness in my heart."

"I want you to remember," she murmured brokenly. "Oh, this has meant more to me than it has to you—much more."

She was standing so close to him that he felt her warm young breath on his face. Once again they swayed together. He pressed her hands and wrists between his as it seemed right to do, and kissed her lips. It was the right kiss, he thought, the romantic kiss—not too little or too much. Yet there was a sort of promise in it of other kisses he might have had, and it was with a slight sinking of his heart that he heard the rowboat close to the yacht and realized that her family had returned. The evening was over.

"And this is only the beginning," he told himself. "All my life will be like this night."

She was saying something in a low quick voice and he was listening tensely.

"You must know one thing—I am married. Three months ago. That was the mistake that I was thinking about when the moon brought you out here. In a moment you will understand."

She broke off as the boat swung against the companionway and a man's voice floated up out of the darkness.

"Is that you, my dear?"

"Yes."

"What is this other rowboat waiting?"

"One of Mrs. Jackson's guests came here by mistake and I made him stay and amuse me for an hour."

A moment later the thin white hair and weary face of a man of sixty appeared above the level of the deck. And then Val saw and realized too late how much he cared.

IV

When the Riviera season ended in May the Rostoffs and all the other Russians closed their villas and went north for the summer.

The Russian Orthodox Church was locked up and so were the bins of rarer wine, and the fashionable spring moonlight was put away, so to speak, to wait for their return.

"We'll be back next season," they said as a matter of course.

But this was premature, for they were never coming back anymore. Those few who straggled south again after five tragic years were glad to get work as chambermaids or *valets de chambre* in the great hotels where they had once dined. Many of them, of course, were killed in the war or in the revolution; many of them faded out as spongers and small cheats in the big capitals, and not a few ended their lives in a sort of stupefied despair.

When the Kerensky government collapsed in 1917, Val was a lieutenant on the eastern front, trying desperately to enforce authority in his company long after any vestige of it remained. He was still trying when Prince Paul Rostoff and his wife gave up their lives one rainy morning to atone for the blunders of the Romanoffs—and the enviable career of Morris Hasylton's daughter ended in a city that bore even more resemblance to a butcher shop than had Chicago in 1892.

After that Val fought with Denikin's army for a while until he realized that he was participating in a hollow farce and the glory of Imperial Russia was over. Then he went to France and was suddenly confronted with the astounding problem of keeping his body and soul together.

It was, of course, natural that he should think of going to America. Two vague aunts with whom his mother had quarreled many years ago still lived there in comparative affluence. But the idea was repugnant to the prejudices his mother had implanted in him, and besides he hadn't sufficient money left to pay for his passage over. Until a possible counter-revolution should restore to him the Rostoff properties in Russia he must somehow keep alive in France.

So he went to the little city he knew best of all. He went to Cannes. His last two hundred francs bought him a third-class ticket and when he arrived he gave his dress-suit to an obliging party who dealt in such things and received in return money for food and bed. He was sorry afterward that he had sold the dress-suit, because it might have helped him to a position as a waiter. But he obtained work as a taxi-driver instead and was quite as happy, or rather quite as miserable, at that.

Sometimes he carried Americans to look at villas for rent, and when the front glass of the automobile was up, curious fragments of conversation drifted out to him from within.

"——heard this fellow was a Russian prince." . . . "Sh!" . . . "No, this one right here." . . . "Be quiet, Esther!"—followed by subdued laughter.

When the car stopped, his passengers would edge around to have a look at him. At first he was desperately unhappy when girls did this; after awhile he didn't mind anymore. Once a cheerfully intoxicated American asked him if it were true and invited him to lunch, and another time an elderly woman seized his hand as she got out of the taxi, shook it violently and then pressed a hundred-franc note into his hand.

"Well, Florence, now I can tell 'em back home I shook hands with a Russian prince."

The inebriated American who had invited him to lunch thought at first that Val was a son of the czar, and it had to be explained to him that a prince in Russia was simply the equivalent of a British courtesy lord. But he was puzzled that a man of Val's personality didn't go out and make some real money.

"This is Europe," said Val gravely. "Here money is not made. It is inherited or else it is slowly saved over a period of many years and maybe in three generations a family moves up into a higher class."

"Think of something people want—like we do."

"That is because there is more money to want with in America. Everything that people want here has been thought of long ago."

But after a year and with the help of a young Englishman he had played tennis with before the war, Val managed to get into the Cannes branch of an English bank. He forwarded mail and bought railroad tickets and arranged tours for impatient sight-seers. Sometimes a familiar face came to his window; if Val was recognized he shook hands; if not he kept silence. After two years he was no longer pointed out as a former prince, for the Russians were an old story now—the splendor of the Rostoffs and their friends was forgotten.

He mixed with people very little. In the evenings he walked for awhile on the promenade, took a slow glass of beer in a café, and went early to bed. He was seldom invited anywhere because people thought that his sad, intent face was depressing—and he never accepted anyhow. He wore cheap French clothes now instead of the rich tweeds and flannels that had been ordered with his father's from England. As for women, he knew none at all. Of the many things he had been certain about at seventeen, he had been most certain about this—that his life would be full of romance. Now after eight years he knew that it was not to be. Somehow he had never had time for love—the war, the revolution and now his poverty had conspired against his expectant heart. The springs of his emotion which had first poured forth one April night had dried up immediately and only a faint trickle remained.

His happy youth had ended almost before it began. He saw himself growing older and more shabby, and living always more and more in the memories of his gorgeous boyhood. Eventually he would become absurd, pulling out an old heirloom of a watch and showing it to amused young fellow clerks who would listen with winks to his tales of the Rostoff name.

He was thinking these gloomy thoughts one April evening in 1922 as he walked beside the sea and watched the never-changing magic of the awakening lights. It was no longer for his benefit, that magic, but it went on, and he was somehow glad. Tomorrow he was going away on his vacation, to a cheap hotel farther down the shore where he could bathe and rest and read; then he would come back and work some more. Every year for three years he had taken his vacation during the last two weeks in April, perhaps because it was then that he felt the most need for remembering. It was in April that what was destined to be the best part of his life had come to a culmination under a romantic moonlight. It was sacred to him—for what he had thought of as an initiation and a beginning had turned out to be the end.

He paused now in front of the Café des Étrangers and after a moment crossed the street on an impulse and sauntered down to the shore. A dozen yachts, already turned to a beautiful silver color, rode at anchor in the bay. He had seen them that afternoon, and read the names painted on their bows—but only from habit. He had done it for three years now, and it was almost a natural function of his eye.

"*Un beau soir*," remarked a French voice at his elbow. It was a boatman who had often seen Val here before. "Monsieur finds the sea beautiful?"

"Very beautiful."

"I too. But a bad living except in the season. Next week, though, I earn something special. I am paid well for simply waiting here and doing nothing more from eight o'clock until midnight."

"That's very nice," said Val politely.

"A widowed lady, very beautiful, from America, whose yacht always anchors in the harbor for the last two weeks in April. If the Privateer comes tomorrow it will make three years."

V

All night Val didn't sleep—not because there was any question in his mind as to what he should do, but because his long stupefied emotions were suddenly awake and alive. Of course he must not see her—not he, a poor failure with a name that was now only a shadow—but it would make him a little happier always to know that she remembered. It gave his own memory another dimension, raised it like those stereopticon glasses that bring out a picture from the flat paper. It made him sure that he had not deceived himself—he had been charming once upon a time to a lovely woman, and she did not forget.

An hour before train time next day he was at the railway station with his grip, so as to avoid any chance encounter in the street. He found himself a place in a third-class carriage of the waiting train.

Somehow as he sat there he felt differently about life—a sort of hope, faint and illusory, that he hadn't felt twenty-four hours before. Perhaps there was some way in these next few years in which he could make it possible to meet her once again—if he worked hard, threw himself passionately into whatever was at hand. He knew of at least two Russians in Cannes who had started over again with nothing except good manners and ingenuity and were now doing surprisingly well. The blood of Morris Hasylton began to throb a little in Val's temples and made him remember something he had never before cared to remember— that Morris Hasylton, who had built his daughter a palace in St. Petersburg, had also started from nothing at all.

Simultaneously another emotion possessed him, less strange, less dynamic but equally American—the emotion of curiosity. In case he did—well, in case life should ever make it possible for him to seek her out, he should at least know her name.

He jumped to his feet, fumbled excitedly at the carriage handle and jumped from the train. Tossing his valise into the check room he started at a run for the American consulate.

"A yacht came in this morning," he said hurriedly to a clerk, "an American yacht—the Privateer. I want to know who owns it."

"Just a minute," said the clerk, looking at him oddly. "I'll try to find out."

After what seemed to Val an interminable time he returned.

"Why, just a minute," he repeated hesitantly. "We're—it seems we're finding out."

"Did the yacht come?"

"Oh, yes—it's here all right. At least I think so. If you'll just wait in that chair."

After another ten minutes Val looked impatiently at his watch. If they didn't hurry he'd probably miss his train. He made a nervous movement as if to get up from his chair.

"Please sit still," said the clerk, glancing at him quickly from his desk. "I ask you. Just sit down in that chair."

Val stared at him. How could it possibly matter to the clerk whether or not he waited?

"I'll miss my train," he said impatiently. "I'm sorry to have given you all this bother——"

"Please sit still! We're glad to get it off our hands. You see, we've been waiting for your inquiry for—ah—three years."

Val jumped to his feet and jammed his hat on his head.

"Why didn't you tell me that?" he demanded angrily.

"Because we had to get word to our—our client. Please don't go! It's—ah, it's too late."

Val turned. Someone slim and radiant with dark frightened eyes was standing behind him, framed against the sunshine of the doorway.

"Why——"

Val's lips parted, but no words came through. She took a step toward him.

"I——" She looked at him helplessly, her eyes filling with tears. "I just wanted to say hello," she murmured. "I've come back for three years just because I wanted to say hello."

Still Val was silent.

"You might answer," she said impatiently. "You might answer when I'd—when I'd just about begun to think you'd been killed in the war." She turned to the clerk. "Please introduce us!" she cried. "You see, I can't say hello to him when we don't even know each other's names."

It's the thing to distrust these international marriages, of course. It's an American tradition that they always turn out badly, and we are accustomed to such headlines as: "Would Trade Coronet for True American Love, Says Duchess," and "Claims Count Mendicant Tortured Toledo Wife." The other sort of headlines are never printed, for who would want to read: "Castle is Love Nest, Asserts Former Georgia Belle," or "Duke and Packer's Daughter Celebrate Golden Honeymoon."

So far there have been no headlines at all about the young Rostoffs. Prince Val is much too absorbed in that string of moonlight-blue taxi-cabs which he manipulates with such unusual efficiency, to give out interviews. He and his wife only leave New York once a year—but there is still a boatman who rejoices when the Privateer steams into Cannes harbor on a mid-April night.

One of My Oldest Friends

A LL afternoon Marion had been happy. She wandered from room to room of their little apartment, strolling into the nursery to help the nurse-girl feed the children from dripping spoons, and then reading for awhile on their new sofa, the most extravagant thing they had bought in their five years of marriage.

When she heard Michael's step in the hall she turned her head and listened; she liked to hear him walk, carefully always as if there were children sleeping close by.

"Michael."

"Oh—hello." He came into the room, a tall, broad, thin man of thirty with a high forehead and kind black eyes.

"I've got some news for you," he said immediately. "Charley Hart's getting married."

"No!"

He nodded.

"Who's he marrying?"

"One of the little Lawrence girls from home." He hesitated. "She's arriving in New York tomorrow and I think we ought to do something for them while she's here. Charley's about my oldest friend."

"Let's have them up for dinner—"

"I'd like to do something more than that," he interrupted. "Maybe a theatre party. You see—" Again he hesitated. "It'd be a nice courtesy to Charley."

"All right," agreed Marion, "but we mustn't spend much—and I don't think we're under any obligation."

He looked at her in surprise.

"I mean," went on Marion, "we—we hardly see Charley anymore. We hardly ever see him at all."

"Well, you know how it is in New York," explained Michael apologetically. "He's just as busy as I am. He has made a big name for himself and I suppose he's pretty much in demand all the time."

They always spoke of Charley Hart as their oldest friend. Five years before, when Michael and Marion were first married,

514

the three of them had come to New York from the same western city. For over a year they had seen Charley nearly every day and no domestic adventure, no uprush of their hopes and dreams, was too insignificant for his ear. His arrival in times of difficulty never failed to give a pleasant, humorous cast to the situation.

Of course Marion's babies had made a difference, and it was several years now since they had called up Charley at midnight to say that the pipes had broken or the ceiling was falling in on their heads; but so gradually had they drifted apart that Michael still spoke of Charley rather proudly as if he saw him every day. For awhile Charley dined with them once a month and all three found a great deal to say; but the meetings never broke up anymore with, "I'll give you a ring tomorrow." Instead it was, "You'll have to come to dinner more often," or even, after three or four years, "We'll see you soon."

"Oh, I'm perfectly willing to give a little party," said Marion now, looking speculatively about her. "Did you suggest a definite date?"

"Week from Saturday." His dark eyes roamed the floor vaguely. "We can take up the rugs or something."

"No." She shook her head. "We'll have a dinner, eight people, very formal and everything, and afterwards we'll play cards."

She was already speculating on whom to invite. Charley of course, being an artist, probably saw interesting people every day.

"We could have the Willoughbys," she suggested doubtfully. "She's on the stage or something—and he writes movies."

"No—that's not it," objected Michael. "He probably meets that crowd at lunch and dinner every day until he's sick of them. Besides, except for the Willoughbys, who else like that do we know? I've got a better idea. Let's collect a few people who've drifted down here from home. They've all followed Charley's career and they'd probably enjoy seeing him again. I'd like them to find out how natural and unspoiled he is after all."

After some discussion they agreed on this plan and within an hour Marion had her first guest on the telephone:

"It's to meet Charley Hart's fiancée," she explained. "Charley Hart, the artist. You see, he's one of our oldest friends."

As she began her preparations her enthusiasm grew. She rented a serving-maid to assure an impeccable service and persuaded the neighborhood florist to come in person and arrange the flowers. All the "people from home" had accepted eagerly and the number of guests had swollen to ten.

"What'll we talk about, Michael?" she demanded nervously on the eve of the party. "Suppose everything goes wrong and everybody gets mad and goes home?"

He laughed.

"Nothing will. You see, these people all know each other—"

The phone on the table asserted itself and Michael picked up the receiver.

"Hello . . . why, hello, Charley."

Marion sat up alertly in her chair.

"Is that so? Well, I'm very sorry. I'm very, very sorry. . . . I hope it's nothing serious."

"Can't he come?" broke out Marion.

"Sh!" Then into the phone, "Well, it certainly is too bad, Charley. No, it's no trouble for us at all. We're just sorry you're ill."

With a dismal gesture Michael replaced the receiver.

"The Lawrence girl had to go home last night and Charley's sick in bed with grippe."

"Do you mean he can't come?"

"He can't come."

Marion's face contracted suddenly and her eyes filled with tears.

"He says he's had the doctor all day," explained Michael dejectedly. "He's got fever and they didn't even want him to go to the telephone."

"I don't care," sobbed Marion. "I think it's terrible. After we've invited all these people to meet him."

"People can't help being sick."

"Yes they *can*," she wailed illogically. "They can help it some way. And if the Lawrence girl was going to leave last night why didn't he let us know *then*?"

"He said she left unexpectedly. Up to yesterday afternoon they both intended to come."

"I don't think he c-cares a bit. I'll bet he's glad he's sick. If he'd cared he'd have brought her to see us long ago."

She stood up suddenly.

"I'll tell you one thing," she assured him vehemently. "I'm just going to telephone everybody and call the whole thing off."

"Why, Marion—"

But in spite of his half-hearted protests she picked up the phone book and began looking for the first number.

They bought theatre tickets next day hoping to fill the hollowness which would invest the evening. Marion had wept when the unintercepted florist arrived at five with boxes of flowers and she felt that she must get out of the house to avoid the ghosts who would presently people it. In silence they ate an elaborate dinner composed of all the things that she had bought for the party.

"It's only eight," said Michael afterwards. "I think it'd be sort of nice if we dropped in on Charley for a minute, don't you?"

"Why, no," Marion answered, startled. "I wouldn't think of it."

"Why not? If he's seriously sick I'd like to see how well he's being taken care of."

She saw that he had made up his mind, so she fought down her instinct against the idea and they taxied to a tall pile of studio apartments on Madison Avenue.

"You go on in," urged Marion nervously. "I'd rather wait out here."

"Please come in."

"Why? He'll be in bed and he doesn't want any women around."

"But he'd like to see you—it'd cheer him up. And he'd know that we understood about tonight. He sounded awfully depressed over the phone."

He urged her from the cab.

"Let's only stay a minute," she whispered tensely as they went up in the elevator. "The show starts at half-past eight."

"Apartment on the right," said the elevator man.

They rang the bell and waited. The door opened and they walked directly into Charley Hart's great studio room.

It was crowded with people; from end to end ran a long lamp-lit dinner table strewn with ferns and young roses, from which a gay murmur of laughter and conversation arose into the faintly smoky air. Twenty women in evening dress sat on one side in a row chatting across the flowers at twenty men, with an elation born of the sparkling burgundy which dripped from many bottles into thin chilled glass. Up on the high narrow balcony which encircled the room a string quartet was playing something by Stravinski in a key that was pitched just below the women's voices and filled the air like an audible wine.

The door had been opened by one of the waiters, who stepped back deferentially from what he thought were two belated guests—and immediately a handsome man at the head of the table started to his feet, napkin in hand, and stood motionless, staring toward the newcomers. The conversation faded into half silence and all eyes followed Charley Hart's to the couple at the door. Then, as if the spell was broken, conversation resumed, gathering momentum word by word—the moment was over.

"Let's get out!" Marion's low, terrified whisper came to Michael out of a void and for a minute he thought he was possessed by an illusion, that there was no one but Charley in the room after all. Then his eyes cleared and he saw that there were many people here—he had never seen so many! The music swelled suddenly into the tumult of a great brass band and a wind from the loud horns seemed to blow against them; without turning he and Marion each made one blind step backward into the hall, pulling the door to after them.

"Marion—!"

She had run toward the elevator, stood with one finger pressed hard against the bell which rang through the hall like a last high note from the music inside. The door of the apartment opened suddenly and Charley Hart came out into the hall.

"Michael!" he cried, "Michael and Marion, I want to explain! Come inside. I want to *explain*, I tell you."

He talked excitedly—his face was flushed and his mouth formed a word or two that did not materialize into sound.

"Hurry up, Michael," came Marion's voice tensely from the elevator.

"Let me explain," cried Charley frantically. "I want—"

Michael moved away from him—the elevator came and the gate clanged open.

"You act as if I'd committed some crime." Charley was following Michael along the hall. "Can't you understand that this is all an accidental situation?"

"It's all right," Michael muttered, "I understand."

"No, you don't." Charley's voice rose with exasperation. He was working up anger against them so as to justify his own intolerable position. "You're going away mad and I asked you to come in and join the party. Why did you come up here if you won't come in? Did you—?"

Michael walked into the elevator.

"Down, please!" cried Marion. "Oh, I want to go down, *please!*"

The gate clanged shut.

They told the taxi-man to take them directly home—neither of them could have endured the theatre. Driving uptown to their apartment, Michael buried his face in his hands and tried to realize that the friendship which had meant so much to him was over. He saw now that it had been over for some time, that not once during the past year had Charley sought their company and the shock of the discovery far outweighed the affront he had received.

When they reached home, Marion, who had not said a word in the taxi, led the way into the living room and motioned for her husband to sit down.

"I'm going to tell you something that you ought to know," she said. "If it hadn't been for what happened tonight I'd probably never have told you—but now I think you ought to hear the whole story." She hesitated. "In the first place, Charley Hart wasn't a friend of yours at all."

"What?" He looked up at her dully.

"He wasn't your friend," she repeated. "He hasn't been for years. He was a friend of mine."

"Why, Charley Hart was—"

"I know what you're going to say—that Charley was a friend to both of us. But it isn't true. I don't know how he considered you at first but he stopped being your friend three or four years ago."

"Why—" Michael's eyes glowed with astonishment. "If that's true, why was he with us all the time?"

"On account of me," said Marion steadily. "He was in love with me."

"What?" Michael laughed incredulously. "You're imagining things. I know how he used to pretend in a kidding way—"

"It wasn't kidding," she interrupted, "not underneath. It began that way—and it ended by his asking me to run away with him."

Michael frowned.

"Go on," he said quietly. "I suppose this is true or you wouldn't be telling me about it—but it simply doesn't seem real. Did he just suddenly begin to—to—"

He closed his mouth suddenly, unable to say the words.

"It began one night when we three were out dancing," Marion hesitated. "And at first I thoroughly enjoyed it. He had a faculty for noticing things—noticing dresses and hats and the new ways I'd do my hair. He was good company. He could always make me feel important, somehow, and attractive. Don't get the idea that I preferred his company to yours—I didn't. I knew how completely selfish he was, and what a will-o'-the-wisp. But I encouraged him, I suppose—I thought it was fine. It was a new angle on Charley, and he was amusing at it, just as he was at everything he did."

"Yes—" agreed Michael with an effort. "I suppose it was—hilariously amusing."

"At first he liked you just the same. It didn't occur to him that he was doing anything treacherous to you. He was just following a natural impulse—that was all. But after a few weeks he began to find you in the way. He wanted to take me to dinner without you along—and it couldn't be done. Well, that sort of thing went on for over a year."

"What happened then?"

"Nothing happened. That's why he stopped coming to see us anymore."

Michael rose slowly to his feet.

"Do you mean—"

"Wait a minute. If you'll think a little you'll see it was bound to turn out that way. When he saw that I was trying to let him down easily so that he'd be simply one of our oldest friends again, he broke away. He didn't want to be one of our oldest friends—that time was over."

"I see."

"Well—" Marion stood up and began biting nervously at her lip, "that's all. I thought this thing tonight would hurt you less if you understood the whole affair."

"Yes," Michael answered in a dull voice, "I suppose that's true."

Michael's business took a prosperous turn, and when summer came they went to the country, renting a little old farmhouse where the children played all day on a tangled half acre of grass and trees. The subject of Charley was never mentioned between them and as the months passed he receded to a shadowy background in their minds. Sometimes, just before dropping off to sleep, Michael found himself thinking of the happy times the three of them had had together five years before—then the reality would intrude upon the illusion and he would be repelled from the subject with almost physical distaste.

One warm evening in July he lay dozing on the porch in the twilight. He had had a hard day at his office and it was welcome to rest here while the summer light faded from the land.

At the sound of an automobile he raised his head lazily. At the end of the path a local taxi-cab had stopped and a young man was getting out. With an exclamation Michael sat up. Even in the dusk he recognized those shoulders, that impatient walk—

"Well, I'm damned," he said softly.

As Charley Hart came up the gravel path Michael noticed in a glance that he was unusually disheveled. His handsome face was drawn and tired, his clothes were out of press and he had the unmistakable look of needing a good night's sleep.

He came up on the porch, saw Michael and smiled in a wan, embarrassed way.

"Hello, Michael."

Neither of them made any move to shake hands but after a moment Charley collapsed abruptly into a chair.

"I'd like a glass of water," he said huskily. "It's hot as hell."

Without a word Michael went into the house—returned with a glass of water which Charley drank in great noisy gulps.

"Thanks," he said, gasping. "I thought I was going to pass away."

He looked about him with eyes that only pretended to take in his surroundings.

"Nice little place you've got here," he remarked; his eyes returned to Michael. "Do you want me to get out?"

"Why—no. Sit and rest if you want to. You look all in."

"I am. Do you want to hear about it?"

"Not in the least."

"Well, I'm going to tell you anyhow," said Charley defiantly. "That's what I came out here for. I'm in trouble, Michael, and I haven't got anybody to go to except you."

"Have you tried your friends?" asked Michael coolly.

"I've tried about everybody—everybody I've had time to go to. God!" He wiped his forehead with his hand. "I never realized how hard it was to raise a simple two thousand dollars."

"Have you come to me for two thousand dollars?"

"Wait a minute, Michael. Wait till you hear. It just shows you what a mess a man can get into without meaning any harm. You see, I'm the treasurer of a society called the Independent Artists' Benefit—a thing to help struggling students. There was a fund, thirty-five hundred dollars, and it's been lying in my bank for over a year. Well, as you know, I live pretty high—make a lot and spend a lot—and about a month ago I began speculating a little through a friend of mine—"

"I don't know why you're telling me all this," interrupted Michael impatiently. "I—"

"Wait a minute, won't you—I'm almost through." He looked at Michael with frightened eyes. "I used that money sometimes without even realizing that it wasn't mine. I've always had plenty of my own, you see. Till this week." He hesitated. "This week there was a meeting of this society and they asked me to turn over the money. Well, I went to a couple of men to try and borrow it and as soon as my back was turned one of them blabbed. There was a terrible blow-up last night. They told me unless I handed over the two thousand this morning they'd send me to jail—" His voice rose and he looked around wildly. "There's a warrant out for me now—and if I can't get the money I'll kill myself, Michael; I swear to God I will; I won't go to prison. I'm an artist—not a business man. I—"

He made an effort to control his voice.

"Michael," he whispered, "you're my oldest friend. I haven't got anyone in the world but you to turn to."

"You're a little late," said Michael uncomfortably. "You didn't think of me four years ago when you asked my wife to run away with you."

A look of sincere surprise passed over Charley's face.

"Are you mad at me about that?" he asked in a puzzled way. "I thought you were mad because I didn't come to your party."

Michael did not answer.

"I supposed she'd told you about that long ago," went on Charley. "I couldn't help it about Marion. I was lonesome and you two had each other. Every time I went to your house you'd tell me what a wonderful girl Marion was and finally I—I began to agree with you. How could I help falling in love with her, when for a year and a half she was the only decent girl I knew?" He looked defiantly at Michael. "Well, you've got her, haven't you. I didn't take her away. I never so much as kissed her—do you have to rub it in?"

"Look here," said Michael sharply, "just why should I lend you this money."

"Well—" Charley hesitated, laughed uneasily, "I don't know any exact reason. I just thought you would."

"Why should I?"

"No reason at all, I suppose, from your way of looking at it."

"That's the trouble. If I gave it to you it would just be because I was slushy and soft. I'd be doing something that I don't want to do."

"All right." Charley smiled unpleasantly. "That's logical. Now that I think, there's no reason why you should lend it to me. Well—" he shoved his hands into his coat pocket and throwing his head back slightly seemed to shake the subject off like a cap, "I won't go to prison—and maybe you'll feel differently about it tomorrow."

"Don't count on that."

"Oh, I don't mean I'll ask you again. I mean something— quite different."

He nodded his head, turned quickly and walking down the gravel path was swallowed up in the darkness. Where the path met the road Michael heard his footsteps cease as if he were hesitating. Then they turned down the road toward the station a mile away.

Michael sank into his chair, burying his face in his hands. He heard Marion come out of the door.

"I listened," she whispered. "I couldn't help it. I'm glad you didn't lend him anything."

She came close to him and would have sat down in his lap but an almost physical repulsion came over him and he got up quickly from his chair.

"I was afraid he'd work on your sentiment and make a fool of you," went on Marion. She hesitated. "He hated you, you know. He used to wish you'd die. I told him that if he ever said so to me again I'd never see him anymore."

Michael looked up at her darkly.

"In fact, you were very noble."

"Why, Michael—"

"You let him say things like that to you—and then when he comes here, down and out, without a friend in the world to turn to, you say you're glad I sent him away."

"It's because I love you, dear—"

"No it isn't!" he interrupted savagely. "It's because hate's cheap in this world. Everybody's got it for sale. My God! What do you suppose I think of myself now?"

"He's not worth feeling that way about."

"Please go away!" cried Michael passionately. "I want to be alone."

Obediently she left him and he sat down again in the darkness of the porch, a sort of terror creeping over him. Several times he made a motion to get up but each time he frowned and remained motionless. Then after another long while he jumped suddenly to his feet, cold sweat starting from his forehead. The last hour, the months just passed, were washed away and he was swept years back in time. Why, they were after Charley Hart, his old friend. Charley Hart who had come to him because he had no other place to go. Michael began to run hastily about the porch in a daze, hunting for his hat and coat.

"Why Charley!" he cried aloud.

He found his coat finally and, struggling into it, ran wildly down the steps. It seemed to him that Charley had gone out only a few minutes before.

"Charley!" he called when he reached the road. "Charley, come back here. There's been a mistake!"

He paused, listening. There was no answer. Panting a little he began to run doggedly along the road through the hot night.

It was only half past eight o'clock but the country was very quiet and the frogs were loud in the strip of wet marsh that ran along beside the road. The sky was salted thinly with stars and after a while there would be a moon, but the road ran among dark trees and Michael could scarcely see ten feet in front of him. After awhile he slowed down to a walk, glancing at the phosphorous dial of his wrist watch—the New York train was not due for an hour. There was plenty of time.

In spite of this he broke into an uneasy run and covered the mile between his house and the station in fifteen minutes. It was a little station, crouched humbly beside the shining rails in the darkness. Beside it Michael saw the lights of a single taxi waiting for the next train.

The platform was deserted and Michael opened the door and peered into the dim waiting room. It was empty.

"That's funny," he muttered.

Rousing a sleepy taxi-driver, he asked if there had been anyone waiting for the train. The taxi-driver considered—yes, there had been a young man waiting, about twenty minutes ago. He had walked up and down for awhile, smoking a cigarette, and then gone away into the darkness.

"That's funny," repeated Michael. He made a megaphone of his hands and facing toward the woods across the track shouted aloud.

"Charley!"

There was no answer. He tried again. Then he turned back to the driver.

"Have you any idea what direction he went."

The man pointed vaguely down the New York road which ran along beside the railroad track.

"Down there somewhere."

With increasing uneasiness Michael thanked him and started swiftly along the road which was white now under the risen moon. He knew now as surely as he knew anything that Charley had gone off by himself to die. He remembered the expression on his face as he had turned away and the hand tucked down close in his coat pocket as if it clutched some menacing thing.

"Charley!" he called in a terrible voice.

The dark trees gave back no sound. He walked on past a dozen fields bright as silver under the moon, pausing every few minutes to shout and then waiting tensely for an answer.

It occurred to him that it was foolish to continue in this direction—Charley was probably back by the station in the woods somewhere. Perhaps it was all imagination; perhaps even now Charley was pacing the station platform waiting for the train from the city. But some impulse beyond logic made him continue. More than that—several times he had the sense that someone was in front of him, someone who just eluded him at every turning, out of sight and earshot, yet leaving always behind him a dim, tragic aura of having passed that way. Once he thought he heard steps among the leaves on the side of the road but it was only a piece of vagrant newspaper blown by the faint hot wind.

It was a stifling night—the moon seemed to be beating hot rays down upon the sweltering earth. Michael took off his coat and threw it over his arm as he walked. A little way ahead of him now was a stone bridge over the tracks and beyond that an interminable line of telephone poles which stretched in diminishing perspective toward an endless horizon. Well, he would walk to the bridge and then give up. He would have given up before except for this sense he had that someone was walking very lightly and swiftly just ahead.

Reaching the stone bridge he sat down on a rock, his heart beating in loud exhausted thumps under his dripping shirt. Well, it was hopeless—Charley was gone, perhaps out of range of his help forever. Far away beyond the station he heard the approaching siren of the nine-thirty train.

Michael found himself wondering suddenly why he was here. He despised himself for being here. On what weak chord in his nature had Charley played in those few minutes, forcing him into this senseless, frightened run through the night? They had discussed it all and Charley had been unable to give a reason why he should be helped.

He got to his feet with the idea of retracing his steps but before turning he stood for a minute in the moonlight looking down the road. Across the track stretched the line of telephone poles and, as his eyes followed them as far as he could see, he heard again, louder now and not far away, the siren of the New York train which rose and fell with musical sharpness on the still night. Suddenly his eyes, which had been traveling down the tracks, stopped and were focused suddenly upon one spot in the line of poles, perhaps a quarter of a mile away. It was a pole just like the others and yet it was different—there was something about it that was indescribably different.

And watching it as one might concentrate on some figure in the pattern of a carpet, something curious happened in his mind and instantly he saw everything in a completely different light. Something had come to him in a whisper of the breeze, something that changed the whole complexion of the situation. It was this: He remembered having read somewhere that at some point back in the dark ages a man named Gerbert had all by himself summed up the whole of European civilization. It became suddenly plain to Michael that he himself had just now been in a position like that. For one minute, one spot in time, all the mercy in the world had been vested in him.

He realized all this in the space of a second with a sense of shock and instantly he understood the reason why he should have helped Charley Hart. It was because it would be intolerable to exist in a world where there was no help—where any human being could be as alone as Charley had been alone this afternoon.

Why, that was it, of course—he had been trusted with that chance. Someone had come to him who had no other place to go—and he had failed.

All this time, this moment, he had been standing utterly motionless staring at the telephone pole down the track, the one that his eye had picked out as being different from the others. The moon was so bright now that near the top he could see a white bar set crosswise on the pole and as he looked the pole and the bar seemed to have become isolated as if the other poles had shrunk back and away.

Suddenly a mile down the track he heard the click and clamor of the electric train when it left the station, and as if the sound had startled him into life he gave a short cry and set off at a swaying run down the road, in the direction of the pole with the crossed bar.

The train whistled again. Click—click—click—it was nearer now, six hundred, five hundred yards away and as it came under the bridge he was running in the bright beam of its searchlight. There was no emotion in his mind but terror—he knew only that he must reach that pole before the train, and it was fifty yards away, struck out sharp as a star against the sky.

There was no path on the other side of the tracks under the poles but the train was so close now that he dared wait no longer or he would be unable to cross at all. He darted from the road, cleared the tracks in two strides and with the sound of the engine at his heels raced along the rough earth. Twenty feet, thirty feet—as the sound of the electric train swelled to a roar in his ears he reached the pole and threw himself bodily on a man who stood there close to the tracks, carrying him heavily to the ground with the impact of his body.

There was the thunder of steel in his ear, the heavy clump of the wheels on the rails, a swift roaring of air, and the nine-thirty train had gone past.

"Charley," he gasped incoherently, "Charley."

A white face looked up at him in a daze. Michael rolled over on his back and lay panting. The hot night was quiet now—there was no sound but the faraway murmur of the receding train.

"Oh, God!"

Michael opened his eyes to see that Charley was sitting up, his face in his hands.

"S'all right," gasped Michael, "s'all right, Charley. You can have the money. I don't know what I was thinking about. Why—why, you're one of my oldest friends."

Charley shook his head.

"I don't understand," he said brokenly. "Where did you come from—how did you get here?"

"I've been following you. I was just behind."

"I've been here for half an hour."

"Well, it's good you chose this pole to—to wait under. I've been looking at it from down by the bridge. I picked it out on account of the crossbar."

Charley had risen unsteadily to his feet and now he walked a few steps and looked up the pole in the full moonlight.

"What did you say?" he asked after a minute, in a puzzled voice. "Did you say this pole had a crossbar?"

"Why, yes. I was looking at it a long time. That's how—"

Charley looked up again and hesitated curiously before he spoke.

"There isn't any crossbar," he said.

A Penny Spent

THE Ritz Grill in Paris is one of those places where things happen—like the first bench as you enter Central Park South, or Morris Gest's office, or Herrin, Illinois. I have seen marriages broken up there at an ill-considered word and blows struck between a professional dancer and a British baron, and I know personally of at least two murders that would have been committed on the spot but for the fact that it was July and there was no room. Even murders require a certain amount of space, and in July the Ritz Grill has no room at all.

Go in at six o'clock of a summer evening, planting your feet lightly lest you tear some college boy bag from bag, and see if you don't find the actor who owes you a hundred dollars or the stranger who gave you a match once in Red Wing, Minnesota, or the man who won your girl away from you with silver phrases just ten years ago. One thing is certain—that before you melt out into the green-and-cream Paris twilight you will have the feel of standing for a moment at one of the predestined centers of the world.

At seven-thirty, walk to the center of the room and stand with your eyes shut for half an hour—this is a merely hypothetical suggestion—and then open them. The grey and blue and brown and slate have faded out of the scene and the prevailing note, as the haberdashers say, has become black and white. Another half hour and there is no note at all—the room is nearly empty. Those with dinner engagements have gone to keep them and those without any have gone to pretend they have. Even the two Americans who opened up the bar that morning have been led off by kind friends. The clock makes one of those quick little electric jumps to nine. We will too.

It is nine o'clock by Ritz time, which is just the same as any other time. Mr. Julius Bushmill, manufacturer; b. Canton, Ohio, June 1, 1876; m. 1899, Jessie Pepper; Mason; Republican; Congregationalist; Delegate M. A. of A. 1908; pres. 1909–1912; director Grimes, Hansen Co. since 1911; director Midland R. R. of Indiana—all that and more—walks in, moving a silk handkerchief over a hot scarlet brow. It is his own brow. He wears a handsome dinner coat but has no vest on because the hotel valet has sent both his vests to the dry-cleaners by mistake, a fact which has been volubly explained to Mr. Bushmill for half an hour. Needless to say the prominent manufacturer is prey to a natural embarrassment at this discrepancy in his attire. He has left his devoted wife and attractive daughter in the lounge while he seeks something to fortify his entrance into the exclusive and palatial dining room.

The only other man in the bar was a tall, dark, grimly handsome young American, who slouched in a leather corner and stared at Mr. Bushmill's patent-leather shoes. Self-consciously Mr. Bushmill looked down at his shoes, wondering if the valet had deprived him of them too. Such was his relief to find them in place that he grinned at the young man and his hand went automatically to the business card in his coat pocket.

"Couldn't locate my vests," he said cordially. "That blamed valet took both my vests. See?"

He exposed the shameful overexpanse of his starched shirt.

"I beg your pardon?" said the young man, looking up with a start.

"My vests," repeated Mr. Bushmill with less gusto—"lost my vests."

The young man considered.

"I haven't seen them," he said.

"Oh, not here!" exclaimed Bushmill. "Upstairs."

"Ask Jack," suggested the young man and waved his hand toward the bar.

Among our deficiencies as a race is the fact that we have no respect for the contemplative mood. Bushmill sat down, asked the young man to have a drink, obtained finally the grudging admission that he would have a milk shake; and after explaining the vest matter in detail, tossed his business card across the table. He was not the frock-coated-and-impressive type of millionaire which has become so frequent since the war. He was rather the 1910 model—a sort of cross between Henry VIII and "our Mr. Jones will be in Minneapolis on Friday." He was much louder and more provincial and warm-hearted than the new type.

He liked young men, and his own young man would have been about the age of this one, had it not been for the defiant stubbornness of the German machine-gunners in the last days of the war.

"Here with my wife and daughter," he volunteered. "What's your name?"

"Corcoran," answered the young man, pleasantly but without enthusiasm.

"You American—or English?"

"American."

"What business you in?"

"None."

"Been here long?" continued Bushmill stubbornly.

The young man hesitated.

"I was born here," he said.

Bushmill blinked and his eyes roved involuntarily around the bar.

"*Born* here!" he repeated.

Corcoran smiled.

"Up on the fifth floor."

The waiter set the two drinks and a dish of Saratoga chips on the table. Immediately Bushmill became aware of an interesting phenomenon—Corcoran's hand commenced to flash up and down between the dish and his mouth, each journey transporting a thick layer of potatoes to the eager aperture, until the dish was empty.

"Sorry," said Corcoran, looking rather regretfully at the dish. He took out a handkerchief and wiped his fingers. "I didn't think what I was doing. I'm sure you can get some more."

A series of details now began to impress themselves on Bushmill—that there were hollows in this young man's cheeks that were not intended by the bone structure, hollows of undernourishment or ill health; that the fine flannel of his unmistakably Bond Street suit was shiny from many pressings—the elbows were fairly gleaming—and that his whole frame had suddenly collapsed a little as if the digestion of the potatoes and milk shake had begun immediately instead of waiting for the correct half hour.

"Born here, eh?" he said thoughtfully. "Lived a lot abroad, I guess."

"Yes."

"How long since you've had a square meal?"

The young man started.

"Why, I had lunch," he said. "About one o'clock I had lunch."

"One o'clock last Friday," commented Bushmill skeptically. There was a long pause.

"Yes," admitted Corcoran, "about one o'clock last Friday."

"Are you broke? Or are you waiting for money from home?"

"This is home." Corcoran looked around abstractedly. "I've spent most of my life in the Ritz hotels of one city or another. I don't think they'd believe me upstairs if I told them I was broke. But I've got just enough left to pay my bill when I move out tomorrow."

Bushmill frowned.

"You could have lived a week at a small hotel for what it costs you here by the day," he remarked.

"I don't know the names of any other hotels."

Corcoran smiled apologetically. It was a singularly charming and somehow entirely confident smile, and Julius Bushmill was filled with a mixture of pity and awe. There was something of the snob in him, as there is in all self-made men, and he realized that this young man was telling the defiant truth.

"Any plans?"

"No."

"Any abilities—or talents?"

Corcoran considered.

"I can speak most languages," he said. "But talents—I'm afraid the only one I have is for spending money."

"How do you know you've got that?"

"I can't very well help knowing it." Again he hesitated. "I've just finished running through a matter of half a million dollars."

Bushmill's exclamation died on its first syllable as a new voice, impatient, reproachful and cheerfully anxious, shattered the seclusion of the grill.

"Have you seen a man without a vest named Bushmill? A very old man about fifty? We've been waiting for him about two or three hours."

"Hallie," called Bushmill, with a groan of remorse, "here I am. I'd forgotten you were alive."

"Don't flatter yourself it's *you* we missed," said Hallie, coming up. "It's only your money. Mama and I want food—and we must look it: two nice French gentlemen wanted to take us to dinner while we were waiting in the hall!"

"This is Mr. Corcoran," said Bushmill. "My daughter."

Hallie Bushmill was young and vivid and light, with boy's hair and a brow that bulged just slightly, like a baby's brow, and under it small perfect features that danced up and down when she smiled. She was constantly repressing their tendency toward irresponsible gaiety, as if she feared that, once encouraged, they would never come back to kindergarten under that childish brow anymore.

"Mr. Corcoran was born here in the Ritz," announced her father. "I'm sorry I kept you and your mother waiting, but to tell the truth we've been fixing up a little surprise." He looked at Corcoran and winked perceptibly. "As you know, I've got to go to England day after tomorrow and do some business in those ugly industrial towns. My plan was that you and your mother should make a month's tour of Belgium and Holland and end up at Amsterdam, where Hallie's—where Mr. Nosby will meet you—"

"Yes, I know all that," said Hallie. "Go on. Let's have the surprise."

"I had planned to engage a courier," continued Mr. Bushmill, "but fortunately I ran into my friend Corcoran this evening and he's agreed to go instead."

"I haven't said a word—" interrupted Corcoran in amazement, but Bushmill continued with a decisive wave of his hand:

"Brought up in Europe, he knows it like a book; born in the Ritz, he understands hotels; taught by experience"—here he looked significantly at Corcoran—"taught by experience, he can prevent you and your mother from being extravagant and show you how to observe the happy mean."

"Great!" Hallie looked at Corcoran with interest. "We'll have a regular loop, Mr.—"

She broke off. During the last few minutes a strange expression had come into Corcoran's face. It spread suddenly now into a sort of frightened pallor.

"Mr. Bushmill," he said with an effort, "I've got to speak to you alone—at once. It's very important. I—"

Hallie jumped to her feet.

"I'll wait with Mother," she said with a curious glance. "Hurry—both of you."

As she left the bar, Bushmill turned to Corcoran anxiously.

"What is it?" he demanded. "What do you want to say?"

"I just wanted to tell you that I'm going to faint," said Corcoran. And with remarkable promptitude he did.

II

In spite of the immediate liking that Bushmill had taken to young Corcoran, a certain corroboratory investigation was, of course, necessary. The Paris branch of the New York bank that had handled the last of the half-million told him what he needed to know. Corcoran was not given to drink, heavy gambling or vice; he simply spent money—that was all. Various people, including certain officers of the bank who had known his family, had tried to argue with him at one time or another, but he was apparently an incurable spendthrift. A childhood and youth in Europe with a wildly indulgent mother had somehow robbed him of all sense of value or proportion.

Satisfied, Bushmill asked no more—no one knew what had become of the money and, even if they had, a certain delicacy would have prevented him from inquiring more deeply into Corcoran's short past. But he did take occasion to utter a few parting admonitions before the expedition boarded the train.

"I'm letting you hold the purse strings because I think you've learned your lesson," he said, "but just remember that this time the money isn't your own. All that belongs to you is the seventy-five dollars a week that I pay you in salary. Every other expenditure is to be entered in that little book and shown to me."

"I understand."

"The first thing is to watch what you spend—and prove to me that you've got the common sense to profit by your mistake. The second and most important thing is that my wife and daughter are to have a good time."

With the first of his salary Corcoran supplied himself with histories and guidebooks of Holland and Belgium, and on the night before their departure, as well as on the night of their arrival in Brussels, he sat up late absorbing a mass of information that he had never, in his travels with his mother, been aware of before. They had not gone in for sight-seeing. His mother had considered it something which only school-teachers and vulgar tourists did, but Mr. Bushmill had impressed upon him that Hallie was to have all the advantages of travel; he must make it interesting for her by keeping ahead of her every day.

In Brussels they were to remain five days. The first morning Corcoran took three seats in a touring bus, and they inspected the guild halls and the palaces and the monuments and the parks, while he corrected the guide's historical slips in stage whispers and congratulated himself on doing so well.

But during the afternoon it drizzled as they drove through the streets and he grew tired of his own voice, of Hallie's conventional "Oh, isn't that interesting," echoed by her mother, and he wondered if five days wasn't too long to stay here after all. Still he had impressed them, without doubt; he had made a good start as the serious and well-informed young man. Moreover he had done well with the money. Resisting his first impulse to take a private limousine for the day, which would certainly have cost twelve dollars, he had only three bus tickets at one dollar each to enter in the little book. Before he began his nightly reading he put it down for Mr. Bushmill to see. But first of all he took a steaming hot bath—he had never ridden in a rubber-neck wagon with ordinary sightseers before and he found the idea rather painful.

The next day the tour continued, but so did the drizzling rain, and that evening, to his dismay, Mrs. Bushmill came down with a cold. It was nothing serious, but it entailed two doctor's visits at American prices, together with the cost of the dozen remedies which European physicians order under any circumstances, and it was a discouraging note which he made in the back of his little book that night:

One ruined hat (She claimed it was an old hat, but it didn't look old to me)	$10.00
3 bus tickets for Monday	3.00
3 bus " " Tuesday	2.00
Tips to incompetent guide	1.50
2 doctor's visits	8.00
Medicines	2.25
Total for two days sightseeing	$26.75

And, to balance that, Corcoran thought of the entry he might have made had he followed his first instinct:

One comfortable limousine for two days, including tip to chauffeur	$26.00

Next morning Mrs. Bushmill remained in bed while he and Hallie took the excursion train to Waterloo. He had diligently mastered the strategy of the battle, and as he began his explanations of Napoleon's maneuvers, prefacing it with a short account of the political situation, he was rather disappointed at Hallie's indifference. Luncheon increased his uneasiness. He wished he had brought along the cold-lobster luncheon, put up by the hotel, that he had extravagantly considered. The food at the local restaurant was execrable and Hallie stared desolately at the hard potatoes and vintage steak, and then out the window at the melancholy rain. Corcoran wasn't hungry either, but he forced himself to eat with an affectation of relish. Two more days in Brussels! And then Antwerp! And Rotterdam! And The Hague! Twenty-five more days of history to get up in the still hours of the night, and all for an unresponsive young person who did not seem to appreciate the advantages of travel.

They were coming out of the restaurant, and Hallie's voice, with a new note in it, broke in on his meditations.

"Get a taxi; I want to go home."

He turned to her in consternation.

"What? You want to go back without seeing the famous indoor panorama, with paintings of all the actions and the life-size figures of the casualties in the foreground—"

"There's a taxi," she interrupted. "Quick!"

"A taxi!" he groaned, running after it through the mud. "And these taxis are robbers—we might have had a limousine out and back for the same price."

In silence they returned to the hotel. As Hallie entered the elevator she looked at him with suddenly determined eyes.

"Please wear your dinner coat tonight. I want to go out somewhere and dance—and please send flowers."

Corcoran wondered if this form of diversion had been included in Mr. Bushmill's intentions—especially since he had gathered that Hallie was practically engaged to the Mr. Nosby who was to meet them in Amsterdam.

Distraught with doubt he went to a florist and priced orchids. But a corsage of three would come to twenty-four dollars, and this was not an item he cared to enter in the little book. Regretfully, he compromised on sweet peas and was relieved to find her wearing them when she stepped out of the elevator at seven in a pink-petaled dress.

Corcoran was astounded and not a little disturbed by her loveliness—he had never seen her in full evening dress before. Her perfect features were dancing up and down in delighted anticipation, and he felt that Mr. Bushmill might have afforded the orchids after all.

"Thanks for the pretty flowers," she cried eagerly. "Where are we going?"

"There's a nice orchestra here in the hotel."

Her face fell a little.

"Well, we can start here—"

They went down to the almost-deserted grill, where a few scattered groups of diners swooned in midsummer languor, and only half a dozen Americans arose with the music and stalked defiantly around the floor. Hallie and Corcoran danced. She was surprised to find how well he danced, as all tall, slender men should, with such a delicacy of suggestion that she felt as though she were being turned here and there as a bright bouquet or a piece of precious cloth before five hundred eyes.

But when they had finished dancing she realized that there were only a score of eyes—after dinner even these began to melt apathetically away.

"We'd better be moving on to some gayer place," she suggested.

He frowned.

"Isn't this gay enough?" he asked anxiously. "I rather like the happy mean."

"That sounds good. Let's go there!"

"It isn't a café—it's a principle I'm trying to learn. I don't know whether your father would want—"

She flushed angrily.

"Can't you be a little human?" she demanded. "I thought when father said you were born in the Ritz you'd know something about having a good time."

He had no answer ready. After all, why should a girl of her conspicuous loveliness be condemned to desolate hotel dances and public-bus excursions in the rain?

"Is this your idea of a riot?" she continued. "Do you ever think about anything except history and monuments? Don't you know anything about having fun?"

"Once I knew quite a lot."

"What?"

"In fact—once I used to be rather an expert at spending money."

"Spending money!" she broke out. "For these?"

She unpinned the corsage from her waist and flung it on the table. "Pay the check, please. I'm going upstairs to bed."

"All right," said Corcoran suddenly, "I've decided to give you a good time."

"How?" she demanded with frozen scorn. "Take me to the movies?"

"Miss Bushmill," said Corcoran grimly, "I've had good times beyond the wildest flights of your very provincial, Middle-Western imagination. I've entertained from New York to Constantinople—given affairs that have made Indian rajahs weep with envy. I've had prima donnas break ten-thousand-dollar engagements to come to my smallest dinners. When you were still playing who's-got-the-button back in Ohio I entertained on a cruising trip that was so much fun that I had to sink my yacht to make the guests go home."

"I don't believe it. I—" Hallie gasped.

"You're bored," he interrupted. "Very well. I'll do my stuff. I'll do what I know how to do. Between here and Amsterdam you're going to have the time of your life."

III

Corcoran worked quickly. That night, after taking Hallie to her room, he paid several calls—in fact he was extraordinarily busy up to eleven o'clock next morning. At that hour he tapped briskly at the Bushmills' door.

"You are lunching at the Brussels Country Club," he said to Hallie directly, "with Prince Abrisini, Countess Perimont and Major Sir Reynolds Fitz-Hugh, the British attaché. The Bolls-Ferrari landaulet will be ready at the door in half an hour."

"But I thought we were going to the culinary exhibit," objected Mrs. Bushmill in surprise. "We had planned—"

"*You* are going," said Corcoran politely, "with two nice ladies from Wisconsin. And afterwards you are going to an American tea room and have an American luncheon with American food.

At twelve o'clock a dark conservative town car will be waiting downstairs for your use."

He turned to Hallie.

"Your new maid will arrive immediately to help you dress. She will oversee the removal of your things in your absence so that nothing will be mislaid. This afternoon you entertain at tea."

"Why, how can I entertain at tea?" cried Hallie. "I don't know a soul in the place—"

"The invitations are already issued," said Corcoran.

Without waiting for further protests he bowed slightly and retired through the door.

The next three hours passed in a whirl. There was the gorgeous landaulet with a silk-hatted, satin-breeched, plum-colored footman beside the chauffeur, and a wilderness of orchids flowering from the little jars inside. There were the impressive titles that she heard in a daze at the country club as she sat down at a rose-littered table; and out of nowhere a dozen other men appeared during luncheon and stopped to be introduced to her as they went by. Never in her two years as the belle of a small Ohio town had Hallie had such attention, so many compliments—her features danced up and down with delight. Returning to the hotel, she found that they had been moved dexterously to the royal suite, a huge high salon and two sunny bedrooms overlooking a garden. Her capped maid—exactly like the French maid she had once impersonated in a play—was in attendance, and there was a new deference in the manner of all the servants in the hotel. She was bowed up the steps—other guests were gently brushed aside for her—and bowed into the elevator, which clanged shut in the faces of two irate Englishwomen and whisked her straight to her floor.

Tea was a great success. Her mother, considerably encouraged by the pleasant two hours she had spent in congenial company, conversed with the clergyman of the American Church, while Hallie moved enraptured through a swarm of charming and attentive men. She was surprised to learn that she was giving a dinner dance that night at the fashionable Café Royal—and even the afternoon faded before the glories of the night. She was not aware that two specially hired entertainers had left Paris for Brussels on the noon train until they bounced hilariously in upon the shining floor. But she knew that there were a dozen partners for every dance, and chatter that had nothing to do with monuments or battlefields. Had she not been so thoroughly and cheerfully tired, she would have protested frantically at midnight when Corcoran approached her and told her he was taking her home.

Only then, half asleep in the luxurious depths of the town car, did she have time to wonder.

"How on earth—? How did you do it?"

"It was nothing—I had no time," said Corcoran disparagingly. "I knew a few young men around the embassies. Brussels isn't very gay, you know, and they're always glad to help stir things up. All the rest was—even simpler. Did you have a good time?"

No answer.

"Did you have a good time?" he repeated a little anxiously. "There's no use going on, you know, if you didn't have a—"

"The Battle of Wellington was won by Major Sir Corcoran Fitz-Hugh Abrisini," she muttered, decisively but indistinctly.

Hallie was asleep.

IV

After three more days Hallie finally consented to being torn away from Brussels, and the tour continued through Antwerp, Rotterdam and The Hague. But it was not the same sort of tour that had left Paris a short week before. It traveled in two limousines, for there were always at least one pair of attentive cavaliers in attendance—not to mention a quartet of hirelings who made the jumps by train. Corcoran's guidebooks and histories appeared no more. In Antwerp they did not stay at a mere hotel, but at a famous old shooting box on the outskirts of the city which Corcoran hired for six days, servants and all.

Before they left, Hallie's photograph appeared in the Antwerp papers over a paragraph which spoke of her as the beautiful American heiress who had taken Brabant Lodge and entertained so delightfully that a certain Royal Personage had been several times in evidence there.

In Rotterdam, Hallie saw neither the Boompjes nor the Groote Kerk—they were both obscured by a stream of pleasant young Dutchmen who looked at her with soft blue eyes. But when they reached The Hague and the tour neared its end, she was aware of a growing sadness—it had been such a good time and now it would be over and put away. Already Amsterdam and a certain Ohio gentleman, who didn't understand entertaining on the grand scale, were sweeping toward her—and though she tried to be glad she wasn't glad at all. It depressed her too that Corcoran seemed to be avoiding her—he had scarcely spoken to her or danced with her since they left Antwerp. She was thinking chiefly of that on the last afternoon as they rode through the twilight toward Amsterdam and her mother drowsed sleepily in a corner of the car.

"You've been so good to me," she said. "If you're still angry about that evening in Brussels, please try to forgive me now."

"I've forgiven you long ago."

They rode into the city in silence and Hallie looked out the window in a sort of panic. What would she do now with no one to take care of her, to take care of that part of her that wanted to be young and gay forever? Just before they drew up at the hotel, she turned again to Corcoran and their eyes met in a strange disquieting glance. Her hand reached out for his and pressed it gently, as if this was their real good-bye.

Mr. Claude Nosby was a stiff, dark, glossy man, leaning hard toward forty, whose eyes rested for a hostile moment upon Corcoran as he helped Hallie from the car.

"Your father arrives tomorrow," he said portentously. "His attention has been called to your picture in the Antwerp papers and he is hurrying over from London."

"Why shouldn't my picture be in the Antwerp papers, Claude?" inquired Hallie innocently.

"It seems a bit unusual."

Mr. Nosby had had a letter from Mr. Bushmill which told him of the arrangement. He looked upon it with profound disapproval. All through dinner he listened without enthusiasm to the account which Hallie, rather spiritedly assisted by her mother, gave of the adventure; and afterwards when Hallie and her mother went to bed he informed Corcoran that he would like to speak to him alone.

"Ah—Mr. Corcoran," he began, "would you be kind enough to let me see the little account book you are keeping for Mr. Bushmill?"

"I'd rather not," answered Corcoran pleasantly. "I think that's a matter between Mr. Bushmill and me."

"It's the same thing," said Nosby impatiently. "Perhaps you are not aware that Miss Bushmill and I are engaged."

"I had gathered as much."

"Perhaps you can gather too that I am not particularly pleased at the sort of good time you chose to give her."

"It was just an ordinary good time."

"That is a matter of opinion. Will you give me the notebook?"

"Tomorrow," said Corcoran, still pleasantly, "and only to Mr. Bushmill. Good-night."

Corcoran slept late. He was awakened at eleven by the telephone, through which Nosby's voice informed him coldly that Mr. Bushmill had arrived and would see him at once. When he rapped at his employer's door ten minutes later, he found Hallie and her mother also were there, sitting rather sulkily on a sofa. Mr. Bushmill nodded at him coolly but made no motion to shake hands.

"Let's see that account book," he said immediately.

Corcoran handed it to him, together with a bulky packet of vouchers and receipts.

"I hear you've all been out raising hell," said Bushmill.

"No," said Hallie, "only Mama and me."

"You wait outside, Corcoran. I'll let you know when I want you."

Corcoran descended to the lobby and found out from the porter that a train left for Paris at noon. Then he bought a "New York Herald" and stared at the headlines for half an hour. At the end of that time he was summoned upstairs.

Evidently a heated discussion had gone on in his absence. Mr. Nosby was staring out the window with a look of patient resignation. Mrs. Bushmill had been crying, and Hallie, with a triumphant frown on her childish brow, was making a camp stool out of her father's knee.

"Sit down," she said sternly.

Corcoran sat down.

"What do you mean by giving us such a good time?"

"Oh, drop it, Hallie!" said her father impatiently. He turned to Corcoran: "Did I give you any authority to lay out twelve thousand dollars in six weeks? Did I?"

"You're going to Italy with us," interrupted Hallie reassuringly. "We——"

"Will you be quiet?" exploded Bushmill. "It may be funny to you, but I don't like to make bad bets, and I'm pretty sore."

"What nonsense!" remarked Hallie cheerfully. "Why, you were laughing a minute ago!"

"Laughing! You mean at that idiotic account book? Who wouldn't laugh? Four titles at five hundred francs a head! One baptismal font to American Church for presence of clergyman at tea. It's like the log book of a lunatic asylum!"

"Never mind," said Hallie. "You can charge the baptismal font off your income tax."

"That's consoling," said her father grimly. "Nevertheless, this young man will spend no more of my money for me."

"But he's still a wonderful guide. He knows everything— don't you? All about the monuments and catacombs and the Battle of Waterloo."

"Will you please let me talk to Mr. Corcoran?" Hallie was silent. "Mrs. Bushmill and my daughter and Mr. Nosby are going to take a trip through Italy as far as Sicily, where Mr. Nosby has some business, and they want you—that is, Hallie and her mother think they would get more out of it if you went along. Understand—it isn't going to be any royal fandango this time. You'll get your salary and your expenses and that's all you'll get. Do you want to go?"

"No, thanks, Mr. Bushmill," said Corcoran quietly. "I'm going back to Paris at noon."

"You're not!" cried Hallie indignantly. "Why—why how am I going to know which is the Forum and the—the Acropolis and all that?" She rose from her father's knee. "Look here, Daddy, I can persuade him." Before they guessed her intentions she had seized Corcoran's arm, dragged him into the hall and closed the door behind her.

"You've got to come," she said intensely. "Don't you understand? I've seen Claude in a new light and I can't marry him and I don't dare tell Father, and I'll go mad if we have to go off with him alone."

The door opened and Mr. Nosby peered suspiciously out into the hall.

"It's all right," cried Hallie. "He'll come. It was just a question of more salary and he was too shy to say anything about it."

As they went back in Bushmill looked from one to the other. "Why do you think you ought to get more salary?"

"So he can spend it, of course," explained Hallie triumphantly. "He's got to keep his hand in, hasn't he?"

This unanswerable argument closed the discussion. Corcoran was to go to Italy with them as courier and guide at three hundred and fifty dollars a month, an advance of some fifty dollars over what he had received before. From Sicily they were to proceed by boat to Marseilles, where Mr. Bushmill would meet them. After that Mr. Corcoran's services would be no longer required—the Bushmills and Mr. Nosby would sail immediately for home.

They left next morning. It was evident even before they reached Italy that Mr. Nosby had determined to run the expedition in his own way. He was aware that Hallie was less docile and less responsive than she had been before she came abroad, and when he spoke of the wedding a curious vagueness seemed to come over her, but he knew that she adored her father and that in the end she would do whatever her father liked. It was only a question of getting her back to America before any silly young men, such as this unbalanced spendthrift, had the opportunity of infecting her with any nonsense. Once in the factory town and in the little circle where she had grown up, she would slip gently back into the attitude she had held before.

So for the first four weeks of the tour he was never a foot from her side, and at the same time he managed to send Corcoran on a series of useless errands which occupied much of his time. He would get up early in the morning, arrange that Corcoran should take Mrs. Bushmill on a day's excursion and say nothing to Hallie until they were safely away. For the opera in Milan, the concerts in Rome, he bought tickets for three, and on all automobile trips he made it plain to Corcoran that he was to sit with the chauffeur outside.

In Naples they were to stop for a day and take the boat trip to the Island of Capri in order to visit the celebrated Blue Grotto. Then, returning to Naples, they would motor south and cross to Sicily. In Naples Mr. Nosby received a telegram from Mr. Bushmill, in Paris, which he did not read to the others, but folded up and put into his pocket. He told them, however, that on their way to the Capri steamer he must stop for a moment at an Italian bank.

Mrs. Bushmill had not come along that morning, and Hallie and Corcoran waited outside in the cab. It was the first time in four weeks that they had been together without Mr. Nosby's stiff, glossy presence hovering near.

"I've got to talk to you," said Hallie in a low voice. "I've tried so many times, but it's almost impossible. He got Father to say that if you molested me, or even were attentive to me, he could send you immediately home."

"I shouldn't have come," answered Corcoran despairingly. "It was a terrible mistake. But I want to see you alone just once—if only to say good-bye."

As Nosby hurried out of the bank, he broke off and bent his glance casually down the street, pretending to be absorbed in some interesting phenomenon that was taking place there. And suddenly, as if life were playing up to his subterfuge, an interesting phenomenon did immediately take place on the corner in front of the bank. A man in his shirt-sleeves rushed suddenly out of the side street, seized the shoulder of a small, swarthy hunchback standing there and, swinging him quickly around, pointed at their taxi-cab. The man in his shirt-sleeves had not even looked at them—it was as if he had known that they would be there.

The hunchback nodded and instantly both of them disappeared—the first man into the side street which had yielded him up, the hunchback into nowhere at all. The incident took place so quickly that it made only an odd visual impression upon Corcoran—he did not have occasion to think of it again until they returned from Capri eight hours later.

The Bay of Naples was rough as they set out that morning, and the little steamer staggered like a drunken man through the persistent waves. Before long Mr. Nosby's complexion was running through a gamut of yellows, pale creams and ghostly whites, but he insisted that he scarcely noticed the motion and forced Hallie to accompany him in an incessant promenade up and down the deck.

When the steamer reached the coast of the rocky, cheerful little island, dozens of boats put out from shore and swarmed about dizzily in the waves as they waited for passengers to the

Blue Grotto. The constant Saint Vitus' dance which they performed in the surf turned Mr. Nosby from a respectable white
to a bizarre and indecent blue and compelled him to a sudden
decision.

"It's too rough," he announced. "We won't go."

Hallie, watching fascinated from the rail, paid no attention.
Seductive cries were floating up from below:

"Theesa a good boat, lady an' ge'man!"

"I spik American—been America two year!"

"Fine, sunny day for go to see Blue Grotte!"

The first passengers had already floated off, two to a boat, and
now Hallie was drifting with the next batch down the gangway.

"Where are you going, Hallie?" shouted Mr. Nosby. "It's too
dangerous today. We're going to stay on board."

Hallie, half down the gangway, looked back over her shoulder.

"Of course I'm going!" she cried. "Do you think I'd come all
the way to Capri and miss the Blue Grotto?"

Nosby took one more look at the sea—then he turned hurriedly away. Already Hallie, followed by Corcoran, had stepped
into one of the small boats and was waving him a cheerful
good-bye.

They approached the shore, heading for a small dark opening
in the rocks. When they arrived, the boatman ordered them to
sit on the floor of the boat to keep from being bumped against
the low entrance. A momentary passage through darkness, then
a vast space opened up around them and they were in a bright
paradise of ultramarine, a cathedral cave where the water and
air and the high-vaulted roof were of the most radiant and opal-
escent blue.

"Ver' pret'," sing-songed the boatman. He ran his oar through
the water and they watched it turn to an incredible silver.

"I'm going to put my hand in!" said Hallie, enraptured. They
were both kneeling now, and as she leaned forward to plunge
her hand under the surface the strange light enveloped them
like a spell and their lips touched—then all the world turned to
blue and silver, or else this was not the world but a delightful
enchantment in which they would dwell forever.

"Ver' beaut'ful," sang the boatman. "Come back see Blue
Grotte tomorrow, next day. Ask for Frederico, fine man for Blue
Grotte. Oh, chawming!"

Again their lips sought each other and blue and silver seemed to soar like rockets above them, burst and shower down about their shoulders in protective atoms of color, screening them from time, from sight. They kissed again. The voices of tourists were seeking echoes here and there about the cave. A brown naked boy dived from a high rock, cleaving the water like a silver fish, and starting a thousand platinum bubbles to churn up through the blue light.

"I love you with all my heart," she whispered. "What shall we do? Oh, my dear, if you only had a little common sense about money!"

The cavern was emptying, the small boats were feeling their way out, one by one, to the glittering restless sea.

"Good-bye, Blue Grotte!" sang the boatman. "Come again soo-oon!"

Blinded by the sunshine they sat back apart and looked at each other. But though the blue and silver was left behind, the radiance about her face remained.

"I love you," rang as true here under the blue sky.

Mr. Nosby was waiting on the deck, but he said not a word—only looked at them sharply and sat between them all the way back to Naples. But for all his tangible body, they were no longer apart. He had best be quick and interpose his four thousand miles.

It was not until they had docked and were walking from the pier that Corcoran was jerked sharply from his mood of rapture and despair by something that sharply recalled to him the incident of the morning. Directly in their path, as if waiting for them, stood the swarthy hunchback to whom the man in the shirt-sleeves had pointed out their taxi. No sooner did he see them, however, than he stepped quickly aside and melted into a crowd. When they had passed, Corcoran turned back, as if for a last look at the boat, and saw in the sweep of his eye that the hunchback was pointing them out in his turn to still another man.

As they got into a taxi Mr. Nosby broke the silence.

"You'd better pack immediately," he said. "We're leaving by motor for Palermo right after dinner."

"We can't make it tonight," objected Hallie.

"We'll stop at Cosenza. That's halfway."

It was plain that he wanted to bring the trip to an end at the first possible moment. After dinner he asked Corcoran to come to the hotel garage with him while he engaged an automobile for the trip, and Corcoran understood that this was because Hallie and he were not to be left together. Nosby, in an ill humor, insisted that the garage price was too high; finally he walked out and up to a dilapidated taxi in the street. The taxi agreed to make the trip to Palermo for twenty-five dollars.

"I don't believe this old thing will make the grade," ventured Corcoran. "Don't you think it would be wiser to pay the difference and take the other car?"

Nosby stared at him, his anger just under the surface.

"We're not all like you," he said dryly. "We can't all afford to throw it away."

Corcoran took the snub with a cool nod.

"Another thing," he said. "Did you get money from the bank this morning—or anything that would make you likely to be followed?"

"What do you mean?" demanded Nosby quickly.

"Somebody's been keeping pretty close track of our movements all day."

Nosby eyed him shrewdly.

"You'd like us to stay here in Naples a day or so more, wouldn't you?" he said. "Unfortunately you're not running this party. If you stay, you can stay alone."

"And you won't take the other car?"

"I'm getting a little weary of your suggestions."

At the hotel, as the porters piled the bags into the high old-fashioned car, Corcoran was again possessed by a feeling of being watched. With an effort he resisted the impulse to turn his head and look behind. If this was a product of his imagination, it was better to put it immediately from his mind.

It was already eight o'clock when they drove off into a windy twilight. The sun had gone behind Naples, leaving a sky of pigeon's-blood and gold, and as they rounded the bay and climbed slowly toward Torre Annunziata, the Mediterranean momentarily toasted the fading splendor in pink wine. Above them loomed Vesuvius and from its crater a small persistent fountain of smoke contributed darkness to the gathering night.

"We ought to reach Cosenza about twelve," said Nosby.

No one answered. The city had disappeared behind a rise of ground, and now they were alone, tracing down the hot mysterious shin of the Italian boot where the Maffia sprang out of rank human weeds and the Black Hand rose to throw its ominous shadow across two continents. There was something eerie in the sough of the wind over these grey mountains, crowned with the decayed castles. Hallie suddenly shivered.

"I'm glad I'm American," she said. "Here in Italy I feel that everybody's dead. So many people dead and all watching from up on those hills—Carthaginians and old Romans and Moorish pirates and medieval princes with poisoned rings—"

The solemn gloom of the countryside communicated itself to all of them. The wind had come up stronger and was groaning through the dark massed trees along the way. The engine labored painfully up the incessant slopes and then coasted down winding spiral roads until the brakes gave out a burning smell. In the dark little village of Eboli they stopped for gasoline, and while they waited for their change another car came quickly out of the darkness and drew up behind.

Corcoran looked at it closely, but the lights were in his face and he could distinguish only the pale blots of four faces which returned his insistent stare. When the taxi had driven off and toiled a mile uphill in the face of the sweeping wind, he saw the lamps of the other car emerge from the village and follow. In a low voice he called Nosby's attention to the fact—whereupon Nosby leaned forward nervously and rapped on the front glass.

"*Più presto!*" he commanded. "*Il sera sono tropo tarde!*"

Corcoran translated the mutilated Italian and then fell into conversation with the chauffeur. Hallie had dozed off to sleep with her head on her mother's shoulder. It might have been twenty minutes later when she awoke with a start to find that the car had stopped. The chauffeur was peering into the engine with a lighted match, while Corcoran and Mr. Nosby were talking quickly in the road.

"What is it?" she cried.

"He's broken down," said Corcoran, "and he hasn't got the proper tools to make the repair. The best thing is for all of you to start out on foot for Agropoli. That's the next village—it's about two miles away."

"Look!" said Nosby uneasily. The lights of another car had breasted a rise less than a mile behind.

"Perhaps they'll pick us up?" asked Hallie.

"We're taking no such chances," answered Corcoran. "This is the special beat of one of the roughest gangs of holdup men in Southern Italy. What's more, we're being followed. When I asked the chauffeur if he knew that car that drove up behind us in Eboli, he shut right up. He's afraid to say."

As he spoke he was helping Hallie and her mother from the car. Now he turned authoritatively to Nosby.

"You better tell me what you got in that Naples bank."

"It was ten thousand dollars in English bank notes," admitted Nosby in a frightened voice.

"I thought so. Some clerk tipped them off. Hand over those notes to me!"

"Why should I?" demanded Nosby. "What are you going to do with them?"

"I'm going to throw them away," said Corcoran. His head went up alertly. The complaint of a motor car taking a hill in second speed was borne toward them clearly on the night. "Hallie, you and your mother start on with the chauffeur. Run as fast as you can for a hundred yards or so and then keep going. If I don't show up, notify the carabinieri in Agropoli." His voice sank lower. "Don't worry, I'm going to fix this thing. Good-bye."

As they started off he turned again to Nosby.

"Hand over that money," he said.

"You're going to—"

"I'm going to keep them here while you get Hallie away. Don't you see that if they got her up in these hills they could ask any amount of money they wanted?"

Nosby paused irresolute. Then he pulled out a thick packet of fifty-pound notes and began to peel half a dozen from the top.

"I want *all* of it," snapped Corcoran. With a quick movement he wrested the packet violently from Nosby's hand. "Now go on!"

Less than half a mile away, the lights of the car dipped into sight. With a broken cry Nosby turned and stumbled off down the road.

Corcoran took a pencil and an envelope from his pocket and worked quickly for a few minutes by the glow of the headlights.

Then he wet one finger and held it up tentatively in the air as if he were making an experiment. The result seemed to satisfy him. He waited, ruffling the large thin notes—there were forty of them—in his hands.

The lights of the other car came nearer, slowed up, came to a stop twenty feet away.

Leaving the engine running idle, four men got out and walked toward him.

"*Buona séra!*" he called, and then continued in Italian, "We have broken down."

"Where are the rest of your people?" demanded one of the men quickly.

"They were picked up by another car. It turned around and took them back to Agropoli," Corcoran said politely. He was aware that he was covered by two revolvers, but he waited an instant longer, straining to hear the flurry in the trees which would announce a gust of wind. The men drew nearer.

"But I have something here that may interest you." Slowly, his heart thumping, he raised his hand, bringing the packet of notes into the glare of the headlight. Suddenly out of the valley swept the wind, louder and nearer—he waited a moment longer until he felt the first cold freshness on his face. "Here are two hundred thousand lire in English bank notes!" He raised the sheaf of paper higher as if to hand it to the nearest man. Then he released it with a light upward flick and immediately the wind seized upon it and whirled the notes in forty directions through the air.

The nearest man cursed and made a lunge for the closest piece. Then they were all scurrying here and there about the road while the frail bills sailed and flickered in the gale, pirouetting like elves along the grass, bouncing and skipping from side to side in mad perversity.

From one side to the other they ran, Corcoran with them—crumpling the captured money into their pockets, then scattering always farther and farther apart in wild pursuit of the elusive beckoning symbols of gold.

Suddenly Corcoran saw his opportunity. Bending low, as if he had spotted a stray bill beneath the car, he ran toward it, vaulted over the side and hitched into the driver's seat. As he plunged the lever into first, he heard a cursing cry and then a sharp report, but the warmed car had jumped forward safely and the shot went wide.

In a moment, his teeth locked and muscles tense against the fusillade, he had passed the stalled taxi and was racing along into the darkness. There was another report close at hand and he ducked wildly, afraid for an instant that one of them had clung to the running board—then he realized that one of their shots had blown out a tire.

After three-quarters of a mile he stopped, cut off his motor and listened. There wasn't a sound, only the drip from his radiator onto the road.

"Hallie!" he called. "Hallie!"

A figure emerged from the shadows not ten feet away, then another figure and another.

"Hallie!" he said.

She clambered into the front seat with him—her arms went about him.

"You're safe!" she sobbed. "We heard the shots and I wanted to go back."

Mr. Nosby, very cool now, stood in the road.

"I don't suppose you brought back any of that money," he said.

Corcoran took three crumpled bank notes from his pocket.

"That's all," he said. "But they're liable to be along here any minute and you can argue with them about the rest."

Mr. Nosby, followed by Mrs. Bushmill and the chauffeur, stepped quickly into the car.

"Nevertheless," he insisted shrilly, as they moved off, "this has been a pretty expensive business. You've flung away ten thousand dollars that was to have bought goods in Sicily."

"Those are English bank notes," said Corcoran. "Big notes too. Every bank in England and Italy will be watching for those numbers."

"But we don't know the numbers!"

"I took all the numbers," said Corcoran.

The rumor that Mr. Julius Bushmill's purchasing department keeps him awake nights is absolutely unfounded. There are those who say that a once conservative business is expanding in a way that is more sensational than sound, but they are probably small, malevolent rivals with a congenital disgust for the Grand

Scale. To all gratuitous advice, Mr. Bushmill replies that even when his son-in-law seems to be throwing it away, it all comes back. His theory is that the young idiot really has a talent for spending money.

"Not in the Guidebook"

THIS story began three days before it got into the papers. Like many other news-hungry Americans in Paris this spring, I opened the "Franco-American Star" one morning and having skimmed the hackneyed headlines (largely devoted to reporting the sempiternal "Lafayette-love-Washington" bombast of French and American orators) I came upon something of genuine interest.

"Look at that!" I exclaimed, passing it over to the twin bed. But the occupant of the twin bed immediately found an article about Leonora Hughes, the dancer, in another column, and began to read it. So of course I demanded the paper back.

"You don't realize—" I began.

"I wonder," interrupted the occupant of the twin bed, "if she's a real blonde."

However, when I issued from the domestic suite a little later I found other men in various cafés saying "Look at that!" as they pointed to the Item of Interest. And about noon I found another writer (whom I have since bribed with champagne to hold his peace) and together we went down into Franco-American officialdom to see. We discovered that the story began about three days before it got into the papers.

It began on a boat, and with a young woman who, though she wasn't even faintly uneasy, was leaning over the rail. She was watching the parallels of longitude as they swam beneath the keel, and trying to read the numbers on them, but of course the *S. S. Olympic* travels too fast for that, and all that the young woman could see was the agate-green, foliage-like spray, changing and complaining around the stern. Though there was little to look at except the spray and a dismal Scandinavian tramp in the distance and the admiring millionaire who was trying to catch her eye from the first-class deck above, Milly Cooley was perfectly happy. For she was beginning life over.

Hope is a usual cargo between Naples and Ellis Island, but on ships bound east for Cherbourg it is noticeably rare. The first-class passengers specialize in sophistication and the steerage

554

passengers go in for disillusion (which is much the same thing) but the young woman by the rail was going in for hope raised to the ultimate power. It was not her own life she was beginning over, but someone else's, and this is a much more dangerous thing to do.

Milly was a frail, dark, appealing girl with the spiritual, haunted eyes that so frequently accompany South European beauty. By birth her mother and father had been respectively Czech and Roumanian, but Milly had missed the overshort upper lip and the pendulous, pointed nose that disfigure the type—her features were regular and her skin was young and olive-white and clear.

The good-looking, pimply young man with eyes of a bright marbly blue who was asleep on a dunnage bag a few feet away was her husband—it was his life that Milly was beginning over. Through the six months of their marriage he had shown himself to be shiftless and dissipated, but now they were getting off to a new start. Jim Cooley deserved a new start, for he had been a hero in the war. There was a thing called "shell shock" which justified anything unpleasant in a war hero's behavior— Jim Cooley had explained that to her on the second day of their honeymoon when he had gotten abominably drunk and knocked her down with his open hand.

"I get crazy," he said emphatically next morning, and his marbly eyes rolled back and forth realistically in his head. "I get started, thinkin' I'm fightin' the war, an' I take a poke at whatever's in front of me, see?"

He was a Brooklyn boy, and he had joined the marines. And on a June twilight he had crawled fifty yards out of his lines to search the body of a Bavarian captain that lay out in plain sight. He found a copy of German regimental orders, and in consequence his own brigade attacked much sooner than would otherwise have been possible, and perhaps the war was shortened by so much as a quarter of an hour. The fact was appreciated by the French and American races in the form of engraved slugs of precious metal which Jim showed around for four years before it occurred to him how nice it would be to have a permanent audience. Milly's mother was impressed with his martial achievement, and a marriage was arranged—Milly didn't realize her mistake until twenty-four hours after it was too late.

At the end of several months Milly's mother died and left her daughter two hundred and fifty dollars. The event had a marked effect on Jim. He sobered up and one night came home from work with a plan for turning over a new leaf, for beginning life over. By the aid of his war record he had obtained a job with a bureau that took care of American soldier graves in France. The pay was small but then, as everyone knew, living was dirt cheap over there. Hadn't the forty a month that he drew in the war looked good to the girls and the wine-sellers of Paris? Especially when you figured it in French money.

Milly listened to his tales of the land where grapes were full of champagne and then thought it all over carefully. Perhaps the best use for her money would be in giving Jim his chance, the chance that he had never had since the war. In a little cottage in the outskirts of Paris they could forget this last six months and find peace and happiness and perhaps even love as well.

"Are you going to try?" she asked simply.

"Of course I'm going to try, Milly."

"You're going to make me think I didn't make a mistake?"

"Sure I am, Milly. It'll make a different person out of me. Don't you believe it?"

She looked at him. His eyes were bright with enthusiasm, with determination. A warm glow had spread over him at the prospect—he had never really had his chance before.

"All right," she said finally. "We'll go."

They were there. The Cherbourg breakwater, a white stone snake, glittered along the sea at dawn—behind it red roofs and steeples and then small, neat hills traced with a warm, orderly pattern of toy farms. "Do you like this French arrangement?" it seemed to say. "It's considered very charming, but if you don't agree just shift it about—set this road here, this steeple there. It's been done before, and it always comes out lovely in the end!"

It was Sunday morning, and Cherbourg was in flaring collars and high lace hats. Donkey carts and diminutive automobiles moved to the sound of incessant bells. Jim and Milly went ashore on a tug-boat and were inspected by customs officials and immigration authorities. Then they were free with an hour before the Paris train, and they moved out into the bright thrilling world of French blue. At a point of vantage, a pleasant square that continually throbbed with soldiers and innumerable dogs and the clack of wooden shoes, they sat down at a café.

"Du vaah," said Jim to the waiter. He was a little disappointed when the answer came in English. After the man went for the wine he took out his two war medals and pinned them to his coat. The waiter returned with the wine, seemed not to notice the medals, made no remark. Milly wished Jim hadn't put them on—she felt vaguely ashamed.

After another glass of wine it was time for the train. They got into the strange little third-class carriage, an engine that was out of some boy's playroom began to puff and, in a pleasant informal way, jogged them leisurely south through the friendly lived-over land.

"What are we going to do first when we get there?" asked Milly.

"First?" Jim looked at her abstractedly and frowned. "Why, first I got to see about the job, see?" The exhilaration of the wine had passed and left him surly. "What do you want to ask so many questions for? Buy yourself a guidebook, why don't you?"

Milly felt a slight sinking of the heart—he hadn't grumbled at her like this since the trip was first proposed.

"It didn't cost as much as we thought, anyhow," she said cheerfully. "We must have over a hundred dollars left anyway."

He grunted. Outside the window Milly's eyes were caught by the sight of a dog drawing a legless man.

"Look!" she exclaimed. "How funny!"

"Aw, dry up. I've seen it all before."

An encouraging idea occurred to her: it was in France that Jim's nerves had gone to pieces; it was natural that he should be cross and uneasy for a few hours.

Westward through Caen, Lisieux and the rich green plains of Calvados. When they reached the third stop Jim got up and stretched himself.

"Going out on the platform," he said gloomily. "I need to get a breath of air; hot in here."

It was hot, but Milly didn't mind. Her eyes were excited with all she saw—a pair of little boys in black smocks began to stare at her curiously through the windows of the carriage.

"American?" cried one of them suddenly.

"Hello," said Milly. "What place is this?"

"Pardon?"

They came closer.

"What's the name of this place?"

Suddenly the two boys poked each other in the stomach and went off into roars of laughter. Milly didn't see that she had said anything funny.

There was an abrupt jerk as the train started. Milly jumped up in alarm and put her head out the carriage window.

"Jim!" she called.

She looked up and down the platform. He wasn't there. The boys, seeing her distraught face, ran along beside the train as it moved from the station. He must have jumped for one of the rear cars. But—

"Jim!" she cried wildly. The station slid past. "Jim!"

Trying desperately to control her fright, she sank back into her seat and tried to think. Her first supposition was that he had gone to a café for a drink and missed the train—in that case she should have got off too while there was still time, for otherwise there was no telling what would happen to him. If this were one of his spells he might just go on drinking, until he had spent every cent of their money. It was unbelievably awful to imagine—but it was possible.

She waited, gave him ten, fifteen minutes to work his way up to this car—then she admitted to herself that he wasn't on the train. A dull panic began—the sudden change in her relations to the world was so startling that she thought neither of his delinquency nor of what must be done, but only of the immediate fact that she was alone. Erratic as his protection had been, it was something. Now—why, she might sit in this strange train until it carried her to China and there was no one to care!

After a long while it occurred to her that he might have left part of the money in one of the suitcases. She took them down from the rack and went feverishly through all the clothes. In the bottom of an old pair of pants that Jim had worn on the boat she found two bright American dimes. The sight of them was somehow comforting and she clasped them tight in her hand. The bags yielded up nothing more.

An hour later, when it was dark outside, the train slid in under the yellow misty glow of the Gare du Nord. Strange, incomprehensible station cries fell on her ears, and her heart was beating loud as she wrenched at the handle of the door. She took her own bag with one hand and picked up Jim's suitcase in the other, but it was heavy and she couldn't get out the door with both, so in a rush of anger she left the suitcase in the carriage.

On the platform she looked left and right with the forlorn hope that he might appear, but she saw no one except a Swedish brother and sister from the boat whose tall bodies, straight and strong under the huge bundles they both carried, were hurrying out of sight. She took a quick step after them and then stopped, unable to tell them of the shameful thing that had happened to her. They had worries of their own.

With the two dimes in one hand and her suitcase in the other, Milly walked slowly along the platform. People hurried by her, baggage-smashers under forests of golf sticks, excited American girls full of the irrepressible thrill of arriving in Paris, obsequious porters from the big hotels. They were all walking and talking very fast, but Milly walked slowly because ahead of her she saw only the yellow arc of the waiting room and the door that led out of it and after that she did not know where she would go.

II

By 10 P.M. Mr. Bill Driscoll was usually weary, for by that time he had a full twelve-hour day behind him. After that he only went out with the most celebrated people. If someone had tipped off a multi-millionaire or a moving-picture director—at that time American directors were swarming over Europe looking for new locations—about Bill Driscoll, he would fortify himself with two cups of coffee, adorn his person with his new dinner coat and show them the most dangerous dives of Montmartre in the very safest way.

Bill Driscoll looked good in his new dinner coat, with his reddish brown hair soaked in water and slicked back from his attractive forehead. Often he regarded himself admiringly in the mirror, for it was the first dinner coat he had ever owned. He had earned it himself, with his wits, as he had earned the swelling packet of American bonds which awaited him in a New York bank. If you have been in Paris during the past two years you must have seen his large white auto-bus with the provoking legend on the side:

WILLIAM DRISCOLL
HE SHOWS YOU THINGS NOT IN THE GUIDEBOOK

When he found Milly Cooley it was after three o'clock and he had just left Director and Mrs. Claude Peebles at their hotel after escorting them to those celebrated apache dens, Zelli's and *Le Rat Mort* (which are about as dangerous, all things considered, as the Biltmore Hotel at noon), and he was walking homeward toward his pension on the Left Bank. His eye was caught by two disreputable-looking parties under the lamp post who were giving aid to what was apparently a drunken girl. Bill Driscoll decided to cross the street—he was aware of the tender affection which the French police bore toward embattled Americans, and he made a point of keeping out of trouble. Just at that moment Milly's subconscious self came to her aid and she called out "Let me go!" in an agonized moan.

The moan had a Brooklyn accent. It was a Brooklyn moan.

Driscoll altered his course uneasily and, approaching the group, asked politely what was the matter, whereat one of the disreputable parties desisted in his attempt to open Milly's tightly clasped left hand.

The man answered quickly that she had fainted. He and his friend were assisting her to the gendarmerie. They loosened their hold on her and she collapsed gently to the ground.

Bill came closer and bent over her, being careful to choose a position where neither man was behind him. He saw a young, frightened face that was drained now of the color it possessed by day.

"Where did you find her?" he inquired in French.

"Here. Just now. She looked to be so tired—"

Bill put his hand in his pocket and when he spoke he tried very hard to suggest by his voice that he had a revolver there.

"She is American," he said. "You leave her to me."

The man made a gesture of acquiescence and took a step backward, his hand going with a natural movement to his coat as if he intended buttoning it. He was watching Bill's right hand, the one in his coat-pocket, and Bill happened to be left-handed. There is nothing much faster than an untelegraphed left-hand blow—this one traveled less than eighteen inches and the recipient staggered back against a lamp post, embraced it transiently and regretfully and settled to the ground. Nevertheless Bill Driscoll's successful career might have ended there, ended with the strong shout of "*Voleurs!*" which he raised into the Paris night, had the other man had a gun. The other man indicated that he had no gun by retreating ten yards down the street. His prostrate companion moved slightly on the sidewalk and, taking a step toward him, Bill drew back his foot and kicked him full in the head as a football player kicks a goal from placement. It was not a pretty gesture, but he had remembered that he was wearing his new dinner coat and he didn't want to wrestle on the ground for the piece of poisonous hardware.

In a moment two gendarmes in a great hurry came running down the moonlit street.

III

Two days after this it came out in the papers—"*War hero deserts wife en route to Paris,*" I think, or "*American Bride arrives penniless, Husbandless at Gare du Nord.*" The police were informed, of course, and word was sent out to the provincial departments to seek an American named James Cooley who was without *carte d'identité*. The newspapers learned the story at the American Aid Society and made a neat pathetic job of it, because Milly was young and pretty and curiously loyal to her husband. Almost her first words were to explain that it was all because his nerves had been shattered in the war.

Young Driscoll was somewhat disappointed to find that she was married. Not that he had fallen in love at first sight—on the contrary, he was unusually level-headed—but after the moonlight rescue, which rather pleased him, it didn't seem appropriate that she should have a heroic husband wandering over France. He had carried her to his own pension that night, and his landlady, an American widow named Mrs. Horton, had taken a fancy to Milly and wanted to look after her, but before eleven o'clock on the day the paper appeared, the office of the American Aid Society was literally jammed with Samaritans. They were mostly rich old ladies from America who were tired of the Louvre and the Tuileries and anxious for something to do. Several eager but sheepish Frenchmen, inspired by a mysterious and unfathomable gallantry, hung about outside the door.

The most insistent of the ladies was a Mrs. Coots, who considered that Providence had sent her Milly as a companion. If she
had heard Milly's story in the street she wouldn't have listened
to a word, but print makes things respectable. After it got into
the "Franco-American Star," Mrs. Coots was sure Milly wouldn't
make off with her jewels.

"I'll pay you well, my dear," she insisted shrilly. "Twenty-five
a week. How's that?"

Milly cast an anxious glance at Mrs. Horton's faded, pleasant
face.

"I don't know—" she said hesitantly.

"I can't pay you anything," said Mrs. Horton, who was confused by Mrs. Coots' affluent, positive manner. "You do as you
like. I'd love to have you."

"You've certainly been kind," said Milly, "but I don't want
to impose—"

Driscoll, who had been walking up and down with his hands
in his pockets, stopped and turned toward her quickly.

"I'll take care of that," he said quickly. "You don't have to
worry about that."

Mrs. Coots' eyes flashed at him indignantly.

"She's better with me," she insisted. "Much better." She
turned to the secretary and remarked in a pained, disapproving
stage whisper, "Who is this forward young man?"

Again Milly looked appealingly at Mrs. Horton.

"If it's not too much trouble I'd rather stay with you," she
said. "I'll help you all I can—"

It took another half hour to get rid of Mrs. Coots, but finally
it was arranged that Milly was to stay at Mrs. Horton's pension,
until some trace of her husband was found. Later the same day
they ascertained that the American Bureau of Military Graves
had never heard of Jim Cooley—he had no job promised him
in France.

However distressing her situation, Milly was young and she
was in Paris in mid-June. She decided to enjoy herself. At Mr.
Bill Driscoll's invitation she went on an excursion to Versailles
next day in his rubberneck wagon. She had never been on such
a trip before. She sat among garment buyers from Sioux City
and school teachers from California and honeymoon couples
from Japan and was whirled through fifteen centuries of Paris,

while Bill stood up in front with the megaphone pressed to his voluble and original mouth.

"Building on our left is the Louvre, ladies and gentlemen. Excursion number twenty-three leaving tomorrow at ten sharp takes you inside. Sufficient to remark now that it contains fifteen thousand works of art of every description. The oil used in its oil paintings would lubricate all the cars in the state of Oregon over a period of two years. The frames alone if placed end to end—"

Milly watched him, believing every word. It was hard to remember that he had come to her rescue that night. Heroes weren't like that—she knew; she had lived with one. They brooded constantly on their achievements and retailed them to strangers at least once a day. When she had thanked this young man he told her gravely that Mr. Carnegie had been trying to get him on the ouija board all that day.

After a dramatic stop before the house in which Landru, the Bluebeard of France, had murdered his fourteen wives, the expedition proceeded on to Versailles. There, in the great hall of mirrors, Bill Driscoll delved into the forgotten scandal of the eighteenth century as he described the meeting between "Louie's girl and Louie's wife."

"Du Barry skipped in, wearing a creation of mauve georgette, held out by bronze hoops over a tablier of champagne lace. The gown had a ruched collarette of Swedish fox, lined with yellow satin fulgurante which matched the hansom that brought her to the party. She was nervous, ladies. She didn't know how the queen was going to take it. After awhile the queen walked in wearing an oxidized silver gown with collar, cuffs and flounces of Russian ermine and strappings of dentist's gold. The bodice was cut with a very long waistline and the skirt arranged full in front and falling in picot-edged points tipped with the crown jewels. When Du Barry saw her she leaned over to King Louie and whispered: 'Royal Honeyboy, who's that lady with all the laundry on that just came in the door?'

"'That isn't a lady,' said Louie. 'That's my wife.'

"Most of the Court almost broke their contracts laughing. The ones that didn't died in the Bastille."

That was the first of many trips that Milly took in the rubber-neck wagon—to Malmaison, to Passy, to St-Cloud. The weeks passed, three of them, and still there was no word from Jim

Cooley, who seemed to have stepped off the face of the earth when he vanished from the train.

In spite of a sort of dull worry that possessed her when she thought of her situation, Milly was happier than she had ever been. It was a relief to be rid of the incessant depression of living with a morbid and broken man. Moreover, it was thrilling to be in Paris when it seemed that all the world was there, when each arriving boat dumped a new thousand into the pleasure ground, when the streets were so clogged with sight-seers that Bill Driscoll's buses were reserved for days ahead. And it was pleasantest of all to stroll down to the corner and watch the blood-red sun sink like a slow penny into the Seine while she sipped coffee with Bill Driscoll at a café.

"How would you like to go to Château-Thierry with me tomorrow?" he asked her one evening.

The name struck a chord in Milly. It was at Château-Thierry that Jim Cooley, at the risk of his life, had made his daring expedition between the lines.

"My husband was there," she said proudly.

"So was I," he remarked. "And I didn't have any fun at all."

He thought for a moment.

"How old are you?" he asked suddenly.

"Eighteen."

"Why don't you go to a lawyer and get a divorce?"

The suggestion shocked Milly.

"I think you'd better," he continued, looking down at the pavement. "It's easier here than anywhere else. Then you'd be free."

"I couldn't," she said, frightened. "It wouldn't be fair. You see, he doesn't—"

"I know," he interrupted. "But I'm beginning to think that you're spoiling your life with this man. Is there anything except his war record to his credit?"

"Isn't that enough?" answered Milly gravely.

"Milly—" He raised his eyes. "Won't you think it over carefully?"

She got up uneasily. He looked very honest and safe and cool sitting there, and for a moment she was tempted to do what he said, to put the whole thing in his hands. But looking at him she saw now what she hadn't seen before, that the advice was not disinterested—there was more than an impersonal care for her future in his eyes. She turned away with a mixture of emotions.

Side by side, and in silence, they walked back towards the pension. From a high window the plaintive wail of a violin drifted down into the street, mingling with practice chords from an invisible piano and a shrill incomprehensible quarrel of French children over the way. The twilight was fast dissolving into a starry blue Parisian evening, but it was still light enough for them to make out the figure of Mrs. Horton standing in front of the pension. She came towards them swiftly, talking as she came.

"I've got some news for you," she said. "The secretary of the American Aid Society just telephoned. They've located your husband, and he'll be in Paris the day after tomorrow."

IV

When Jim Cooley, the war hero, left the train at the small town of Evreux, he walked very fast until he was several hundred yards from the station. Then, standing behind a tree, he watched until the train pulled out and the last puff of smoke burst up behind a little hill. He stood for several minutes, laughing and looking after the train, until abruptly his face resumed his normal injured expression and he turned to examine the place in which he had chosen to be free.

It was a sleepy provincial village with two high lines of silver sycamores along its principal street, at the end of which a fine fountain purred crystal water from a cat's mouth of cold stone. Around the fountain was a square and on the sidewalks of the square several groups of small iron tables indicated open-air cafés. A farm wagon drawn by a single white ox was toiling toward the fountain and several cheap French cars, together with a 1910 Ford, were parked at intervals along the street.

"It's a hick town," he said to himself with some disgust. "Reg'lar hick town."

But it was peaceful and green, and he caught sight of two stockingless ladies entering the door of a shop—and the little tables by the fountain were inviting. He walked up the street and at the first café sat down and ordered a large beer.

"I'm free," he said to himself. "Free, by God!"

His decision to desert Milly had been taken suddenly—in Cherbourg, as they got on the train. Just at that moment he had seen a little French girl who was the real thing, and he realized that he didn't want Milly "hanging on him" anymore. Even on the boat he had played with the idea, but until Cherbourg he had never quite made up his mind. He was rather sorry now that he hadn't thought to leave Milly a little money, enough for one night—but then somebody would be sure to help her when she got to Paris. Besides, what he didn't know didn't worry him, and he wasn't going ever to hear about her again.

"Cognac this time," he said to the waiter.

He needed something strong. He wanted to forget. Not to forget Milly, that was easy, she was already behind him; but to forget himself. He felt that he had been abused. He felt that it was Milly who had deserted him, or at least that her cold mistrust was responsible for driving him away. What good would it have done if he had gone on to Paris anyways? There wasn't enough money left to keep two people for very long—and he had invented the job on the strength of a vague rumor that the American Bureau of Military Graves gave jobs to veterans who were broke in France. He shouldn't have brought Milly, wouldn't have if he had had the money to get over. But, though he was not aware of it, there was another reason why he had brought Milly. Jim Cooley hated to be alone.

"Cognac," he said to the waiter. "A big one. *Très grand.*"

He put his hand in his pocket and fingered the blue notes that had been given him in Cherbourg in exchange for his American money. He took them out and counted them. Crazy-looking kale. It was funny you could buy things with it just like you could do with the real mazuma.

He beckoned to the waiter.

"Hey!" he remarked conversationally. "This is funny money you got here, ain't it?"

But the waiter spoke no English and was unable to satisfy Jim Cooley's craving for companionship. Never mind. His nerves were at rest now—body was glowing triumphantly from top to toe.

"This is the life," he muttered to himself. "Only live once. Might as well enjoy it." And then aloud to the waiter, "'Nother one of those big cognacs. Two of them. I'm set to go."

He went—for several hours. He awoke at dawn in a bedroom of a small inn, with red streaks in his eyes and fever pounding in his head. He was afraid to look in his pockets until he had ordered and swallowed another cognac, and then he found that his worst fears were justified. Of the ninety-odd dollars with which he had got off the train only six were left.

"I must have been crazy," he whispered to himself.

There remained his watch. His watch was large and methodical, and on the outer case two hearts were picked out in diamonds from the dark solid gold. It had been part of the booty of Jim Cooley's heroism, for when he had located the paper in the German officer's pocket he had found it clasped tight in the dead hand. One of the diamond hearts probably stood for some human grief back in Friedland or Berlin, but when Jim married he told Milly that the diamond hearts stood for their hearts and would be a token of their everlasting love. Before Milly fully appreciated this sentimental suggestion their enduring love had been tarnished beyond repair and the watch went back into Jim's pocket where it confined itself to marking time instead of emotion.

But Jim Cooley had loved to show the watch, and he found that parting with it would be much more painful than parting with Milly—so painful, in fact, that he got drunk in anticipation of his sorrow. Late that afternoon, already a reeling figure at which the town boys jeered along the streets, he found his way into the shop of a *bijoutier*, and when he issued forth into the street he was in possession of a ticket of redemption and a note for two thousand francs which, he figured dimly, was about one hundred and twenty dollars. Muttering to himself, he stumbled back to the square.

"One American can lick three Frenchmen!" he remarked to three small stout bourgeois drinking their beer at a table.

They paid no attention. He repeated his jeer.

"One American—" tapping his chest, "can beat up three dirty frogs, see?"

Still they didn't move. It infuriated him. Lurching forward, he seized the back of an unoccupied chair and pulled at it. In what seemed less than a minute there was a small crowd around him and the three Frenchmen were all talking at once in excited voices.

"Aw, go on, I meant what I said!" he cried savagely. "One American can wipe up the ground with three Frenchmen!"

And now there were two men in uniform before him—two men with revolver holsters on their hips, dressed in red and blue.

"You heard what I said," he shouted. "I'm a hero—I'm not afraid of the whole damn French army!"

A hand fell on his arm, but with blind passion he wrenched it free and struck at the black mustached face before him. Then there was a rushing, crashing noise in his ears as fists and then feet struck at him, and the world seemed to close like water over his head.

v

When they located him and, after a personal expedition by one of the American vice consuls, got him out of jail, Milly realized how much these weeks had meant to her. The holiday was over. But even though Jim would be in Paris tomorrow, even though the dreary round of her life with him was due to recommence, Milly decided to take the trip to Château-Thierry just the same. She wanted a last few hours of happiness that she could always remember. She supposed they would return to New York—what chance Jim might have had of obtaining a position had vanished now that he was marked by a fortnight in a French prison.

The bus, as usual, was crowded. As they approached the little village of Château-Thierry, Bill Driscoll stood up in front with his megaphone and began to tell his clients how it had looked to him when his division went up to the line five years before.

"It was nine o'clock at night," he said, "and we came out of a wood and there was the Western Front. I'd read about it for three years back in America, and here it was at last—it looked like the line of a forest fire at night except that fireworks were blazing up instead of grass. We relieved a French regiment in new trenches that weren't three feet deep. At that, most of us were too excited to be scared until the top sergeant was blown to pieces with shrapnel about two o'clock in the morning. That made us think. Two days later we went over and the only reason I didn't get hit was that I was shaking so much they couldn't aim at me."

The listeners laughed and Milly felt a faint thrill of pride. Jim hadn't been scared—she'd heard him say so, many times. All he'd thought about was doing a little more than his duty. When others were in the comparative safety of the trenches he had gone into no-man's land alone.

After lunch in the village the party walked over the battlefield, changed now into a peaceful undulating valley of graves. Milly was glad she had come—the sense of rest after a struggle soothed her. Perhaps after the bleak future, her life might be quiet as this peaceful land. Perhaps Jim would change someday. If he had risen once to such a height of courage there must be something deep inside him that was worth while, that would make him try once more.

Just before it was time to start home Driscoll, who had hardly spoken to her all day, suddenly beckoned her aside.

"I want to talk to you for the last time," he said.

The last time— Milly felt a flutter of unexpected pain. Was tomorrow so near?

"I'm going to say what's in my mind," he said, "and please don't be angry. I love you, and you know it; but what I'm going to say isn't because of that—it's because I want you to be happy."

Milly nodded. She was afraid she was going to cry.

"I don't think your husband's any good," he said.

She looked up.

"You don't know him," she exclaimed quickly. "You can't judge."

"I can judge from what he did to you. I think this shell-shock business is all a plain lie. And what does it matter what he did five years ago?"

"It matters to me," cried Milly. She felt herself growing a little angry. "You can't take that away from him. He acted brave."

Driscoll nodded.

"That's true. But other men were brave."

"You weren't," she said scornfully. "You just said you were scared to death—and when you said it all the people laughed. Well, nobody laughed at Jim—they gave him a medal because he wasn't afraid."

When Milly had said this she was sorry, but it was too late now. At his next words she leaned forward in surprise.

"That was a lie too," said Bill Driscoll slowly. "I told it because I wanted them to laugh. I wasn't even in the attack."

He stared silently down the hill.

"Well then," said Milly contemptuously, "how can you sit here and say things about my husband when—when you didn't even—"

"It was only a professional lie," he said impatiently. "I happened to be wounded the night before."

He stood up suddenly.

"There's no use," he said. "I seem to have made you hate me, and that's the end. There's no use saying any more."

He stared down the hill with haunted eyes.

"I shouldn't have talked to you here," he cried. "There's no luck here for me. Once before I lost something I wanted, not a hundred yards from this hill. And now I've lost you."

"What was it you lost," demanded Milly bitterly. "Another girl?"

"There's never been any other girl but you."

"What was it then?"

He hesitated.

"I told you I was wounded," he said. "I was. For two months I didn't know I was alive. But the worst of it was that some dirty sneak thief had been through my pockets, and I guess he got the credit for a copy of German orders that I'd just brought in. He took a gold watch too. I'd pinched them both off the body of a German officer out between the lines."

Mr. and Mrs. William Driscoll were married the following spring and started off on their honeymoon in a car that was much larger than the King of England's. There were two dozen vacant places in it, so they gave many rides to tired pedestrians along the white poplar-lined roads of France. The wayfarers, however, always sat in the back seat as the conversation in front was not for profane ears. The tour progressed through Lyons, Avignon, Bordeaux, and smaller places not in the guidebook.

Presumption

SITTING by the window and staring out into the early autumn dusk, San Juan Chandler remembered only that Noel was coming tomorrow; but when, with a romantic sound that was half gasp, half sigh, he turned from the window, snapped on the light and looked at himself in the mirror, his expression became more materially complicated. He leaned closer. Delicacy balked at the abominable word "pimple," but some such blemish had undoubtedly appeared on his cheek within the last hour, and now formed, with a pair from last week, a distressing constellation of three. Going into the bathroom adjoining his room—Juan had never possessed a bathroom to himself before—he opened a medicine closet, and after peering about, carefully extracted a promising-looking jar of black ointment and covered each slight protuberance with a black gluey mound. Then, strangely dotted, he returned to the bedroom, put out the light and resumed his vigil over the shadowy garden.

He waited. That roof among the trees on the hill belonged to Noel Garneau's house. She was coming back to it tomorrow; he would see her there. . . . A loud clock on the staircase inside struck seven. Juan went to the glass and removed the ointment with a handkerchief. To his chagrin, the spots were still there, even slightly irritated from the chemical sting of the remedy. That settled it—no more chocolate malted milks or eating between meals during his visit to Culpepper Bay. Taking the lid from the jar of talcum he had observed on the dressing table, he touched the laden puff to his cheek. Immediately his brows and lashes bloomed with snow and he coughed chokingly, observing that the triangle of humiliation was still observable upon his otherwise handsome face.

"Disgusting," he muttered to himself. "I never saw anything so disgusting." At twenty, such childish phenomena should be behind him.

Downstairs three gongs, melodious and metallic, hummed and sang. He listened for a moment, fascinated. Then he wiped the powder from his face, ran a comb through his yellow hair and went down to dinner.

Dinner at Cousin Cora's he had found embarrassing. She was so stiff and formal about things like that, and so familiar about Juan's private affairs. The first night of his visit he had tried politely to pull out her chair and bumped into the maid; the second night he remembered the experience—but so did the maid, and Cousin Cora seated herself unassisted. At home Juan was accustomed to behave as he liked; like all children of deferent and indulgent mothers, he lacked both confidence and good manners.

Tonight there were guests.

"This is San Juan Chandler, my cousin's son—Mrs. Holyoke—and Mr. Holyoke."

The phrase "my cousin's son" seemed to explain him away, seemed to account for his being in Miss Chandler's house: "You understand—we must have our poor relations with us occasionally." But a tone which implied that would be rude—and certainly Cousin Cora, with all her social position, couldn't be rude.

Mr. and Mrs. Holyoke acknowledged the introduction politely and coolly, and dinner was served. The conversation, dictated by Cousin Cora, bored Juan. It was about the garden and about her father, for whom she lived and who was dying slowly and unwillingly upstairs. Toward the salad Juan was wedged into the conversation by a question from Mr. Holyoke and a quick look from his cousin.

"I'm just staying for a week," he answered politely; "then I've got to go home, because college opens pretty soon."

"Where are you at college?"

Juan named his college, adding almost apologetically, "You see, my father went there."

He wished that he could have answered that he was at Yale or Princeton, where he had wanted to go. He was prominent at Henderson and belonged to a good fraternity, but it annoyed him when people occasionally failed to recognize his alma mater's name.

"I suppose you've met all the young people here," supposed Mrs. Holyoke—"my daughter?"

"Oh, yes"—her daughter was the dumpy, ugly girl with the thick spectacles—"oh, yes." And he added, "I knew some people who lived here before I came."

"The little Garneau girl," explained Cousin Cora.

"Oh, yes. Noel Garneau," agreed Mrs. Holyoke. "Her mother's a great beauty. How old is Noel now? She must be—"

"Seventeen," supplied Juan; "but she's old for her age."

"Juan met her on a ranch last summer. They were on a ranch together. What is it that they call those ranches, Juan?"

"Dude ranches."

"Dude ranches. Juan and another boy worked for their board." Juan saw no reason why Cousin Cora should have supplied this information; she continued on an even more annoying note: "Noel's mother sent her out there to keep her out of mischief, but Juan says the ranch was pretty gay itself."

Mr. Holyoke supplied a welcome change of subject.

"Your name is—" he inquired, smiling and curious.

"San Juan Chandler. My father was wounded in the battle of San Juan Hill and so they called me after it—like Kenesaw Mountain Landis."

He had explained this so many times that the sentences rolled off automatically—in school he had been called Santy, in college he was Don.

"You must come to dinner while you're here," said Mrs. Holyoke vaguely.

The conversation slipped away from him as he realized freshly, strongly, that Noel would arrive tomorrow. And she was coming because he was here. She had cut short a visit in the Adirondacks on receipt of his letter. Would she like him now—in this place that was so different from Montana? There was a spaciousness, an air of money and pleasure about Culpepper Bay for which San Juan Chandler—a shy, handsome, spoiled, brilliant, penniless boy from a small Ohio city—was unprepared. At home, where his father was a retired clergyman, Juan went with the nice people. He didn't realize until this visit to a fashionable New England resort that where there are enough rich families to form a self-sufficient and exclusive group, such a group is invariably formed. On the dude ranch they had all dressed alike; here his ready-made Prince of Wales suit seemed exaggerated in style, his hat correct only in theory—an imitation hat—his very ties only projections of the ineffable Platonic ties which were worn here at Culpepper Bay. Yet all the differences were so small that he was unable quite to discern them.

But from the morning three days ago when he had stepped off the train into a group of young people who were waiting at the station for some friend of their own, he had been uneasy; and Cousin Cora's introductions, which seemed to foist him horribly upon whomever he was introduced to, did not lessen his discomfort. He thought mechanically that she was being kind, and considered himself lucky that her invitation had coincided with his wild desire to see Noel Garneau again. He did not realize that in three days he had come to hate Cousin Cora's cold and snobbish patronage.

Noel's fresh, adventurous voice on the telephone next morning made his own voice quiver with nervous happiness. She would call for him at two and they would spend the afternoon together. All morning he lay in the garden, trying unsuccessfully to renew his summer tan in the mild lemon light of the September sun, sitting up quickly whenever he heard the sound of Cousin Cora's garden shears at the end of a neighboring border. He was back in his room, still meddling desperately with the white powder puff, when Noel's roadster stopped outside and she came up the front walk.

Noel's eyes were dark blue, almost violet, and her lips, Juan had often thought, were like very small, very soft, red cushions—only cushions sounded all wrong, for they were really the most delicate lips in the world. When she talked they parted to the shape of "Oo!" and her eyes opened wide as though she was torn between tears and laughter at the poignancy of what she was saying. Already, at seventeen, she knew that men hung on her words in a way that frightened her. To Juan, her most indifferent remarks assumed a highly ponderable significance and begot an intensity in him—a fact which Noel had several times found somewhat of a strain.

He ran downstairs, down the gravel path toward her.

"Noel, my dear," he wanted so much to say, "you are the loveliest thing—the loveliest thing. My heart turns over when I see your beautiful face and smell that sweet fresh smell you have around you." That would have been the precious, the irreplaceable truth. Instead he faltered, "Why, hello, Noel! How are you? . . . Well, I certainly am glad. Well, is this your car? What kind is it? Well, you certainly look fine."

And he couldn't look at her, because when he did his face seemed to him to be working idiotically—like someone else's face. He got in, they drove off and he made a mighty effort to compose himself; but as her hand left the steering wheel to fall lightly on his, a perverse instinct made him jerk his hand away. Noel perceived the embarrassment and was puzzled and sorry.

They went to the tennis tournament at the Culpepper Club. He was so little aware of anything except Noel that later he told Cousin Cora they hadn't seen the tennis, and believed it himself.

Afterward they loitered about the grounds, stopped by innumerable people who welcomed Noel home. Two men made him uneasy—one a small handsome youth of his own age with shining brown eyes that were bright as the glass eyes of a stuffed owl, the other a tall, languid dandy of twenty-five who was introduced to her, Juan rightly deduced, at his own request.

When they were in a group of girls he was more comfortable. He was able to talk, because being with Noel gave him confidence before these others, and his confidence before others made him more confident with Noel. The situation improved.

There was one girl, a sharp, pretty blonde named Holly Morgan, with whom he had spent some facetiously sentimental hours the day before, and in order to show Noel that he had been able to take care of himself before her return he made a point of talking aside to Holly Morgan. Holly was not responsive. Juan was Noel's property, and though Holly liked him, she did not like him nearly well enough to annoy Noel.

"What time do you want me for dinner, Noel?" she asked.

"Eight o'clock," said Noel. "Billy Harper'll call for you."

Juan felt a twinge of disappointment. He had thought that he and Noel were to be alone for dinner; that afterward they would have a long talk on the dark verandah and he would kiss her lips as he had upon that never-to-be-forgotten Montana night, and give her his D.K.E. pin to wear. Perhaps the others would leave early—he had told Holly Morgan of his love for Noel; she should have sense enough to know.

At twilight Noel dropped him at Miss Chandler's gate, lingered for a moment with the engine cut off. The promise of the evening—the first lights in the houses along the bay, the sound of a remote piano, the little coolness in the wind—swung them both up suddenly into that paradise which Juan, drunk with ecstasy and terror, had been unable to evoke.

"Are you glad to see me?" she whispered.

"Am I glad?" The words trembled on his tongue. Miserably he struggled to bend his emotion into a phrase, a look, a gesture, but his mind chilled at the thought that nothing, nothing, nothing could express what he felt in his heart.

"You embarrass me," he said wretchedly. "I don't know what to say."

Noel waited, attuned to what she expected, sympathetic, but too young quite to see that behind that mask of egotism, of moody childishness, which the intensity of Juan's devotion compelled him to wear, there was a tremendous emotion.

"Don't be embarrassed," Noel said. She was listening to the music now, a tune they had danced to in the Adirondacks. The wings of a trance folded about her and the inscrutable someone who waited always in the middle distance loomed down over her with passionate words and dark romantic eyes. Almost mechanically, she started the engine and slipped the gear into first.

"At eight o'clock," she said, almost abstractedly. "Good-bye, Juan."

The car moved off down the road. At the corner she turned and waved her hand and Juan waved back, happier than he had ever been in his life, his soul dissolved to a sweet gas that buoyed up his body like a balloon. Then the roadster was out of sight and, all unaware, he had lost her.

II

Cousin Cora's chauffeur took him to Noel's door. The other male guest, Billy Harper, was, he discovered, the young man with the bright brown eyes whom he had met that afternoon. Juan was afraid of him; he was on such familiar, facetious terms with the two girls—toward Noel his attitude seemed almost irreverent—that Juan was slighted during the conversation at dinner. They talked of the Adirondacks and they all seemed to know the group who had been there. Noel and Holly spoke of boys at Cambridge and New Haven and of how wonderful it was that they were going to school in New York this winter. Juan meant to invite Noel to the autumn dance at his college, but he thought that he had better wait and do it in a letter, later on. He was glad when dinner was over.

The girls went upstairs. Juan and Billy Harper smoked.

"She certainly is attractive," broke out Juan suddenly, his repression bursting into words.

"Who? Noel?"

"Yes."

"She's a nice girl," agreed Harper gravely.

Juan fingered the D.K.E. pin in his pocket.

"She's wonderful," he said. "I like Holly Morgan pretty well—I was handing her a sort of line yesterday afternoon—but Noel's really the most attractive girl I ever knew."

Harper looked at him curiously, but Juan, released from the enforced and artificial smile of dinner, continued enthusiastically: "Of course it's silly to fool with two girls. I mean, you've got to be careful not to get in too deep."

Billy Harper didn't answer. Noel and Holly came downstairs. Holly suggested bridge, but Juan didn't play bridge, so they sat talking by the fire. In some fashion Noel and Billy Harper became involved in a conversation about dates and friends, and Juan began boasting to Holly Morgan, who sat beside him on the sofa.

"You must come to a prom at college," he said suddenly. "Why don't you? It's a small college, but we have the best bunch in our house and the proms are fun."

"I'd love it."

"You'd only have to meet the people in our house."

"What's that?"

"D.K.E." He drew the pin from his pocket. "See?"

Holly examined it, laughed and handed it back.

"I wanted to go to Yale," he went on, "but my family always go to the same place."

"I love Yale," said Holly.

"Yes," he agreed vaguely, half hearing her, his mind moving between himself and Noel. "You must come up. I'll write you about it."

Time passed. Holly played the piano, Noel took a ukulele from the top of the piano, strummed it and hummed. Billy Harper turned the pages of the music. Juan listened, restless, unamused. Then they sauntered out into the dark garden, and finding himself beside Noel at last, Juan walked her quickly ahead until they were alone.

"Noel," he whispered, "here's my Deke pin. I want you to have it."

She looked at him expressionlessly.

"I saw you offering it to Holly Morgan," she said.

"Noel," he cried in alarm, "I wasn't offering it to her. I just showed it to her. Why, Noel, do you think—"

"You invited her to the prom."

"I didn't. I was just being nice to her."

The others were close behind. She took the Deke pin quickly and put her finger to his lips in a facile gesture of caress.

He did not realize that she had not been really angry about the pin or the prom, and that his unfortunate egotism was forfeiting her interest.

At eleven o'clock Holly said she must go, and Billy Harper drove his car to the front door.

"I'm going to stay a few minutes if you don't mind," said Juan, standing in the door with Noel. "I can walk home."

Holly and Billy Harper drove away. Noel and Juan strolled back into the drawing room, where she avoided the couch and sat down in a chair.

"Let's go out on the verandah," suggested Juan uncertainly.

"Why?"

"Please, Noel."

Unwillingly she obeyed. They sat side by side on a canvas settee and he put his arm around her.

"Kiss me," he whispered. She had never seemed so desirable to him before.

"No."

"Why not?"

"I don't want to. I don't kiss people anymore."

"But—me?" he demanded incredulously.

"I've kissed too many people. I'll have nothing left if I keep on kissing people."

"But you'll kiss me, Noel?"

"Why?"

He could not even say, "Because I love you." But he could say it, he knew that he could say it, when she was in his arms.

"If I kiss you once, will you go home?"

"Why, do you want me to go home?"

"I'm tired. I was traveling last night and I can never sleep on a train. Can you? I can never—"

Her tendency to leave the subject willingly made him frantic.

"Then kiss me once," he insisted.

"You promise?"

"You kiss me first."

"No, Juan, you promise first."

"Don't you want to kiss me?"

"Oh-h-h!" she groaned.

With gathering anxiety Juan promised and took her in his arms. For one moment at the touch of her lips, the feeling of her, of Noel, close to him, he forgot the evening, forgot himself—rather became the inspired, romantic self that she had known. But it was too late. Her hands were on his shoulders, pushing him away.

"You promised."

"Noel—"

She got up. Confused and unsatisfied, he followed her to the door.

"Noel—"

"Good-night, Juan."

As they stood on the doorstep her eyes rose over the line of dark trees toward the ripe harvest moon. Some glowing thing would happen to her soon, she thought, her mind far away. Something that would dominate her, snatch her up out of life, helpless, ecstatic, exalted.

"Good-night, Noel. Noel, please—"

"Good-night, Juan. Remember we're going swimming tomorrow. It's wonderful to see you again. Good-night."

She closed the door.

III

Toward morning he awoke from a broken sleep, wondering if she had not kissed him because of the three spots on his cheek. He turned on the light and looked at them. Two were almost invisible. He went into the bathroom, doused all three with the black ointment and crept back into bed.

Cousin Cora greeted him stiffly at breakfast next morning.

"You kept your great-uncle awake last night," she said. "He heard you moving around in your room."

"I only moved twice," he said unhappily. "I'm terribly sorry."

"He has to have his sleep, you know. We all have to be more considerate when there's someone sick. Young people don't always think of that. And he was so unusually well when you came."

It was Sunday, and they were to go swimming at Holly Morgan's house, where a crowd always collected on the bright easy beach. Noel called for him, but they arrived before any of his half-humble remarks about the night before had managed to attract her attention. He spoke to those he knew and was introduced to others, made ill at ease again by their cheerful familiarity with one another, by the correct informality of their clothes. He was sure they noticed that he had worn only one suit during his visit to Culpepper Bay, varying it with white flannel trousers. Both pairs of trousers were out of press now, and after keeping his great-uncle awake, he had not felt like bothering Cousin Cora about it at breakfast.

Again he tried to talk to Holly, with the vague idea of making Noel jealous, but Holly was busy and she eluded him. It was ten minutes before he extricated himself from a conversation with the obnoxious Miss Holyoke. At the moment he managed this he perceived to his horror that Noel was gone.

When he last saw her she had been engaged in a light but somehow intent conversation with the tall well-dressed stranger she had met yesterday. Now she wasn't in sight. Miserable and horribly alone, he strolled up and down the beach, trying to look as if he were having a good time, seeming to watch the bathers, but keeping a sharp eye out for Noel. He felt that his self-conscious perambulations were attracting unbearable attention, and sat down unhappily on a sand dune beside Billy Harper. But Billy Harper was neither cordial nor communicative, and after a minute hailed a man across the beach and went to talk to him.

Juan was desperate. When, suddenly, he spied Noel coming down from the house with the tall man, he stood up with a jerk, convinced that his features were working wildly.

She waved at him.

"A buckle came off my shoe," she called. "I went to have it put on. I thought you'd gone in swimming."

He stood perfectly still, not trusting his voice to answer. He understood that she was through with him; there was someone else. Immediately he wanted above all things to be away. As they came nearer, the tall man glanced at him negligently and

resumed his vivacious, intimate conversation with Noel. A group
suddenly closed around them.

Keeping the group in the corner of his eye, Juan began to move
carefully and steadily toward the gate that led to the road. He
started when the casual voice of a man behind him said "Going?"
and he answered "Got to" with what purported to be a reluctant
nod. Once behind the shelter of the parked cars, he began to run,
slowed down as several chauffeurs looked at him curiously. It was
a mile and a half to the Chandler house and the day was broiling,
but he walked fast lest Noel, leaving the party—"with that man,"
he thought bitterly—should overtake him trudging along the
road. That would be more than he could bear.

There was the sound of a car behind him. Immediately Juan
left the road and sought concealment behind a convenient
hedge. It was no one from the party, but thereafter he kept an
eye out for available cover, walking fast, or even running, over
unpromising open spaces.

He was within sight of his cousin's house when it happened.
Hot and disheveled, he had scarcely flattened himself against
the back of a tree when Noel's roadster, with the tall man at the
wheel, flashed by down the road. Juan stepped out and looked
after them. Then, blind with sweat and misery, he continued on
toward home.

IV

At luncheon, Cousin Cora looked at him closely.

"What's the trouble?" she inquired. "Did something go
wrong at the beach this morning?"

"Why, no," he exclaimed in simulated astonishment. "What
made you think that?"

"You have such a funny look. I thought perhaps you'd had
some trouble with the little Garneau girl."

He hated her.

"No, not at all."

"You don't want to get any idea in your head about her," said
Cousin Cora.

"What do you mean?" He knew with a start what she meant.

"Any ideas about Noel Garneau. You've got your own way
to make." Juan's face burned. He was unable to answer. "I say

that in all kindness. You're not in any position to think anything serious about Noel Garneau."

Her implications cut deeper than her words. Oh, he had seen well enough that he was not essentially of Noel's sort, that being nice in Akron wasn't enough at Culpepper Bay. He had that realization that comes to all boys in his position that for every advantage—that was what his mother called this visit to Cousin Cora's—he paid a harrowing price in self-esteem. But a world so hard as to admit such an intolerable state of affairs was beyond his comprehension. His mind rejected it all completely, as it had rejected the dictionary name for the three spots on his face. He wanted to let go, to vanish, to be home. He determined to go home tomorrow, but after this heart-rending conversation he decided to put off the announcement until tonight.

That afternoon he took a detective story from the library and retired upstairs to read on his bed. He finished the book by four o'clock and came down to change it for another. Cousin Cora was on the verandah arranging three tables for tea.

"I thought you were at the club," she exclaimed in surprise. "I thought you'd gone up to the club."

"I'm tired," he said. "I thought I'd read."

"Tired!" she exclaimed. "A boy your age! You ought to be out in the open air playing golf—that's why you have that spot on your cheek"—Juan winced; his experiments with the black salve had irritated it to a sharp redness—"instead of lying around reading on a day like this."

"I haven't any clubs," said Juan hurriedly.

"Mr. Holyoke told you you could use his brother's clubs. He spoke to the caddie master. Run on now. You'll find lots of young people up there who want to play. I'll begin to think you're not having a good time."

In agony Juan saw himself dubbing about the course alone—seeing Noel coming under his eye. He never wanted to see Noel again except out in Montana—some bright day, when she would come saying, "Juan, I never knew—never understood what your love was."

Suddenly he remembered that Noel had gone into Boston for the afternoon. She would not be there. The horror of playing alone suddenly vanished.

The caddie master looked at him disapprovingly as he displayed his guest card, and Juan nervously bought a half dozen balls at a dollar each in an effort to neutralize the imagined hostility. On the first tee he glanced around. It was after four and there was no one in sight except two old men practicing drives from the top of a little hill. As he addressed his ball he heard someone come up on the tee behind him, and he breathed easier at the sharp crack that sent his ball a hundred and fifty yards down the fairway.

"Playing alone?"

He looked around. A stout man of fifty, with a huge face, high forehead, long wide upper lip and great undershot jaw, was taking a driver from a bulging bag.

"Why—yes."

"Mind if I go 'round with you?"

"Not at all."

Juan greeted the suggestion with a certain gloomy relief. They were evenly matched, the older man's steady short shots keeping pace with Juan's occasional brilliancy. Not until the seventh hole did the conversation rise above the fragmentary boasting and formalized praise which forms the small talk of golf.

"Haven't seen you around before."

"I'm just visiting here," Juan explained, "staying with my cousin, Miss Chandler."

"Oh, yes—know Miss Chandler very well. Nice old snob."

"What?" inquired Juan.

"Nice old snob, I said. No offense. . . . Your honor, I think."

Not for several holes did Juan venture to comment on his partner's remark.

"What do you mean when you say she's a nice old snob?" he inquired with interest.

"Oh, it's an old quarrel between Miss Chandler and me," answered the older man brusquely. "She's an old friend of my wife's. When we were married and came out to Culpepper Bay for the summer, she tried to freeze us out. Said my wife had no business marrying me—I was an outsider."

"What did you do?"

"We just let her alone. She came 'round, but naturally I never had much love for her. She even tried to put her oar in before we were married." He laughed. "Cora Chandler of Boston—how she used to boss the girls around in those days! At twenty-five she had the sharpest tongue in Back Bay. They were old people there, you know—Emerson and Whittier to dinner and all that. My wife belonged to that crowd too. I was from the Middle West. . . . Oh, too bad. I should have stopped talking. That makes me two up again."

Suddenly Juan wanted to present his case to this man—not quite as it was, but adorned with a dignity and significance it did not so far possess. It began to round out in his mind as the sempiternal struggle of the poor young man against a snobbish, purse-proud world. This new aspect was comforting, and he put out of his mind the less pleasant realization that, superficially at least, money hadn't entered into it. He knew in his heart that it was his unfortunate egotism that had repelled Noel, his embarrassment, his absurd attempt to make her jealous with Holly. Only indirectly was his poverty concerned; under different circumstances it might have given a touch of romance.

"I know exactly how you must have felt," he broke out suddenly as they walked toward the tenth tee. "I haven't any money and I'm in love with a girl who has—and it just seems as if every busybody in the world is determined to keep us apart."

For a moment Juan believed this. His companion looked at him sharply.

"Does the girl care about you?" he inquired.

"Yes."

"Well, go after her, young man. All the money in this world hasn't been made by a long shot."

"I'm still in college," said Juan, suddenly taken aback.

"Won't she wait for you?"

"I don't know. You see, the pressure's pretty strong. Her family want her to marry a rich man"—his mind visualized the tall well-dressed stranger of this morning and invention soared—"an easterner that's visiting here, and I'm afraid they'll all sweep her off her feet. If it's not this man, it's the next."

His friend considered.

"You can't have everything, you know," he said presently. "I'm the last man to advise a young man to leave college, especially when I don't know anything about him or his abilities; but if it's going to break you up not to get her, you better think about getting to work."

"I've been considering that," said Juan, frowning. The idea was ten seconds old in his mind.

"All the girls are crazy now, anyhow," broke out the older man. "They begin to think of men at fifteen, and by the time they're seventeen they've run off with the chauffeur next door."

"That's true," agreed Juan absently. He was absorbed in the previous suggestion. "The trouble is that I don't live in Boston. If I left college I'd want to be near her, because it might be a few months before I'd be able to support her. And I don't know how I'd go about getting a position in Boston."

"If you're Cora Chandler's cousin, that oughtn't to be difficult. She knows everybody in town. And the girl's family will probably help you out, once you've got her—some of them are fools enough for anything in these crazy days."

"I wouldn't like that."

"Rich girls can't live on air," said the older man grimly.

They played for awhile in silence. Suddenly, as they approached a green, Juan's companion turned to him frowning.

"Look here, young man," he said. "I don't know whether you are really thinking of leaving college or whether I've just put the idea in your head. If I have, forget it. Go home and talk it over with your family. Do what they tell you to."

"My father's dead."

"Well, then ask your mother. She's got your best interest at heart."

His attitude had noticeably stiffened, as if he were sorry he had become even faintly involved in Juan's problem. He guessed that there was something solid in the boy, but he suspected his readiness to confide in strangers and his helplessness about getting a job. Something was lacking—not confidence, exactly—"It might be a few months before I was able to support her"—but something stronger, fiercer, more external. When they walked together into the caddie house he shook hands with him and was about to turn away, when impulse impelled him to add one word more.

"If you decide to try Boston come and see me," he said. He pressed a card into Juan's hand. "Good-bye. Good luck. Remember, a woman's like a street car—"

He walked into the locker room. After paying his caddie, Juan glanced down at the card which he still held in his hand.

"Harold Garneau," it read, "23–27 State Street."

A moment later Juan was walking nervously and hurriedly from the grounds of the Culpepper Club, casting no glance behind.

V

One month later San Juan Chandler arrived in Boston and took an inexpensive room in a small downtown hotel. In his pocket was two hundred dollars in cash and an envelope full of Liberty Bonds aggregating fifteen hundred dollars more— the whole being a fund which had been started by his father when he was born, to give him his chance in life. Not without argument had he come into possession of this—not without tears had his decision to abandon his last year at college been approved by his mother. He had not told her everything, simply that he had an advantageous offer of a position in Boston; the rest she guessed and was tactfully silent. As a matter of fact, he had neither a position nor a plan; but he was twenty-one now, with the blemishes of youth departed forever. One thing Juan knew—he was going to marry Noel Garneau. The sting and hurt and shame of that Sunday morning ran through his dreams, stronger than any doubts he might have felt, stronger even than the romantic boyish love for her that had blossomed one dry, still Montana night. That was still there, but locked apart; what had happened later overlay it, muffled it. It was necessary now to his pride, his self-respect, his very existence, that he have her, in order to wipe out his memory of the day on which he had grown three years.

He hadn't seen her since. The following morning he had left Culpepper Bay and gone home.

Yes, he had a wonderful time. Yes, Cousin Cora had been very nice.

Nor had he written, though a week later a surprised but somehow flippant and terrible note had come from her, saying how pleasant it was to have seen him again and how bad it was to leave without saying good-bye.

"Holly Morgan sends her best," it concluded, with kind, simulated reproach. "Perhaps she ought to be writing instead of me. I always thought you were fickle, and now I know it."

The poor effort which she had made to hide her indifference made him shiver. He did not add the letter to a certain cherished package tied with blue ribbon, but burned it up in an ash tray—a tragic gesture which almost set his mother's house on fire.

So he began his life in Boston, and the story of his first year there is a fairy tale too immoral to be told. It is the story of one of those mad, illogical successes upon whose substantial foundations ninety-nine failures are later reared. Though he worked hard, he deserved no special credit for it—no credit, that is, commensurate with the reward he received. He ran into a man who had a scheme, a preposterous scheme, for the cold storage of sea food which he had been trying to finance for several years. Juan's inexperience allowed him to be responsive and he invested twelve hundred dollars. In the first year this appalling indiscretion paid him 400 per-cent. His partner attempted to buy him out, but they reached a compromise and Juan kept his shares.

The inner sense of his own destiny which had never deserted him whispered that he was going to be a rich man. But at the end of that year an event took place which made him think that it didn't matter after all.

He had seen Noel Garneau twice—once entering a theatre and once riding through a Boston street in the back of her limousine, looking, he thought afterwards, bored and pale and tired. At the time he had thought nothing; an overwhelming emotion had seized his heart, held it helpless, suspended, as though it were in the grasp of material fingers. He had shrunk back hastily under the awning of a shop and waited trembling, horrified, ecstatic, until she went by. She did not know he was in Boston—he did not want her to know until he was ready. He followed her every move in the society columns of the papers. She was at school, at home for Christmas, at Hot Springs for Easter, coming out in the fall. Then she was a debutante, and every day he read of her at dinners and dances and assemblies and balls and charity functions and theatricals of the Junior League. A dozen blurred newspaper unlikenesses of her filled a drawer of his desk. And still he waited. Let Noel have her fling.

When he had been sixteen months in Boston, and when Noel's first season was dying away in the hum of the massed departure for Florida, Juan decided to wait no longer. So on a raw, damp February day, when children in rubber boots were building dams in the snow-filled gutters, a blond, handsome, well-dressed young man walked up the steps of the Garneaus' Boston house and handed his card to the maid. With his heart beating loud, he went into a drawing room and sat down.

A sound of a dress on the stairs, light feet in the hall, an exclamation—Noel!

"Why, Juan," she exclaimed, surprised, pleased, polite, "I didn't know you were in Boston. It's so good to see you. I thought you'd thrown me over forever."

In a moment he found voice—it was easier now than it had been. Whether or not she was aware of the change, he was a nobody no longer. There was something solid behind him that would prevent him ever again from behaving like a self-centered child.

He explained that he might settle in Boston, and allowed her to guess that he had done extremely well; and though it cost him a twinge of pain, he spoke humorously of their last meeting, implying that he had left the swimming party on an impulse of anger at her. He could not confess that the impulse had been one of shame. She laughed. Suddenly he grew curiously happy.

Half an hour passed. The fire glowed in the hearth. The day darkened outside and the room moved into that shadowy twilight, that weather of indoors, which is like a breathless starshine. He had been standing; now he sat down beside her on the couch.

"Noel—"

Footsteps sounded lightly through the hall as the maid went through to the front door. Noel reached up quickly and turned up the electric lamp on the table behind her head.

"I didn't realize how dark it was growing," she said, rather quickly, he thought. Then the maid stood in the doorway.

"Mr. Templeton," she announced.

"Oh, yes," agreed Noel.

Mr. Templeton, with a Harvard-Oxford drawl, mature, very much at home, looked at him with just a flicker of surprise, nodded, mumbled a bare politeness and took an easy position in front of the fire. He exchanged several remarks with Noel which indicated a certain familiarity with her movements. Then a short silence fell. Juan rose.

"I want to see you soon," he said. "I'll phone, shall I, and you tell me when I can call?"

She walked with him to the door.

"So good to talk to you again," she told him cordially. "Remember, I want to see a lot of you, Juan."

When he left he was happier than he had been for two years. He ate dinner alone at a restaurant, almost singing to himself; and then, wild with elation, walked along the waterfront till midnight. He awoke thinking of her, wanting to tell people that what had been lost was found again. There had been more between them than the mere words said—Noel's sitting with him in the half darkness, her slight but perceptible nervousness as she came with him to the door.

Two days later he opened the "Transcript" to the society page and read down to the third item. There his eyes stopped, became like china eyes:

> Mr. and Mrs. Harold Garneau announce the engagement of their daughter Noel to Mr. Brooks Fish Templeton. Mr. Templeton graduated from Harvard in the class of 1912 and is a partner in—

VI

At three o'clock that afternoon Juan rang the Garneaus' doorbell and was shown into the hall. From somewhere upstairs he heard girls' voices, and another murmur came from the drawing room on the right, where he had talked to Noel only the week before.

"Can you show me into some room that isn't being used?" he demanded tensely of the maid. "I'm an old friend—it's very important—I've got to see Miss Noel alone."

He waited in a small den at the back of the hall. Ten minutes passed—ten minutes more; he began to be afraid she wasn't coming. At the end of half an hour the door bounced open and Noel came hurriedly in.

"Juan!" she cried happily. "This is wonderful! I might have known you'd be the first to come." Her expression changed as she saw his face, and she hesitated. "But why were you shown in here?" she went on quickly. "You must come and meet everyone. I'm rushing around today like a chicken without a head."

"Noel!" he said thickly.

"What?"

Her hand was on the door knob. She turned, startled.

"Noel, I haven't come to congratulate you," Juan said, his face white and firm, his voice harsh with his effort at self-control. "I've come to tell you you're making an awful mistake."

"Why—Juan!"

"And you know it," he went on. "You know no one loves you as I love you, Noel. I want you to marry me."

She laughed nervously.

"Why, Juan, that's silly! I don't understand your talking like that. I'm engaged to another man."

"Noel, will you come here and sit down?"

"I can't, Juan—there're a dozen people outside. I've got to see them. It wouldn't be polite. Another time, Juan. If you come another time I'd love to talk to you."

"Now!" The word was stark, unyielding, almost savage. She hesitated. "Ten minutes," he said.

"I've really got to go, Juan."

She sat down uncertainly, glancing at the door. Sitting beside her, Juan told her simply and directly everything that had happened to him since they had met, a year and a half before. He told her of his family, his Cousin Cora, of his inner humiliation at Culpepper Bay. Then he told her of coming to Boston and of his success, and how at last, having something to bring to her, he had come only to find he was too late. He kept back nothing. In his voice, as in his mind, there was no pretense now, no self-consciousness, but only a sincere and overmastering emotion. He had no defense for what he was doing, he said, save this—that he had somehow gained the right to present his case, to have her know how much his devotion had inspired him, to have her look once, if only in passing, upon the fact that for two years he had loved her faithfully and well.

When Juan finished, Noel was crying. It was terrible, she said, to tell her all this—just when she had decided about her life. It hadn't been easy, yet it was done now, and she was really going to marry this other man. But she had never heard anything like this before—it upset her. She was—oh, so terribly sorry, but there was no use. If he had cared so much he might have let her know before.

But how could he let her know? He had had nothing to offer her except the fact that one summer night out west they had been overwhelmingly drawn together.

"And you love me now," he said in a low voice. "You wouldn't cry, Noel, if you didn't love me. You wouldn't care."

"I'm—I'm sorry for you."

"It's more than that. You loved me the other day. You wanted me to sit beside you in the dark. Didn't I feel it—didn't I know? There's something between us, Noel—a sort of pull. Something you always do to me and I to you—except that one sad time. Oh, Noel, don't you know how it breaks my heart to see you sitting there two feet away from me, to want to put my arms around you and know you've made a senseless promise to another man?"

There was a knock outside the door.

"Noel!"

She raised her head, putting a handkerchief quickly to her eyes.

"Yes?"

"It's Brooks. May I come in?" Without waiting for an answer, Templeton opened the door and stood looking at them curiously. "Excuse me," he said. He nodded brusquely at Juan. "Noel, there are lots of people here—"

"In a minute," she said lifelessly.

"Aren't you well?"

"Yes."

He came into the room, frowning.

"What's been upsetting you, dear?" He glanced quickly at Juan, who stood up, his eyes blurred with tears. A menacing note crept into Templeton's voice. "I hope no one's been upsetting you."

For answer, Noel flopped down over a hill of pillows and sobbed aloud.

"Noel"—Templeton sat beside her and put his arm on her shoulder—"Noel." He turned again to Juan. "I think it would be best if you left us alone, Mr. ——" The name escaped his memory. "Noel's a little tired."

"I won't go," said Juan.

"Please wait outside then. We'll see you later."

"I won't wait outside. I want to speak to Noel. It was you who interrupted."

UNCOLLECTED STORIES

"And I have a perfect right to interrupt." His face reddened angrily. "Just who the devil are you, anyhow?"

"My name is Chandler."

"Well, Mr. Chandler, you're in the way here—is that plain? Your presence here is an intrusion and a presumption."

"We look at it in different ways."

They glared at each other angrily. After a moment Templeton raised Noel to a sitting posture.

"I'm going to take you upstairs, dear," he said. "This has been a strain today. If you lie down till dinnertime—"

He helped her to her feet. Not looking at Juan, and still dabbing her face with her handkerchief, Noel suffered herself to be persuaded into the hall. Templeton turned in the doorway.

"The maid will give you your hat and coat, Mr. Chandler."

"I'll wait right here," said Juan.

VII

He was still there at half-past six, when, following a quick knock, a large broad bulk which Juan recognized as Mr. Harold Garneau came into the room.

"Good evening, sir," said Mr. Garneau, annoyed and peremptory. "Just what can I do for you?"

He came closer and a flicker of recognition passed over his face.

"Oh!" he muttered.

"Good evening, sir," said Juan.

"It's you, is it?" Mr. Garneau appeared to hesitate. "Brooks Templeton said that you were—that you insisted on seeing Noel"—he coughed—"that you refused to go home."

"I want to see Noel, if you don't mind."

"What for?"

"That's between Noel and me, Mr. Garneau."

"Mr. Templeton and I are quite entitled to represent Noel in this case," said Mr. Garneau patiently. "She has just made the statement before her mother and me that she doesn't want to see you again. Isn't that plain enough?"

"I don't believe it," said Juan stubbornly.

"I'm not in the habit of lying."

"I beg your pardon. I meant—"

"I don't want to discuss this unfortunate business with you," broke out Garneau contemptuously. "I just want you to leave right now—and not come back."

"Why do you call it an unfortunate business?" inquired Juan coolly.

"Good-night, Mr. Chandler."

"You call it an unfortunate business because Noel's broken her engagement."

"You are presumptuous, sir!" cried the older man. "Unbearably presumptuous."

"Mr. Garneau, you yourself were once kind enough to tell me—"

"I don't give a damn what I told you!" cried Garneau. "You get out of here now!"

"Very well, I have no choice. I wish you to be good enough to tell Noel that I'll be back tomorrow afternoon."

Juan nodded, went into the hall and took his hat and coat from a chair. Upstairs, he heard running footsteps and a door opened and closed—not before he had caught the sound of impassioned voices and a short broken sob. He hesitated. Then he continued on along the hall toward the front door. Through a portière of the dining room he caught sight of a manservant laying the service for dinner.

He rang the bell the next afternoon at the same hour. This time the butler, evidently instructed, answered the door.

Miss Noel was not at home. Could he leave a note? It was no use; Miss Noel was not in the city. Incredulous but anxious, Juan took a taxi-cab to Harold Garneau's office.

"Mr. Garneau can't see you. If you like, he will speak to you for a moment on the phone."

Juan nodded. The clerk touched a button on the waiting-room switchboard and handed an instrument to Juan.

"This is San Juan Chandler speaking. They told me at your residence that Noel had gone away. Is that true?"

"Yes." The monosyllable was short and cold. "She's gone away for a rest. Won't be back for several months. Anything else?"

"Did she leave any word for me?"

"No! She hates the sight of you."

"What's her address?"

"That doesn't happen to be your affair. Good-morning."

Juan went back to his apartment and mused over the situation. Noel had been spirited out of town—that was the only expression he knew for it. And undoubtedly her engagement to Templeton was at least temporarily broken. He had toppled it over within an hour. He must see her again—that was the immediate necessity. But where? She was certainly with friends, and probably with relatives. That latter was the first clue to follow—he must find out the names of the relatives she had most frequently visited before.

He phoned Holly Morgan. She was in the South and not expected back in Boston till May.

Then he called the society editor of the "Boston Transcript." After a short wait, a polite, attentive, feminine voice conversed with him on the wire.

"This is Mr. San Juan Chandler," he said, trying to intimate by his voice that he was a distinguished leader of cotillions in the Back Bay. "I want to get some information, if you please, about the family of Mr. Harold Garneau."

"Why don't you apply directly to Mr. Garneau?" advised the society editor, not without suspicion.

"I'm not on speaking terms with Mr. Garneau."

A pause; then—"Well, really, we can't be responsible for giving out information in such a peculiar way."

"But there can't be any secret about who Mr. and Mrs. Garneau's relations are!" protested Juan in exasperation.

"But how can we be sure that you—"

He hung up the receiver. Two other papers gave no better results, a third was willing, but ignorant. It seemed absurd, almost like a conspiracy, that in a city where the Garneaus were so well known he could not obtain the desired names. It was as if everything had tightened up against his arrival on the scene. After a day of fruitless and embarrassing inquiries in stores, where his questions were looked upon with the suspicion that he might be compiling a sucker list, and of poring through back numbers of the Social Register, he saw that there was but one resource—that was Cousin Cora. Next morning he took the three-hour ride to Culpepper Bay.

It was the first time he had seen her for a year and a half, since the disastrous termination of his summer visit. She was offended—that he knew—especially since she had heard from his mother of the unexpected success. She greeted him coldly and reproachfully; but she told him what he wanted to know, because Juan asked his questions while she was still startled and surprised by his visit. He left Culpepper Bay with the information that Mrs. Garneau had one sister, the famous Mrs. Morton Poindexter, with whom Noel was on terms of great intimacy. Juan took the midnight train for New York.

The Morton Poindexters' telephone number was not in the New York phone book, and Information refused to divulge it; but Juan procured it by another reference to the Social Register. He called the house from his hotel.

"Miss Noel Garneau—is she in the city?" he inquired, according to his plan. If the name was not immediately familiar, the servant would reply that he had the wrong number.

"Who wants to speak to her, please?"

That was a relief; his heart sank comfortably back into place.

"Oh—a friend."

"No name?"

"No name."

"I'll see."

The servant returned in a moment.

No, Miss Garneau was not there, was not in the city, was not expected. The phone clicked off suddenly.

Late that afternoon a taxi dropped him in front of the Morton Poindexters' house. It was the most elaborate house that he had ever seen, rising to five stories on a corner of Fifth Avenue and adorned even with that ghost of a garden which, however minute, is the proudest gesture of money in New York.

He handed no card to the butler, but it occurred to him that he must be expected, for he was shown immediately into the drawing room. When, after a short wait, Mrs. Poindexter entered he experienced for the first time in five days a touch of uncertainty.

Mrs. Poindexter was perhaps thirty-five, and of that immaculate fashion which the French describe as *bien soignée*. The inexpressible loveliness of her face was salted with another quality which for want of a better word might be called dignity. But it was more than dignity, for it wore no rigidity, but instead a softness so adaptable, so elastic, that it would withdraw from any attack which life might bring against it, only to spring back at the proper moment, taut, victorious and complete. San Juan saw that even though his guess was correct as to Noel's being in the house, he was up against a force with which he had had no contact before. This woman seemed to be not entirely of America, to possess resources which the American woman lacked or handled ineptly.

She received him with a graciousness which, though it was largely external, seemed to conceal no perturbation underneath. Indeed, her attitude appeared to be perfectly passive, just short of encouraging. It was with an effort that he resisted the inclination to lay his cards on the table.

"Good-evening." She sat down on a stiff chair in the center of the room and asked him to take an easy-chair nearby. She sat looking at him silently until he spoke.

"Mrs. Poindexter, I am very anxious to see Miss Garneau. I telephoned your house this morning and was told that she was not here." Mrs. Poindexter nodded. "However, I know she is here," he continued evenly. "And I'm determined to see her. The idea that her father and mother can prevent me from seeing her, as though I had disgraced myself in some way—or that you, Mrs. Poindexter, can prevent me from seeing her"—his voice rose a little—"is preposterous. This is not the year 1500—nor even the year 1910."

He paused. Mrs. Poindexter waited for a moment to see if he had finished. Then she said, quietly and unequivocally, "I quite agree with you."

Save for Noel, Juan thought he had never seen anyone so beautiful before.

"Mrs. Poindexter," he began again, in a more friendly tone, "I'm sorry to seem rude. I've been called presumptuous in this matter, and perhaps to some extent I am. Perhaps all poor boys who are in love with wealthy girls are presumptuous. But it happens that I am no longer a poor boy, and I have good reason to believe that Noel cares for me."

"I see," said Mrs. Poindexter attentively. "But of course I knew nothing about all that."

Juan hesitated, again disarmed by her complaisance. Then a surge of determination went over him.

"Will you let me see her?" he demanded. "Or will you insist on keeping up this farce a little longer?"

Mrs. Poindexter looked at him as though considering.

"Why should I let you see her?"

"Simply because I ask you. Just as, when someone says 'Excuse me,' you step aside for him in a doorway."

Mrs. Poindexter frowned.

"But Noel is concerned in this matter as much as you. And I'm not like a person in a crowd. I'm more like a bodyguard, with instructions to let no one pass, even if they say 'Excuse me' in a most appealing voice."

"You have instructions only from her father and mother," said Juan, with rising impatience. "She's the person concerned."

"I'm glad you begin to admit that."

"Of course I admit it," he broke out. "I want you to admit it."

"I do."

"Then what's the point of all this absurd discussion?" he demanded heatedly.

She stood up suddenly.

"I bid you good-evening, sir."

Taken aback, Juan stood up too.

"Why, what's the matter?"

"I will not be spoken to like that," said Mrs. Poindexter, still in a low cool voice. "Either you can conduct yourself quietly or you can leave this house at once."

Juan realized that he had taken the wrong tone. The words stung at him and for a moment he had nothing to say—as though he were a scolded boy at school.

"This is beside the question," he stammered finally. "I want to talk to Noel."

"Noel doesn't want to talk to you."

Suddenly Mrs. Poindexter held out a sheet of notepaper to him. He opened it. It said:

Aunt Jo: As to what we talked about this afternoon: If that intolerable bore calls, as he will probably do, and begins his presumptuous whining, please speak to him frankly. Tell him I never loved him, that I never at any time claimed to love him and that his persistence is revolting to me. Say that I am old enough to know my own mind and that my greatest wish is never to see him again in this world.

Juan stood there aghast. His universe was suddenly about him. Noel did not care, she had never cared. It was all a preposterous joke on him, played by those to whom the business of life had been such jokes from the beginning. He realized now that fundamentally they were all akin—Cousin Cora, Noel, her father, this cold, lovely woman here—affirming the prerogative of the rich to marry always within their caste, to erect artificial barriers and standards against those who could presume upon a summer's philandering. The scales fell from his eyes and he saw his year and a half of struggle and effort not as progress toward a goal but only as a little race he had run by himself, outside, with no one to beat except himself—no one who cared.

Blindly he looked about for his hat, scarcely realizing it was in the hall. Blindly he stepped back when Mrs. Poindexter's hand moved toward him half a foot through the mist and Mrs. Poindexter's voice said softly, "I'm sorry." Then he was in the hall, the note still clutched in the hand that struggled through the sleeve of his overcoat, the words which he felt he must somehow say choking through his lips.

"I didn't understand. I regret very much that I've bothered you. It wasn't clear to me how matters stood—between Noel and me—"

His hand was on the door knob.

"I'm sorry, too," said Mrs. Poindexter. "I didn't realize from what Noel said that what I had to do would be so hard—Mr. Templeton."

"Chandler," he corrected her dully. "My name's Chandler."

She stood dead still; suddenly her face went white.

"What?"

"My name—it's Chandler."

Like a flash she threw herself against the half-open door and it bumped shut. Then in a flash she was at the foot of the staircase.

"Noel!" she cried in a high, clear call. "Noel! Noel! Come down, Noel!" Her lovely voice floated up like a bell through the long high central hall. "Noel! Come down! It's Mr. Chandler! It's Chandler!"

The Adolescent Marriage

C HAUNCEY Garnett, the architect, once had a miniature city constructed, composed of all the buildings he had ever designed. It proved to be an expensive and somewhat depressing experiment, for the toy, instead of resulting in a harmonious whole, looked like a typical cross-section of Philadelphia. Garnett found it depressing to be reminded that he himself had often gone in for monstrosities, and even more depressing to realize that his architectural activities had extended over half a century. In disgust, he distributed the tiny houses to his friends and they ended up as the residences of undiscriminating dolls.

Garnett had never—at least not yet—been called a nice old man; yet he was both old and nice. He gave six hours a day to his offices in Philadelphia or to his branch in New York, and during the remaining time demanded only a proper peace in which to brood quietly over his crowded and colorful past. In several years no one had demanded a favor that could not be granted with pen and check book, and it seemed that he had reached an age safe from the intrusion of other people's affairs. This calm, however, was premature, and it was violently shattered one afternoon in the summer of 1925 by the shrill clamor of a telephone bell.

George Wharton was speaking. Could Chauncey come to his house at once on a matter of the greatest importance?

On the way to Chestnut Hill, Garnett dozed against the grey duvetyn cushions of his limousine, his sixty-eight-year-old body warmed by the June sunshine, his sixty-eight-year-old mind blank save for some vivid unsubstantial memory of a green branch overhanging green water. Reaching his friend's house, he awoke placidly and without a start. George Wharton, he thought, was probably troubled by some unexpected surplus of money. He would want Garnett to plan a church—one of these modern churches with a cabaret on the twentieth floor, car-cards in every pew and a soda-fountain in the sanctuary. He was of a younger generation than Garnett—a modern man.

Wharton and his wife were waiting in the gilt-and-morocco intimacy of the library.

"I couldn't come to your office," said Wharton immediately. "In a minute you'll understand why."

Garnett noticed that his friend's hands were slightly trembling.

"It's about Lucy," Wharton added.

It was a moment before Garnett placed Lucy as their daughter. "What's happened to Lucy?"

"Lucy's married. She ran up to Connecticut about a month ago and got married."

A moment's silence.

"Lucy's only sixteen," continued Wharton. "The boy's twenty."

"That's very young," said Garnett considerately, "but then—my grandmother married at sixteen and no one thought much about it. Some girls develop much quicker than others—"

"We know all that, Chauncey." Wharton waved it aside impatiently. "The point is, these young marriages don't work nowadays. They're not normal. They end in a mess."

Again Garnett hesitated.

"Aren't you a little premature in looking ahead for trouble? Why don't you give Lucy a chance? Why not wait and see if it's going to turn out a mess?"

"It's a mess already," cried Wharton passionately. "And Lucy's life's a mess. The one thing her mother and I cared about—her happiness—that's a mess, and we don't know what to do—what to do."

His voice trembled and he turned away to the window—came back again impulsively.

"Look at us, Chauncey. Do we look like the kind of parents who would drive a child into a thing like this? She and her mother have been like sisters—just like sisters. She and I used to go on parties together—football games and all that sort of thing—ever since she was a little kid. She's all we've got, and we always said we'd try to steer a middle course with her—give her enough liberty for her self-respect and yet keep an eye on where she went and who she went with—at least till she was eighteen. Why, by God, Chauncey, if you'd told me six weeks ago that this thing could happen—" He shook his head helplessly. Then he continued in a quieter voice. "When she came and told us what she'd done it just about broke our hearts, but we tried to make the best of it. Do you know how long the marriage—if you can call it that—lasted? Three weeks. It lasted three weeks. She came home with a big bruise on her shoulder where he'd hit her."

"Oh, dear!" said Mrs. Wharton in a low tone. "Please—"

"We talked it over," continued her husband grimly, "and she decided to go back to this—this young"—again he bowed his head before the insufficiency of expletives—"and try to make a go of it. But last night she came home again, and now she says it's definitely over."

Garnett nodded. "Who's the man?" he inquired.

"Man!" cried Wharton. "It's a boy. His name's Llewellyn Clark."

"What's that?" exclaimed Garnett in surprise. "Llewellyn Clark? Jesse Clark's son? The young fellow in my office?"

"Yes."

"Why, he's a nice young fellow," Garnett declared. "I can't believe he'd—"

"Neither could I," interrupted Wharton quietly. "I thought he was a nice young fellow too. And what's more, I rather suspected that my daughter was a pretty decent young girl."

Garnett was astonished and annoyed. He had seen Llewellyn Clark not an hour before in the small drafting room he occupied in the Garnett & Linquist offices. He understood now why Clark wasn't going back to Boston Tech this fall. And in the light of this revelation he remembered that there had been a change in the boy during the past month—absences, late arrivals, a certain listlessness in his work.

Mrs. Wharton's voice broke in upon the ordering of his mind.

"Please do something, Chauncey," she said. "Talk to him. Talk to them both. She's only sixteen and we can't bear to see her life ruined by a divorce. It isn't that we care what people will say; it's only Lucy we care about, Chauncey."

"Why don't you send her abroad for a year?"

Wharton shook his head.

"That doesn't solve the problem. If they have an ounce of character between them they'll make an attempt to live together."

"But if you think so badly of him—"

"Lucy's made her choice. He's got some money—enough. And there doesn't seem to be anything vicious in his record so far."

"What's his side of it?"

Wharton waved his hands helplessly.

"I'm damned if I know. Something about a hat. Some bunch of rubbish. Elsie and I have no idea why they ran away, and now we can't get a clear idea why they won't stick together. Unfortunately his father and mother are dead." He paused. "Chauncey, if you could see your way clear—"

An unpleasant prospect began to take shape before Garnett's eyes. He was an old man with one foot, at least, in the chimney corner. From where he stood, this youngest generation was like something infinitely distant, and perceived through the large end of a telescope.

"Oh, of course—" he heard himself saying vaguely. So hard to think back to that young time. Since his youth such a myriad of prejudices and conventions had passed through the fashion show and died away with clamour and acrimony and commotion. It would be difficult even to communicate with these children. How hollowly and fatuously his platitudes would echo on their ears. And how bored he would be with their selfishness and with their shallow confidence in opinions manufactured day before yesterday.

He sat up suddenly. Wharton and his wife were gone, and a slender dark-haired girl whose body hovered delicately on the last edge of childhood had come quietly into the room. She regarded him for a moment with a shadow of alarm in her intent brown eyes; then sat down on a stiff chair near him.

"I'm Lucy," she said. "They told me you wanted to talk to me."

She waited. It occurred to Garnett that he must say something, but the form his speech should take eluded him.

"I haven't seen you since you were ten years old," he began uneasily.

"Yes," she agreed, with a small, polite smile.

There was another silence. He must say something to the point before her young attention slipped utterly away.

"I'm sorry you and Llewellyn have quarreled," he broke out. "It's silly to quarrel like that. I'm very fond of Llewellyn, you know."

"Did he send you here?"

Garnett shook his head. "Are you—in love with him?" he inquired.

"Not anymore."

"Is he in love with you?"

"He says so, but I don't think he is—anymore."

"You're sorry you married him?"

"I'm never sorry for anything that's done."

"I see."

Again she waited.

"Your father tells me this is a permanent separation."

"Yes."

"May I ask why?"

"We just couldn't get along," she answered simply. "I thought he was terribly selfish and he thought the same about me. We fought all the time, from almost the first day."

"He hit you?"

"Oh, that!" She dismissed that as unimportant.

"How do you mean—selfish?"

"Just selfish," she answered childishly. "The most selfish thing I ever saw in my life. I never saw anything so selfish in my life."

"What did he do that was selfish?" persisted Garnett.

"Everything. He was so stingy—Gosh!" Her eyes were serious and sad. "I can't stand anybody to be so stingy. About money," she explained contemptuously. "Then he'd lose his temper and swear at me and say he was going to leave me if I didn't do what he wanted me to." And she added, still very gravely, "Gosh!"

"How did he happen to hit you?"

"Oh, he didn't mean to hit me. I was trying to hit him on account of something he did, and he was trying to hold me and so I bumped into a still."

"A still!" exclaimed Garnett, startled.

"The woman had a still in our room because she had no other place to keep it. Down on Beckton Street, where we lived."

"Why did Llewellyn take you to such a place?"

"Oh, it was a perfectly good place except that the woman had this still. We looked around two or three days and it was the only apartment we could afford." She paused reminiscently and then added, "It was very nice and quiet."

"H'm. You never really got along at all?"

"No." She hesitated. "He spoiled it all. He was always worrying about whether we'd done the right thing. He'd get out of bed at night and walk up and down worrying about it. I wasn't complaining. I was perfectly willing to be poor if we could get along and be happy. I wanted to go to cooking school, for instance, and he wouldn't let me. He wanted me to sit in the room all day and wait for him."

"Why?"

"He was afraid that I wanted to go home. For three weeks it was one long quarrel from morning till night. I couldn't stand it."

"It seems to me that a lot of this quarreling was over nothing," ventured Garnett.

"I haven't explained it very well, I guess," she said with sudden weariness. "I knew a lot of it was silly and so did Llewellyn. Sometimes we'd apologize to each other, and be in love like we were before we were married. That's why I went back to him. But it wasn't any use." She stood up. "What's the good of talking about it any more? You wouldn't understand."

Garnett wondered if he could get back to his office before Llewellyn Clark went home. He could talk to Clark, while the girl only confused him as she teetered disconcertingly between adolescence and disillusion. But when Clark reported to him just as the five o'clock bell rang, the same sensation of impotence stole over Garnett, and he stared at his apprentice blankly for a moment, as if he had never seen him before.

Llewellyn Clark looked older than his twenty years—a tall, almost thin young man with dark red hair of a fine, shiny texture, and auburn eyes. He was of a somewhat nervous type, talented and impatient, but Garnett could find little of the egotist in his reserved, attentive face.

"I hear you've been getting married," Garnett began abruptly.

Clark's cheeks deepened to the color of his hair.

"Who told you that?" he demanded.

"Lucy Wharton. She told me the whole story."

"Then you know it, sir," said Clark almost rudely. "You know all there is to know."

"What do you intend to do?"

"I don't know." Clark stood up, breathing quickly. "I can't talk about it. It's my affair, you see. I—"

"Sit down, Llewellyn."

The young man sat down, his face working—suddenly it crinkled uncontrollably and two great tears, stained faintly with the dust of the day's toil, gushed from his eyes.

"Oh, hell!" he said brokenly, wiping his eyes with the back of his hand.

"I've been wondering why you two can't make a go of it after all." Garnett looked down at his desk. "I like you, Llewellyn, and I like Lucy. Why not fool everybody and—"

Llewellyn shook his head emphatically.

"Not me," he said. "I don't care a snap of my finger about her. She can go jump in the lake for all I care."

"Why did you take her away?"

"I don't know. We'd been in love for almost a year and marriage seemed a long way off. It came over us all of a sudden—"

"Why couldn't you get along?"

"Didn't she tell you?"

"I want your version."

"Well, it started one afternoon when she took all our money and threw it away."

"Threw it away?"

"She took it and bought a new hat. It was only thirty-five dollars, but it was all we had. If I hadn't found forty-five cents in an old suit we wouldn't have had any dinner."

"I see," said Garnett dryly.

"Then—oh, one thing happened after another. She didn't trust me, she didn't think I could take care of her, she kept saying she was going home to her mother. And finally we began to hate each other. It was a great mistake, that's all, and I'll probably spend a good part of my life paying for it. Wait till it leaks out!" He laughed bitterly. "I'll be the Leopold and Loeb of Philadelphia—you'll see."

"Aren't you thinking about yourself a little too much?" suggested Garnett coldly.

Llewellyn looked at him in unfeigned surprise.

"About myself?" he repeated. "Mr. Garnett, I'll give you my word of honor, this is the first time I've ever thought about that side of it. Right now I'd do anything in the world to save Lucy any pain—except live with her. She's got great things in her, Mr. Garnett." His eyes filled again with tears. "She's just as brave and honest, and sweet sometimes—I'll never marry anybody else, you can bet your life on that, but—we were just poison to each other. I never want to see her anymore."

After all, thought Garnett, it was only the old human attempt to get something for nothing—neither of them had brought to the marriage any trace of tolerance or moral experience. However trivial the reasons for their incompatibility, it was firmly established now in both their hearts, and perhaps they were wise in realizing that the wretched voyage, too hastily embarked upon, was over.

That night Garnett had a long and somewhat painful talk with George Wharton, and on the following morning he went to New York, where he spent several days. When he returned to Philadelphia, it was with the information that the marriage of Lucy and Llewellyn Clark had been annulled by the state of Connecticut on the ground of their minority. They were free.

II

Almost everyone who knew Lucy Wharton liked her, and her friends rose rather valiantly to the occasion. There was a certain element, of course, who looked at her with averted eyes; there were slights, there were the stares of the curious; but since it was wisely given out, upon Chauncey Garnett's recommendation, that the Whartons themselves had insisted upon the annulment, the burden of the affair fell less heavily upon Lucy than upon Llewellyn. He became not exactly a pariah—cities live too quickly to linger long over any single scandal—but he was cut off entirely from the crowd in which he had grown up, and much bitter and unpleasant comment reached his ears.

He was a boy who felt things deeply, and in the first moment of depression he contemplated leaving Philadelphia. But gradually a mood of defiant indifference took possession of him—try as he might he wasn't able to feel in his heart that he had done anything morally wrong. He hadn't thought of Lucy as being sixteen, but only as the girl whom he loved beyond understanding. What did age matter? Hadn't people married as children, almost, one hundred—two hundred years ago? The day of his elopement with Lucy had been like an ecstatic dream—he the young knight, scorned by her father, the baron, as a mere youth, bearing her away, and all willing, on his charger, in the dead of the night.

And then the realization, almost before his eyes had opened from their romantic vision, that marriage meant the complicated adjustment of two lives to each other, and that love is a small part only of the long, long marriage day. Lucy was a devoted child whom he had contracted to amuse—an adorable and somewhat frightened child, that was all.

As suddenly as it had begun it was over. Doggedly Llewellyn went his way, alone with his mistake. And so quickly had his romance bloomed and turned to dust that after a month a merciful unreality began to clothe it as if it were something vaguely sad that had happened long ago.

One day in July he was summoned to Chauncey Garnett's private office. Few words had passed between them since their conversation the month before, but Llewellyn saw that there was no hostility in the older man's attitude. He was glad of that, for now that he felt himself utterly alone, cut off from the world in which he had grown up, his work had come to be the most important thing in his life.

"What are you doing, Llewellyn?" asked Garnett, picking up a yellow pamphlet from the litter of his desk.

"Helping Mr. Carson with the Municipal Country Club."

"Take a look at this." He handed the pamphlet to Llewellyn. "There isn't a gold mine in it—but there's a good deal of this gilt-edge hot air they call publicity. It's a syndicate of twenty papers, you see. The best plans for—what is it?—a neighborhood store—you know, a small drug store or grocery store that could fit into a nice street without being an eye-sore. Or else for a suburban cottage—that'll be the regular thing. Or thirdly for a small factory recreation house."

Llewellyn read over the specifications.

"The last two aren't so interesting," he said. "Suburban cottage—that'll be the usual thing, as you say—recreation house, no. But I'd like to have a shot at the first, sir—the store."

Garnett nodded. "The best part is that the plan which wins each competition materializes as a building right away. And therein lies the prize. The building is yours. You design it, it's put up for you, then you sell it and the money goes into your own pocket. Matter of six or seven thousand dollars—and there won't be more than six or seven hundred other young architects trying."

Llewellyn read it over again carefully.

"I like it," he said. "I'd like to try the store."

"Well, you've got a month. I wouldn't mind it a bit, Llewellyn, if that prize came into this office."

"I can't promise you that." Again Llewellyn ran his eyes over the conditions, while Garnett watched him with quiet interest.

"By the way," he asked suddenly, "what do you do with yourself all the time, Llewellyn?"

"How do you mean, sir?"

"At night. Over the week-ends. Do you ever go out?"

Llewellyn hesitated. "Well, not so much—now."

"You mustn't let yourself brood over this business, you know."

"I'm not brooding."

Mr. Garnett put his glasses carefully away in their case.

"Lucy isn't brooding," he said suddenly. "Her father told me that she's trying to live just as normal a life as possible."

Silence for a moment.

"I'm glad," said Llewellyn in an expressionless voice.

"You must remember that you're free as air now," said Garnett. "You don't want to let yourself dry up and get bitter. Lucy's father and mother are encouraging her to have callers and go to dances—behave just as she did before—"

"Before Rudolph Rassendale came along," said Llewellyn grimly. He held up the pamphlet. "May I keep this, Mr. Garnett?"

"Oh, yes." His employer's hand gave him permission to retire. "Tell Mr. Carson that I've taken you off the country club for the present."

"I can finish that too," said Llewellyn promptly. "In fact—"

His lips shut. He had been about to remark that he was doing practically the whole thing himself anyhow.

"Well—?"

"Nothing, sir. Thank you very much."

Llewellyn withdrew, excited by his opportunity and relieved by the news of Lucy. She was herself again, so Mr. Garnett had implied; perhaps her life wasn't so irrevocably wrecked after all. If there were men to come and see her, to take her out to dances, then there were men to care for her. He found himself vaguely pitying them—if they knew what a handful she was, the absolute impossibility of dealing with her, even of talking to her.

At the thought of those desolate weeks he shivered, as though recalling a nightmare.

Back in his room that night, he experimented with a few tentative sketches. He worked late, his imagination warming to the set task, but next day the result seemed "arty" and pretentious—like a design for a tea shop. He scrawled "Ye Olde-Fashioned Butcher Shoppe. Veree Unsanitaree" across the face of it and tore it into pieces, which he tossed into the wastebasket.

During the first weeks in August he continued his work on the plans for the country club, trusting that for the more personal venture some burst of inspiration would come to him toward the end of the allotted time. And then one day occurred an incident which he had long dreaded in the secret corners of his mind—walking home along Chestnut Street he ran unexpectedly into Lucy.

It was about five o'clock, when the crowds were thickest. Suddenly they found themselves in an eddy facing each other and then borne along side by side as if fate had pressed into service all these swarming hundreds to throw them together.

"Why, Lucy!" he exclaimed, raising his hat automatically. She stared at him with startled eyes. A woman laden with bundles collided with her and a purse slipped from Lucy's hand.

"Thank you very much," she said as he retrieved it. Her voice was tense, breathless. "That's all right. Give it to me. I have a car right here."

Their eyes joined for a moment, cool, impersonal, and he had a vivid memory of their last meeting—of how they had stood, like this, hating each other with a cold fury.

"Are you sure I can't help you?"

"Quite sure. Our car's at the curb."

She nodded quickly. Llewellyn caught a glimpse of an unfamiliar limousine and a short smiling man of forty who helped her inside.

He walked home—for the first time in weeks he was angry, excited, confused. He must get away tomorrow. It was all too recent for any such casual encounter as this—the wounds she had left on him were raw and they opened easily.

"The little fool!" he said to himself bitterly. "The selfish little fool! She thought I wanted to walk along the street with her as if nothing had ever happened. She dares to imagine that I'm made of the same flimsy stuff as herself!"

He wanted passionately to spank her, to punish her in some way like an insolent child. Until dinnertime he paced up and down in his room, going over in his mind the forlorn and useless arguments, reproaches, imprecations, furies, that had made up their short married life. He rehearsed every quarrel from its trivial genesis down to the time when a merciful exhaustion intervened and brought them, almost hysterical, into each other's arms. A brief moment of peace—then again the senseless, miserable human battle.

"Lucy," he heard himself saying, "listen to me. It isn't that I want you to sit here waiting for me. It's your hands, Lucy—suppose you went to cooking school and burned your pretty hands. I don't want your hands coarsened and roughened, and if you'll just have patience till next week when my money comes in—I won't stand it! Do you hear? I'm not going to have my wife doing that! No use of being *stubborn*—"

Wearily, just as he had been made weary by those arguments in reality, he dropped into a chair and reached listlessly for his drawing materials. Laying them out, he began to sketch, crumpling each one into a ball before a dozen lines marred the paper. It was her fault, he whispered to himself, it was all her fault. "If I'd been fifty years old I couldn't have changed her."

Yet he could not rid himself of her dark young face set sharp and cool against the August gloaming, against the hot hurrying crowds of that afternoon.

"Quite sure. Our car's at the curb."

Llewellyn nodded to himself and tried to smile grimly.

"Well, I've got one thing to be thankful for," he told himself. "My responsibility will be over before long."

He had been sitting for a long while looking at a blank sheet of drawing paper, but presently his pencil began to move in light strokes at the corner. He watched it idly, impersonally, as though it were a motion of his fingers imposed on him from outside. Finally he looked at the result with disapproval, scratched it out and then blocked it in again in exactly the same way.

Suddenly he chose a new pencil, picked up his ruler and made a measurement on the paper, and then another. An hour passed. The sketch took shape and outline, varied itself slightly, yielded in part to an eraser and appeared in an improved form. After two hours he raised his head, and catching sight of his tense, absorbed face he started with surprise. There were a dozen half-smoked cigarettes in the tray beside him.

When he turned out his light at last it was half-past five. The milk wagons were rumbling through the twilit streets outside, and the first sunshine streaming pink over the roofs of the houses across the way fell upon the board which bore his night's work. It was the plan of a suburban bungalow.

III

As the August days passed, Llewellyn continued to think of Lucy with a certain anger and contempt. If she could accept so lightly what had happened just two months ago, he had wasted his emotion upon a girl who was essentially shallow. It cheapened his conception of her, of himself, of the whole affair. Again the idea came to him of leaving Philadelphia and making a new start farther west, but his interest in the outcome of the competition decided him to postpone his departure for a few weeks more.

The blueprints of his design were made and dispatched. Mr. Garnett cautiously refused to make any prophecies, but Llewellyn knew that everyone in the office who had seen the drawing felt a vague excitement about it. Almost literally he had drawn a bungalow in the air—a bungalow that had never been lived in before. It was neither Italian, Elizabethan, New England or California Spanish, nor a mongrel form with features from each one. Someone dubbed it "the tree house," and there was a certain happiness in the label, but its charm proceeded less from any bizarre quality than from the virtuosity of the conception as a whole—an unusual length here and there, an odd, tantalizingly familiar slope of the roof, a door that was like the door to the secret places of a dream. Chauncey Garnett remarked that it was the first skyscraper he had ever seen built with one story—but he recognized that Llewellyn's unquestionable talent had matured overnight. Except that the organizers of the competition were probably seeking something more adapted to standardization, it might have had a chance for the award.

Only Llewellyn was sure. When he was reminded that he was only twenty-one, he kept silent, knowing that, whatever his years, he would never again be twenty-one at heart. Life had betrayed him. He had squandered himself on a worthless girl and the world had punished him for it—as ruthlessly as though he had spent spiritual coin other than his own. Meeting Lucy on the street again, he passed her without a flicker of his eye—and returned to his room, his day spoiled by the sight of that young distant face, the insincere reproach of those dark haunting eyes.

Early in September arrived a letter from New York informing him that from four hundred plans submitted the judges of the competition had chosen his for the prize. Llewellyn walked into Mr. Garnett's office without excitement, but with a strong sense of elation, and laid the letter on his employer's desk.

"I'm especially glad," he said, "because before I go away I wanted to do something to justify your belief in me."

Mr. Garnett's face assumed an expression of concern.

"It's this business of Lucy Wharton, isn't it?" he demanded. "It's still on your mind?"

"I can't stand meeting her," said Llewellyn. "It always makes me feel—like the devil."

"But you ought to stay till they put up your house for you."

"I'll come back for that, perhaps. I want to leave tonight."

Garnett looked at him thoughtfully.

"I don't like to see you go away," he said. "I'm going to tell you something I didn't intend to tell you. Lucy needn't worry you a bit anymore—your responsibility is absolutely over."

"Why's that?" Llewellyn felt his heart quicken.

"She's going to marry another man."

"Going to marry another man!" repeated Llewellyn mechanically.

"She's going to marry George Hemmick, who represents her father's business in Chicago. They're going out there to live."

"I see."

"The Whartons are delighted," continued Garnett. "I think they've felt this thing pretty deeply—perhaps more deeply than it deserves. And I've been sorry all along that the brunt of it fell on you. But you'll find the girl you really want one of these days, Llewellyn, and meanwhile the sensible thing for everyone concerned is to forget that it happened at all."

"But I can't forget," said Llewellyn in a strained voice. "I don't understand what you mean by all that—you people—you and

Lucy, and her father and mother. First it was such a tragedy, and now it's something to forget! First I was this vicious young man and now I'm to go ahead and 'find the girl I want.' Lucy's going to marry somebody and live in Chicago. Her father and mother feel fine because our elopement didn't get in the newspapers and hurt their social position. It came out 'all right'!"

Llewellyn stood there speechless, aghast and defeated by this manifestation of the world's indifference. It was all about nothing—his very self-reproaches had been pointless and in vain.

"So that's that," he said finally in a new, hard voice. "I realize now that from beginning to end I was the only one who had any conscience in this affair after all."

IV

The little house, fragile yet arresting, all aglitter like a toy in its fresh coat of robin's-egg blue, stood out delicately against the clear sky. Set upon new-laid sod between two other bungalows, it swung your eye sharply toward itself, held your glance for a moment, then turned up the corners of your lips with the sort of smile reserved for children. Something went on in it, you imagined; something charming and not quite real. Perhaps the whole front opened up like the front of a doll's house; you were tempted to hunt for the catch because you felt an irresistible inclination to peer inside.

Long before the arrival of Llewellyn Clark and Mr. Garnett a small crowd had gathered—the constant efforts of two police-men were required to keep people from breaking through the strong fence and trampling the tiny garden. When Llewellyn's eye first fell upon it, as their car rounded a corner, a lump rose in his throat. That was his own—something that had come alive out of his mind. Suddenly he realized that it was not for sale, that he wanted it more than anything in the world. It could mean to him what love might have meant, something always bright and warm where he could rest from whatever disappointments life might have in store. And unlike love it would set no traps for him. His career opened up before him in a shining path and for the first time in half a year he was radiantly happy.

The speeches, the congratulations, passed in a daze. When he got up to make a stumbling but grateful acknowledgment, even the sight of Lucy standing close to another man on the edge of the crowd failed to send a pang through him as it would have a month before. That was the past and only the future counted. He hoped with all his heart, without reservations now, or bitterness, that she would be happy.

Afterwards when the crowd melted away he felt the necessity of being alone. Still in a sort of trance he went inside the house again and wandered from room to room, touching the walls, the furniture, the window casements, with almost a caress. He pulled aside curtains and gazed out; he stood for awhile in the kitchen and seemed to see the fresh bread and butter on the white boards of the table and hear the kettle, murmurous on the stove. Then back through the dining room—the remembered planning that the summer evening light should fall through the window just so—and into the bedroom, where he watched a breeze ruffle the edge of a curtain faintly, as if someone already lived here. He would sleep in this room tonight, he thought. He would buy things for a cold supper from a corner store. He was sorry for everyone who was not an architect, who could not make their own houses—he wished he could have set up every stick and stone with his own hands.

The September dusk fell. Returning from the store he set out his purchases on the dining-room table—cold roast chicken, bread and jam, and a bottle of milk. He ate lingeringly—then he sat back in his chair and smoked a cigarette, his eyes wandering about the walls. This was home. Llewellyn, brought up by a series of aunts, scarcely remembered ever having had a home before. Except of course where he had lived with Lucy. Those barren rooms in which they were so miserable together had been, nevertheless, a sort of home. Poor children—he looked back on them both, himself as well as her, from a great distance. Little wonder their love had made a faint, frail effort, a gesture, and then, unprepared for the oppression of those stifling walls, starved quickly to death.

Half an hour passed. Outside the silence was heavy except for the complaint of some indignant dog far down the street. Llewellyn's mind, detached by the unfamiliar, almost mystical surroundings, drifted away from the immediate past; he was thinking of the day when he had first met Lucy a year before.

Little Lucy Wharton—how touched he had been by her trust in him, by her confidence that, at twenty, he was experienced in the ways of the world.

He got to his feet and began to walk slowly up and down the room—starting suddenly as the front doorbell pealed through the house for the first time. He opened the door and Mr. Garnett stepped inside.

"Good evening, Llewellyn," he said. "I came back to see if the king was happy in his castle."

"Sit down," said Llewellyn tensely. "I've got to ask you something. Why is Lucy marrying this man? I want to know."

"Why, I think I told you that he's a good deal older," answered Garnett quietly. "She feels that he understands."

"I want to see her!" Llewellyn cried. He leaned miserably against the mantelpiece. "Oh God—I don't know what to do. Mr. Garnett, we're in love with each other, don't you realize that? Can you stay in this house and not realize it? It's her house and mine—why, every room in it is haunted with Lucy! She came in when I was at dinner and sat with me—just now I saw her in front of the mirror in the bedroom brushing her hair—"

"She's out on the porch," interrupted Garnett quietly. "I think she wants to talk to you. In a few months she's going to have a child."

For a few minutes Chauncey Garnett moved about the empty room, looking at this feature or that, here and there, until the walls seemed to fade out and melt into the walls of the little house where he had brought his own wife over forty years ago. It was long gone, that house—the gift of his father-in-law, it would have seemed an atrocity to this generation. Yet on many a forgotten late afternoon when he had turned in at its gate and the gas had flamed out at him cheerfully from its windows he had got from it a moment of utter peace that no other house had given him since—

—until this house. The same quiet secret thing was here. Was it that his old mind was confusing the two, or that love had built this out of the tragedy in Llewellyn's heart? Leaving the question unanswered he found his hat and walked out on the dark porch, scarcely glanced at the single shadow on the porch chair a few yards away.

"You see, I never bothered to get that annulment after all," he said, as if he were talking to himself. "I thought it over carefully and I saw that you two were good people. And I had an idea that eventually you'd do the right thing. Good people—so often do."

When he reached the curb he looked back at the house. Again his mind, or his eyes, blurred and it seemed to him that it was that other house of forty years ago. Then, feeling vaguely ineffectual and a little guilty because he had meddled in other people's affairs, he turned and walked off hastily down the street.

The Dance

A LL my life I have had a rather curious horror of small towns: not suburbs—they are quite a different matter—but the little lost cities of New Hampshire and Georgia and Kansas, and upper New York. I was born in New York City, and even as a little girl I never had any fear of the streets or the strange foreign faces—but on the occasions when I've been in the sort of place I'm referring to, I've been oppressed with the consciousness that there was a whole hidden life, a whole series of secret implications, significances and terrors, just below the surface, of which I knew nothing. In the cities everything good or bad eventually comes out, comes out of people's hearts, I mean. Life moves about, moves on, vanishes. In the small towns—those of between five and twenty-five thousand people—old hatreds, old and unforgotten affairs, ghostly scandals and tragedies, seem unable to die, but live on all tangled up with the natural ebb and flow of outward life.

Nowhere has this sensation come over me more insistently than in the South. Once out of Atlanta and Birmingham and New Orleans, I often have the feeling that I can no longer communicate with the people around me. The men and the girls speak a language wherein courtesy is combined with violence, fanatic morality with corn-drinking recklessness, in a fashion which I can't understand. In "Huckleberry Finn" Mark Twain described some of those towns perched along the Mississippi River, with their fierce feuds and their equally fierce revivals—and some of them haven't fundamentally changed beneath their new surface of flivvers and radios. They are deeply uncivilized to this day.

I speak of the South because it was in a small southern city of this type that I once saw the surface crack for a minute and something savage, uncanny and frightening rear its head. Then the surface closed again—and when I have gone back there since, I've been surprised to find myself as charmed as ever by the magnolia trees and the singing darkies in the street and the sensuous warm nights. I have been charmed too by the bountiful hospitality and the languorous easy-going outdoor life and the almost universal good manners. But all too frequently I am the prey of a vivid nightmare that recalls what I experienced in that town five years ago.

Davis—that is not its real name—has a population of about twenty thousand people, one-third of them colored. It is a cotton-mill town and the workers of that trade, several thousand gaunt and ignorant "poor whites," live together in an ill-reputed section known as "Cotton Hollow." The population of Davis has varied in its seventy-five years. Once it was under consideration for the capital of the state, and so the older families and their kin form a proud little aristocracy, even when individually they have sunk to destitution.

That winter I'd made the usual round in New York until about April, when I decided I never wanted to see another invitation again. I was tired and I wanted to go to Europe for a rest, but the Baby Panic of 1921 hit Father's business, and so it was suggested that I go South and visit Aunt Musidora Hale instead.

Vaguely I imagined that I was going to the country, but on the day I arrived, the Davis "Courier" published an hilarious old picture of me on its society page, and I found I was in for another season. On a small scale, of course: there were Saturday-night dances at the little country club with its nine-hole golf course and some informal dinner parties and several attractive and attentive boys. I didn't have a dull time at all and when after three weeks I wanted to go home, it wasn't because I was bored. On the contrary I wanted to go home because I'd allowed myself to get rather interested in a good-looking young man named Charley Kincaid, without realizing that he was engaged to another girl.

We'd been drawn together from the first because he was almost the only boy in town who'd gone north to college, and I was still young enough to think that America revolved around Harvard and Princeton and Yale. He liked me too—I could see that—but when I heard that his engagement to a girl named Marie Bannerman had been announced six months before, there was nothing for me except to go away. The town was too small to avoid people, and though so far there hadn't been any talk, I was sure that—well, that if we kept meeting the emotion we were beginning to feel would somehow get into words. I'm not mean enough to take a man away from another girl.

Marie Bannerman was almost a beauty. Perhaps she would have been a beauty if she'd had any clothes, and if she hadn't used bright pink rouge in two high spots on her cheeks and powdered her nose and chin to a funereal white. Her hair was shining black, her features were lovely, and an affliction of one eye kept it always half-closed and gave an air of humorous mischief to her face.

I was leaving on a Monday, and on Saturday night a crowd of us dined at the country club as usual before the dance. There was Joe Cable, the son of a former governor, a handsome, dissipated and yet somehow charming young man; Catherine Jones, a pretty, sharp-eyed girl with an exquisite figure, who under her rouge might have been any age from eighteen to twenty-five; Marie Bannerman; Charley Kincaid; myself and two or three others.

I loved to listen to the genial flow of bizarre neighborhood anecdote at this kind of party. For instance one of the girls, together with her entire family, had that afternoon been evicted from her house for non-payment of rent. She told the story wholly without self-consciousness, merely as something troublesome but amusing. And I loved the banter which presumed every girl to be infinitely beautiful and attractive, and every man to have been secretly and hopelessly in love with every girl present from their respective cradles.

"—we liked to die laughin'" . . . "—said he was fixin' to shoot him without he stayed away." The girls "'clared to heaven"; the men "took oath" on inconsequential statements. "How come you nearly about forgot to come by for me—" and the incessant Honey, Honey, Honey, Honey until the word seemed to roll like a genial liquid from heart to heart.

Outside, the May night was hot, a still night, velvet, soft-pawed, splattered thick with stars. It drifted heavy and sweet into the large room where we sat and where we would later dance, with no sound in it except the occasional long crunch of an arriving car on the drive. Just at that moment I hated to leave Davis as I never had hated to leave a town before—I felt that I wanted to spend my life in this town, drifting and dancing forever through these long, hot, romantic nights.

Yet horror was already hanging over that little party, was waiting tensely among us, an uninvited guest, and telling off the hours until it could show its pale and blinding face. Beneath the chatter and laughter something was going on, something secret and obscure that I didn't know.

Presently the colored orchestra arrived, followed by the first trickle of the dance crowd. An enormous red-faced man in muddy knee boots, and with a revolver strapped around his waist, clumped in and paused for a moment at our table before going upstairs to the locker room. It was Bill Abercrombie, the sheriff, the son of Congressman Abercrombie. Some of the boys asked him half-whispered questions, and he replied in an attempt at an undertone.

"Yes. . . . He's in the swamp all right; farmer saw him near the crossroads store. . . . Like to have a shot at him myself."

I asked the boy next to me what was the matter.

"Nigger case," he said, "over in Kisco, about two miles from here. He's hiding in the swamp and they're going in after him tomorrow."

"What'll they do to him?"

"Hang him, I guess."

The notion of the forlorn darky crouching dismally in a desolate bog waiting for dawn and death depressed me for a moment. Then the feeling passed and was forgotten.

After dinner Charley Kincaid and I walked out on the verandah—he had just heard that I was going away. I kept as close to the others as I could, answering his words but not his eyes—something inside me was protesting against leaving him on such a casual note. The temptation was strong to let something flicker up between us here at the end. I wanted him to kiss me—my heart promised that if he kissed me, just once, it would accept with equanimity the idea of never seeing him anymore; but my mind knew it wasn't so.

The other girls began to drift inside and upstairs to the dressing room to improve their complexions, and with Charley still beside me, I followed. Just at that moment I wanted to cry—perhaps my eyes were already blurred, or perhaps it was my haste lest they should be, but I opened the door of a small card room by mistake, and with my error the tragic machinery of the night began to function. In the card room, not five feet from us, stood Marie Bannerman, Charley's fiancée, and Joe Cable. They were in each other's arms, absorbed in a passionate and oblivious kiss.

I closed the door quickly, and without glancing at Charley opened the right door and ran upstairs.

II

A few minutes later Marie Bannerman entered the crowded dressing room. She saw me and came over, smiling in a sort of mock despair, but she breathed quickly and the smile trembled a little on her mouth.

"You won't say a word, Honey, will you?" she whispered.

"Of course not." I wondered how that could matter, now that Charley Kincaid knew.

"Who else was it that saw us?"

"Only Charley Kincaid and me."

"Oh!" She looked a little puzzled. Then she added: "He didn't wait to say anything, honey. When we came out he was just going out the door. I thought he was going to wait and romp all over Joe."

"How about his romping all over you?" I couldn't help asking.

"Oh, he'll do that." She laughed wryly. "But honey, I know how to handle him. It's just when he's first mad that I'm scared of him—he's got an awful temper." She whistled reminiscently. "I know, because this happened once before."

I wanted to slap her. Turning my back, I walked away on the pretext of borrowing a pin from Katie, the negro maid. Catherine Jones was claiming the latter's attention with a short gingham garment which needed repair.

"What's that?" I asked.

"Dancing-dress," she answered shortly, her mouth full of pins. When she took them out, she added, "It's all come to pieces, I've used it so much."

"Are you going to dance here tonight?"

"Going to try."

Somebody had told me that she wanted to be a dancer—that she had taken lessons in New York.

"Can I help you fix anything?"

"No, thanks—unless—can you sew? Katie gets so excited Saturday night that she's no good for anything except fetching pins. I'd be everlasting grateful to you, honey."

I had reasons for not wanting to go downstairs just yet, and so I sat down and worked on her dress for half an hour. I wondered if Charley had gone home, if I would ever see him again—I scarcely dared to wonder if what he had seen would set him free, ethically. When I went down finally he was not in sight.

The room was now crowded; the tables had been removed and dancing was general. At that time, just after the war, all Southern boys had a way of agitating their heels from side to side, pivoting on the ball of the foot as they danced, and to acquiring this accomplishment I had devoted many hours. There were plenty of stags, almost all of them cheerful with corn-liquor; I refused on an average at least two drinks a dance. Even when it is mixed with a soft drink, as is the custom, rather than gulped from the neck of a warm bottle, it is a formidable proposition. Only a few girls like Catherine Jones took an occasional sip from some boy's flask down at the dark end of the verandah.

I liked Catherine Jones—she seemed to have more energy than these other girls, though Aunt Musidora sniffed rather contemptuously whenever Catherine stopped for me in her car to go to the movies, remarking that she guessed "the bottom rail had gotten to be the top rail now." Her family were "new and common," but it seemed to me that perhaps her very commonness was an asset. Almost every girl in Davis confided in me at one time or another that her ambition was to "get away and come to New York," but only Catherine Jones had actually taken the step of studying stage dancing with that end in view.

She was often asked to dance at these Saturday night affairs, something "classic" or perhaps an acrobatic clog—on one memorable occasion she had annoyed the governing board by a "shimmy" (then the scapegrace of jazz), and the novel and somewhat startling excuse made for her was that she was "so tight she didn't know what she was doing anyhow." She impressed me as a curious personality, and I was eager to see what she would produce tonight.

At twelve o'clock the music always ceased, as dancing was forbidden on Sunday morning. So at eleven-thirty a vast fanfaronade of drum and cornet beckoned the dancers and the couples on the verandahs, and the ones in the cars outside, and the stragglers from the bar, into the ballroom. Chairs were brought in and galloped up *en masse* and with a great racket to the slightly raised platform. The orchestra had evacuated this and taken a place beside. Then, as the rearward lights were lowered, they began to play a tune accompanied by a curious drum-beat that I had never heard before, and simultaneously Catherine Jones appeared upon the platform. She wore the short, country girl's dress upon which I had lately labored, and a wide sunbonnet under which her face, stained yellow with powder, looked out at us with rolling eyes and a vacant negroid leer. She began to dance.

I had never seen anything like it before, and until five years later I wasn't to see it again. It was the Charleston—it must have been the Charleston. I remember the double drum-beat like a shouted "*Hey! Hey!*" and the unfamiliar swing of the arms and the odd knock-kneed effect. She had picked it up, heaven knows where.

Her audience, familiar with negro rhythms, leaned forward eagerly—even to them it was something new, but it is stamped on my mind as clearly and indelibly as though I had seen it yesterday. The figure on the platform swinging and stamping, the excited orchestra, the waiters grinning in the doorway of the bar, and all around through many windows the soft languorous southern night seeping in from swamp and cottonfield and lush foliage and brown, warm streams. At what point a feeling of tense uneasiness began to steal over me I don't know. The dance could scarcely have taken ten minutes; perhaps the first beats of the barbaric music disquieted me—long before it was over I was sitting rigid in my seat, and my eyes were wandering here and there around the hall, passing along the rows of shadowy faces as if seeking some security that was no longer there.

I'm not a nervous type, nor am I given to panic, but for a moment I was afraid that if the music and the dance didn't stop I'd be hysterical. Something was happening all about me. I knew it as well as if I could see into these unknown souls. Things were happening, but one thing especially was leaning over so close that it almost touched us, that it did touch us. . . . I almost screamed as a hand brushed accidentally against my back.

The music stopped. There was applause and protracted cries of encore, but Catherine Jones shook her head definitely at the orchestra leader and made as though to leave the platform. The appeals for more continued—again she shook her head, and it seemed to me that her expression was rather angry. Then a strange incident occurred. At the protracted pleading of someone in the front row, the colored orchestra leader began the vamp of the tune, as if to lure Catherine Jones into changing her mind. Instead she turned toward him, snapped out, "Didn't you hear me say no?" and then, surprisingly, slapped his face. The music stopped and an amused murmur terminated abruptly as a muffled but clearly audible shot rang out.

Immediately we were on our feet, for the sound indicated that it had been fired within or near the house. One of the chaperones gave a little scream, but when some wag called out "Caesar's in that henhouse again," the momentary alarm dissolved into laughter. The club manager, followed by several curious couples, went out to have a look around, but the rest were already moving around the floor to the strains of "Good Night, Ladies," which traditionally ended the dance.

I was glad it was over. The man with whom I had come went to get his car. I called a waiter and sent him for my golf clubs, which were in the stack upstairs. I strolled out on the porch and waited, wondering again if Charley Kincaid had gone home.

Suddenly I was aware, in that curious way in which you become aware of something that has been going on for several minutes, that there was a tumult inside. Women were shrieking; there was a cry of "Oh, my God!" then the sounds of a stampede on the inside stairs and footsteps running back and forth across the ballroom. A girl appeared from somewhere and pitched forward in a dead faint—almost immediately another girl did the same, and I heard a frantic male voice shouting into a telephone. Then, hatless and pale, a young man rushed out on the porch, and with hands that were cold as ice, seized my arm.

"What is it?" I cried. "A fire? What's happened?"

"Marie Bannerman's dead upstairs in the women's dressing room. Shot through the throat!"

III

The rest of that night is a series of visions that seem to have no connection with one another, that follow each other with the sharp instantaneous transitions of scenes in the movies. There was a group who stood arguing on the porch, in voices now raised, now hushed, about what should be done and how every waiter in the club, "even old Moses," ought to be given the third degree tonight. That a "nigger" had shot and killed Marie Bannerman was the instant and unquestioned assumption—in the first unreasoning instant, anyone who doubted it would have been under suspicion. The guilty one was said to be Katie Golstien, the colored maid, who had discovered the body and fainted. It was said to be "that nigger they were looking for over near Kisco." It was any darky at all.

Within half an hour people began to drift out, each with his little contribution of new discoveries. The crime had been committed with Sheriff Abercrombie's gun—he had hung it, belt and all, in full view on the wall before coming down to dance. It was missing—they were hunting for it now. Instantly killed, the doctor said—bullet had been fired from only a few feet away.

Then a few minutes later another young man came out and made an announcement in a loud, grave voice:

"They've arrested Charley Kincaid."

My head reeled. Upon the group gathered on the verandah fell an awed, stricken silence.

"—arrested Charley Kincaid!"

"Charley *Kincaid?*"

Why, he was one of the best, one of themselves.

"That's the craziest thing I ever heard of!"

The young man nodded, shocked like the rest but self-important with his information.

"He wasn't downstairs when Catherine Jones was dancing—he says he was in the men's locker room. And Marie Bannerman told a lot of girls that they'd had a row, and she was scared of what he'd do."

Again an awed silence.

"That's the craziest thing I ever heard!" someone said again. "Charley *Kincaid!*"

The narrator waited a moment. Then he added:

"He caught her kissing Joe Cable—"

I couldn't keep silence a minute longer.

"What about it?" I cried out. "I was with him at the time. He wasn't—he wasn't angry at all."

They looked at me, their faces startled, confused, unhappy. Suddenly the footsteps of several men sounded loud through the ballroom and a moment later Charley Kincaid, his face dead white, came out the front door between the sheriff and another man. Crossing the porch quickly they descended the steps and disappeared in the darkness. A moment later there was the sound of a starting car.

When an instant later far away down the road I heard the eerie scream of an ambulance, I got up desperately and called to my escort, who formed part of the whispering group.

"I've got to go," I said. "I can't stand this. Either take me home or I'll find a place in another car." Reluctantly he shouldered my clubs—the sight of them made me realize that I now couldn't leave on Monday after all—and followed me down the steps just as the black body of the ambulance curved in at the gate—a ghastly shadow on the bright, starry night.

IV

The situation, after the first wild surmises, the first burst of unreasoning loyalty to Charley Kincaid, had died away, was outlined by the Davis "Courier" and by most of the state newspapers in this fashion: Marie Bannerman died in the women's dressing room of the Davis Country Club from the effects of a shot fired at close quarters from a revolver just after eleven forty-five o'clock on Saturday night. Many persons had heard the shot; moreover it had undoubtedly been fired from the revolver of Sheriff Abercrombie, which had been hanging in full sight on the wall of the next room. Abercrombie himself was down in the ballroom when the murder took place, as many witnesses could testify. The revolver was not found.

So far as was known, the only man who had been upstairs at the time the shot was fired was Charles Kincaid. He was engaged to Miss Bannerman, but according to several witnesses they had quarreled seriously that evening. Miss Bannerman herself had mentioned the quarrel, adding that she was afraid and wanted to keep away from him until he cooled off.

Charles Kincaid asserted that at the time the shot was fired he was in the men's locker room—where, indeed, he was found, immediately after the discovery of Miss Bannerman's body. He denied having had any words with Miss Bannerman at all. He had heard the shot but it had had no significance for him—if he thought anything of it, he thought that "someone was potting cats outdoors."

Why had he chosen to remain in the locker room during the dance?

No reason at all. He was tired. He was waiting until Miss Bannerman wanted to go home.

The body was discovered by Katie Golstien, the colored maid, who herself was found in a faint when the crowd of girls surged upstairs for their coats. Returning from the kitchen, where she had been getting a bite to eat, Katie had found Miss Bannerman, her dress wet with blood, already dead on the floor.

Both the police and the newspapers attached importance to the geography of the country club's second story. It consisted of a row of three rooms—the women's dressing room and the men's locker room at either end, and in the middle a room which was used as a cloak-room and for the storage of golf clubs. The women's and men's rooms had no outlet except into this chamber, which was connected by one stairs with the ballroom below, and by another with the kitchen. According to the testimony of three negro cooks and the white caddy master, no one but Katie Golstien had gone up the kitchen stairs that night.

As I remember it after five years, the foregoing is a pretty accurate summary of the situation when Charley Kincaid was accused of first-degree murder and committed for trial. Other people, chiefly negroes, were suspected (at the loyal instigation of Charley Kincaid's friends), and several arrests were made, but nothing ever came of them, and upon what grounds they were based I have long forgotten. One group, in spite of the disappearance of the pistol, claimed persistently that it was a suicide and suggested some ingenious reasons to account for the absence of the weapon.

Now when it is known how Marie Bannerman happened to die so savagely and so violently, it would be easy for me, of all people, to say that I believed in Charley Kincaid all the time. But I didn't. I thought that he had killed her, and at the same time I knew that I loved him with all my heart. That it was I who first happened upon the evidence which set him free was due not to any faith in his innocence but to a strange vividness with which, in moods of excitement, certain scenes stamp themselves on my memory, so that I can remember every detail and how that detail struck me at the time.

It was one afternoon early in July, when the case against Char-ley Kincaid seemed to be at its strongest, that the horror of the actual murder slipped away from me for a moment and I began to think about other incidents of that same haunted night. Something Marie Bannerman had said to me in the dress-ing room persistently eluded me, bothered me—not because I believed it to be important, but simply because I couldn't remember. It was gone from me, as if it had been a part of the fantastic undercurrent of small-town life which I had felt so strongly that evening, the sense that things were in the air, old secrets, old loves and feuds and unresolved situations that I, an outsider, could never fully understand. Just for a minute it seemed to me that Marie Bannerman had pushed aside the curtain; then it had dropped into place again—the house into which I might have looked was dark now forever.

Another incident, perhaps less important, also haunted me. The tragic events of a few minutes after had driven it from every-one's mind, but I had a strong impression that for a brief space of time I wasn't the only one to be surprised. When the audience had demanded an encore from Catherine Jones, her unwilling-ness to dance again had been so acute that she had been driven to the point of slapping the orchestra leader's face. The discrep-ancy between his offense and the venom of the rebuff recurred to me again and again. It wasn't natural—or, more important, it hadn't *seemed* natural. In view of the fact that Catherine Jones had been drinking, it was explicable; but it worried me now as it had worried me then. Rather to lay its ghost than to do any investigating, I pressed an obliging young man into service and called on the leader of the band.

His name was Thomas, a very dark, very simple-hearted vir-tuoso of the traps, and it took less than ten minutes to find out that Catherine Jones' gesture had surprised him as much as it had me. He had known her a long time, seen her at dances since she was a little girl—why, the very dance she did that night was one she had rehearsed with his orchestra a week before. And a few days later she had come to him and said she was sorry.

"I knew she would," he concluded. "She's a right good-hearted girl. My sister Katie was her nurse from when she was born up to the time she went to school."

"Your sister—?"

"Katie. She's the maid out the country club. Katie Golstien. You been reading 'bout her in the papers in 'at Charley Kincaid case. She's the maid. Katie Golstien. She's the maid at the country club what found the body of Miss Bannerman."

"So Katie was Miss Catherine Jones' nurse?"

"Yes ma'am."

Going home, stimulated but unsatisfied, I asked my companion a quick question.

"Were Catherine and Marie good friends?"

"Oh, yes," he answered without hesitation. "All the girls are good friends here, except when two of them are tryin' to get hold of the same man. Then they warm each other up a little."

"Why do you suppose Catherine hasn't married? Hasn't she got lots of beaux?"

"Off and on. She only likes people for a day or so at a time. That is—all except Joe Cable."

Now a scene burst upon me, broke over me like a dissolving wave. And suddenly, my mind shivering from the impact, I remembered what Marie Bannerman had said to me in the dressing room: "Who else was it that saw?" She had caught a glimpse of someone else, a figure passing so quickly that she could not identify it, out of the corner of her eye.

And suddenly, simultaneously, I seemed to see that figure, as if I too had been vaguely conscious of it at the time, just as one is aware of a familiar gait or outline on the street long before there is any flicker of recognition. On the corner of my own eye was stamped a hurrying figure—that might have been Catherine Jones.

But when the shot was fired Catherine Jones was in full view of over fifty people. Was it credible that Katie Golstien, a woman of fifty, who as a nurse had been known and trusted by three generations of Davis people, would shoot down a young girl in cold blood at Catherine Jones' command?

"But when the shot was fired Catherine Jones was in full view of over fifty people."

That sentence beat in my head all night, taking on fantastic variations, dividing itself into phrases, segments, individual words.

"*But when the shot was fired* . . . Catherine Jones was in full view . . . of over fifty people."

When the shot was fired! What shot? The shot we heard. When the shot was fired. . . . When the shot was fired. . . .

The next morning at nine o'clock, with the pallor of sleeplessness buried under a quantity of paint such as I had never worn before or have since, I walked up a rickety flight of stairs to the sheriff's office.

Abercrombie, engrossed in his morning's mail, looked up curiously as I came in the door.

"Catherine Jones did it," I cried, struggling to keep the hysteria out of my voice. "She killed Marie Bannerman with a shot we didn't hear because the orchestra was playing and everybody was pushing up the chairs. The shot we heard was when Katie fired the pistol out the window after the music was stopped. To give Catherine an alibi!"

V

I was right—as everyone now knows—but for a week, until Katie Golstien broke down under a fierce and ruthless inquisition, nobody believed me. Even Charley Kincaid, as he afterward confessed, didn't dare to think it could be true.

What had been the relations between Catherine and Joe Cable no one ever knew, but evidently she had determined that his clandestine affair with Marie Bannerman had gone too far.

Then Marie chanced to come into the women's room while Catherine was dressing for her dance—and there again there is a certain obscurity, for Catherine always claimed that Marie got the revolver, threatened her with it and that in the ensuing struggle the trigger was pulled. In spite of everything I always rather liked Catherine Jones, but in justice it must be said that only a simple-minded and very exceptional jury would have let her off with five years. And in just about five years from her commitment my husband and I are going to make a round of the New York musical shows and look hard at all the members of the chorus from the very front row.

After the shooting she must have thought quickly. Katie was told to wait until the music stopped, fire the revolver out the window and then hide it—Catherine Jones neglected to specify where. Katie, on the verge of collapse, obeyed instructions but she was never able to specify where she had hid the revolver.

And no one ever knew until a year later when Charley and I were on our honeymoon and Sheriff Abercrombie's ugly weapon dropped out of my golf bag onto a Hot Springs golf links. The bag must have been standing just outside the dressing room door; Katie's trembling hand had dropped the revolver into the first aperture she could see.

We live in New York. Small towns make us both uncomfortable. Every day we read about the crime waves in the big cities, but at least a wave is something tangible that you can provide against. What I dread above all things is the unknown depths, the incalculable ebb and flow, the secret shapes of things that drift through opaque darkness under the surface of the sea.

NONFICTION
1920–1926

Copyright by White.

The Author's Apology

I don't want to talk about myself because I'll admit I did that somewhat in this book. In fact, to write it took three months; to conceive it—three minutes; to collect the data in it—all my life. The idea of writing it came on the first of last July: it was a substitute form of dissipation.

My whole theory of writing I can sum up in one sentence: An author ought to write for the youth of his own generation, the critics of the next, and the schoolmasters of ever afterward.

So, gentlemen, consider all the cocktails mentioned in this book drunk by me as a toast to the American Booksellers Association.

MAY, 1920

An Interview with Mr. Fitzgerald

by F. Scott Fitzgerald

WITH the distinct intention of taking Mr. Fitzgerald by surprise I ascended to the twenty-first floor of the Biltmore and knocked in the best waiter-manner at the door. On entering my first impression was one of confusion—a sort of rummage sale confusion. A young man was standing in the center of the room turning an absent glance first at one side of the room and then at the other.

"I'm looking for my hat," he said dazedly. "How do you do. Come on in and sit on the bed."

The author of *This Side of Paradise* is sturdy, broad-shouldered and just above medium height. He has blond hair with the suggestion of a wave and alert green eyes—the mélange somewhat Nordic—and good-looking too, which was disconcerting as I had somehow expected a thin nose and spectacles.

We had preliminaries—but I will omit the preliminaries. They consisted in searching for things: cigarettes, a blue tie with white dots, an ash tray. But as he was obviously quite willing to talk, and seemed quite receptive to my questions, we launched off directly on his ideas of literature.

"How long did it take to write your book?" I began.

"To write it—three months, to conceive it—three minutes. To collect the data in it—all my life. The idea of writing it occurred to me on the first of last July. It was sort of a substitute form of dissipation."

"What are your plans now?" I asked him.

He gave a long sigh and shrugged his shoulders.

"I'll be darned if I know. The scope and depth and breadth of my writings lie in the laps of the gods. If knowledge comes naturally, through interest, as Shaw learned his political economy or as Wells devoured modern science—why, that'll be slick. On study itself—that is in 'reading up' a subject—I haven't anthill-moving faith. Knowledge must cry out to be known—cry out that only I can know it, and then I'll swim in it to satiety as I've swum in—in many things."

637

"Please be frank."

"Well, you know if you've read my book. I've swum in various seas of adolescent egotism. But what I meant was that if big things never grip me—well, it simply means I'm not cut out to be big. This conscious struggle to find bigness outside, to substitute bigness of theme for bigness of perception, to create an objective *magnum opus* such as *The Ring and the Book*—well, all that's the antithesis of my literary aims.

"Another thing," he continued. "My idea is always to reach my generation. The wise writer, I think, writes for the youth of his own generation, the critic of the next and the schoolmasters of ever afterward. Granted the ability to improve what he imitates in the way of style, to choose from his own interpretation of the experiences around him what constitutes material, and we get the first-water genius."

"Do you expect to be—to be—well, part of the great literary tradition?" I asked, timidly.

He became excited. He smiled radiantly. I saw he had an answer for this. "There's no great literary tradition," he burst out. "There's only the tradition of the eventual death of every literary tradition. The wise literary son kills his own father."

After this he began enthusiastically on style.

"By style, I mean color," he said. "I want to be able to do anything with words: handle slashing, flaming descriptions like Wells, and use the paradox with the clarity of Samuel Butler, the breadth of Bernard Shaw and the wit of Oscar Wilde. I want to do the wide sultry heavens of Conrad, the rolled-gold sundowns and crazy-quilt skies of Hichens and Kipling as well as the pastel dawns and twilights of Chesterton. All that is by way of example. As a matter of fact I am a professed literary thief, hot after the best methods of every writer in my generation."

The interview terminated about then. Four young men with philistine faces and conservative ties appeared and, looking at each other, exchanged broad winks. Mr. Fitzgerald faltered and seemed to lose his stride.

"Most of my friends are—are like those," he whispered as he showed me to the door. "I don't care for literary people much—they make me nervous."

It was really rather a good interview, wasn't it!

Who's Who—and Why

THE history of my life is the history of the struggle between an overwhelming urge to write and a combination of circumstances bent on keeping me from it.

When I lived in St. Paul and was about twelve I wrote all through every class in school in the back of my geography book and first year Latin and on the margins of themes and declensions and mathematic problems. Two years later a family congress decided that the only way to force me to study was to send me to boarding school. This was a mistake. It took my mind off my writing. I decided to play football, to smoke, to go to college, to do all sorts of irrelevant things that had nothing to do with the real business of life, which, of course, was the proper mixture of description and dialogue in the short story.

But in school I went off on a new tack. I saw a musical comedy called "The Quaker Girl," and from that day forth my desk bulged with Gilbert & Sullivan librettos and dozens of notebooks containing the germs of dozens of musical comedies.

Near the end of my last year at school I came across a new musical-comedy score lying on top of the piano. It was a show called "His Honor the Sultan," and the title furnished the information that it had been presented by the Triangle Club of Princeton University.

That was enough for me. From then on the university question was settled. I was bound for Princeton.

I spent my entire freshman year writing an operetta for the Triangle Club. To do this I failed in algebra, trigonometry, coördinate geometry and hygiene. But the Triangle Club accepted my show, and by tutoring all through a stuffy August I managed to come back a sophomore and act in it as a chorus girl. A little after this came a hiatus. My health broke down and I left college one December to spend the rest of the year recuperating in the West. Almost my final memory before I left was of writing a last lyric on that year's Triangle production while in bed in the infirmary with a high fever.

The next year, 1916–17, found me back in college, but by this time I had decided that poetry was the only thing worth while, so with my head ringing with the meters of Swinburne and the matters of Rupert Brooke I spent the spring doing sonnets, ballads and rondels into the small hours. I had read somewhere that every great poet had written great poetry before he was twenty-one. I had only a year and, besides, war was impending. I must publish a book of startling verse before I was engulfed.

By autumn I was in an infantry officers' training camp at Fort Leavenworth, with poetry in the discard and a brand-new ambition—I was writing an immortal novel. Every evening, concealing my pad behind "Small Problems for Infantry," I wrote paragraph after paragraph on a somewhat edited history of me and my imagination. The outline of twenty-two chapters, four of them in verse, was made; two chapters were completed; and then I was detected and the game was up. I could write no more during study period.

This was a distinct complication. I had only three months to live—in those days all infantry officers thought they had only three months to live—and I had left no mark on the world. But such consuming ambition was not to be thwarted by a mere war. Every Saturday at one o'clock when the week's work was over I hurried to the Officers' Club, and there, in a corner of a roomful of smoke, conversation and rattling newspapers, I wrote a one-hundred-and-twenty-thousand-word novel on the consecutive week-ends of three months. There was no revising; there was no time for it. As I finished each chapter I sent it to a typist in Princeton.

Meanwhile I lived in its smeary pencil pages. The drills, marches and "Small Problems for Infantry" were a shadowy dream. My whole heart was concentrated upon my book.

I went to my regiment happy. I had written a novel. The war could now go on. I forgot paragraphs and pentameters, similes and syllogisms. I got to be a first lieutenant, got my orders overseas—and then the publishers wrote me that though "The Romantic Egotist" was the most original manuscript they had received for years they couldn't publish it. It was crude and reached no conclusion.

It was six months after this that I arrived in New York and presented my card to the office boys of seven city editors asking to be taken on as a reporter. I had just turned twenty-two, the war was over, and I was going to trail murderers by day and do short stories by night. But the newspapers didn't need me. They sent their office boys out to tell me they didn't need me. They decided definitely and irrevocably by the sound of my name on a calling card that I was absolutely unfitted to be a reporter.

Instead I became an advertising man at ninety dollars a month, writing the slogans that while away the weary hours in rural trolley cars. After hours I wrote stories—from March to June. There were nineteen altogether, the quickest written in an hour and a half, the slowest in three days. No one bought them, no one sent personal letters. I had one hundred and twenty-two rejection slips pinned in a frieze about my room. I wrote movies. I wrote song lyrics. I wrote complicated advertising schemes. I wrote poems. I wrote sketches. I wrote jokes. Near the end of June I sold one story for thirty dollars.

On the Fourth of July, utterly disgusted with myself and all the editors, I went home to St. Paul and informed family and friends that I had given up my position and had come home to write a novel. They nodded politely, changed the subject and spoke of me very gently. But this time I knew what I was doing. I had a novel to write at last, and all through two hot months I wrote and revised and compiled and boiled down. On September fifteenth "This Side of Paradise" was accepted by special delivery.

In the next two months I wrote eight stories and sold nine. The ninth was accepted by the same magazine that had rejected it four months before. Then, in November, I sold my first story to the editors of the "Saturday Evening Post." By February I had sold them half a dozen. Then my novel came out. Then I got married. Now I spend my time wondering how it all happened.

In the words of the immortal Julius Caesar: "That's all there is; there isn't any more."

The Credo of F. Scott Fitzgerald

D EAR Boyd: It seems to me that the overworked art-form at present in America is the "history of a young man." Frank Norris began it with "Vandover and the Brute," then came Stephen French Whitman with "Predestined" and of late my own book and Floyd Dell's "Moon Calf." In addition I understand that Stephen Benét has also delved into his past. This writing of a young man's novel consists chiefly in dumping all your youthful adventures into the readers' lap with a profound air of importance, keeping carefully within the formulas of Wells and James Joyce. It seems to me that when accomplished by a man without distinction of style it reaches the depth of banality as in the case of "Moon Calf." * * * Up to this year the literary people of any pretensions—Mencken, Cabell, Wharton, Dreiser, Hergesheimer, Cather and Charles Norris—have been more or less banded together in the fight against intolerance and stupidity, but I think that a split is due. On the romantic side Cabell, I suppose, would maintain that life has a certain glamour that reporting—especially this reporting of a small Midwestern town—cannot convey to paper. On the realistic side Dreiser would probably maintain that romanticism tends immediately to deteriorate to the Zane Grey–Rupert Hughes level, as it has in the case of Tarkington, fundamentally a brilliant writer. * * *

It is encouraging to notice that the number of pleasant sheep, i.e., people who think they're absorbing culture if they read Blasco Ibanez, H. G. Wells and Henry Van Dyke—are being rounded into shape. This class, which makes up the so-called upper class in every American city, will read what they're told and now that at last we have a few brilliant men like Mencken at the head of American letters, these amiable sheep will pretend to appreciate the appreciable of their own country instead of rushing to cold churches to hear noble but unintelligible words, and meeting once a week to read papers on the aforementioned Blasco Ibanez. Even the stupidest people are reading "Main

Street," and pretending they thought so all the time. I wonder how many people in St. Paul ever read "The Titan" or "Salt" or even "McTeague." All this would seem to encourage insincerity of taste. But if it does it would at least have paid Dreiser for his early struggles at the time when such cheapjacks as Robert Chambers were being hailed as the "Balzacs of America."

Three Cities

IT began in Paris, that impression—fleeting, chiefly literary, unprofound—that the world was growing darker. We carefully reconstructed an old theory and, blond both of us, cast supercilious Nordic glances at the play of the dark children around us. We had left America less than one half of one per cent American, but the pernicious and sentimental sap was destined to rise again within us. We boiled with ancient indignations toward the French. We sat in front of Anatole France's house for an hour in hope of seeing the old gentleman come out—but we thought simultaneously that when he dies, the France of flame and glory dies with him. We drove in the Bois de Boulogne—thinking of France as a spoiled and revengeful child which, having kept Europe in a turmoil for two hundred years, has spent the last forty demanding assistance in its battles, that the continent may be kept as much like a bloody sewer as possible.

In Brentano's near the Café de la Paix, I picked up Dreiser's suppressed "Genius" for three dollars. With the exception of "The Titan" I liked it best among his five novels, in spite of the preposterous Christian Science episode near the end. We stayed in Paris long enough to finish it.

Italy, which is to the English what France is to the Americans, was in a pleasant humor. As a French comedy writer remarked we inevitably detest our benefactors, so I was glad to see that Italy was casting off four years of unhealthy suppressed desires. In Florence you could hardly blame a squad of Italian soldiers for knocking down an Omaha lady who was unwilling to give up her compartment to a Colonel. Why, the impudent woman could not speak Italian! So the *Carabinieri* can hardly be blamed for being incensed. And as for knocking her around a little—well, boys will be boys. The American ambassadorial tradition in Rome having for some time been in the direct line of sentimental American literature, I do not doubt that even they found some compensating sweetness in the natures of the naughty *Bersaglieri*.

We were in Rome two weeks. You can see the fascination of the place. We stayed two weeks even though we could have left in two days—that is we *could* have left if we had not run out of money. I met John Carter, the author of "These Wild Young People," in the street one day and he cashed me a check for a thousand lira. We spent this on ointment. The ointment trust thrives in Rome. All the guests at the two best hotels are afflicted with what the proprietors call "mosquitoes too small for screens." We do not call them that in America.

John Carter lent us "Alice Adams" and we read it aloud to each other under the shadow of Caesar's house. If it had not been for Alice we should have collapsed and died in Rome as so many less fortunate literary people have done. "Alice Adams" more than atones for the childish heroics of "Ramsey Milholland" and for the farcical spiritualism in "The Magnificent Ambersons." After having made three brave attempts to struggle through "Moon-Calf" it was paradise to read someone who knows how to write.

By bribing the ticket agent with one thousand lira to cheat some old General out of his compartment—the offer was the agent's, not ours—we managed to leave Italy.

"*Vous avez quelque chose pour déclarer?*" asked the border customs officials early next morning (only they asked it in better French).

I awoke with a horrible effort from a dream of Italian beggars.

"*Oui!*" I shrieked. *"Je veux déclare que je suis très, très heureux a partir d'Italie!"* I could understand at last why the French loved France. They have seen Italy.

We had been to Oxford before—after Italy we went back there, arriving gorgeously at twilight when the place was fully peopled for us by the ghosts of ghosts—the characters, romantic, absurd or melancholy, of "Sinister Street," "Zuleika Dobson" and "Jude the Obscure." But something was wrong now—something that would never be right again. Here was Rome—here on The High were the shadows of the Via Appia. In how many years would our descendents approach this ruin with supercilious eyes to buy postcards from men of a short, inferior race—a race that once were Englishmen. How soon—for money follows the rich lands and the healthy stock, and art follows begging after money. Your time will come, New York, fifty years, sixty. Apollo's head is peering crazily, in new colors that our generation will never live to know, over the tip of the next century.

What I Think and Feel at 25

THE man stopped me on the street. He was ancient, but not a mariner. He had a long beard and a glittering eye. I think he was a friend of the family's, or something.

"Say, Fitzgerald," he said, "say! Will you tell me this: What in the blinkety-blank-blank has a—has a man of your age got to go saying these pessimistic things for? What's the idea?" I tried to laugh him off. He told me that he and my grandfather had been boys together. After that, I had no wish to corrupt him. So I tried to laugh him off.

"Ha-ha-ha!" I said determinedly. "Ha-ha-ha!" And then I added, "Ha-ha! Well, I'll see you later."

With this I attempted to pass him by, but he seized my arm firmly and showed symptoms of spending the afternoon in my company.

"When I was a boy—" he began, and then he drew the picture that people always draw of what excellent, happy, care-free souls they were at twenty-five. That is, he told me all the things he liked to *think* he thought in the misty past.

I allowed him to continue. I even made polite grunts at intervals to express my astonishment. For I will be doing it myself some day. I will concoct for my juniors a Scott Fitzgerald that, it's safe to say, none of my contemporaries would at present recognize. But they will be old themselves then; and they will respect my concoction as I shall respect theirs. . . .

"And now," the happy ancient was concluding; "you are young, you have good health, you have made money, you are exceptionally happily married, you have achieved considerable success while you are still young enough to enjoy it—will you tell an innocent old man just why you write those—"

I succumbed. I would tell him. I began:

"Well, you see, sir, it seems to me that as a man gets older he grows more vulner—"

But I got no further. As soon as I began to talk he hurriedly shook my hand and departed. He did not want to listen. He did not care why I thought what I thought. He had simply felt the need of giving a little speech, and I had been the victim. His receding form disappeared with a slight wobble around the next corner.

"All right, you old bore," I muttered; "*don't* listen, then. You wouldn't understand, anyhow." I took an awful kick at a curbstone, as a sort of proxy, and continued my walk.

Now, that's the first incident. The second was when a man came to me not long ago from a big newspaper syndicate, and said:

"Mr. Fitzgerald, there's a rumor around New York that you and—ah—you and Mrs. Fitzgerald are going to commit suicide at thirty because you hate and dread middle age. I want to give you some publicity in this matter by getting it up as a story for the feature sections of five hundred and fourteen Sunday newspapers. In one corner of the page will be—"

"Don't!" I cried. "I know: In one corner will stand the doomed couple, she with an arsenic sundae, he with an Oriental dagger. Both of them will have their eyes fixed on a large clock, on the face of which will be a skull and crossbones. In the other corner will be a big calendar with the date marked in red."

"That's it!" cried the syndicate man enthusiastically. "You've grasped the idea. Now, what we—"

"Listen here!" I said severely. "There is nothing in that rumor. Nothing whatever. When I'm thirty I won't be *this* me—I'll be somebody else. I'll have a different body, because it said so in a book I read once, and I'll have a different attitude on everything. I'll even be married to a different person—"

"Ah!" he interrupted, with an eager light in his eye, and produced a notebook. "That's very interesting."

"No, no, no!" I cried hastily. "I mean my wife will be different."

"I see. You plan a divorce."

"No! I mean—"

"Well, it's all the same. Now, what we want, in order to fill out this story, is a lot of remarks about petting-parties. Do you think the—ah—petting-party is a serious menace to the Constitution? And, just to link it up, can we say that your suicide will be largely on account of past petting-parties?"

"See here!" I interrupted in despair. "Try to understand. I don't know what petting-parties have to do with the question. I have always dreaded age, because it invariably increases the vulner—"

But, as in the case of the family friend, I got no further. The syndicate man grasped my hand firmly. He shook it. Then he muttered something about interviewing a chorus girl who was reported to have an anklet of solid platinum, and hurried off.

That's the second incident. You see, I had managed to tell two different men that "age increased the vulner—" But they had not been interested. The old man had talked about himself and the syndicate man had talked about petting-parties. When I began to talk about the "vulner—" they both had sudden engagements.

So, with one hand on the Eighteenth Amendment and the other hand on the serious part of the Constitution, I have taken an oath that I will tell somebody my story.

As a man grows older it stands to reason that his vulnerability increases. Three years ago, for instance, I could be hurt in only one way—through myself. If my best friend's wife had her hair torn off by an electric washing-machine, I was grieved, of course. I would make my friend a long speech full of "old mans," and finish up with a paragraph from Washington's Farewell Address; but when I'd finished I could go to a good restaurant and enjoy my dinner as usual. If my second cousin's husband had an artery severed while having his nails manicured, I will not deny that it was a matter of considerable regret to me. But when I heard the news I did *not* faint and have to be taken home in a passing laundry wagon.

In fact I was pretty much invulnerable. I put up a conventional wail whenever a ship was sunk or a train got wrecked; but I don't suppose, if the whole city of Chicago had been wiped out, I'd have lost a night's sleep over it—unless something led me to believe that St. Paul was the next city on the list. Even then I could have moved my luggage over to Minneapolis and rested pretty comfortably all night.

But that was three years ago when I was still a young man. I was only twenty-two. When I said anything the book reviewers didn't like, they could say, "Gosh! That certainly is callow!" And that finished me. Label it "callow," and that was enough.

Well, now I'm twenty-five I'm not callow any longer—at least not so that I can notice it when I look in an ordinary mirror. Instead, I'm vulnerable. I'm vulnerable in every way.

For the benefit of revenue agents and moving-picture directors who may be reading this magazine I will explain that vulnerable means easily wounded. Well, that's it. I'm more easily
wounded. I can not only be wounded in the chest, the feelings,
the teeth, the bank account; but I can be wounded in the *dog*.
Do I make myself clear? In the dog.

No, that isn't a new part of the body just discovered by
the Rockefeller Institute. I mean a real dog. I mean if anyone gives my family dog to the dog-catcher he's hurting *me*
almost as much as he's hurting the dog. He's hurting me
in the dog. And if our doctor says to me tomorrow, "That
child of yours isn't going to be a blonde after all," well, he's
wounded me in a way I couldn't have been wounded in
before, because I never before had a child to be wounded in.
And if my daughter grows up and when she's sixteen elopes
with some fellow from Zion City who believes the world is
flat—I wouldn't write this except that she's only six months
old and can't quite read yet, so it won't put any ideas in her
head—why, then I'll be wounded again.

About being wounded through your wife I will not enter
into, as it is a delicate subject. I will not say anything about my
case. But I have private reasons for knowing that if anybody said
to your wife one day that it was a shame she *would* wear yellow
when it made her look so peaked, you would suffer violently,
within six hours afterward, for what that person said.

"Attack him through his wife!" "Kidnap his child!" "Tie a tin
can to his dog's tail!" How often do we hear those slogans in life,
not to mention in the movies. And how they make me wince!
Three years ago, you could have yelled them outside my window
all through a summer night, and I wouldn't have batted an eye.
The only thing that would have aroused me would have been:
"Wait a minute. I think I can pot him from here."

I used to have about ten square feet of skin vulnerable to
chills and fevers. Now I have about twenty. I have not personally
enlarged—the twenty feet includes the skin of my family—but
I might as well have, because if a chill or fever strikes any bit of
that twenty feet of skin *I* begin to shiver.

And so I ooze gently into middle age; for the true middle age
is not the acquirement of years, but the acquirement of a family. The incomes of the childless have wonderful elasticity. Two

people require a room and a bath; couple with child requires the millionaire's suite on the sunny side of the hotel.

So let me start the religious part of this article by saying that if the Editor thought he was going to get something young and happy—yes, and callow—I have got to refer him to my daughter, if she will give dictation. If anybody thinks that I am callow they ought to see her—she's so callow it makes me laugh. It even makes her laugh, too, to think how callow she is. If any literary critics saw her they'd have a nervous breakdown right on the spot. But, on the other hand, anybody writing to me, an editor or anybody else, is writing to a middle-aged man.

Well, I'm twenty-five, and I have to admit that I'm pretty well satisfied with *some* of that time. That is to say, the first five years seemed to go all right—but the last twenty! They have been a matter of violently contrasted extremes. In fact, this has struck me so forcibly that from time to time I have kept charts, trying to figure out the years when I was closest to happy. Then I get mad and tear up the charts.

Skipping that long list of mistakes which passes for my boyhood I will say that I went away to preparatory school at fifteen, and that my two years there were wasted, were years of utter and profitless unhappiness. I was unhappy because I was cast into a situation where everybody thought I ought to behave just as they behaved—and I didn't have the courage to shut up and go my own way, anyhow.

For example, there was a rather dull boy at school named Percy, whose approval, I felt, for some unfathomable reason, I must have. So, for the sake of this negligible cipher, I started out to let as much of my mind as I had under mild cultivation sink back into a state of heavy underbrush. I spent hours in a damp gymnasium fooling around with a muggy basket-ball and working myself into a damp, muggy rage, when I wanted, instead, to go walking in the country.

And all this to please Percy. He thought it was the thing to do. If you didn't go through the damp business every day you were "morbid." That was his favorite word, and it had me frightened. I didn't want to be morbid. So I became muggy instead.

Besides, Percy was dull in classes; so I used to pretend to be dull also. When I wrote stories I wrote them secretly, and felt like a criminal. If I gave birth to any idea that did not appeal to

Percy's pleasant, vacant mind I discarded the idea at once and felt like apologizing.

Of course Percy never got into college. He went to work and I have scarcely seen him since, though I understand that he has since become an undertaker of considerable standing. The time I spent with him was wasted; but, worse than that, I did not enjoy the wasting of it. At least, he had nothing to give me, and I had not the faintest reasons for caring what he thought or said. But when I discovered this it was too late.

The worst of it is that this same business went on until I was twenty-two. That is, I'd be perfectly happy doing just what I wanted to do, when somebody would begin shaking his head and saying:

"Now see here, Fitzgerald, you mustn't go on doing that. It's—it's morbid."

And I was always properly awed by the word "morbid," so I quit what I wanted to do and what it was good for me to do, and did what some other fellow wanted me to do. Every once in awhile, though, I used to tell somebody to go to the devil; otherwise I never would have done anything at all.

In officers' training camp during 1917 I started to write a novel. I would begin work at it every Saturday afternoon at one and work like mad until midnight. Then I would work at it from six Sunday morning until six Sunday night, when I had to report back to barracks. I was thoroughly enjoying myself.

After a month three friends came to me with scowling faces:

"See here, Fitzgerald, you ought to use the weekends in getting some good rest and recreation. The way you use them is—is morbid!"

That word convinced me. It sent the usual shiver down my spine. The next weekend I laid the novel aside, went into town with the others and danced all night at a party. But I began to worry about my novel. I worried so much that I returned to camp, not rested, but utterly miserable. I *was* morbid then. But I never went to town again. I finished the novel. It was rejected; but a year later I rewrote it and it was published under the title "This Side of Paradise."

But before I rewrote it I had a list of "morbids," chalked up against people that, placed end to end, would have reached to the nearest lunatic asylum. It was morbid:

1st. To get engaged without enough money to marry

2d. To leave the advertising business after three months

3d. To want to write at all

4th. To think I could

5th. To write about "silly little boys and girls that nobody wants to read about."

And so on, until a year later, when I found to my surprise that everybody had been only kidding—they had believed all their lives that writing was the only thing for me, and had hardly been able to keep from telling me all the time.

But I am really not old enough to begin drawing morals out of my own life to elevate the young. I will save that pastime until I am sixty; and then, as I have said, I will concoct a Scott Fitzgerald who will make Benjamin Franklin look like a lucky devil who loafed into prominence. Even in the above account I have managed to sketch the outline of a small but neat halo. I take it all back. I am twenty-five years old. I wish I had ten million dollars, and never had to do another lick of work as long as I live.

But as I *do* have to keep at it, I might as well declare that the chief thing I've learned so far is: If you don't know much— well, nobody else knows much more. And nobody knows half as much about your own interests as *you* know.

If you believe in anything very strongly—including yourself— and if you go after that thing alone, you end up in jail, in heaven, in the headlines, or in the largest house in the block, according to what you started after. If you *don't* believe in anything very strongly—including yourself—you go along, and enough money is made out of you to buy an automobile for some other fellow's son, and you marry if you've got time, and if you do you have a lot of children, whether you have time or not, and finally you get tired and you die.

If you're in the second of those two classes you have the most fun before you're twenty-five. If you're in the first, you have it afterward.

You see, if you're in the first class you'll frequently be called a darn fool—or worse. That was as true in Philadelphia about 1727 as it is today. Anybody knows that a kid that walked around town munching a loaf of bread and not caring what anybody thought was a darn fool. It stands to reason! But there are a lot of darn fools who get their pictures in the schoolbooks—with their names under the pictures. And the sensible fellows, the ones that had time to laugh, well, their pictures are in there, too. But their *names* aren't—and the laughs look sort of frozen on their faces.

The particular sort of darn fool I mean ought to remember that he's *least* a darn fool when he's being *called* a darn fool. The main thing is to be your own kind of a darn fool.

(The above advice is of course only for darn fools *under* twenty-five. It may be all wrong for darn fools over twenty-five.)

I don't know why it is that when I start to write about being twenty-five I suddenly begin to write about darn fools. I do not see any connection. Now, if I were asked to write about darn fools, I would write about people who have their front teeth filled with gold, because a friend of mine did that the other day, and after being mistaken for a jewelry store three times in one hour he came up and asked me if I thought it showed too much. As I am a kind man, I told him I would not have noticed it if the sun hadn't been so strong on it. I asked him why he had it done.

"Well," he said, "the dentist told me a porcelain filling never lasted more than ten years."

"Ten years! Why, you may be dead in ten years."

"That's true."

"Of course it'll be nice that all the time you're in your coffin you'll never have to worry about your teeth."

And it occurred to me that about half the people in the world are always having their front teeth filled with gold. That is, they're figuring on twenty years from now. Well, when you're young it's all right figuring your success a long ways ahead—if you don't make it *too* long. But as for your pleasure—your front teeth!—it's better to figure on today.

And that's the second thing I learned while getting vulnerable and middle-aged. Let me recapitulate:

1st. I think that compared to what you know about your own business nobody else knows *any*thing. And if anybody knows more about it than you do, then it's *his* business and you're *his* man, not your own. And as soon as your business becomes *your* business you'll know more about it than anybody else.

2d. Never have your front teeth filled with gold.

And now I will stop pretending to be a pleasant young fellow and disclose my real nature. I will prove to you, if you have not found it out already, that I have a mean streak and nobody would like to have me for a son.

I do not like old people. They are always talking about their "experience"—and very few of them have any. In fact, most of them go on making the same mistakes at fifty and believing in the same white list of approved twenty-carat lies that they did at seventeen. And it all starts with my old friend vulnerability.

Take a woman of thirty. She is considered lucky if she has allied herself to a multitude of things; her husband, her children, her home, her servant. If she has three homes, eight children, and fourteen servants, she is considered luckier still. (This, of course, does not generally apply to more husbands.)

Now, when she was young she worried only about herself; but now she must be worried by *any* trouble occurring to *any* of these people or things. She is ten times as vulnerable. Moreover, she can never break one of these ties or relieve herself of one of these burdens except at the cost of great pain and sorrow to herself. They are the things that break her, and yet they are the most precious things in life.

In consequence, everything which doesn't go to make her secure, or at least to give her a sense of security, startles and annoys her. She acquires only the useless knowledge found in cheap movies, cheap novels, and the cheap memoirs of titled foreigners.

By this time her husband also has become suspicious of anything gay or new. He seldom addresses her, except in a series of profound grunts, or to ask whether she has sent his shirts out to the laundry. At the family dinner on Sunday he occasionally gives her some fascinating statistics on party politics, some opinions from that morning's newspaper editorial.

But after thirty, both husband and wife know in their hearts that the game is up. Without a few cocktails social intercourse becomes a torment. It is no longer spontaneous; it is a convention by which they agree to shut their eyes to the fact that the other men and women they know are tired and dull and fat, and yet must be put up with as politely as they themselves are put up with in their turn.

I have seen many happy young couples—but I have seldom seen a happy home after husband and wife are thirty. Most homes can be divided into four classes:

1st. Where the husband is a pretty conceited guy who thinks that a dinky insurance business is a lot harder than raising babies, and that everybody ought to kow-tow to him at home. He is the kind whose sons usually get away from home as soon as they can walk.

2d. When the wife has got a sharp tongue and the martyr complex, and thinks she's the only woman in the world that ever had a child. This is probably the unhappiest home of all.

3d. Where the children are always being reminded how nice it was of the parents to bring them into the world, and how they ought to respect their parents for being born in 1870 instead of 1902.

4th. Where everything is for the children. Where the parents pay much more for the children's education than they can afford, and spoil them unreasonably. This usually ends by the children being ashamed of the parents.

And yet I think that marriage is the most satisfactory institution we have. I'm simply stating my belief that when Life has used us for its purposes it takes away all our attractive qualities and gives us, instead, ponderous but shallow convictions of our own wisdom and "experience."

Needless to say, as old people run the world, an enormous camouflage has been built up to hide the fact that only young people are attractive or important.

Having got in wrong with many of the readers of this article, I will now proceed to close. If you don't agree with me on any minor points you have a right to say: "Gosh! He certainly is callow!" and turn to something else. Personally I do not consider that I am callow, because I do not see how anybody of my age could be callow. For instance, I was reading an article in this magazine a few months ago by a fellow named Ring Lardner that says he is thirty-five, and it seemed to me how young and happy and carefree he was in comparison with me.

Maybe he is vulnerable, too. He did not say so. Maybe when you get to be thirty-five you do not *know* any more how vulnerable you *are*. All I can say is that if he ever gets to be twenty-five again, which is very unlikely, maybe he will agree with me. The older I grow the more I get so I don't know anything. If I had been asked to do this article about five years ago it might have been worth reading.

How to Live on $36,000 a Year

"YOU ought to start saving money," The Young Man With a Future assured me just the other day. "You think it's smart to live up to your income. Someday you'll land in the poorhouse."

I was bored, but I knew he was going to tell me anyhow, so I asked him what I'd better do.

"It's very simple," he answered impatiently; "only you establish a trust fund where you can't get your money if you try."

I had heard this before. It is System Number 999. I tried System Number 1 at the very beginning of my literary career four years ago. A month before I was married I went to a broker and asked his advice about investing some money.

"It's only a thousand," I admitted, "but I feel I ought to begin to save right now."

He considered.

"You don't want Liberty Bonds," he said. "They're too easy to turn into cash. You want a good, sound, conservative investment, but also you want it where you can't get at it every five minutes."

He finally selected a bond for me that paid 7 per cent and wasn't listed on the market. I turned over my thousand dollars, and my career of amassing capital began that day.

On that day, also, it ended.

My wife and I were married in New York in the spring of 1920, when prices were higher than they had been within the memory of man. In the light of after events it seems fitting that our career should have started at that precise point in time. I had just received a large check from the movies and I felt a little patronizing toward the millionaires riding down Fifth Avenue in their limousines—because my income had a way of doubling every month. This was actually the case. It had done so for several months—I had made only thirty-five dollars the previous August, while here in April I was making three thousand—and it seemed as if it was going to do so forever. At the end of the year it must reach half a million. Of course with such a state of affairs, economy seemed a waste of time. So we went to live at the most expensive hotel in New York, intending to wait there until enough money accumulated for a trip abroad.

To make a long story short, after we had been married for three months I found one day to my horror that I didn't have a dollar in the world, and the weekly hotel bill for two hundred dollars would be due next day.

I remember the mixed feelings with which I issued from the bank on hearing the news.

"What's the matter?" demanded my wife anxiously, as I joined her on the sidewalk. "You look depressed."

"I'm not depressed," I answered cheerfully; "I'm just surprised. We haven't got any money."

"Haven't got any money," she repeated calmly, and we began to walk up the Avenue in a sort of trance. "Well, let's go to the movies," she suggested jovially.

It all seemed so tranquil that I was not a bit cast down. The cashier had not even scowled at me. I had walked in and said to him, "How much money have I got?" And he had looked in a big book and answered, "None."

That was all. There were no harsh words, no blows. And I knew that there was nothing to worry about. I was now a successful author, and when successful authors ran out of money all they had to do was to sign checks. I wasn't poor—they couldn't fool me. Poverty meant being depressed and living in a small remote room and eating at a *rôtisserie* on the corner, while I— why, it was impossible that I should be poor! I was living at the best hotel in New York!

My first step was to try to sell my only possession—my $1000 bond. It was the first of many times I made the attempt. In all financial crises, I dig it out and with it go hopefully to the bank, supposing that, as it never fails to pay the proper interest, it has at last assumed a tangible value. But as I have never been able to sell it, it has gradually acquired the sacredness of a family heirloom. It is always referred to by my wife as "your bond," and it was once turned in at the Subway offices after I left it by accident on a car seat!

This particular crisis passed next morning when the discovery that publishers sometimes advance royalties sent me hurriedly to mine. So the only lesson I learned from it was that my money

usually turns up somewhere in time of need, and that at the
worst you can always borrow—a lesson that would make Benjamin Franklin turn over in his grave.

For the first three years of our marriage our income averaged
a little more than $20,000 a year. We indulged in such luxuries
as a baby and a trip to Europe, and always money seemed to
come easier and easier with less and less effort, until we felt
that with just a little more margin to come and go on we could
begin to save.

We left the Middle West and moved east to a town about
fifteen miles from New York, where we rented a house for $300
a month. We hired a nurse for $90 a month; a man and his
wife—they acted as butler, chauffeur, yard man, cook, parlor
maid and chambermaid—for $160 a month; and a laundress,
who came twice a week, for $36 a month. This year of 1923, we
told each other, was to be our saving year. We were going to
earn $24,000, and live on $18,000, thus giving us a surplus of
$6000 with which to buy safety and security for our old age. We
were going to do better at last.

Now as everyone knows, when you want to do better you
first buy a book and print your name in the front of it in capital
letters. So my wife bought a book, and every bill that came to
the house was carefully entered in it, so that we could watch
living expenses and cut them away to almost nothing—or at
least to $1500 a month.

We had, however, reckoned without our town. It is one of
those little towns springing up on all sides of New York which
are built especially for those who have made money suddenly
but have never had money before.

My wife and I are, of course, members of this newly rich class.
That is to say, five years ago we had no money at all, and what we
now do away with would have seemed like inestimable riches to
us then. I have at times suspected that we are the only newly rich
people in America, that in fact we are the very couple at whom
all the articles about the newly rich were aimed.

Now when you say "newly rich" you picture a middle-aged
and corpulent man who has a tendency to remove his collar at
formal dinners and is in perpetual hot water with his ambitious
wife and her titled friends. As a member of the newly rich class,
I assure you that this picture is entirely libelous. I myself, for

example, am a mild, slightly used young man of twenty-seven, and what corpulence I may have developed is for the present a strictly confidential matter between my tailor and me. We once dined with a bona fide nobleman, but we were both far too frightened to take off our collars or even to demand corned beef and cabbage. Nevertheless we live in a town especially prepared for keeping money in circulation.

When we came here, a year ago, there were, all together, seven merchants engaged in the purveyance of food—three grocers, three butchers and a fishman. But when the word went around in food-purveying circles that the town was filling up with the recently enriched as fast as houses could be built for them, the rush of butchers, grocers, fishmen and delicatessen men became enormous. Trainloads of them arrived daily with signs and scales in hand to stake out a claim and sprinkle sawdust upon it. It was like the gold rush of '49, or a big bonanza of the '70's. Older and larger cities were denuded of their stores. Inside of a year eighteen food dealers had set up shop in our main street and might be seen any day waiting in their doorways with alluring and deceitful smiles.

Having long been somewhat overcharged by the seven previous food purveyors we all naturally rushed to the new men, who made it known by large numerical signs in their windows that they intended practically to give food away. But once we were snared, the prices began to rise alarmingly, until all of us scurried like frightened mice from one new man to another, seeking only justice, and seeking it in vain.

What had happened, of course, was that there were too many food purveyors for the population. It was absolutely impossible for eighteen of them to subsist on the town and at the same time charge moderate prices. So each was waiting for some of the others to give up and move away; meanwhile the only way the rest of them could carry their loans from the bank was by selling things at two or three times the prices in the city fifteen miles away. And that is how our town became the most expensive one in the world.

Now in magazine articles people always get together and found community stores, but none of us would consider such a step. It would absolutely ruin us with our neighbors, who would suspect that we actually cared about our money. When I suggested one day to a local lady of wealth—whose husband, by the way, is reputed to have made his money by vending illicit liquids—that I start a community store known as "F. Scott Fitzgerald—Fresh Meats," she was horrified. So the idea was abandoned.

But in spite of the groceries, we began the year in high hopes. My first play was to be presented in the autumn, and even if living in the East forced our expenses a little over $1500 a month, the play would easily make up for the difference. We knew what colossal sums were earned on play royalties, and just to be sure, we asked several playwrights what was the maximum that could be earned on a year's run. I never allowed myself to be rash. I took a sum halfway between the maximum and the minimum, and put that down as what we could fairly count on its earning. I think my figures came to about $100,000.

It was a pleasant year; we always had this delightful event of the play to look forward to. When the play succeeded we could buy a house, and saving money would be so easy that we could do it blindfolded with both hands tied behind our backs.

As if in happy anticipation we had a small windfall in March from an unexpected source—a moving picture—and for almost the first time in our lives we had enough surplus to buy some bonds. Of course we had "my" bond, and every six months I clipped the little coupon and cashed it, but we were so used to it that we never counted it as money. It was simply a warning never to tie up cash where we couldn't get at it in time of need.

No, the thing to buy was Liberty Bonds, and we bought four of them. It was a very exciting business. I descended to a shining and impressive room downstairs, and under the chaperonage of a guard deposited my $4000 in Liberty Bonds, together with "my" bond, in a little tin box to which I alone had the key.

I left the bank, feeling decidedly solid. I had at last accumulated a capital. I hadn't exactly accumulated it, but there it was anyhow, and if I had died next day it would have yielded my wife $212 a year for life—or for just as long as she cared to live on that amount.

"That," I said to myself with some satisfaction, "is what is called providing for the wife and children. Now all I have to do is to deposit the $100,000 from my play and then we're through with worry forever."

I found that from this time on I had less tendency to worry about current expenses. What if we did spend a few hundred too much now and then? What if our grocery bills did vary mysteriously from $85 to $165 a month, according as to how closely we watched the kitchen? Didn't I have bonds in the bank? Trying to keep under $1500 a month the way things were going was merely niggardly. We were going to save on a scale that would make such petty economies seem like counting pennies.

The coupons on "my" bond are always sent to an office on lower Broadway. Where Liberty Bond coupons are sent I never had a chance to find out, as I didn't have the pleasure of clipping any. Two of them I was unfortunately compelled to dispose of just one month after I first locked them up. I had begun a new novel, you see, and it occurred to me it would be much better business in the end to keep at the novel and live on the Liberty Bonds while I was writing it. Unfortunately the novel progressed slowly, while the Liberty Bonds went at an alarming rate of speed. The novel was interrupted whenever there was any sound above a whisper in the house, while the Liberty Bonds were never interrupted at all.

And the summer drifted too. It was an exquisite summer and it became a habit with many world-weary New Yorkers to pass their weekends at the Fitzgerald house in the country. Along near the end of a balmy and insidious August I realized with a shock that only three chapters of my novel were done—and in the little tin safety-deposit vault, only "my" bond remained. There it lay—paying storage on itself and a few dollars more. But never mind; in a little while the box would be bursting with savings. I'd have to hire a twin box next door.

But the play was going into rehearsal in two months. To tide over the interval there were two courses open to me—I could sit down and write some short stories or I could continue to work on the novel and borrow the money to live on. Lulled into a sense of security by our sanguine anticipations I decided on the latter course, and my publishers lent me enough to pay our bills until the opening night.

So I went back to my novel, and the months and money melted away; but one morning in October I sat in the cold interior of a New York theatre and heard the cast read through the first act of my play. It was magnificent; my estimate had been too low. I could almost hear the people scrambling for seats, hear the ghostly voices of the movie magnates as they bid against one another for the picture rights. The novel was now laid aside; my days were spent at the theatre and my nights in revising and improving the two or three little weak spots in what was to be the success of the year.

The time approached and life became a breathless affair. The November bills came in, were glanced at, and punched onto a bill file on the bookcase. More important questions were in the air. A disgusted letter arrived from an editor telling me I had written only two short stories during the entire year. But what did that matter? The main thing was that our second comedian got the wrong intonation in his first-act exit line.

The play opened in Atlantic City in November. It was a colossal frost. People left their seats and walked out, people rustled their programs and talked audibly in bored impatient whispers. After the second act I wanted to stop the show and say it was all a mistake but the actors struggled heroically on.

There was a fruitless week of patching and revising, and then we gave up and came home. To my profound astonishment the year, the great year, was almost over. I was $5000 in debt, and my one idea was to get in touch with a reliable poorhouse where we could hire a room and bath for nothing a week. But one satisfaction nobody could take from us. We had spent $36,000, and purchased for one year the right to be members of the newly rich class. What more can money buy?

The first move, of course, was to get out "my" bond, take it to the bank and offer it for sale. A very nice old man at a shining table was firm as to its value as security, but he promised that if I became overdrawn he would call me up on the phone and give me a chance to make good. No, he never went to lunch with depositors. He considered writers a shiftless class, he said, and assured me that the whole bank was absolutely burglarproof from cellar to roof.

Too discouraged even to put the bond back in the now yawning deposit box, I tucked it gloomily into my pocket and went home. There was no help for it—I must go to work. I had exhausted my resources and there was nothing else to do. In the train I listed all our possessions on which, if it came to that, we could possibly raise money. Here is the list:

1 Oil stove, damaged.
9 Electric lamps, all varieties.
2 Bookcases with books to match.
1 Cigarette humidor, made by a convict.
2 Framed crayon portraits of my wife and me.
1 Medium-priced automobile, 1921 model.
1 Bond, par value $1000; actual value unknown.

"Let's cut down expenses right away," began my wife when I reached home. "There's a new grocery in town where you pay cash and everything costs only half what it does anywhere else. I can take the car every morning and—"

"Cash!" I began to laugh at this. "Cash!"

The one thing it was impossible for us to do now was to pay cash. It was too late to pay cash. We had no cash to pay. We should rather have gone down on our knees and thanked the butcher and grocer for letting us charge. An enormous economic fact became clear to me at that moment—the rarity of cash, the latitude of choice that cash allows.

"Well," she remarked thoughtfully, "that's too bad. But at least we don't need three servants. We'll get a Japanese to do general housework, and I'll be nurse for awhile until you get us out of danger."

"Let them go?" I demanded incredulously. "But we can't let them go! We'd have to pay them an extra two weeks each. Why, to get them out of the house would cost us $125—in cash! Besides, it's nice to have the butler; if we have an awful smash we can send him up to New York to hold us a place in the bread line."

"Well, then, how can we economize?"

"We can't. We're too poor to economize. Economy is a luxury. We could have economized last summer—but now our only salvation is in extravagance."

"How about a smaller house?"

"Impossible! Moving is the most expensive thing in the world; and besides, I couldn't work during the confusion. No," I went on, "I'll just have to get out of this mess the only way I know how, by making more money. Then when we've got something in the bank we can decide what we'd better do."

Over our garage is a large bare room whither I now retired with pencil, paper and the oil stove, emerging the next afternoon at five o'clock with a 7000-word story. That was something; it would pay the rent and last month's overdue bills. It took twelve hours a day for five weeks to rise from abject poverty back into the middle class, but within that time we had paid our debts, and the cause for immediate worry was over.

But I was far from satisfied with the whole affair. A young man can work at excessive speed with no ill effects, but youth is unfortunately not a permanent condition of life.

I wanted to find out where the $36,000 had gone. Thirty-six thousand is not very wealthy—not yacht-and-Palm-Beach wealthy—but it sounds to me as though it should buy a roomy house full of furniture, a trip to Europe once a year, and a bond or two besides. But our $36,000 had bought nothing at all.

So I dug up my miscellaneous account books, and my wife dug up her complete household record for the year 1923, and we made out the monthly average. Here it is:

HOUSEHOLD EXPENSES

	APPORTIONED PER MONTH
Income tax	$198.00
Food	202.00
Rent	300.00
Coal, wood, ice, gas, light, phone and water	114.50
Servants	295.00
Golf clubs	105.50
Clothes—three people	158.00
Doctor and dentist	42.50
Drugs and cigarettes	32.50
Automobile	25.00
Books	14.50
All other household expenses	112.50
Total	$1,600.00

"Well, that's not bad," we thought when we had got thus far. "Some of the items are pretty high, especially food and servants.

But there's about everything accounted for, and it's only a little more than half our income."

Then we worked out the average monthly expenditures that could be included under pleasure.

Hotel bills—this meant spending the night or
  charging meals in New York $51.00
Trips—only two, but apportioned per month 43.00
Theatre tickets 55.00
Barber and hairdresser.. 25.00
Charity and loans 15.00
Taxis 15.00
Gambling—this dark heading covers bridge,
  craps and football bets 33.00
Restaurant parties.. 70.00
Entertaining... 70.00
Miscellaneous.. 23.00

Total $400.00

Some of these items were pretty high. They will seem higher to a Westerner than to a New Yorker. Fifty-five dollars for theatre tickets means between three and five shows a month, depending on the type of show and how long it's been running. Football games are also included in this, as well as ringside seats to the Dempsey-Firpo fight. As for the amount marked "restaurant parties"—$70 would perhaps take three couples to a popular after-theatre cabaret—but it would be a close shave.

We added the items marked "pleasure" to the items marked "household expenses," and obtained a monthly total.

"Fine," I said. "Just $3000. Now at least we'll know where to cut down, because we know where it goes."

She frowned; then a puzzled, awed expression passed over her face.

"What's the matter?" I demanded. "Isn't it all right? Are some of the items wrong?"

"It isn't the items," she said staggeringly; "it's the total. This only adds up to $2000 a month."

I was incredulous, but she nodded.

"But listen," I protested; "my bank statements show that we've spent $3000 a month. You don't mean to say that every month we lose $1000?"

"This only adds up to $2000," she protested, "so we must have."

"Give me the pencil."

For an hour I worked over the accounts in silence, but to no avail.

"Why, this is impossible!" I insisted. "People don't lose $12,000 in a year. It's just—it's just missing."

There was a ring at the doorbell and I walked over to answer it, still dazed by these figures. It was the Banklands, our neighbors from over the way.

"Good heavens!" I announced. "We've just lost $12,000!"

Bankland stepped back alertly.

"Burglars?" he inquired.

"Ghosts," answered my wife.

Mrs. Bankland looked nervously around.

"Really?"

We explained the situation, the mysterious third of our income that had vanished into thin air.

"Well, what we do," said Mrs. Bankland, "is, we have a budget."

"We have a budget," agreed Bankland, "and we stick absolutely to it. If the skies fall we don't go over any item of that budget. That's the only way to live sensibly and save money."

"That's what we ought to do," I agreed.

Mrs. Bankland nodded enthusiastically.

"It's a wonderful scheme," she went on. "We make a certain deposit every month, and all I save on it I can have for myself to do anything I want with."

I could see that my own wife was visibly excited.

"That's what I want to do," she broke out suddenly. "Have a budget. Everybody does it that has any sense."

"I pity anyone that doesn't use that system," said Bankland solemnly. "Think of the inducement to economy—the extra money my wife'll have for clothes."

"How much have you saved so far?" my wife inquired eagerly of Mrs. Bankland.

"So far?" repeated Mrs. Bankland. "Oh, I haven't had a chance so far. You see we only began the system yesterday."

"Yesterday!" we cried.

"Just yesterday," agreed Bankland darkly. "But I wish to heaven I'd started it a year ago. I've been working over our accounts all week, and do you know, Fitzgerald, every month there's $2000 I can't account for to save my soul."

Our financial troubles are now over. We have permanently left the newly rich class and installed the budget system. It is simple and sensible, and I can explain it to you in a few words. You consider your income as an enormous pie all cut up into slices, each slice representing one class of expenses. Somebody has worked it all out; so you know just what proportion of your income you can spend on each slice. There is even a slice for founding universities, if you go in for that.

For instance, the amount you spend on the theatre should be half your drug-store bill. This will enable us to see one play every five and a half months, or two and a half plays a year. We have already picked out the first one, but if it isn't running five and a half months from now we shall be that much ahead. Our allowance for newspapers should be only a quarter of what we spend on self-improvement, so we are considering whether to get the Sunday paper once a month or to subscribe for an almanac.

According to the budget we will be allowed only three-quarters of a servant, so we are on the lookout for a one-legged cook who can come six days a week. And apparently the author of the budget book lives in a town where you can still go to the movies for a nickel and get a shave for a dime. But we are going to give up the expenditure called "Foreign missions, etc.," and apply it to the life of crime instead. Altogether, outside of the fact that there is no slice allowed for "missing" it seems to be a very complete book, and according to the testimonials in the back, if we make $36,000 again this year, the chances are that we'll save at least $35,000.

"But we can't get any of that first $36,000 back," I complained around the house. "If we just had something to show for it I wouldn't feel so absurd."

My wife thought a long while.

"The only thing you can do," she said finally, "is to write a magazine article and call it 'How to Live on $36,000 a Year.'"

"What a silly suggestion!" I replied coldly.

How to Live on Practically Nothing a Year

"ALL right," I said hopefully, "what did it come to for the month?" "Two thousand three hundred and twenty dollars and eighty-two cents."

It was the fifth of five long months during which we had tried by every device we knew of to bring the figure of our expenditures safely below the figure of our income. We had succeeded in buying less clothes, less food and fewer luxuries— in fact, we had succeeded in everything except in saving money.

"Let's give up," said my wife gloomily. "Look—here's another bill I haven't even opened."

"It isn't a bill—it's got a French stamp."

It was a letter. I read it aloud and when I finished we looked at each other in a wild expectant way.

"I don't see why everybody doesn't come over here," it said. "I am now writing from a little inn in France where I just had a meal fit for a king, washed down with champagne, for the absurd sum of sixty-one cents. It costs about one-tenth as much to live over here. From where I sit I can see the smoky peaks of the Alps rising behind a town that was old before Alexander the Great was born—"

By the time we had read the letter for the third time we were in our car bound for New York. As we rushed into the steamship office half an hour later, overturning a rolltop desk and bumping an office boy up against the wall, the agent looked up with mild surprise.

"Don't utter a word," he said. "You're the twelfth this morning and I understand. You've just got a letter from a friend in Europe telling you how cheap everything is and you want to sail right away. How many?"

"One child," we told him breathlessly.

"Good!" he exclaimed, spreading out a deck of cards on his flat table. "The suits read that you are going on a long unexpected journey, that you have illness ahead of you and that you will soon meet a number of dark men and women who mean you no good."

As we threw him heavily from the window his voice floated up to us from somewhere between the sixteenth story and the street:

"You sail one week from tomorrow."

II

Now when a family goes abroad to economize, they don't go to the Wembley exhibition or the Olympic games—in fact they don't go to London and Paris at all but hasten to the Riviera, which is the southern coast of France and which is reputed to be the cheapest as well as the most beautiful locality in the world. Moreover we were going to the Riviera *out of season,* which is something like going to Palm Beach for July. When the Riviera season finishes in late spring, all the wealthy British and Americans move up to Deauville and Trouville, and all the gambling houses and fashionable milliners and jewelers and second-story men close up their establishments and follow their quarry north. Immediately prices fall. The native Rivierans, who have been living on rice and fish all winter, come out of their caves and buy a bottle of red wine and splash about for a bit in their own blue sea.

For two reformed spendthrifts the Riviera in summer had exactly the right sound. So we put our house in the hands of six real-estate agents and steamed off to France amid the deafening applause of a crowd of friends on the dock—both of whom waved wildly until we were out of sight.

We felt that we had escaped—from extravagance and clamor and from all the wild extremes among which we had dwelt for five hectic years, from the tradesman who laid for us and the nurse who bullied us and the "couple" who kept our house for us and knew us all too well. We were going to the Old World to find a new rhythm for our lives, with a true conviction that we had left our old selves behind forever,—and with a capital of just over seven thousand dollars.

The sun coming through high French windows woke us one week later. Outside we could hear the high clear honk of strange auto-horns and we remembered that we were in Paris. The baby was already sitting up in her cot ringing the bells which summoned the different *fonctionnaires* of the hotel as though she had determined to start the day immediately. It was indeed *her* day, for we were in Paris for no other reason than to get her a nurse.

"*Entrez!*" we shouted together as there was a knock at the door.

A handsome waiter opened it and stepped inside whereupon our child ceased her harmonizing upon the bells and regarded him with marked disfavor.

"Iss a madamoselle who waited out in the street," he remarked.

"Speak French," I said sternly. "We're all French here."

He spoke French for some time.

"All right," I interrupted after a moment. "Now say that again very slowly in English; I didn't quite understand."

"His name's Entrez," remarked the baby helpfully.

"Be that as it may," I flared up, "his French strikes me as very bad."

We discovered finally that an English governess was outside to answer our advertisement in the paper.

"Tell her to come in."

After an interval a tall, languid person in a Rue de la Paix hat strolled into the room and we tried to look as dignified as is possible when sitting up in bed.

"You're Americans?" she said, seating herself with scornful care.

"Yes."

"I understand you want a nurse. Is this the child?"

"Yes, ma'am."

(Here is some high-born lady of the English court, we thought, in temporarily reduced circumstances.)

"I've had a great deal of experience," she said, advancing upon our child and attempting unsuccessfully to take her hand. "I'm practically a trained nurse; I'm a lady born and I never complain."

"Complain of what?" demanded my wife.

The applicant waved her hand vaguely.

"Oh, the food, for example."

"Look here," I asked suspiciously, "before we go any further, let me ask what salary you've been getting."

"For you," she hesitated, "one hundred dollars a month."

"Oh, you wouldn't have to do the cooking too," we assured her; "it's just to take care of one child."

She arose and adjusted her feather boa with fine scorn.

"You'd better get a French nurse," she said, "if you're *that* kind of people. She won't open the windows at night and your baby will never learn the French word for 'tub' but you'll only have to pay her ten dollars a month."

"Good-bye," we said together.

"I'll come for fifty."

"Good-bye," we repeated.

"For forty,—and I'll do the baby's washing."

"We wouldn't take you for your board."

The hotel trembled slightly as she closed the door.

"Where's the lady gone?" asked our child.

"She's hunting Americans," we said. "She looked in the hotel register and thought she saw Chicago written after our names."

We are always witty like that with the baby—she considers us the most amusing couple she has ever known.

After breakfast I went to the Paris branch of our American bank to get money, but I had no sooner entered it than I wished myself at the hotel, or at least that I had gone in by the back way, for I had evidently been recognized and an enormous crowd began to gather outside. The crowd grew and I considered going to the window and making them a speech but I thought that might only increase the disturbance so I looked around intending to ask someone's advice. I recognized no one, however, except one of the bank officials and a Mr. and Mrs. Douglas Fairbanks from America, who were buying francs at a counter in the rear. So I decided not to show myself and, sure enough, by the time I had cashed my check the crowd had given up and melted away.

I think now that we did well to get away from Paris in nine days—which, after all, was only a week more than we had intended. Every morning a new boat-load of Americans poured into the boulevards and every afternoon our room at the hotel was filled with familiar faces until, except that there was no faint taste of wood-alcohol in the refreshments, we might have been in New York. But at last, with six thousand five hundred dollars remaining and with an English nurse whom we engaged for twenty-six dollars a month, we boarded the train for the Riviera, the hot sweet South of France.

When your eyes first fall upon the Mediterranean you know at once why it was here that man first stood erect and stretched out his arms toward the sun. It is a blue sea—or rather it is too blue for that hackneyed phrase which has described every muddy pool from pole to pole. It is the fairy blue of Maxfield Parrish's pictures, blue like blue books, blue oil, blue eyes, and in the shadow of the mountains a green belt of land runs along the coast for a hundred miles and makes a playground for the world. The Riviera! The names of its resorts, Cannes, Nice, Monte Carlo, call up the memory of a hundred kings and princes who have lost their thrones and come here to die, of mysterious rajahs and beys flinging blue diamonds to English dancing girls, of Russian millionaires tossing away fortunes at roulette in the lost caviar days before the war.

From Charles Dickens to Catherine de Medici, from Prince Edward of Wales in the height of his popularity to Oscar Wilde in the depth of his disgrace, the whole world has come here to forget or to rejoice, to hide its face or have its fling, to build white palaces out of the spoils of oppression or to write the books which sometimes batter those palaces down. Under striped awnings beside the sea grand dukes and gamblers and diplomats and noble courtesans and Balkan czars smoked their slow cigarettes while 1913 drifted into 1914 without a quiver of the calendar, and the fury gathered in the north that was to sweep three-fourths of them away.

We reached Hyères, the town of our destination, in the blazing noon, aware immediately of the tropic's breath as it oozed out of the massed pines. A cabby with a large egg-shaped carbuncle in the center of his forehead struggled with a uniformed hotel porter for the possession of our grips.

"Je suis a stranger here," I said in flawless French. "Je veux aller to le best hotel dans le town."

The porter pointed to an imposing autobus in the station drive. On the side was painted "GRAND HÔTEL DE PARIS ET DE ROME."

"Which is the best?" I asked.

For answer he picked up our heaviest grip, balanced it a moment in his hand, hit the cabby a crashing blow on the forehead—I immediately understood the gradual growth of the carbuncle—and then pressed us firmly toward the car. I tossed several nickels—or rather francs—upon the prostrate carbuncular man.

"Isn't it hot," remarked the nurse.

"I like it very much indeed," I responded, mopping my forehead and attempting a cool smile. I felt that the moral responsibility was with me—I had picked out Hyères for no more reason than that a friend had once spent a winter there. Besides we hadn't come here to keep cool—we had come here to economize, to live on practically nothing a year.

"Nevertheless, it's hot," said my wife, and a moment later the child shouted "Coat off!" in no uncertain voice.

"He must think we want to see the town," I said when, after driving for a mile along a palm-lined road, we stopped in an ancient, Mexican-looking square. "Hold on!"

This last was in alarm for he was hurriedly disembarking our baggage in front of a dilapidated quick-lunch emporium. On a ragged awning over its door were the words "GRAND HÔTEL DE PARIS ET DE ROME."

"Is this a joke?" I demanded. "Did I tell you to go to the best hotel in town?"

"Here it is," he said.

"No it isn't. This is the worst one. This is the worst hotel I ever saw."

"I am the proprietor," he said.

"I'm sorry, but we've got a baby here"—the nurse obligingly held up the baby—"and we want a more modern hotel, with a bath."

"We have a bath."

"I mean a private bath."

"We will not use while you are here. All the big hotels have shut up themselves for during the summer."

"I don't believe him for a minute," said my wife.

I looked around helplessly. Two scanty, hungry women had come out of the door and were looking voraciously at our baggage. Suddenly I heard the sound of slow hoofs and glancing up I beheld the carbuncular man driving disconsolately up the dusty street.

"What's le best hotel dans le town?" I shouted at him.

"Non, non, non, non!" he cried, waving his reins excitedly. "Jardin Hôtel open!"

"As the proprietor of the Grand Hotel of Paris and of Rome dropped my grip and started toward the cabby at a run, I turned to the hungry women accusingly.

"What do you mean by having a bus like this?" I demanded.

I felt very American and superior; I intimated that if the morals of the French people were in this decadent state I regretted that we had ever entered the war.

"Daddy's hot too," remarked the baby irrelevantly.

"I am not hot!"

"Daddy had better stop talking and find us a hotel," remarked the English nurse, "before we all melt away."

It was the work of but an hour to pay off the proprietor of the Hôtel de Paris et de Rome, to add damages for his wounded feelings and to install ourselves in the Hôtel du Jardin, on the edge of town.

"Hyères," says my guidebook, "is the very oldest and warmest of the Riviera winter resorts and is now frequented almost exclusively by the English." But when we arrived there late in May, even the English, except the very oldest and warmest, had moved away. The Hôtel du Jardin bore traces of having been inhabited—the halls were littered with innumerable old copies of the "Illustrated London News"—but now, as we found at dinner, only a superannuated dozen, a slowly decaying dozen, a solemn and dispirited dozen remained.

But we were to be there merely while we searched for a villa, and it had the advantage of being amazingly cheap for a first-class hotel—the rate for four of us, including meals, was one hundred and fifty francs, less than eight dollars a day.

The real-estate agent, an energetic young gentleman with his pants buttoned snugly around his chest, called on us next morning.

"Dozens of villas," he said enthusiastically. "We will take the horse and buggy and go see."

It was a simmering morning but the streets already swarmed with the faces of Southern France—dark faces, for there is an Arab streak along the Riviera, left from turbulent, forgotten centuries. Once the Moors harried the coast for gain, and later, as they swept up through Spain in mad glory, they threw out frontier towns along the shores as outposts for their conquest of the world. They were not the first people, or the last, that have tried to overrun France—all that remains now for proud Moslem hopes is an occasional Moorish tower and the tragic glint of black Eastern eyes.

"Now this villa rents for thirty dollars a month," said the real-estate agent as we stopped at a small house on the edge of town.

"What's the matter with it?" asked my wife suspiciously.

"Nothing at all. It is superb. It has six rooms and a well."

"A well?"

"A fine well."

"Do you mean it has no bathroom?"

"Not what you would call an actual bathroom."

"Drive on," we said.

It was obvious by noon that there were no villas to be let in Hyères. They were all too hot, too small, too dirty, or too *triste*, an expressive word which implies that the mad marquis still walks through the halls in his shroud.

"Yes, we have no villas today," remarked the agent, smiling.

"That's a very old played-out joke," I said, "and I am too hot to laugh."

Our clothes were hanging on us like wet towels but when I had established our identity by a scar on my left hand we were admitted to the hotel. I decided to ask one of the lingering Englishmen if there was perhaps another quiet town nearby.

Now, asking something of an American or a Frenchman is a definite thing—the only difference is that you can understand the American's reply. But getting an answer from an Englishman is about as complicated as borrowing a match from the Secretary of State. The first one I approached dropped his paper, looked at me in horror and bolted precipitately from the room. This disconcerted me for a moment but luckily my eyes fell on a man whom I had seen being wheeled in to dinner.

"Good morning," I said. "Could you tell me—" He jerked spasmodically, but to my relief, he was unable to leave his seat. "I wonder if you know a town where I could get a villa for the summer."

"Don't know any at all," he said coldly. "And I wouldn't tell *you* if I did."

He didn't exactly pronounce the last sentence but I could read the words as they issued from his eyes.

"I suppose you're a newcomer too," I suggested.

"I've been here every winter for sixteen years."

Pretending to detect an invitation in this, I drew up my chair. "Then you must know some town," I assured him.

"Cannes, Nice, Monte Carlo."

"But they're too expensive. I want a quiet place to do a lot of work."

"Cannes, Nice, Monte Carlo. All quiet in summer. Don't know any others. Wouldn't tell you if I did. Good day."

Upstairs the nurse was counting the mosquito bites on the baby, all received during the night, and my wife was adding them up in a big book.

"Cannes, Nice, Monte Carlo," I said.

"I'm glad we're going to leave this broiling town," remarked the nurse.

"I think we'd better try Cannes."

"I think so too," said my wife eagerly. "I hear it's very gay—I mean, it's no economy to stay where you can't work, and I don't believe we can get a villa here after all."

"Let's go on the big boat," said the baby suddenly.

"Silence! We've come to the Riviera and we're here to stay."

So we decided to leave the nurse and baby in Hyères and run up to Cannes, which is a more fashionable town in a more northerly situation along the shore. Now when you "run up" to somewhere, you have to have an automobile, so we bought the only new one in town next day. It had the power of six horses— the age of the horses was not stated—and it was so small that we loomed out of it like giants; so small that you could run it under the verandah for the night. It had no lock, no speedometer, no gauge, and its cost, including the parcel-post charge, was seven hundred and fifty dollars. We started for Cannes in it and, except for the warm exhaust when other cars drove over us, we found the trip comparatively cool.

All the celebrities of Europe have spent a season in Cannes— even the Man with the Iron Mask whiled away twelve years on an island off its shore. Its gorgeous villas are built of stone so soft that it is sawed instead of hewed. We looked at four of them next morning. They were small, neat and clean—you could have matched them in any suburb of Los Angeles. They rented at sixty-five dollars a month.

"I like them," said my wife firmly. "Let's rent one. They look awfully easy to run."

"We didn't come abroad to find a house that was easy to run," I objected. "How could I write looking out on a—" I glanced out the window and my eyes met a splendid view of the sea, "—where I'd hear every whisper in the house."

So we moved on to the fourth villa, the wonderful fourth villa, the memory of which still causes me to lie awake and hope that some bright day will find me there. It rose in white marble out of a great hill, like a chateau, like a castle of old. The very taxi-cab that took us there had romance in its front seat.

"Did you notice our driver?" said the agent, leaning toward me. "He used to be a Russian millionaire."

We peered through the glass at him—a thin dispirited man who ordered the gears about with a lordly air.

"The town is full of them," said the agent. "They're glad to get jobs as chauffeurs, butlers or waiters—the women work as *femmes de chambre* in the hotels."

"Why don't they open tea rooms like Americans do?"

"Most of them aren't fit for anything. We're awfully sorry for them, but—" He leaned forward and tapped on the glass. "Would you mind driving a little faster? We haven't got all day!"

"Look," he said when we reached the chateau on the hill. "There's the Grand Duke Michael's villa next door."

"You mean he's the butler there?"

"Oh, no. He's got money. He's gone north for the summer."

When we had entered through scrolled brass gates that creaked massively as gates should for a king, and when the blinds had been drawn we were in a high central hall hung with ancestral portraits of knights in armor and courtiers in satin and brocade. It was like a movie set. Flights of marble stairs rose in solid dignity to form a grand gallery into which light dropped through blue figured glass upon a mosaic floor. It was modern too,—with huge clean beds and a model kitchen and three bathrooms and a solemn, silent study overlooking the sea.

"It belonged to a Russian general," said the agent; "killed in Silesia during the war."

"How much is it?"

"For the summer—one hundred and ten dollars a month."

"Done!" I said. "Fix up the lease right away. My wife will go to Hyères immediately to get the—"

"Just a minute," she said, frowning. "How many servants will it take to run this house?"

"Why, I should say—" the agent glanced at us sharply and hesitated. "About five."

"I should say about eight." She turned to me. "Let's go to Newport and rent the Vanderbilt house instead."

"Remember," said the agent, "you've got the Grand Duke Michael on your left."

"Will he come to see us?" I inquired.

"He would, of course," explained the agent, "only, you see, he's gone away."

We held debate upon the mosaic floor. My theory was that I couldn't work in the little houses and that this would be a real investment because of its romantic inspiration. My wife's theory was that eight servants eat a lot of food and that it simply wouldn't do. We apologized to the agent, shook hands respectfully with the millionaire taxi-driver, and gave him five francs, and in a state of great dejection returned to Hyères.

"Here's the hotel bill," said my wife as we went despondently in to dinner.

"Thank heaven it's only fifty-five dollars."

I opened it. To my amazement, tax after tax had been added beneath the bill—government tax, city tax, a ten per cent tax to re-tip the servants and the special tax for Americans besides—and the fifty-five dollars had swollen to one hundred and twenty-seven.

I looked gloomily at a nameless piece of meat soaked in a lifeless gravy which reclined on my plate.

"I think it's goat's meat," said the nurse, following my eyes. She turned to my wife. "Did you ever taste goat's meat, Mrs. Fitzgerald?"

But Mrs. Fitzgerald had never tasted goat's meat and Mrs. Fitzgerald had fled.

As I wandered dismally about the hotel next day, hoping that our house on Long Island hadn't been rented so that we could go home for the summer, I noticed that the halls were even more deserted than usual. There seemed to be more old copies of the "Illustrated London News" about, and more empty chairs. At dinner we had the goat again. As I looked around the empty dining room I suddenly realized that the last Englishman had taken his cane and his conscience and fled to London. No wonder there was goat—it would have been a miracle had there been anything else but goat. The management was keeping open a two-hundred-room hotel for us alone!

III

Hyères grew warmer and we rested there in a helpless daze. We knew now why Catherine de Medici had chosen it for her favorite resort. A month of it in the summer and she must have returned to Paris with a dozen St. Bartholomew's sizzling in her head. In vain we took trips to Nice, to Antibes, to Ste. Maxime—we were worried now; a fourth of our seven thousand had slipped away. Then one morning just five weeks after we had left New York we got off the train at a little town called St. Raphaël that we had never considered before.

It was a red little town built close to the sea, with gay red-roofed houses and an air of repressed carnival about it, carnival that would venture forth into the streets before night. We knew that we would love to live in it and we asked a citizen the whereabouts of the real-estate agency.

"Ah, for that you had far better ask the King!" he exclaimed.

A principality! A second Monaco! We had not known there were two of them along the French shore.

"And a bank that will cash a letter of credit?"

"For that, too, you must ask the King."

He pointed the way toward the palace down a long shady street, and my wife hurriedly produced a mirror and began powdering her face.

"But our dusty clothes?" I said modestly. "Do you think the King will—"

He considered.

"I'm not sure about clothes," he answered. "But I think—yes, I think the King will attend to that for you too."

I hadn't meant that, but we thanked him and with much inward trepidation proceeded toward the imperial domain. After half an hour, when royal turrets had failed to rise against the sky, I stopped another man.

"Can you tell us the way to the imperial palace?"

"The *what?*"

"We want to get an interview with His Majesty—His Majesty the King."

The word "King" caught his attention. His mouth opened understandingly and he pointed to a sign over our heads:

"W.F. King," I read, "Anglo-American Bank, Real-Estate Agency, Railroad Tickets, Insurance, Tours and Excursions, Circulating Library."

The potentate turned out to be a brisk efficient Englishman of middle age who had gradually acquired St. Raphaël to himself over a period of twenty years.

"We are Americans come to Europe to economize," I told him. "We've combed the Riviera from Nice to Hyères and haven't been able to find a villa. Meanwhile our money is leaking gradually away."

He leaned back and pressed a button and almost immediately a lean, gaunt woman appeared in the door.

"This is Marthe," he said, "your cook."

We could hardly believe our ears.

"Do you mean you have a villa for us?"

"I have already selected one," he said. "My agents saw you getting off the train."

He pressed another button and a second woman stood respectfully beside the first.

"This is Jeanne, your *femme de chambre*. She does the mending, too, and waits on the table. You pay her thirteen dollars a month and you pay Marthe sixteen dollars. Marthe does the marketing, however, and expects to make a little on the side for herself."

"But the villa?"—

"The lease is being made out now. The price is seventy-nine dollars a month and your check is good with me. We move you in tomorrow."

Within an hour we had seen our home, a clean cool villa set in a large garden on a hill above town. It was what we had been looking for all along. There was a summerhouse and a sand pile and two bathrooms and roses for breakfast and a gardener who called me milord. When we had paid the rent, only thirty-five hundred dollars, half our original capital, remained. But we felt that at last we could begin to live on practically nothing a year.

IV

In the late afternoon of September 1st, 1924, a distinguished-looking young man, accompanied by a young lady in a short, bright blue bathing suit, might have been seen lying on a sandy beach in France. Both of them were burned to a deep chocolate brown so that at first they seemed to be of Egyptian origin; but closer inspection showed that their faces had an Aryan cast and that their voices, when they spoke, had a faintly nasal, North American ring. Near them played a small black child with cotton-white hair who from time to time beat a tin spoon upon a pail and shouted, "*Regardez-moi!*" in no uncertain voice.

Out of the casino nearby drifted weird rococo music—a song dealing with the non-possession of a specific yellow fruit in a certain otherwise well-stocked store. Waiters, both Senegalese and European, rushed around among the bathers with many-colored drinks, pausing now and then to chase away the children of the poor, who were dressing and undressing with neither modesty nor self-consciousness, upon the sand.

"Hasn't it been a good summer!" said the young man, lazily. "We've become absolutely French."

"And the French are such an aesthetic people," said the young lady, listening for a moment to the banana music. "They know how to live. Think of all the nice things they have to eat!"

"Delicious things! Heavenly things!" exclaimed the young man, spreading some American deviled ham on some biscuits marked Springfield, Illinois. "But then they've studied the food question for two thousand years."

"And things are so cheap here!" cried the young lady enthusiastically. "Think of perfume! Perfume that would cost fifteen dollars in New York, you can get here for five."

The young man struck a Swedish match and lit an American cigarette.

"The trouble with most Americans in France," he remarked sonorously, "is that they won't lead a real French life. They hang around the big hotels and exchange opinions fresh from the States."

"I know," she agreed. "That's exactly what it said in the 'New York Times' this morning."

The American music ended and the English nurse arose, implying that it was time the child went home to supper. With a sigh, the young man arose too and shook himself violently, scattering a great quantity of sand.

"We've got to stop on the way and get some Arizon-oil gasoline," he said. "That last stuff was awful."

"The check, suh," said a Senegalese waiter with an accent from well below the Mason-Dixon Line. "That'll be ten francs fo' two glasses of beer."

The young man handed him the equivalent of seventy cents in the gold-colored hat-checks of France. Beer was perhaps a little higher than in America, but then he had had the privilege of hearing the historic banana song on a real, or almost real, jazz band. And waiting for him at home was a regular French supper—baked beans from the quaint old Norman town of Akron, Ohio, an omelette fragrant with la Chicago bacon and a cup of English tea.

But perhaps you have already recognized in these two cultured Europeans the same barbaric Americans who had left America just five months before. And perhaps you wonder that the change could have come about so quickly. The secret is that they had entered fully into the life of the Old World. Instead of patronizing "tourist" hotels they had made excursions to quaint little out-of-the-way restaurants, with the real French atmosphere, where supper for two rarely came to more than ten or fifteen dollars. Not for them the glittering capitals—Paris, Brussels, Rome—they were content with short trips to beautiful historic old towns, such as Monte Carlo, where they once left their automobile with a kindly garage man who paid their hotel bill and bought them tickets home.

Yes, our summer had been a complete success. And we had lived on practically nothing—that is, on practically nothing except our original seven thousand dollars. It was all gone!

The trouble is that we had come to the Riviera out of season,—that is, out of one season but in the middle of another. For in summer the people who are "trying to economize" come south and the shrewd French know that this class is the very easiest game of all—as people who are trying to get something for nothing are very liable to be.

Exactly where the money went we don't know—we never do. There were the servants for example; I was very fond of Marthe and Jeanne (and afterwards of their sisters Eugénie and Serpolette, who came in to help) but on my own initiative it would never have occurred to me to insure them all. Yet that was the law. If Jeanne suffocated in her mosquito netting, if Marthe tripped over a bone and broke her thumb I was responsible. I wouldn't have minded so much except that the "little on the side" that Marthe made in doing our marketing amounted, as I figure, to about forty-five per cent.

Our weekly bills at the grocer's and the butcher's averaged sixty-five dollars—or higher than they had ever been in an expensive Long Island town. Whatever the meat actually cost it was almost invariably inedible, while as for the milk every drop of it had to be boiled because the cows were tubercular in France. For fresh vegetables we had tomatoes and a little asparagus, that was all—the only garlic that can be put over on us must be administered in sleep. I wondered often how the Riviera middle class—the bank clerk, say, who supports a family on from forty to seventy dollars a month—manages to keep alive.

"It's even worse in winter," a little French girl told us on the beach. "The English and Americans drive the prices up until we can't buy and we don't know what to do. My sister had to go to Marseilles and find work and she's only fourteen. Next winter I'll go too."

There simply isn't enough to go around—and the Americans who, because of their own high standard of material comfort, want the best obtainable, naturally have to pay. And in addition, the sharp French tradesmen are always ready to take advantage of a careless American eye.

"I don't like this bill," I said to the food-and-ice deliverer. "I arranged to pay you five francs and not eight francs a day."

He became unintelligible for a moment to gain time.

"My wife added it up," he said.

Those valuable Riviera wives! Always they are adding up their husbands' accounts and the dear ladies simply don't know one figure from another. Such a talent in the wife of a railroad president would be an asset worth many million dollars.

It is twilight as I write this and out of my window darkening banks of trees, set one clump behind another in many greens, slope down to the evening sea. The flaming sun has collapsed behind the peaks of the Estérels and the moon already hovers over the Roman aqueducts of Fréjus, five miles away. In half an hour Renée and Bobbé, officers of aviation, are coming to dinner in their white ducks and Renée, who is only twenty-three and has never recovered from having missed the war, will tell us romantically how he wants to smoke opium in Peking and how he writes a few things "for myself alone." Afterwards in the garden their white uniforms will grow dimmer as the more liquid dark comes down, until they, like the heavy roses and the nightingales in the pines, will seem to take an essential and indivisible part in the beauty of this proud gay land.

And though we have saved nothing we have danced the *carmagnole* and, except for the day when my wife took the mosquito lotion for a mouth wash and the time when I tried to smoke a French cigarette and, as Ring Lardner would say, "swooned," we haven't yet been sorry that we came.

The dark-brown child is knocking at the door to bid me good-night.

"Going on the big boat, Daddy?" she says in broken English.

"No."

"Why?"

"Because we're going to try it for another year, and besides—think of perfume!"

We are always like that with the baby. She considers us the wittiest couple she has ever known.

How to Waste Material

A NOTE ON MY GENERATION

EVER since Irving's preoccupation with the necessity for an American background, for some square miles of cleared territory on which colorful varia might presently arise, the question of material has hampered the American writer. For one Dreiser who made a single-minded and irreproachable choice there have been a dozen like Henry James who have stupid-got with worry over the matter, and yet another dozen who, blinded by the fading tail of Walt Whitman's comet, have botched their books by the insincere compulsion to write "significantly" about America.

Insincere because it is not a compulsion found in themselves—it is "literary" in the most belittling sense. During the past seven years we have had at least half a dozen treatments of the American farmer, ranging from New England to Nebraska; at least a dozen canny books about youth, some of them with surveys of the American universities for background; more than a dozen novels reflecting various aspects of New York, Chicago, Washington, Detroit, Indianapolis, Wilmington and Richmond; innumerable novels dealing with American politics, business, society, science, racial problems, art, literature and moving pictures, and with Americans abroad at peace or in war; finally several novels of change and growth, tracing the swift decades for their own sweet lavender or protesting vaguely and ineffectually against the industrialization of our beautiful old American life. We have had an Arnold Bennett for every five towns—surely by this time the foundations have been laid! Are we competent only to toil forever upon a never completed first floor whose specifications change from year to year?

In any case we are running through our material like spendthrifts—just as we have done before. In the nineties there began a feverish search for any period of American history that hadn't been "used," and once found it was immediately debauched into a pretty and romantic story. These past seven years have seen the same sort of literary gold rush and for all our boasted sincerity and sophistication, the material is being turned out raw and undigested in much the same way. One author goes to a midland farm for three months to obtain the material for an epic of the American husbandman! Another sets off on a like errand to the Blue Ridge Mountains, a third departs with a Corona for the West Indies—one is justified in the belief that what they get hold of will weigh no more than the journalistic loot brought back by Richard Harding Davis and John Fox, Jr., twenty years ago.

Worse, the result will be doctored up to give it a literary flavor. The farm story will be sprayed with a faint dilution of ideas and sensory impressions from Thomas Hardy; the novel of the Jewish tenement block will be festooned with wreaths from "Ulysses" and the later Gertrude Stein; the document of dreamy youth will be prevented from fluttering entirely away by means of great and half-great names—Marx, Spencer, Wells, Edward Fitzgerald—dropped like paper-weights here and there upon the pages. Finally the novel of business will be cudgeled into being satire by the questionable but constantly reiterated implication that the author and his readers don't partake of the American commercial instinct.

And most of it—the literary beginnings of what was to have been a golden age—is as dead as if it had never been written. Scarcely one of those who put so much effort and enthusiasm, even intelligence, into it, got hold of any material at all.

To a limited extent this was the fault of two men—one of whom, H. L. Mencken, has yet done more for American letters than any man alive. What Mencken felt the absence of, what he wanted, and justly, back in 1920, got away from him, got twisted in his hand. Not because the "literary revolution" went beyond him but because his idea had always been ethical rather than aesthetic. In the history of culture no pure aesthetic idea has ever served as an offensive weapon. Mencken's invective, sharp as Swift's, made its point by the use of the most forceful prose style now written in English. Immediately, instead of committing himself to an infinite series of pronouncements upon the American novel, he should have modulated his tone to the more urbane, more critical one of his early essay on Dreiser.

But perhaps it was already too late. Already he had begotten a family of hammer and tongs men—insensitive, suspicious of glamour, preoccupied exclusively with the external, the contemptible, the "national" and the drab, whose style was a debasement of his least effective manner and who, glib children, played continually with his themes in his maternal shadow. These were the men who manufactured enthusiasm when each new mass of raw data was dumped on the literary platform—mistaking incoherence for vitality, chaos for vitality. It was the "new poetry movement" over again, only that this time its victims were worth the saving. Every week some new novel gave its author membership in "that little band who are producing a worthy American literature." As one of the charter members of that little band I am proud to state that it has now swollen to seventy or eighty members.

And through a curious misconception of his work, Sherwood Anderson must take part of the blame for this enthusiastic march up a blind alley in the dark. To this day reviewers solemnly speak of him as an inarticulate, fumbling man, bursting with ideas—when, on the contrary, he is the possessor of a brilliant and almost inimitable prose style, and of scarcely any ideas at all. Just as the prose of Joyce in the hands of, say, Waldo Frank becomes as insignificant and idiotic as the automatic writing of a Kansas Theosophist, so the Anderson admirers set up Hergesheimer as an antichrist and then proceed to imitate Anderson's lapses from that difficult simplicity they are unable to understand. And here again critics support them by discovering merits in the very disorganization that is to bring their books to a timely and unregretted doom.

Now the business is over. "Wolf" has been cried too often. The public, weary of being fooled, has gone back to its Englishmen, its memoirs and its prophets. Some of the late brilliant boys are on lecture tours (a circular informs me that most of them are to speak upon "the literary revolution"!), some are writing pot-boilers, a few have definitely abandoned the literary life—they were never sufficiently aware that material, however closely observed, is as elusive as the moment in which it has its existence unless it is purified by an incorruptible style and by the catharsis of a passionate emotion.

Of all the work by the young men who have sprung up since 1920 one book survives—"The Enormous Room" by E. E. Cummings. It is scarcely a novel; it doesn't deal with the American scene; it was swamped in the mediocre downpour, isolated—forgotten. But it lives on, because those few who cause books to live have not been able to endure the thought of its mortality. Two other books, both about the war, complete the possible salvage from the work of the younger generation—"Through the Wheat" and "Three Soldiers," but the former despite its fine last chapters doesn't stand up as well as "Les Croix de Bois" and "The Red Badge of Courage," while the latter is marred by its pervasive flavor of contemporary indignation. But as an augury that someone has profited by this dismal record of high hope and stale failure comes the first work of Ernest Hemingway.

II

"In Our Time" consists of fourteen stories, short and long, with fifteen vivid miniatures interpolated between them. When I try to think of any contemporary American short stories as good as "Big Two-Hearted River," the last one in the book, only Gertrude Stein's "Melanctha," Anderson's "The Egg," and Lardner's "Golden Honeymoon" come to mind. It is the account of a boy on a fishing trip—he hikes, pitches his tent, cooks dinner, sleeps and next morning casts for trout. Nothing more—but I read it with the most breathless unwilling interest I have experienced since Conrad first bent my reluctant eyes upon the sea.

The hero, Nick, runs through nearly all the stories, until the book takes on almost an autobiographical tint—in fact "My Old Man," one of the two in which this element seems entirely absent, is the least successful of all. Some of the stories show influences but they are invariably absorbed and transmuted, while in "My Old Man" there is an echo of Anderson's way of thinking in those sentimental "horse stories," which inaugurated his respectability and also his decline four years ago.

But with "The Doctor and the Doctor's Wife," "The End of Something," "The Three Day Blow," "Mr. and Mrs. Elliot" and "Soldier's Home" you are immediately aware of something temperamentally new. In the first of these a man is backed down by a half-breed Indian after committing himself to a fight. The quality of humiliation in the story is so intense that it immediately calls up every such incident in the reader's past. Without a comment or a pointing finger one knows exactly the sharp emotion of young Nick who watches the scene.

The next two stories describe an experience at the last edge of adolescence. You are constantly aware of the continual snapping of ties that is going on around Nick. In the half-stewed, immature conversation before the fire you watch the awakening of that vast unrest that descends upon the emotional type at about eighteen. Again there is not a single recourse to exposition. As in "Big Two-Hearted River," a picture—sharp, nostalgic, tense—develops before your eyes. When the picture is complete a light seems to snap out, the story is over. There is no tail, no sudden change of pace at the end to throw into relief what has gone before.

Nick leaves home penniless; you have a glimpse of him lying wounded in the street of a battered Italian town, and later of a love affair with a nurse on a hospital roof in Milan. Then in one of the best of the stories he is home again. The last glimpse of him is when his mother asks him, with all the bitter world in his heart, to kneel down beside her in the dining room in Puritan prayer.

Anyone who first looks through the short interpolated sketches will hardly fail to read the stories themselves. "The Garden at Mons" and "The Barricade" are profound essays upon the English officer, written on a postage stamp. "The King of Greece's Tea Party," "The Shooting of the Cabinet Ministers" and "The Cigar-store Robbery" particularly fascinated me, as they did when Edmund Wilson first showed them to me in an earlier pamphlet, over two years ago.

Disregard the rather ill-considered blurbs upon the cover. It is sufficient that here is no raw food served up by the railroad restaurants of California and Wisconsin. In the best of these dishes there is not a bit to spare. And many of us who have grown weary of admonitions to "watch this man or that" have felt a sort of renewal of excitement at these stories wherein Ernest Hemingway turns a corner into the street.

CHRONOLOGY

NOTE ON THE TEXTS

NOTES

Chronology

1896   Born September 24 at his parents' home at 481 Laurel Avenue, in St. Paul, Minnesota, first surviving child of Mollie McQuillan Fitzgerald and Edward Fitzgerald. Named Francis Scott Key Fitzgerald after the author of "The Star-Spangled Banner," his father's second cousin three times removed. Mother, born 1860 in St. Paul, is the eldest of five children of successful grocery wholesaler who at his death in 1877 left an estate of more than $250,000 and a large Victorian home on Summit Avenue, St. Paul's most fashionable street. Father, born in 1853 in Rockville, Maryland, is a furniture manufacturer. They had two daughters who died, aged three and one, earlier in 1896.

1898   When furniture business fails, family moves to Buffalo, New York, where father takes a job as a wholesale grocery salesman for Procter & Gamble.

1901   Father transferred by Procter & Gamble to Syracuse, New York, and family moves in January. Sister Annabel born in July.

1902   Enrolls in Miss Goodyear's School in September.

1903   Family moves back to Buffalo. Attends school at Holy Angels Convent.

1905   Transfers to Miss Nardin's private Catholic school. Reads *The Scottish Chiefs*, *Ivanhoe*, and the adventure novels of G. A. Henty.

1908   Father loses his job at Procter & Gamble in March and in July family moves back to St. Paul, where at first they live with the McQuillans and then in a series of rented homes, eventually settling at 599 Summit Avenue. Enters St. Paul Academy in September.

1909   Publishes first story, "The Mystery of the Raymond Mortgage," in *Now and Then*, the St. Paul Academy school paper, in October.

1910   Publishes two more stories in *Now and Then*, "Reade, Substitute Right Half" (February) and "A Debt of Honor" (March).

693

1911   Publishes story "The Room with the Green Blinds" in the
            June *Now and Then*. In August, writes and plays the lead in
            a play, *The Girl from Lazy J,* for the Elizabethan Dramatic
            Club, local amateur theatrical group. Because of poor grades
            at St. Paul Academy, is sent in September to boarding school
            at the Newman School in Hackensack, New Jersey, where
            his boastful and domineering personality makes him unpop-
            ular. Takes frequent trips to New York City and attends
            theater often, seeing Ina Claire in *The Quaker Girl* and Ger-
            trude Bryant in *Little Boy Blue.* Publishes poem "Football"
            in Christmas issue of the school magazine, the *Newman
            News.*

1912–13   Writes another play, *The Captured Shadow,* which is pro-
            duced by the Elizabethan Dramatic Club in the summer of
            1912. Publishes three stories in the *Newman News* during
            the 1912–13 school year. Meets Father Cyril Sigourney Web-
            ster Fay, prominent Catholic priest, who becomes a mentor.
            During a visit to Father Fay in Washington, meets Henry
            Adams and Anglo-Irish writer Shane Leslie. Despite failing
            four courses in two years at the Newman School, Fitzgerald
            takes entrance examination for Princeton University in May
            1913. Writes play *Coward* for Elizabethan Dramatic Club
            in July. Grandmother McQuillan dies in August, leaving
            his mother enough money for his college tuition. Enters
            Princeton in September as member of Class of 1917.

1914   Meets John Peale Bishop and Edmund Wilson, fellow stu-
            dents at Princeton. In January his book and lyrics for *Fie!
            Fie! Fi-Fi!* win the competition for the 1914–15 Triangle
            Club show. Contributes to the *Princeton Tiger,* the college
            humor magazine. Reads and admires the social reform writ-
            ings of H. G. Wells and George Bernard Shaw and Compton
            Mackenzie's novel *Sinister Street.* Writes fourth and last play
            for the Elizabethan Dramatic Club, *Assorted Spirits,* during
            summer. Returns to Princeton in September but is ineligi-
            ble for extracurricular activities because of poor grades and
            cannot act in *Fie! Fie! Fi-Fi!* during the fall semester.

1915   Meets Ginevra King, sixteen-year-old from socially promi-
            nent Lake Forest, Illinois, family, while home for Christmas
            vacation. Falls in love with her and writes to her almost daily
            after he returns to Princeton. Elected secretary of the Tri-
            angle Club in February after his grades improve; later in the
            term is selected for the Cottage Club and for the editorial

board of the *Tiger.* Story "Shadow Laurels" is published in the *Nassau Literary Magazine* (the *Lit*) in April, followed in June by "The Ordeal." Writes the lyrics (Edmund Wilson writes the book) for *The Evil Eye,* the 1915–16 Triangle Club show. Takes Ginevra King to the Princeton prom in June. In the fall, his low grades again make him ineligible for campus activities. Takes French literature course taught by Christian Gauss and begins lifelong friendship with Gauss, who later becomes Dean of the College. Continues to write for the *Tiger.* In November, falls ill and leaves college for the remainder of the semester to recuperate (illness is diagnosed as malaria, but may have been mild case of tuberculosis).

1916   Spends the spring in St. Paul on a leave of absence from Princeton; publishes poem "To My Unused Greek Book" in the *Lit.* Continues courtship of Ginevra King, whom he visits in Lake Forest in August. Returns to Princeton in September to repeat his junior year and writes the lyrics for the Triangle Club show, *Safety First,* in which he is again ineligible to perform. Attends Princeton–Yale football game with King in November.

1917   Courtship of Ginevra King ends in January. Publishes play "The Debutante," whose title character is modeled on King, in the *Lit.* During spring semester, his writing appears another twelve times in the *Lit* (four stories, three poems, and five reviews of books by Shane Leslie, E. F. Benson, H. G. Wells, and Booth Tarkington). In May, a month after the U.S. enters World War I, signs up for three weeks of intensive military training and takes exam for infantry commission. During summer in St. Paul, reads William James, Schopenhauer, and Bergson. While waiting for his commission, returns to Princeton in September and rooms with John Biggs, Jr., editor of the *Tiger,* and continues to contribute to both the *Tiger* and the *Lit.* Receives commission as second lieutenant in the infantry and in November reports for training to Fort Leavenworth, Kansas. Expecting that he will eventually be killed in combat, begins writing a novel.

1918   On leave from the army in February, finishes novel, "The Romantic Egotist," at the Cottage Club in Princeton and sends it to Shane Leslie, who has agreed to recommend it to his publisher, Charles Scribner's Sons. Reports in March to 45th Infantry Regiment at Camp Zachary Taylor, near

Louisville; in April, regiment is transferred to Camp Gordon in Georgia, and in June, to Camp Sheridan, outside Montgomery, Alabama. In July, at a dance at the Country Club of Montgomery, meets Zelda Sayre, eighteen-year-old daughter of a justice of the Alabama Supreme Court. Scribner's rejects "The Romantic Egotist" in August; Fitzgerald submits a revised version, which is rejected in October. War ends on November 11, as Fitzgerald is waiting to embark for France with his regiment. Continues courtship of Zelda Sayre, who is reluctant to commit to marriage because of his lack of income and prospects.

1919   Father Fay dies on January 10. Fitzgerald is discharged from the army, moves to New York in February, and takes job at Barron Collier advertising agency writing trolley-car ads. Writes fiction and poetry at night, accumulating 112 rejection slips. *The Smart Set* accepts "Babes in the Woods," revised version of story published in 1917 issue of the *Lit,* paying him $30 (story appears in September). Sends Zelda his mother's engagement ring in March, but cannot convince her to marry him during visits to Montgomery, April–June. During his last visit, Zelda breaks off the engagement. Quits job and returns to parents' house in St. Paul, determined to rewrite novel and have it accepted for publication. Sends novel, now titled *This Side of Paradise,* to editor Maxwell Perkins at Scribner's in September. Perkins writes on September 16 that firm has accepted it: "The book is so different that it is hard to prophesy how it will sell but we are all for taking a chance and supporting it with vigor." Revises several of his rejected stories; four are accepted by *The Smart Set,* two by *Scribner's Magazine,* and one by *The Saturday Evening Post.* Earns $879 from his writing by the end of the year. During a trip to New York in November, engages Harold Ober as his agent. Visits Zelda in Montgomery.

1920   With Harold Ober's assistance, begins to sell stories regularly to *The Saturday Evening Post,* which pays $400 each for them; by February, they have bought six. Reads Samuel Butler's *Note-Books* and H. L. Mencken's essays. Spends January in New Orleans writing stories and reading proofs of his novel, then moves back to New York in February. Sells story "Head and Shoulders" to Metro Films for $2,500. *This Side of Paradise* is published March 26; it sells three thousand copies in three days, and makes its author a celebrity. Marries Zelda in vestry of New York's St. Patrick's Cathedral on April 3. Develops friendships with Mencken and George Jean Nathan, editors of *The Smart Set*. Reads Mark Twain. In May, *Metropolitan Magazine* takes option on his stories at $900 per story and, eventually, publishes four. Rents house in Westport, Connecticut, and in July takes car trip to Montgomery. Scribner's publishes *Flappers and Philosophers*, collection of eight stories, September 10. Rents apartment on West 59th Street in New York in October and works on second novel.

1921   Zelda discovers she is pregnant in February. In May, they sail for Europe, visiting England (where they have tea with John Galsworthy), Paris, Venice, Florence, and Rome, returning in July to the U.S., where they live in St. Paul. Second novel, *The Beautiful and Damned*, begins to run serially in *Metropolitan Magazine* in September. Daughter Frances Scott (Scottie) Fitzgerald is born on October 26.

1922   *The Beautiful and Damned* published by Scribner's March 4; it receives mixed reviews and sells forty thousand copies in a year. Begins work on play. Moves to Great Neck, Long Island, where he begins close friendships with Ring Lardner and John Dos Passos. *Tales of the Jazz Age,* short-story collection, published by Scribner's on September 22. Reads Dostoevsky and Dickens.

1923   Sells first option on his stories to Hearst organization for $1,500 per story. Receives $10,000 for film rights to *This Side of Paradise*. Play *The Vegetable* is published by Scribner's on April 27. Begins work on third novel. *The Vegetable* opens for pre-Broadway tryout in Atlantic City, New Jersey, on November 19, is received badly, and closes almost immediately, leaving its author in debt. Starts selling stories to *The Saturday Evening Post* for $1,250 each. Earns $28,759.78 from his writing for the year, but spends more.

1924   Sails for France in May to complete novel, settling on the Riviera. Zelda becomes romantically involved with French naval aviator Edouard Jozan in July; although the relationship ends quickly, Fitzgerald later writes, "I knew something had happened that could never be repaired." Meets Gerald and Sara Murphy during the summer. In October, recommends the work of Ernest Hemingway to Perkins and Scribner's. After sending manuscript of new novel to Scribner's in late October, goes to Rome and Capri for winter. Drinks heavily and quarrels constantly with Zelda.

1925   Extensively revises novel in galley proof in January and February, changing title to *The Great Gatsby*. Moves to Paris in April. *The Great Gatsby* is published by Scribner's on April 10, receives mostly favorable reviews, but sales are disappointing. Meets Hemingway for first time at the Dingo bar in Montparnasse and subsequently takes trip to Lyon with him. Has tea with Edith Wharton at her home outside Paris in July. Through Hemingway, meets Gertrude Stein, Robert McAlmon (founder of Contact Editions publishers), and Sylvia Beach (owner of Shakespeare & Co. bookstore in Paris). Spends part of summer ("1000 parties and no work") on the Riviera, where his friends include writers Dos Passos, Max Eastman, Archibald MacLeish, and Floyd Dell and movie star Rudolph Valentino. Returns to Paris in September and spends a great deal of time with Hemingway.

1926   *All the Sad Young Men*, short-story collection, is published by Scribner's on February 26. Returns to the Riviera in March and begins work on new novel. Encourages Scribner's to publish Hemingway's novels *The Torrents of Spring* and *The Sun Also Rises*. Reads draft of *The Sun Also Rises* in July and convinces Hemingway to eliminate the first two chapters. Returns to U.S. in December, spending Christmas in Montgomery.

1927   Spends first two months of year in Hollywood, under contract to United Artists to write flapper comedy for Constance Talmadge; script, "Lipstick," is eventually rejected. Meets and is infatuated with seventeen-year-old Hollywood starlet Lois Moran; also meets producer Irving Thalberg, Lillian Gish, John Barrymore, and Richard Barthelmess. With help of Princeton roommate John Biggs, Jr., rents Ellerslie, Greek Revival–style mansion outside Wilmington, Delaware. Zelda begins ballet lessons with director of Philadelphia Opera Ballet and also writes magazine articles. Fitzgerald's income from writing for year totals $29,757.87, a new high.

1928   Goes to Paris for the summer in April. Zelda continues ballet studies there with Lubov Egorova. Writes nine Basil Duke Lee stories for *The Saturday Evening Post*, which earn him $31,500. Meets James Joyce at dinner given by Sylvia Beach in June. Later in summer, meets Thornton Wilder and heavyweight boxing champion Gene Tunney, who are on a walking tour of Europe together. Returns to U.S. in

October and resumes work on novel. Attends Princeton–Yale football game in Princeton on November 19 with Hemingway and his wife, Pauline.

1929   Gives up lease on Ellerslie in spring and returns to Europe, renting apartment in Paris in April. Zelda resumes ballet lessons with Egorova and also publishes series of short stories in *College Humor*. Fitzgerald reads typescript of Hemingway's novel *A Farewell to Arms* in June and offers suggestions for revisions, all of which Hemingway ridicules but some of which he takes. Rents villa in Cannes from July to September. Now is paid $4,000 per story by *The Saturday Evening Post*. Returns to Paris in October and lives in rented apartment. Works on novel, while Zelda continues her ballet lessons and writing.

1930   Travels with Zelda to North Africa in February. Her behavior shows signs of extreme stress, and on April 23, she enters Malmaison clinic outside Paris. Discharges herself on May 11 to resume ballet lessons, then attempts suicide and enters Val-Mont clinic in Glion, Switzerland, on May 22. After being diagnosed as schizophrenic by Dr. Oscar Forel, she is transferred in June to Forel's Les Rives de Prangins clinic on Lake Geneva. Fitzgerald spends summer traveling between Paris and Switzerland. Meets Thomas Wolfe in Paris and later spends time with him in Switzerland. In order to pay for Zelda's treatment, writes and sells stories to *The Saturday Evening Post,* earning $32,000 for the year from eight stories, among them "Babylon Revisited," published in December. Spends fall at Hotel de la Paix in Lausanne and has brief affair with Englishwoman Bijou O'Conor.

1931   Father dies in January in Washington and Fitzgerald goes home for funeral. After visits to Montgomery and New York, returns to Europe and finds Zelda's condition improved; she becomes an outpatient and is allowed to take trips to Paris and the Austrian Tyrol, then is discharged from Prangins on September 15. Sails for U.S. with Zelda on September 19, and settles in Montgomery. Goes to Hollywood in November after being offered $1,200 a week by M-G-M to work on a Jean Harlow movie, leaving Zelda in Montgomery to be with her ailing father, who dies on November 17. Returns to Montgomery for Christmas.

1932   Takes Zelda in January on vacation to Florida and she works on a novel. Zelda has relapse on trip back to Montgomery,

and enters Henry Phipps Psychiatric Clinic in Baltimore on
February 12. Fitzgerald remains in Montgomery to work on
his novel. Zelda finishes her novel while at the Phipps Clinic
and, after Fitzgerald comes to Baltimore to help her revise
it, Scribner's accepts it. Rents La Paix, Victorian-style house
on the Turnbull estate in Towson, just outside Baltimore,
in May. Zelda is discharged from Phipps on June 26. In
August, Fitzgerald spends time at Johns Hopkins Hospital with what is diagnosed as typhoid fever (will eventually
be hospitalized there eight more times from 1933 to 1937
for alcoholism and chronic inactive fibroid tuberculosis).
Zelda's novel *Save Me the Waltz* is published October 7; it
receives bad reviews and sells very poorly. Resumes serious work on his novel, while Zelda paints and writes play,
Scandalabra.

1933   *Scandalabra* is produced by the Junior Vagabonds, Baltimore amateur little theater, in the spring. In September,
Ring Lardner dies and Fitzgerald writes tribute for *The New
Republic*. Sends new novel, *Tender Is the Night*, to Scribner's
in late October.

1934   *Tender Is the Night* serialized in *Scribner's Magazine*, January–April, and is published on April 12, receiving largely
favorable reviews and selling well. While working on revising
the book in New York in January and February, spends time
with John O'Hara and with Dorothy Parker. Zelda reen-
ters Phipps Clinic on February 12 and later is transferred to
Craig House in Beacon, New York ("I left my capacity for
hoping on the little roads that led to Zelda's sanitarium").
Fitzgerald arranges showing of her paintings at art gallery
in New York in March and April, and she is permitted to
attend opening. When her condition deteriorates, Zelda is
admitted to the Sheppard and Enoch Pratt Hospital outside
Baltimore on May 19. Fitzgerald begins to sell stories and
articles to recently established magazine *Esquire*, which pays
$250 per piece.

1935   Travels to Tryon, North Carolina, in February in attempt to
improve his health. *Taps at Reveille*, short-story collection,
published by Scribner's on March 10. Spends summer in
Asheville, North Carolina, at the Grove Park Inn, where
he has affair with Beatrice Dance, who is married. Returns
to Baltimore in September and lives in rented apartment.
Spends winter in Hendersonville, North Carolina.

1936   Writes three confessional articles, "The Crack-Up," "Pasting It Together," and "Handle With Care," which appear in *Esquire,* February–April, and arouse considerable consternation among his friends. Zelda is transferred to Highland Hospital in Asheville on April 6, and Fitzgerald spends summer at Grove Park Inn to be near her. Mother dies in August, but Fitzgerald is unable to attend funeral. Daughter enters Ethel Walker School in Simsbury, Connecticut, in September. On his fortieth birthday in September is interviewed by Michel Mok of the New York *Post.* Subsequent article is headlined "Scott Fitzgerald, 40, Engulfed in Despair"; after it appears, Fitzgerald attempts suicide with overdose of morphine. Through Perkins, meets Marjorie Kinnan Rawlings when she comes to Asheville. Spends Christmas holidays in Johns Hopkins Hospital recovering from influenza and heavy drinking.

1937   Spends first months of year at Oak Hall Hotel in Tryon, North Carolina. Has great difficulty selling stories; his debts exceed $40,000, with $12,000 owed to his agent, Harold Ober. Hired as a screenwriter by M-G-M in July for six months at $1,000 per week. Rents small apartment at Garden of Allah, 8152 Sunset Boulevard, in Hollywood. Meets Sheilah Graham, twenty-eight-year-old Englishwoman who writes a Hollywood gossip column, at a party soon after his arrival, and they begin an affair. Works on film adaptation of Erich Maria Remarque's novel *Three Comrades.* Though it is extensively altered by producer Joseph Mankiewicz, his work on it contributes to renewal of his M-G-M contract (will be only screenplay for which he receives on-screen credit).

1938   Visits Zelda in January and takes her to Florida and Montgomery. Returns to Hollywood, and works from February to May on "Infidelity," movie for Joan Crawford, which is never produced. During daughter's spring vacation, takes her and Zelda to Virginia Beach and Norfolk, Virginia, but gets drunk and behaves badly. Moves to house at 114 Malibu Beach in April. Daughter is accepted at Vassar College. Fitzgerald works from May to October on screenplay of Claire Booth Luce's play *The Women* but is eventually replaced. Moves to Encino in November and rents small house on Belly Acres estate of actor Edward Everett Horton. Hires Frances Kroll as his secretary. Plans educational curriculum, "College of One," for Sheilah Graham, a two-year course in the arts and humanities that he participates in by tutoring her as well as assigning readings. Begins work in November on *Madame Curie,* film for Greta Garbo.

1939   Plans for *Madame Curie* are shelved in January, and after he is loaned to David O. Selznick to work very briefly on *Gone With the Wind,* Fitzgerald learns that M-G-M is dropping its option after eighteen months. Becomes freelance screenwriter and socializes in Hollywood with, among others, Nathanael West and S. J. Perelman. Hired by producer Walter Wanger of United Artists to collaborate with recent Dartmouth graduate Budd Schulberg on screenplay of *Winter Carnival*; they take a disastrous trip to Dartmouth College in February, during which Fitzgerald is drunk the entire time, and they are both fired. Goes on trip to Cuba with Zelda in April, and is so drunk and ill that she has to take him to New York, where he is hospitalized before returning to California. Begins work on a novel about Hollywood, with main character, Monroe Stahr, based on Irving Thalberg (never completed, it is edited by Edmund Wilson and published posthumously in 1941 as *The Last Tycoon*). Receives intermittent but brief screenwriting assignments but falls deeper in debt, eventually severing ties with longtime agent Harold Ober because Ober refuses to lend him any more money; becomes his own agent.

1940   Begins to publish series of stories in *Esquire* about Pat Hobby, a hack Hollywood writer, for which he receives $250 per story; ultimately, *Esquire* publishes seventeen Pat Hobby stories, one in each monthly number from January 1940 to July 1941. Writes "Cosmopolitan," screen adaptation of his story "Babylon Revisited," but it is never used. Moves in May to apartment at 1403 Laurel Avenue in Hollywood, a block from Sheilah Graham's apartment, and works intensively on his novel through the summer and fall. Suffers heart attack in late November and is ordered to rest in bed. Moves to Sheilah Graham's apartment, where he dies, apparently of a second heart attack, on December 21. With Zelda's approval, decision is made to bury Fitzgerald with his father's family in Rockville, Maryland, but he is refused burial at St. Mary's Church cemetery because he was not a practicing Catholic at his death. Buried December 27 at Rockville Union Cemetery.

Note on the Texts

This volume brings together F. Scott Fitzgerald's third novel, *The Great Gatsby* (1925); his third collection of short stories, *All the Sad Young Men* (1926); and a selection of magazine work—sixteen short stories and nine pieces of nonfiction—published from 1920 to 1926 and not collected by Fitzgerald. New, corrected texts of *The Great Gatsby*, *All the Sad Young Men*, and the uncollected magazine work selected for this volume have been prepared for Library of America by James L. W. West III. The texts for all selections are described below.

In the late spring of 1922, while living at the resort town of White Bear Lake, near his hometown of St. Paul, Minnesota, Fitzgerald began work on the novel that was to become *The Great Gatsby*. He had recently finished correcting the proofs of *Tales of the Jazz Age*, his second collection of short stories, and was keen to get to work on a new book. In a letter dated June 20, 1922, he wrote to Maxwell Perkins, his editor at Scribner's, informing him that the novel would have a "catholic element" and would be set in "the middle west and New York of 1885." Four months later, Fitzgerald moved his family to Great Neck, Long Island, where he worked sporadically on the manuscript during the next year and a half. His progress was interrupted by other creative projects—first by the writing and production of his play, *The Vegetable*, and then, after its pre-Broadway flop in November 1923, by the composition of magazine stories to get himself out of debt.

In the early spring of 1924, Fitzgerald reconceived the novel, changing its omniscient narration to Nick Carraway's not always reliable first-person reminiscences and placing most of the action in a fictionalized version of contemporary Great Neck. He drafted three chapters in March and April. The following month, he and his wife and daughter sailed to France for an extended stay. They settled on the French Riviera, where Fitzgerald continued to work on the novel through the summer and early fall of that year. He composed in longhand on sheets of foolscap and worked with stenographers, through two or three drafts, to produce a typescript setting copy of the novel. This document he sent to Perkins via transatlantic mail on October 27, 1924.

In a letter of November 14, 1924, and in a subsequent, much longer letter of November 20, 1924, to Fitzgerald, Perkins praised the new novel but offered suggestions about how to bring Jay Gatsby's character and physical appearance into sharper focus. Perkins's advice prompted Fitzgerald to revise his novel heavily. The text was now in galley proofs, two sets of which had been sent to him in late December. Fitzgerald supplied more information about the early years of Jay Gatsby's life and the origins of his money, but he went far beyond addressing Perkins's criticisms, almost rewriting the novel. He made Nick into a more sympathetic character, moved material about, reordered chapters, deleted long sections of exposition, provided fresh passages of description and dialogue, and polished the prose throughout. And Fitzgerald seemed to settle at last on *The Great Gatsby* as the title. He had previously tried out several possibilities, including "Among the Ash Heaps and Millionaires," "Gold-Hatted Gatsby," "Trimalchio," "Trimalchio in West Egg," "The High-Bouncing Lover," "On the Road to West Egg," and "Gatsby." In December 1924, Fitzgerald and Perkins agreed to contractual terms, though there was never any doubt that Fitzgerald would publish the novel with Scribner's, which had published all of his books.

In February 1925, Fitzgerald sent a set of galleys bearing his handwritten revisions to Perkins (the other set, his working galleys, he kept for himself). He was now living in Italy, and there was not enough time for the publisher to send another round of proofs. Three weeks before publication, he cabled his editor: "CRAZY ABOUT TITLE UNDER THE RED WHITE AND BLUE STOP WHART WOULD DELAY BE." Perkins cabled back on the following day: "Advertised and sold for April tenth publication. Change suggested would mean some weeks delay, very great psychological damage. Think irony is far more effective under less leading title. Everyone likes present title. Urge we keep it." Fitzgerald conceded in a March 22 cable: "YOURE RIGHT." Fitzgerald continued to send revisions to Perkins, by letter and cable, until almost the day of publication.

The job of incorporating Fitzgerald's revisions into the text and seeing the novel through the press fell to Perkins. The novel was published on schedule by Scribner's, with few textual errors, on April 10, 1925.

The Great Gatsby had an initial print run of 20,870 copies; a second printing of 3,000 copies followed in August 1925. Reviews were generally favorable, but sales were modest, disappointing the expectations of both author and publisher. Harold Ober, Fitzgerald's literary agent, sold the subsidiary rights for both a stage adaptation and a movie version of the novel for the considerable sum (in total) of $26,000, but the 1926 Broadway play and the silent movie of the same year failed to boost book sales. Fitzgerald felt that *The Great Gatsby* had not succeeded commercially because, as he explained to Perkins in a letter of late April 1925, the title was "only fair" and because the novel lacked any important female characters. In 1926, Chatto & Windus published the novel in London, using duplicate plates cast in the Scribner's printing plant.

This volume presents the text of the first printing of the 1925 Scribner's edition of *The Great Gatsby*, emended to account for typographical errors and other obvious mistakes that require correction, for

Fitzgerald's preferred American spellings, and for subsequent alterations authorized by Fitzgerald. The first printing has been collated with Fitzgerald's composite manuscript, his working galleys, and his personal reading copy of the novel as well as all printings of the novel in the author's lifetime. Additionally, Fitzgerald's correspondence with Perkins has been consulted. The typescript setting copy is not known to be extant, nor is the set of galleys that Fitzgerald sent back to Scribner's (which evidently contained revisions not entered on his working galleys and may have omitted some he had previously made on those galleys). These materials were likely discarded soon after the novel's publication.

It was Scribner's practice up until the 1930s to impose British spelling on the texts of its American authors. Fitzgerald was not an exception in this regard, nor was Scribner's unique among American publishers in this practice, intended to encourage British publishers to purchase sheets from American publishers or to use their plates for a fee. Instances of this British orthography in *The Great Gatsby* include "defence," "centre," and "criticising." This volume restores Fitzgerald's preferred American spellings, with a few exceptions (for example, "theatre"), in deference to Fitzgerald's own long-standing habit. Hyphenated spellings introduced by Fitzgerald's editors (for example, "to-day" and "week-end") have been replaced by the unhyphenated spellings found in the author's manuscripts.

As evidenced by Fitzgerald's manuscript and the extensive revisions he made to the working galleys, he tended to punctuate more lightly than his editors; however, with the exception of the correction of typographical errors, no attempt has been made to restore the punctuation in the composite manuscript, which constitutes a working draft of the novel, not a fair copy.

Fitzgerald sometimes mispunctuated split speech in dialogue, and his pointing was inconsistently corrected by his typists or by the copyeditors at Scribner's. For example, in Chapter I, the 1925 Scribner's text reads as follows:

> "I'm stiff," she complained, "I've been lying on that sofa for as long as I can remember."

In this edition, the comma following the verb has been emended to a period in this and other similar instances. Where necessary, the first word of the second clause has been capitalized.

Six alterations were introduced into the plates for the second printing of *The Great Gatsby* in August 1925. Four of these revisions are changes authorized by Fitzgerald; the other two are corrections of typographical errors. All six plate changes have been adopted for the present edition. These emendations are found in the 1926 Chatto & Windus printing. A single additional emendation appears in the British text;

that emendation has been adopted ("self-absorbtion" has been corrected to "self-absorption"). In black pencil, Fitzgerald marked about three dozen revisions into the text of his personal reading copy of *The Great Gatsby* (a first impression of the 1925 Scribner's text), including corrections in spelling, capitalization, and punctuation as well as substantive alterations. These altered readings from the marked copy are incorporated into the present edition. Tom Buchanan's "God Damn" and "God Damned," from the manuscript and galleys, are adopted for this edition instead of the milder "God damned" of the first edition. An alternative reading adopted from an April 10, 1925, letter from Fitzgerald to Perkins has been adopted for this edition and is noted in the list of emendations.

Within a few weeks after the publication of *The Great Gatsby*, Fitzgerald—now living in Paris—began to assemble and edit the nine stories that comprise *All the Sad Young Men*. All the stories had been previously published in magazines, but Fitzgerald now heavily reworked them for book publication. Given the scope of his revisions, he likely submitted new typescripts rather than marked-up tearsheets to Scribner's. In the case of "Winter Dreams," he wrote several new passages of descriptive prose and substituted them for passages he had incorporated into *The Great Gatsby*. This was a common practice for Fitzgerald; he identified passages of good description and dialogue from his stories, copied them into his notebooks, and often used them again in his novels. In a letter of June 1925 to Perkins, Fitzgerald reported that the setting copy "will reach you by July 15th." In the same letter, he proposed language for the flap copy of the jacket: the collection shows the "transition from his early exuberant stories of youth which created a new type of American girl and the later and more serious mood which produced *The Great Gatsby* and marked him as one of the half dozen masters of English prose now writing in America."

Based on Fitzgerald's reported progress, Perkins scheduled *All the Sad Young Men* for publication in the fall of 1925, but Fitzgerald did not mail the setting copy until late August. And there was another problem: Harold Ober had sold "The Rich Boy" to *Red Book* magazine for publication in two parts, and the editors at *Red Book* were unable to clear the necessary space in the monthly magazine until January and February 1926. *Red Book* had paid $3,500 for "The Rich Boy," a high price at the time, and insisted the collection not be released until after the publication of the February issue. Fitzgerald had originally agreed not to see galleys of the book so that it might pass quickly into print and be available for the Christmas bookselling season, but the postponement in publication now made it possible for galleys to be mailed to him in mid-October. He corrected the galleys and sent them back to Perkins by the end of November. Scribner's published *All the Sad Young Men* on February 26, 1926, to favorable reviews. An initial printing of 10,100 copies was soon followed by two smaller printings of 3,020 and 3,050 copies, in March and May 1926.

This volume presents the text of the first printing of the 1926 Scribner's edition of *All the Sad Young Men*, emended in consultation with the published magazine versions of the stories and, when they exist, with typescripts, to account for Fitzgerald's preferred American spellings, typographical errors, and other mistakes requiring correction. No copy of the printed book bearing revisions by Fitzgerald is known to survive, nor are any galleys extant. No plate changes were introduced into subsequent printings of the collection. There was no British printing of the collection during the author's lifetime. Details of the first publication of the stories in *All the Sad Young Men* are given below.

The Rich Boy. *The Red Book Magazine*, January and February 1926.

Winter Dreams. *Metropolitan Magazine*, December 1922.

The Baby Party. *Hearst's International*, February 1925.

Absolution. *The American Mercury*, June 1924.

Rags Martin-Jones and the Pr-nce of W-les, *McCall's*, July 1924.

The Adjuster. *The Red Book Magazine*, September 1925.

Hot and Cold Blood. *Hearst's International*, August 1923.

"The Sensible Thing." *Liberty*, July 5, 1924.

Gretchen's Forty Winks. *The Saturday Evening Post*, March 15, 1924.

Fitzgerald published more than 150 stories in mass-circulation magazines during his career, beginning with one called "Head and Shoulders" in *The Saturday Evening Post* for February 21, 1920. As a professional writer, he depended on the substantial income that he could earn for his magazine work. Fitzgerald received almost $5,500 in royalties from the sales of *All the Sad Young Men*, but the serial income he had earned from the nine stories in the collection was a considerably larger sum—$14,200, minus a 10 percent commission to his agent. The uncollected stories and items of nonfiction selected for this volume were all published in magazines; like much of his magazine work, these pieces were not reprinted during his lifetime. For these items Fitzgerald earned in total approximately $37,500 before commission. Fitzgerald came to think of his work as divided between serious writing and commercial magazine fiction, but the line between artistic respectability and commercial success was never an absolute one in the author's mind. Details of the first publication of the uncollected stories selected for this volume are given below.

Myra Meets His Family. *The Saturday Evening Post*, March 20, 1920.

The Smilers. *The Smart Set*, June 1920.

The Popular Girl. *The Saturday Evening Post*, February 11 and 18, 1922.

Dice, Brassknuckles and Guitar. *Hearst's International*, May 1923.

Diamond Dick and the First Law of Woman. *Hearst's International*, April 1924.

The Third Casket. *The Saturday Evening Post*, May 31, 1924.

The Unspeakable Egg. *The Saturday Evening Post*, July 12, 1924.

John Jackson's Arcady. *The Saturday Evening Post*, July 26, 1924.

The Pusher-in-the-Face. *Woman's Home Companion*, February 1925.

Love in the Night. *The Saturday Evening Post*, March 14, 1925.

One of My Oldest Friends. *Woman's Home Companion*, September 1925.

A Penny Spent. *The Saturday Evening Post*, October 10, 1925.

"Not in the Guidebook." *Woman's Home Companion*, November 1925.

Presumption. *The Saturday Evening Post*, January 9, 1926.

The Adolescent Marriage. *The Saturday Evening Post*, March 6, 1926.

The Dance. *The Red Book Magazine*, June 1926.

Details of the first publication of the uncollected nonfiction selected for this volume follow.

An Interview with Mr. Fitzgerald. In Heywood Broun's "Books" column in the *New York Herald-Tribune* on May 7, 1920, and in a longer, uncut version in *Saturday Review*, November 5, 1960.

Who's Who—and Why. *The Saturday Evening Post*, September 18, 1920.

The Credo of F. Scott Fitzgerald. *Chicago Daily News*, March 9, 1921.

Three Cities. *Brentano's Book Chat*, September–October 1921.

What I Think and Feel at 25. *American Magazine*, September 1922.

How to Live on $36,000 a Year. *The Saturday Evening Post*, April 5, 1924.

How to Live on Practically Nothing a Year. *The Saturday Evening Post*, September 20, 1924.

How to Waste Material: A Note on My Generation. *The Bookman*, May 1926.

With the two exceptions noted below, the texts of the uncollected stories and nonfiction presented here are those of their first magazine publication, emended with reference to manuscripts and typescripts, when they survive, to account for typographical errors, other obvious mistakes that require correction, and revisions intended by the author. The text of "Dice, Brassknuckles and Guitar" is that of a set of tearsheets heavily revised by Fitzgerald and preserved among his papers at Princeton. It is not known why Fitzgerald revised this story after its serial publication, but he may have considered including it in *All the Sad Young Men*. The text has been emended to account for typographical and other small errors requiring correction. Parts of "An Interview with Mr. Fitzgerald" were published on May 7, 1920, in Heywood Broun's "Books" column in the *New York Herald-Tribune*, and, in a longer, uncut version, based on Fitzgerald's manuscript (which has not been located), in *Saturday Review*, on November 5, 1960; the text presented here is that of the later printing. After the publication of "Diamond Dick and the First Law of Woman" in *Hearst's International*, Fitzgerald shortened the title to "Diamond Dick" on tearsheets that survive among his papers; that change is accepted here (he made no further revisions on the tearsheets). For "'Not in the Guidebook,'" two excisions made for space by the editors at *Woman's Home Companion* have been restored. For "How to Live on Practically Nothing a Year," cuts made at *The Saturday Evening Post* to remove references to hotels and businesses in France have been reinstated.

The texts presented in this volume reproduce those of the selected sources, altered only in the ways described above. Substantive alterations to *The Great Gatsby*, *All the Sad Young Men*, and the uncollected magazine publications are indicated in the list of emendations below. The three lists record, by page and line number, the changes incorporated into the respective texts. A key to the abbreviations used to indicate the source of a particular reading precedes the list of emendations for each text.

THE GREAT GATSBY

MS   *The Great Gatsby*, composite manuscript, March–September 1924, F. Scott Fitzgerald Papers, Department of Rare Books and Special Collections, Princeton University Library.

G   Fitzgerald's working galleys, January–February 1925, F. Scott Fitzgerald Papers, Department of Rare Books and Special Collections, Princeton University Library.

Ai   *The Great Gatsby*. New York: Scribner's, 1925. Copy-text.

Ai2   *The Great Gatsby*, second printing (August 1925). New York: Scribner's, 1925.

Aib   *The Great Gatsby*. London: Chatto & Windus, 1926.

FC   Fitzgerald's marked copy of *The Great Gatsby* (first printing).

L   Letter from Fitzgerald to Perkins, April 10, 1925, Archives of Charles Scribner's Sons, Department of Rare Books and Special Collections, Princeton University Library.

ed   Editor.

7.40   confusion] FC; wonder

8.1   arresting] FC; interesting

11.40   Damn] MS; damned

15.14   said] FC; began

15.38   startlingly] MS; startingly

19.33   been at] ed; been

20.8   men] FC; ash-gray men

20.33   restaurants] FC; cafés

21.39   surplus flesh] FC; flesh

23.33   so warm] FC; warm

23.34   afternoon that I] FC; afternoon. I

24.34   disappeared] FC; both disappeared

28.38–39   had played no part in her past] FC; expected no affection

29.2–3   out." She looked to see who was listening. "'Oh] FC; out: 'Oh

29.19   was him] FC; saw him

33.1   shorn] FC; bobbed

33.32–33   amusement parks] FC; an amusement park

35.39   sometime] MS; sometimes

38.10   Third] FC; First

38.11   Ninth Machine-Gun Battalion] FC; Twenty-eighth Infantry

38.12   Seventh Infantry] FC; Sixteenth

38.38   external] FC; eternal

40.2   echolalia] Ai2; chatter

40.4   Vladimir] ed; Vladmir

40.9   Vladimir] ed; Vladmir

40.25   formed with] MS; formed for

44.12   them little] MS; them a little

45.26   five] FC; lined five

45.29   outlined] FC; made

45.29–30   gestures] FC; circles

50.11–12   work or rigid sitting] FC; work

51.39   two machine-gun detachments] FC; the remains of my machine-gun battalion

54.36   asked Gatsby] MS; asked

59.6   Seelbach] FC; Muhlbach

60.30   Victoria] MS; victoria

61.19   he's a regular] FC; he's regular

64.1   looked] FC; looked down

68.28–29   occasionally willing] FC; willing, even eager,

68.35   a large] FC; the large

70.35   Adam] ed; Adam's

74.13   will store] FC; can store

76.11   self-absorp-|tion] Aib; self-absorb-|tion

76.24   southern] Ai2; northern

91.9–11   expectantly. ¶"Pardon me?" ¶"Have] G; expectantly. ¶"Have

93.11   stop] MS; spot

97.1–2   added, as if she might have sounded irreverent,] FC; added,

99.36   God Damned] G; God damned

104.8   Michaelis] FC; Mavromichaelis

104.11   its] Ai2; it's

104.18   ripped] FC; ripped a little

104.21   away.] Ai2; away

104.35   wire] FC; metal

105.1   disarranged] MS; deranged

106.16   him, seized] ed; him seized

106.16   him] MS; him,

107.18   God Damn] MS; God damned

107.29   moonlit] MS; moonlight

113.30   finger] MS; fingers

117.26   Central] ed; central

117.27   Long Distance] ed; long distance

121.18   thereabouts] MS; thereabout

122.24   compass] L; transit

124.24   as] FC; though

124.25   unmoved] FC; shocked

128.25   sickantired] Ai2; sick in tired

128.28   at me all] MS; at me

128.30   Wolfshiem] MS; Wolfsheim

132.5–6   Owl Eyes] ed; Owl-eyes

132.16   Union Station] Ai2; Union Street station

ALL THE SAD YOUNG MEN

MS   Early holograph manuscript for "Rags Martin-Jones and the Pr-nce of W-les," December 1923, F. Scott Fitzgerald Papers,

Department of Rare Books and Special Collections, Princeton University Library.

TS   Typescript for "The Rich Boy" from Harold Ober files, bearing Fitzgerald's final revisions for serial publication, August 1925, F. Scott Fitzgerald Papers, Department of Rare Books and Special Collections, Princeton University Library.

ser   Serial text for "'The Sensible Thing,'" *Liberty*, July 5, 1924.

Ai   *All the Sad Young Men*. New York: Scribner's, 1926. Copy-text.

ed   Editor.

142.14   De Soto] ed; De Sota

143.17   bridesmaids] TS; bridesmaid

155.4   Vanderbilt] ed; Madison

156.39–40   imminent] ed; eminent

157.14   out] TS; on

157.18   that] TS; they

159.19   in] TS; of

181.7   these] ed; this

198.24–25   hiding the] ed; hiding up the

210.23   thoughts] ed; thought

213.23   interrogator] ed; interrogation

216.33   Hamline] ed; Hamlin

217.4   shoulders] ed; shoulder

221.36   *Die*] ed; *Dei*

227.31   1912] ed; 1913

230.30   elusive] ed; illusive

234.11   after] MS; after a

234.29   with a] MS; with

237.21   laid] MS; had laid

240.19   bunch over] MS; bunch across over

284.28   ground] ser; grounds

288.19   O'Kelly] ed; Rollins

UNCOLLECTED STORIES AND NONFICTION

TS1   Typescript of "A Penny Spent" bearing Fitzgerald's handwritten revisions, July 1925, F. Scott Fitzgerald Papers, Department of Rare Books and Special Collections, Princeton University Library.

TS2   Typescript of "'Not in the Guidebook,'" with light handwritten revisions by Fitzgerald, February 1925, F. Scott Fitzgerald Papers, Department of Rare Books and Special Collections, Princeton University Library.

TS3   Carbon typescript of "The Adolescent Marriage," December 1925, private collection (Fitzgerald's grandchildren).

TS4   Early Typescript of "The Dance," with heavy revisions by Fitzgerald, January 1926, F. Scott Fitzgerald Papers, Department of Rare Books and Special Collections, Princeton University Library.

TS5   Typescript of "How to Live on Practically Nothing a Year," August 1924, F. Scott Fitzgerald Papers, Department of Rare Books and Special Collections, Princeton University Library.

ser   Serial texts. Copy-texts.

TRS1   Tearsheets of "Dice, Brassknuckles and Guitar," F. Scott Fitzgerald Papers, Department of Rare Books and Special Collections, Princeton University Library. Copy-text.

TRS2   Tearsheets of "Diamond Dick and the First Law of Woman," F. Scott Fitzgerald Papers, Department of Rare Books and Special Collections, Princeton University Library.

ed   Editor

315.13   Rose] ed; Red

319.14   telegram] ed; telegraph

347.4   to a] ed; to

411.1   *Diamond Dick*] TRS2; *Diamond Dick and the First Law of Woman*

443.18   or] ed; nor

523.35   out of] ed; out

525.19   woods] ed; wood

529.2   Ritz] TS1; Brix

529.4   or Morris Gest's office, or Herrin] TS1; or Herrin

529.10   Ritz] TS1; Brix

529.30   Ritz] TS1; Brix

532.6   Ritz] TS1; Brix

533.8   Ritz] TS1; Brix

533.25   Ritz] TS1; Brix

537.15   half a dozen] TS1; a half dozen

537.33   Ritz] TS1; Brix

543.15   he's still] TS1; still he's

543.35   off] TS1; away

545.7   a low] ed; low

547.40   at Cosenza. That's halfway.] TS1; halfway.

548.8   trip to Palermo] TS1; trip

548.36   Torre Annunziata] TS1; Torre dell' Annunziata

549.1   Cosenza] TS1; our destination

554.1   "Not in the Guidebook"] TS2; Not in the Guidebook

554.21–23   to see. We discovered that the story began about three days before it got into the papers. ¶ It began] TS2; to see. ¶ It began

558.40   loud] TS2; loudly

559.30   good] ed; well

562.12   anything," said Mrs. Horton, who] ed; anything." Mrs. Horton

563.1   Bill] ed; their guide

563.18   proceeded on] TS2; proceeded

563.35–38   my wife.' ¶ "Most of the Court almost broke their contracts laughing. The ones that didn't died in the Bastille." ¶ That was] TS2; my wife.'" ¶ That was

564.24   you go to a lawyer and] TS2; you

564.26–27   down at the pavement] TS2; down

565.31   a 1910 Ford] TS2; an ancient American one

565.31   parked at intervals] TS2; parked

567.7   whispered to himself] TS2; whispered

572.39   lived] ed; live

599.5–6   toy, instead of resulting in a harmonious whole, looked like a typical cross-section of Philadelphia] TS3; toy did not result in a harmonious whole

599.31–33   plan a church—one of these modern churches with a cabaret on the twentieth floor, car-cards in every pew and a soda-fountain in the sanctuary] TS3; plan one of those modern churches, perhaps

600.36   Why, by God,] TS3; Why,

605.27–28   bitterly. "I'll be the Leopold and Loeb of Philadelphia—you'll see."] TS3; bitterly.

607.8   alone] TS3; along

612.8   Early in September] TS3; A week or so later

613.17   your] ed; the

613.36   half a year] TS3; months

614.14   summer evening] TS3; evening

615.15   Oh God—I] TS3; I

615.27   over] TS3; more than

618.20   an hilarious] TS4; a hilarious

619.5   affliction] ed; affection ser, affition TS

621.3   me] TS4; I

624.13   around] TS4; about

624.16   car. I called a waiter and sent] ed; car, and calling a waiter, I sent

625.15   made an] TS4; made the

629.1   out] TS4; out at

676.20–23   away. The Hôtel du Jardin bore traces of having been inhabited—the halls were littered with innumerable old copies of the "Illustrated London News"—but now, as we found at dinner] TS5; away. At dinner

680.12–13   Ste. Maxime] TS5; St. Maximin

680.15–16   town called St. Raphaël] TS5; a little town

681.11   St. Raphaël] TS5; the little town

686.5   varia] variants.

Notes

In the notes below, the reference numbers denote page and line of this volume (the line count includes chapter headings). For further biographical information than is contained in the Chronology, see David S. Brown, *Paradise Lost: A Life of F. Scott Fitzgerald* (Cambridge, MA: Belknap Press, 2017); Matthew J. Bruccoli, *Some Sort of Epic Grandeur: The Life of F. Scott Fitzgerald*, 1981, second revised edition (Columbia: University of South Carolina Press, 2002); Scott Donaldson, *Fool for Love: A Biography of F. Scott Fitzgerald*, 1983, revised edition (Minneapolis: University of Minnesota Press, 2012); André Le Vot, *F. Scott Fitzgerald: A Biography*, translated by William Byron (Garden City, NY: Doubleday, 1983); James R. Mellow, *Invented Lives: F. Scott and Zelda Fitzgerald* (Boston: Houghton Mifflin, 1984); Arthur Mizener, *The Far Side of Paradise: A Biography of F. Scott Fitzgerald*, 1951, revised edition (Boston: Houghton Mifflin, 1965); Andrew Turnbull, *Scott Fitzgerald* (New York: Scribner, 1962). For a history of the early versions of *The Great Gatsby* see the texts published in The Cambridge Edition of the Works of F. Scott Fitzgerald, 18 vols. (1991–2019): *Trimalchio: An Early Version of* The Great Gatsby, ed. James L. W. West III (New York: Cambridge University Press, 2000) and *The Great Gatsby: An Edition of the Manuscript*, ed. James L. W. West III and Don C. Skemer (New York: Cambridge University Press, 2018). A detailed account of the making of *The Great Gatsby* and a history of its publication are included in the final volume of The Cambridge Edition of the Works of F. Scott Fitzgerald: *The Great Gatsby: A Variorum Edition*, ed. James L. W. West III (New York: Cambridge University Press, 2019).

THE GREAT GATSBY

3.1–3 ONCE AGAIN TO ZELDA] Fitzgerald had previously dedicated his second book, *Flappers and Philosophers* (1920), to his wife, Zelda Sayre Fitzgerald.

6.15 the Dukes of Buccleuch] Ducal house of the Scotts of Buccleuch, granted land by King James II of Scotland in the fifteenth century. The title "Duke of Buccleuch" was created for James Scott, Duke of Monmouth (1649–1685).

6.17 sent a substitute . . . Civil War] The Enrollment Act of 1863 allowed men in the Northern states who were eligible for conscription to avoid service in the Civil War by hiring a substitute.

6.21 New Haven] Yale University, located in New Haven, Connecticut.

6.39   eighty a month] In 1922, the year in which *The Great Gatsby* is set, eighty dollars would have had the approximate buying power of thirteen hundred dollars in 2022.

7.3   an old Dodge] The Dodge Brothers Company of Hamtramck, Michigan, began making cars in 1914. Their Model 30, a four-cylinder passenger vehicle, was meant to compete with the Ford Model T.

7.21   Midas and Morgan and Maecenas] Midas, in Greek and Roman mythology, a king of Phrygia, who was granted his wish that everything he touched be turned to gold. John Pierpont Morgan (1837–1913), American financier and banker of the Gilded Age. Gaius Macenas (c. 70–8 B.C.E.), Roman statesman, friend and confidant of Augustus, and great literary patron of the "golden" Augustan era who fostered the careers of both Horace and Vergil.

7.37–38   the egg in the Columbus story] Apocryphal story concerning Christopher Columbus. Columbus is said to have challenged detractors of his discovery of the "New World" to stand an egg on its end. After they all had failed in the attempt, Columbus smashed one end of the egg against the table.

8.3   West Egg . . . less fashionable of the two] East Egg and West Egg suggest, respectively, Manhasset Neck (old money) and Great Neck (new money) on Long Island. In the manuscript version of the novel, Jordan gives Tom this description of West Egg: "Most expensive town on Long Island. Full of moving picture people, playrites, singers and cartoonists and kept women. You'd love it." From October 1922 until April 1924, Fitzgerald and his wife and daughter lived in a rented house on Great Neck.

8.32   Lake Forest.] A suburb of Chicago on the North Shore of Lake Michigan. Ginevra King, Fitzgerald's first serious romantic interest, lived in Lake Forest for much of the summer season. Her father, Charles Garfield King, was a successful stockbroker; he kept a string of polo ponies and played in matches at Onwentsia, a country club for the wealthy near Lake Forest.

11.24   She's three years old.] The Buchanans were married in June 1919; according to Jordan, their daughter was born ten months later, in April 1920. The child must therefore be two years old when this scene takes place in June 1922. The reading "three years old" originated in the manuscript, where the action of the novel was set at a later date and "three years old" was correct. Fitzgerald failed to adjust the child's age when he shifted the year to 1922.

12.1   Miss Baker] Before World War I, young men and women of the haute bourgeoisie addressed each other as "Mr." and "Miss"—at least until they became friends. These customs began to fade after the war, but Nick still observes them in the novel.

13.33   'The Rise of the Colored Empires' by . . . Goddard?"] Tom misremembers the title and author of *The Rising Tide of Color against White World-Supremacy* (1920), by the American historian and white supremacist Lothrop Stoddard (1883–1950). According to Stoddard's thesis, a racial world war was inevitable if Africans and Asians were not prevented from migrating to Western nations.

15.33–34 Cunard or White Star Line.] The two major British transatlantic passenger lines of Fitzgerald's era. (In 1934, the two rivals merged to form the Cunard–White Star Line.) The Cunard liners included the *Mauretania*, the *Aquitania*, and the *Berengaria*; the White Star liners, which were known for their black-topped funnels, included the *Olympic*, the *Britannic*, and the ill-fated *Titanic*.

16.33–34 I woke up . . . ether] During the 1920s, halogenated ether was a commonly used anesthetic. Daisy would have been unconscious during childbirth.

17.14 the Saturday Evening Post—] The most popular middle-class magazine of the period and Fitzgerald's most dependable market for short fiction during the peak years of his career.

17.29 *Jor*dan Baker."] Jordan Baker's name combines the titles of two early automobile manufacturers, both of which produced vehicles aimed at female buyers. The Jordan Motor Car Company (1916–1931) in Cleveland was known for its stylish runabouts; the Baker Motor Vehicle Company (1899–1914), also based in Cleveland, specialized in electric two-seaters, ideal for use in town.

17.31–32 rotogravure pictures] Rotogravure was a printing process using intaglio cylinders on a rotary press. Here, "rotogravure" refers to the illustrated supplement found in most Sunday newspapers of the day, featuring printed images of celebrities, society people, stage and movie stars, and sports figures.

17.32–33 Asheville and Hot Springs and Palm Beach.] Luxury resorts known for their golf courses, in North Carolina, Arkansas, and Florida.

20.15–16 the eyes . . . T. J. Eckleburg] Likely suggested by a painting, a gouache on paper by the illustrator Francis Cugat, that Fitzgerald saw in the Scribner's offices before departing for France in May 1924. In late August, while at work on the manuscript of the novel, he wrote to Maxwell Perkins: "For Christs sake don't give anyone that jacket you're saving for me. I've written it into the book." Cugat's painting, which depicts a woman's eyes hovering over an amusement-park scene, was used on the front panel of the first-edition dust jacket.

22.36 Town Tattle] A fictional magazine. Cf. *Town Topics,* a New York gossip rag known for printing scandalous stories about the rich and celebrated, published from 1885 to 1937.

23.6 John D. Rockefeller] American business magnate and wealthiest American of the twentieth century (1839–1937), known for his philanthropy and for his Social Darwinist beliefs. He founded the Standard Oil Company in 1870.

24.20 "Simon Called Peter,"] Scandalous best-selling novel of 1921 by British author Robert Keable (1887–1927). The protagonist is an army chaplain who loses his morals and ideals while serving on the front during World War I. In letters to Maxwell Perkins, Fitzgerald expressed nervousness about the reference.

27.5   Kaiser Wilhelm's.] Kaiser Wilhelm II (1859–1941), the last German emperor, who abdicated in November 1918 at the end of World War I after losing the support of the German army. He spent the rest of his life in exile in the Netherlands.

31.7   the morning Tribune] The *New-York Tribune*, founded by Horace Greeley in 1841, the leading Republican newspaper in the country and the chief rival of *The New York Times*. The *Tribune* merged with the *New York Herald* in 1924 to form the *New York Herald-Tribune*.

32.8   aquaplanes] Aquaplaning was a water sport popular before the advent of waterskiing. The participant, either standing or kneeling, rode a flat board towed behind a motorboat.

33.20–21   moving her hands like Frisco] In the dancing style of Joe Frisco (1889–1958), a comedian popular during the 1920s. Frisco was famous for a soft-shoe shuffle, of his own invention, called the "Frisco Dance." Beginning in 1918, he was featured in *The Midnight Frolic*, a late-night floor show staged by the impresario Florenz Ziegfeld (1867–1932) on the rooftop of Broadway's New Amsterdam Theatre. He performed also in *Vanities*, a Broadway girly-leggy variety show produced by Earl Carroll (1893–1948).

33.24–25   Gilda Gray's understudy from the Follies.] Gilda Gray (1901–1959), born Marianna Michalska, was a Polish American dancer and cabaret singer who popularized the "shimmy" in the 1920s when she performed in the Ziegfeld Follies, a Broadway review with revealing costumery and elaborate sets. The shimmy was characterized by movement of the shoulders and hips ("I'm shaking my shimmy, that's what I'm doing," Gray explained).

37.5   "Stoddard Lectures."] John L. Stoddard (1850–1931), an American author and popular performer on the lecture circuit. He was among the first to use the stereopticon in his presentations. His travelogues, comprising ten volumes and five supplements, were issued in a uniform edition beginning in 1897.

37.7   a regular Belasco] David Belasco (1853–1931), a Broadway dramatist and producer, was known for creating lifelike illusions onstage. Among his best-known productions were *Lord Chumley* in 1888 and *The Girl of the Golden West* in 1905.

37.9   didn't cut the pages.] In the early twentieth century, some books were still issued with untrimmed edges. Progressing through the book, the reader separated the leaves from one another with a paper knife or letter-opener.

38.16   hydroplane] Here, a fixed-wing aircraft that could take off and land on water.

40.4–5 Mr. Vladimir Tostoff's . . . Carnegie Hall] The Russian jazz musician Vladimir Tostoff is a fictional invention. George Gershwin's *Rhapsody in Blue* (1923) and other works of serious jazz made their world premieres at New York's Carnegie Hall.

43.7 a long duster] A lightweight overcoat worn by drivers and passengers for protection against engine exhaust and dirt from the roads.

45.3 the Yale Club—] A private New York club for graduates and faculty of Yale University. It was located at the corner of Vanderbilt and East 44th Street.

45.9 the old Murray Hill Hotel] Late Victorian New York hotel that was razed in 1947. The Murray Hill Hotel had one entrance on Park Avenue opposite Grand Central Station and another entrance on 40th Street. According to one 1920s guidebook, the atmosphere inside was "heavily gracious."

48.7–8 Von Hindenburg] Paul von Hindenburg (1847–1934), field marshal of the German armed forces during World War I. After the war he served as president of the Weimar Republic (1925–1934).

50.9 the dashboard] Narrow platform fixed beneath each car door. Later, it was called a "running-board."

51.33–34 the Bois de Boulogne] Wooded area of over two thousand acres, lying just west of Paris, originally designated by Napoleon III in the 1850s as a recreational space for the upper classes. By the early 1900s "Le Bois" had been transformed into a public park for the bourgeoisie, with areas for rowing, riding, and picnicking.

51.38 Argonne Forest] Forest in northeastern France, 135 miles east of Paris, through which American troops pushed in the final offensive of World War I, known as the Meuse-Argonne Offensive, which lasted from September 26, 1918, until the Armistice on November 11, 1918. American troops sustained more than 110,000 casualties.

51.38–52.4 so far forward . . . of dead.] Gatsby's exploits are based on the story of the "Lost Battalion," a unit of the 77th Division that advanced well beyond its flank support during the Meuse-Argonne Offensive. The battalion held its ground but at a heavy cost. Of some 554 men, there were only 194 survivors. The Lewis gun, a standard weapon in most American units, was a one-man air-cooled machine gun with a circular cartridge drum.

52.9–10 Montenegro's troubled history] Montenegro was among the Allied Powers during the First World War. After the Treaty of Versailles, it was absorbed by Yugoslavia as part of a newly unified Montenegro and Serbia; however, the unification was contested by the exiled king of Montenegro and his supporters.

52.24 Trinity Quad—] Trinity College, Oxford, founded in 1555, is one of the constituent colleges of the University of Oxford. On his first trip to Europe, during the spring of 1921, Fitzgerald and his wife, Zelda, visited Trinity.

52.31   the Grand Canal] A major waterway through the city of Venice, lined with opulent palaces belonging to the wealthiest Venetian families.

54.28   "Highballs?"] A whiskey drink, usually mixed with soda water or ginger ale, and served with ice in a tall glass.

54.38–55.5   "The old Metropole . . . outside.] Fitzgerald based Wolfshiem's recollections on the murder of the gangster and bookmaker Herman Rosenthal. The shooting took place on July 16, 1912, in New York, at the Metropole Hotel, 147 West 43rd Street, near Times Square. Accounts of the killing stayed on the front pages of metropolitan newspapers for the rest of the summer.

57.8–9   the man who fixed the World's Series] Racketeer Arnold Rothstein (1882–1928), on whom Wolfshiem is based, is said to have fixed the 1919 World's Series in the infamous "Black Sox" scandal. Rothstein got wind of a plan by several players on the Chicago White Sox team to throw the series; he therefore bet heavily on the Cincinnati Reds, their opponents. The White Sox lost the series, and Rothstein won more than $300,000. Rothstein was never formally charged with involvement in the swindle, but eight members of the Chicago White Sox, including star outfielder "Shoeless Joe" Jackson and pitcher Eddie Cicotte, were banned for lifetime from baseball for their participation.

57.39   the Plaza Hotel] The Plaza, among the most fashionable of the New York caravansaries, stands across from the southeast corner of Central Park at Fifth Avenue and 59th Street.

59.2   the armistice] The agreement that ended hostilities between the Allies and Germany in World War I specified that fighting should cease on November 11, 1918, at 11:00 A.M.—the eleventh hour of the eleventh day of the eleventh month (Matthew 20:1–16). Here, "after the armistice" means "after the war."

59.6–7   the Seelbach Hotel] A grand hotel in downtown Louisville, designed in the opulent European style, that was operated by immigrant brothers from Bavaria named Louis and Otto Seelbach.

60.31   a Victoria] A low, light, horse-drawn carriage that had a calash top and, in front, a perch for the driver.

60.35–38   "I'm the Sheik . . . I'll creep—"] Lyrics from "The Sheik of Araby," a hit tune in 1921, with words by Harry B. Smith and Francis Wheeler and music by Ted Snyder. Contemporary readers might also have been reminded of *The Sheik*, a silent movie of 1921 starring Rudolph Valentino (1895–1926), the first "Latin lover" screen idol. During the early 1920s, romantic young men were often called "sheiks."

65.21   The Journal.] The *New York Evening Journal*, a Hearst newspaper known for its racy, sensationalist reporting. It carried a daily comic-strip page and sold for one cent in 1922. Columnists included O. O. McIntyre and Nellie

Bly, with society news provided by Maury Henry Biddle Paul (a.k.a. "Cholly Knickerbocker").

65.31 Clay's "Economics,"] *Economics: An Introduction for the General Reader* (1916) by British economist and lecturer Henry Clay (1883–1954). Among Clay's concerns was the redistribution of wealth for the public good.

66.18 Castle Rackrent.] The ancestral home of the Irish Rackrent family in the novel of the same name by Anglo-Irish novelist Maria Edgeworth (1767–1849). *Castle Rackrent* recounts the adventures of three generations of Rackrents. They squander their wealth and eventually lose their tumbledown castle.

68.21 like Kant at his church steeple] The German philosopher Immanuel Kant (1724–1804) was said to gaze at a church steeple visible from the window of his writing room in Königsberg.

70.26 "the Merton College Library"] Merton College, which dates from 1264, was among the first colleges to be founded at Oxford. Its library is considered one of the most beautiful at the university. The library at Cottage Club (Fitzgerald's club at Princeton) is modelled on the Merton College Library.

70.35 an Adam study] The "Adam style" was a neoclassical furniture style developed by the Scottish brothers Robert and James Adam, an ornate choice for a man of Gatsby's age during the 1920s.

72.20 "The pompadour!] A hairstyle in which the hair is swept upward from the sides and forehead and fixed in place with hair oil or gel. The pompadour was popular during the 1910s but would have been passé by 1922.

73.23 "The Love Nest"] Popular song from the 1920 Broadway musical comedy *Mary*, with music by Louis A. Hirsch (1887–1924) and lyrics by Otto Harbach (1873–1963). The lyrics read in part: "Just a love nest, / Cozy with charm, / Like a dove nest, / Down on a farm . . . Better than a palace with a gilded dome, / Is a love nest / You can call home."

73.29–74.2 "In the morning . . . in between time—"] The seven lines are from "Ain't We Got Fun?" (1921), with music by Richard A. Whiting (1891–1938) and lyrics by Gus Kahn (1886–1941) and Raymond B. Egan (1890–1952). In the third-from-last line, Klipspringer sings the variant "children" for "poorer."

75.15–16 "underground pipe-line to Canada"] Illegal alcohol entered the U.S. from Canada, but a popular myth of the Prohibition era held that liquor flowed southward across the border through an underground pipeline.

76.24 Lutheran college of St. Olaf's] St. Olaf College in Northfield, Minnesota, founded in 1874 by Norwegian Lutherans.

76.38 Madame de Maintenon] Françoise d'Aubigné (1635–1719), known as Madame de Maintenon, who was secretly married in 1683 to Louis XIV, king of France. She was said to be pious and narrow-minded; she exercised much influence over the king during the last years of his reign.

83.30   "Three o'Clock in the Morning,"] Popular song of the 1920s with music by Julián Robledo (1887–1940) and lyrics by Dorothy Terriss (1883–1953). An instrumental version by Paul Whiteman's orchestra was released on the Victor label in 1922 and sold more than three million copies.

86.4   Trimalchio] A wealthy freed slave in the *Satyricon,* a Latin fiction likely written by the Roman author Petronius (c. A.D. 27–66). Trimalchio, who appears in a section of the work called "Trimalchio's Feast," throws ostentatious parties for his guests. The narrator of the *Satyricon* is a layabout named Encolpius. Fitzgerald considered "Trimalchio" and "Trimalchio in West Egg" as possible titles for *The Great Gatsby.*

87.10–11   National Biscuit Company] A sprawling Nabisco plant located in Long Island City in the borough of Queens.

89.26   gin rickeys] A hot-weather drink made with gin, lime juice, fruit syrup or sugar, and seltzer water. It is served over ice, usually with a wedge of lime, in a lowball glass.

91.40–41   You can . . . drug-store nowadays."] During Prohibition some drugstores were fronts for bootlegging, the suggestion by Tom being that Gatsby is a bootlegger.

93.10   both brakes] During the 1920s most automobiles were equipped with two mechanisms for stopping: hand brakes, which acted on the rear wheels, and pedal-operated brakes, which acted on the transmission shaft.

96.29   Mendelssohn's Wedding March] Fitzgerald refers to the march from the incidental music for *A Midsummer Night's Dream* (1842), by Felix Mendelssohn (1809–1847), usually played as a recessional at weddings. The ceremony downstairs appears to be beginning; the music one might expect to hear would be the "Bridal Chorus" ("Here comes the bride . . .") from *Lohengrin,* by Richard Wagner (1813–1883).

96.37   Biloxi, Tennessee."] Biloxi is a city in Harrison County, Mississippi, on the Gulf Coast. Daisy is perhaps confused.

97.36   New Haven."] See note 6.21.

100.20   Kapiolani?"] A three hundred-acre park in Honolulu, Hawaii.

100.24   the Punch Bowl] Extinct volcano crater in Honolulu.

113.33   the Argonne battles] See note 51.38.

114.8   "Beale Street Blues"] Early blues tune by American songwriter and pianist W. C. Handy (1873–1958), first published in 1917.

117.26   an exasperated Central] Telephones during the early 1920s were not equipped with mechanisms for dialing. An operator at a central office placed the call through a switchboard. For long-distance calls the line had to be cleared in advance through several interchanges.

127.5–6   James J. Hill.] A Canadian American railroad executive and financier (1838–1916) whose base of operations was in St. Paul, Minnesota, Fitzgerald's hometown. A self-made man, Hill was a hero to many midwestern boys. His thirty-two-room mansion, which contains a ballroom and an art gallery, still stands on Summit Avenue in St. Paul.

128.14   "The Rosary,"] Popular sentimental tune written by American composer and pianist Ethelbert Nevin (1862–1901), with words by Robert Cameron Rogers (1862–1912): "The hours I spent with thee, dear heart, / Are as a string of pearls to me; / I count them over, every one apart, / My rosary, my rosary!"

130.22   "Hopalong Cassidy."] One in a series of novels and stories by American writer Clarence E. Mulford (1883–1956) that featured the rough-talking but upright cowboy of the same name. The novel is an anachronism, since Jimmy Gatz's list is dated September 12, 1906—and the book was not published until 1910.

132.2–3   "Blessed are the dead . . . falls on"] Paraphrase of a line from "Rain" (1916), by the British war poet Edward Thomas (1878–1917), killed on the Western Front during World War I.

133.12   El Greco] Doménikos Theotokópoulos (1541–1614), a Greek painter and sculptor.

ALL THE SAD YOUNG MEN

138.1   TO RING AND ELLIS LARDNER] Ringgold Wilmer "Ring" Lardner (1885–1933), American sports columnist and short-story writer, and his wife, Ellis Lardner (1887–1960). The Fitzgeralds and Lardners spent considerable time together from October 1922 to April 1924 when both couples lived in Great Neck.

141.3   New Haven] See note 6.21.

141.34   Pensacola] Pensacola, Florida, the location of the U.S. Naval Air Station during World War I. There, trainees learned to fly seaplanes, dirigibles, and kite balloons.

141.35   "I'm Sorry, Dear"] A war song with music by N. J. Clesi (1880–1950) and lyrics by Harry Tobias (1895–1994), popularized by Fats Waller in a 1918 recording. "I'm sorry dear, so sorry dear, / I'm sorry I made you cry. / Won't you forget, won't you forgive, / Don't let us say goodbye."

143.28   The Ritz] The Ritz-Carlton Hotel, located in the 1920s at Madison and 46th Street, famous for its elegantly appointed Palm Room.

145.34   bromo-seltzer] Bromo-Seltzer, a bromide. The granules were mixed with water before ingesting.

145.42   in Dutch] In trouble.

146.3   the Links."] Exclusive New York club located on East 62nd Street, about a block from Central Park.

149.4–5   the Breakers . . . the Royal Poinciana] Gilded Age luxury hotels built by American oil, real estate, and railroad tycoon Henry Flagler. The two hotels occupied the same property in Palm Beach.

149.11   the double-shuffle] A three-step dance—a variation on the polka, with extra steps interpolated for syncopated music. By convention, dancers performing the double-shuffle moved counterclockwise around the floor.

149.13   the Everglades Club] Exclusive Palm Beach club that opened in 1919.

149.26–29   "*Rose of Washington Square . . . basement air*—"] Three lines from the popular 1920 song "Rose of Washington Square," with music by the vaudeville accompanist James F. Hanley (1892–1942) and lyrics by Princeton alumnus Ballard MacDonald (1882–1935). The song has two versions, one serious and the other comic. The lyrics here are from the comic rendition: "Rose of Washington Square, she's withering there; / In basement air she's fading . . . / She's got those Broadway vampires lashed to the mast; / She's got no future, but oh! What a past; / She's Rose of Washington Square."

149.32   Mr. Conan Doyle] Sir Arthur Conan Doyle (1859–1930), British author of the Sherlock Holmes detective stories.

151.17   a cutaway coat] A coat with the front cut back to curve toward the tails, worn with striped trousers, vest, winged collar, and ascot. The ensemble was worn for formal daytime occasions, such as weddings and Sunday morning churchgoing.

151.24–25   Wheatley Hills.] Exclusive club on Long Island, in East Williston, New York.

152.30–31   Junior League . . . the Plaza . . . the Assembly] The Junior League and the Assembly, social organizations for women of wealth who wanted to do civic good works and help the indigent and poor. Dolly's debutante ball was held at New York's Plaza Hotel (see also note 57.39).

159.18   Celliniesque] Resembling the extravagant escapades of the Florentine goldsmith and writer Benvenuto Cellini (1500–1571), recounted in *The Auto-biography of Benvenuto Cellini* (English translation 1791).

164.28–29   St. Thomas's church.] Protestant Episcopal church at 53rd Street and Fifth Avenue. Its congregation was drawn from the ranks of the rich and socially prominent. One of the ornaments above its "marriage door," situated to the left of the main entrance, resembles a dollar sign—a matter for joking among some of the parishioners.

166.31   continuities for pictures] In the motion-picture business, a "continuity" is a written plan, set down in advance of filming. It details the order and connection of the scenes.

167.9 Homeric] Big, formal send-off.

169.15–16 'God Save the King'?"] British national anthem, adopted in 1745 during the reign of George III.

170.3 the exchange existed no longer.] Telephone numbers of the time were preceded by lettered prefixes that stood for exchanges or central offices—Plaza or Rhinelander, for example. Certain exchanges were more prestigious than others. See also note 117.26.

174.8 the *Paris*] Luxury transatlantic French liner that entered service in 1921. It was decorated in a combination of Art Deco, Art Nouveau, and Moorish styles. The Fitzgeralds traveled to France on the *Paris* in April 1928.

176.20 Black Bear Lake] Cf. White Bear Lake, a town on the lake of the same name, near Fitzgerald's hometown of St. Paul, Minnesota. As a youth Fitzgerald attended dances at the White Bear Yacht Club; after their marriage, he and Zelda lived at the lake in August 1921 and again during the summer of 1922.

177.1 Pierce-Arrow] Large luxury automobile with a powerful thirteen-liter engine. It was the most elegant car of the period.

182.1 mashie shot] The mashie, a standard club for most golfers. It had the approximate loft of a five-iron and was used for medium-length shots.

183.6–7 "Chin-Chin" and "The Count of Luxembourg" and "The Chocolate Soldier"—] "Chin-Chin Chinaman," a comic song from the 1896 musical *The Geisha*, by Sidney Jones (which enjoyed a Broadway revival in 1913). *The Count of Luxembourg* (1912), a two-act Broadway operetta with English lyrics and libretto by Basil Hood and Adrian Ross, adapted from Austro-Hungarian composer Franz Lehár's three-act operetta *Der Graf von Luxembourg* (1909). *The Chocolate Soldier* (1909), an English-language adaptation of an operetta by Viennese composer Oscar Straus, based on George Bernard Shaw's play *Arms and the Man* (1894). Prior to the manufacture of high-quality record discs and phonographs, hits from Broadway shows circulated as sheet music.

190.17 when he was twenty-five.] The only date provided in the story is February 1917, just before Dexter enters the war. Here, Dexter should be twenty-six, not twenty-five.

195.6–7 the war came to America in March] U.S. diplomatic relations with Germany ceased in February 1917, and entrance into World War I seemed certain by March. On April 6, 1917, the United States formally declared war on Germany and its allies.

212.8 the Sixth and Ninth Commandments.] As numbered by the Roman Catholic Church, the commandments, respectively, against adultery and the coveting of one's neighbor's wife.

213.18 'Twenty-three Skidoo'] Slang term (early twentieth century) of uncertain origin, meaning "Beat it!" or "Scram!"

216.14   James J. Hill] See note 127.5–6.

216.32   Alger books] American author Horatio Alger, Jr. (1832–1899), wrote
Ragged Dick (1868) and numerous other rags-to-riches stories extolling honesty, hard work, and perseverance.

216.33   "Hamline,"] Hamline University, a small Methodist institution in
Fitzgerald's native St. Paul.

220.39–40   *Dómini, non sum dignus . . . ánima mea*] From the Ordinary
of the Roman Catholic Mass (c.1910): "Lord, I am not worthy that Thou
shouldst come under my roof; but only say the word, and my soul will be
healed."

221.9–10   *Corpus Dómini . . . vitam ætérnam*] See note 220.39–40. "May the
Body of our Lord Jesus Christ preserve (my/your) soul unto life everlasting."

221.36   "*Sagitta Volante in Die*"] Latin: Flies by day. See Psalms 90:5–7 (the
Douay version, 1914): "His truth shall compass thee with a shield: thou shalt
not be afraid of the terror of the night. / Of the arrow that flieth in the day,
of the business that walketh about in the dark: of invasion, or of the noonday
devil."

224.24–25   the German cuirassiers at Sedan] During the Franco-Prussian
War, Sedan, on the Meuse River in northeastern France, was the site of a battle
on September 1–2, 1870, that resulted in the capture of Napoleon III and the
effective defeat of the French. The Prussian cuirassiers, a unit of heavy cavalry,
wore breastplates and plumed or spiked helmets.

226.2   The *Majestic*] Luxurious White Star liner that began life as the partly
built German liner *Bismarck*. Under the reparations agreements in the Treaty
of Versailles, the ship was awarded to the British as compensation for the sinking of the *Britannic* by a German mine. The *Majestic* was completed in 1921
and worked the transatlantic service between New York and Southampton.

226.15–16   Gloria Swanson . . . Lord & Taylor . . . Graustark] Gloria Swanson
(1899–1983), American actress who became famous in the 1920s while under
contract with Paramount Pictures. Lord & Taylor, the department store chain,
whose New York flagship store and headquarters had moved in 1914 from
Broadway and 20th Street in the "Ladies' Mile" to a new building at Fifth
Avenue and 38th Street. Graustark, a fictional Balkan kingdom that is the setting of several novels by popular American writer George Barr McCutcheon
(1866–1928), including *Graustark* (1901), *Beverly of Graustark* (1904), and
The Prince of Graustark (1914)—all adapted for the screen as silent films.

228.4   "American Magazine"] *The American Magazine* (1906–1956), a
monthly magazine that began as a vehicle for muckraking journalism. Under
the editorship of John M. Siddall (1915–23), the magazine expanded its market
by focusing on female readers.

229.22   the Ritz] See note 143.28.

232.11–14 See who? . . . the Prince of Wales."] Edward, Prince of Wales (1894–1972), toured the U.S. and Canada during the summer and fall of 1919. The press regarded him as the world's most eligible bachelor. While in New York City, he was given a ticker-tape parade and attended the Ziegfeld Follies.

243.9–11 Wessex . . . a Guelph] Wessex, an Anglo-Saxon kingdom in southern England, famous as the setting for many of Thomas Hardy's novels. The Guelphs, a European (and primarily German) dynasty from which the British House of Hanover was descended.

244.17–18 Rue de la Paix.] Parisian street on the Right Bank near the Place de l'Opera, famous for its women's clothing stores and jewelry shops.

245.33 *Hausfrau—*] German: Housewife.

248.1 "Ladies' Home Journal"] *The Ladies' Home Journal* (1883–2016), a leading monthly women's magazine. "LHJ" had a circulation of one million copies by 1903. Fitzgerald's essay "Imagination—and a Few Mothers" was published there in June 1923.

256.26 incredible cherub . . . "Lux" advertisement] Lux was a widely used bath soap, introduced to Americans in 1925 by Lever Brothers. Lux Soaps' first national advertising campaign of 1926 featured fat cherub-like babies.

266.6–7 Bessemer] High-grade steel, smooth to the touch, made by forcing air through molten iron, thus removing carbon and other impurities.

267.39 car cards.] Advertisements posted above the side windows in buses and subway cars.

280.18 car-card] See note 267.39.

285.29–30 evening pianos . . . street outside.] In middle-class homes of the period, a favorite after-dinner activity was to play popular songs on the piano.

288.10 Cuzco, Peru] City in southern Peru, known as a trading center for agricultural produce and textiles, and famous for its Incan ruins.

295.9 Titian-haired] Possessing brownish orange hair, like that of the female subjects depicted by the Italian painter Titian (c. 1488/90–1576).

308.16 Biltmore Hotel.] Luxury New York hotel that stood across from Grand Central Station at 43rd Street and Madison Avenue. Its main restaurant, The Cascades, featured an indoor waterfall; the hotel was said to have the finest Turkish baths in the city.

UNCOLLECTED STORIES 1920–1926

315.10 Biltmore lobby.] See note 308.16.

315.12–13 Club de Vingt or the Plaza Rose Room.] Club de Vingt, a fashionable New York City club, located in the Waldorf-Astoria, 42 East 58th Street. Club de Vingt opened its doors in November 1921. There, young women (always with chaperones) came to meet young men and to learn the latest dance steps. The Rose Room, located in New York's Plaza Hotel, at 59th Street and Fifth Avenue, was used for dinner-dances and other formal entertainments.

315.28   Derby School in Connecticut] Cf. Derby Academy, established in 1840 in Derby, Vermont.

316.11   Kelly Field] U.S. military installation, south of San Antonio, Texas, constructed during World War I and used for training aviation recruits.

316.16–17   "Midnight Frolic" and "Cocoanut Grove" and "Palais Royal."] Trendy postwar New York City nightspots. Midnight Frolic, a nightclub on the roof garden above the New Amsterdam Theatre, owned and operated by theater impresario Florenz Ziegfeld. Cocoanut Grove, a nightclub on the roof of the Century Theatre. Palais Royal, an exclusive and pricey nightclub at 1580 Broadway.

319.40   regelar Hoover."] Before Herbert Hoover (1874–1964) became the thirty-first president of the United States from 1929 to 1933, he was known for managing the Food Administration during World War I. He encouraged voluntary conservation and asked citizens to observe meatless and wheatless days. The word "Hooverize" during the war meant to save or economize.

320.6   flivver] Slang: a small, inexpensive automobile.

324.28–29   putting the tonneau before the radiator] Fitzgerald reworks the clichéd expression "putting the cart before the horse": the tonneau in automobiles of the period was an enclosed passenger compartment in the rear, and the radiator was in the front.

328.16–17   buck-and-wing dance.] A step dance originating from African American and Irish clog dances, marked by high kicks, clicking of heels, and complex steps such as the shuffle and slide.

329.28   East Side snarl] Rough, working-class accent from the Lower East Side of Manhattan, where many recent immigrants lived.

329.28–29   she ragged . . . shimmied . . . did a tickle-toe step] The Rag, the Shimmy, and the Tickle-Toe were current dances seen on Broadway and in the theater-district cafés. See also note 33.24–25.

329.31   an Al Jolson position] Jolson (1886–1950), a popular actor and singer on Broadway, often finished his performances on one knee with arms outstretched.

330.29   floppity Gainsborough hats] Some of the best-known portraits by the English painter Thomas Gainsborough (1727–1788) are of women wearing large-brimmed straw hats adorned with drooping feathers or flowers.

332.24   supes] A shortened form of *supernumeraries*—actors with small parts in stage shows or movies.

337.28   the Broadway Limited.] Luxury express train connecting New York and Chicago that began service in 1912. It departed from New York's Penn Station every afternoon at three o'clock, going south to take on passengers in Philadelphia before heading west to Chicago.

338.10   the marble dome.] The waiting room in New York's Penn Station had high marble vaulted arches; the walls were decorated with murals by the artist Jules Guerin.

339.34–35   left hand . . . offending him] See Matthew 5:30: "And if thy right hand offend thee, cut it off, and cast it from thee: for it is profitable for thee that one of thy members should perish, and not that thy whole body should be cast into hell."

340.5   Tiffany's] The jewelry store Tiffany and Co., founded in 1837, then located at 37th Street and Fifth Avenue in a building modelled on the Palazzo Grimani di San Luca in Venice, Italy. In 1940, Tiffany's moved farther uptown to its present location at 57th Street.

341.6   Corona."] A type of cigar, between five and six inches long, with a rounded head and cut foot; also, the brand name of a popular Cuban cigar.

341.9   Larchmont] Affluent suburb and summer playground for the wealthy, in southern Westchester County, on the Long Island Sound. Mary Pickford, Douglas Fairbanks, the Barrymores, and other celebrities of the era had summer houses in Larchmont. J. P. Morgan and Andrew Carnegie kept their steam yachts at the Larchmont Yacht Club.

341.37   'Smile, Smile, Smile' or 'The Smiles that You Gave to Me.'] Likely references to "Pack Up Your Troubles in Your Old Kit Bag and Smile, Smile, Smile" (1915), with lyrics by George Asaf and music by Felix Powell, and "Smiles" (1918), with lyrics by J. Will Callahan and music by Lee G. Roberts.

347.33   Fabian maneuver] A military strategy that avoids pitched battles and frontal assaults in favor of harassment of the enemy and disruption of supply lines, so named for the Roman general Quintus Fabius Maximus Verrucosus (c. 280–203 B.C.E.), who frustrated Hannibal with such tactics during the Second Punic War.

348.20   Bones man at Yale] A member of Skull and Bones, the most prestigious of the secret senior societies at Yale.

355.10   Montmartre] Club de Montmartre, an upmarket New York nightspot with faux French décor ("The rendezvous of the smart New Yorker"), located at 50th and Broadway. Montmartre had only an orchestra and dance floor—no cabaret.

355.19–20   The Manhattan . . . torn down.] The Manhattan, a large, moderately priced New York hotel that occupied an entire block between 42nd and 43rd Streets, was torn down in 1922. It stood across the street from the more ornate Biltmore at 43rd Street and Madison Avenue.

356.26   his cut-out resounding] An automobile's cutout switch allowed the driver to pull a lever and let the exhaust bypass the muffler, thereby producing a loud racket. Many sports cars of the era were rigged with cutouts.

359.18–19   Crest Avenue—that's our show street] "The Popular Girl" is set in a fictional version of St. Paul, Minnesota, never mentioned by name in the story. Scott and Yanci are traveling down Summit Avenue (Crest Avenue in the story)—past many impressive homes, churches, and other buildings— toward its terminus at the Mississippi River.

359.34–360.1   Nathan Hale . . . slow Mississippi.] A source of civic pride, the larger-than-life bronze statue of Revolutionary War hero Nathan Hale (1755– 1776) stands in St. Paul's Nathan Hale Park. With his hands tied behind his back, Hale stands on the scaffold awaiting sentencing. The statue was given to the city in 1906 by the Daughters of the American Revolution.

360.7   the Petit Trianon.] Country house erected by Louis XV at the sugges- tion of Mme. de Pompadour. Le Petit Trianon still stands in Versailles.

374.19–20   Plaza, Circle and Rhinelander] Telephone exchanges for presti- gious residential sections of New York City.

375.22   Tuxedo] Tuxedo Park, an exclusive, gated enclave in Orange County, some forty miles outside New York City. The men's black dinner jacket known as a tuxedo was worn first at Tuxedo Park.

378.34   Mae Murray] American dancer and movie actress (1889–1965) who first came to the attention of the public in the late 1910s as a performer in Manhattan cafés and ballrooms. Later, she starred in movies at Universal Pic- tures, where she drew a weekly salary of $10,000. Publicists called her "The Girl with Bee-stung Lips."

379.18–20   the floor clerk . . . her key.] Room keys at first-class urban hotels of the period were kept by a clerk stationed on each floor. One left the key with the clerk when away from the hotel.

380.3   'Dulcy'] *Dulcy: A Comedy in Three Acts*, by American playwrights George S. Kaufman and Marc Connelly. The show had 241 performances at the Frazee Theatre on West 42nd Street, opening on August 13, 1921 and closing on March 11, 1922.

382.6–7   "Manhattan Transfer] Busy transfer station in Harrison, New Jersey, in operation from 1910 to 1937.

382.17   the Charter Club."] Undergraduate eating club at Princeton. Eat- ing clubs maintained dining establishments and influenced student dress and behavior.

385.21   the Hippodrome.] The largest theater in New York City in its day, seating over five thousand and noted for its lavish spectacles; it opened in 1905 on Sixth Avenue between 43rd and 44th Streets.

391.17 Mrs. Humphry Ward] Mary Augusta Ward (1851–1920), English novelist.

391.21 Diana] Goddess in Roman religion, patroness of wild animals and the hunt.

392.18 motometer] Automobile instrument that measured the number of revolutions made by the motor.

400.20–21 the Boodlin' Bend—and the Mississippi Sunrise.] Southern dances of African American origin, performed to ragtime or jazz music.

401.35 banjo tom-tom] Musical instrument, a combination of the tambourine and the stringed banjo.

405.40 "All Alone" and "Tea for Two"] "All Alone" (1924), popular song written by Irving Berlin (lyrics and music) and recorded by Al Jolson, Paul Whiteman, and John McCormack. "Tea for Two," a duet with lyrics by Irving Caesar and music by Vincent Youmans, first performed by Louise Groody and John Barker in the Broadway musical *No, No, Nanette* (1924).

408.10 flivver] See note 320.6.

413.14–15 the Ritz.] See note 143.28.

413.23 "Beale Street Blues,"] Popular 1916 blues tune by W. C. Handy (1873–1958), named for Beale Street in Memphis, Tennessee. Fitzgerald's readers would have known the recordings by Ernest Hare and Marion Harris.

422.31–38 "*Lis*-sen *while . . . don't repeat.*"] Lyrics from "I Ain't Gonna Give Nobody None o' This Jelly Roll" (1919), a jazz song played by many artists, including Sidney Bechet and His New Orleans Feet Warmers.

427.36 Fontenay in the late fall?"] Abbey of Fontenay, a former Cistercian abbey in Burgundy, France, that underwent a major restoration during Fitzgerald's lifetime. The phrase "in the late fall," however, suggests that Fitzgerald was thinking of Fontaine, a commune in southwestern France. During the battle of Cambrai (November 20 to December 5, 1917), tanks were used to great advantage by British forces at Fontaine.

430.7 stock ticker] Telegraph instrument, quite noisy, that received current prices from the stock exchange and printed the information on paper strip called ticker tape.

430.25 Circassian leather] Leather from Circassia, a region on the Black Sea in southern Russia.

431.9 Telamonian Ajax] Warrior of Greek mythology, the son of King Telamon, large and slow of speech but possessed of great courage and strength. In Book VII of the *Iliad*, he fights Hector to a draw.

434.3–4 Tuxedo Park] See note 375.22.

443.29   the *Aquitania*] British ocean liner of the Cunard Line sister ship of the *Lusitania*. Launched in 1914, the *Aquitania* was used as both a hospital ship and a troopship during World War I.

444.11   double-dummy mah-jongg.] Normally there are four players in mah-jongg, a game of Chinese origin involving tiles, counters, and dice; double-dummy mah-jongg can be played by two people.

445.25   Mr. Trotzky to Mr. Rockefeller.] Leon Trotsky (1879–1940), theorist of socialism and one of the chief architects of the Russian Revolution, and at the time Fitzgerald wrote "The Unspeakable Egg" minister of war for the Soviet Union. John D. Rockefeller, see note 23.6.

454.33   'The Sheik'?"] Popular "desert romance" novel of 1919 by English novelist Edith Maud Hull (1880–1947).

454.39   "'Little Lord Fauntleroy.'"] Popular children's novel of 1885–1886 by American author Frances Hodgson Burnett (1849–1924).

458.29   wireless] Here, a verb, meaning to send a message via radiotelegraph.

462.9   college at New Haven] See note 6.21.

488.20   a few days on the Island] A few days in prison. New York City penitentiaries were located on Welfare Island (originally Blackwell's Island and now Roosevelt Island) and Hart Island.

497.15–16   Chicago World's Fair] The World's Columbian Exposition, popularly known as the Chicago World's Fair, held in Chicago from May to November 1893.

497.25   Bernini—] Gian Lorenzo Bernini (1598–1680), Baroque sculptor and architect whose works include many fountains in Rome and the colonnade outside St. Peter's at the Vatican.

498.9–10   Peter the Great] Peter I, the Great (1672–1725), tzar of Russia who reigned with his half-brother Ivan V from 1682 to 1696 and alone thereafter until his death.

508.12–14   When the Kerensky government . . . it remained.] After the abdication of Nicholas II, Aleksander Kerensky (1881–1970) led the short-lived Russian Provisional Government, which was toppled in November 1917 by the Bolsheviks, led by Lenin and Trotsky. Val appears to have served on the eastern front between Russia and Germany, a confrontation that Kerensky wanted to prolong.

508.17   the Romanoffs—] The ruling dynasty of Russia from 1613 to 1917, when Czar Nicholas II abdicated. Nicholas II was executed in 1918 along with his wife and children.

508.20 Denikin's army] Val's commander was Anton Denikin (1872–1947), who commanded the White army in southern Russia and Ukraine, April 1918–April 1920.

511.16 stereopticon glasses] Spectacles that give the illusion of depth to flat images. The stereoscope, a similar invention, was used with double-image slides for home entertainment.

518.5 Stravinski] Igor Stravinsky (1882–1971), Russian-born American composer, conductor, and pianist.

527.7 Gerbert] Pope Sylvester II (c. 946–1003), originally known as Gerbert of Aurillac, a French-born scholar and teacher who became archbishop of Rheims and then pope in 999.

529.4 Morris Gest's . . . Herrin, Illinois.] Morris Gest (1881–1942), one of Broadway's most successful theatrical producers in the 1910s and 1920s. His 1919 production of *Aphrodite*, featuring scantily clad exotic dancers, drew criticism. Herrin, a small city in the coal-mining region of southern Illinois, the site of a battle between striking miners and scabs in 1922. The clash, known as the Herrin Massacre, resulted in more than twenty deaths.

531.17 Saratoga chips] Potato chips, or crisps, said to have been invented in 1853 by a cook in the resort town of Saratoga Springs, New York.

531.30 Bond Street suit] A fashionable suit, one purchased on Bond Street, home to many of London's finest men's clothiers.

539.36 Café Royal] Perhaps the café at Le Royal, a hotel on the Boulevard M. Lemonnier, in Old Brussels.

540.28 shooting box] Small lodge or house used only during the hunting season.

540.36–37 Boompjes . . . Groote Kerk] Boompjes, a large sea dike, constructed in south-central Rotterdam along the Nieuwe Maas. Groote Kerk, the familiar name given to the church of St. Laurenskerk, also in Rotterdam.

542.27–28 "New York Herald"] New York City newspaper published from 1835 to 1924, when it merged with the *New York Tribune* to form the *New York Herald Tribune*. Americans abroad would have read the European edition.

546.17 Blue Grotto] La Grotta Azzura, a natural sea cave with brilliant blue or emerald light, one of the chief attractions on the island of Capri.

549.5 the Black Hand] Likely reference to the Italian Mano Nera, a collective name for several extortion rackets in New York, Chicago, New Orleans, and Kansas City run by immigrant Sicilian gangsters. The Black Hand was also a byname for the Serbian terrorist group that planned the assassination of Archduke Francis Ferdinand in 1914—the event that precipitated the First World War.

549.18   Eboli] A town in the Cilento region of Italy.

549.39   Agropoli . . . two miles away."] Agropoli, one of the highest towns on the Cilento coast, is in fact some thirty miles distant from Eboli.

554.11   Leonora Hughes] American dancer (1897–1978) who enjoyed great success with her dancing partner Maurice Mouvet ("Maurice the Dancer") from 1919 to 1924.

554.27   *S. S. Olympic*] British luxury liner in the White Star Line, sister ship of the *Britannic* and the *Titanic*. Launched in 1911, the *Olympic* was favored by wealthy travelers, including the Prince of Wales and Charlie Chaplin.

557.3   "Du vaah,"] Jim means "*Du vin*"—"Some wine."

560.5   apache] Kinetic and sometimes violent dance associated with the ruffian street culture of fin-de-siècle Paris.

560.5–6   Zelli's and *Le Rat Mort*] Chic dinner restaurants in the 1920s, located near the Place Pigalle in Montmartre.

561.3   "*Voleurs!*"] French: Thieves!

561.20–21   American Aid Society] Organization founded in 1922 to help destitute Americans in France. In 1926, some 2,800 U.S. citizens applied to the society for help.

562.31   American Bureau of Military Graves] Likely Fitzgerald had in mind the American Battle Monuments Commission, an independent agency established by the U.S. Congress in 1923.

563.16–17   Landru, the Bluebeard of France] Henri-Désiré Landru (1869–1922), French serial killer who murdered at least ten wives from 1915 to 1919. Bluebeard, a character in a French folktale of the same name, in which a wealthy man murders his wives and deposits their corpses in an underground chamber that each new bride is forbidden to enter.

563.20–21   "Louie's girl and Louie's wife."] Jeanne Bécu (1743–1793), Comtesse Du Barry, was mistress of Louis XV from 1768 to 1774. His queen was Marie Leszcynska of Poland.

563.39   Malmaison . . . Passy . . . St-Cloud.] Château de Malmaison, the residence of Empress Josephine from 1809 to 1814 after her divorce from Napoleon Bonaparte. Passy, a Parisian residential district favored by writers and artists. Parc de St. Cloud, Parisian gardens and site of former Château de Saint Cloud, where Henri III was assassinated in 1589 and where the marriage of Napoleon to Marie Louise took place in 1810.

573.14–16   the battle of San Juan Hill . . . Kenesaw Mountain Landis."] The battle of San Juan Hill, fought on July 1, 1898, was a U.S. victory in the short-lived Spanish-American War. American troops assaulted and captured the San Juan heights east of Santiago, Cuba. Kenesaw Mountain Landis, an

American judge, was appointed commissioner of baseball following the "Black Sox" scandal in the 1919 World's Series, with orders to restore the integrity of the game. Landis was named after the Civil War battle of Kennesaw Mountain, in which Landis's father, a Union soldier, was wounded. See also note 57.8–9.

573.35–36   Prince of Wales suit] The influence of Edward, Prince of Wales (1894–1972), on the men's fashion industry was especially significant in the 1920s: he believed in "soft dressing" and favored unlined double-breasted jackets, woolly sweaters, and side-creased wide trousers.

575.31   D.K.E. pin] Delta Kappa Epsilon, a social fraternity, with chapters at many American colleges. Asking a young woman to wear one's fraternity pin was an important step toward marriage.

584.3   Emerson and Whittier.] Ralph Waldo Emerson (1803–1882), Boston-born American essayist, poet, and lecturer associated with transcendentalism. John Greenleaf Whittier (1807–1892), American poet who wrote about rural New England life.

586.9   Liberty Bonds] U.S. government bonds, issued to help finance American participation in World War I. The bonds paid 3.5 percent interest.

589.14   the "Transcript"] The *Boston Evening Transcript*, published from 1830 to 1941, the most conservative and traditional of Boston's newspapers in its day.

595.35   *bien soignée*] French: well-groomed.

599.24   Chestnut Hill] Affluent neighborhood in northwest Philadelphia, with many grand homes.

605.27   Leopold and Loeb] On May 21, 1924, Nathan Leopold and Richard Loeb, two nineteen-year-olds from Chicago, murdered fourteen-year-old Bobby Franks. Their trial, in which they were represented by Clarence Darrow, resulted in convictions and life sentences for both. Sons of wealthy, respectable South Side Jewish families, both were attending the University of Chicago at the time of the murder; Leopold in particular was interested in philosophy, especially the ideas of Friedrich Nietzsche, whose "influence" on the killing was emphasized by Darrow in his defense and in press accounts of the trial.

608.23   Rudolf Rassendale] Llewellyn has in mind Rudolf Rassendyll, the hero of *The Prisoner of Zenda* (1894), a popular novel by English author Anthony Hope, later adapted for the stage by Edward Rose. Rudolf bears a marked resemblance to the king of Ruritania, whom he impersonates, becoming involved with Flavia, the king's betrothed.

617.23   corn-drinking recklessness] Bootleg corn liquor, also called moonshine or white lightning, was a potent concoction responsible for much bad behavior among southern men.

617.28   flivvers] See note 320.6.

618.17   Baby Panic of 1921] Brief but severe postwar recession caused by defense cuts and industrial overproduction. Unemployment during the Baby Panic reached 5.7 million in the U.S.

622.28   "shimmy"] See note 33.24–25.

623.9–12   the Charleston . . . knock-kneed effect.] The Charleston was a jazz dance in the 1920s and later, popularized by its appearance in the 1923 Broadway musical *Runnin' Wild*, where it was set to the rhythms of James P. Johnson's song of the same title. The dance involved turning the knees inward and kicking out the legs.

624.2   the vamp] A simple accompaniment improvised to fit a song, played in preparation for the entry of a soloist.

624.13–14   "Good Night, Ladies,"] Nineteenth-century folk song attributed to American composer Edwin Pearce Christy (1815–1862).

NONFICTION 1920–1926

635.1   *The Author's Apology*] Five hundred copies of "The Author's Apology" were printed for the American Booksellers Association meeting in 1920, when *This Side of Paradise*, Fitzgerald's first book, was high on the best sellers lists. It was tipped into copies of the third trade printing of the novel, which was distributed to those who attended the annual meeting. Fitzgerald used part of "The Author's Apology" in "An Interview with Mr. Fitzgerald."

637.1   *An Interview with Mr. Fitzgerald*] Parts of "An Interview with Mr. Fitzgerald" appeared in Heywood Broun's column in the *New York Herald-Tribune*, May 7, 1920. The full text of the self-interview was published for the first time, from Fitzgerald's surviving manuscript, in the *Saturday Review*, November 5, 1960.

638.1–2   Shaw . . . Wells] George Bernard Shaw (1856–1950), Irish playwright and critic. H. G. Wells (1866–1946), English writer who worked in many genres but is best known for his works of speculative fiction, including *The Time Machine* (1895).

638.13   *The Ring and the Book*—] Long narrative poem (1868–1869) by English poet Robert Browning (1812–1889).

638.31–35   Samuel Butler . . . Chesterton.] Samuel Butler (1835–1902), English novelist whose many works include *Erewhon* (1872) and *The Way of All Flesh* (1903). Oscar Wilde (1854–1900), Irish playwright, poet, wit, and fiction writer. Joseph Conrad (1857–1924), Polish-born English novelist whose many works include *Heart of Darkness* (1899) and *Lord Jim* (1900). Robert Hichens (1864–1950), prolific English novelist whose writing was inspired by travel to Egypt. Rudyard Kipling (1865–1936), English novelist and story writer born in India, the setting for his most celebrated books. Gilbert K.

Chesterton (1874–1936), English journalist, literary critic, Catholic theologian, and fiction writer.

639.17 "The Quaker Girl,"] British musical comedy, which opened in New York in October 1911. The lead role was played by the comic actress Ina Claire (1892–1985), one of Fitzgerald's favorite performers. In the play she wins the heart of an American visitor to an English town.

639.18 Gilbert & Sullivan] Theatrical partnership of English dramatist and librettist W. S. Gilbert (1836–1911) and English composer Arthur Sullivan (1842–1900), whose comic operas include *H.M.S. Pinafore*, *The Pirates of Penzance*, and *The Mikado*.

639.22–24 "His Honor the Sultan" . . . Princeton University.] *His Honor the Sultan*, a musical comedy, presented at Princeton's Triangle Club for 1909–10. The plot involves an attempt to overthrow Sultan Murad VI of Tanjocco and replace him with Herr Heinrich Schlitz, a correspondent for *Die Fliegende Blatter*, a German newspaper. Founded in 1891, the Triangle Club produced an annual musical comedy written and performed by Princeton undergraduates. The shows were given first on campus and then taken on the road over the Christmas holidays. All of the parts, including the female roles, were played by members of the then all-male student body. The productions always included a dance number with a kick-line. Fitzgerald collaborated on three Triangle shows during his time at Princeton: *Fie! Fie! Fi-Fi!*, *The Evil Eye*, and *Safety First!*

639.32 My health broke down] Fitzgerald suffered from recurrent tuberculosis throughout his life. After a flare-up in December 1915, he withdrew from Princeton for the remainder of that academic year, though part of his motivation was poor performance in his coursework.

640.3–4 Swinburne . . . Rupert Brooke] Algernon Charles Swinburne (1837–1909) and Rupert Brooke (1887–1915), English poets under whose influence the young Fitzgerald fell. Brooke's poems conveyed the idealism that many young men felt at the beginning of the war. His death from septicemia on his way to military service transformed him into an iconic figure. Brooke had a strong influence on *This Side of Paradise*. Fitzgerald took the title of *This Side of Paradise* from Brooke's poem "Tiare Tahiti."

640.9–10 officers' training camp . . . Fort Leavenworth] Fitzgerald attended army staff school at Fort Leavenworth, in northeastern Kansas, from November 1917 to February 1918.

640.35–36 "The Romantic Egotist"] Fitzgerald's unpublished novel was narrated in the first person by a quasi-autobiographical character named Stephen Palms. Parts of the novel were incorporated into Book I of *This Side of Paradise*. Typescript fragments survive in Fitzgerald's papers at Princeton.

641.28–29 Then, in November . . . "The Saturday Evening Post."] Fitzgerald's "Head and Shoulders" appeared in the February, 21, 1920, issue of

The Saturday Evening Post and was later collected in *Flappers and Philosophers* (1920). The *Post* claimed the highest circulation among popular magazines in the United States; Fitzgerald published sixty-five stories and articles in its pages.

641.32–33   "That's all . . . any more."] Spoken not by Julius Caesar but by American actress Ethel Barrymore (1879–1959), who recited these words at the end of each performance.

642.1   *The Credo of F. Scott Fitzgerald*] Published in the Chicago *Daily News* on March 9, 1921. It is taken from a letter by Fitzgerald to his friend Thomas Boyd, a novelist and literary journalist in St. Paul.

642.7   Stephen Benét . . . his past.] A reference to Benét's forthcoming auto-biographical campus novel *The Beginning of Wisdom* (1921), published shortly after the author's graduation from Yale University. In reviews, it was frequently compared to *This Side of Paradise*.

642.35–643.3   "Main Street," . . . "The Titan" . . . "Salt" . . . "McTeague."] *Main Street* (1920), a novel by American fiction writer and playwright Sinclair Lewis. *The Titan* (1914), part of the Trilogy of Desire, based on the life of financier Charles Tyson Yerkes, by American novelist Theodore Dreiser. *Salt* (1919), a novel by American author Charles Gilman Norris, brother of novelist Frank Norris. *McTeague* (1899), a novel by Frank Norris.

643.5–7   Robert Chambers . . . "Balzacs of America."] Robert W. Chambers (1865–1933), prolific American novelist and short-story writer whose works included historical fiction and romance. H. L. Mencken called him "the boudoir Balzac."

644.1   *Three Cities*] Published in *Brentano's Book Chat* (September–October 1921). The article is based on Fitzgerald's notes from his and Zelda's first trip to Europe, May–July 1921.

645.10   "Alice Adams" . . . "Ramsey Milholland" . . . "The Magnificent Ambersons"] Three novels by American novelist and playwright Booth Tarkington (1869–1946).

645.17   "Moon-Calf"] An autobiographical novel of 1920 by American novelist and playwright Floyd Dell (1887–1969).

645.32–33   "Sinister Street," "Zuleika Dobson" and "Jude the Obscure"] *Sinister Street* (1914), a novel by Scottish writer Compton Mackenzie (1883–1972). *Zuleika Dobson* (1911), the only novel by English essayist, parodist, and caricaturist Max Beerbohm (1872–1956). *Jude the Obscure* (1895), a novel by English poet and novelist Thomas Hardy (1840–1928).

645.35   The High . . . Via Appia.] Fitzgerald refers to High Street in Oxford, England. Via Appia, the Appian Way, was an important road in ancient Rome.

647.2–3   The man . . . not a mariner.] See "The Rime of the Ancient Mariner" (1798) by Samuel Taylor Coleridge, in which a gray-bearded mariner stops a man on his way to a wedding ceremony and relays a fantastic tale.

649.12   the Eighteenth Amendment] Ratified on January 16, 1919, the Eighteenth Amendment prohibited the manufacture, sale, or transportation of alcohol in the United States.

649.17–18   her hair torn off by an electric washing-machine] Early automatic washing machines had roller wringers attached to the tubs; wet clothes were fed by hand through these wringers—in which hair and fingers could be caught.

649.20   Washington's Farewell Address] President George Washington's valedictory speech, delivered on September 17, 1796, before his retirement to Mount Vernon.

650.2   this magazine] *The American Magazine*. "What I Think and Feel at 25" appeared in the September 1922 issue. See also note 228.4.

650.16–17   Zion City . . . world is flat—] Zion, a city in Illinois, was established in 1901 by John Alexander Dowie (1847–1907). Dowie believed that prayer, by itself, could heal the sick. Initially, Dowie governed Zion alone; he was deposed in 1905, but the city maintained its theocratic government until 1935.

653.36–38   in Philadelphia about 1727 . . . munching a loaf of bread] In *The Autobiography of Benjamin Franklin* (1793), Franklin relates how, after arriving in Philadelphia, he stopped in at a bakery and purchased "three great Puffy Rolls." The young Franklin then walked about the streets "with a Roll under each Arm, and eating the other."

656.30–31   an article . . . by a fellow named Ring Lardner] Fitzgerald refers to Ring Lardner's "General Symptoms of Being 35—Which Is What I Am," first published in *The American Magazine* (May 1921). See also note 138.1.

657.17   Liberty Bonds] See note 586.9.

657.28   received a large check from the movies] In February 1920, Fitzgerald's short story "Head and Shoulders" was sold to Metro Films for $2,500.

659.10–11   a town about fifteen miles from New York] The Fitzgeralds lived at 6 Gateway Drive in Great Neck, Long Island, from October 1922 to April 1924.

659.37   remove his collar] During the 1910s and 1920s, men wore shirts with detachable collars, which were held to the body of the shirt by collar buttons or studs.

660.16   the gold rush of '49, or a big bonanza of the '70's.] In 1848, when gold was discovered in California, the flood of would-be prospectors transformed San Francisco from a village to a city of 35,000 people in five years.

In the 1860s and 1870s, several significant "bonanzas," or rich deposits of precious metals, were discovered in the West.

661.6   My first play . . . the autumn] *The Vegetable, or from President to Postman*. In hope of stirring interest among New York producers, Fitzgerald published his play in book form in April 1923, but *The Vegetable* never made it to Broadway.

661.19–20   a small windfall . . . a moving picture—] In March 1923, Fitzgerald received $10,000 for film rights to *This Side of Paradise*.

662.14–15   a new novel] The earliest version of *The Great Gatsby*, which Fitzgerald began in the late spring of 1923. Only two pages of this attempt survive; they are narrated in the third person.

664.7   2 Framed crayon portraits of my wife and me.] The crayon portraits were made by American illustrator James Montgomery Flagg and published with the Fitzgeralds' cowritten article "Looking Back Eight Years," in *College Humor*, June 1928.

666.23   ringside seats to the Dempsey-Firpo fight] Jack Dempsey, the heavyweight champion, successfully defended his title against the Argentinian Luis Firpo at the Polo Grounds in New York City on September 14, 1923. The crowd numbered more than 88,000. Ringside seats would have been expensive.

670.7   Wembley exhibition] The British Empire Exposition (1924–25), in Wembley, near London. Wembley Stadium was constructed for the exhibition, which highlighted industry and the arts.

670.14   Deauville and Trouville] Seaside resorts in the Normandy region of northwestern France.

671.21   Rue de la Paix hat] See note 244.17–18.

672.27   Mr. and Mrs. Douglas Fairbanks] Douglas Elton Fairbanks (1883–1939) and Mary Pickford (1892–1979), American stars of the silent film era. Fairbanks and Pickford married in 1920. Pickford was known as "America's Sweetheart," and Fairbanks was famous for his swashbuckler roles.

672.35–36   no faint taste of wood-alcohol] During Prohibition, American bootleggers were reputed to lace their products with wood alcohol.

673.5–6   fairy blue of Maxfield Parrish's pictures] American painter and illustrator Maxfield Parrish (1870–1966) frequently used cobalt blue—also called "Parrish blue"—in his work.

673.15   Charles Dickens to Catherine de Medici] Charles Dickens (1812–1870), prolific novelist of the Victorian—sometimes called the Dickensian—era. Catherine de Medici (1519–1589), queen of France during the reign of Henry II.

673.15–17   Prince Edward . . . Oscar Wilde . . . his disgrace] Prince Edward, see note 232.11–14. The Irish playwright and wit Oscar Wilde went from being one of Britain's most celebrated literary figures to a notorious sexual criminal when he was found guilty of "gross indecency" between men on May 25, 1895, in one of the most publicized trials of the century.

675.22 the "Illustrated London News"—] Popular international newspaper and the first weekly newsmagazine, in operation from 1842 to 2003.

676.18 "Yes, we have no villas today,"] Cf. "Yes, We Have No Bananas!" (1923), one of the most popular American novelty songs of the 1920s, by Frank Silver and Irving Cohn.

677.35–36 the Man with the Iron Mask . . . its shore.] The French prisoner known as the Man in the Iron Mask, probably Count Girolamo Mattioli, was incarcerated for more than thirty years by Louis XIV. For a time, he was held in a fortress prison on Île Sainte-Marguerite, off the coast of Cannes.

678.24 Grand Duke Michael's] Grand Duke Michael Alexandrovich of Russia (1878–1918), youngest brother to Nicholas II, the last emperor of Russia.

680.9–12 Catherine de Medici . . . St. Bartholomew's sizzling in her head.] While serving as regent for her second son, Catherine de Medici (1519–1589) helped to plan the infamous 1572 massacre of St. Bartholomew's Day, an attack on Protestant leaders that resulted in civil war in France. See also note 674.15.

683.15 the historic banana song] See note 677.18.

685.5 white ducks] Uniforms made of white duck, a lightweight cotton or linen cloth similar to canvas.

685.14 *carmagnole*] Lively song and round dance, popular during the French Revolution. It was named after Carmagnola, a town in the Piedmont occupied by the revolutionaries.

686.3–4 Irving's preoccupation . . . American backgrounds] Washington Irving (1783–1859), American story writer, historian, and biographer, was among the first American authors to use native scenes and settings.

687.5 Corona] The Corona typewriter, a popular portable typewriter. Fitzgerald himself could not type.

687.7–8 journalistic loot . . . Richard Harding Davis and John Fox, Jr.] American fiction writers Richard Harding Davis (1864–1916) and John Fox, Jr. (1862–1919), had significant careers as war correspondents. Fox reported on the Spanish-American War while serving as a Rough Rider and later traveled to Asia to cover the Russo-Japanese War; Davis covered the Spanish-American War, the Second Boer War, and World War I.

687.26–37 H. L. Mencken . . . pronouncements . . . essay on Dreiser.] Henry Louis Mencken (1880–1956), American journalist, prominent literary and social critic. Two years before the appearance of "How to Waste Material" in the May 1926 issue of *The Bookman*, Mencken and his co-editor George Jean Nathan launched the influential magazine *The American Mercury*, in which many of Mencken's "pronouncements" appeared. In his article "The Dreiser Bugaboo" (1917), Mencken predicts Dreiser's books will survive because of their honesty, courage, and Greek-like sense of tragedy.

688.13–18   Sherwood Anderson . . . at all.] Sherwood Anderson (1876–1941), American writer best remembered for his story collections, especially *Winesburg, Ohio* (1919). Fitzgerald was one of the few writers to express admiration for Anderson's novel *Many Marriages* (1923), which, together with his subsequent, best-selling novel, *Dark Laughter* (1925), was parodied by Ernest Hemingway in *The Torrents of Spring* (1926).

688.19–21   Waldo Frank . . . a Kansas Theosophist] Waldo Frank (1889–1967), American novelist, social historian, and political activist. His fiction is marked by mysticism and a poeticized style.

688.21   Hergesheimer] Joseph Hergesheimer (1880–1954), prominent American novelist of the 1920s, whose books include *The Three Black Pennys* (1917) and *Cytherea* (1922).

689.5   "Through the Wheat" and "Three Soldiers,"] *Through the Wheat* (1923), a novel by American writer Thomas Alexander Boyd (1898–1935), about the experiences of a young Marine during World War I. Fitzgerald reviewed the novel in the New York *Evening Post*: "To my mind, this is not only the best combatant story of the Great War, but also the best war book since *The Red Badge of Courage.*" *Three Soldiers* (1921), an antiwar novel by American writer John Dos Passos (1896–1970), set during World War I. Fitzgerald reviewed *Three Soldiers* in the *St. Paul Daily News*, calling it "the first war book by an American which is worthy of serious notice."

689.7   "Les Croix de Bois" and "The Red Badge of Courage."] *Les croix de bois*, French novel of 1919 by Roland Dorgelès (1886–1973), based on the author's experiences in trench fighting during World War I. Likely Fitzgerald read the English translation, *Wooden Crosses*, published the same year in the U.S. by G. P. Putnam's Sons. *The Red Badge of Courage* (1895), by American author Stephen Crane (1871–1900).

689.13   "In Our Time"] "How to Waste Material" was written on the occasion of the American publication of *In Our Time* (Boni & Liveright, 1925).

690.17–20   The last glimpse . . . in Puritan prayer.] Fitzgerald is mistaken: "Soldier's Home," the Hemingway story to which he alludes, concerns Harold Krebs, not Nick Adams.

*This book is set in 10 point ITC Galliard, a face designed
for digital composition by Matthew Carter and based
on the sixteenth-century face Granjon. The paper is acid-free
lightweight opaque that will not turn yellow or brittle with age.
The binding is sewn, which allows the book to open easily and lie flat.
The binding board is covered in Brillianta, a woven rayon cloth
made by Van Heek–Scholco Textielfabrieken, Holland.
Composition by Neuwirth & Associates, Inc.
Printing by Sheridan Grand Rapids, Grand Rapids, MI.
Binding by Dekker Bookbinding, Wyoming, MI.
Designed by Bruce Campbell.*

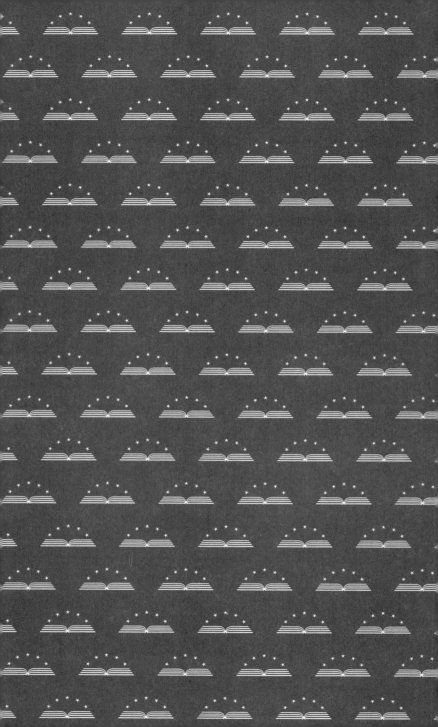